ANDERSON W. FROST'S

THORNS

FEATHERS & BONES

THE PENDANT EDITION

For my wife,

whose love is the quiet strength beneath every page.

Your unwavering support, your patience, your belief in me—

they are the reasons this book exists.

Without you, there would be no story,

no courage to tell it,

no light to see it through.

Always, and forever.

Edited by Bonnie Jayne Murphy
Map by: Melissa Nash

ISBN: 979-8-218-88511-3

Author's Note

This book is a work of fiction. While it explores themes like magic and other forces, these elements are used solely as narrative devices to examine aspects of the human condition—such as fear, desire, power, identity, and belief.

The story does **not** endorse or promote any occult practices, spiritual belief systems, or esoteric doctrines. Any resemblance to real-world ideologies or systems of belief is purely metaphorical and unintentional. Readers are encouraged to approach this tale as an imaginative exploration of morality, emotion, and choice—through the lens of fantasy.

Names, characters, places, and incidents are either the product of the author's imagination or used fictitiously. Any resemblance to actual persons, living or dead, events, or locales is entirely coincidental.

Content Warning

This novel contains material that may be disturbing or triggering
for some readers, including: violence, strong language, themes of
abuse, self-harm, implied sexual content, and death.

Reader discretion is advised.

Pronunciation Guide

Character Names:

1. Aghor – AH-gor
2. Balfour – BAL-for
3. Brüg – BROOG
4. Caelithor – KAY-lih-thor
5. Connerh Manthil – CON-ner MAN-thil
6. Curzon – KUR-zon
7. Darros – DAIR-ohs
8. Egress – EE-gress or EH-gress
9. Elarion – eh-LAIR-ee-on
10. Elisceryn - Eh-lis-ser-in
11. Farrah - Fair-Uh
12. Glendrake – GLEN-drayk
13. Gregor – GREG-or
14. Hammul – HAM-ul
15. Hargatha – HAR-gah-thah
16. Illithor - Ill-uh-thor
17. Io - Eye-Oh
18. Ioelena (Lena) – eye-oh-LEH-nah (LEH-nah)
19. Joriah – jor-EYE-ah
20. Madika – mah-DEE-kah
21. Niko Hargrave – NEE-koh HAR-grayv
22. Oleander – OH-lee-an-der
23. Reh'gara – RAY-gah-rah
24. Sevryn – SEV-rin
25. Thaetra – THAY-trah
26. Toke – TOHK
27. Torinir - Tore-uh-near

28.Vidar — VEE-dar
29.Yuri — YOO-ree

Location Names:

1.Aelthoria — ay-el-THOR-ee-ah
2.Cyraxis — sigh-RAK-sis
3.Hildeheim — HIL-duh-hyme
4.Khazmyr — KAZ-meer
5.Mount Sankari — mount san-KAR-ee
6.Nyradhal — Near-rah-dahl
7.Stallhearth — STALL-harth
8.Tu'Chauri — too-CHOW-ree
9.Uridar — OOR-ee-dar

THE FREE ISLANDS
N
W
E
S
Nyradhal
Duringar's Peak
Castle Corvidae
Aragath
Gryphon's Rest
HILDEHEIM
Mount Sankari
Solmara
Virelen Thael
Life Garden
The Golden Pass
Aylren
BROOKEHAVEN
OSTREGAL
THE FAR SANDS
THE WESTWOOD
UTREDEN
SUNSPIRE GORGE
TU'CHAURIA
The Seat of Darros
EMBRAVALE
VYRUNE
KHAZMYR
THE RIM

PART ONE

CHAPTER ONE

A BEAUTIFUL VIOLENT ARRAY OF NOTHINGNESS

LENA

Lena approached the edge of the world…

The secluded balcony off the throne room was her sanctuary. In the absence of courtiers, amidst the hushed silence of polished floors, she found solace in solitary reflection. Unlike the bustling view from her chambers, this panorama offered the uninterrupted expanse of the North Sea – no scurrying servants, no ornate temples, no clamorous city squares.

Instead, just a beautiful, violent array of nothingness.

The massive churning waves crashed into the tall, natural rock structures protruding from the sea, instantly erupting into mist and foam. Their debris gently returned to the ocean, re-joining the repeating patterns that stretched far beyond the horizon. And yet from her perspective, high up on the balcony's edge, the chaos moved in delicate, slow motion, like a rhythmic dance. She always wondered what lay just beyond.

She removed the crown perched atop her head before setting it down on the cold marble railing. The polished stone was worn and scuffed there. Her hand lagged behind her as she walked, drifting from her crown to drag along the cold, smooth slab. She released the cloak where it was attached to her gown via clasps on each shoulder. Her gloves were then pulled away from her fingers with a furious intensity and tossed to a watery demise as a blood-curdling scream escaped her lungs. She braced her tongue against her teeth…but it didn't matter. The silent tears burned with a pulsating intensity. She didn't try to stop them. The acidic liquid demanded its liberation after being held at bay for so long. She pursed her lips, blowing air through them as her cheeks ballooned. The tears weren't releasing her internal pressure fast enough, making it difficult to breathe. She felt herself reach for sanity as it tore itself from her grasp. She tried to hold on to it, to convince it to stay, but she could not. Her legs gave out. She crumpled to the floor, emitting a nonsensical bleat from her diaphragm. Her chest pulsed angrily with each breath. Her lungs forgot their process, causing her gasps for air to gracefully suffocate her. Still, it was not enough to satiate.

A low-pitched cry broke through, back-feeding air into her lungs and making her sound human once more. She'd lost the will to move, despite her awkward and uncomfortable pose, eventually curling her torso over her knees to form a tight ball. There was a noise in the distance, but she couldn't find the will to investigate, to break the loop of shaking her head back and forth, to stop mumbling in a tone phasing in and out of comprehensibility while weeping with a tempered cry. The only answers she could rationalise to her internal questions were too devastating to process. The realised feelings of isolation and betrayal had become overwhelming. She opened her eyes, her gaze fixed upon the railing. It wasn't so far.

Yet the balcony's edge, while a convenient escape, seemed insurmountable.

Eventually, her anger won out, drying the tears. She sat up and began fiddling with her fingers in her lap. She thought about what to do next while practising pairing each deep breath with a controlled exhale. The pitter-patter of hurried bare feet echoed before a tight embrace jostled her forward. A pair of arms and hands wrapped around her, causing an anguished smile to twist across her face. Farrah collapsed next to Lena, her hands rapidly moving over her eyes and cheeks, futilely wiping away tears only for them to be replaced anew. Lena grabbed Farrah's hands and brought them down to rest in her lap, knowing it was a losing battle. They stared quietly into one another's eyes for a moment, exchanging an unspoken dialogue with furrowed brows. Farrah nodded continually as she herself began to loosen her grip, giving Lena the unrequired permission to let go.

They sat there, quietly comforting each other until the morning hours.

CHAPTER TWO

LITTLE BIRD

LENA

Earlier that day…

The queen's chalice never had the chance to run dry. Farrah, the Queen's Handmaiden, stood nearby, clinging to the edge of shadow and holding a freshly filled amphora of wine. For most of the evening, she'd pretended not to listen, offering empty glances to random, uninhabited corners of the room and occasionally staring at the floor as if it held the secrets to eternal life. A random thought would quickly distract her before a key word or phrase drew her back into the conversation. All was going well until she heard his name: Connerh. Like paper left too long in warm water, slowly rotating in place, her pitiful façade disintegrated.

Her professional etiquette abandoned her.

She stood there, awkwardly staring back and forth between the queen and her aunt, Hargatha, her mouth open. Her discreet intrusion was noticed but casually ignored. Farrah was more to the queen than a mere servant. She not only held a special position but was also, by all accounts, the queen's companion and loyal friend, separate only in station and lineage. Her eyes followed Ioelena—affectionately called Lena by those close to her—as she slowly approached the large, ornate glass window framed in heavy wood. Lena's eyes were heavy, her cheeks limp. She hadn't made a sound, but her expression was louder than the roaring fireplace in the background. Farrah wished to break decorum and run to her, but her feet felt cemented to the floor. The self-imposed restraint was anguishing.

The evening sun struggled to maintain its hold over the horizon. A faint, orange glaze was cast through the windows of Lena's personal chambers, illuminating her raven-coloured hair and rich, olive skin tone in the dying light. The crackle and hiss of the fireplace, though subtle, provided an audible distraction from the awkward silence. Hargatha lay casually across a long crimson chaise lounge, her even longer body still reaching beyond the beginning and end of it. Her eyes carefully analysed Lena's body language, no longer able to read her facial expressions directly. Lena gazed intently at her own reflection, circling the rim of her chalice with a finger. The small lights at street level danced about like fireflies in the night's sky, moving ever so slowly in the late hour, unaware of her royal observance from her ivory tower.

Her gaze broke free, having had no success in finding clarity.

She turned to the velvet liquid contained by her cup, where her reflection still lay in wait. It looked foreign. The hairs on her neck stood on end. Her focus snapped, locking eyes with Hargatha. The exceptionally large centrepiece of the woman still lay, devoid of expression, save for the twitching muscles in the top innermost portion of her cheek. Her chiselled features were framed by hair as white as the rising moon, contrasting her piercing, pale-blue eyes under naturally arched brows. Her jaw shifted beneath porcelain skin.

"Could it really be true, Gatty?" Lena uttered quietly, unwilling and unbelieving. While she was an intimidating figure to most, she would always be simply '*Aunt Gatty*' to her beloved niece. And until she passed on, she would expect to be called nothing less.

Please be a joke... she thought while silently mouthing the words.

Her brow began to sink, realising how preposterous her proposition appeared. Hargatha was not known for her sense of humour, nor would she have brought the information to her had it not been confirmed at least three times over. Still, it felt unbelievable, if not entirely impossible. Lena had spent ten agonising years convincing herself of a lie that she thought she'd accepted, only to now realise how desperately she *needed* it to be true. The weight of the resulting questions, were it not, would be...unbearable. The scab had been ripped from a forgotten wound. Fresh blood now bubbled up to the surface, making it new again. Her breathing hastened;

her heart sped up its rhythm.

Hargatha nodded, carefully and deliberately acknowledging her worst fears. The confirmation was a stinging blow, adding salt to the refurbished sore. Lena's face crumpled against her will. There was a brief pause as she gazed into memories, long forced from her mind, that now rushed back with an overwhelming intensity. She was thrust into an emotional loop of anger, happiness, and sadness, then back again. She conjured her self-proclaimed closure, the happy thoughts that had sustained her over the better part of a decade, but the feeling of betrayal was sharply overwhelming. The memories stole her breath. Her faith in him to stay alive under any circumstances denied every possibility that this was a fluke, or some…accident. A red-hot pool of tears welled in her eyes. She felt the urge to vomit, and she tried locking her jaw to regain control of her thoughts. The acid in her stomach churned. Her expression deformed into anger as tears liberated themselves to run freely down her face. They left a trail which the subsequent could easily follow, yet they seemed to flow with such ferocity that they forged new tracks with abandon. She uttered no sound, but her body began to convulse, steadily increasing in rhythm and intensity.

Hargatha, overwhelmed with pity, stood quickly, discarded her drink on a side table, and pulled Ioelena into a firm embrace just as her body went limp. She looked down, caressing her face and hair before finally resting her head upon her upper abdomen.

"Oh, child." Hargatha's voice cracked as they embraced. The embrace was lasting. Wiping Lena's face, Hargatha eventually fussed, "Gather yourself. Do not let this control you. You're stronger than this."

She had grown tired of *being strong*. Her façade was thoroughly saturated. It wouldn't be long now.

"Say it, and I will see it done," Hargatha added with eager sharpness, her own dark wishes filling the inflection of her tone. Her grooming of Lena – the wiping, flattening, and straightening – grew more forceful by the minute.

A steeled reserve washed over Lena. Her spine stretched and straightened. She gently pushed away.

"I will see him for myself," she commanded. Hargatha's brow raised. Her hands lingered in mid-air, tracing the ghostly outline of where Lena had previously stood.

"Dead…or alive?" she insisted. Her eyes flashed upwards, examining

Lena's face.

"Alive!" Her words shot out like a reflex, incensed by the absurdity of the question. She folded her arms, pulling tight the furs draped over her shoulders. No matter how angry she felt, killing him seemed an inappropriate response. Sure, she'd joked about this day, about how she would kill him if he ever reappeared after burying him. But now...they were just words. They were nonsensical sounds that didn't make sense.

Weren't they?

She struggled to maintain eye contact with Hargatha. Surely there were reasons for him to still be alive. Surely, he wouldn't have abandoned her without good reason, should it be true. Her logical mind put up a valiant fight, to the point that acceptance began to feel...achievable.

"We don't know what happened yet; how could you jump to such conclusions? No...just, no. Alive. Obviously," she argued.

"As you wish, little bird," Hargatha's accent added a forced, endearing inflection to her words, though she was far from agreeable on the matter. It was resignation. It was not the response she preferred, far from desired, but she'd already had her time to argue her philosophy regarding the man, and it'd had little effect. It hadn't worked up until now, and it certainly had no basis for working going forward. But it was worth a shot. She looked up at Farrah with a scoured expression. Her sniffling was not as quiet as she perhaps thought it was. Farrah startled at the giant's gaze, stepping backwards into shadow, hands clasped over her mouth while still sobbing profusely.

"Where's Bjorn? Does he know?" Lena eventually asked, wiping her running nose and turning to face Hargatha with anticipation.

"Still on his quest to find your mother's killer. He's sent us his usual check-in, received just this morning. I hadn't crossed paths with you yet to tell you, until now. He reports that he's well, but nothing more. This is his pattern. We should get a more detailed update in the coming days," she replied, then added, "and it's doubtful that he knows anything of this, as you're the only person I've shared it with."

"And it should stay that way for now. Tell only who you absolutely must," Lena instructed; Hargatha acknowledged her command. Then, second-guessing herself, Lena quietly remarked, "Though he should be here...and I there."

She drifted to the window, returning her gaze to the city below.

"There's no crime in dreaming..." Hargatha sharply quipped. She moved closer, resting her hands upon Lena's shoulders.

"Your place is here. Bjorn…" She paused at the thought of him.

"Bjorn has yet to find his place in the world." Hargatha tilted her head to gauge Lena's expression.

"Let him have this. Perhaps he will find a small bit of purpose along the way. Besides, you don't need the distraction – not now, this is bad enough. I would see it handled and out of your view, if you would let me. You need to remain focused…as focused as you've ever been," Hargatha pressed, leaning in.

"I will not let you, and I know. I know," Lena fussed, changing gears. She snapped out of her mental fog for long enough to realise Farrah had been crying, and she walked over to physically console her. Hargatha followed her with her eye, barely rotating her body. Lena held Farrah's head to her chest and rocked her back and forth. She pondered a minute before looking up at Gatty.

"You're right. Let him have it. Do your best to keep it from him, for as long as you can. He'll march right back here and stir up trouble. I can't deal with that right now," Lena conceded.

Hargatha nodded in her small victory.

"Tell me, what is your plan to secure Connerh's passage here?" Lena asked.

CHAPTER THREE

NEITHER HERE NOR THERE

CONNERH

Connerh's gaze wandered over the horizon's edge. The faint auburn glow of hand-held torches sauntered in the distance, their patterns fringing on familiar. He mumbled to himself while stalking their movements, staring through shoddy glasses that barely clung to the bridge of his nose. He steadied his sword across his lap as he leaned over to make notes in a small leather-bound journal, taking care not to knock over the fragile glass inkwell. He set the quill down and removed his glasses, placing them on the stump next to him before retrieving the whetstone he'd previously held.

Connerh's right hand moved in a gentle downstroke. The whetstone met his blade, producing a low, raspy, metallic scrape that melded with the calming ambience of the evening. The soft crackle of burning firewood battled against the rising wind, composing the perfect setting for his mind to wander. Countless nights like this one had come before, each bearing the same breeze, temperature, and scent of the air – a blend of grass, charred hay, and wood. The locations and company might have varied, but the essence remained: Connerh, seated before a fire on a cool night, methodically honing his blade, forever poised for what lay ahead.

As his gaze lingered on the dancing flame, his expression and presence in the moment faded with each stroke. His eyes began to glaze over as he mentally retreated to the *other place* – the place that had become a sanctuary for him over the years. It was a dark and familiar realm, free from the burdens imposed upon him by the world. Here, time slowed, his surroundings dimmed, and he could reflect on the past, present, and future…or nothing at all. Memories played out before him like apparitions, performing in vivid detail. Though he could not pinpoint when it began, this potent dream state was a fourth-dimensional experience. Sometimes he relived moments that had already transpired, and on rare occasions, he witnessed blurred events that would eventually come to pass. He was a mere observer in these dreams, lacking any control over what he saw; at times, the visions were so intense they caused him to physically perspire or shed tears.

With a deep exhale, Connerh's breathing and movements slowed.

Rose observed his drifting from the nearby doorway of their home, standing a mere five metres away. Her curly brown hair jostled in the breeze as she sipped from a steaming cup of tea, her piercing hazel eyes reflecting a portion of the fire's flickering light. She wrestled with the idea of going out to him but waited for his subtle cues. Connerh could be a temporary isolationist at best; a practitioner of over-analysing and brooding at the least. As it stood, he seemed satisfied in his solitude. In the early years, Rose had been horrified upon first finding him in this state, mistaking him for dead. When he drifted, his pulse and breath became barely detectable, his skin grew pale, and his body temperature dropped. Still, he always returned to her, usually with a better countenance than before. She didn't understand it fully – and for that matter, neither did he – but they had both grown to accept it.

The best she could do was support him when he came to. As much as she disliked the condition and the toll it took on him, the dreams tended to benefit them, albeit at a cost. They often helped them elude danger, which was a welcome side effect in this day and age. As a superstitious woman, Rose could find meaning in even the most mundane of things, and this was far from mundane. Ultimately, his well-being was her priority.

She felt she owed him at least that much.

Rose was kind and motherly in nature to those she cared for, then fiery and direct with those unfortunate enough to encounter her bad side, which included Connerh at times. She was a balance of beauty and grace, though she paid little mind to appearances, often wearing close to no makeup. Her eyes were what most people noticed first, and it would come as no surprise that green was her favourite colour; she frequently adorned herself in clothing primarily of that hue. Her beauty was of the natural variety: crafted yet delicate, defined by full cheekbones, naturally arched eyebrows, a button nose, and soft, inviting lips – Connerh's favourite feature, next to her hair. She did not believe in abstaining from good food, but she was far from a portly woman, being short in stature but curvy where it mattered.

As the sun methodically sank into its evening nook, it cast an orange hue on everything its light touched, extending rays across the landscape as far as the topography allowed. The wind noticeably cooled, carrying a chilled undertone that signalled the impending arrival of Hildeheim's unrelenting winter. The days would be brief, and the nights would lengthen unendingly the further north one travelled, with snow blanketing everything in sight.

Connerh preferred this time of year, but Rose, not being native to this land, hadn't quite adapted to its extreme seasons. Accustomed to warmth, humidity, and copious amounts of rain her entire life, she had essentially exchanged a paradise-like, tropical climate for wherever the winds took them. They were currently settled in the western province of Hildeheim, Connerh's native country, yet winter's first snowfall remained a spectacle to behold and a highlight of the year for her. Ultimately, her whereabouts mattered little if she was with Connerh. Their nomadic lifestyle took them to the ends of the world, but they always returned to Hildeheim for a time. After all, its inhospitable nature to outsiders made it the perfect retreat from those seeking to locate them.

Connerh's exploits, both past and present, made them easy targets for savoury and unsavoury kinds alike, each desiring to collect him. He preferred anonymity, perhaps even death, to ever again being an owned man.

After roughly one hour, he slowly transitioned from the places within his mind to the present moment. He looked around, slightly dazed, taking stock of his surroundings. His colour returned, and a light steam emanated from his skin as blood fuelled warmth. He looked disturbed. Rose began to gather her things to go to him, as her cue had arrived.

Connerh sighed loudly before setting down the whetstone in favour of lifting his chalice. Peering down into his near-empty silver cup, its golden rim glinting, he watched the semi-translucent pool of velvet wine as it rocked back and forth, briefly revealing glimmers of metal. He ignored the eyes staring back at him from the reflection. They were always watching him from seemingly nondescript locations, apparently unaware of his own noticing.

Connerh poorly convinced himself that he was losing his grip on reality – that the eyes were, in fact, his own. He forced himself to reject the gaze of the stranger as being anything other than a fractured reflection of himself, regardless of his conviction that it blinked independently of him. He shook his head, consumed what remained in his cup, and promptly discarded it on the ground. It was easier not to think about it. His dream state was overwhelming on its own, and he was running out of excuses for that which he could not explain.

As if the universe wished to offer him relief, motion in the distance triggered Connerh's peripheral vision, clearing his thoughts and snapping him into a defensive posture. His hand gripped the hilt of his sword tightly. Suddenly, a large wolf with a reddish hue to its fur calmly walked out from the tall grass and sat on its hind legs. It stared at him, not in a predatory or stalking way but with peaceful, observatory intent. The creature's tail dusted the ground repeatedly, and its ears pivoted in place from left to right and back again, as did its head occasionally. It was as if it was trying to work out what exactly Connerh was doing there. Connerh's guard lowered with a sigh, and he removed his grip from the blade. It was an appropriate response; they were, after all, acquainted.

There was a calming energy about the beast. It always seemed to want something, but Connerh could never figure out exactly what it was. It had no interest in food, going so far as to walk away from a perfectly well-roasted chicken leg Connerh threw at it on one occasion, which notably marked the last time he offered it food. It just watched and patiently expected…something. The creature was always alert and inquiring, as if it were waiting for Connerh to give it a command. Out of all the things he had shouted at the beast (profanity-laden remarks aside), an actual, wilful command was oddly never among them. In his semi-lucid state, he pondered going over and trying to touch it. It was something he'd never done before, as it seemed ridiculously absurd to touch such a foreboding monster.

He'd imagined how he would fight a beast of this size, should the need arise. Having worked out the imaginary confrontation, he was confident he could kill it, though undoubtedly not without sustaining serious injury. Fortunately, the creature had never shown a violent will – not that Connerh was in any rush to test his strategies.

Connerh thought for a second, then raised his hand towards the creature in a beckoning motion. The wolf stood but delayed, as if pondering the invitation. It began to walk towards him, albeit slowly and cautiously, before suddenly freezing dead in its tracks.

A growing warmth heated Connerh's backside, causing the hairs on his neck to stand. A familiar scent, a mix of vanilla, pomegranate, and a hint of jasmine, engulfed his nostrils. Rose's arm slid down his neck and around his chest as a smile creased his cheek. Her curls tickled his nose as he looked up at her, their lips embracing for an audible peck. He closed his eyes briefly as his tension began to dissipate, and his shoulders dropped when she caressed his face. Connerh raised his hand to embrace her arm just as it slid away. She retrieved the chalice he'd discarded, wiping it clean with her apron and promptly refilling it with the amphora she was holding.

"You looked bothered, and I thought to relieve you," her heavily accented voice offered.

Connerh turned his attention to the wolf, just in time to see the last quarter of its tail retreating into the tall grass.

'Perhaps another time,' he thought.

Rose gently rested her hand on his shoulder as she returned his chalice to his hand.

"Has the night brought you good news?" she asked, seeking to satisfy her own anxious curiosity.

They seldom discussed the content of his visions these days. They'd grown dark and grim, and their details kept her up at night not only due to their subject matter but also because they were sometimes nonsensical. Trying to assign meaning or a timeline to nonsensical things drove a person like her mental. Connerh rarely slept much and willingly accepted the burden alone. He would do his best to answer her questions in generic terms, protecting her peace of mind while still involving her in potentially life-altering decisions. The arrangement was not perfect, typically leaving her curiosity unsatiated, but it worked for them.

"Tonight was the same as it has been, but at the same time different, ever so slightly. But not enough to matter," his expression returned to frustration and disappointment. She kneeled to lock eyes with him.

"Is there anything I can do?" she inquired calmly. He shook his head, not wanting to speak further on it, gripping his chalice and pouring the wine down his throat as fast as gravity would allow. Rose took hold of his chalice hand and refilled the cup once more, all the while studying his face. Concern washed over her as she again attempted to lock eyes with him.

"Do you think it's avoidable? Or does it feel set in stone?" she pressed in a low tone. Her eyes attempted to dive into his mind as her personal desire for reassurance bled through, but he wouldn't look at her. She knew something was wrong. Her heart beat a little faster, but she tried her best not to grow flustered; he would shut down if she panicked.

He shook his head once more, looking down into his cup but hesitating to drink. He cleared his throat loudly. The acid in his stomach had shot up into his throat from drinking too fast, causing it to burn. The discomfort was momentarily unbearable.

Connerh cleared his throat again, loudly, which she took to mean he was holding back his emotions. She was not entirely wrong. She kept touching and rubbing him in an attempt to draw his attention, but it all became too much, like a bag being pulled tight over his head. He quickly stood and put some small distance between them, staring off into the night. It was easily the worst reaction she could have hoped for, and her internal panic heightened.

"Connerh…" Her soft voice broke the silence as she stood calmly. He acknowledged her but refused to turn and face her. Then, barely uttering the words, such that they almost came out as a whisper, she asked, "Is it…is it about me?"

He lowered his head but said nothing. She fought an expression which sought to prune her face. The desire for answers – and her frustration with his avoidance – aided her in winning the battle. She quickly set the amphora on the ground and ran to him, grabbing him by the arm once more, much to his ire. He looked at the hand that clutched him and then to her, indicating that he wished to be released. A coldness had overtaken him; he had seemingly put the darkness out of his mind already, for the moment anyway. His cold way was off-putting to her, and her head lurched back as she observed *the soldier* take control. It was an undesirable version of him.

As far as he was concerned, he had no choice other than to end the conversation; he'd already crossed a line he shouldn't have. Even with the little she knew compared to the towering mountain she had yet to comprehend, she still knew too much. Any further details would only be cruel.

"You don't get to do that," she scolded him.

He'd already promised himself that he would not argue with her – a decision that would only serve to inflame her further. He looked at the ground as he collected his thoughts. His face softened, and he realised he couldn't blame her. He reached out and pulled her into an embrace.

"Don't think on it. I just need to work it out, that's all," he tried to reassure her. The effect of his efforts was like pouring a glass of water on a forest fire, but she appreciated his attempt.

She went to speak, but he stopped her.

"There's time, don't worry," he continued.

"Should we break camp? Are we safe here? Is it time to relocate?"

Her mind hadn't slowed an inch – and then there was that subject. It was a sore one for Connerh. He had grown tired of relocating; he longed for the day they would no longer need to look over their shoulders, constantly running from prying eyes that sought to find them. They were both weary from the chase. It had been ten long years, and a part of him wished she would just leave and take the boy to start a new life elsewhere, in some place where his mere presence would not attract unwanted attention. They both knew that she and the boy deserved a better life. However, Connerh's own difficult childhood prevented him from forcing her away or abandoning the child. It was a course of action he could never rationalise. The last thing the world needed was another version of him roaming the land: a bastard with anger in his heart and a weapon in his hand. He seldom let his emotions, particularly fear, dictate his actions, but at present, nothing pushed him forward more than the fear of being unable to protect those dear to him. It seemed that their adversaries were closing in more swiftly than before, and each day that passed only brought the enemy nearer.

Perhaps running was not the answer, he thought.

"No," he replied finally, with firmness.

She looked up at him, confused about which question he was responding to.

He grabbed her hand and made full eye contact with her as he stated, "We're not running anymore." He paused, still processing the words as they came out of his mouth. Her excitement and confusion toppled over each other before he continued, motioning to their modest hut, "We don't have to stay here, but surely we can do better than this. Let's find a plot in the north, close to Nyradhal. We'll build something larger. We'll keep animals…perhaps start a farm. Give a normal life a try?"

Her eyes widened as she tried to ascertain whether he was being serious. Rose had dreamt of this moment for years but had long put it out of her mind. She'd become accustomed to finding contentment in being a nomad.

"But what about—" she started. He shook his head.

"Whatever comes, comes. I have kin there, and they will offer aid, should I ask it," he interjected. His energy level increased as his mind raced with the potential of his plan. What he needed was time. He also needed additional eyes to watch over Rose and the boy while he dealt with the enemy, but she didn't need to know that. What she needed was a distraction.

She squeezed him tightly and buried her head into his chest. Rose was optimistic, ecstatic, and anxious. The idea of having a home – a place to return to, that did not change every few months – was exciting. At the same time, the fear of the unknown, should they be found, worried her. His confidence in the matter was reassuring and silenced the panic within her…at least for the moment. Still, she resisted the urge to give in to emotion. She wanted to believe, but it felt too good to be true. Could they deserve such a thing? She turned her head for air, still resting on him.

He ran his hand through her hair. Her response was not what he had counted on, and the lack of excitement upset him a little, in truth. He lifted her chin to look at him. There was both hope and despair in her eyes. They stood quietly, an unspoken dialogue going on. Neither of them wished to utter words that might spoil the moment; that would be an unfortunate thing. Connerh knew what she was thinking by her facial expression and body language, and she him. His calm, confident, and reserved smile confirmed to her that his mind and heart were at least in a good place, and that was good enough for her. It would have to be.

Rose nodded her head repeatedly.

"We'll go," she agreed, smiling and giggling as he suddenly squeezed her and kissed her neck in celebration.

"Aeryk will want dogs…and a cave to explore. And his own room. With a door, preferably. I'm tired of having to bite my tongue in the twilight hours, good sir," she continued.

Connerh paused for a moment, then let out a loud laugh.

"Perhaps we start with just one dog, and there's no shortage of caves in Hildeheim. I may know a few experts… And there will be so many doors, you can scream as loud as your lungs will allow," he chuckled. She flared her eyebrows seductively as he held her from behind, facing the fire. Though some trepidation remained, her trust in him far outweighed the fear.

The fire in front of them crackled and snapped loudly as it consumed the wood in its belly. It offered a new focal point for both Connerh and Rose, and they gazed into the churning flame together, each one lost in their own thoughts, each one enraptured in a separate element. For Connerh, it was the ember. It destroyed even when the fire was extinguished. Memories of the past gave chase more ferociously than the soldiers he observed on the horizon. In order to free them from their tether, he would have to delve into his old ways. The familiar mantle of death and devastation was weightless for him, one he wielded with cold, careless precision.

That was, of course, before Rose and Aeryk entered the picture. It had been easier when he'd had nothing to lose, but now he had everything. For Rose, it was the ash. It clung to everything. The thought of having a normal life again was all-consuming, though some would debate that her past life was anything but normal. Despite having forged countless, priceless memories together over the past ten years, the thought of being able to settle down was priceless. It felt like she could stop running from her past, and finally, her life with Connerh would be allowed to begin. She never talked much about her life before Connerh, partly out of shame and partly out of not knowing how he would react. It helped matters that he never asked; she would hate very much to lie to him.

She, too, had a past, but unlike Connerh's, hers was shrouded in darkness, waiting for the most inopportune time to strike. It always lingered in the back of her mind. A sense of impending doom haunted her, likely the cause of her constant anxiety. Rose looked up at him, caressing his face once more as the guilt soured her stomach. She excused herself on the premise of needing to check on their dinner, but she already felt the vomit rising in her throat. She required privacy to expel her contrition.

He released her with a kiss and without complaint, as he, too, wished to consult his demons alone. Connerh maintained a smile until the door closed behind her. His shoulders raised, and his chest tightened as a dark spirit resumed within him.

He had thinking to do.

He lifted his arm and then extended it, his hand semi-cupped. His eyes slowly drifted closed. A spear made of gold and blackwood floated effortlessly towards him, rotating eerily in place. His eyes opened, observing it for a moment before it suddenly snapped into his grip. He expelled the air in his lungs loudly.

His breathing slowed.

His skin grew pale.

His temperature lowered.

CHAPTER FOUR

A Familiar Stranger

Elarion

Soft golden shafts of light pierced the shadow of the lush green canopy. A sea of fireflies painted the space between the leaves and the ground, offering their temporary light in an inaudible, asynchronous symphony. They appeared as stars drifting towards the ground, captured in a vast, invisible web. The wind carried the low echo of a melodic chorus throughout the forest. The sound bounced from tree to tree, making its origin impossible to detect while surrounding one from all directions. The forest's song was pleasantly encompassing, bringing comfort and tranquillity to all who chose to listen.

"They offer their thanks for sanctuary here and bid their farewell until the leaves fall and warmth returns." Elarion's deep voice resonated throughout the space.

"Absolutely breathtaking, Elarion. We have them in our forests, too, but never like this. They're considered pests where I come from," Curzon, his human guest, replied in awe. He almost seemed to take pride in his misinformed arrogance.

"They are noble and loyal creatures," Elarion passively corrected him.

"Everything here is heaven-sent. Hell, even the water smells good. I see why your people fight to protect its secrets. Just think of what we could do…one day…cohabiting in this place," the man continued, leaning over the balcony and ingesting the majesty the Wood Elves called home. He smiled as his eyes glazed over, inebriated by his own imagination.

To outsiders, it was called the Westwood; to the elves, it was just the Forest. Their home towered high above the forest floor, forming a magnificent tapestry woven amidst the branches of ancient trees. From small homes to massive structures, all intricately crafted from living wood and adorned with delicate carvings, they seemed to grow seamlessly from the trunks and limbs, as if an extension of the very trees that cradled them. The structures were connected by slender and gracefully arched bridges, forming a sprawling network among the treetops.

"The forest is far from a secret; many have known of and visited its splendour for as long as the elves have dwelled within its borders. We welcome all to enjoy the beauty it has to offer. We protect not secrets but the forest itself from those who seek to corrupt it. You would do well to remember that in your discussions with King Galathir," Elarion replied plainly, his posture stiffening.

Curzon turned to look at him, attempting to understand his meaning and change in demeanour. Elarion's stoic nature often made him hard to read. He meant nothing of ill will by the statement; it was purely factual, meant as helpful advice. The man smiled and reached up to pat Elarion on the shoulder.

"You're right. Thank you, my friend," he replied. Elarion nodded, pleased to have provided him with much-needed clarification.

Elarion was a tall male with chiselled features and a strong jaw, looking no older than forty years. He had long white hair that was held back by a wooden ornamental circlet. He kept one side of his head shaved low as an ode to his non-elf mother, who had died a few hundred or so years prior. Muscularly larger and slightly taller than an average Wood Elf on account of his being a half-blood, his darker complexion primarily betrayed that fact. Elven blood was thick, metaphorically speaking, and no amount of human blood could taint or water down his elven genes. On the contrary, the merger of his parents created rare mutations not seen in an age, his white hair and muscular physique being chief among them. By comparison, Wood Elves had dark chestnut hair and slim, athletic builds. His rarity was praised by his people. For this fact, along with their having higher sensibilities, Wood Elves didn't follow suit in looking down on what other races deemed half-breeds. Other noticeable features he had inherited from his mother were a portion of her pigment and some facial characteristics — the small dimple in his cheek, a human trait, was a feature easily missed since he smiled so rarely. Not in public, anyway.

Two armoured guards with spears and shields approached.

"The Lord King would see you now," the shorter of the two spoke in a hurried manner. Curzon's attention was redirected from a waterfall in the distance to the soldier who spoke to him. His smile widened. He took Elarion's hand and shook it, thanking him repeatedly.

"May you find what you seek," Elarion responded. He'd little faith in the fulfilment of his offering; it was simply the customary thing to say.

Elarion had granted him a rare audience with the king purely as a favour he and Galathir fully intended to collect on at a later time. The bigger the ask, the bigger the favour required to grease the palm…and this favour ranked highly in the 'big' category.

"I will await you in the garden below," he continued, bowing with a nod before slowly walking away, his hands folded behind his back. Elarion's ward moved from the shadows, following a few feet behind him. The older man bowed and went with the soldiers. Elarion paused before descending the ramp that led to the forest floor, remembering that he was being dutifully followed.

"Go, commune with the forest. I will send for you in the morning."

His tone had softened. He was fond of his ward, and not only because she, too, was a half-breed. Her elven mother had taken pity on a ginger halfling after an evening of indulgent drinking, ultimately marrying the lucky sap. The resulting breeding resulted in a human-sized, spritely young woman with fiery, red, curly hair and freckles painted across her face. Her optimistic energy kept him feeling young and hopeful. Elarion had lived an extended, fulfilled life through some good and some very dark times. Now, he longed to move on from this world as he waited for the Forest to take him. The winds of change had blown a dark spirit into the land that found comfort there, and with each generation, it grew darker. The world had drifted far from the way things had been before. Thaetra, born amidst the darkness, offered him a sliver of hope that things could change.

"Yes, Master," she bowed with a nod and quietly disappeared into the night.

Elarion waited a moment, then descended to the forest floor himself. He walked into the secluded garden and wandered around, checking on his favourite flowers — most of which he had planted himself. Most elves had a general green thumb, but he took a special interest in growing plants and vegetation not naturally found in these parts. The soil in the Forest had special properties and could successfully grow any seed, regardless of its origin. He plucked a pink lily and took it to a stone bench, where he sat, removing his circlet and setting it on the smooth surface next to him. He took a deep breath as he inhaled its fragrance, his eyes drifting closed. It was her favourite. He revealed a gold band attached to a necklace from under his shirt and held it tight, rubbing it with the pad of his thumb. A hundred or so fireflies descended upon him, sensing his discomfort, and he opened his eyes after seeing the introduction of light through his eyelids. He smiled at the display of respect and concern they offered him. Their synchronised flashing mimicked the pattern of calm breathing, and he studied them for a moment before understanding their meaning. Taking another deep breath, he synchronised his breathing with their display.

"Thank you for the honour you have given me. I wish you well on your journey," he spoke softly to them. They grew very bright, then, one by one, unsynchronised their pattern, accepting his appreciation. They lingered a while longer with him, and Elarion sat quietly, observing the fireflies as they flew in patterns to entertain him. Suddenly, a chill wind blew, causing the creatures to stifle their lights into abrupt darkness.

Elarion's smile faded as he covertly returned the band to under his shirt. His posture stiffened as he returned the circlet to sit atop his head.

"To what do I owe the honour of this visit?" he asked coldly as he moved to kneel upon the ground.

A cloaked figure shifted into the garden from the shadows. It moved quietly and spoke nothing, instead communicating telepathically. Elarion nodded, then stood.

"As you wish," he continued. He had the ability to converse with thought, but he refused to. Call it subtle defiance or silent protest, the feelings he felt were the same. They walked together through the garden. Elarion nodded from time to time as he listened, his hands folded behind his back, his eyes always looking forward.

The stranger stopped and looked at him, waiting for a response.

"I will do as you ask, but I will not betray him," Elarion sighed and replied sternly.

"I'm not asking you to," the stranger responded vocally, their voice morphing eerily from masculine to feminine. The stranger turned their attention to a nearby rosebush and pulled a stem from it. They marvelled at the sharp, nasty thorns hidden behind the bloom of the flower.

"Isn't it ironic that, hidden behind beauty, one often finds painful secrets?" they scoffed and discarded the rose on the ground. Their voice deepening to a masculine tone, the stranger continued, "See it done, my friend."

They walked off hurriedly and vanished into the shadows. Warmth returned to the garden.

Elarion sighed forcefully, kneeling to retrieve the discarded rose stem. He carefully lifted the flower, smelling it. Removing a dagger from his waistband, he trimmed the stem and found a place for it before planting it into the ground.

"We all deserve second chances," he whispered.

His quiet companions began to glow again. He could barely offer a smile; his mood was ruined. Elarion said his goodbyes in Elvish and departed from them.

Elarion stood on the balcony outside the king's throne room. The large metal doors thundered as they opened. Curzon walked out, clearly excited.

"Elarion! I thought I would find you in your garden," he announced.

"I found it difficult…to find peace there. I needed a walk," Elarion responded. Pointedly changing the subject, he asked, "Did you find what you were seeking?"

"Perhaps…perhaps, my good man!" Curzon's chubby cheeks blushed with elation.

Elarion raised an eyebrow in disbelief but quickly composed himself, washing the expression from his face.

"I hate to cut my visit short, but I need to return home to make preparations. I hope you will allow me to take you up on your offer of dinner another time," Curzon seemed genuinely disappointed, disorienting Elarion momentarily.

"Of course. Your journey is a long one, and I understand your eagerness to return," he responded. "Would you like me to see you out?"

"That's not necessary. You seem…preoccupied. I can find my own way," Curzon replied, displaying concern. Elarion raised his hand and summoned a nearby guard.

"Very well. I will provide a guide, just in case." Elarion motioned to the guard who approached, commanding, "Accompany our guest to retrieve his belongings and to rejoin those who came with him. Replenish any supplies they may need for the journey."

The guard acknowledged the order. Elarion wasn't overly concerned with Curzon getting lost; rather, the elves were generally distrusting of strangers, even familiar ones, wandering about.

"Thank you, Elarion. Please give my regards to your ward. I thoroughly enjoyed her company," Curzon said, expressing his gratitude. They exchanged their farewells, and Curzon departed, guard in tow. Elarion watched them grow smaller in the distance before entering the king's chamber.

"Why do they always want something that isn't being offered?" Galathir's voice echoed off the massive walls. He removed his crown and placed it on the throne, exchanging it for the chalice of wine he was being offered. His cupbearer bowed and left the room as Elarion approached, his brow arched once again.

"You're sending soldiers to Brookehaven?" Elarion disregarded the offer in favour of bantering.

"I never agreed to such a thing. Is that what he told you?" Galathir responded with a smirk.

"Well, no…not exactly," Elarion replied, suddenly feeling slightly sheepish. His human emotions briefly betrayed him.

"I told him what he needed to hear. Besides, would it really be so bad to send a detachment to patrol Brookehaven's borders as a courtesy among allies?" Galathir questioned. Elarion scowled at the word 'allies.' Galathir motioned for Elarion to follow him to the balcony before he offered Elarion a chalice of his own, which Elarion declined with an upright palm.

"I'd rather we not get involved in territory disputes or the inner squabbles of outsiders," Elarion countered.

"That's all this is about, cousin: territory. That's all it ever is with men. Violent arguments over invisible lines drawn in the sand; battles and wars over stones and rocks they have no more control over than the direction in which the ocean flows. And what if the Mountain Queen, the golden goat lover, and the two pathetic dirt piles they call kingdoms to their south take offence at our…little stroll?" he smirked slyly. "What would they do? March against us? We would destroy them in open battle. We outnumber them twenty to one!"

Galathir spread his arms, drawing Elarion's attention to the endless tree city. Elarion listened quietly, giving thought to Galathir's reasoning.

"I would beg them to try it," his tone twisted nefariously.

Elarion frowned as he looked upon his cousin, asking, "Since when does the forest beg for blood?"

He crossed his arms, taking a slow step backwards. Galathir took notice, glancing away before regaining his composure. He slid closer to Elarion and wrapped an arm around his shoulder.

"Worry not; I understand your concern. That's why this temporary alliance is necessary. We need to expand and adapt," Galathir's tone turned sombre.

"Men and dwarves' fascination with machines and fire will one day threaten to destroy this place..." He ran his hand over the tree trunk near them, drifting briefly into despair before pulling himself back and continuing, "We need to expand to the south, spread out, and grow even greater in numbers. Then, and only then, can we protect the forest in its entirety. In just two generations, we will absorb Curzon's kingdom." He stared into Elarion's eyes, which avoided his own, before he concluded, "It will all be ours, without needing a single drop of blood to be spilt."

Sensing he was about to voice something negative, Galathir moved quickly to put his finger over Elarion's mouth.

"What is that to us? A generation for them is but a cycle to our kind. They come and go like the desires of the wind, but the will of the elves stands through time," he lectured. Then, pleading playfully, Galathir pressed, "You could attend another human wedding ceremony...or four, couldn't you?"

Elarion frowned and folded his arms, beginning to protest, "I am not..."

"Relax," Galathir interrupted, offering relief to his beloved cousin as he continued, "I wouldn't ask that much of you. I have many sons to offer the daughters of Curzon."

Elarion relaxed his guard...slightly.

"There's always the second option." A devilish grin crept onto Galathir's face as he turned his back on him.

"What now?" Elarion inquired, fresh out of patience with Galathir's nonsense.

"You could allow me to retire... Take the crown yourself and do things your way," he turned to reveal his smile. Elarion rolled his eyes.

"You will not rest until I am sufficiently tortured, is that it?" he sniped.

"I will not. You will give me what I want, whether in this era or the next," Galathir playfully demanded. Elarion shook his head in silent protest, although an eventual smile – the kind never seen in public – tugged at his lips. Galathir sat on the balcony next to his cousin, and both looked out over the city, enjoying a moment of quiet reflection.

Elarion looked down at his feet, then back again.

"Because it's always easier to want…even lust after what one doesn't have, in favour of what one deserves," he mused introspectively.

"What?" Galathir replied.

"You asked…why do they always want what is not being offered? Or in other words…what they can't have," he replied, including Galathir in his ongoing thought experiment. Then, with a twinge of guilt, he continued, "That is your answer. The heart wants what it wants, absent the mind. Absent logic."

Galathir gazed into the pool of nothingness, contemplating his words.

"I suppose…" he eventually uttered, caught off guard and clueless as to how to proceed.

"I know in my heart you intend to do what's right. I'm just…" Elarion started. Galathir began to understand.

"Tired? Like an hourglass almost fully spent?" Galathir finished his sentence. Elarion nodded in agreement.

"Yes," he replied. It was all he could muster.

"You wear your indifference like a badge of honour as of late, cousin. I often wonder what keeps you by my side."

His words stung Elarion, disarming him. His mouth fell agape as he thought on how to respond to the implication.

"Still your heart. It is because you have given up on this world. Be patient; there is more to see, more to be done. But first, this age must pass. It is the process of life, death, and rebirth. You keep dwelling on the middle, but it is not the end," Galathir replied, running his hand over the shaved portion of Elarion's head before sliding it down to his chest, just above the hidden ring. Galathir patted it once before retracting his hand. Elarion looked up at him with defeated eyes before turning his attention to the city once more. He found it difficult to refute Galathir's words.

Galathir turned away from him, staring into the forest.

"Go. I give you leave from your obligation. Roam the land for a generation and come back to me once you have found the fire you once had. Take a bride…or three. Sire children, start a new city, and re-join me at my side. I'll send twenty thousand with you. Perhaps fifty? Tell me what it is you desire, and I will see it done," Galathir pretended not to care, bordering on no longer amused with the direction of the conversation. In reality, he was hoping to stave his cousin from the obvious eventuality of their separation.

"It is ironic that you should say that…" Elarion replied, delivering a wounding blow.

"Oh?" Galathir struggled to maintain his composure.

"I need to take my leave for a time," Elarion said. Galathir raised his brow for a moment before it sunk into a devious smirk.

"What is her name, cousin?" he pressed. Elarion looked away.

"Ioelena the Fourth, Queen of Hildeheim," he replied plainly.

"The Mountain Queen?" Galathir responded in shock, his voice ascending an octave. He continued jokingly, "Quite the overachiever, aren't we? Though I admittedly admire your confidence."

Elarion rolled his eyes as he replied, "It is not of a romantic nature."

"Pity," Galathir replied, playfully disappointed. Then, facetiously, "Is everything alright? Do you run to betray my confidence so quickly?"

Elarion thought for a moment.

"No, not at all. This was my intent prior to knowing yours. The winds compel me north," he replied.

It was an Elvish expression meant to convey that his reasons were private or unknown. It was an expression the king was not accustomed to hearing, but as his cousin, Elarion enjoyed a special privilege. Still, it made Galathir no less uncomfortable in not knowing. He could demand the truth, but he would not.

"Very well. Keep your secrets," he said suspiciously, his brows raised with a smirk and his palms turned upwards. Truth be told, he was slightly offended. While they were only cousins, they were much closer to brothers in bond.

"I mean not to bother you with…" Elarion began, sensing his cousin's discomfort.

"No, it's alright," Galathir cut him off, raising his hand. Then, pointing towards Elarion's face, he demanded, "As long as you come back in good spirits and are ready to provide me seven nephews and three nieces! Only then will you have my blessing."

"Will you settle for good spirits?" Elarion smiled.

"It's a start. I suppose I find your terms acceptable — adding that you take your ward with you. She needs to see the world. Besides, I need someone to keep an eye on you," he smiled. Elarion thought to protest but resisted, knowing it to be futile.

"Very well. I will depart after the Elderharts' visit," he replied.

"There's no need to delay; I can very much handle the visit myself," Galathir replied. He could see Elarion was troubled by the thought of skipping the tradition, so he continued, "I will inform them of your quest."

"Do we know yet who of the elders come this way?" Elarion questioned. Galathir gently shook his head.

"Lysand and Oroben have been seen wandering a day or two away, so it is likely them, but I cannot say for sure," he replied.

Elarion's eyes dropped in thought. His focus was interrupted by Galathir's hand on his shoulder.

"I will free you from your internal turmoil: I order you to leave on your quest," he announced, somewhat forcefully.

Elarion grinned with a nod.

"Keep your ears to the dirt and your back to the wind," Galathir whispered into his ear, then pressed a kiss to Elarion's brow. He drew back and started toward his chamber. At the doorway, he paused and turned—watching Elarion stand exactly where he'd left him, motionless, eyes fixed on the void.

There was an obvious conflict within him.

Galathir looked to the guard standing by the door.

"Quietly send for his ward. Bring her to me."

CHAPTER FIVE

THE HAND THAT ROCKS THE CRADLE

HARGATHA

The rhythmic and thunderous tapping of Hargatha's heeled boots did slightly more to announce her arrival than her striking features or stature, though they were no less successful. Her flowing bone-white hair, blue eyes, and pale skin were illuminated against her eye-catching attire. Unlike her husband and kin, who preferred their tribal garments, she dressed in a more progressive manner. She was typically adorned in blood-coloured gowns, laced and bordered in black, fitted underneath a black, armoured bodice affixed with silver ornaments...and matching gauntlets. It was a fashionable choice that projected a battle-ready appearance, appropriately befitting the Hand of the Queen.

Despite her height reaching seven feet and five inches, she found moving around the castle to be an effortless affair. In its formative years, Hildeheim was built by the giants that once ruled over it. With the elder giants averaging ten to twelve feet tall, the younger and smaller generations found the rooms and corridors within the capital's castle quite spacious. Years of inbreeding, specifically with humans, had resulted in the giants becoming smaller with each era, much to the ire of older traditionalists. While Hargatha was far from a traditionalist herself, she certainly respected the old ways – but she also recognised their flaws, going so far as to view some as potential vulnerabilities.

She opened the large metal doors to her official chamber and took inventory of who awaited her inside. Upon seeing several viceroys seated, their attention now focused on her, she offered a brief smile and turned to one of the guards stationed nearby.

"I will speak with my husband now. Send him in immediately," she declared, not allowing time for them to acknowledge her order.

She casually entered the room, closing the doors behind her. Hargatha walked slowly to her seat at the head of the table, the vibration of her steps causing concentric circles to emerge in the wine held within the viceroys' chalices. Her scent filled the air, a combination of freshly muddled juniper berries and bergamot, which added an additional layer to the ongoing mental fantasies of some of the men. Their effort to conceal their thoughts was feeble, bordering on patently pathetic. The slightly agape mouths, slow-roaming tongues, and low-slung eyes that tracked specific parts of her anatomy with each passing second painted a very specific picture of what preoccupied their thoughts.

She didn't blame them for their inwards lack of dignity. After all, they were not decorated court officials but mere rats plucked from the trash heap for a singular purpose. They were tasked with serving as intermediaries between the crown and the local bureaucracy, including esteemed governors and governesses, often assuming a more forceful role when needed. Men of their station understood that they were both readily disposable and replaceable. The realisation and acceptance of this fact came with a price, and thus, a certain calibre of man emerged – albeit a low one.

Hargatha was fully aware of how the desire to possess that which one could not have could be so tempting. Giants had an innately violent nature towards all things non-giant. It was an insatiable thirst that took ages to control, but by now, living in a more civilised age, they had learned to suppress those urges – for the most part. Since she had to contain and conceal her primal desire to savagely dismember them all, she too expected a certain level of decorum in her presence. After all, even rats could be trained to assemble in an orderly manner.

She deliberately pulled her large chair away from the table, letting it scrape against the black stone ground as if to snap them out of their delusions. The scraping continued just long enough to cause physical discomfort, the sound causing their eyes to squint and their faces to wrinkle. She sat gracefully and began to unfasten her gauntlets, leaning back in her chair.

"Now that I have your attention, here is what you are going to do for me, gentlemen," she asserted, unfastening the leather straps around her wrists and forearms. "I am going to fill every single one of your crevices..."

As she paused for effect, Hamish, the Queen's Clergy Master, frowned, shaking his head as it descended into his palm. He'd long given up on encouraging her to speak in a statelier manner when addressing the viceroys, and at this point, she knew that he was convinced she purposely thought of new ways to make him uncomfortable.

There may have been some truth to that theory.

"I will be sending my little spiders to every corner of your provinces. I want to know when you open a new cask of wine and when you dispose of it in your chamber pot. It is information that I seek, and it is information that you will provide. You will furnish my representatives with whatever resources they require, ensuring you stay out of their way. It might get loud and become quite messy. However, it would be in your best interests to avert your gaze. Be patient; once my prey has been retrieved, I will soon be out of your hair," she snarled.

The term "spiders" was metaphorical in nature, symbolising her spies and eyes across the kingdom. Men-for-hire who were loyal only to her and the crown, willing to report or undertake whatever she deemed necessary. The term was first coined due to an initially unappealing nickname she earned, the Black Widow, which she later embraced and incorporated into her attire.

Hargatha hurled her large gauntlets onto the centre of the table, the resonant clash of metal-on-metal echoing and seizing the viceroys' attention. The size of her gauntlets dwarfed their own forearms. Occasionally, she possessed a flair for the dramatic, deeming it necessary to ignite the hearts of men.

"Can we humbly ask what it is that you are looking for?" one of the viceroys asked.

"Or who?" another added before the first could finish. Hargatha leaned forward in her chair.

"No," she said plainly, an eyebrow raised. However, her tone drifted into a seductive half-whisper when she continued, "But when I am done, I will pay you for your silence...and you will thank me."

Hamish rolled his eyes, crossing his arms.

"How will we know who these men are?" yet another piped up.

"Men, women, children...they will be everyone and everywhere... You will know who they are when and only when the need arises," she countered. The viceroys grumbled to one another.

The large metal doors to her chamber opened; Galabrand's head and white hair entered the room before he did. There wasn't a need for him to duck through the doorway, but he had been accustomed to doing so.

"Consider yourself formally dismissed," she ordered as she stood. The viceroys quickly evacuated their chairs and filed out of the room. Galabrand snarled at them as they skittered by him. Unlike his wife, he'd been known to indulge his baser nature – and, as he typically appeared to be in a sour mood most of the time, non-giants did their best to avoid him, if at all possible. He walked towards Hargatha as the doors closed.

"Husband, come, help me out of this thing," she requested, turning around and scooping her hair over her shoulder, exposing the laces of her bodice. He sighed loudly, as he famously did in response to most things.

"Surely you did not summon me to attend to your wardrobe," his deep voice echoed lightly.

"Surely you aren't complaining about undressing me," she playfully frowned as she peeked over her shoulder. Galabrand shook his head and began undoing the clasps and laces of her bodice.

"That is not what I said," he protested, arching a brow.

She cupped the bodice with one hand as it broke free from the last clasp, instantly stretching her back. He took a step back to give her room to extend her limbs.

"Thank you, Brand," she leaned in to kiss him. He smirked, unsure of what she was getting at.

"I'll never understand why you wear these things. There's nothing like the comfort of a good bearskin and some leather," he smiled while patting his own attire.

"You don't think I look good in red?" she flirted with him, still cupping her chest and glancing over her shoulder coquettishly.

"I think you look smashing in anything you wear, and definitely better taking it off."

He smiled once more, and she couldn't help but laugh. She turned fully to him and dropped her bodice to the ground. The metal ornaments clanked loudly on the floor. She lifted her foot to rest on the seat of her chair and began removing her boots. Her full curves, previously suppressed by the confines of her armour, now spilt out of her top, naturally catching his glance. He shook his head; none of this made sense to him. She looked up, noticing that he was watching, and smirked at the focus of his attention as she fought to loosen her boots. Suddenly, it clicked for him.

"I see…" he said as his smile faded. She stepped out of her boots, her height lowering noticeably. Though she was not intentionally trying to seduce him, she was aware of the potential and, in truth, had hopes that watching her would put him in a more malleable mood. Hargatha thought to play innocent for a moment, but she quickly abandoned the idea due to its futility. They hadn't been newlyweds in over seventy human years. Her shoulders sank. Galabrand folded his arms, sighed again, and leaned against a nearby column.

"What am I getting involved in at the behest of my niece on this day?" he asked, insulted by what he perceived to be her approach to the topic. Her brow sunk and her eyes widened. She was overwhelmed with thoughts – fears and problems she hadn't quite worked out yet. Unaware of how to begin, she looked away and instead turned to walk towards her small balcony. Galabrand frowned and pushed off from the pillar, following her. He'd not seen her like this in a long time.

"What is it, my sweet?" he quickly closed the gap and rested his hands on her waist, pulling her into a rear hug.

Aside from him being the love of her life, it was calming to be engulfed by him. It was not often she felt small, living and working in the castle surrounded by humans, dwarves, and halflings.

"Don't be angry, but I don't believe it would be a good idea to give you all the details. In fact, I mean not to," she turned her head up to look at him but settled on his neck, not wanting to make eye contact. He studied her face and remained quiet as she ran her hand through his shaped, grey beard. Galabrand carefully pulled away from her and stood to her side.

"Come, now. Lay it on me – or, that is to say, tell me what you feel I can handle," he replied flippantly.

She went to speak to defend herself; he raised his hand to silence her. She stopped abruptly and paused.

"Very well," she stared him in the eye now, slightly angered. Her head snapped back and forth, and she prepared herself for his reaction. Fussing, she said, "You want the full, raw truth…so be it. Don't say I didn't warn you."

Galabrand's eyes squinted, realising that perhaps he was asking for something he really didn't want. Hargatha had a record of being right when she ended a sentence with that phrase – even their two children had grown to hate the expression. He held up his hand again to stop her, closed his eyes, and took a deep breath. He subtly shook his fist in the air, then opened his eyes and motioned for her to continue.

"Don't. Ruin. My. Chamber!" she pointed her finger sharply towards him, punctuating each word with a sharp jab in the air. He canted his head, now thoroughly engaged.

"What coul—" he started.

"Connerh is alive. And she knows!" she shouted, cutting him off.

Galabrand's eyes shot wide. His fists curled as he immediately looked around to smash something, the internal fight to show restraint apparent.

"Don't you dare!" she shouted at him.

He marched back into her chamber and grabbed her chair.

"Not mine!" she yelled, folding her arms and moving out of his way.

He snarled and grabbed another chair, dragging it to the balcony and throwing it as far as he could into the air and distance, shouting all the while. They both stood in silence and watched as the chair fell slowly into the crashing waves far below the balcony.

"Feel better?" she asked sarcastically.

"Barely," he replied, chest heaving.

She grabbed his hand and pulled him back into her chamber, then over to a giant map sprawled across a table.

"She wants to bring him here."

"Of course she does," he interrupted in one frustrated exhale.

"We can do it, quietly," she continued.

"He will ruin her…again," he frowned, his tone dramatically lowered. Galabrand held a special disgust for menfolk, disliking even his twin brother's wife. However, he had an undeniable soft spot for her daughter, his niece, often showing her preferential treatment over his own children.

"I don't believe so. But this is obviously a delicate situation. We can't let Vidar find out; you know what he'll do," she looked at him with a concerned expression.

"Oh, he'd try, but he would fail miserably. Our son may have my temper, but he lacks the brain to control it," he remarked. Continuing, he said, "You'll not be able to hide it from him indefinitely. But, when the time comes, I will be the one to handle him."

Hargatha caressed his face, pleased with his reasonableness as she murmured, "I need your help looking over my plan. Time will be working against us, if we are to do this correctly."

And with a flip of the switch, she became the Hand of the Queen again, grabbing little figurines from nearby to position on the map.

CHAPTER SIX

BLOOD OF THE MOTHER

ELARION

Thaetra quietly observed Elarion as they made their gradual traversal of the eastern edge of the forest on horseback. Their pace had slowed in the last hour from a steady gallop to deliberate pathing. He'd altered their route, oddly without making a single mention of it – not that his station required that he should. She'd been silently stalking his expressions, movements, and demeanour from a distance for the better part of an hour. He exuded nothing. There was nothing she could extrapolate; nothing she could determine to be out of place. Her focus was so intense that she barely noticed as his steed came to a complete stop, and she narrowly avoided crashing into him. He lowered his head to the left, in her direction, stopping just short of turning to face her.

"Go ahead and ask your questions." His calm and assertive voice barely broke the ambience of the deepwood. Her head sank into her shoulders like a pup being scolded.

"Why are we travelling so close to the border? Passage through Tu'Chauri lands is forbidden, let alone the unnecessary risk posed by being so close," her voice pushed and pulled as she navigated concern, insistence, and curiosity.

Elarion listened patiently at first, then turned to look at her to confirm the source of her tone. She was genuinely conflicted and confused.

"I know my cousin has commissioned you to report on me," he said plainly, staring her in the eyes while casually studying her face. He broke eye contact for a few moments, allowing her the dignity and privacy to decide how she would react. Her mind raced, despite her decision being clearly made.

"He did, Master, but I would never…" she began. He held up his hand to stop her.

"I would never presume to ask you to violate your oath," he countered.

Further confusion overwhelmed her desire to express relief. He beckoned for her to approach, and she complied, heel-kicking her steed.

"I want to prepare you for the potential that perhaps I will. I sense your conflict and would not want to put you in a position that would bring you dishonour," he frowned, breaking eye contact with her.

Thaetra took quick inventory of his change in expression before she, too, avoided looking at him directly. She thought quietly for a moment, reaching out to touch his arm as she murmured, "My report will not change."

He looked up at her.

"We rode through the forest to the border of Hildeheim," she offered him a slight smirk. A small crease imprinted into his cheek in return.

"Very well," he conceded. Then, his eyes dropped as he continued, "There's something you may not know about me, Thaetra."

Her brow raised in curiosity.

"My mother was Tu'Chauri…" He felt the urge to reach for his hidden necklace at the sudden resurgence of memories, but he resisted. He looked back at her, then finished, "…as was my mate. But that was a very, very long time ago."

His eyes squinted as he quickly dismissed the attached feelings. His lungs involuntarily filled with air, expelling it again almost immediately. She stared at him intently, unsure of how to proceed in the conversation. She was aware of his mother and mate not being of elven descent, but the details of their origin were not a common topic of discussion, even among the private circles she would occasionally and unintentionally eavesdrop on while she waited for him in the shadows.

Or at least, that was what she'd convinced herself had happened.

Elves had never placed importance on that sort of issue, yet the Tu'Chauri were mortal enemies of the Forest. The elves were virtuous, but they were not perfect. In some ways, it was shocking to her that this small but important detail would have been so obscured from public knowledge, though in reality, most things Tu'Chauri were not discussed.

"I seek information; nothing more. If at any point you find yourself uncomfortable, depart to the west, and I will meet with you at the turning stone near the Hildeheim border in just a few hours. Do you understand my meaning?" His tone went through a spectrum of change as he worked out possible outcomes.

"Yes. Yes, Master, I understand," she replied after a brief lag, finding displeasure in the thought of being sent away.

"We will encounter shadows from my past. I take great self-risk in exposing you to such darkness, but I fear my personal discretion is no longer a priority. The winds are blowing aggressively in a new direction, and I must do what I must for my people," he thought meaningfully while speaking in an unrehearsed manner. "Do you understand my meaning?" he asked again.

She nodded heavily. He wished to ask more of her. However, the potential impropriety of doing so prevented him.

"And what are you to do, should you feel the inclination? Or if I should ask it of you?" he sought to validate the plan. For the first time, she could feel his anxiety. In the moment, she felt honoured that he would lower his guard in front of her, but the significance of it made her fearful for him. In the moment, she never thought to consider her own safety.

"I'll depart to the northwest, where I will meet you in a few hours' time," she hesitantly confirmed. Regurgitating the words only increased her desire and intent to disregard them completely, staying with him no matter the outcome or consequence.

He nodded in agreement as his mind wandered, struggling with a crawling regret to include her. She had no idea the lengths his cousin's jealousy would reach, should he discover her disloyalty, yet the internal voice driving him was louder and more insistent than any potential dangers. He quietly heel-kicked his steed and proceeded deeper into the forest.

Thaetra now followed closely behind him, her focus sharply tuned to the shadows lurking across and beyond the border, where there was movement she had not noticed before. They were being watched.

The scenery was changing. The lush green foliage of the elven forest had begun to fade. The soil was different; the air was different. A rolling fog permeated the ground as plants and trees emerged in an almost alien colour palette of purple, black, auburn, and yellow. It seemed as if the life force of the forest had been drained here. Large breaks in the canopy allowed the sunlight to penetrate the layer of fog and water vapour, giving it a thick, opaque appearance. Still, despite the landscape's off-putting appearance, there was a sweet aroma hanging in the air – that promptly turned bitter at the back of your tongue, like poison.

Elarion came to a standstill.

"We'll cross over shortly. Cover your mouth and nose; protect your breathing. It will buy you some time to see what was meant to be concealed. Use this knowledge at your discretion. This fog is not of nature's creation, and while it will soon overtake your attempts to shield yourself from it, do not fear; it will not cause you harm. The mist will manipulate your mind to make you see many things, some of which will be frightening, some of which will not be real. Trust only my voice," he paused for a moment, making sure she had absorbed his words, "and my way of speaking."

He locked eyes with her. She looked terrified as she hurried to put on a mask that covered her face, leaving only her eyes exposed. She retrieved two sprigs, one of an orange flower and one of a red flower, from a pouch around her waist and placed them between the layers of her mask.

"Don't worry; we are protected by the blood of my mother. Stay close," he continued.

As if on cue, thirty steed-mounted shadows emerged from the nearby treeline across the border. The riders approached rapidly, as if to intercept them. Their horses were black and muscular, with yellow eyes shielded behind blinders that focused their attention forward. The lead rider came to a sudden stop at the physical border; those with him spread out in a semicircle. His horse breathed heavily, stomping its front legs in place. Thaetra's bow was drawn with an arrow nocked, though she aimed it at the ground.

The rider's face was concealed with a war mask resembling a boar's head. He was quite muscular, tall, and covered in tattoos down his neck and across his mostly exposed body. His dark brown and auburn hair was braided, with four threads of a golden colour woven in among them. They all wore long purple earrings resembling a cluster of dark flowers.

He and Elarion slowly approached each other, face to face. The foliage beneath them was just as juxtaposed: half green, half a palish purple. Thaetra quietly pulled her bowstring back a few inches.

"Are you two alone?" the rider asked. His accented voice was slightly muffled behind the mask.

"We are," Elarion replied.

"Is she going to try to kill me the entire time?" he asked with a tinge of humour.

Elarion looked back at Thaetra and waved his hand towards the ground, signalling her to relax. She hesitantly obliged, returning her bow to its place and opting instead to rest her hand on the hilt of her sword. Elarion returned his gaze to his counterpart.

"Most likely," he replied.

The rider laughed loudly, nodding to himself. He twirled his finger up in the air, and his men slowly backed off a few feet, as did his own horse.

"Well, then, welcome home, brother," he splayed his fingers, his hand outstretched towards the dark woodland.

Thaetra's eyes grew wide, and she and Elarion crossed over into the dark forest. Their horses' slow trot quickly progressed into a violent gallop, kicking up swirls of the mist beneath them. Thaetra tucked her head close to her steed, looking behind them as her own forest shrank in the distance, eventually disappearing altogether. She returned her focus to Elarion and increased in speed to catch up to him.

After nearly an hour, the once-bitter aftertaste of the aroma that engulfed this place began to taste pleasant to her.

"The smell has altered," she whispered to him as she matched speed alongside him. His eyes dropped for a moment.

"You don't have much longer. Remain strong. Remember what I have told you," he said calmly, although his brow was heavy.

They rode aggressively for another half hour before slowing in pace, then eventually stopping. The rider circled a spot with his horse and dismounted. Elarion followed suit, helping Thaetra down from her own steed; she was struggling to maintain focus and thoroughly appreciated his assistance. The rider's men circled them, still mounted, but they quickly turned in place, facing away from the trio at the centre.

The rider removed his mask and set it upon his horse. Thaetra fought her eyes' desire to wander, settling on observing him as he secured his belongings to his steed. The tips of his ears were noticeably mangled. She instinctively ran a hand over her own ear as the sight triggered a phantom pain. A thought occurred to her; her brows furrowed as she dismissed it immediately. The foliage around them seemed to grow in brightness and vibrancy, while those surrounding her became muted in colour.

"The horses need to rest," the rider announced, still facing away from Elarion and Thaetra.

Elarion rolled his eyes, knowing full well that this was not the reason for their stopping.

"She's of strong will to have lasted this long," the rider continued.

Elarion helped Thaetra into a sitting position on the ground. The words were a blur to her; her focus shifted to her hands, which seemed to be distorting in shape and size.

"Lover?" he asked as he turned to face Elarion. Elarion stared back, expressionless, and he continued, "No, of course not. They would never allow you to indulge in such pleasurable pursuits." He probed Elarion's face, but upon seeing that his attempt to provoke him was futile, he changed the conversation by asking, "So, what is it you have come to tell us?"

Thaetra's hearing began to clarify, though she was still distracted by her warped surroundings.

"I will share it in the presence of your king, Bakaru. I'll not get involved in your quest for glory. That is not why I am here," Elarion quipped sharply. Bakaru pursed his lips with a raised brow.

"That's what you do best, is it not? Not get involved," he replied to a non-responsive Elarion.

Again, Elarion stared blankly back at Bakaru without so much as a blink of his eyes. His stoicism not-so-secretly brought discomfort to his brother.

"Is that an act?" Bakaru started, gesturing to Elarion's expressionless face. "Or do you truly not care? Are you really so cold?"

His face grew saddened. A part of Elarion wanted to reply to him sincerely, despite being convinced Bakaru's emotions were just a ruse. Though in truth, the sibling emotions within him rather enjoyed watching Bakaru pitifully pivot his technique. Either way, they were wasting time here.

"Why are you talking to yourself? Did they leave us?" Thaetra unintentionally muttered. Her eyes darted back and forth as her world continued to spin. She squinted and forced herself to focus on Elarion. Bakaru smiled and scoffed.

"You don't talk about me? I'm offended, Elarion. Of course, I suppose I shouldn't be surprised; I am the better-looking one," he commented, amusing himself.

Elarion kneeled next to Thaetra and rested his hand on her shoulder. Bakaru walked closer and kneeled in front of her.

"Hello," he spoke slowly, drawing out the word.

Her head rocked to rest on her opposite shoulder as she looked up at him. His full-body tattoos and the markings above and below his eyes appeared to glow to her. His face was familiar. The ring in his nose reflected real sunlight and drew her attention from his face for a brief moment. She refocused, immediately letting loose a blood-curdling scream and crawling backwards with her hands. Elarion and Bakaru both stood, appearing as mirror images of one another. Her head shot back and forth as she observed them both. Elarion had a restful aura glowing about his body, while Bakaru appeared as his luminescent evil twin, albeit with mutilated ears. Bakaru's devious smirk did little to help his distorted appearance.

"Be still. The choice is yours," Elarion said calmly, reminding her of his earlier words.

She gathered herself, doing her best to avoid looking at Bakaru directly. She shook her head quietly, declining to leave him.

Turning his attention to his brother, Elarion spoke sternly, "Enough of this. I will not help you betray your king, no matter how many are with you. Trust me, I am here on behalf of you all." He grabbed Bakaru's arm and leaned into his ear, whispering, "For what's coming, that is not a seat it would be wise to occupy, brother."

He pulled back and stared into Bakaru's widened eyes. Bakaru processed his meaning and nodded slowly as his shoulders relaxed.

"She has suffered enough," Elarion continued, gently scolding them.

Bakaru nodded again, then spoke in his native language to one of his riders. The rider reached into his saddlebags and tossed Bakaru a small flask, which he handed to Elarion.

"Thank you," he replied sincerely. He walked over to Thaetra and kneeled next to her, then instructed in a low tone, "Drink; it will reduce the effects of the mist."

She complied, enamoured by his glow.

"We'll head to the capital. It will be nightfall when we arrive, so you will stay with me and mine. I'll take you to see the king when the sun rises. Does this please you?" Bakaru asked as he mounted his horse. Elarion nodded in agreement, and he continued in a softened tone, "Your nephews look forward to seeing you, by the way."

A gentle smile crept onto Elarion's face.

FROZEN DEVOTION

VIDAR

A steady stream of snowflakes descended slowly from the holes in the breached ceiling. Light shafts protruded through the cracked openings, catching and illuminating the delicate wisps of frozen platelets as they accumulated into little piles on the ground. The air was frigid but calm inside the dilapidated temple at Gryphon's Rest, providing eerie yet resolute shelter from the windstorm outside. The once-consecrated holy ground now played host to a variety of flying creatures seeking shelter from inclement weather, mostly clinging to the darkest and most isolated corners of the massive structure. Loose bones and partially decomposed skeletons littered the ground among broken and splintered pieces of wood and metal, originating from broken burglary equipment and pews that were once affixed to the floor. Decades of bandits and scavengers had been judiciously efficient at looting any and everything of value that could be dragged safely down the mountainside.

The destruction and desolation abruptly ended roughly thirty feet from the centre of the temple, where an object stood surrounded by pristine ornaments of gold, silver, and brilliantly coloured gemstones. Unsurprisingly, the closest accumulation of bones was around the twenty-nine-foot mark, and this object, just like the gold, silver, and gemstones encircling it, stood unwaveringly through time, peacefully untouched. It was an immense black sphere that floated a few inches above the ground. It had a liquid but solid appearance, somewhat shining with a portion of the room's light captured at its ridge, but not truly showing the reflection of anything in the room around it. It emitted a physical presence while at the same time appearing to reflect the real object it represented.

Vidar stood in the doorway, his focus fixed on the ethereal orb hovering some sixty yards away. Behind him, on the other side of a pair of massive wooden doors, two of his men stood exchanging glances with one another, waiting for him to advance. Eventually, he turned slightly towards them.

"I do not wish to be disturbed here," he paused, waiting for their acknowledgement. The men looked up at him and offered a couple of grunts underneath their heavily layered garb of leather and fur. He placed his giant hand on the door, pushing it closed.

The impact of wood hitting the frame echoed throughout the chamber, startling less resilient birds to take flight from the rafters. Vidar entered the temple and looked around in awe, taking in its intricate construction. The hand-painted ceilings soared high overhead, and while it was not often he needed to look up, he welcomed the change. He felt small in the shadow of his ancestors' legacy. Even for a nine-foot giant, the first temple in Hildeheim was an immense vision to behold, dwarfing him with relative ease.

Vidar removed his cloak of fur, bear hide, and raven feathers, resting it upon a broken column before venturing deeper into the temple. His heavy footsteps reverberated, liberating loose pebbles and rocks from the stone walls and scattering rodents near his path. He removed a rolled-up scroll containing the original layout of the temple from his waistband, unfurling it and examining its content. His expression soured as he compared what was with what is: everything had been stripped to its core, valueless materials, with even the candleholders having been ravaged, their core wooden sticks all that remained.

He felt a noticeable warmth through his garb, stopping him in his tracks. The moisture from his once snow-covered clothing had evaporated, and steam rose from his wet hair.

He knew there were few who could safely approach the Orb. For most, its unique properties made it physically impossible to get close to it. The relic gave off extraordinary heat, its intensity increasing the closer one came. There were many scattered around the known world, varying in size and the properties they exhibited, yet legend insisted that this one — at Gryphon's Rest on the peak of Mount Sankari — was the first to arrive. They rained from the sky with violent, fiery fury, yet they did not crash. The orbs simply stopped moving, without sound or fanfare, coming to rest just above the very spots at which they still stood. These immovable relics remained in place for all of time, like watchful observers frozen in their devotion to their original purpose, whatever that may be.

As they could not be moved, the orbs became the foundation of the temples built around them, slowly becoming centrepieces to the religious and political world. Their presence sparked a frenzy of speculation and intrigue across the known world, with the most prominent scholars, priests, and shamans having devoted their lives to unravelling the secrets of the relics. Unfortunately, their efforts proved futile, only adding to the mysterious and enigmatic qualities of the mystical orbs. Originally having had unique names depending on the kingdom, during a brief time of unity, the leaders of the known world termed them the Uridar.

The Uridar became the foci of numerous religious ceremonies and rituals, attracting pilgrims from far and wide, eager to witness their power. Over time, they collectively transformed into the ultimate symbol of power and mystique, sparking attempts by many rulers to claim them as their own. Wars were waged and alliances were formed and dissolved over these coveted orbs. Some believed they held the key to eternal life, while others feared the potential destruction they could unleash. Despite the danger and uncertainty surrounding them, the Uridar remained objects of fascination and worship for generations. Viewed as divine gifts – manifestations of the gods' will – they were believed to hold the secrets of the universe. As centuries passed, however, their true purpose remained undiscovered.

With the number of people who could safely approach the Uridar having drastically declined due to their potent and unpredictable energies, and with their popularity as revered artefacts gradually being lost, their temples were repurposed as grim places for carrying out executions. The once-sacred orbs, once drawing in devoted pilgrims from all corners, now struck fear into the hearts of those who bore witness to the dreadful judgments delivered within their eerie glow. With the passing of time, the Uridar's mystique faded even further into obscurity, leaving behind tales of their enigmatic history, lost powers, and the unsettling echoes of their past significance.

Vidar felt unsure of how to proceed. He considered removing his clothes, but he hadn't quite thought it through. He felt a force delicately pushing against his skin, yet he felt drawn to it. He heard whispers calling to him. The conflict was enthralling to him, causing fear to churn in his belly. Fear was an emotion he felt rarely. It made his adrenaline flow; it felt…exciting. He obliged the whispers and pressed onwards. The warmth increased, as did the pressure against his skin. His eyes fixated on the large piles of bones stacked on top of one another just a few steps away. Some had been crawling towards the Uridar, while others had been trying to escape. His stomach churned even more strongly. The smell of charred paper curled upwards through the air as the edges of his map began to smoke.

He ventured onwards.

Vidar was only a few steps from the relic, and for the first time, he felt burning. The blue scar on his face, thought by most to be tattoos of runes, began to glow with an eerie iridescence. It burned, but it was not unbearable. As he took his final steps towards the Uridar, he was compelled to collapse to one knee.

Suddenly, the pressure he felt pushing against him dissipated. He raised his hand in front of his face, only to witness his flesh in a constant state of disintegrating and reconstituting itself. Skin, muscle, bone, ash, and back again. The curiosity of it all overrode his innate terror. He rotated it, observing the unnatural event from all angles as it played out in real time. Though there was warmth throughout his limb, he felt no pain. He felt the same warmth on his face and chest but dared not look for a reflection. It was, after all, a bad omen to see one's own heart.

"Vidar."

His eyes flared upon hearing his name come clearly from the orb. He looked at its surface. His glowing birthmark was reflected, yet he was not. His brow raised at the realisation.

"Vidar…" it repeated to him, as if to break his focus.

He felt compelled to reach out and touch it.

And so, eagerly, he obliged.

"How long is he going to be in there?" Gunnar whispered to his compatriot waiting with him by the door, his tone clearly exasperated.

"I don't know, but I'm not going to be the one to ask him. Why don't you go in there and see for yourself?" Olaf responded, glancing at his counterpart with furrowed brows.

Gunnar tried to peek through the thick wooden doors that had slightly slid open. He was outwardly anxious, stuck in a mental loop of what to do next, and he pressed, "The hairs on the back of my neck are standing up. I hate coming to this place, Olaf. It feels like insects are crawling on my skin."

"Maybe you should try bathing more often," Olaf replied.

"Very funny, you half-wit. This land is cursed. We do not belong here, as implied by the giant death ball in there. It will kill us all," Gunnar continued to fret, still fidgeting about the doors, trying to get a good look inside. Olaf flashed his brows; his counterpart wasn't wrong, after all. However, he didn't find any sense in rousing his friend further.

"You think he's dead? It's been a few hours now," Olaf replied.

Gunnar turned to look at him, locking eyes. Olaf dwelled on the thought a little longer than perhaps he should have. He turned around and opted to peek through the door himself. He pushed his shoulder up against the large wooden door…

"Help me open it," he grunted as he pushed with all he could muster. Gunnar obliged. They stopped once it opened sufficiently to peek their heads inside.

"Are you alive, Lord Vidar?!" he shouted. His voice echoed in the large structure.

After a brief delay, a grunt was his only response.

"What does that mean?" Gunnar whispered, hoping for more.

"Means he's not dead. Which means we get to wait, right…here," Olaf responded. Gunnar nodded with relief, smiling at another who stood nearby, waiting for entry.

Vidar remained kneeled and naked in front of the Uridar, marvelling at his hand as the process of his reconstitution occurred ever more rapidly.

"Lord Vidar!" Gunnar's voice echoed. Vidar heard the noise but ignored it, choosing to remain otherwise distracted.

"Lord Vidar!" he increased in volume, shouting repeatedly.

"WHAT!?" Vidar snapped, turning to look behind him.

"Apologies, but there is someone here to see you. He says it is important, and that your attendant told him where to find you. Do you want us to send him in?" Gunnar responded, eager to wash his hands of the visitor.

Vidar looked pensively back at the Uridar, then towards his guard.

"Send him," he replied in a low tone.

He sat on the ground and crossed his legs. His joints were sore. Rapidly approaching footsteps echoed, slowing before they came to an abrupt halt. Vidar smiled to himself as he heard them take several steps backwards.

"A little warm?" Vidar asked, amused. The man stumbled over his words, apparently unfamiliar with what he was observing.

"Lord Vidar, I come with news." The man did his best to sound composed. He failed, taking notice of the enormous relic in the background while doing his best to ignore Vidar's large, silhouetted backside.

"Go on…" the giant replied.

"The traitor is alive…" he announced with glee. Vidar remained still.

"You'll have to be more specific than that." His low tone bounced around the interior.

The messenger looked around, as if spies might be lurking in the shadows. He leaned his head further forward with a deep smirk on his face.

"Connerh Mer…" he gleefully began. Vidar raised his hand in the air, signalling him to stop as a look of disgust crossed his face. He could not be bothered to even hear the name. His deep sigh was very much audible.

"And you're sure of it?" Vidar responded.

"Yes, milord. Our spies in the field have caught sight of the traitor on multiple occasions in or around the marketplaces on the southwest of the mountain. He's getting careless, making mistakes."

The man was overtly invested. Vidar's interest was piqued, but he refused to give in so easily.

"And how is this any different from the last four times he was allegedly sighted? I need more than that. The bastard commander has been seen in your grandmother's stew, last I heard." The sarcasm could not be mistaken; he'd grown restless with this routine.

"Yes, I understand, but these sightings were also confirmed by—"

"By whom?" Vidar impatiently cut him off.

"Your mother's personal cadre…"

Vidar quickly stood to his feet and began walking towards the man.

"What are you saying, exactly?" His volume increased noticeably.

Yamil quickly looked away, trying his best to ignore Vidar's indecency.

"Are you saying the Hand of the Queen is aware of the traitor's enduring existence?" His tone was threatening.

"Yes...I am, milord," Yamil began to fidget, looking for a place to avert his eyes to as Vidar now towered over him.

"I didn't know we were in the business of keeping information from one another," Vidar mused to himself in a low rumble. He raised his hand to his chin and ran his fingers through his beard, then turned away from the man.

"Who else knows?" he asked with a half-look tossed over his shoulder.

"Your mother has notified the half-breed..."

Vidar turned quickly, lifting the man off the ground as he shouted, "What did you say!?"

"I'm sorry, Lord Vidar! I said your mother has notified the hal—" he started just as he was hurled into a nearby wall.

"My cousin may be a half-blood to *me*. However, to you, she is a god with the blood of the raven coursing through her veins!" Vidar bellowed. His chest heaving, he threatened, "Don't get too comfortable, Yamil. Had it not been for the news you bring me, I would have crushed your skull into your chest."

Yamil softly spoke over him, profusely apologising as he picked himself up, ignoring his obvious concussion. He felt something wet on his face, and he wiped it to discover blood running down his nose and eyes. He used his own garments to clean it up.

"You may continue your report," Vidar instructed, denying him a quiet recovery.

"Yes, of course. Your mother has informed...the queen...of the traitor's whereabouts and will be sending a detachment to retrieve him," Yamil explained as he struggled to ignore his pain and discomfort.

Vidar turned to ponder.

"Do you want me to send men to intercept?" Yamil asked.

"It has to be done correctly. Send a detachment of your men from the Sands...make it look random. Commission them through two others, and pay some disposable men to cause a delay for my mother's troops... Buy your own some time."

"Only send one?" Yamil asked almost unintentionally, still focused on that detail. Vidar looked away, then back at him.

"Make it two. Now, make haste," he replied, shooing the man away.

Yamil bowed several times as he ran towards the doors.

Vidar stood and pondered for a moment, then walked back towards the sphere.

CHAPTER EIGHT

GOODBYE BROTHER

ELARION

Elarion sat quietly on a bed of straw and animal hide, his back pressed firmly against a terra-cotta-coloured wall. His eyes wandered across the thatched roof above him, noting imperfections in its weave while silently judging its creator's craftsmanship. The white and caramel pattern of dried leaves contrasted with the muted orange pigment of the walls surrounding him. A growing, sweet smell of petrichor captured his attention, inviting him to draw a breath. The rain's natural perfume paired perfectly with the audible pitter-patter of its drops, and its scent brought him comfort while mentally transporting him to the one place he'd rather be – his homeland.

He took the wooden pipe sandwiched between his right thumb and index finger and brought it to the crest of his lips, inhaling sharply. He held the warm, charred, herbaceous vapours in his lungs for a moment before exhaling. His shoulders relaxed as his pursed lips released opaque clouds that tumbled into the air. His long, slender ears twitched and pivoted in place as he listened to low whispering voices outside of his room, and his near-black eyes lowered to focus on nothing as he processed the individual sounds. A distant chirping was gently layered atop a running river, accentuating the audible quiet. These woods differed from the Westwood: these trees were quiet…soulless. The animals did not seek to communicate, instead opting to commune only with their own.

Morning was approaching, and his hosts had already begun to stir.

It wouldn't be long before he could deliver his message to the local bureaucracy and continue with his travels to Hildeheim. Anticipation for what was to come unfortunately overshadowed the brief, remedial joy he felt upon reuniting with his kin. Instead, the creeping feeling of futility surrounding his reasons for being here grew heavier with every passing minute, and each minute felt more wasted than the one that came before it. And yet, he would wait a while longer. The elves considered it an ill gesture to rise before your host; therefore, he would be sure to delay before leaving his room. The individual variations in footsteps told a story about who was in the home. A smirk visibly washed onto his face as the gentle tumble of small footsteps sounded off. He welcomed a break from the night's long silence – which he had endured alone, staring into complete darkness and listening to Thaetra's subtle snoring in the neighbouring room.

He watched as the smoke from his pipe pooled in an inverted pond, slowly expanding to a lake as it nestled in the concave roof. Without warning, the room suddenly felt small – and growing smaller by the second. An unwelcoming air overcame him, causing a warmth behind his ears and neck. Elarion stood quickly and dressed himself with a newly found urgency. He nestled a short blade in his waistband, its silver and gold decorative hilt peaking just above the fabric. The smell of fire and wood permeated the air, redirecting his thoughts and overriding the peaceful aromas of his burning herbs. He slid open the door to his room and paused long enough to observe his surroundings before crossing over the threshold.

"I trust you slept well?" Bakaru's voice carried from the darkened corner of the common room. He was somewhat distracted, his attention still focused on lighting the stout, chestnut-coloured pipe nestled firmly between his lips. The peaks of his face flickered with an eerily dim orange hue, and his black eyes reflected the animation of the flame before him. Elarion nodded, opting for courtesy over honesty. In truth, he hadn't slept much and found the bed *more* than mildly uncomfortable. Bakaru's eyes quickly darted up towards him before returning to his own hands.

"Join me?" he asked, pointing to a chair across from him near the fire pit in the centre of the space. The rapid puffs of his pipe let out a discreet smacking sound. Elarion nodded and made himself comfortable, although his nose wrinkled at the smell of tobacco; it was such a harsh and abrasive odour compared to ashpetal, the smoking herb of choice for elves. A calm settled as each one took silent drags of their herb of choice, both internally trying to decide how to start a peaceable conversation with the other.

"Where did the kits run off to?" Elarion asked.

Children and women were easy topics.

"Along with their mother, fetching a few things for furstmeal. They'll return shortly."

The awkward silence resumed.

"And my ward? How is she recovering?"

"Ward?" Bakaru's left brow raised.

"I'll never understand why you insist on talking like *them*," he continued. The embers of his pipe grew bright before dimming again. Bakaru's contempt for his brethren had unfortunately become a defining characteristic of his personality, and it was a point of contention that both disappointed and aggravated Elarion. He ignored the bait. It was not the time to discuss heritage, politics, or alleged racial disparity – topics with which, in his opinion, his brother had an unhealthy obsession.

"She's over there, in the second room from the right, still in slumber. The addition of the Kingsfoil root fortifies the old mixture, but with it comes lethargy. It's for the better. A deep sleep gives the mind the proper rest it needs to cleanse itself of the mists' effects." Bakaru's scornful tone had softened.

"That is a rather interesting choice…" Elarion folded his arms, pipe still in hand. His brows furrowed as he pondered, and his lower lip became puckered, growing more pronounced. The two had held a keen interest in herbology as far back as younglings. Common ground.

"Why not use something a bit more…passive? Perhaps lilyweed, or scorchvine? They would both fortify the mixture and keep the mind nimble, with little to no side effects… Perhaps a sour stomach and a bitter tongue for a time…with the use of scorchvine, that is," he continued. Bakaru grunted and nodded in agreement.

"We've not gotten the rains necessary to grow lilyweed, so it's in short supply." He let out a deep exhale, and his eyes darted around, giving the secondary suggestion some thought. His improved mood was slightly suppressed.

"Scorchvine would work. However, as you're well aware, it isn't native to these lands…and, to be blunt, the comfort of trespassers and outsiders is *not* a priority of the Tu'Chauri people. Even less at the expense of doing business with the elves."

"Nonsense. There would be no need for diplomats and ambassadors; I could have three wagons filled to the brim delivered in a fortnight. Use the new version of the brew for special occasions. Consider it..."

"A favour? Favours come with expectations..." Bakaru interrupted with a glare.

"Done. Consider it done," Elarion continued with a firm but peaceable tone. He *was* the fixer and caretaker of the family. There was no cost too high, no task too low that he would not undertake if it were for his family. Bakaru, on the other hand, was – as most siblings to a fixer were – the fighter, the resister of most everything not originating from his own mind. Trust was a hard thing to come by, even in his old age. It was an even harder thing to extend.

"...Thank you." His reply was measured.

The fire between them had doubled in size, illuminating the area. The orange flame flickered, refracting off of Bakaru's mangled ears. The tips were coated in a salve, giving them a wet, shiny appearance. Elarion's gaze lasted perhaps a little too long, and his eyes lost focus as he dwelt on the shame he felt for his brother. Bakaru noticed.

"Don't start with me," Bakaru angrily muttered under his breath, rising to his feet. The unfortunate truth was that the cause of his mutilation was not some punishment for crime, but merely adolescent rebellion gone too far. He had done it to himself. When he and Elarion had been around the age of sixteen, their father had been given a choice: A life sentence with his Tu'Chauri wife and children, or the *Forest*. He and Elarion had chosen *the Forest*. Their mother had refused to leave. She'd become quite the proficient healer, having gone as far as her tutelage would allow in mastering the elven healing arts, as taught to her by her husband. Her purpose in life had become clear; her people had needed her. Bakaru, finding nobility in her charge, had stayed with her.

And so, the family had splintered.

Not understanding the charged political reasons for his father's decision, he had taken it at its face value, as a child would see it. Abandonment. As a show of defiance, he had changed his name and cut his ears, hoping to make them more human-like. While he had been able to reject his elven lineage externally, internal matters were more complex.

An unfortunate consequence of Bakaru's half-elven blood was rapid healing.

Every six months, he would repeatedly re-cut his ears, maintaining their twisted, misshapen state. Following decades of self-mutilation, the culmination of his wounds had finally taken a permanent hold. Worse, with time, his reasons for his actions had lost their potency. As his ears had become less a symbol and more of a spectacle, his pride had dwindled into shame. What once had been proudly displayed was now typically concealed under hood and cloak.

"It's not as if they would take me back anyway..." he continued, mumbling the words under his breath. The truth in his statement was as mangled as his ears. Elarion closed his eyes, squeezing them tightly as he canted his head slightly to the left and fought the urge to engage. He took a pronounced breath. His ear twitched as the sound of rain faded.

"You should leave this place. Take your wife and children and move east. Only tell who you must. A turbulent storm approaches these lands. If you stay, I fear I alone cannot ensure your survival." Elarion's pace varied as he spoke. Bakaru laughed in short bursts. He opened his mouth to respond but took a puff of the pipe instead. Elarion braced for his rebuttal.

"A storm, is it? Tell only who I must?" Bakaru's tone was mocking. "Then I must tell everyone! I know *they* are cold and unfeeling, lacking empathy for anyone who doesn't look like them, but here, we look out for everyone. If there really is danger, then I *must* warn *everyone*, mustn't I?"

"Not *everyone* will believe you..." Elarion replied, leaning forward. It wasn't his best choice of words, but he stood by it. There were too many fallacies in Bakaru's accusations, most of them intentional, and therefore there was no use in countering them...and Elarion felt his time running short.

"So, what...? You want me to pick and choose who lives or who dies?"

"No, you intentionally misconstrue my words. I came to warn you and your people, but you must acknowledge reality, Bakaru. I wish them all to be saved, but many...*most* will not listen." Elarion began losing his patience. There was a pause. Bakaru stroked his scraggly, peppered beard.

"And where exactly would you lead them?"

"What do you mean?" Elarion's bewilderment became evident. He was beginning to believe they were having two very different conversations. In reality, they were.

"You said you came to warn the Tu'Chauri, so where would you lead them, if you are leading them to their salvation?"

"I wouldn't *lead* them anywhere." The words shot out, seasoned with frustration. "It's not that kind of situation."

"Not grand enough to justify making a claim to the throne?"

"I should've never come here," Elarion replied in disbelief and stood, shaking his head to himself. He continued, "I said I would not help your quest for the throne, not because I want it for myself—"

"Then why are you here?" Bakaru shouted, interrupting him.

"To save you!"

"Have you ever considered, perhaps, that I don't need saving?" Bakaru shot back snidely.

"Well, you've certainly never stopped to consider that you are, in fact, the one who needs it most of all! Never in all my span have I met a self-ostracised martyr. How, exactly, is that working out for you?" Elarion quickly shed what little patience he had remaining.

His abruptness silenced Bakaru, ill-prepared for the truth as he was.

And then, "Spoken like an elf. All those years pretending to be one have finally paid off."

It was a weak defence, but it was the best he could come up with on the spot. Elarion's words had unexpectedly wounded his ego.

"What are we, then, *Bakaru*?!" Elarion replied, mocking his self-given name. "I am no more an elf than you are Tu'Chauri. And yet, how many generations do you have to watch *die* before you accept the curse of our reality? For us, there are no elves, and there are no Tu'Chauri, or dwarves, or gnomes! They are all but meaningless titles and names! There is only life and death, and there are those who run from it and those who long for it."

Elarion's temper flared, but Bakaru remained quiet, his head tilted downwards as he listened.

"How many sons and daughters have you outlived? And yet you cling to this...identity," Elarion sneered as he pointed towards Bakaru's tribal wardrobe and markings in succinct disgust.

An internal voice screaming for restraint finally won the better of him; he bridled his tongue, sighed loudly, and gazed across the room. There was a palpable pause in the argument. The crackling fireplace seemed to grow louder.

"Three," Bakaru finally replied.

"What?" Elarion snapped back, still in the process of holding back bitter speech.

"Three. I've outlived...three generations. Nine children, sixteen grandchildren, eight great grandchildren, and..."

He spoke matter-of-factly, the sour taste of regret tightening his upper cheek muscles and giving the awkward appearance of a slight smile. The nuance of joyful memories outlined his painful reflection.

"The eight and their children were killed in a skirmish...victims of a squabble between dwarves and the... It doesn't matter," he sighed. "So that's four. I now sire my fifth."

As his volume trailed off, Elarion's gaze drifted towards the ground. A creeping sorrow for his dead relatives weighed heavily on his heart. A few loose tears pooled in the corner of Bakaru's eyes; looking away released them into a stream trickling down his face.

"I *should* be growing old, Elarion..." His voice grew weaker. He looked up at his brother with a creased face, desiring relief.

Elarion's brow sunk, having no relief to offer despite his want to do so. He sighed as he reflected on his own wish.

"Wondering what the future will bring for those that come after you. Wanting to feel content in your accomplishment – and in the mystery of not knowing what comes next," Elarion continued his brother's sentiment, staring blankly into the air. Then, with a grimace, he continued, "Only...there is no mystery. Not for you."

He locked eyes with Bakaru, an unspoken offer for peace that was accepted with a glance. Their focus shifted to the fire. The dancing flame offered a proper distraction from the flood of memories that overwhelmed them both.

"What good is it, if we face it alone?" Bakaru replied.

"No one said we had to."

"What else is there for us, Elarion?"

"Nothing the Tu'Chauri can provide. Come home," he replied, trying once more to recruit him to his senses.

"What aren't you telling me?" Bakaru pleaded.

"I was not entirely truthful...and, in fact, you were right at the outset. From a certain point of view," Elarion confessed. Bakaru raised a brow and looked at him with curiosity, so Elarion went on, "I came to warn the others because I felt it was the only way to make you listen. To be honest, I do not care what number of them are lost tomorrow. And many *will* perish." For the first time in a long time, he was being honest...with himself. "I only care about my family," he concluded.

Bakaru stared at him, mouth partially open.

"I have deciphered that the King of the Forest means to trap the Tu'Chauri into a confrontation. One that will quickly escalate into a slaughter…as it was designed to. Hermod is a predictable and prideful fool, and he will march your people to their destruction." Elarion stopped staring into the fire and made eye contact with Bakaru to reemphasise, "They will *not* listen to me."

Bakaru's eyes fell towards the ground. He knew his brother was right, and there was nothing for him to argue. He slowly began to feel the weight of Elarion's warning. His demeanour changed.

'So, how—" he began to ask.

"Tell all who will heed the warning. Get away from the interior. Go as far east as possible, as soon as possible," Elarion interrupted.

"I, also, was not entirely truthful," Bakaru confessed. Elarion's face remained still, waiting as he admitted, "I did not arrange for your audience with King Hermod; he does not know you are here."

Elarion's head tilted involuntarily. They locked eyes for a brief second. Bakaru started upon Elarion bursting into momentary laughter.

"I suppose it's for the better," he replied.

"Master Elarion?" Thaetra's voice was a pleasant change, sounding just before she slid open the door to her room. Bakaru stood upon her arrival.

"Are you well?" Elarion asked.

"Steadily but surely," she affirmed, nodding.

"I am glad for it. Thaetra, this is my brother…" He paused, fighting his inclination, then continued, "Bakaru."

They exchanged a short bow.

"Pleasure to meet you," she said, unintentionally staring for too long. It was disconcerting to see a twisted, disfigured clone of her master. He was skinnier, darker, and grizzled, all the descriptions befitting the stereotypical evil twin. And yet, somewhere in the middle was Elarion's likeness – but the soul behind his black eyes was…different. His own gaze drifted away, his brow furrowing lightly. He was used to the stares, but it made them no less irritating.

"I am happy to see you awake, Thaetra. Please give us a moment; my kin is waiting to receive you just outside," Elarion replied to her, indicating towards the door. Thaetra nodded and left, although not before offering another a bow.

"What will you do now?" Bakaru asked after the door had closed behind her.

"I will continue heading north," Elarion began, holding an internal debate over allowing full disclosure.

Bakaru nodded. He was curious, but he decided not to pry.

"The Seer would have me wait there." Elarion had chosen full disclosure, his tone highlighting the sensitivity of the information. Bakaru's eyes opened widely.

"Wait there for what reason?"

"I don't know yet," he replied, reflecting on the lie as it left his lips.

"I'll leave in a day…*or two*, since I'd like to get to know my nephews… If that's alright?" he continued. Bakaru nodded weakly, again with intent.

"I would…they would like that," he replied.

CHAPTER NINE

NORTH BY NORTHWEST

CONNERH

Three months later…

Connerh and Aeryk lay among the tall grass, their hands cradled behind their heads. The glittering fabric of space twinkled and shimmered, like diamonds strewn across black velvet, and the dying stalks of grass swayed in an overactive wind, mimicking the sound of the ocean cresting upon the shore. A small fire crackled behind them. Together, they swam in an independent stream of thought and fantasy.

"It's hard to believe all those rocks stay up there for so long. Do you think they'll all fall to the ground eventually?" Aeryk's young voice pierced the ambience. His accent was a charming mix of southern Hildeheim and western Piikani…the Hs and Rs were a tad strong.

Connerh withdrew from his mental wandering. He took a deep breath and pondered a moment on the boy's question.

"Oh, sure…I don't see why not…one day. Long after you and I are gone, that's for sure. We'll be long-forgotten ancestors before the last star falls." He cleared his throat.

"I wonder how many of 'em have fallen without anyone noticing? Maybe we could go find and collect them all! They could be scattered anywhere. Man, they'd be worth a lot of coin!" Aeryk's enthusiasm brought a smile to Connerh's face. The boy could turn just about anything into an 'adventure'. Collecting *special* rocks in the wilderness would be no exception.

"I suppose you're right. There must be hundreds of them on the mountain's peak. Countless more in the sea."

"Oh, can we go!? Can we? Please?" The boy could hardly contain himself.

"Settle down, now. First, we need to make sure you can endure the cold. Winter in the north is unlike anything you're accustomed to." He thought of a quick excuse.

"I'll stay out all night every night until I get used to it, and then we can go," the boy promised. Connerh chuckled lightly.

"Something like that. It'll take some time. Be patient. It'll also take some convincing your mother."

"I'll take care of that." The confidence in his voice caught Connerh by surprise, spurring on more laughter.

"Oh, will you now? I'm not scared to admit that I'm glad to hear it, lad," he continued. "But before we can even plan our expedition, there's a little matter left unresolved, good sir," Connerh smirked.

Aeryk rolled to his side with an inquisitive look spreading across his face.

"I do believe you owe me coin." Connerh's brow raised playfully. "Let's hear it…"

"This is the best view I've ever seen," Aeryk replied mockingly. Connerh grunted.

"I believe there was also a promissory regarding one chicken dance, if I remember correctly." He barely managed a straight face.

"There was not!" Aeryk protested. When he finally stopped laughing and grew quiet, he said, "I have something to admit."

"Well, what is it?" Connerh sat up, thinking the boy had some weight to relieve from his shoulders.

"I've not two silver to my name," Aeryk snickered.

"You little rat! I should have you thrown into stocks for making an illegal wager," Connerh joked, falling to his back again.

"You'd have to catch me first, old man," he chuckled. Connerh grew quiet.

"You're right. I'm not as fast as I used to be. I'd have to spear you in the kneecap first. Maybe sever the tendon above and behind your ankle…removing your will or desire to walk, let alone run… It's quite painful…very long recovery."

Connerh trailed off as his morbid joke ran on slightly too long. He looked over at Aeryk, who looked horrified. Connerh excused himself with a laugh.

"For three silver?!" Aeryk shouted at him. Connerh shrugged.

"A contract is a contract. You should always be a man of your word." He paused abruptly after the words slipped from his lips – the words of his father, coming out like it was second nature. His smile faded as he ruminated on their meaning.

"Though there can…I suppose we should leave room…for some exceptions." He cleared his throat.

"What are you boys up to?" Rose approached cheerfully with a small lantern in her hand. She plopped herself on the ground between them. The gold rim of her green dress sparkled in the fire's light.

"Enjoying my last days walking upright, I guess," Aeryk giggled.

"What?" Rose forced a smile, not understanding the inside joke.

"And he's loose of the tongue, too. These charges just keep racking up, boy." Connerh smirked at Aeryk's silent protest. Rose pulled Aeryk to her, resting his head in her lap and running her hands through his curly hair. Connerh glanced at them and smiled before quickly looking away.

"I underestimated you, Connerh. This place…is breathtaking. I can only imagine it in the spring," she said.

"That's the good thing: you won't have to. Spring is the reward for enduring the North's winter. Anywhere near the coast is lovely in spring. There's plenty of trouble for the boy to get into should he desire it," he replied.

"Yes!" Aeryk whispered.

"I wouldn't celebrate just yet. I'm not sure how much time you'll have tending to the farm, the garden, and caring for your…dog," he continued.

Aeryk shot up.

"I'm getting a dog?!" he could barely contain himself.

"Oh, sure, you heard that part."

Aeryk ran on, making promises as children do when trying to sweeten the deal. He aggressively hugged both Rose and Connerh while profusely thanking them.

"Every boy needs a companion. Show them care, love, and respect, and they will offer their life on behalf of yours, should you ask it."

Connerh found himself reaching into his pocket and rubbing a bracelet made of braided horsehair and silver beads between his fingers. His eyes lost focus in the flames. Rose observed but opted to rub his shoulder instead of drawing attention to it. He cleared his throat and sat up.

"I will," Aeryk promised.

"You'll need a good name, too, so start thinking of something *strong*," he continued. Aeryk's lip puckered as he thought good and hard.

"What about Frog?" he asked.

"Oh, that's absolutely dreadful…" Connerh chuckled.

"Perhaps you should come up with a few of them and choose from those," Rose suggested, flaring her eyes at Connerh.

He shook his head with disapproval in return. It *was* a terrible name for a dog.

"Are you still wanting to go into the city tomorrow?" Rose offered a break in the conversation.

"I'll get up before the sunrise and climb the peak. I'd like to get a lay of the land before we descend. I imagine much has changed in fifteen years," he replied. Rose smiled with glee.

"We've not been to a proper city in some time. I'll have to prepare. Aeryk, you should bathe," she rambled on.

"Mother, it's a fishing port. I'm sure I'm ahead of the competition," he replied sarcastically.

"Not from where we're sitting," Connerh countered.

"Ha. Ha. Ha."

She pulled Connerh back to lie with her, curling up into his side and regaling them with all the things she wanted to see and do in the city. Connerh mentally trailed off, still rubbing the horsehair bracelet in his pocket. He smiled, quietly recalling memories of observing the night sky with his companion, the large black horse named Whisper. The two of them would sit in the middle of the wilderness staring endlessly, while Connerh mused about the day's events. Whisper's tail would dust the ground while he stared at Connerh in turn, as if hanging on to every word. Connerh's smile slowly drifted.

The stars were entrancing.

The sounds, sights, and smells of the mountain air, the sea, the jasmine and rosemary gave him an overwhelming sense of comfort. He felt no need to be on alert, to fight…to run.

His breathing slowed.

His shoulders relaxed.

There were many nights like this one.

A light snore emanated from the bridge of his nose. Rose stopped speaking upon hearing the gentle rumble. Startled at first, she smiled, motioning for Aeryk to remain quiet. She couldn't remember the last time she had witnessed him sleeping. The old warrior had earned his rest. Together, they lay there until the morning hours.

WHERE THE WIND BLOWS

ELARION

It had been a fairly quiet trek for the first week after leaving the Tu'Chauri people, save for pleasant conversation when they camped at sundown. Elarion had seemed content to quietly ruminate otherwise, leaving Thaetra to assume he had been reflecting on his time spent with family. By the second week, it seemed that he'd mostly returned to normal, jovial in nature and actively carrying on conversation during the day. Having doubled back into elven territory and his feeling reconnected with the forest had likely had some effect, but now, at the beginning of the third week, there was a noticeable change within him. His reservation and internal preoccupation had returned, stronger this time.

They sat, motionless atop their steeds, under the shade of a willow tree. Before them stood a carved stone bridge spanning a gorge. Intricate Elvish runes decorated the bridge's pillars, etching the tale of its construction alongside a few fabled events that occurred a very long time ago. The gentle roar of an active waterfall nearly drowned out all other sounds as it split the mountainside and rushed under the ancient bridge's sturdy arch. They were stood at the edge of the Westwood, a symbolic foothold of peace and tranquillity. Elarion stared across the bridge into Hildeheim; it was grim, cold, and painted in hues of brown, blue, and white. The path shifted from carefully placed cobblestone to snow-covered gravel.

His gaze was not on the landscape but something beyond. His trance broke as he heard Thaetra's steed quietly approach, and his own horse shuffled in place. A sigh escaped his lips.

"I've never seen a more befitting contrast," he said solemnly. He found it difficult to cross over; a non-descript hesitation bound him in place.

She looked up, attempting to see what he saw.

"I know I must go, but…something feels…wrong." He struggled to put his finger on it.

Thaetra studied his face and began, "Should we cross over a different way? If we head south…"

"No…it's not that."

He half-rotated in his saddle and observed the path behind them. It was empty but endless, winding through massive, over-slung trees bearing red and orange foliage. Winter was slow to invade the Westwood.

"We should get off the road. We'll camp there for the evening, then attempt again in the morning." He pointed to a spot in the near distance. He grabbed the reins of his horse and trotted in the direction he had identified before she could reply.

Thaetra followed quickly.

"It would be a good time to prepare additional layers. It will be drastically colder in Hildeheim. Have you ever been?" he asked as he dismounted and hitched his horse to a tree.

"I've not. I've been as east as the Far Sands, but I've never stepped into the Mountain Queen's domain," she replied.

"It was once a beautiful land. In some ways, I suppose its charm still remains, despite lacking the spirit it once had," he offered.

"What happened?" she asked.

"Death. Far too much of it, and even further, the acceptance of it." It was a brief reply, but it encapsulated the deluge of memories he navigated. He noticed her staring at him but continued to unpack supplies to make camp before saying, "The forest is alive; it gives to us freely. It withholds nothing, including its secrets. It speaks to those who are disposed to listen. We, in turn, give back to it freely. We protect it and all who reside under its canopy. It is a symbiotic relationship." He gestured as if describing waves of the ocean. "The mountain, however…it takes, selfishly and freely. No one listens to it because it speaks to no one. It is a virus with a blatant disregard for the living; the spirit it once had is dead."

He spoke pointedly and, as elves were oft to do, in riddles clear only to those who already knew the cypher. She understood enough for her not to question it. In summary, it was a grim warning of what lay ahead, and that was all she decided she needed to know. Her grip tightened around the hilt of her fastened sword; her eyes fixed sharply on the bridge.

A steady, modest fire provided them light as darkness descended on the forest. An unsettling wind blew, causing the horses to stir.

"These human steeds are weak and pathetic," Thaetra grumbled, then sighed, thinking of her own companion, Ethil, who she'd left behind. The elves, renowned for their deep bonds with nature, often chose to ride alternative beasts over the typical option of horses. These wild creatures would become loyal mounts when they forged a connection with an elf. Ethil was a nightshade, a rare cat-like creature and the larger cousin to the human panther. Only a few hundred nightshades were born each year, and their intelligence made them highly selective when imprinting on their riders. To have one as a companion was considered good fortune. As the energetic runt of her litter, Ethil was a natural match for Thaetra.

"I don't think they're so bad. The humans possess some rather impressive, oftentimes large and powerful breeds..." Elarion countered.

"It would seem our horse trader ran out of those, then," she scowled.

"Perhaps," he replied.

"This is the longest I've been away from her, you know?" she continued, lamenting.

"The stablemaster will take good care of your companion; you need not worry. Besides, our need for discretion imposed the need for more...discrete travel arrangements," he countered. After a moment of her silence lingered, he realised that this was an appropriate time for compassion and, looking at her to gauge her response, he said, "I, too, miss...Stag."

Stag was a silvercrown – a large-antlered creature and a cousin of the human's much smaller elk or deer.

Thaetra rolled her eyes and laughed at his attempt to soothe her with absurdity.

"I understand not wanting for this world, Master, but you should really give him a name," she remarked.

He smiled.

"He does not need a name. He answers when I call; that is sufficient," he replied quickly.

She shook her head again. Elarion retrieved his pipe from his satchel, inspiring Thaetra to retrieve her own. He grunted as he extended his hand, offering her the ashpetal he had wrapped delicately in a linen cloth.

"Inka?" she asked.

His face wrinkled and recoiled.

"No…ashpetal," he replied.

She held up her palm to deny the offer, instead retrieving a small wooden box from her belongings. Elarion observed while lighting his own pipe. She lifted the small clasp that bound the box shut, pinched a bundle of the dried leaf, packed it into her pipe, and lit it with a stick from the fire. While ashpetal had a calming and soothing effect, Inka heightened the senses. Typically smoked in higher potencies before battle, it had since become the preferred option for the younger generation.

"I'll never understand how you manage to still fall asleep after," he remarked, his interest evident.

"You get used to it after a while. Mind you, it's not full strength," she replied, lighting her pipe. After a few puffs, her pupils dilated to an extreme degree.

"I've not done it in a very long time. Even a small amount would have me running from coast to coast," he smiled.

After their light banter, a calm permeated their modest campsite. Semi-translucent clouds of blue-rimmed pipe smoke were illuminated by the bands of moonlight piercing the thick tree cover. The large branches and boughs of the forest creaked and groaned with the ebb and flow of the wind. Thaetra retreated into a small leather-backed binding of poetry that she kept in the front pocket of her riding pack. Her hand wrapped delicately around the long stem of her pipe as she puffed and exhaled its vapours. Elarion quietly observed their surroundings, glancing occasionally over at her. He thought it a peculiar way to hold the instrument, but he dismissed the critique as his mind wandered. Her sometimes-unorthodox ways made him smirk, recalling memories of his *own* youth. The *song of the forest* was distant here, at the north-eastern tip of the Westwood, like the longing call of a mother gone too far over the horizon. Here, the source of the song was clearly behind them, and it stirred a not-so-pleasant feeling in the pit of his stomach. Thaetra, on the other hand, seemed unfazed by the diminished chorus.

Elarion glanced at the soft-white, glowing runes etched into the pillars of the bridge. Their light peeked through the leaves fluttering in the breeze.

"I imagine I owe you some sort of explanation." His low tone broke the silence between them. He cleared his throat.

"Nonsense, you owe me nothing. That's the ashpetal talking," she replied quickly, before fully breaking eye contact with her poetry. She looked at him with a partial frown, unsure of what he was referring to.

"Be that as it may, I feel compelled," he insisted.

She folded the edge of the page she was reading and closed her book, offering him her full attention as she patiently replied, "Whatever brings you comfort."

"I fear the truth concerning my lineage has been kept quiet since long before you were born," he began.

She had the urge to stop him, feeling unworthy of the information he was about to share, but her curiosity was stronger.

"Even a curse can spawn from something beautiful," he said as his focus wandered. "I am Elarion, illegitimate son of Aemithil the Patient, Eighth King of the Forest."

Her eyes widened dramatically. "And rightful heir to…" she ecstatically began.

He raised his hand to stop her and said plainly, "No."

"Why would you not…? There are no laws that prohibit…" she continued to protest, as if it were news to him. He laughed quietly.

"Nonsense. I have no interest in staking any claim. Even if I *were* to set my heart upon it, only…ten thousand out of the millions would accept a half-breed as king," he replied, shaking his head. She frowned.

"Why do you keep using that term? We care not for…" she protested. It began to feel like a scripted response, even to her. He smiled and continued to mildly shake his head. She paused.

"The elves are a passionate people, that is true. Tolerant, patient, enduring…but not perfect. Elves accept their divergent offspring purely…because we cannot reproduce. Otherwise, we would be stamped out, plucked from the root, and destroyed. Make no mistake about it," he replied while staving off his body's attempt to yawn.

She returned a lost and confused gaze as his yawn finally escaped.

"I'm sorry, that is to say…we cannot produce elves. While, yes, we can produce offspring, the reality that has not been shared with you…is that they will share the same death sentence of mortality as the humans. And thus, the elven bloodline remains pure. Think of it as a built-in failsafe of sorts. A cure contained within the disease."

He looked at the ground to mask his displeasure. While he may have had hundreds of years to accept this simple fact, it never lost its potency. Thaetra remained silent, unaware that her mouth was hanging ever-so slightly open.

"It's not *you* they hate. It is what we represent. Even then, *hate* is such a strong, perhaps inappropriate word," he continued, feeling as if she desired more information but could not yet utter the words to request it.

"Somehow that does not offer solace…" she finally replied.

"It should," he rebutted and frowned.

She returned a raised eyebrow.

"You are free to have children, and they will be accepted by our people. They will not be treated as something less," he continued.

"But they will be *viewed* as something less," she replied. Again, he frowned.

"Are you?" He was quick-footed.

"Well…perhaps not," she hesitated to admit.

"And yet, you *are…*" he quickly rebutted. Thaetra stood out of frustration.

"What are you saying? You agree with this…bigotry?" She struggled to find the appropriate word, instead settling for a human one. His eyes raced back and forth between the both of hers, trying to understand the disconnect.

"The elven bloodline is over ten thousand years old – one of the oldest in existence. We have ascended to a level that no other kind in this world has, and we stand to ascend yet again. Beyond this…this." He drew attention to the flesh of his hands with a frustrated look. "With such a gift, it is important that we move forward, not backwards. Introducing weaker blood weakens the line. To put it another way…it grants a gift to those who did not earn it, and from those without the authority to give it. Imagine a kingdom of immortal dwarves or humans in their current state," he continued.

They both made disgusted expressions.

"Or giants."

Her eyes flared, and her face crumpled further.

"Or *giants*," he repeated with a lower volume.

Thaetra's shoulders slumped. She felt defeated as far as reasoning was concerned. She sat down again, still struggling with acceptance.

"I understand, but it does not provide comfort. I confess I suddenly feel alone. Perhaps, less than whole," she stated.

"Understanding can be logical, or it can be emotional. I would imagine you reside somewhere in the middle. As I do," he replied.

They exchanged a warm, affirming glance.

"Bakaru does not understand," he continued, then paused, realising she may be deficient in the details. "Bakaru…" He quietly snorted and shook his head. "Illithor was his name…Bakaru is who he has become. And yet, he is still my brother." He glanced at her after getting lost in thought. "Illithor could not grasp our role in this grand scheme. He thought it a cruel and undesirable state of being. Although, there is no one alive who could fail to find a great number of those who would not trade with him in an instant, yet he refuses to accept it." He ran his hand through his beard as he spoke candidly.

She listened attentively.

"He'd always been the difficult one." His thoughts bounced around. "Yes, I suppose I should start near the beginning. It begins with my father. He was a decorated leader; Aemithil the Patient is what they called him. Broker of the Iron Core Accords, the treaty that unified the five kingdoms of the mountain," he began.

She counted on her fingers, then asked, "Five kingdoms? But there are only four. Giants, dwarves, humans, and halflings."

"There were five, and now there are four. They may have changed the records of their history, but we have not. At least, not regarding those sorts of matters," he replied. "My father may have been a patient man with regards to his allies and enemies, but he was not with his mate. Failing to provide an heir put a stain on his name, or so they allowed themselves to believe. They felt an elven surrogate would bring them shame, as word among the forest travels quickly. The plan was simple, really: find a Tu'Chaurian woman who closely resembled his wife, impregnate her, and pass the offspring as their own."

"Why would that make any sense? Why the Tu'Chauri?" she asked.

"Because they are our closest relative…" A puzzled look ran across his face, and then he admitted, "I suppose we are also guilty of editing the history books. The Tu'Chauri and the elves were once the same people…a very long time ago. They were the first divergent group, in a manner of speaking. Essentially, they were those who did not ascend as we did, leaving our two peoples to share a common ancestor. In those days, the elves did not mingle with others. There were no half-bloods at the time, and so discretion was required, you understand. A Tu'Chauri woman from some remote village would ensure the secret could be kept, whether they succeeded or failed…"

"They could kill the woman and the child," she replied. He nodded.

"Initially, the plan worked. He was rewarded with not one but two male heirs. Basking in their joy, they decided to let the Tu'Chauri woman live, even allowing her to aid in the care of the children. But eventually the truth was discovered, as it always is." He paused as he reflected on the solemn details. Thaetra's eyes were widened in the suspense. "They were not prepared for the shared traits of the mixed blood to reveal themselves, some three months later. For Illithor and me, our skin darkened past the range common for our kind. A minor detail, in the grand scheme of things, but enough to draw attention. And, unfortunately, enough for his wife to assume the worst. She took her own life shortly thereafter, out of fear of public scandal," he continued.

Thaetra quietly covered her mouth with her hand.

"Irony has a…funny way of rearing its ugly head." The words were bitter on his tongue. He stared into the void. "In the end, it was the suicide that marred his reign…not the twin illegitimate sons. And eventually history would present a more…palatable version of what actually happened," he continued, grim in tone.

"The twins of Mare's Point!" she shouted while snapping her fingers. "The sons of Aemithil and their mother were killed in Tu'Chauri territory at Mare's Point! There's allegedly still a monument there, and it's why we entered into a second war with them." For a moment, she was proud of her recollected history lesson. He closed his eyes and shook his head.

"Just lies to cover for the sins of the ruling class," he replied.

"Illithor was quite close to our mother. He took the betrayal to our kin rather personally, and in hindsight, rightfully so," he said.

She stared at him but said nothing, her gaze asking the question that she wanted to voice. He picked up on her cues.

"Sadly, I couldn't be bothered with emotions at the time. I was still in the first stage of life. The wisdom that comes with longevity had not yet settled upon me."

He stared at his hands, where they sat cradled inside his lap, as he tried his best to process his embarrassment with humility and grace. Thaetra's eyes were glazed, and she stood frozen in the moment, unaware of how to proceed, battling the desire to console rooted in her non-elven blood.

"All this to say…I could not stand by and let his future be written by elven history…again." He paused to swallow the unpleasant-to-utter verbiage.

Thaetra continually shook her head in agreement, despite not finding the appropriate words to reply.

"In doing so, I am unaware of the consequences I have prepared for us. And for that, I am sorry. You weren't supposed to accompany me on this venture…it was not a part of the plan," he admitted. She froze as the final dot connected. He continued, "It is the most human thing I've ever done. Frankly, it's rather terrifying, but it's energising at the same time. How do they live like this?"

They both erupted into nervous laughter, and he looked up at her with a hopeful gaze.

"There's so much I wish to tell you, but I cannot. *All of this* only works if there is honest intent," he uttered while looking intimately disturbed. His gaze trailed away. Water pooled in the corners of his eyes.

Thaetra's head pivoted as she took notice of the unreleased tears, and her face crumpled as he quickly wiped them away.

"I must go for a walk now. Should I not return by morning, return home. Tell them that I sent you away," he said, refusing to make eye contact with her.

Thaetra's confusion was plainly broadcast. He stood hurriedly, nodding before walking into the shadow of the night. She managed to get out a nod of her own, although she did not quite fully agree or understand. It was all unfolding faster than she could adapt. Before she could process it all, he was gone. The howling wind forced its way through the trees, signalling an audible cue that she was now cold and alone.

Elarion walked amongst the trees, guided by the sound of the wind. He wandered aimlessly towards the song of the forest, stopping only once he noticed two glowing eyes that were focused on him from the shadows. A smile warmed his face. He bowed as they began to move closer to him.

"I was filled with regret not being able to see you, Lysand," Elarion said softly.

She stepped out of the shadow and into the light of the full moon.

CHAPTER ELEVEN

TRAPPED IN AMBER

CONNERH

He found himself here again, immobile and disconnected from his body. A captive within the constraints of his peripheral vision, he observed as glowing particles descended at a snail's pace, akin to raindrops, frozen and illuminated during their journey towards a ground adorned with smooth, wet, dark river stones. In the distance, a sea of black rippled, while everything under the sky was bathed in the amber hue of a burning sunset. Streaks of stars adorned the blue and purple sky, with a sun-like star divided by the horizon, blazing intensely, casting ripples of heat across the ground. However, its light offered no warmth. A deep, low hum reverberated in the background – audible, but not intrusive to the ear. Next to him stood a large tree with long, spiny branches stretching out from its trunk. Its appearance shifted with each experience, sprouting leaves that changed colour before eventually withering and falling to the ground. It served as both a temporal marker and a means of tethering him to time.

Alone, he sat, legs crossed and frozen in place, like a mosquito suspended in tree sap.

This realm sidestepped reality. He called it *the Amber.*

He hated this place, yet amidst its delicate chaos, its familiarity provided an odd solace. He felt like a stranger in someone else's home, forever waiting in a sort of…lobby. An uninvited guest who, for reasons beyond his ken, was allowed to stay. The duration of his entrapment here varied based on the experience – some lasted hours, others days, and a few remained indeterminately prolonged. His experiences were vivid visions of past and potential future events unfolding in three dimensions, here on a cosmic coastal side. Yet, regardless of the experience, he remained a passenger in an already moving vehicle. When here, he relinquished control – not by choice but through acceptance. This also meant avoiding fixation on the mechanics of this plane, which would trigger a cycle of panic and fear seemingly unending until his awakening.

The Amber was a peculiar and unusual place – it was his personal paradise, purgatory, and hell.

A long time had passed, and he was growing tired. Exactly how long, he could not be sure, but he knew that the black sea had crested and retracted roughly four hundred and sixteen times…for whatever measurement that was worth. His focus waned, and his eyelids dropped as he slipped into a restful state. Eventually, the sound of whispers reawakened his consciousness. He felt cold, but he struggled to attribute the sensation to any specific limb. His physical form was still present from what he could see, but it still refused to respond to his demands. A fog rolled in, obscuring his vision.

A feminine silhouette emerged from the white mist. The face was featureless, but her shape and gait were all too familiar. His heart sank.

No…no…no, he protested mentally. He'd seen this vision many times before. He felt anxious. *I don't want to see this again. Why do you keep showing me this!?*

His temper flared.

Why doesn't she run?! he shouted internally.

The feminine figure kneeled, arms outstretched, and embraced the child who ran to her.

"Take him and run!" he screamed.

His eyes darted away, yet he could not avoid the scene captured in his peripheral vision. He felt the sensation of tears running down his face, yet he could not observe them. A burning star scorched across the sky, emanating smoke as it crashed into the ground and took the shape of a man.

"Run!" Connerh shouted again. The shadowy figure of the man approached the woman and child. They acknowledged him. It was this part that always confused Connerh: the man sank to one knee as the child ran to him.

In this moment, Connerh could feel what they felt. The child was excited, happy, and optimistic. She was doubtful. The man sat the child on his knee, pointing at the stars. The woman approached and seemed to look up towards the sky along with them. The man pointed towards something and traced a path from the sky towards the horizon. The child clapped excitedly at its conclusion. The feminine figure seemed displeased with the climax of the story and backed away. The man grabbed the child by the shoulders and removed them from his knee as he stood.

"Grab him and go! NOW!" Connerh became more impatient.

The man approached the woman, wrapping an arm around her shoulder and pointing to the sky once more. She shook her head in protest. He insisted, grabbing her tighter. She broke away from his grasp. He moved to the child, wrapping his arm around the child instead. The woman became visibly uncomfortable and ran to the child to intervene – but the child raised its hand in protest at her advance. She stopped and froze in place.

"Why do you keep showing me this? What more do you want me to do?" Connerh asked in an undertone, remaining calm for the first time. The man stood as the child ran off, no longer visible. He wrapped his arm around the woman once more, pointing to the stars again. She patiently observed as he told an animated tale. After a while, he stopped, moving to stand opposite her. Her hand raised to her mouth, as if contemplating it all. She turned away, looking towards the stars. He waited patiently. When she turned to him and shook her head calmly, his head dropped in disappointment.

"It's too late!" Connerh shouted. "You should have run!"

He felt himself emotionally break without any physical manifestation. The man approached the woman calmly. Producing a blade, he stabbed her repeatedly until her figure crumpled into a pile of ash that dissipated and faded with the wind. It was always in this moment that Connerh felt especially helpless. If only he had hands and legs, he would've saved her at least once out of the hundreds of times he'd watched her die. His metaphorical stomach soured. He would have thrown up, had he the ability.

"I'm sorry."

He continued weeping.

The man approached the child, who reappeared, still distracted. He kneeled behind the child, dissipating into a fog that poured into the child.

"No!" Connerh shouted, finally awakening into the real world, covered in sweat and tears. His face and shirt were drenched. Rose approached quickly, embracing him as she wiped the tears from his eyes.

"I'm sorry, Rose! I couldn't stop it!" he apologised as tears ran down his face, still caught between the here and there.

She did her utmost to comfort him, but to no immediate resolution. She'd been there for him when he awoke from night terrors before, but this time was notably different. He was inconsolable, particularly bothered by what he'd seen, unable to break from it.

"I'm here!" she shouted as panic and anxiety began to overtake her.

He reacted by grasping wildly for her. His eyes rammed shut as he took a loud, audible inhale. It was as if he was taking his first breath.

Connerh's eyes opened.

Her blurry shape took focus. His lungs forcibly expelled the air they contained, and he smiled at her with deep-seated relief. She returned the gaze with pity for him. They remained in the moment, and for him, time slowed into the here and now. He traced the details of her face with his eyes, raising his hands as he had wished to do for what felt like weeks. Finally, he caressed her face.

CHAPTER TWELVE

FOREVER IN THE NIGHT SKY

LENA

"…It is unfortunate that you persist in entangling yourself in such a twisted and sordid affair. All I'll say is consider the cost before you act. What would this grant you? What is it worth? You know it pains me to be cliché and melodramatic, but really, you've not given me much choice. I hope you realise that I am doing all that I can for you…even when it comes at great personal risk. However, this…this I cannot do. Surely you understand why I cannot support you in this endeavour.

Should it count towards easing your mind…you are right. If only all matters in your world could be resolved by the scales of right and wrong. Oh, how simple it would all be.

…You know, there's an infinitely fine line between Justice and Revenge…

For what it's worth, I am sorry…and that it took so long to reply. Sadly, I'll be delayed longer than originally anticipated. But I am en route. A few hurdles have arisen…but worry not. It isn't anything that I cannot resolve. In the meantime, keep your ear to the wind. I am always a whisper away. I may be far, but I can still make my presence felt where it matters.

-R

P.S. Don't hold a grudge."

The black words were still damp on the parchment. Lena's brow grew heavy and furrowed. A frown pushed her bottom lip upwards, bracing for the loud, exacerbated sigh to follow. She lay draped over a rather stiff and uncomfortable chair, holding the spread-out letter between her thumbs and forefinger. She'd done her best to pad her body with a few pillows, and for the moment, it was providing some relief. She thought to move to more comfortable accommodations but lacked the energy or will to act on it, especially not after this.

"Damn," she whispered under her breath.

The disappointing nature of the letter came as no surprise; she had, in fact, been anticipating it, thinking that doing so would somehow cushion the blow of disappointment. It did not, but it had been worth a try.

"How convenient," she muttered and flared a brow before her arms crashed into her lap. Her head and eyes lowered as the words on the parchment began to fade. The ink was absorbed into the page, as if the words had never been written.

"*It hasn't ever been about convenience. You don't honestly believe that; you're just angry. Don't beg for reassurance. It's unbecoming.*" Freshly inked script appeared as if written by the hand of an invisible penman. The ink was dark blue, with metallic specks that sparkled when they caught the light.

"I'm not angry, just…disappointed," she replied, opting to take the mature route. The version playing in her head, however, took a much different path. She glanced away before looking back to read the reply.

"*We all have our own course to plot. You cannot always depend upon others to intervene on your behalf; otherwise, you risk losing your way.*"

"I don't always depend on others…and that's easy for you to say! You have the power of the cosmos at your fingertips," Lena replied. She watched as the ink dissolved.

"*Not so much. But if I could swap places with you, I would.*"

"No, you wouldn't," she replied with a scornful laugh.

"*You're right…I wouldn't. Lying isn't really my thing — it was an attempt to comfort you. Did it work? Kudos for effort?*"

"I hardly call that an effort," Lena retorted. "A half-hearted bunch of sentences on a piece of parchment is supposed to make me feel better about you isolating me?"

"*You're begging for reassurance again…*"

She growled out of frustration.

"*You act as if what you request is a small thing.*"

"For you, it is." Her voice lowered.

"*Power isn't about getting what you want all the time. Those who possess it still experience disappointment and failure; they still feel sadness and pain. Power does not exempt you from these burdens, and revenge does not free you of them.*"

She frowned, looking away. There was a pause as she thought, quickly brushing away the angry tears that escaped the clutches of her ducts. Her room was quiet, dark, and gloomy. It was snowing outside. The gentle, crisp flakes of snowfall made delicate impacts on the ground, their soft white glow illuminating the highlights of the bluish metal décor. Ravens were gathered on her patio as they played with one another. She glanced at them, then back again.

"You're quiet. What troubles you?"

"That…that I am alone." She could barely finish the words. Her tears barraged the parchment. The words vanished, taking the marks of her sorrow with them.

"Don't cry; you are not alone."

"Why? Because he's allegedly alive? If it even *is* him – with my fortune, it is yet another lookalike," she anguished, setting the parchment down as the words faded. She paced. "Even if it were, why would I bring him here? He knows where to find me, so obviously it was a conscious decision. But what if he's injured? Perhaps he's lost his memory in the battle… What's the word for it? Amnesia?"

Her thoughts raced aloud as she sought to navigate the waves of an emotional spectrum. She looked down, realising she had dropped the parchment. She ran to retrieve it, the echo of her footsteps resonating.

"Who?"

Her head lurched backwards.

"Connerh. I thought you would have known?" she asked, caught off guard. The words faded.

She waited. And waited.

Lena frowned.

"Reh'gara?" she asked.

The parchment began to glow, bringing a smile to her face. She set the parchment on the ground, taking a step back and crossing her hands at the waist. Once the glow subsided, her frown returned with it. When she could see the words being written again, she retrieved the parchment once more.

"I cannot come to you at this time."

"I understand," she said, disappointed but accepting.

"When did you hear of this? Regarding…the man?"

"Not long ago. It was confirmed by Gatty's spiders," she replied.

"He cannot be alive; this is a farce."

"Why?" she asked.

There was a delay.

"Because I looked for him, and he was nowhere to be found."

"She wouldn't have brought this to me unless she was sure," she retorted, confused and unwilling to accept it as a false report.

"This troubles me."

"Why?" Her breathing hastened.

"He does not have the capacity for change. The two of you together spell disaster. It was better for you when he was dead."

"I don't think he has a reunion in mind."

"Explain."

"Either it is true, and he was killed, meaning this is an impostor. Or…" she paused and shook her head. "Or the rumours of his death were false, and he has hidden from me."

"Perhaps he knows what is best."

She grimaced. His words stung.

"I am sorry. I do what I must, even if it may cause you temporary discomfort. It brings me sadness to see you affected in this way. But even as I do what I must, there is something that fights me. I took no pleasure in seeing you in anguish when he vanished from your life, but in some ways…with the future in mind…it was good for you."

She finally screamed, having had enough of what she did not want to hear. She tore the parchment into pieces and threw it on the ground before marching out to her balcony. A raven landed on the railing of the balcony and stared at her.

"Am I so limited by paper and ink?"

His voice spoke to her in her mind, older and calming.

"Running away never absolves you of your responsibility. It only delays the inevitable, adding with it pain and distress you need not accrue," he went on.

"It is not my *responsibility* to listen to you berate me," she replied sharply.

"I am not berating you, my dear. I am only trying to spare you further pain…but I see that this is beyond my reach. Even *my* power has limitations," he said, resigned. The raven seemed to revert back to being simply a bird, finding a new focus for its gaze and hopping around the railing. She grew concerned.

"Don't leave me," she whimpered, rapidly coming down from her anger. The raven jumped on an insect and ate it before flying quickly back to her side and re-establishing its gaze.

"I have not left you; it was hungry," he assured her. His voice sighed, and he continued, "What am I to do with you?" he continued.

She stared blankly over the balcony. The crashing waves below sang to her, calling to her. Her eyes welled with tears, and she finally cried, "I don't want to play this game anymore."

"Enough," he demanded.

The distance between her and the sea seemed to expand, making her dizzy. She shrank back as the doors swung open with a loud crash, and Farrah ran in, out of breath.

"I'm here, I'm here," she shouted.

"What?" Lena asked.

Farrah looked confused.

"You called for me?" Farrah asked, struggling to regain her breath. "It sounded important. Did you not?"

"I did not," Lena said, looking at the raven. She offered a timid smile. Keeping her gaze on the bird, she assured, "You must be hearing things. Go back to what you were doing. I am… I'll be fine."

Farrah acknowledged her and left, still confused, gently closing the doors behind herself.

There was a drawn-out silence before Reh'gara pressed, "Even while trying to convince me otherwise, the mere discussion of him drives you to madness. Did those thoughts seem reasonable to you?"

"When is sorrow reasonable, considerate, or kind?" she retorted, and he sighed again.

"I will do a portion of what you ask…within reason. The rest we will discuss when I arrive," he began.

She sniffled, rushing to wipe her eyes.

"I have tried for an eternity to shield you from what it is you are so eager to run towards. Perhaps it is I who am running away from what is inevitable?" he said. She frowned, but before she could respond, he went on. "Review the exploits of your ancestor, Archemond. There you will find what it is you need to sway Darros to your mission. I will not force him to aid you, but be cautious; Darros is neither friend nor ally to anyone but himself."

She nodded and ran to get a quill and paper to take notes.

"The elf will be of much aid. Persuade him to stay with you a while. Keep those closest to you even closer," he continued. Then, almost second-guessing his decision, he pressed, "Lena… This will come at a cost, even to those not involved. Is it worth that cost? Even when they come to you for repayment? And you know they will come. Is *he* worth it?"

"Yes," she replied quickly, without hesitation.

"I was afraid you might say that," he remarked. "If it is true, then hold him until I arrive. Don't speak a word to him. Promise me."

Her eyes dropped, and as her brows lowered and crumpled, she whispered, "…I promise."

His responding laughter caught her off guard.

"Even now, you make a promise you already intend to break. Very well, daughter of Ioelena. I relinquish you to your fate. Carve it well. Find where your heart and mind converge. Failing to find balance in the end will cost you a great deal…as it often does…for everyone." Then, his voice waning, he said, "It does pain me when I can't be there for you."

A piece of parchment appeared in front of her. The raven squawked loudly, having grown frustrated with being suspended in place. It flapped its wings at her, first attempting to make her move away before choosing to fly off when she did not. She picked up the parchment, reading its words aloud, but quietly.

"*Remember my words. Forever in the night's sky. —R*"

The words were blotted onto the page in black ink. The abrupt end of the conversation saddened her.

"Hurry to me," she whispered, gripping the parchment tightly.

The words eventually faded. She was reluctant to let go but finally gave in. She set the paper on the ground and whispered a phrase in another tongue, focusing on its correct pronunciation, before lurching backwards with a smile as a gentle blue flame erupted. It consumed the parchment until nothing remained.

She quickly ran to retrieve her journal and began to write down as much as she could remember.

CHAPTER THIRTEEN

A NORMAL LIFE

CONNERH

Connerh sat at the mountain's summit, isolated by the thin fog that surrounded him. His legs were crossed in just the same way as when he used to idle here in his younger days. He toyed with a picturesque sprig of rosemary, a souvenir he had acquired on his hike. Herbs like jasmine and rosemary grew in abundance in this part of the north, often blooming into expansive fields of intertwining bushes. The relaxing scent carried for miles, but the fragrant air was thin and chilled. It nipped at his lungs with each breath and stung the drying walls of his nostrils, but he could not bring himself to be bothered by it.

The dead grass spread out under him, alongside petite yellow flowers too stubborn to die before winter took full hold. Delicate petals littered the ground, shining through the mist and varying in density along the path he had taken to get here. The journey up had been predictably uneventful, though no less charming. He'd spent the majority of it identifying boulders he had once climbed as a boy, with the scars received and lessons learned from them. He'd spent his formative years in Nyradhal. Most of them were good, some were bad…a few dark. But it was what he considered to be his home. He'd been born there, and he had been thoroughly convinced that he'd die there.

Still might, he thought.

If only he could go back to when the times were simpler, when colours were more vivid and the days twice in length. Before the days seemed dark and when the night was brighter. However, he was running low on room for regret and just wanted to start anew. As he saw it, the only way to blot out a smudge was with new ink. It was an unoriginal sentiment coming from a man like him, but it was no less true. It's not that he would take it *all* back – what's done was done. But to be able to experience the better days, *truly* appreciate them, with informed eyes…it was the soldier's lament. They all felt it, sooner or later. Still, despite being flooded with nostalgia, the trek had succeeded in the much-needed task of cleansing his mind. His therapeutic silence had been rarely disturbed, except by his own damp footsteps or the bleating of goats too far in the distance to know he was there. Even the birds had kept the volume of their discussions to a minimum.

The rising sun now burned brightly at this elevation. The fiery sphere cast diagonal pillars embellished by the mist, illuminating the city below like a beacon of resonant remembrance. Its ambience carried with impunity – dock workers scuttled over wooden planks, seagulls bickered with fluctuating intensity, and the deep tone of bells melded into a quintessential backdrop. He couldn't help but smile as the salty aroma of the sea danced at the tip of his tongue. As the sun began to dissolve the mist, his attention fell towards the sprig. Its powerful aroma was linked to enduring memories not relegated to the recesses of his mind. He rolled the sprig between his fingers, inhaling the concentrated scent released by the oils. A rush of images flooded his mind, finally coalescing into a single lasting scene.

Lena's silken hair flowed across his face, tickling his neck. His mind filled in the missing pieces, like the sweet scent of her sweat mixed with her perfume. It was as if she were right in front of him. He wanted to open his eyes to confirm she was there, waiting for him, but he didn't want to risk losing the moment. The images were so vivid, but they, too, eventually faded.

His widened eyes opened to an upwards gaze. He struggled to refocus his scattered thoughts, desperately wanting to return to the conjured moment. It was a losing battle. His breathing hastened. He took a moment to gather himself, plunging his face into his hands before they slid along the sides of his head and back again. Perhaps he needed to start over. He looked at his hand longingly, like a fiend in desperate need of *more*. He discarded the sprig in favour of grasping another, assuming its magic had been expended. He vigorously crushed it between his palms, engulfing his face with his cupped hands, surrounding his nose and mouth. His shoulders released as she returned to the place somewhere between dreaming and being awake. He smiled as she twirled around the summit. Her laughter echoed against the dense ambience, and her face...

Her face was obscured. Somehow, only the essence of her features remained. It was all that he could remember. He frowned. A subtle panic began to spread. He could not recall, and the inability to do so was maddening. His closed-eye frown deepened as he attempted to force details onto her face, to superimpose what fragments he could coerce together. However, the amalgamation felt foreign. Those were not her eyes staring back at him; they belonged to someone else. They were missing that certain spark – the spark that made the pit of his stomach a little heavy and caused his chest to flutter. These eyes were familiar, but they were not hers. His own instinctively drifted open for a moment before he squeezed them shut once more.

But it was too late.

She was gone.

It was all gone.

He had, after all, left it all behind.

All that remained was a glowing, red blur at the back of his eyelids. He exhaled, blinking the accumulated moisture from his eyes. The absurdity of how he must have looked to an onlooker, as if the summit was full to the brim with tourists, brought about an abrupt suspension to his endeavour of longing. It was only his pride trying to salvage what it could, but it was enough for him to regain sufficient composure. The chapters of life replayed in his head.

It had gone by so quickly. He'd last seen her just over ten years ago, and he had last set foot here in Nyradhal in no less than fifteen. He looked out over the city without the rosy monocle of nostalgia.

Nyradhal, the small fishing village he remembered, was no more. Now, it thrived as a city of commerce. Modest shacks and shops had been replaced with grand buildings of stone, and a bustling harbour lined a fjord that, once embraced by nature, was now filled with large ships and their towering masts. The place was damned-near unrecognisable, he thought. He released a grunt. So much had changed.

Had she?

Time had been such a brief eternity.

He thought about a moment in time in which a simple flicker of choice would have changed everything. Had he known then what he had now, *should* he have changed anything? He suddenly felt like a leaf being carried by the wind. He was twirling about in a specific direction, having thought it was he who chose the path – a path that was supposed to be some great journey he'd been destined to undertake.

Hadn't it, though?

"Is he back yet?" Aeryk asked upon walking into the house.

"No, not yet," Rose replied as she continued to pack a few satchels. The question had grown tiresome, but she understood his excitement. He'd never been inside a large city before, or at least he had been far too young to remember. The last time they took such a risk, he was a baby. It was a different time then, when the thrill of being on the run was still new. Stressful, of course, but exciting in a way that got the blood flowing.

It only took one close call of being discovered before such adventures were scrubbed from future possibility. Connerh had even said goodbye to his favourite horse, Whisper, as he feared harm coming to him. He was a sweet horse with a human-like disposition; a true companion. They were inseparable much of the time, so much so that the risk of being identified because of Whisper was always a concern. He was somewhat unique, standing at least twice the size of a normal horse and solid black except for a spot of white on his forehead.

It was such a sad day.

But it was too risky, especially with a little one in tow. She was still reeling in disbelief that Connerh had even suggested going into Nyradhal, let alone was carrying through with it. Having spent her life accustomed to city life, the past ten years of living in the countryside had required time to acclimate, making it seem impossible to return to that previous life. Not full-time, anyway. Life was quieter now, less rushed, less…everything. Simple. It seemed a diminutive word, but it was no less succinct. There was always the belief that life needed to be chaotic and stressful in order for it to be rewarding, or even normal. What silly little lies we convince ourselves of. She caught herself daydreaming and returned to packing their satchels for the trip, leaving Aeryk's words a blur.

"What?" she asked, then nodded as her thoughts caught up, registering what he had said as he repeated them.

"How much longer?" he asked. Her eyes flared.

"If you go outside now, you'll be the first to know, my love." She smiled with a chuckle.

He shrugged and left, finding her terms agreeable. He was an easy child most of the time. As long as he had something to focus on, he kept out of trouble. Most of the time. She smirked.

She rubbed her chin, now faced with a dilemma. The white cloak or the green? Oh, who was she kidding? Obviously the green. It was a velvet cloak in the shade of crushed emerald and complemented her gold necklace. Stunning. She could still remember a time when she didn't have to make such choices, let alone pack her own bags; it was always done for her. She had servants to attend to her every whim and need. It was a memory that now felt silly to recall. She would never share such things aloud; a tinge of embarrassment flushed her cheeks. Had she only known the sense of agency something as simple as attending to oneself provided, she would have excused…well, the majority of them. There was nothing wrong with a little help, after all. Today, however, was not one of those days. She enjoyed the quiet and the time it gave her to mentally prepare. Connerh would be sure to be on high alert. Probably a little bit grumpy. Understandably so, but he was trying.

For their sakes.

Connerh's arrival was without much fanfare, a grin strewn across his lips. She admired him from a distance, hesitating to distract him from whatever – or whoever – he was pondering. Rose approached, embraced him, and then paused upon being assaulted by the aroma of rosemary that emanated from him.

She understood its significance.

She took his hands and caressed her face with them, identifying the source of the fragrance. It was petty to confirm her suspicions in this way, but she was only human, after all. She pushed past the feelings of jealousy, closing her eyes and basking in his touch. His hands were warm to her chilled cheeks. He kissed her head and pulled away.

"Well…how was the scout?" she asked. He seemed pensive, but it quickly washed away in a genuine fashion, not forced.

"Everything is so different. It might as well be called something else," he said. She could sense his disappointment and followed him.

"New Nyradhal, perhaps?" she offered to his laughter.

"That is the practice, isn't it? Slapping *New* in front of everything," he said.

She tugged at his arm, turning him around to face her once more before she said, "I'm sure much has remained the same. Besides, this is good news."

"Oh?"

"It means the memory of what it once was will remain. Better it evolve into something better than be lost to ruin and forgotten in time," she replied. His head tilted with a flash of his brow.

"I hadn't looked at it that way. I suppose you're right," he said. She smiled, having succeeded in mollifying his spirits.

"Still, I can't help but feel a bit of me has been erased. I was hoping to show Aeryk where I grew up…as I saw it," he said remorsefully.

She offered a tender smile while holding his hands and replied, "I'm sure he'll find it fascinating all the same."

He smiled. Her words hadn't swayed his feelings on the matter, but he appreciated the effort. He took a deep breath and looked around.

"What?" she asked, sensing his sudden discomfort.

"How's it feel? The house, that is. Does it feel permanent?" he asked. She grinned, also taking a look around.

"I think so. I'm having to relearn the meaning of the word…but it fits," she chuckled. He was happy for her, as evidenced by his sincere expression.

Her brows furrowed, although she was still wearing a smile as she murmured, "You really mean it, don't you?"

"Mean what?"

"You mean to stay here," she said. He looked at her as if she were ridiculous.

"Yes, of course," he replied.

"I mean…we always talk about it, I just thought…" she said.

"That I was joking?"

"No, that we'd…I don't know, give it a try first? I just didn't think it would be so…easy?" She became flustered, but he squeezed her hands.

"I'm sorry that it took so long…" he said.

"No, no, that's not what I meant—" she protested.

"I know, but I meant it. It's important to me that he gets a proper life. My past is not his responsibility to bear. It chases me, not him. After a while, I began to wonder if I was imagining the ghosts on the horizon. I still don't know the answer…" he said, trailing off.

Her eyes averted at the mention of the past. Her ghosts never came, and she'd not settled on how to feel about it.

"And what if they come after all?" she let slip.

"Then *I* will deal with them," he replied. She wanted to smile, but it was the way he said it. It didn't sit right with her.

"Hurry, let's go! The horses are waiting!" Aeryk shouted as he burst through the door, rushing over to break up their embrace. He pulled a giggling Connerh outside. She lingered a moment, looking around the empty home.

It all took on new meaning.

CHAPTER FOURTEEN

THANKSGIVING & EMANCIPATION

VIDAR

The crunching sound of old snow being forcibly compressed under Vidar's colossal boot reverberated along the mountainside, sending nearby creatures scrambling to their preferred place of concealment. He, on the other hand, made no effort to conceal his presence. He was not a stranger here, nor an uninvited guest, and there would be nothing that could frighten him. He used to live here, play here, eat here…even hunt here. Vidar paused mid-stride, grimaced, and tilted his head back, watching his semi-transparent breath float quietly towards the sky. He swore the incline increased in gradient with each year. It most certainly had nothing to do with his increasing age, as he was far too young to begin feeling its effects…or so he thought. At eighty years, he still felt generally spritely and limber – for the most part. Though, in truth, perhaps not in this exact moment. More specifically, his lower back was proving a problem. Giants were prone to diminished mobility as they aged, often fuelling the slow-moving, grunting stereotype that depicted them as cursing in incoherent, slow speech.

Actually, the joint pain could be rather excruciating – especially for the older, much larger generations.

He twisted his torso back and forth, trying to release the tight band of tension around his lower back, managing to loosen only the snow from his cloak and long beard. It was perpetually winter this high in the mountains, just the way his kind preferred it. Giants lived on top of the mountain, dwarves below, gnomes within, and men beside it. It was an equitable arrangement. *The mountain stands for strength and provides protection*, his father, Galabrand, would always say…still said, often. He sarcastically mouthed the words with a scowl. Vidar hated the mountain, or at least climbing it, enduring it…and the general reverence the elders placed upon such an inanimate *thing* filled him with a palpable distaste.

Despite this silent revolt, the ambience and humility it provided were hard to dispute, even for him. The mountain had a way of making him feel small in the world – a task not easily accomplished, even in these uncertain times.

Vidar looked out over Furstholm in the near distance, its spires piercing the light cloud cover that attempted to conceal the city. He took a deep breath and sighed as his frustration melted away. His gaze dropped upon realising he did this every year at just about this point in the trek. He shook his head as fleeting thoughts of the inevitable dinner-table arguments crossed his mind. Vidar cursed aloud, wondering why he continued to put up with and support this custom, yet he continued pressing onwards. This, too, was by all accounts a custom of its own. His frustration resumed as if it had never been interrupted. While his parents had accommodations within the castle, his father insisted on maintaining a traditional cavern dwelling, often staying there alone when Hargatha had business in the capital. He had admired his father's unrelenting adherence to the old ways in his younger years, but now they seemed more trouble than they were worth. And ignorantly blind to progress.

His visit with the Uridar had only made his frustration with the way of things exponentially worse. He'd been shown what was, what is, and what could be. Yet he was unsure of what version of existence was better or worse: knowing the truth or living in blissful ignorance. He'd not yet come to terms with it, only aware that his impatience was growing beyond his control. What was once a localised discomfort was now mutating into a sharp pain, a quiet disdain into a roaring rage. As he grew closer to his destination, a familiar rush of…something…coursed through his veins.

He quickly pulled his sleeve down and inspected his hand from all angles. There was no change to its appearance, yet the feeling in the limb was…familiar.

Could it be?

Vidar opened the immense wooden door to his parents' home and slipped inside, quietly closing it behind him. He hoped he would have a moment to mentally prepare in relative silence. Pressing his head against the door, he closed his eyes; air escaped his lungs with a suppressed sigh. It was then and there that he determined this would be the last time he observed this…*absurd tradition*. After all, what was in it for him anyway? The last remaining strand of what he once considered loyalty was the only motivation for him to make the best of it. However, he'd slowly begun to realise that the tug he felt was not loyalty but a learned guilt imposed upon him by his parents, specifically his mother. Even at his current age, an old man by human standards, he fought the instinctive call to regress to the childlike dynamic when he visited his old home. Perhaps it was the scents, the sights, or just the instinctive familiarity of it all that quickly transported him to a time of being a youngling. His mother's perfume, his father's sometimes overpowering, sweaty musk…the odours her meals gave off, or maybe just the ambient sounds. It was like he had never left, and for a fleeting moment, he felt like a child again.

He *hated* himself for it.

His hatred was powerful, even more so since his visit with the Uridar. Now seemingly malleable, it overpowered the remnants of generational guilt, the preferred tool of his forefathers for exerting their control. His rage would no longer be suppressed in order to make *others* feel good…not after today.

His nose wrinkled at the pungent body odours that permeated the chamber, barely masked by the smell of burning wood, smoke, and seared meat. These were not the scents that spurred pleasant, nostalgic memories. The realisation of who the odours represented made his shoulders sink and his head rock back and forth. His relatives from his father's side were the epitome of Mountainfolk: barely clothed, hairy, unhygienic, and lacking decorum or any sort of manners befitting the era. It'd been many years since most of them had descended from the High Mountain, seemingly about the same time they had last bathed. Vidar began to discard his outer cloak on the already mountainous pile of hides and furs, but the stench emanating from them dissuaded him. He did his best to subdue the disgust that sauntered across his face, but it was a losing battle from the start.

Hargatha quietly approached from around the corner, a chalice of wine in one hand. Her face softened upon seeing him, and her arms quickly extended as she walked towards him. He looked at her without moving, receiving an embrace he did not want if only to placate her. She began to giggle quietly; his expression was an open book, though she took it to be directed to their relatives rather than herself.

"I was rather hoping you were a burglar here to put me out of my misery," she whispered. He smirked and relaxed his posture slightly as he finally returned her embrace, even if it was lacking in warmth and enthusiasm.

"Sorry to disappoint. Though I do have a dagger here, somewhere," he replied, pretending to search his pockets.

Hargatha laughed as she took his cloak and, to his relief, set it neatly on a nearby bench. He kissed the top of her head as she took his arm in her own and began to walk him over to the main dining area.

"Your father's kin deemed it appropriate and timely to invite themselves for dinner," she offered.

He looked back at her with a frown.

"I couldn't say no… They were all here already," she said by way of an explanation, excusing herself of blame, *just as she always did*, he thought.

"I suppose I owe them a token of my gratitude. Anything to spare me from the ramblings and musings of the great Galabrand," he replied mockingly. She ran her hand across his cheek.

"Still your heart, my son. He's promised to be on his best behaviour this night," she assured him, hardly believing the words herself as they came out of her mouth.

"You say that every year, Mother."

He was not impressed, but hearing him call her that sent her mind back in time, to before the politics, to before…the secrets. Her eyes darted around his face. There was much she wanted to say to him, but this was neither the time nor the place. They locked eyes, both trapped in a time that no longer was.

"We should talk later."

"I think we should speak—"

They spoke at the same time, immediately disarming the other.

"What is it?" she whispered with a hint of concern in her voice, suddenly incapable of waiting to satiate her curiosity. The idea that her child was withholding something from her pulled at strings she was incapable of defending against.

Then the childlike face she'd mentally superimposed over his true visage grew older before her eyes. It was tired…and seething.

Her expression collapsed into pity. His refusing to look her in the eye stole her breath, suggesting his topic of conversation was serious. Hargatha knew she had a way of making her children feel guilty, regardless of whether there was reason to be found. It was a fragment of childhood trauma that had managed to retain itself even until now. Hargatha shook her head, breaking eye contact and dismissing her own thoughts. She looked down at his wardrobe and started to adjust his necklace, then noticed his right pinky finger flexing back and forth. Her hands slowed; his nervous twitch had betrayed him.

"What's going on in here?" asked Egress, his younger sister, quickly bounding out of the corner and into the reception area. She did her best to speak quietly, although she was mostly unsuccessful.

"Oh, piss off," Vidar replied quickly.

"How dare you two leave me alone in there! And why are you so late?" She folded her arms in protest.

Hargatha smirked.

"We should go; I'm sure we're not being as quiet as we think we are," she interrupted them, leading them both by the hand into the dining chamber. Inside, a long, rectangular table was surrounded by large pillows with even larger relatives splayed across them. In the centre was a fire pit with a plethora of skewered animals and vegetables roasting above it.

Galabrand quietly tracked Vidar with his eyes as he entered the room. "Cousin!"

A few of his younger kin rushed up to embrace Vidar; his eyes rolled in the back of his head at the odour. He nodded out of respect, not daring to inhale the stench through his mouth by returning a verbal greeting. Vidar patted their heads in an awkward gesture of endearment.

"Vidar," Galabrand's sharp, deep voice elevated above the loud conversations. He motioned to an empty spot next to him. While Galabrand was showing him respect in traditional terms by offering the position beside him, as Vidar saw it, it was still a position beneath him. The smile Galabrand wore made the upper left side of his lip begin to writhe. He raised a palm, declining the offer before he chose to sit instead at the opposite end of the table to Galabrand. The move was partly purposefully symbolic, partly purely strategic. After all, it was far enough from the closest vomit-inducing relative. Hargatha and Galabrand locked eyes; she was already warning him with a look as she returned to sit to the left of him.

"Good fortune, cousin," Vidar's much larger relative greeted him. The High Mountain Clan, being the borderline-feral isolationists that they were, had retained an almost pure-giant bloodline. Where Vidar, Galabrand, and his brother were some of the tallest in their line, the High Mountains towered over them by some two to three feet.

"And to you," he returned the gesture. Then, failing to make pleasantries in a sincere manner, Vidar asked, "What brings the lot of you this way?"

"We're going to see dwarves!" one of the younger ones shouted. Most of the table laughed at the innocent outburst. Vidar, still encumbered by the odour of his relatives, failed to find amusement in the little one's words.

"The High Mountain Clan has much to discuss with the Iron-Borne. We decided to bring the little ones, as a chance to see the world below," Sigherd, the eldest, replied. Vidar exchanged glances with his mother, now very much interested in what information he could gather.

"Is that so? Servants, feed us; I'm famished after climbing this forsaken mountain."

Vidar snapped his fingers, trailing off from the original conversation. Human attendants, vastly smaller by comparison, quickly rushed to the fire pit and began carving slabs of meat from the skewered animals.

"Now, then: family does not keep secrets from one another, do they?" Vidar continued as he slouched into a more comfortable posture, grabbed some of the food being served to him, and began eating it.

Sigherd first looked to Galabrand, seeking approval to continue. He nodded in agreement and returned his gaze to Vidar.

"We seek to remove the half-breed from the throne. She is not worthy of the honour; it is time we return to the old ways," Sigherd continued.

Vidar's eyes widened as he looked at Hargatha in disbelief, then back again.

"I find it peculiar that you would be so bold as to say this in front of the hand of the very queen you seek to usurp. That typically spells disaster for rebellions, last I checked," Vidar replied. He knew his relatives had a touch of the mad, but this...this was another matter in its entirety. Sigherd looked around the room with a vacant smile, not understanding the disconnect.

"Is the House of Galabrand no longer…a safe place?" Sigherd asked in sudden doubt.

"It is, and it always will be," Hargatha responded stoically, catching Vidar by surprise. His brow raised as he cleared the food debris from his teeth with his tongue. He lifted the chalice of wine in front of him, inhaling its aroma while maintaining his gaze where it was fixed on his cousin, still swirling it around in his cup as he held it from beneath.

"Forgive me; I forget where I am. I spend entirely too much time with bureaucrats. Go on, cousin," he offered a borderline-insincere smile, the top of his cheek muscles pulling upwards, like a facial curtsy of sorts. He took a sip from his cup as he politically pivoted, quickly; he had learned from the best. Galabrand quietly snorted in approval, still brandishing the smile that gave Vidar particularly violent inclinations. Hargatha observed quietly. Added to Vidar's frustrations was the fact that *she* always defended the impropriety of the old fool, often despite her duty. In a sense, he wasn't all that surprised that the *old neanderthal* and his relatives were planning a coup at the very same dinner table as his mother, the person responsible for quelling such a thing.

It fits, he thought. He looked towards his sister, where she sat with her arms folded. She looked uncomfortable, *as she should*. He didn't always see eye-to-eye with her, but she could at least be counted on to be sensible…consistent. She had a good heart, though she was sometimes self-inclined – but really, who wasn't in this day and age? Her only glaring flaw, as best he could see, was the ease with which she was manipulated by Hargatha and intimidated by Galabrand. It was a weakness Vidar could not simply overlook. Her lack of strength and self-agency put him at odds with her. She was smarter than this, yet he could not identify *why* she persisted in being an instrument to her own demise.

Sigherd went on with their supposed discontent with Lena's service to the kingdom. Their imagined grievances fell upon his deaf ears. He had stopped listening beyond the first twelve words, instead focusing his eyes upon each family member in turn. For the first time, he felt like he was staring at strangers playing a game with no possible winners. There was a time when he would have gladly engaged in political intrigue – he used to love playing the game alongside his mother. She had taught him everything, but this time, it felt…meaningless.

"The Brothers of Cree also express displeasure…" Galabrand offered.

Vidar laughed.

"Those half-wit zealots? The very ones who tried to burn down a brothel," he laughed in disbelief, "*with* the whores still in it! You can't be serious."

"Granted, their methods lean towards the extreme, but they are at least principled. Determined in their cause," Hargatha cut in.

"This is not serious. This is a prank. It has to be," Vidar mumbled to himself, half laughing.

"It's not just the zealots, Vidar; it's the governors, the clergy, and the guilds. I love her dearly, but Little Bird does not have the strength in her wings anymore. Honestly, I'm not quite sure she ever did," she replied. Then, almost as if she were trying to comfort him, she continued, "There's nothing wrong with not being cut out for leadership. Always distracted, that one, with her head in the clouds instead of performing her duty."

Vidar's gaze dropped. He couldn't quite disagree with the assessment – and in some ways, he agreed with it – but something about it also felt wrong. He didn't like his family's insistence upon *control*. He loved his cousin… It was Connerh he hated, even more so for what he had done to her. But now he was beginning to question *why* he originally hated him. Were they his own reasons? He paused for a moment.

"Surely it's not *all of them*. She's quite favoured in the capital… Besides, isn't it your job to bring her down from said clouds? Or is that shiny medallion you've got just for fashion's sake?" His brow furrowed.

"That would be a fair question if you were inferring I'd not done my job…and at times, hers. And no, it's not *all* of them, but it is a sizeable…" she replied, not appreciating his sarcasm.

"Rebellion? Coup? Hostile takeover? What *is* this, exactly?" Vidar cut her off.

"It's just talk, *son*," Galabrand intervened. *That* word made Vidar's eye twitch.

"The word you're looking for is sedition," Vidar shot back, swirling the wine in his cup.

"It takes more than popularity with lackies in the capital to run a kingdom. You know this. As cliché as it sounds, there's a storm brewing to our south. What we do is to ensure everyone's safety. Times are going to get hard; we need a strong leader who will do what is right by everyone. We're not talking about killing her, just moving her aside," Hargatha replied. Vidar's brow sunk. He lightly shook his head to himself.

"That's what they always say, isn't it? It's for *your* protection…as they slide the knife into your back," he mused to himself.

"What's gotten into you?" Galabrand replied.

Vidar locked eyes with him and muttered, "You…have no idea," quietly laughing to himself.

"All this talk of protecting the kingdom… *Who*, exactly, will be ushering in this new era of peace and security for all to enjoy?" he asked cynically.

"I think your mother will be a fine queen. It could have been you, had you listened," Galabrand replied, grabbing her hand to kiss it.

Hargatha felt a wave of embarrassment wash over her. She knew exactly how it sounded to Vidar. She would have felt the same, had she been in his shoes.

"It has been far too long since one of *us* has worn the crown! No more half-breeds and *others*!" Sigherd shouted.

"Long live Hargatha, daughter of Ragnar and Ylva, blessed be their names!" Galabrand, Sigherd, and his wife shouted repeatedly. Even their children eventually joined in.

"This is madness," Vidar said aloud to himself. He looked at Egress as she sat there quietly, arms still folded and mind far removed from the conversation.

"Don't you have anything to say to this?" Vidar insisted.

She stared at him blankly, silent, regardless of what she actually thought.

"Of course you don't." He scowled at her. The cheering and shouting continued in what felt like slow motion. He felt disconnected from the family hive mind, finally cured of the virus that had once infected him.

He felt…free.

Vidar stood and refilled his cup.

"You're absolutely right. Storm the castle; send your zealot minions to burn everything in sight. Kill anyone who stands in your way!" he joked with sharp sarcasm. The table grew quiet as he swigged his wine.

A frown overtook his face. He was done.

"The dwarves will never join your cause," he began. "They are, in fact, loyal to the crown, much thanks to her *once-deceased fiancé*."

Hargatha locked eyes with Galabrand.

Vidar continued uninterrupted, "You'll be lucky if they don't cut you at the knee and toss you into the fire at the mere *suggestion* of betraying their queen! Although it's nothing more than what you deserve; aligning with your whore murders will cause you to lose the support of the east *and* the south. They're far too conservative for such extremist methods. So, forget peace, since you'll turn the kingdom on its backside, inciting a civil war." He laughed at the ignorance, yet he was confused by it. "And then, the elves…" His empty gaze focused on Hargatha. "They would descend upon you like flies on the trash heap! Demanding justice…and balance. They may not outright ally with us, but they respect *her*. Again…thanks to her *once-deceased fiancé*."

He paused to gather his thoughts, and he suddenly found himself staring into the void once again.

"What have I done?" he whispered.

One of Sigherd's children passed wind and erupted into laughter, breaking the awkward silence. However, it only angered Vidar.

"You would know this information if you stopped eating goat shit and descended the mountain more than once in a generation, you *fucking filthy feral fungoids!*" he shouted directly towards his cousins.

Galabrand stood in protest.

Vidar pointed directly at him, locking eyes as he declared, "I pray to the gods you *would* provoke me. I would wear your entrails as decoration at my coronation as the newly appointed Hand. I *beg* you to do what you do best."

His eyes pierced through Galabrand. For the first time in what felt like his entire life, he spoke freely and candidly, without restraint. The hatred, while burning and acidic in nature, left relief in its wake. It was cathartic.

Hargatha stood and put her hand on Galabrand's chest, as if to restrain his tongue. Galabrand himself wasn't sure of how to react; he'd always relegated Vidar's emotions in a condescending manner, but now, he felt substance behind his son's words. He also felt a streak of pride at Vidar standing up for himself, though it was drowned out amidst his anger.

Vidar imagined the feelings of hurt and betrayal his mother would undergo if he murdered Galabrand in hateful respite. It was only her theoretical pain that troubled him, no matter the consequence. He could envision it so clearly: the relief he would receive as Galabrand drew his last breath. He was sure of it. The peripheral sight of his mother's shock was the only thing keeping him from lunging across the table and engulfing his hands in Galabrand's blood. The *injustice* of his continual existence haunted Vidar, and he would not be satiated until the deed was done.

Egress' hand reached out and touched him, causing a break in his train of thought. He looked at her. She shook her head, encouraging him to stop.

She sought to return to the way of things, he thought. Vidar scoffed loudly.

There would be no going back.

"You *disgust* me." His eyes lowered as his lip curled, and he reprimanded her, "You're strong, capable of thinking for yourself, yet you succumb to those weaker than you."

Vidar thought to strike her, but she looked pathetic…weak. He raised his head, looking back at Hargatha instead.

"I *loved* you…" He shook his head. Vidar swallowed the remainder of his wine, threw the chalice into the fire, looked around the room, and concluded, "And the wine is shit."

There was silence as he gathered his things to leave.

Then, just before he slammed the door shut behind himself, he said in a low tone, "I pray *he* kills you all."

And then he was gone.

They all looked at one another, unsure of how to proceed.

"Vidar is no longer one of us." Galabrand broke the silence.

Hargatha's eyes dropped. It pained her to hear it, but Galabrand was right. Still, her first move was to approach Egress, leaning into her ear.

"I have a job for you," she whispered.

Egress' brow crumpled.

Vidar stood on the other side of the door, catching his breath. The cold, sharp air filled his lungs, purging the lingering stench of his relatives. His stomach churned anyway, causing him to vomit.

As he wiped his mouth, he looked out over the mountainside, gathering his thoughts, unsure of what caused the episode. His pinky finger and hand shook violently. He grabbed it with his left hand, keeping them steady.

"It's time for things to change," he said to himself.

He took a deep breath, gathering himself to begin his descent down the mountain.

CHAPTER FIFTEEN

The Head that Wears the Crown

LENA

"I am Ioelena the Fourth, Queen of Hildeheim, the Northern Isles, and the High Mountain. I stand before you as your rightful queen and a daughter of this great nation. It is the blood of the raven that courses through my veins, the same blood as that of the conquerors who built these walls and the grand pillars that have kept them standing for eras. It has come to my attention that some of you are wavering in your oath to me – and, therefore, to Hildeheim. The whispers of those too cowardly to face me directly seek to spread doubt, to divide us…to weaken us. Need I remind you that deeds written in stone outweigh words whispered in shadow?" Lena took a breath and sighed while looking around the room full of clergy and politicians. Farrah watched attentively from the shadows, mouthing the words to the speech they had rehearsed ad nauseam.

Lena's voice softened as she stood in the centre of the grand parliamentary chamber. It was a rather large room with ten elevated rows of twenty seats to her left, housing representatives of the north, and ten rows of twenty seats to her right, housing representatives of the south.

"Judge me by my actions, not baseless accusations spoken by those who only seek to enrich and empower themselves and those loyal to them.

I have sacrificed much for Hildeheim. I have bled for it, buried loved ones for it, almost died for it on more than nine occasions, just as all of you have," she continued.

She paused as she noticed Hargatha doing her utmost to slip quietly into the chamber. Surely a futile effort, as there was no room in existence that the towering woman could quietly invade. Attention turned briefly towards her before returning to Lena, her shuffling loud amidst the deafening silence. Lena offered her a cold glance when they briefly locked eyes. It was a fleeting exchange, but its impact caused confusion to override Hargatha's expression; her head recoiled to the side.

"We all make sacrifices, as that is the price we pay to secure our way of life…our survival," Lena continued. She slowly paced the oval-shaped floor as she spoke to them, her heeled boots echoing with each step.

"When diplomacy fails, the price of victory is sealed with blood. Thus, I could never rightfully claim victory alone. It is by the strength and sacrifice of each and every one of you that we vanquish our enemies…past, present…future, both foreign and domestic." She scanned the room, looking at each individual in turn. "Who sent General Akanni of the Far Sands scurrying to his master after failing to annexe our eastern borders?"

A low, harmonious rumble of laughter reverberated in the chamber, causing a smirk to drift across her face. The positive reaction caught Hargatha's attention, and her eyes darted around the room.

"Houses Breivik, Astrid, and Ivar: Hildeheim does not forget your bravery or your sacrifice." Ioelena bowed towards them; they all stood and returned the respectful gesture. A thunderous stomp sounded off in triplicate. Lena momentarily lost focus – she was already winning them over. She hadn't expected it to start so quickly.

'*Mustn't get cocky; there's still a long road*,' she thought to herself.

"Though we must admit, it was the Far Sands who sacrificed the majority." She dropped her brow and snarled with a devious smirk.

A louder, even deeper rumble of laughter erupted, along with a quieter intermingling of voices as they exchanged quips. Hargatha noticed Farrah across the room and slowly walked in her direction while keeping her focus on Lena. She stopped near a familiar face. Nikolas Hargrave, the queen's Master of the Interior, was professional bureaucracy in its purest form. He was both the nicest man one could meet and the bluntest, though he meant no ill will by it. Nikolas acknowledged her arrival with a curt smile and a nod. While his thinly shaved moustache and sharply groomed beard gave him a villainous appearance, this was not representative of who he really was. Hargatha maintained a frown, not inspired enough to attempt to hide it.

"And who guarded our southern trade routes during the endless summer four years prior? Who sent the Tu'Chauri six satchels of the heads of those who dared to lust after what was ours?" She stomped her foot on the ground three times. A loud roar went up as they replied with three stomps of their own. Her tone sharpened as she declared, "Torunn, Runa, Alrik, Einar...Hildeheim remembers."

The four named stood and bowed to a symphony of stomps. She waited until quiet resumed.

"We would be here for days if I were to recount the heroic service every one of you has offered. No matter the storm, just know..."

"Hildeheim remembers!" the chorus of men and women shouted.

"...Hildeheim remembers," she echoed softly in delayed agreement. "This kingdom has survived worse storms than the childish scheming and ambition of a vocal minority. Remain with me. Cling to me as you did when my mother passed into *the other*," she paused for effect, allowing them to stew in the mournful groans that replied. She then went on, "Continue to lend me your *wisdom*, your strength, and most of all, your patience. Together, we *will* weather the winds, as we have done before. I ask not for blind loyalty but for faith in the vision we share of a powerful Hildeheim that will stand for another thousand years. You pledged to serve this realm just as I pledged to lead it, justly and well. Trust in me and in each other. Stay true to your vow, and let no splintering divide us. If we stand united, no force can destroy that which we have created. Hildeheim's greatest days lie still ahead. Together, let us march boldly to meet them. Have faith in me...in Hildeheim."

The room erupted into applause. The majority were standing, with a few *familiar* disputants remaining in their seats, arms crossed or otherwise openly not taking part in the applause.

Lena smiled at them anyway.

"What just happened?" Hargatha muttered quietly to Nikolas. She pretended to clap with a forced smile as Nikolas offered measured applause. He turned towards her, still wearing his humorous smirk.

"It seems as if your student has just graduated." His eyes flared at her before he turned his attention back to the queen, noting, "You're losing your touch, Hargatha – though for you, I suppose *grip* would be the more appropriate word." He shook his head lightly.

She gazed at Lena as the queen approached, patiently awaiting the moment they would lock eyes; it would be that moment in which she could read what was truly going on with her, she thought.

The moment, however, would never come.

Lena passed directly in front of her, engaged in conversation with politicians who were doing their best to capitalise on the opportunity. She not once looked up or so much as acknowledged Hargatha's existence, which was something that normally required great effort to accomplish. Farrah, dependably, noticed her and discreetly waved with a few fluttering fingers. Hargatha nodded in return, feeling somehow appreciative of the acknowledgement.

"Hargatha, walk with me." Lena's voice carried over the chaotic ambience of the room, shedding her professional tone in the process.

Hargatha followed quickly, still tumbling through the overwhelming show unfolding around her. Her mind raced as she tried to get ahead of the *play*, to figure out the angle at which she should pivot.

"What did I just walk into? And why the short notice? That's not like you to leave me in the dark." She spoke first in an attempt to gain control of the conversation. Even towering over Lena, she somehow felt beneath her. It was both an unusual and uncomfortable position to be in for her. Lena stopped walking in unison with the small crowd that swelled around her as she turned to probe Hargatha's face.

"For far too long, I have used you as a crutch. Through the loss of the Crown Mother…through Connerh…" She maintained sharp eye contact with Hargatha. "Yet no more. I appreciate that you have always offered your shoulder to cry on, that you have supported me through dark and unfamiliar times, but enough is enough. It is time I moved on from these…*tragedies* that I've allowed myself to be consumed with…defined by. I could never repay you for what you've done for me, though I *shall* try. But it is time to move on, towards a brighter future," she concluded.

Hargatha's eyes flared unintentionally as her mouth dangled open. She smiled; it was the most she could do to seem supportive of this…new direction.

"I've heard some disturbing reports I wish to discuss with you, but first, I need some time to myself. I will send for you later," Lena continued, grabbing Hargatha's hand with two of her own. She kissed the large appendage before promptly departing with Farrah and the others. Hargatha stood alone, marinating in shock and disbelief.

The stinging itch of someone else's eyes burned into her shoulder.

Nikolas observed from where he stood still near the parliament chamber. His eyes were squinting as he tried to read their lips, but they relaxed as he offered a nod upon realising he'd been discovered.

The smell of wet soil and lavender induced a restful state of mind as they were inhaled. Lena plopped onto the ground in her white-and-blue-patterned gardening dress, digging her hands deep into the rich, black dirt. It was her therapy of choice and favourite place to escape from the mundane, second only to a tall chalice of plum and apricot wine. She went to loosen her hair from its over-tightened bun but stopped short upon seeing her hands covered in damp dirt.

"Should I fetch the slop?" Farrah asked, barely keeping her composure – before losing it altogether and erupting into a giggle. Lena joined her.

"Come free my hair so that I may roll in the muck properly," she replied playfully.

Farrah removed her hands from the tiny pockets sewn into the front of her dress and quickly sauntered over to her, releasing Lena's hair from the black ribbon that had captured it.

Farrah's small, rapid footsteps always caused Lena to chuckle; the miniature clapping sound of her heeled boots only added to the amusement. Farrah was a petite young woman with a large bouquet of tightly curled, light-brown hair that sort of bounced when she walked. She also had a darker, tanned complexion in a different shade from those whose ancestry never strayed from Hildeheim. Her green eyes were piercing where they looked out from within a slightly round, pleasant face. While she had a natural prettiness, she was completely unaware of it, never being the sort to dwell upon herself.

Lena's silky black hair slid gracefully from the ribbon as it was removed, falling just below her shoulder blades. She twisted her head back and forth, letting her hair loosen and *stretch* in the breeze. Lena leaned forward, pretending to dive into the wet soil in front of her.

"I can hear Sonora dying inside as you track mud through the castle…all the way to your chamber," Farrah shouted. Lena laughed loudly as Farrah physically impersonated the grumpy old chambermaid.

"The look on her face would be well worth the speech!" Lena declared, and her laugh re-fired but faded quickly. The word made her think of her own, spoken earlier that day. She beckoned for Farrah with her dirty hands. "Anyway, quickly now, bring me my babies; they won't plant themselves."

Farrah quickly lifted her dress and exaggeratedly shuffled her small feet as she went to retrieve the cart of seeds and seedlings. Lena quietly chuckled as she futilely tried to clean her hands with her apron, then manoeuvred herself into a kneeling position in front of a row of dirt and soil, leaning back to rest her bottom on the heels of her feet. The loud scuffing of stiff, wooden wheels echoed through the greenhouse as Farrah approached.

"I want a row of carrots with a row of cabbage right behind it," Lena announced, her hand outstretched over the vegetable plot. Farrah nodded, finding the correct cup of seeds from the cart and handing it to her. Lena's eyes moved across the dirt for a minute before resting upon Farrah, who hadn't realised she was a part of the plan. Her focus shifted from Farrah to the cup, then back again.

"Well, get down here and join me, you heifer," she demanded playfully.

"Only if I must," she replied, quickly finding her place next to Lena. They began to dig little holes, plant a single seed in each, and pack soil over them again before moving on to the next spot.

"Okay, out with it… Thoughts on the assembly today?" Lena asked, eager to discuss the topic at the forefront of her mind. Farrah's eyes flared as she leaned her head towards the dirt beneath them.

"I think you successfully identified those who support you, those who pretend to, and those who perhaps desire their palms to be greased," she replied after a moment.

"Or their heads lopped off." Lena rolled her eyes.

Farrah shook her head in amusement.

"I'd kick them down the great hall, through the gates, and into the courtyard," she continued with a smirk, causing Farrah to giggle.

"You're all talk," Farrah nudged her, grinning ear to ear.

"Is that so?" Faux indignation washed across Lena's face.

"It is, very much so."

"I will order their heads be delivered to me by dinner…golden platter and all. I'll even have one sent to you, just to show you how serious I am,"

Lena decreed, her furrowed brow undercut by her smile.

"You *will not*," Farrah replied, the depth of her laughter increasing as she feigned disgust.

Lena's eyes widened as she stared at her unbelieving counterpart. Her brow lowered, and she insisted, "You're right, I might not do it… But I *could*." Still, she somehow sounded defeated as she returned to planting more seeds. Then, with a faint smile triggered by a secret thought, she mumbled to herself, "I could've had Connerh do it."

The pleasant thought faded quickly, and the muscles in her face grew slack. Farrah's laughter cautiously came to a still as she chose, at first, not to acknowledge it. Instead, she quietly watched from the corner of her eye as Lena's head drifted to the side, and she gazed beyond the soil, then the universe behind it. Farrah reached out slowly and rested her left hand on top of Lena's. They locked eyes for a moment, exchanging a hopeful smile.

Lena was the first to break eye contact.

"Did you see Aghor and Vaelen? Sitting during your ovation? I wanted to go over to them and punch them in their stupid faces," Farrah exclaimed. Hoping Lena would take the bait, she added, "They looked like complete fools."

"Purely for attention, no doubt. It's the only motivation for which they seem to muster energy these days. I understand they represent the smallest houses in Hildeheim, but that is precisely the reason to *embrace* the majority, not make a show of rebelling against it. Pick your battles… Standing out isn't always a good thing. And it is most definitely not the way to make friends in *this* court," Lena stoically fussed.

"More likely to make everyone suspicious of you," Farrah agreed. "I mean, if you're going to rebel, at least be smart about it."

"Right? I hate to say it, but be more like Alrik and Torunn. At least they had the decency *to play the game*. Do you know how hard it was to call them out by name…and offer commendation, no less?" Lena continued. Farrah pretended to dry heave.

"I can only imagine," she replied, smiling at the fact her bait had been taken. She stood, wiped her hands on her apron, and quietly walked over to the seedling cart.

"Please tell me you're retrieving us large vessels of wine," Lena called, stretching her fingers under the crumbly dirt. Farrah retrieved a small cask and two cups from the middle shelf of the cart before she returned to her spot.

"Of course. You know me too well." She handed Lena a cup and filled it promptly before doing the same to her own and plopping back down onto the ground. Her dress puffed out as the air shot up her legs.

"No, it is you who knows me too well – and of this, I am appreciative," Lena returned as she smiled sincerely.

"We can both be right." Farrah rested her hand on Lena's one more before delving into the contents of her cup.

Lena took a deep swig from her chalice. There was a moment of silence between them during which Farrah sat next to her, quietly waiting after having fully abandoned her gardening charade. She was, as in all things, supportive of Lena and her wishes and interests, but the thought of making a mess of herself and her outfit was far from her idea of a relaxing evening.

"How will you handle Hargatha?" she eventually enquired from behind the rim of her cup. Lena's eyes flared.

"As I must: straight and to the point. I don't know whom I can trust anymore, and I need space to think. As Copernium said, *trust no one, and trust those closest to you even less.*" Her lips puckered as she reflected on the words.

"Copernium was a paranoid, lonely, cynical old philosopher. I understand the gist of the sentiment, but it's a bit much, don't you think?" Farrah frowned.

"It was just an expression; obviously, you are not included in that grouping." Lena shook her head as she tried to soothe Farrah's injured ego.

In reality, her assurances were only skin-deep. Lena had been betrayed by someone, at one time or another, at almost every stage in her life. Despite never giving her any reason for doubt…even Farrah was not above suspicion at this point. Lena shared most things with her, *but not everything.* One prominent example would be the visitor she had received just days ago.

Three days prior…

Lena sat alone at a table just off to the right side of her balcony, her body draped across a large chair covered with a thick fur. The average evening's temperature was dropping, signalling that the season's first snow would soon come. She rifled through scrolls and flattened out pieces of parchment while nibbling on strips of dried meat, her chalice not far off. The soundscape for the afternoon was an ensemble of gulls' cries and the crashing waves below.

She paused at the sound of rocks crumbling.

On its own, it wasn't unusual, but the frequency with which it had been occurring *was*. She leaned back and stared at the stone railing, unsure of what to expect but not sufficiently concerned to stop eating. She went back to reading the stuffy report titled *Concerning Elves*. Apparently, they were sending patrols near the Tu'Chauri border, and their neighbours to the south didn't much care for it. As stuffy as the phrasing was, it was still a particularly enthralling report compared to most – the unusual behaviour of the elves, with them outwardly provoking war, had captured her attention.

The crumbling echoed again.

Her brow arched, but she reached for her chalice as she tried to convince herself not to investigate.

'*I should call the guard…*' The fleeting thought crossed her mind, but she batted it away with, '*Nonsense! What could it even be? There's no way an assassin could endure the climb.*'

The inner battle raged on, and as she glanced down for a moment, her eyes focused intently on the centre of the table. She quickly converged upon it, rapidly shoving the mountain of paperwork onto the floor as she revealed her sword underneath.

The crumbling sounded again, closer this time.

Her bare feet quietly pattered across the smooth stone floor, sword high and at the ready. She carefully peered over the edge, only to find…rocks, water, and waves.

She sighed with relief.

'*That* is *a long way down*,' she thought to herself as she lowered her sword, letting it dangle in the grip of her right hand.

She started as a large hand appeared, grabbing onto the edge of the balcony. She jumped backwards and raised her sword, ready to plunge it into whatever face belonged to the hand.

When she suddenly recognised the ruby ring adorning the hand, she realised who it belonged to but was left no less confused. A second hand appeared just before Vidar's head popped into view, almost recoiling in shock at the sight of her staring directly at him. He whispered to her to remain silent, fighting the urge to cover his lips with a finger – giving in and releasing his grip might have been a deadly mistake, after all. With a final grunt and a strain, he raised himself high enough to clamber over the railing. She initially dropped her guard upon seeing him, but lingering suspicions urged her to keep her sword at the low ready. Vidar collapsed onto the balcony floor and fought to catch his breath, doing his best to control his volume.

"Thank you for unlocking a new fear, cousin," she sarcastically offered as she returned to the table and leaned against it, facing him. She wasn't quite ready to relinquish her blade. "We'll have to install some new countermeasures."

Vidar couldn't help but laugh while still struggling to catch his breath, assuring her, "That was not my intent. Trust me, I'll never be doing that again. It is not for the faint of heart, and even with no heart, that was terrifying." He splayed out, letting his skin cool on the cold stone floor.

She laughed.

"If it's any consolation, you weren't supposed to be here," he continued.

Her brow raised, head canted, she replied, "No...no, it does not."

"Well..." he paused, still processing what to say in reply.

"I must say," she interrupted his thinking, "this is quite possibly the worst assassination attempt I've ever seen...and that's saying something."

Vidar erupted into laughter as he connected the dots. He sat up and looked at her in disbelief.

"Wait, did you *really* think I did all that just to try and...?" he began, noticing the sword gripped in her hand and the way her eyes still focused on him with a raised brow. He laughed again. "Point taken, I suppose. But do you really take me for the hands-on type? I do all my killing through proxy. Come, now; you know this."

She thought for a moment, then shrugged... He had a point. She tossed her sword on the table behind her, causing a loud, metallic thud.

"Point returned," she replied, exchanging her weapon for the pitcher of water next to it. She took it to him.

"Thank you." He barely uttered the words before he chugged the water rather obnoxiously. Then, still fighting to control his volume, he discarded the pitcher and insisted, "I apologise for the theatrics, but it is urgent I speak with you with anonymity."

"Vidar, what is it?" Her interest was piqued.

"There's no other way to cushion it… Your life is in danger." He stood and perched himself on the balcony railing. She huffed out a breath that resembled a laugh and stood next to him.

"Vidar, I hate to break it to you, but my life is always in danger. You'll have to be more specific than that." Sarcasm was how they often communicated, but this time, she used it to mask her growing concern.

Obviously, it's serious enough for him to risk his life, she thought, her mind running rampant with questions. *Who is he concerned about seeing him?*

A knot formed in her stomach, understanding the implication of his warning, defined by his commitment to bring it to her. He unslung a satchel that was wrapped around his chest and retrieved a once-sealed scroll, now tied with a thin string to keep it closed. He reached across the table and handed it to her.

Her frown deepened at the sight of whose signet it bore, and her head raised as her eyes lowered.

"I see," was all she could muster as she took the document from him. She carefully unfurled it and examined it in its entirety. Once she finished reading it, her eyes drifted downwards before she rolled it back up and threw it on the table between them.

"Is there no one left loyal to me?" she asked herself, albeit loud enough that he could hear it. Still, she left him no time to comment on it, continuing, "What's in this for you? And why risk your life to bring it to me?"

"Let's get one thing straight: I don't think you're cut out for this. I think you'd rather be elsewhere, living a boring life with four children swinging from your tit and a husband who waits on you hand and foot… And, to put it plainly, that shows in how you rule. You'd much rather be far away from politics and the fear of death every waking moment," he began.

"I don't fear it…not anymore," she interrupted him.

"No matter," he disregarded her answer, deeming it irrelevant. "You *are* the Queen of Hildeheim, and until *you* decide to relinquish the mantle, it is rightfully yours. And as long as *I* breathe, I will not stand by and let conspiracy be the rule of law. That will be the way of things." His tone deepened to match his conviction. "I took that risk in order to provide you with the unadulterated *choice*…of where we go from here."

He motioned for the clay vessel of wine. She thought for a moment, then pushed it towards him. He topped off her chalice before swigging directly from the source.

"What would you do if you were me?" Her curiosity got the better of her.

"If it were me…the blood would pour until the mountain drowned in crimson. But that is not *my* choice to make, nor is it your style. I'd also ask for more proof before making such a…*life-altering* decision," he continued almost scornfully.

She nodded, feeling slightly embarrassed at being rebuked for her haste.

"And since we think so much alike, cousin…I have brought you just that." He removed the satchel and threw it on the table. The flap opened, and a variety of scrolls splayed across the surface, all with varying signets, some of them duplicates. Lena's eyes grew wide. He leaned in towards her to pose his question once again.

"So, then, where do we go from here?"

Lena wore the black, metal-adorned gown Connerh had often referred to as her battle gown, though she had never seen a day of it. The matching platinum-and-black crown she wore was luxurious but simple, being less flashy and jewel-encrusted than the one she wore during formal events. She stood over a table covered in maps, carefully combing over each of them.

There was a knock at the door.

"*Enter,*" she ordered.

Hargatha entered, a pitcher of wine in one hand and two chalices in the other. Lena raised an unintentional brow. Hargatha's nervous uncertainty blatantly betrayed her, being both uncharacteristic and slightly alarming. Lena could tell by the way she walked in that she'd already begun drinking. She didn't carry guilt very well, and when she did, the way in which she did so was very unbecoming. As she approached, she leaned in and kissed Lena on the cheek. The endearment it was intended to carry only made the sting of betrayal burn that much more for Lena. Any doubt she had in Vidar quickly melted away.

'*Is this really happening?*' she thought to herself. Hargatha filled the chalices with a white wine from the pitcher she had brought with her, then offered one to Lena. She raised her hand in response, turning down the offer.

Hargatha frowned, too inebriated to fully control herself or her expressions.

"I've heard some rather disturbing reports that I need to discuss with you," Lena began, getting straight to the point. Her words seemed to aid in sobering Hargatha. She quickly put some distance between them, walking to the other side of the table full of maps.

"Well, what is it?" Hargatha pitifully portrayed concern.

"There are whispers…of an uprising…" She paused purposely for effect. Hargatha's eyebrow raised slightly.

"In the Rim… It's partly what inspired my speech earlier this morning. It was a backdrop, of sorts, to quell any pushback for what I am about to do next," she continued.

"I was very surprised by your speech this morning…" Hargatha began, trying to both seize control of the conversation and extract information. She prompted, "Normally, you alert me to such things."

Lena stared at her blankly.

"And…what is it that you intend to do next?" Hargatha enquired cautiously.

"I'm sending you to be my eyes, ears, and fist. My grip on the Rim has slipped. We also need to refurbish the navy – it has fallen into disrepair, for which I take the full blame," Lena replied.

"I've not heard of any such uprising, and I have my spiders everywhere," she interjected promptly. Then, trying to impose her will, she decreed, "I'll dispose of those men and send new ones. We'll get to the bottom of it quickly."

"No," Lena countered, "you will depart for the Isles in the morning. Take Uncle with you and set up a new keep. Use what provisions you need; they are yours for the asking. It will prove difficult for any spark to give rise to flame with my kin breathing down their necks," she countered.

"As you wish…" Hargatha struggled to reply but bowed, once again finding it difficult to pivot. Attempting to regain control, she went on, "There may be some delay, however, as we are currently seeking the whereabouts of Vidar."

"Oh?" Lena prompted.

"Vidar, I fear, has…gone his own way. He has been spending too much *leisure time* with extremists from the east. He's been questioning things. His desire to rule is clouding his judgment. There was a gathering at our home…that did not end very well, to say the least. I'm almost embarrassed to discuss it." Hargatha flared her eyes and fluctuated her tone, trying her best to sell the distraction.

"Go on…" Lena played along, pretending her concern and investment. Hargatha sipped her wine.

"He threatened to kill Brand and Egress in a fit of rage…and in front of Brand's relatives, no less. It was such a distasteful display," she plied.

Lena's brow collapsed briefly before she forced herself to restore it. She was almost insulted at Hargatha's pitiful attempt to manipulate her, though it was clear the giant woman was *heavily* intoxicated. It was, after all, late in the hour…by design. She fought the desire to pity her, rationalising that whatever was motivating Hargatha to betray her must have been insurmountable.

'*It was that kind of thinking that got Mother killed,*' she corrected herself.

"That *is* unfortunate…" Lena replied, pretending to think on it. Her patience had grown weary, and she only hoped it didn't show as she instructed, "Very well…I'll deal with Vidar. Don't let it trouble you. Get your rest, Gatty, and give my best to Galabrand and Egress. I will have six ships on the north shore in the morning as your transport. Send word to me once you've arrived."

Hargatha's head lowered, mirroring the defeat she felt. Her mind was too clouded to process it fully, and she finally capitulated, "As you command."

She began to walk towards the door but stopped and turned towards Lena, who was staring at the maps in front of her. She hesitated before finally accepting her fate and leaving.

The large doors rumbled and closed behind her. Lena's eyes raised to ensure she'd left, and she let out a loud sigh upon receipt of that confirmation. Vidar's words echoed in her mind. She was the Queen of Hildeheim and would remain so until she chose to no longer wear the crown.

But that day was *not* today, nor would it be the day after.

For the first time, she felt emboldened and with purpose. She understood her role: to protect her people from those who sought to *take*. Her speech from earlier had come full circle. Words that once rang hollow, yet were rich with intent, now played back in her mind like a creed.

Hildeheim's greatest days *are* still ahead.
Just as he said they would be.

CHAPTER SIXTEEN

As Luck Would Have It

Connerh

The day had been long. Nyradhal's markets were closing, and its traffic had slowed to a declining trickle. Connerh was tired; his feet hurt, and his arms were aching. He'd forgotten the toll a day of shopping could take. Between carrying purchased goods and balancing Aeryk atop his shoulders, he'd stretched muscles that had long metaphorically atrophied. Despite the discomfort, the looks on their faces made the subtle suffering an agreeable price. They had been happy, lost in moments of careless abandon. They hadn't been looking over their shoulders, down alleyways, or second-glancing shadows. Of course, he had been – he always would be – but they hadn't seemed to give it much thought. It was the way things were supposed to be.

"What do you say, should we be getting back?" Rose asked as they trotted down a dead street on horseback.

"What if…we stay the night? We can head back in the morning." Connerh had a look of whimsy in his eye. Rose's eyes widened.

"Are you sure? Do you think it's safe?" she asked in disbelief. He brushed by his initial thoughts of anxiousness, not wanting their cherished moment to end, and averted his eyes as he quieted the distrustful voices.

"I think we'll be fine. Come on, there's an inn I used to frequent. Let's see if it's still around," he said.

"What kind of inn? And what about Aeryk? Surely, in a city like this, it wouldn't be appropriate for a child?" she replied, her motherly instincts activating. Connerh laughed.

"What do you mean? And a city like what? What are you implying?" he asked. Her head tilted and brows raised.

"Sailors, travellers, and those who pass by in the night. Surely you know my meaning," she blushed. He laughed again.

"It'll be fine," he assured her.

"And what's this inn called?" she pressed.

"It was called the Lucky Lamb's Leg," he replied. She shot him a doubtful look, but he grinned back, saying, "It's fine, come on. Keep up."

The Lucky Lamb's Leg earned its name as it stood, seemingly untouched by progress. Its fading wooden sign still swung by its original, now-rusting hinge. The view through the large bay window was obscured by a dark curtain, its edges gleaming with the glow of the light from inside. The window itself was fogged and smudged, giving it a frosted appearance. There was a time when having such a large window in a storefront caused quite a scandal, as the locals thought it would encourage crime. This had, of course, turned out not to be the case, and despite the rumblings, it gave the building a unique curb appeal and charm.

A lively tune played inside, a man's voice paired to the tune of a lute, but the volume was considerate. The fragrance of herbs and roasted meat permeated the air, making Connerh's mouth water. He stood, hands on his hips, basking in recollection. He'd spent a considerable amount of time here, even worked as a janitor for some time as a young man. He could still remember the layout of the place, where the mops were kept, where he'd sneak off to catch a quick nap – and where Mister Joannes, the then-owner, would shag willing waitresses while his wife wasn't around. He was such a dirty old man.

Fun times.

He was anxious to step inside, almost forgetting to help Rose and Aeryk dismount.

"It's…quaint. The smell is to die for, however," Rose offered as she scanned the building.

He smiled with an eye roll. Her passive-aggressive comments were true to form. She'd already formed an opinion in just a few seconds, having looked past all of the…character the inn had to offer.

She grinned as she took his hand and dismounted, sensing his eyes rolling and adding, "What? It's nice."

"Just give it a chance," he replied as he hitched their horses to a post.

"I will!" she playfully assured him.

A gust of warmth and an even stronger aroma greeted them at the door. There was a bar with tables scattered to one side of the room, with a mezzanine overlooking the ground floor and multiple doors leading to rooms for…short-term stays. Rose's eyes widened as she caught sight of them, and she elbowed Connerh discreetly. He chuckled.

"That's not where we're staying," he whispered to her.

"Find yerself a table, and I'll be right over, hon," the barmaid shouted over.

Connerh nodded in reply. He didn't recognise her, but the thought suddenly sapped his excitement. He hadn't thought about being identified. Surely, no one would recognise him. Right? The chances were slim; he looked nothing like he used to, and the disguise of age and facial hair served him well, or so he quickly convinced himself.

The bar was near capacity, but the dining room was half empty, and shadows were plenty. He opted for a table in the corner, always preferring to have his back to a sturdy wall. It provided a clear view of the entrance. *Preference* was perhaps too weak a word. Required would be more suitable. He'd been known to leave an establishment if he couldn't have his choice in seating arrangement.

"The name's Peg. What can I get fer ya?" the barmaid asked, seemingly having appeared from nowhere.

"Mead," Rose said plainly before Connerh could reply. She exchanged a look of humoured determination with him.

"Right, then, mead it is. And whatever you have for little-kin folk," he replied.

"Hey!" Aeryk shouted.

"We've got small ale. Or goat's milk?" she asked. Aeryk's frown drew Connerh's attention with a smirk.

"Small ale," he said, much to the boy's relief.

"Right. Three legs of lamb, then?" she asked. Connerh nodded. Her stout legs carried an oversized posterior that wobbled as she walked towards the bar. Aeryk noticed and released his infectious giggle. Rose's eyes flared as she went after him.

"The man knows what he likes," Connerh chuckled.

"Don't encourage him," she argued.

"You've got a nice family there," a wiry older voice said, suspending Connerh's laughter. The man, much like the waitress, had seemingly appeared from thin air. Connerh's eyes steadily raised towards him. There was nothing special about him – a typical bar regular dressed in yesterday's fashion. His clothes were kept well enough, but his breath was ripe, even from a seated position. It was probably best he didn't speak near a lit flame.

"Thank you," Connerh replied, his tone a little deeper, the inflection polite but curt. Rose read his body language and distracted herself with Aeryk, paying the man no mind. Connerh shouted for the man to go away in his mind. If only he had Elarion's telepathic ability.

"I've not seen you around here. Most people who venture through here are regulars. Some call it the hidden treasure of Nyradhal; I'm surprised you found it," the man continued. It wasn't clear if he was genuinely asking questions or if he was just unaware, uttering his inner monologue. His inebriation was evident, but Connerh's capacity for politeness was quickly running out.

"We could smell the food as soon as we entered the quarter. I can see why you're a regular. How long have you been coming here?" Rose spoke up. Connerh appreciated the skilful misdirect, and his focus dropped.

"Oh, yes. The food is wonderful. Really good. Me? Seems like forever, Peg, am I right?" he asked, stumbling out of Peg's way as she delivered their drinks.

"Don't remind me. If he's botherin' you nice folks, just let me know. He's harmless, but I understand if you want some peace and quiet," she said, still leaning over the table. Then, turning to face him, she fussed, "Keep it brief, Charlie."

Rose elbowed Aeryk as he watched.

"Oh, I'm not hurting anybody! Gentle as a fly, I am," he replied, fluttering his fingers in her direction. Peg grunted and walked off.

"About as bothersome as one, too," Connerh whispered to Rose.

"You didn't say where you're from," Charlie continued.

"Yes, we did, you silly old goat. It's been twice now; you're not getting me to say it again. Maybe it's time you switched to milk!" Rose replied with a laugh. Connerh's eyes flared. She was good.

"You did? No! Really?" Charlie's brain broke. He looked into his cup and back again with a forgetful grin. With a drunk chuckle, he concluded, "Maybe you're right!"

"Next one's on me, Charlie," Connerh spoke up. "Have a good

evening."

His capacity for patience was officially empty. A chair scraped the floor in the background, followed by a cup hitting the floor. Connerh shot a glance in the direction but didn't gather any details.

"That's mighty kind of you, good sir. Whelp, I'm going back to my spot. I won't take up any more of your time. Let me know if you need anything," he said with a hiccup and a bow.

Connerh shook his head. He felt others staring, and this time, he took his time to investigate. They were casual looks, nothing too alarming. Most of them were probably grateful that Charlie was bothering him instead of them. He nodded their glances away and had just begun to whisper to Rose when Charlie spun around.

"Anyone ever tell you that you look familiar?" Charlie asked.

Connerh froze.

He hesitated to meet Charlie's gaze.

It all flashed before his eyes. He'd retrieve his hidden sword. Slice the neck. Kick over the table. Take Rose and Aeryk by the hand, kick the front door open, and make for the city gate. Timing would be essential. At this hour, the guard would be light. The men would be sluggish, and the night would obscure them.

"Who, me?" Rose asked.

Connerh's expression blanked. He released a silent sigh of relief, but the adrenaline lingered in his veins, eventually making him feel sick.

"Yes, you…I know I've seen you somewhere," he said.

"That's the worst pickup line I've heard in a while. Besides, I'm taken, can't you see?" Rose replied.

Connerh laughed. The door to the inn closed. Connerh tried to investigate, but the old drunk was in the way.

"No, I didn't mean to imply—" Charlie said, visibly racking his brain.

"It's okay, I have a common face. I hear that a lot," she said.

Charlie grunted. He didn't seem fully convinced, but he didn't put up a fuss either. His embarrassment prevented him from pushing the matter. She shot a look at Peg as she approached. The message was received.

"Okay, Charlie, go sit down or go home. The choice is yours," she fussed, elbowing him out of the way as she set a large serving plate on the table. It was enough to feed ten men, with seconds for all. Three roasted legs of lamb sat on a bed of purple carrots and potatoes. The smell was intoxicating. Connerh and Rose stared at the oversized portion, eyes wide;

Peg only chuckled at their expressions.

"I thought it might be too much for ya. Yer definitely not from around here. Don't worry, I'll bring you something to take home the leftovers," she said before grabbing Charlie's arm and leading him away.

"Perhaps we should retire after all," Rose whispered to Connerh. Her heart was racing, and she could only imagine what he'd been feeling. Aeryk was looking around in an attempt to entertain himself, completely unaware of what was transpiring. Connerh agreed hesitantly. He'd been feeling the call to exfiltrate the location, but he didn't want to be the one to spoil the outing.

"Give me a few moments," he whispered to her as he stood, returning the plate of food to Peg. He appeared a ragged, unkempt man of the mountain, but his walk did not match the story told by his appearance. It was different. He walked like a soldier. And not just a normal soldier – a royal one. Back straightened, chest outward, shoulders squared. Rose watched the stares accumulate. The room felt as if it were shrinking. He could feel the eyes peering into the back of his skull as he requested to pay for their food. Everyone at the bar was staring at him, at the side of his face. The stares were warm. Lingering ones. Undesirable ones. Brows began to furrow and arch, and then the whispers began.

Rose stood abruptly. Her chair scraped against the floor, drawing attention to her. She whispered to Aeryk and led him towards the door.

"Everything alright?" Peg asked.

"The boy's feeling a little sick. Probably just needs some fresh air," he assured her.

"Aye. Give me a minute to put this in a crate for ya. The box is going to cost you extra, mind. I can't do much for that; we only have so many at a time," she said. Connerh acknowledged her with a raise of a few fingers.

The door swung open.

"Paddy, you old cunt!" the newcomer shouted to a reply of laughter amidst the palpable quiet. Connerh turned his head slightly to take a glance.

His head snapped back as he closed his eyes, taking a breath. He knew the man.

"Why's everyone so serious this evening?" the man asked, throwing a look around the room. The stares were still fixed on Connerh, and they eventually drew his own.

"What's so special about this bloke?" he asked, not so quietly.

Paddy, or so the other man was affectionately called, whispered something in his ear.

He cast a doubtful glance at Connerh and asked, "Who might you be?"

Connerh remained still, his face quarter-turned away.

His name was Gregor, and he was one of Hargatha's minions. Back then, he had always followed her around like a dog with a bone, except his was in his pants. *Why now? What were the odds?* Connerh thought. Agonised. It had to be a sign. He would always be confronted by this, always followed by his past and present. No matter how much he tried to evade it, it was always there. Lurking in the shadows. Clinging to the horizon, like soot in a chimney. Even when removed, the stain remained. He just wanted to move on.

To close that chapter of his life.

To postpone the inevitable.

To save himself.

He shook his head. The stars had aligned in a different pattern, hadn't they?

"Hey, you! I said, who might you be?" Gregor shouted, sticking his chest out to display his insignia and moving uncomfortably close to Connerh.

Connerh sighed, relinquishing the charade. He stood erect and turned to face the man.

"My name is Connerh Manthil, son of Nyradhal, Commander of the First Battalion of Her Majesty's Army. Cyraxis. The Blight. The Devil. Gargoyle. Judge, jury, and executioner," he pronounced.

A chorus of whispers and chairs erupted. Gregor stood, mouth agape.

Rose silently wept on the other side of the door. Connerh's voice carried, and her ear was pressed against it.

"I've gone by many names. Pick one," he declared, looking around to observe the parade of onlookers. "Thank you, Peg," he continued, taking the crate of food from her frozen hands. "Now, if you will be so kind as to excuse me, I will be escorting my employer to her destination. And then," he leaned into Gregor's face, "I will be waiting for you."

Gregor stammered.

"Run along, Gregor. Tell your master to get on with it," Connerh whispered.

The man hurried out, almost knocking over Rose as he exited. Connerh caught a glimpse of her just before the door swung closed. Her defeated expression dissolved his bravado. She'd already wiped her face, but the redness remained.

The ride out of Nyradhal was quiet. The night was cold. Rose's tears had dried, as had the life behind Connerh's eyes. His mind was preoccupied with the vibration lingering in his mind. He glanced upwards. They'd planned for this moment. For every moment. Every contingency and every backup for every contingency possible. His speech…his self-proclaimed resurrection had swept most of them away. Only one remained.

The end of their journey together.

Rose advanced on her horse, catching up to Connerh. Aeryk had fallen asleep in the cradle of her arms.

"So, it has to be this way, then?" she asked in a whisper, drawing strength from the unfamiliar corners of her soul. He actively shed his stoicism, revealing his concern for her. His face visibly softened.

"I'm sorry that I couldn't do better by you. Perhaps it was always leading to this," he offered. She shook her head in defiance of the thought.

"You've done wonderfully by me, by us. I still search my soul, trying to figure out what I did to deserve your kindness, your mercy. We should have died in that fire," she said reflectively. His brow crumpled.

"You continue to thank the one who set it?" he asked out of frustration.

"Your reasons were just," she replied.

He scoffed loudly, shuffling in his saddle. He fought the urge to engage. It was pointless…at this point.

"You blind yourself. Perhaps you will think differently when I no longer pollute your air. When the stench of me has faded. When the memory of our time together has been replaced. Perhaps then your view of me will be different…clear," he argued.

"You know, it's not too late. We've relocated before, and we can relocate again. The world's a big place; there are still places to go, places to visit," she said, trying to tempt him with the idea despite knowing it was a battle destined to be lost.

"Even if I were to continue to give in to my selfishness, it's not fair to him," he responded with defeat in the undercurrent of his inflection.

He looked at Aeryk, sleeping in blissful ignorance in his mother's arms. The child's innocence caused a puff of air to rush out of his nose.

"He is not my son, and even if he were, my sins are not his to be punished for. I don't believe in that creed," he fussed, turning his face away from her.

"I wanted you to marry me…one day," she blurted out, fearing that she would one day regret this moment for not having laid plain her desires. His hidden expression crumpled with pity for a moment before it rehardened, firmer than before.

"You wish to redeem a monster. Despite your beauty and grace, that is beyond your capability. You love a version of me, not the true me. It is a version I fear will never take hold. Just a cloak. Something to be worn for a time and removed. What's underneath will always remain," he paused, dropping his gaze.

"Connerh…" she begged.

"A normal life was never destined for me. I've accepted it. It would be better for you if you did the same." His head rose. His words were sharp, plunging deep into the heart of her hope. A few tears rolled down her cheek.

"Was this as you saw…in your dreams?" she asked, her soft voice piercing.

He shook his head in small, rapid motions. A heavy frown encumbered his face.

"Then that is a good thing, is it not?" she asked, her hope resisting its quiet death.

"There's still time," he said. His heart sank.

Her eyes raised, and her mouth slipped open. His meaning was elusive, but his facial expression was not.

"Do you remember our plan?" he asked, cutting her off. She glanced at him only to see his face stony, fixed with an expression she was not used to on him: resignation.

"I do," she replied.

"If the house does not burn, we will find you a new place to settle with the boy. And if it should," he said, pausing.

She winced.

He locked eyes with her.

"Then I thank you for your time with me. Especially for your patience," he said, his softer side exposed.

She smiled through her sadness.

"You know where the money is hidden. Seek out your kin and start the life you deserve. Destiny will ensure our paths cross again. Whether it be in this life…or the next."

CHAPTER SEVENTEEN

INDULGENCE

YURI

Considered footsteps echoed softly down the corridor within the emperor's grand dining hall. The delicate, leather-soled impacts were overtaken by the clank and shuffle of the plate armour worn by two men who followed close behind her. Yuri wasn't in a hurry. She moved at what she deemed a comfortable pace, yet the envoys struggled to keep up. These men seemed far from the hardened, cold-steel warriors Hildeheim was legendarily said to have produced. They carried themselves as if they had not travelled fully armoured often, or they were at the least out of practice... severely out of practice. The younger one appeared to be wearing someone else's cuirass, and the older one was injured. His left foot slid a little when walking, causing the metal of his boots to scuff against the smooth stone floor with a loud scrape. He suffered in silence, save for the occasional wince that was not as discreet as he imagined.

The pain was sharp, still fresh, perhaps, she thought. Yuri frowned to herself, feeling slightly disappointed by the anaemic first impression. She had neither been to Hildeheim before nor met its soldiers in any official capacity. Be that as it may, *the old man needed a moment to rest,* she thought.

Approaching the next pillar, she came to an abrupt halt and turned to face them. Her outstretched palm prevented a collision, cushioning their sudden stop. The two men, Glendrake and Hammul by surname, gathered themselves – albeit in a loud and dishevelled manner. She found their way rather clumsy and irritating. Glendrake, the older and more impatient of the two men, looked anxiously around and then back at her. His curt expression spoke volumes. She found it curious, however; most visitors came to the country for business but prioritised the cornucopia of carnal pleasures the country had to offer. As the saying goes, *Khazmyr has few laws and even fewer morals.* The intent to give in to such temptation would consume their thoughts, made visible by a certain *shit-eating* grin that Yuri had grown to despise. But Glendrake, for all his faults, seemed an exception. His desire to conduct his business and depart with haste was overtly evident. He was certainly not enamoured with the potential surrounding him, as most men were…as Hammul was.

Perhaps he was a practising religious man, quickly crossed her mind. It would be a rare thing to see a man with such devout convictions in these parts. Admittedly, a large portion of the country claimed allegiance to one or more deities and professed belief in some code or tenet.

But they were only words.

"We'll wait here a moment," she said in the common tongue, her natural accent seasoning the pronunciation of her words. She was careful not to bring dishonour to the old codger by acknowledging his injuries or apparent need to catch his breath. Instead, they would wait here until she felt it sufficed…until his normal breathing had returned. Though Glendrake and Hammul had not yet earned her respect, the crest displayed on their tabards evoked a feeling of nostalgic honour within her. The embroidered emblem, meticulously stitched, bore the weight of lineage and tradition. Its symbols of a raven, feathers, and bones represented battles fought, oaths sworn, and ancestors long gone. To Yuri, it was more than fabric and thread; it was a bridge to a past she both revered and mourned – a tapestry woven with threads of duty and sacrifice.

"Aye," Glendrake grumbled with a mostly put-on smile.

Meanwhile, Hammul was doing his best to examine her without the truth of his actions being so obvious, and had she not been staring at him, it might have worked. Yuri's sustained eye contact with him – though intended to dissuade him from gazing for too long – only served to focus his attention on her eyes. They were like spheres of honey exuding the light of the evening sun. Sunlight had bronzed her skin to a perfect glow, a complexion earned from her days on the coast, and straps of contrasting brown leather encircled her hair, wound tightly in a high bun and adorned with a decorative ornament. Even the soft white fabric of her tunic seemed to radiate under the shafts of sunlight. Despite her deceptively plain expression, her eyes revealed a blend of amusement and irritation.

"Is this your first visit to the Seat of Darros—the heart of Khazmyr?" she probed, choosing small talk to pass the time and root out whatever feeling wasn't sitting right with her.

Hammul's face lit up.

"No, we…I have been lucky enough to visit once or twice," he said with a flash of *the grin*. He spoke quietly, hinting at his betrayed conscience as if he were sharing a forbidden secret.

She barely offered a nod. His reply was no surprise. Her gaze wandered to Glendrake, who appeared more interested in the silent activities of Yuri's two burly companions trailing behind them.

"And you?" she asked, raising her voice slightly to divert his attention from her reinforcements. She quickly scanned him and noticed the beads of perspiration decorating his brow. He swung his head to acknowledge her once he noticed the conversation had gone quiet.

"What?" he asked exasperatedly.

"Your first time? To Khazmyr?" she repeated.

He nodded, breaking eye contact with her. Her brow arched. She glanced at her companions in the distance, at Glendrake, and back again. The men nodded, having received her cue.

"No…well, technically, yes…" he paused and reclaimed her gaze. "Though I never left port. I wouldn't be caught dead here unless I had to be." He punctuated the sentence with his head, carrying on with his thoughts in a low mumble.

Her brows flashed up in momentary intrigue. His insistence on clarification was…interesting.

"Listen, will this delay last much longer?" he insisted. Yuri's companions quietly moved in closer but left a reasonable gap between them.

"No," she replied. Returning to her topic of choice, she went on, "I would conclude, then, that neither of you has been in the presence of Darros. I'm sure you've heard rumours and stories, as words concerning Darros and Khazmyr travel like wildfire in the outer kingdoms. Khazmyr is, after all, the centre of the explored world."

"You mean the rumours that he looks and acts like a fre—" Hammul began.

The back of Glendrake's hand smacked heavily against Hammul's chest plate, stopping him mid-statement. A stern look accompanied the strike.

"You will find *those* rumours to be unfounded. The appearance of Darros is a gift from the gods. He is kind and merciful. You will be tempted to stare…" She immediately looked at Hammul.

"But if we do, he'll have us hanged," Glendrake cut her off. "Yes, yes, I've heard threats like these before, parroted by every sycophant in every known realm."

Yuri smiled; the thought of him hanging was beginning to paint a pleasant visual.

"It's perfectly natural. Just be mindful of how…you gaze upon Darros. Be sure that it is with the respect and reverence he is due," she countered.

Darros was many things: a title, a family name, a ruler, and that ruler's immediate family members. There were many Darros in a long line of Darros. Each generation brought a new descendant who inherited the mantle from his or her predecessor, while the incestuous nature of the Darros family ensured a close resemblance was maintained throughout the iterations. While concubines and slaves were optional for Darros, inbreeding was not.

Glendrake looked as if she had said something vile and offensive.

"Of course," Hammul offered in his companion's place. She nodded, not minding Glendrake.

"Very well… Right this way," she replied, giving them both another once-over. She turned and walked towards two large doors at the end of the hall.

The unlikely envoys from Hildeheim and her two companions followed.

As the two large doors slowly swung open, the assault of sunlight and sound temporarily disorientated the envoys. The roaring crowd of the coliseum ebbed and flowed like ocean waves.

"Welcome to Darros' personal section. It is a great honour for him to receive you here; he rarely entertains men of…your station…in such an informal setting." She looked them over, satisfied with her choice of words.

Hammul took slight offence.

"You will wait for him to call for you before you approach. This way," Yuri concluded, attempting to maintain her volume over the crowd as she waved them forward.

The men briefly raised their arms to shield their eyes from the onslaught of sunlight, being sure to stay close behind. The coliseum was nothing short of an exhibition of wealth, its towering walls adorned with intricate murals depicting mythical beasts locked in mortal combat with muscular gladiators, their swords held high and clothing absent. Fabrics in shades of crimson covered the seating, growing darker the closer they got to the pit. The cement floor beneath their feet was embedded with sparkling chunks of rubies and seashells that twinkled in the brilliant sunlight streaming through the open-air structure. The only thing to dwarf its spectacle was the sheer number of people crammed within its walls.

And there, in the middle of the eastern side, unsurprisingly juxtaposed, elevated, and painted in white, was Darros' sanctuary. His throne-like seat stood in the centre under a canopy adorned with semi-transparent, billowing draperies.

"There's not an empty seat in the whole house," Hammul shouted as they traversed a small walkway adjoined to the stairs leading to Darros. The crowd cheered and screamed at the carnage unfolding in the ring, affectionately called *the meat pit*.

"Wait here," she called before ascending the stairs.

Glendrake squinted and shielded his eyes in an attempt to sneak a peek at his host, but the sun made it practically impossible. To make matters worse, Darros was surrounded by a host of scantily clad servants. Some were fanning him with large palm fronds, while others were holding golden bowls of fruit and dried meats. There were no less than seven cupbearers, one for each flavour of wine. It was everything expected of the ruler of Khazmyr, yet it was also slightly more ridiculous.

Yuri bowed when she reached the top of the stairway. She approached and leaned into him, just out of view of the envoys. All Glendrake could make out were the golden fingerstalls decorating each of Darros' fingers. His hand extended out of the shroud to point in their direction.

"Can you see anything?" Hammul shouted as quietly as possible in Glendrake's ear.

The noise from the crowd swelled.

Glendrake shook his head, both responding to his counterpart and annoyed with the loud ambience. After a few moments, Yuri appeared at the top of the stairway and called them up to her with a brief waving gesture.

"The moment is here. She calls for us. Steel yourself," Hammul shouted in his ear again, pointing to the woman. Glendrake took a deep breath and began the climb up the stairwell. Hammul cursed quietly at the weight of his armour, then followed.

"Darros will see you now," Yuri said as they reached the top, gave a slight bow, and waved her hand in her master's direction.

Darros raised a languid hand, beckoning the two envoys to approach. Glendrake and Hammul, their steps heavy with trepidation, slowly approached Darros. Hammul's eyes glazed over at the sight of all the eye candy surrounding him, and he secured his tongue with his teeth as the tip protruded out from the corner of his lips. His eyes were fixated on the exposed body parts, and his thoughts were on clear display across his face.

Glendrake's jaw unlocked as the unsettling nature of Darros' appearance became ever more apparent as they approached. The crowned emperor's face was concealed by a feature-fitting skull mask made from pure gold, its permanently carved appearance purely menacing. The eyes were sunken and hollow, while the twisted, malevolent expression around its mouth insinuated a smile. Contrasting the sinister visage were his soft, brown, emotionless eyes. His hair – long and naturally wavy – was kept like that of a woman's, and his gaze was intense and piercing.

Just as Glendrake was about to speak, the crowd roared and stomped their feet. Darros stood, clasping his hands together.

"Kill! Kill! Kill!" they shouted.

"No! Mercy! Mercy!" the remainder of the crowd countered.

Everyone's attention, bar that of Hammul, was focused on the pit. Darros took notice.

The winning gladiator threw his hands into the air to the sound of applause. He lifted his sword. The crowd fell deathly silent. With a forceful and over-exaggerated swing, he stopped just short of his opponent's neck, close enough to break the skin. A few beads of blood swelled up where the sword made contact before collecting together and trickling down the man's neck.

"Mercy!" the winner announced as he helped his counterpart to his feet. The crowd cheered and threw flowers into the pit.

"Always the performer," Darros said disappointedly, resuming his seat. His soothing voice resonated, drawing Glendrake's attention back to him.

"Send Nef'et an extra head of livestock, a bouquet of white, and a cask of my reserve red coastal wine," he announced.

One of the many servants acknowledged his command and shuffled away.

"How was the journey? Did you first take rest, or did you come straight to me?" he continued without a pause.

It took a moment for Glendrake to realise it was he whom Darros was addressing.

"Oh, uh, straight here, Your Highness; I come at the urgency of Queen Ioelena. I have a message that I must hand deliver only to you, my lord." Glendrake gathered his resolve, quickly retrieved a rolled scroll from his waistband, and managed to take a few steps forward. Yuri, the other guards, and the half-naked women surrounding Darros rushed to intercede, all brandishing blades that had been concealed only heartbeats prior. Darros' laughter broke the tension of the moment.

"It's just Darros. I offer my apologies for them… They can all be a little jumpy," he replied.

Glendrake swallowed slowly against the blade pressed against his throat, the several others prodding his back and making him acutely aware of their presence. Hammul was sure not to move, though his hand still rested on his hilt. Darros waved them away with a finger. The servants returned to their duties, although Yuri and the guards remained on high alert.

"Go on…bring it to me," Darros offered.

Glendrake looked around him before he proceeded.

Accepting the scroll, Darros asked, "What was your name again?"

"Sorry?" a very confused Glendrake replied. He stared into the mask.

"Your name…you do have one, don't you? Or is it a secret you intend to keep to yourself?"

"Glenn, Drake, your…it's Glenn Drake, Darros," he replied. Darros exchanged a glance with Yuri.

"No, not your pretend name. Your real name. What are you otherwise called?" he pressed.

Glendrake frowned, asking, "I'm sorry?"

Darros shook his head and said something to Yuri in their native language. She smirked.

"I want to know the name of my would-be killer. Surely I deserve that much," he replied.

A bead of perspiration formed at Glendrake's hairline and began its slow, trickling descent down his forehead as his eyes shot wide. His breathing quickened. His knuckles were white from the pressure of gripping the hilt of his sheathed sword. He instinctively lifted the blade upwards out of its sheath by just an inch with only the movement of his thumb. He thought to draw it fully, but not before Yuri's blade appeared in a flash, lifting his head by his chin. A sudden commotion erupted behind him, only to reach a swift end as a blood-curdling scream from Hammul filled the air. He'd crumpled to the ground, holding his newly minted stump of a bloody arm – sans hand. It seemed he, too, had been slow to the draw. Glendrake tried to look out of the corner of his eye but could only see blurred movement as it eased to a still.

"Did you kill him?" Darros inquired.

"What?"

The adrenaline surge had emptied the assassin's brain. It had all happened so quickly. Khazmyrian soldiers were exceptionally quick-footed; he had no chance to keep up, especially encumbered as he was.

"I am a patient Darros. However, this back-and-forth is growing rather tiresome. So, let's try this: I will speak, and you will listen. Can you manage that?" he asked with a deeper tone.

The assassin nodded nervously.

"Glendrake is the surname of the man you, at the very least, *robbed* for this letter." He waved it in his hand. "I'd grown rather fond of the man. An older fellow, roughly your height, fit, quite muscular. And he would've had to have been…as it is a decently well-known fact that the soldiers of Hildeheim train and fight with overly weighted armour. It builds strength and character. It makes them tough and enduring. You lack two of those things and are not the other." He mimed flexing his muscles while getting comfortable in his seat, a purely mocking gesture. "The training is said to be rather severe…not for those who aren't acclimated to the extreme environments atop harsh mountain peaks. Besides creating a hardened warrior, it provides one tiny, little…minuscule benefit. Would you care to guess what that would be?"

Glendrake pondered a moment before he shook his head, having come up with nothing. Darros stared with disappointment, then offered a glance in Yuri's direction.

"It makes impostors very easy to identify," she answered for him.

"You two could barely make it up my steps without wheezing. Surely that plate doesn't belong to you," Darros continued.

"So, I ask you again: did you kill him? How many of you did it take? It must have taken more than the two of you to subdue him. I assume he almost took your leg?" Darros asked.

The impostor shook his head in defeat and embarrassment. Hammul grimaced and moaned in the background, still holding his stump, still leaching the red from his pallor and spilling it on the ruby-encrusted floor.

"No, milord," the would-be assassin replied. "We bound him with rope and stowed him under the bridge in Stallhearth."

"Oh…good. He's no doubt escaped already and should be halfway back to Hildeheim by now. Good, that has gained you a few more breaths. Take off that plate; it is not yours to equip. You dishonour it," Darros replied with dissatisfaction in his tone. Both men began to shamefully strip to their undergarments.

"That cuirass doesn't even fit him," Yuri said to Darros in their native tongue. He chuckled lightly.

The impostor known as Hammul whimpered pitifully as he struggled to remove the armour with one hand. Darros watched as he caressed the back of the head of the servant sitting at his feet, a woman by the name of Hera. She stood and walked towards the man, her bare ebony breasts glistening and swaying in between her long-braided hair. Her green eyes were somehow more captivating than her figure. She carefully assisted his efforts to disrobe, being considerate of his injuries. In the depths of the pain he was experiencing, her touch was a welcome reprieve that brought tears to his eyes. Once his armour was removed, she stood next to him, holding his head against her breasts.

"Send this remarkable standard of craftsmanship back to its rightful owner. Include word of what happened here today," he ordered.

Another servant approached from behind and gathered both sets of armour before he began to walk away. Darros observed the pair as the man impersonating Hammul, even in great pain, could not control his fantasies. He was intoxicated by Hera and her scent. His behaviour was off-putting, even for Darros.

"Wait, we forgot one thing," Darros said, his focused eyes resting on Hammul's impostor, communicating all that was required. Hera produced a blade and slid it across that man's neck, parting the flesh like butter and releasing a torrent of red. Darros watched with restrained enjoyment as she finished the job.

"Well played," he noted approvingly, locking eyes with Hera as she lifted the man's head and handed it to another servant. Following a mocking glance offered to the man's corpse, he continued, "He almost began to believe you were going to save him." Finally, looking her figure up and down. He concluded, "Such is the touch of a woman."

Young male servants rushed out to clean the mess and remove the corpse. The remaining assassin had grown pale. Darros turned his attention to the man. He'd almost forgotten he was there.

"I'll ask for the last time. What is your name?"

"Joriah, milord!" He was quick to reply this time. Joriah was afraid, but he was also too proud to admit it to himself.

"Oh, look, he found his voice," Darros joked. Then, with a much more serious tone, "Well, Joriah, you work for me now."

"I…I don't understand, Darros," Joriah begged.

"Joriah, you may be many things, but intelligent is not among them. Therefore, someone put you up to this failed endeavour. Even after seeing there was no means of escape, you held steadfast to your mission. Either you possess a steely reserve, or the need for your success outweighs the risk. Either way, there is a small part of me that admires such resolve," he replied.

Joriah's confusion grew.

"That, and…your man could only think about fucking my servants. A distracted man is a useless one. You haven't glanced at a single tit or cunt since you've been here, and that takes a measure of focus, all things considered," Darros continued, gesturing to his harem. "Hera!"

She walked towards Joriah, who trembled where he stood.

"First, she's going to drain that withering sack between your legs," he continued.

She reached into Joriah's undergarments and took hold. Joriah tensed and froze.

"And when your nerves ease and the colour returns to your wrinkled flesh, you will tell her everything there is to know. If I determine what you say to be good and truthful, then, and only then, will we discuss your future in my employ. If, however, I determine your words to be filth and lies…well…Hera will, with the same hand, drain that other precious fluid coursing through your body." A cold, sinister tone overtook his voice. He found his own words arousing. Hera smiled menacingly, and Joriah's eyes grew wide where he was still frozen in place, half crumpled forward on account of her flexing grip.

"No matter how your immediate future unfolds, consider this your last offer of employment in this world. Do we have an understanding?" Darros said, pausing to give the man time to reply.

"Aye, milord," a defeated Joriah replied.

"Also…" He looked Joriah up and down. "You look like a Merith to me. That is your name now."

"As you wish, Darros," he replied.

"Very good. Now then, Merith…fuck off." Darros shooed him off with a nod of his head. Hera's hand slid out of his undergarments and across his bare chest as she escorted the trembling man away.

"Stay close. Once he outlives his usefulness, send his head as an addendum to Ioelena. Or keep him as a plaything; I don't care. Be it sooner or later, I leave that determination to you," he said to Yuri in their native tongue.

She acknowledged him with a nod and began to leave.

"Yuri?" he called out to her, the 'r' in her name rolling off his tongue. She turned to face him.

"Hera has earned her tunic. Arrange the ceremony for the morning," he said.

"Of course, Darros. She will be pleased," she replied and excused herself.

Darros tapped his golden-tipped fingers against the arms of his throne before he handed the scroll to Thane, a rather handsome guard with long, curly hair. He wore garb like Yuri's: a white tunic secured by a leather belt, his body decorated with golden armbands, and a thin circlet resting atop his head. He opened the scroll and read it to himself, then flipped the scroll over to check for anything written on its back.

"It just says *For Goldwyn Pass*," Thane said in confusion, handing the parchment to Darros. Darros took it and inspected it for himself. He, too, examined the back, expecting something to be written there. His eye arched under his mask.

"She can be so strange at times," he muttered. Then, louder, he announced, "We're leaving. Call for my caravan."

Standing, he walked to a hidden doorway behind his throne. The throng of servants and guards followed close behind him.

CHAPTER EIGHTEEN

AND SO WE REMAIN

ELARION

The wind blew, and the tree boughs groaned. Lysand's hands probed his face, tracing every detail and contour. Elarion stood, smiling humbly as her sightless eyes examined him. She was one of the few remaining Elderharts, the original race of elves, and they had long outgrown the use of their ocular organs. Still, despite being physically blind, she saw everything: what was, what is, and what could be. Her appearance was striking, almost alien, with her eyes being wide and curious. Her skin was pale, with hues of purple and green that had an almost transparent delicacy. It was stretched over a muscular and bony frame that stood taller than Elarion, slender but not frail. She had two sets of ears, common for the females of her species, and the larger set was covered in a sort of velvet-like fur that blended into her long white hair. The smaller pair sat below the larger and were much like Elarion's. They were animated as they twitched and flared inwardly and outwardly, listening for anything that made a sound. The larger, more rigid set, called tonals, was for hearing beyond. It was said that female Elderharts could hear the very heartbeat of the forest. Their command of the Gift was unmatched.

Elarion stared into her eyes. A warm rush of happiness filled him as he felt her exploring his mind. Her appearance began to change, growing younger. Her subtle wrinkles faded, and a hint of a smile pulled her cheek muscles upwards. She blinked for the first time since she began staring at him. His head retreated from her gaze.

"You honour me, but I do not wish for you to comfort me," he said aloud, choosing his words carefully. Her head kept moving around as if she were examining every inch of his face while she stared at him. Elderharts lacked the ability to exhibit what most would consider natural emotion, as it was a concept rooted solely in the present moment. Her movement froze.

'Why do you insist on speaking?' Her thoughts echoed in his mind.

His eyes lingered on the forest floor.

'You are more than capable of accepting me. Why do you limit yourself to your weakest parts?' she asked. Elderharts preferred communication that involved a level of telepathy, projecting their entire consciousness onto the other person. Elarion knew it to be a dynamic and transparent form of communication, and it required an advanced telepathic mind to endure the hive-like connection.

'Very well, dear. I will not force it,' she replied to his lack of a response. Her facsimile of a smile faded. Her *voice* was vibrantly expressive, indicating her disappointment, although the accompanying expression was absent from her face.

"Thank you," he said. He felt her mental probing pull away, and his mood returned to its original state. She appeared old again. Attempting to make conversation, he asked, "Did Galathir send you this way?"

'Galathir does not command me. I came to you of my own volition. In fact, I have not seen Galathir; I came straight to you. I saw you from the other side of the forest. Your light burns brightly, like a fire in winter's calm. Your despair concerned me, and so I delayed you until I could arrive,' she said. Elderharts did not leave the forest, never crossing its borders. They instead wandered the Westwood, never sleeping, always observing and listening.

Elarion nodded, now understanding why he had felt unable to cross over into Hildeheim earlier.

'Walk with me,' she said.

He obliged her as she began walking, staring at him all the while. Lysand sensed her unwavering gaze made him uncomfortable, and so she changed her focus.

'How is Illithor? Does he still resist returning to the forest?' she asked.

His eyes flared; he had forgotten the wealth of her abilities. She had limited herself from fully absorbing his thoughts and memories, only sampling that which he was not attempting to shield from her. His visit with his brother was open fodder. She found the trivial and transactional nature of conversation frustrating but engaged in it out of consideration.

"He does," he said regretfully, straightening his posture. She laughed.

'Your desire to save your brother is admirable. It is your defining characteristic. Always testing the limits of possibility for the good of others,' she began, turning to look at him again. *'If only you would do the same for yourself.'*

His posture weakened.

"I know…" he agreed.

Her head lifted sharply as her eyes drifted downwards. Her tonals opened, rotating outward ever so slightly, the hair on them rising. He couldn't help but be enamoured by their awakening and movement. Her hair began to flow as if blown by the wind, but before the spectacle could truly begin, it sadly ended. Her tonals returned to form and stiffened.

'Your brother will heed your counsel and return to the forest, his family along with him. Ease your mind,' she demanded.

He nodded happily, but neither his expression nor his pattern of thoughts changed.

'And yet, you are still in despair,' she fussed. He felt her itching to probe like a cresting wave, animated yet frozen in place. Continuing to scold him, she went on, *'If you could only see what you will become. If you would only embrace it.'*

"I am humbled by your faith in me," he replied.

'It is called faith by those who cannot see the outcome, those who cannot bind certainty to contract. It is a wish for assurance based upon circumstantial evidence. And even then, Elarion, son of Aemethil…yes. If I were so limited, I would still have faith in you; fortune for us, I am not,' she said. Her head began moving about again as she stared. Her cheeks were slightly raised, granting her an eerie expression that almost resembled a smile.

"I wish I could see what it is that you see," he replied as a few tears broke free, forging hot paths down his face.

'You could,' she said, extending her hand.

He took her hand and kissed it. She scoffed.

'What is it you intend to do?' she asked pointedly. His brow raised. She continued, *'Is it the human?'*

"It is, Lysand," he admitted.

She nodded in reply and stopped walking.

"He has returned to the fold. I must go to ensure his survival. I owe him that much," he continued.

'You don't owe anyone anything,' she said.

He grew visibly agitated with her, and her tonals began to move again, halting his tantrum. She looked away from him.

'*I see,*' she said. She looked up at the columns of the bridge to Hildeheim, then ran her hand over the glowing runes.

Elarion started, not having noticed where they had walked.

'*The Candorians are active again, meddling as they should not,*' she said, her tonals stiffening.

He looked sheepish.

'*Is that what you are trying to hide from me?*' she asked.

He looked confused, not having felt her reach deeper into his mind.

'*I saw you talking to one in the Garden before you left for Illithor,*' she continued. '*Do not allow them to drag you into their intrusions, serving as a tool for their corrupted ways,*' she said before erupting into sinister laughter. '*Even they cannot stop what you will become.*'

"It is because of them that I go… For his sake," he replied. Then, looking over her ears, he continued, "I may not have tonals, but even I can sense the darkness that is coming."

She laughed again and replied, '*And you intend to stop it? Alone? Elarion, ever the hero to those who look to destroy themselves. You have given your allegiance to many, yet all have died. Why do you keep limiting yourself to your weakest parts?*'

"I cannot help it, Lysand. They need guidance—" he pleaded.

'*As do you,*' she interrupted.

"But they do not have an eternity, as I do," he argued.

'*And how long will you wait?*' she asked.

He pondered her question. He'd never thought to give himself a timeline.

'*I can see your struggle. It is a noble one. Perhaps we could all learn from your unwavering commitment to altruism,*' she offered.

He blushed at the sincerity and replied, "You flatter me, but there is nothing I could teach you."

'*On the contrary, everyone needs reminders from time to time,*' she said, rubbing his shoulder. He could hear the smile in her voice. There was a pause in the conversation, and as he looked across the bridge, Hildeheim seemed less uninviting.

"Do you ever long to cross over?" he asked. Her head canted as she understood the duality of his question.

'*It is not that I lack the ability. Our people still need the others, as they need me, and so we remain. The time will come, but it is not now,*' she said. '*You will one day learn to stop thinking with your eyes. We Elderharts do not need our physical bodies to leave the forest. I wander everywhere, all the time.'* She could sense he was beginning to understand. He looked at her eyes, and she quipped, *'I think we are beginning to see eye-to-eye.'*

Even an Elderhart enjoyed a good pun. Her raspy laughter echoed, and he laughed along while nodding.

'Very well,' she said, setting aside her intent to persuade him as she glanced back in Thaetra's direction. *'That one has potential, though her path is still unclear. Will you one day aid her as you do the expiring ones?'*

He looked over in Thaetra's direction and affirmed, "I will."

'That would be wise,' she replied. Shifting in tone and focus, she then asked, *'Come, now. When was the last time you slept, dear?'*

"It *has* been some time," he acknowledged after struggling to remember.

'You need rest,' she decided, taking his hand and walking towards his campsite. He suddenly felt tired and agreeable. *'You have not reached the point where you can forgo rest, little one. Not yet.'*

He fought the desire to yawn as they walked together slowly, asking, "I know I am only a fraction of your years, but why is it I feel so…empty? I hesitate to complain to you. You must think me to be so…short-sighted."

'It is because you deny yourself the full scope of your purpose, Elarion. Instead, you fill your days with these…meaningless pursuits. While fulfilling in the moment, the next day holds no lasting effect,' she replied, then stopped walking as they arrived. She released his hand and rested her own on his shoulder, motioning for him to lie down. He obliged.

Thaetra snored gently.

'Do not worry; you are not a lost cause. Complete your quest with the human, and then we will speak again,' she said to him, offering her words as a workaround to his desire to see the future unfold.

"Will it be soon?" he asked, drifting off to sleep.

'To me, yes,' she replied. *'Rest, and I will stay here with you until the morning.'*

He yawned heavily again, and his eyelids began to flutter.

'Elarion. Find your purpose,' she called to him, *'and do not deny me a third time.'*

She tapped her own temple, and his eyes closed. Her tonals began to shift, and her hair flowed with the wind.

Lysand stood over them until the morning hours, at which point he began to rouse. He wakened enough to see the back of her as she walked away, fading into the forest.

CHAPTER NINETEEN

Dark and Familiar Places

Connerh

His gaze was fixed.

He sat alone in the darkened interior, taking calm, silent breaths. The moon was large and bright, and its shafts beamed through the windowpane, softly highlighting his features. The flames of the hearth had subsided some time ago, but their remnant embers were still consuming what could be scavenged from its belly. His spear rotated just before him, ignoring the natural laws of gravity and glimmering in the pale moonlight. Its rhythmic pulse filled the void of his mind, near where the corners of consciousness and choice met. Their deep connection was an exchange of thoughts and inclinations in real time; it was not a voice that Connerh heard echoing in his mind, as a telepath would, but a constant form of dialogue on a completely different plane. Its objective was as clear as that of a weapon: to be wielded with precision and lethality, to accomplish the task no matter what it entailed, and to be devoid of illusions and discussions of morality.

A simple yes or no was all that was required.

When in its presence, Connerh would enjoy an elevation of the senses – below the threshold of nausea but above the nature of what was normal. He had yet to decipher the radius of its influence, as it was never far from him, but he felt no desire to part from it or test the bounds. The thought alone felt undesirable in his core. Despite its arrival being precipitous in nature, its place as a permanent fixture in his life was now assured. The bond had been instantaneous, like puzzle pieces finally being reunited.

The yin to his yang.

He could hear a man outside moving ever closer to his homestead. The measured steps of the heavy-framed brute were accurately matched to the wind and other audible distractions as he navigated the dead cornfield, demonstrating his prowess as a seasoned predator. Sadly for him, his lifetime of training and discipline were rendered inept against Connerh's heightened advantage. He could have saved time by approaching astride the backs of furious equines; his presence would have been no less obvious to Connerh. There were times when he felt his elevated abilities were sort of a cheat…but death held no such honour code, and nor would he. Only fools and dead men chose to reside in such realms of hubris.

Connerh felt a mental tap on the shoulder. The intruder was close.

The spear slowed in its orbit, sliding back into darkness in synchronisation with Connerh.

The man's blurry-edged shadow slid across the windowpane with stealthy silence. His blob-like head scanned the interior through the foggy pane of glass before him while Connerh tracked his movements, his footsteps, his heartbeat. The movement stopped abruptly as the man spotted the shape of someone sleeping in the bed. A sharp elevation in heart rate. The man was nervous. Connerh offered a modest grin in the comfort of his concealment. Even professionals could get nervous from time to time.

The heart often exhibited a truth the exterior sought to hide.

The moonlight and embers cast an uneven glow, revealing just enough detail despite the darkness concealing the rest, making the faux body all the more convincing. It was a quick but efficient job of positioning the perfect amount of pillows and blankets in just the right way. It hadn't been the first time Connerh had constructed such an illusion, and by this point, he'd begun to take pride in how convincing he could make them when he gave it some effort.

The shadow vanished, but he could still hear him. He was making his way around the house, likely seeking another point of entry. He took even more care in his step placement now, though he leaned too heavily into the pads of his feet.

Poor footing is the root of all defeat, he mouthed in the dark, shaking his head; that tenet was beaten into him during his early military training. It was a simple saying, memorable, bordering on profound in its potential application, and he could always find a way to apply it.

Things had changed irrevocably. The man knew someone was inside, yet he still persisted in his activity. This was not meant to be a simple burglary, a crime of convenience.

The window for mercy had expired.

What will you do? he wondered. There was only one other window, which he'd strategically barricaded already. That left the front door and the window next to him, and both made entirely too much noise to breach. The rate at which the man's heart raced remained the same, but it was beating harder. He was frustrated, probably wishing it was a quick and easy job. They always did. Not that it mattered; he would be dead well before Connerh could react to any attempt at forced entry. And even understanding this, he still enjoyed the game. He liked to see how the enemy thought – how they blended improvisation with textbook training. Like watching a rat traverse a maze, all the time knowing the trap was at the end. It added a bit of intrigue to an otherwise dull and macabre affair.

His shadow returned. He stood there a while, thinking. Convincing himself, maybe. Working through his breathing exercises. Connerh crossed a leg at the knee, raised his arms, and interlocked his hands.

The spear desperately craved his permission. The power of its longing could be intoxicating at times.

As it was now.

The man's very existence hung on the knife's edge of Connerh's will. A single, deliberate thought sealed with intent would rejoin him with the cosmos, and Connerh would be free of conscience and consequence. He wouldn't even have to see the body. He would just know that it would be done because he had willed it to be so. If only the fool knew what lay in wait for him: that such thin walls of wood and glass were the demarcation of death.

What is it that talks a man out of a thing? Connerh considered. *Who owns the voice in the back of your head telling you not to do a thing? Does the owner know what's on the other side of the proverbial or literal wall? Why is it so insistent? So pervasive? And why was it usually right?*

The shadow pulled away, vanishing quickly. He was less careful in his retreat.

"Run along," Connerh said aloud.

"Tell them to come. It's about time," the man said from afar.

There were at least thirty of them, as far as Connerh could count. Some people often shared the same beat pattern, making them harder to detect; it was an art more than a science, at least at this stage in his understanding. Connerh sat forward. The ominous red glow of his pipe highlighted the shadows of his face. Thirty was a good number. He was flattered.

"I suppose it's time we prepare," Connerh said, standing. The chill of battle was in the air. Death had arrived in anticipation of the festivities. An old friend from another time — another life — yet Death's greeting was always the same. He lowered the temperature to better preserve the bodies. He stilled the wind to balance the battlefield. And the quiet that was always too quiet…because everything hid from Death. The moon was vibrant and large in the sky, like an engaged spectator. Connerh's armour was already prepared, set out in perfect order next to him, cleaned, oiled, and ready to be worn. And so, he made ready. He danced through the familiar steps of putting it on, piece by piece, in the order he'd always preferred. It still fit, just as on the day he'd last worn it. It held the stench of irony; the thing he'd grown to hate was the one thing he could never seem to abandon. Not fully. He was always somehow brought back here, to battle, in one way or another. He just wanted a normal life, but he was beginning to wonder if he knew what that really meant. Was this, perhaps, normal after all? Had he been chasing a figment of his imagination?

Were 'simple' and 'quiet' not obtainable for him?

He grimaced.

The others were gathering, their rumblings forcing him to refocus. It would be as it used to be.

A familiar ritual.

Earth. A bundle of dry inka leaves tossed on the embers. The opaque white smoke rapidly engulfed the interior of the house, filling his lungs with its toxic terpenes. His pupils dilated, and the sharpness of his hearing increased. Combined with the effects of his spear, his senses elevated beyond the point of comfort, creating a living hell for the next several hours.

Water. A drink known affectionately as Tears of the Angel numbed the pain receptors. It was a very expensive cocktail only afforded by the best — unless, of course, you knew how to make it. It burned going down, staining the skin it touched. His nostrils began to drip with blood.

Fire. There was always fire. There would be no war without fire. He added wood to the pile and used bellows to catch them, quickly getting lost in the ethereal dance of the flame. It focused him amidst the madness running rampant in his body.

He kneeled before the fire, and his eyes watered. It wasn't the men's fault. They were only following orders, but he would not absolve them of the price of a soldier.

"Keep it clean."

He spoke to the spear as if it were his lesser. It acknowledged him in what way it could. It began to move about the house as if it were patrolling or looking for something. Connerh watched while he, for a moment, grew uncomfortable in his comfort. It was a peculiar affair, having this ultimate trust in a thing you couldn't quite explain – a thing that could kill you faster than you could register your own demise. It was exhilarating, actually. A constant touch of danger always kept the blood fresh.

He retrieved a long wooden box and set it on the bed. He paused before opening it. It was all beginning to feel real again.

He opened it.

Elisceryn was the blade's name. It was the blade of his father's forefather, a gift from the then-Elven King of the Forest. It was a fine sword. The weapon was a blending of styles, marrying the elegance and signature curve of the elves with the rigid and enduring spine of men. The blade was a muted grey, with etchings that looked like the outlines of continents on a map. She was a cursed blade now, but she did not complain. She was ready and willing. He watched it as it slid into its sheath at his side. He frowned, realising he had not thought to name the spear. Of course, it was in much the same way you would not think to name someone who has one already, but neither did he know its name.

"Should I want to call you by name? Would you make it known to me, were you to have one? I will think of one, should you not," he said. The spear floated closer to him. The time had arrived. He turned around, fixing his gaze on the mask he had delayed donning and returning the empty stare it offered him. This was the piece of armour that had earned him the nickname of *Gargoyle*. It was meant as a pejorative, but he had accepted it, seeing it as an appropriate moniker. At times, he was forced to become the very thing he sought to destroy.

He unlocked the front door and walked out, vanishing into the cornfield that surrounded his property. The spear followed behind him. It paused, then shot into the sky with a violent rush of air.

They appeared without sound. Shadowy figures crept out of the cornfield like spectres returning to the grave. Three staggered rows of ten men each, spaced eight feet apart, descended on the modest home, their metaphorical net closing in. Their weapons were unsheathed and held forward, consisting mainly of swords and crossbows. Silent gestures and hand movements communicated improvisational orders with precision and clarity. Two fingers raised high, pointing sharply towards their target. The signal was sent. There would be no turning back now.

The designated soldier pushed through the ranks, kneeling on the ground and retrieving specific items from his sack: a clay sphere with a piece of fabric extended from it and a corked vial. The content of the vial was for soaking the fabric, the clay sphere for reducing the chance of conflict. A quick light and a toss preceded the crash and shattering of a glass window. It was louder and echoed a bit more than anticipated. The ranks shuffled. The sound of erupting flames roared within the four walls, smoke beginning to leak out through the single broken pane.

The rate at which their heart rate increased was barely detectable, their resolve unwavering. Connerh watched from the rear as his home burned like a funeral pyre under the night sky, his mask held low in his hand. His eyes watered. It wasn't the material loss that upset him but what it represented. Things could be replaced, and homes could be rebuilt, but dreams could be kept out of reach.

Ferocious blue flames consumed everything in their path. There would be nothing left but the stone pillars when the fire finally subsided, but even they would one day fall, retaking their place among the dirt. The ashes would be scattered to the wind, leaving scorched earth where the home once stood. Years would pass, the weeds would grow, and only memories would remain. Nevertheless, even they had an expiration date. His eyes lowered, resting upon pouting cheeks. Wincing with each crackle and pop, he inhaled the smoke of scorched sulphur and his former possessions.

An eternal death.

Morning began as his mourning concluded. It was cloudy. His dried eyes raised as he returned his mask to his face. He vanished amidst the forest of stalks and husks.

"You didn't even confirm who was inside," he said with a peaceful calm. His voice echoed.

The soldier's shuffling armour was audible. They tightened their formation, with every other man turning to face a new direction, being sure to cover every possible point of ambush. Their chests were drumming loudly.

"That takes a very special disregard," he continued, his voice moving.

"Show yourself, coward!" a soldier shouted. His voice was wrought with fear.

"I'm not the one—" he replied before pausing abruptly.

The passing seconds felt like minutes. The number of glances exchanged among the men increased. They were frozen with confusion and trepidation.

"Your leader is there, hiding in the middle, hoping to blend in and avoid detection. But he is not the strongest of you. Who is it, then?" Connerh asked. His voice originated from the centre of the field.

They instinctively looked at the man designated to command them. His gaze lowered.

"Come, now. Now is not the time for humility. We are *long* past formalities," he said, a tinge of annoyance in his tone. He was closer.

"I am the strongest." A large, burly figure stepped forward. His voice was both deep and powerful enough to carry.

"Very good. And what is your name, soldier?" Connerh asked.

"What's it to you?" he replied to his fellow men's nervous laughter.

Connerh stepped forward, revealing himself. He brought with him a gentle rain as he explained, "Because an example must be made."

His lone presence gave the soldiers a misplaced hope. They bolstered, feeling comfort in their seemingly assured victory.

"I'm glad we're on the same page, then, because that's exactly what we're doing here. However, if you're dying to know, it's Heim," he said. The men chuckled.

Connerh nodded, replying, "It is good that you told me, as they will not be able to identify your remains." His muffled voice was firm, his inflection plain, devoid of emotion. Heim's face flushed with humoured confusion.

A terrifying crack split the sky above, and a rolling thunderclap travelled through the air. The *crescendo of pressure* exploded, rattling the soldiers' armour. Connerh's spear fell like lightning from the heavens, piercing Heim's fleshy form and exploding it into a robust red mist, peppering chunks of flesh, bone, and gristle over his former compatriots. Only a few inches of the golden spear handle protruded from the mud.

Connerh stood motionless.

Unphased.

One of the men vomited violently, while the rest promptly abandoned their weapons and dropped to their knees. Except one. The spear vibrated and jostled as it worked its way out of the mud, drawing the men's gaze. It shot back into the sky upon freeing itself, leaving a vacuum of air that tugged at the men as it sought to fill itself. Connerh's unseen gaze focused on the commander in charge, the lone man still standing. The cause for his defiance was not a steeled bravado as it appeared, but fear. His lower back and knees had simply locked. To them, Connerh looked like a supernatural spectacle, a thing of legend.

And he was.

"Are you the man who ordered these men to their end?" he asked.

The commander shook his head slowly but took off running as soon as he realised control of his limbs had returned. He disappeared into the vegetation, making no effort to conceal the sound of his retreat. Connerh sighed aloud, audible beyond his mask.

A crack. A roll of thunder. Dirt and debris flew violently into the air in the distance. Connerh folded his arms in front of himself as the men's focus snapped to the sound of the eruption.

"Which of you is the youngest?" he asked.

"Aye, I am, Your Grace. William is the name." A quivering young voice spoke up. The boy stood, barely fitting into his armour. Connerh's head shook.

"Grace? I am not a lord or a god. Just a man created for a purpose, which I once again embrace today," he replied.

"Yes, milord," William replied.

Connerh chuckled quietly, then asked, "How old?"

"Eighteen, milord," he replied.

Connerh's head shook, preceding his words. "Too young, despite what you have been told. Remove your armour, keep your dagger, but leave your sword. Do not return to your employ. Find a new life whilst you still can…and tell the story of Haim," he ordered.

The boy nodded intently, although he kept sparing glances upwards, hesitant to retreat because of the spear.

"It will not bother you. Besides, it's still wedged between what remains of your commander and the ground at the moment," he added, dark humour dripping from his words.

The boy failed to find the joke in it. The vacuum of the spear returning to the air sounded.

Connerh waited patiently as the boy frantically removed his armour. His head canted as he received new information, and he asked, "There are others on approach. Are they with you?"

The boy, confused, turned to the others.

"No, milord; we don't work well with others," another said. Connerh's brow raised.

"Go!" Connerh shouted, having lost his patience. The shout sufficiently motivated the boy to take off running.

"What can we do to persuade milord to mercy?" another asked. Connerh casually rested his folded hands on the hilt of his sword. He thought about letting them go, and the thought lasted longer than he realised. As if to jog his memory, a loud pop and crackle from his burning house pulled his attention away. His hands dropped to his sides.

"Did you know if anyone else was in the home?" he asked.

The man shook his head shamefully.

"Women, children…did it not matter?" he asked again.

Another shameful decline.

"Then it would seem you are unworthy of mercy, as you are incapable of giving it," Connerh replied.

"What if we offer you information?" they begged. "Don't you want to know who we work for?"

His head began to shake, again preceding his words: "At this point, it doesn't matter."

The spear descended next to Connerh, eerily and without sound.

"Come. Let's get on with it," he said, motioning towards their swords and taking the first step forward.

The spear began to rotate clockwise, gaining speed by the half-second. After just a matter of moments, the sound it made was deafening. The vibration rattled their teeth, and the wind it produced blinded them.

Connerh unsheathed Elisceryn.

CHAPTER TWENTY

FLUIDS

YURI

Merith failed to notice the extravagant buildings, their pillars ripe with artwork detailing Darros' exploits throughout the millennia. He was not impressed by how clean the city was or how orderly its people were. The lack of visible armed security, other than those who escorted him, escaped his notice. His mind was elsewhere, preoccupied with destiny – his destiny. After what felt like an hour of travelling and climbing a multitude of stairs, he lifted his gaze to take stock of his surroundings. The large, burly soldiers who had cleared the way for them now parted and stood outside the doorway, with the ones behind them following suit. Hera took his hand and led him into a room with Yuri close behind. The room was filled with sheer curtains that hung from a tall ceiling. A large bed stood at the centre with stocks affixed to the wall, while a red-stained bowl sat in the middle of the floor.

Before he could hesitate, Yuri pushed him forward.

"You don't have to do this," he said, his voice shaken.

"Don't you know? Sycophants aren't affected by begging," Yuri snapped, recalling his previous choice of words. They pushed and prodded him over to the wall and fastened his arms and legs with straps.

"I'm not begging; I'm stating a fact," he replied, calm but still downtrodden.

Yuri walked over to the bed and sat, leaning back on her hands and facing them. She crossed her legs at the knee, anxiously waiting for that which needed to be done to be over. Hera kneeled and removed his undergarment, exposing him to the room.

"Well, then…you should have chosen a much different career. You would do well here," Yuri remarked with a flare.

"Wait! Damn you," he shouted. Hera looked back at Yuri with confusion. Yuri sat forward.

"Maybe you're not his type, darling. I'll call for one of the footmen," she said and stood.

"No, it's not that either!" he protested.

"Then what?" Yuri demanded, crossing her arms.

"Maybe he's committed to another?" Hera offered while smiling and groping him.

"No…no, she's long gone. It's my son," he said solemnly.

Both women wore their confusion plainly.

"They have my son!" he shouted at them again.

"I don't want to be here any more than you want me here. It was the Far Sands, a man by the name of Tyreek…" he began.

"The Viper, I know that name… Go on," Yuri interrupted, her interest piqued. She took a few steps in his direction.

"Do you mind?!" he asked Hera, who was still busy fondling him. She giggled at his discomfort.

"Give him a minute," Yuri ordered her. Hera stood, giving his bits a moment of reprieve.

"He's rounding up anyone between there and the Forest of the Elves to do his bidding, meaning anyone not equipped to ward off his band of travelling thugs. My son and I were on a journey to bury the remains of my deceased wife back in her homeland, where she's from. They ambushed us…took my son as insurance, if you will," he said.

"And the armour?" Yuri insisted.

"They ambushed a patrol nearby and forced us to wear their armour. I tried to get away in the chaos with my son, and…I wasn't fast enough. Hence the injury," he explained, disappointed in himself.

"And your wife? Where was she from?" Yuri asked, walking ever closer to him.

"Hildeheim. She was born there; we met and were wed there. It's only right she be buried there," he replied. She squinted her eyes and stared into his. She wanted to believe him. Hera looked to her for guidance.

"Why send you on a suicide mission? Obviously you would be discovered, offence intended," she quipped.

"I don't know," he said, shaking his head.

"Not good enough. Who are you? Who was your wife? Your son? Why punish you in such a way?" she pressed.

"I don't know," he repeated, insistent. Yuri nodded at Hera, who quickly moved in to fill her hands. He recoiled at her touch.

"Why does my touch offend you?" she asked, thoroughly disturbed by him.

"In my eyes and the eyes of my god, I am still betrothed until she is buried. And as I said, it is not necessary; I will tell you all that you wish to know," he responded. Yuri rolled her eyes.

"I accept that I should be punished; what I attempted is unspeakable, but I assure you, I had no choice. Just as you have no choice," he said, resigned. Yuri frowned.

"I have all the choices, as far as you are concerned," she argued back. "You didn't answer my question. Who are you? Why were you sent to your death? How did you draw the Viper's ire? Speak, or Hera will spoil the memory of your dead whore, breaking your vow," she pressed, pulling her dagger from her waistband, "and I will ensure it can never physically happen again."

"I am no one, a sheep herder from Lambshead, just outside of..." he cried.

"Hildeheim," Yuri finished his statement and glanced around the room.

"Yes, at the southwestern edge. It's a small town in comparison to this place, but we supply a large amount of wool and meat to the surrounding cities. We were in the wrong place at the wrong time, I assure you," he pleaded. Yuri thought for a moment.

"And what would you do if I were to release you? Where would you go, empty-handed as you are?" she asked.

"I do not know. I cannot return as long as Darros is alive. There is hope they will keep my son alive until I can..." he began.

"Your son is already dead, sheep herder. Men like the Viper don't get names like that without reason," she laughed in disbelief at his ignorance.

"I can hope," he whispered as the tears ran hot down his face.

She walked up to him and lifted his face.

"He sent you to die just to mock that hope. That is what evil men do. They teach you to rely on hope, all the while knowing there is none," she said with a squint in her eye. She snatched her hand away from his chin and took a few steps back.

"You are correct, however… There is no return for you," she continued.

"What do we do with him?" Hera spoke up, rubbing her hands down his chest.

"You heard Darros. Get the bowl," she said, taking deliberate steps towards him. His head dropped, resigned to his fate.

Yuri took hold of him and squeezed, raising her dagger. Hera held the bowl between his legs.

"May the god of mercies have pity on you; you are only doing what you must," he said as loose tears rolled down his cheeks. He mumbled a proverb in the tongue of Hildeheim. Yuri squinted and listened to the words. They were familiar, and she recalled the words as he finished them. In his prayerful fervour, he hadn't noticed that she had released him or that Hera had stood and placed the bowl on the table next to him.

"Apologies. We had to be sure," Yuri said, taking a deep breath and returning her dagger to its place.

"But if you change your mind, the offer stands," Hera suggested, flaring her eyes as she bent down to draw up his undergarments. Yuri shook her head and unfastened his binds.

"You're not the first poor soul we've captured who has been sent on a suicide run by the Viper. This isn't his first campaign to stir chaos between the ruling kingdoms, either. It only takes one assassination to drive the world into war, eating itself alive," she remarked. Merith rubbed at his sore wrists.

"That's how roaches like him rise to the top: when there's no one left to challenge him," Hera added.

"How many have attempted to kill Darros?" Merith asked.

"Oh, they all *tried*. None ever managed to get within kilometres of him. Darros thought to change that, to see what would come of it," Yuri replied.

"Outsiders don't understand Khazmyrians. We aren't a people to be liberated. We are happy here. Darros is surrounded by millions who are ready to kill and sacrifice for him," Hera continued.

"This is no safe place in Khazmyr for the enemies of Darros," Yuri added as they released his feet from the straps.

"What happened to the others? Were they also released?" Merith asked.

"They didn't pass the test," Hera said, looking at the bowl.

"I'll handle it from here. I'll come find you shortly, once I have news for you," Yuri said. Hera nodded and walked away, but not before winking at Merith. Merith finally gave in and glanced at her bare chest as she turned to leave. Yuri smirked.

"Now I believe you," she said.

"What do you mean?" he asked in a panic, quickly meeting her gaze.

"That you didn't want the footman to replace her," she chuckled.

He blushed, realising he had been caught.

"Apologies to your wife and for your loss. I didn't mean what I said. They were only words," she explained humbly.

He nodded in appreciation, and his eyes dropped.

"Where exactly was she from?" she continued.

"A small, insignificant village outside of Bear Creek. The town barely had a name. Just a bunch of poor blacksmiths and metal workers trying to get by." A warm smile washed across his face. Then, motioning to their surroundings, he wryly remarked, "The complete opposite of a place like this, in fact." After a brief pause, he pushed himself to ask, "What happens now?"

"I do not know the answer to that question yet. But, as I said, there is no return for you. You're safer here. I don't believe the Viper would remember your face, let alone a memorable thought about you, but we'd best be sure. Also, Darros won't let you leave; he finds joy in liberating lost souls," she said while thinking.

"Am I to be your plaything?" he asked, quoting Darros.

"There is a first for everything, I suppose," she replied and motioned towards the bed. "Get some rest…Joriah. We have activities in the morning, and you will accompany me. The guards will be posted just outside…until you earn our trust. I'll have them bring you something to eat," she said.

He smiled at the utterance of his true name, then clenched his jaw to hold back further emotion.

"May I ask a small favour?" he asked.

"Already asking for favours, I see," she joked.

He forced a smile.

"What is it, Joriah?" she asked.

A genuine smile overtook the fake one as she said his name again.

"If it were possible, could you find out if, by chance…" he paused. The seriousness of his request cancelled out her levity.

"Oh, of course. I'll see what is possible. But Joriah," she paused and grabbed his hand, "remember what I said about hope." She was sincere but stern.

"It's all I have," he interrupted her, melancholy in his tone.

Overwhelmed with pity for the man, she walked over to the table, lifted a clay pitcher, and smashed it upon the ground. Picking up one of the sharpest pieces, she brought the shard back to him.

"Write your name at the bottom of your foot. The wound will heal, but the words will remain…your real name. Never forget it," she said, cradling his hand in her own.

He nodded to her, which she returned.

He watched her feet as she left and wondered.

Yuri walked into Darros' bath chamber. It was filled with candles and overpowered by the smell of lavender and eucalyptus. She saw his unmasked silhouette through layers of semi-transparent curtains and immediately dropped her eyes.

"And what did we find?" Darros asked.

"Another pawn," Hera said as she walked past Yuri, who stood open-mouthed and preparing to speak. Hera's white linen skirt dropped to the ground as she approached Darros. Her bare, athletic physique faded behind the curtains.

"Did you call the footman?" Darros asked. Hera giggled.

"He was another victim of the Viper," Yuri spoke up, getting back to the subject at hand.

"And he passed the test?" he asked.

"Yes," Yuri replied.

"Well, that's new," he said, stunned. Yuri glanced up to see Hera throwing herself at him. His chuckle of delight resonated. She rolled her eyes.

"What am I to do with him, Darros?" she demanded.

"It is as I said: kill him or keep him as your pet…I leave that up to you," Darros replied.

"I refer to the Viper," she said, taking on a slightly irate tone. He stopped fondling Hera and moved to the edge of his bath. She saw the outline of his face where he was staring directly at her. His eyes were piercing, causing her to shrink in place.

"I'm sorry, I…" she began.

"Silence." He raised his voice. Hera and Yuri flinched at the echo, shielding their eyes with their brow.

"Here you go again. How many times have I told you to drop your vendetta against a meaningless desert worm?" he said with disappointment. "Tyreek is a useful idiot; you need a few of those from time to time."

She opened her mouth slightly, indicating she wished to speak. He sighed as he caught sight of it.

"Speak the words you always say at this point," he instructed, sighing again.

She opened her mouth but paused, realising he was correct.

"Come," he announced.

She nodded, disrobed quickly, and navigated the maze of curtains of varying colours. He grabbed her hips and lowered her into the water. She released a soothed sigh as she was embraced by both the relaxing, warm waters and his touch, though she still avoided looking at him directly.

"I just want…" she began.

"I will have your revenge when the time is right. I have told you this," he assured her.

"It's not me…" she said, lying.

"Oh?" he replied.

"This man today would have been the three hundred and seventy-fourth to be sent to his death by our hands. Why not end this slow-trickling genocide of the innocent?" she implored him, staring at his chin.

"That is why we have the tests! No innocent man or woman could fail the test. And look, one passed today, proving what I have always told you. Three hundred and seventy-three…against one. Quite terrible odds, wouldn't you say? The world outside is a treacherous one," he replied, twirling her around and pulling her back into his muscular arms.

"That is why you belong here, under my endless embrace." Darros' tone deepened. Her muscles relaxed as she lay her head against him.

"But Darros…" she began. He sighed and moved her away from him.

"What do I care if a thousand – no, a hundred thousand – march in single file to receive their sweet release by means of Khazmyrian steel? They're little more than slaves, are they not? And if they cannot pass the tests, then they do not deserve to be here with us, within these walls," he snarled, then softened.

Her face wrinkled at his casual dismissal of life. She heard the water ripple as he moved closer to her backside. His projected warmth overpowered the warmth emanating from the water, and she dropped her head as he turned her around to face him. His hands lifted out of the water and raised her face to his. A smile crept onto her face as she locked eyes with him.

"It has been a long journey, and still a sliver of the old you fights to remain. What will it take for you to surrender to me completely?" he asked. Hera floated over and massaged his shoulders.

"I *am* trying, Darros," she replied softly.

"I will give you Tyreek's head on a golden platter covered in rubies, I promise. You must just give me time. It is all I ask," he whispered in her ear, his lips grazing her neck and firing off goosebumps.

"Yes, Darros," she said as her eyes slipped closed. He moved away from her just as she turned, intending to lie back against him. He sat on the submerged bench as Hera moved to straddle him. Yuri's eyes dropped.

"Go. You need to rest and clear your mind of these matters. Come to me in the morning," he instructed, gazing into her eyes with an unbreakable glare. Yuri stepped out of the water, taking a towel from a waiting servant.

"And what of the man? What am I to do with him?" she asked as she retrieved her tunic sadly.

"I don't care."

His voice trailed into Hera's laughter.

CHAPTER TWENTY-ONE

DECLARATIONS AND CONSTITUTIONS

HARGATHA

A stiff breeze whistled, accompanying the chorus of the open sea. The loud claps of a distant flag looped infinitely in the background. Hargatha stood in defiance of the wind aboard the bridge of the Resolace. With a furrowed brow and squinted eyes, she stared beyond the water, the focus of her gaze empty as she obsessed over her thoughts. She hadn't moved in hours. Her lips were dry and covered in a thin layer of salt. Had it not been for the occasional squawking of the gulls, she may have forgotten to blink.

"I might have said something clever to break the tension had we been here under different circumstances," Galabrand began as he approached quietly from behind.

Her face remained frozen but for a moment before her gaze broke, her head tilting in his direction. His warm hands rested gently upon her shoulders, warming her earlobes. Her shoulders slowly dropped. She hadn't realised they were pinned so tightly or so high.

"You have to admit, being so far away from everything… Well, it's a pretty good view," he said. She flashed a smile and kissed his hand. She took a moment to actually absorb her surroundings. The Resolace was a

167

beautiful ship, with its rich, dark redwood colour, collared by black metal, sitting in perfect contrast to the bluest waters. The cool, insistent sea breeze forced her to take restful breaths often. She loved the Mountain but had always thought she could live by the sea. Be it another life, another height. She smirked, having enjoyed putting her mind on other matters, even if it were only for a moment.

"I'd say that was pretty clever," she said with the residue of her smile still on her face.

He let out a quiet laugh.

"Thank you, by the way," she quickly continued, looking back in his direction.

"For?" His deep, aged voice growled.

"Letting me think," she replied, returning her gaze to the endless motion of the sea. He nodded.

"It's good for you. I like to let it out, but you…" he said with a small shrug and a wink. "Even when we were young, you were always the quiet thinker. My mother thought you to be strange for it, gods rest her. But I knew…it meant you had your head on your shoulders." He recalled fondly. "You like to think it out so you don't do something stupid like I would."

She rolled her eyes and replied, "She only said that so you wouldn't like me."

His deep laugh was carried by the wind.

"Probably. The only boy to hold on to the old ways… I was her favourite," he admitted.

"A fact she constantly reminded everyone of," she said.

He laughed again, leaning on the guardrail. They were somewhat at home on the Resolace, one of Hildeheim's many ships designed for transporting giants. Everything was at the perfect scale, including the ship itself. The size of everything made humans look like children, but it wasn't designed for them, after all.

Hargatha took a deep breath, sighed, and used a few precious moments to compile her thoughts into something logical – something other than the convoluted thoughts and screams that played out in her mind. He moved around her, placing his back to the sea.

"The way I see it, we have two options," he began, waiting for her to meet his gaze. "The first…we can play along and see where this takes us. Or…"

She looked up at him and asked curiously, "Or what?"

"We send for the rest of ours…and take the Rim. We have the ships, and we'll have solid numbers. Who is she going to send? Would she really waste the men and resources needed to sail around the entire continent and fight a battle when we have the advantage?" he asserted. She raised a brow as the smile melted away.

"Secede? Our kind does not belong on an island. We belong to the Mountain, and it belongs to us," she said. He pinched her chin with a smirk.

"Maybe, but times are changing. Isn't that what you always tell me?" he asked. "Besides, the Mountain isn't going anywhere. Consider it an extended holiday."

"You would pack up and run because your brother's mistake is throwing a temper tantrum?" she scowled.

His brows flared, and he grinned with a chuckle, "I don't think I've seen you this riled up in a long while."

"It was fine when I saw Lena as the little child she once was. Just needing a little smack on the bottom every now and then…a correction of sorts. But now…" Her eyes focused and squinted, and when she continued, her tone had lowered, "Now she plays games with the adults."

He patiently allowed her to vent. Her eyes shot around, finally landing on him.

"And now that Nyradhal bastard is going to fuck everything up…even worse than she's managed to do on her own," she argued. She washed her face with her hands and groaned. "Why can't he just disappear forever!?"

"I thought you sent a solution to that problem?" he asked.

"I've learned to never underestimate his ability to *not* die. I've tried twice to be rid of this problem, and to be frank, I don't have much faith in the third attempt," she snapped.

He nodded. She sighed again out of frustration.

"Were we so easy to cast aside? She claims good intent, but we all see it for what it is. She means to get us out of her way," she said and looked back at him. "Perhaps I was too forceful with her? Did I not show enough concern when she was upset? We were so close…" Her frown faded.

He shook his head, quietly anticipating his moment to speak. "No, no. You're making it personal. It's not… Every generation goes through this. The young get older, they make new young, and then they push out the oldest. It's a cycle."

"That's just it: she hasn't made any offspring. She's not even betrothed.

All we had to do was remove her from the equation, and I would have taken the throne. We could have restored the crown to our blood. No more of these *little people* problems," she said.

"Are you sure that ship has sailed?" he asked.

"We're standing on it, what do you think? You can't rule a country from an island on the other side of the world. That is precisely why she sends me there," she snarled, raising her hands in the air. Then, crossing her arms and leaning over the railing, she finally argued playfully, "Besides, I am *not* old."

He chuckled.

"I'm a very spritely one hundred and ten, I'll have you know," she pouted with a grin.

"You don't look a day over fifty," he flattered. It was cliché banter, but it felt obligatory…and it made her smile. He turned around and faced the sea alongside her.

"What of Vidar?" she asked, her thoughts turning sombre. His eyes dropped for a moment.

"Vidar…Vidar will find his way. It is the cycle of things," he said curtly. "He was always his mother's boy; he can't stay away for long. He won't."

She pouted, invited herself into his embrace, and asked the wind,

"What is happening to us? And when did you become so charismatically wise?" His chuckle vibrated her shoulders.

"Apparently, I've been hanging around you too much," he said.

"Do you really think we could live so far away?" she asked as their laughter subsided. The wind puffed out the sails, drawing their attention upwards for a moment.

"I do. It would take some adjustment, but…home hasn't felt like home for a while."

She grunted in agreement.

"Doesn't it have a small mountain?" he asked.

"It's a dried-up old volcano, and there's never any snow on it," she grumbled, then scoffed in scornful realisation. "A dried-up old volcano for two dried-up old relatives. She's sending us to retirement."

He shook his head.

"Is this what appeals to you? Staying there?" she asked, looking up at him.

"What appeals to me and what is good for me are often different things," he replied coyly. She flashed a frown and studied his face.

"What appeals to you, then?" she asked. He thought a moment.

"What appeals to me is taking back the Mountain that our elders built." He looked sternly forward.

Her gaze trailed down his face, then off to the side.

"But what is good for us is biding our time. We can't go back and just wait, hoping things will work out in our favour," he said.

She thought as her eyes roved over the ship, both men and giants walking about the deck.

"Then we'll do both," she concluded. "We'll play this out until the tide is in our favour. First, we'll take the Rim, and then we'll take back the Mountain."

Her gaze matched her focus. He straightened his posture.

"We'll send word for the others immediately, but we'll do it in stages so as not to draw attention to the sudden exodus," she continued.

"There she is," Galabrand said with pride.

"She wants to play games, so we'll play."

CHAPTER TWENTY-TWO

COMMUNE

VIDAR

The mountain shuddered as a thunderous explosion ripped chunks of rock from its shell. Echoes of the blast rattled through the valleys like the roar of a wounded beast. Stone, dust, and splinters of wood rained down like a summer shower, peppering the white snow with soot and debris. A thick mist of grey billowed from the wounded mountainside, engulfing the surrounding area in a semi-transparent fog. And then it was quiet again. Vidar rested his large pickaxe on the ground, crossing his wrists atop the shaft. A subtle glimpse of pride curled his lips into a fading sneer. He twirled the edges of his beard with his fingers and released an audible grunt. As visibility began to return, a much smaller figure extended past his silhouette, carefully investigating the extent of the damage.

"You've made it through, milord, but you'll have to give it a few more blows before the likes of you will fit through!" the little dwarf shouted and laughed, looking back at his oversized employer. Vidar nodded, releasing another grunt and shooing the little man out of his way.

"Hurry up, Toke; get out of the way," he fussed with an irritated expression.

Toke scampered clear of the opening as fast as he could, finding solitude in Vidar's shadow. Vidar lifted his pickaxe and prepared for another strike. He took a second to choose his target.

"Cover your ears again," Vidar warned. Toke stuffed his stubby fingers into his ears, gritting his teeth in anticipation.

"Just imagine it's someone you loathe, and give it all she's got!" Toke shouted. Vidar offered a grin.

"You don't know me very well yet, do you?" he replied.

He let out a loud grunt as he swung. The point of the pickaxe split the air, cracking like thunder as it impacted the rock face. A grunt, another crack, and one last explosion that sent stone missiles hissing through the air. Toke coughed and choked on the fine particles filling his lungs. He again extended past Vidar's shadow and ran to investigate the opening.

"It's good enough, but a few more blows might make it more comfortable. There're still some jagged and sharp spots," he warned.

"When am I *not* uncomfortable? Have you met my family?" Vidar snarled.

"It's a fair point," Toke replied.

Vidar casually disregarded the tool on the ground and walked over to investigate for himself. The pickaxe made a crunch as it hit the snow.

"I'm tired of waiting. It will have to make do," Vidar decided, looking past the opening where a had door once stood. Glancing back at the short-statured fellow, he asked, "You're sure none of this troubles you? We're desecrating hallowed ground, after all." His subtle grin betrayed the not-so-secret pleasure he found in his participation.

"It's all just rocks and bones, milord," Toke replied, shaking his head. Vidar's eyes lit up.

"Exactly. That's what I like about you, Toke. You're a man free of the burdens of expectation. You go where the wind takes you," Vidar said, turning his gaze back to the cavernous maw they had torn open in the mountainside, his mind's eye conjuring visions of the past. He continued, "It's hard to imagine, but this was once a crowned jewel of your people. Now it is all but invisible to the naked eye, buried by centuries of snow and ignorance."

"Well, this was all before my time. Now it's just where the dead lie," Toke replied. Vidar's glance lingered a moment before taking a deeper look at the cavern. He carefully stepped inside, groaning as the sharp rocks scraped his back.

"Rocks and bones," Vidar whispered to himself.

"You should probably remain. Looks pretty treacherous in here," he continued. Toke gasped, putting his hand to his chest. Vidar frowned.

"I didn't know you cared," he said before erupting into laughter. His deeply accented tone carried inside the corridor.

"I was just being polite. Your stubby little legs will only slow me down, and as I have said, I am tired of waiting," Vidar retorted with a smile.

"That's fair enough. You go down the creepy, haunted ghost hole, and I'll stay here…and eat. Solid plan, milord. That's why you're the boss," Toke replied, leaning in and rubbing his belly.

"On second thought…"

"Nope. No takebacks," Toke said while pretending to run away.

"I'm joking. Hand me a torch, will you?" Vidar replied, holding out his hand in anticipation of receipt.

"Give me a second; I'll light it for you," Toke said, rushing to prepare it. The air rushing out of the cavern whispered like a low, slow-moving whistle. The echoes of falling rock or concealed creatures bounced from somewhere within its expanse. He turned back at the sound of a wavering flame. Toke approached.

"Thanks. Keep your head somehow lower. And if I don't come back…" he began.

"Who? Or something like that," Toke replied, pretending to remember.

"Right," Vidar said, dragging out the word and retreating into the darkness.

"I messed it up, didn't I?" Toke argued with himself, his voice still carrying. "It's *if* someone asks…"

"Toke, would you like to join me?" Vidar poked his head out once more. The dwarf quickly suppressed his initial excitement.

"Are you sure it's safe?" he inquired.

Vidar sighed. He thought about lying, but Toke was a useful companion – and arguably better company than his predecessors. Taking another breath, he began, "I'm not going to lie to you, though in full transparency, I've considered it." He was still considering it. "There *is* a chance this could end badly for you. I suppose we can take it one step at a time. There's always time to turn back…at least, there should be. Though I couldn't say with certainty, as I've never encountered this one. But if the legend of the Temple at Duringar's Peak is to be believed, it is quite safe, up until a point," Vidar replied in a twisting expulsion of thought.

Toke stared at him plainly, one brow raised in a mix of scepticism and amusement before he erupted into a chuckle, declaring, "You are…the worst salesman I've ever met, milord."

Vidar smirked and looked down.

"I'll join you. But if it gets questionable…you'll excuse me if I pull back to camp?" Toke replied.

Vidar's smirk evolved into a smile. He nodded for the dwarf to follow him.

The corridor was short and narrow – for Vidar, anyway. Its partially completed décor was chiselled into the very rock surrounding it. Stalactites hung from the ceiling like fingers eager to scratch his head with violent delight, leaving him no choice but to walk hunched over, as crawling was certainly not an option. No living man would ever see him crawl on all fours. Once intended to be a means of escape from the mountain temple, the cavernous tunnel now served as a home for the spiders, bats, and other creatures that delighted in their isolation from the world. Toke, however, found it quite comfortable. Manageable, at the very least.

"Apparently, your elders were not concerned for the safety of anyone other than their selves," he said, just after growling at scraping his head.

"That is the dwarven way. We've always had to look out for ourselves, cos no one else tends to," he replied.

Vidar frowned, quietly offering, "It is a sad perspective… But I sympathise with the sentiment."

"It's not that sad. We make do. Always have, always will. If it's meant to be, it'll be," Toke added.

"Truer words have never been spoken. I tend to like, *It is what it is*," he said, trying to gesture with his hands. Another scrape of the skull. A growl and a swear. Toke giggled.

"Oh, good one. Good one. What about…such is life?" Toke replied, his hands stretching wide as if releasing the words into the air. Vidar glared at the sight of his physical freedom.

"I've heard of it. A bit lazy, if you ask me. Perhaps if you said it in another language, it would disguise its pitiful resignation to despair…" Vidar replied.

Toke chuckled again. His infectious laughter brought a smirk to Vidar's cheek.

'Such is life' is such a dark cloud over what could be. It is the total acceptance of life taking you forcefully from the rear." He couldn't help but gyrate, his eyes losing focus. "But 'It is what it is' is reverential. It is a declaration that no matter what comes, the purest of good or evil incarnate…" Vidar paused, a face coming to mind and causing his lip to curl in a snarl. "…it doesn't matter," he concluded, shaking his head. His eyes reclaimed their focus. "Because I *will* remain."

His expression and voice softened as he looked at the dwarf. Toke grunted. They had stopped walking and were facing each other.

"It is a middle finger to the powers that be. Simple, yet succinct. Just like this…" he continued, raising his middle finger. The true tone of his voice appeared, calm and low. Resigned to weariness.

"In all my years, I'd never thought I'd be waxing poetic with a giant in the ancient ruins of my forebearers." He paused for a moment to reflect before erupting into laughter. Vidar's gaze dropped, deflated by the non-engagement.

"And in all my years, I've never stopped to consider that what a dwarf calls a short trip might be somehow…longer. We're taking a break here before my lower back gives," he said, plopping down and stretching. He looked up at the ceiling.

"I'm coming back with a hammer, and I'm taking out every single last one of those," he said, pointing. Toke chuckled.

"Seriously, how much longer?" Vidar pressed.

Toke began to speak, paused, and then continued, "About ten or fifteen minutes at the minimum. There's not much to it, really. Just traverse this path right into a side entrance, and we're in. I don't even got a map. Don't need one. There's no maze to navigate, is what I mean."

Vidar nodded. He dusted the ground behind him and lay out flat, letting out a loud, restful sigh. Toke dug furiously into his backpack.

"For what it's worth, they had good taste. These tiles are simply beautiful. I'm surprised this place hasn't been raided yet. Nothing like this would remain for long up top – the scavengers must scavenge," Vidar remarked, his voice echoing off the ceiling.

Toke's smirk went unnoticed. He quietly stuffed and lit his pipe, taking a few puffs.

"What are you thinking?" Vidar asked, growing impatient with the quiet. Toke took a long, deep drag from his pipe.

"I'm thinking…that you talk a lot more than I'd imagined," he replied with another laugh.

"Does it bother you? I suppose I have a weak spot for…little things," he playfully snarled. His gaze drifted inwards. He thought of Lena.

"No, no, not at all. I've just not heard a giant speak as you do," Toke replied.

"What, do you think we all scream *'unga bunga'* and throw boulders at passing villagers?" Vidar quipped.

Toke fell backwards in laughter.

"How incredibly bigoted of you, Toke. I am thoroughly disappointed," Vidar added, eventually joining in the giggling. "Me smash rock. There, is that more to your liking?" Vidar continued, still laughing. His hands were intertwined where they lay on his chest. His feet were interlocked at the ankle, rocking back and forth as his laughter reverberated.

"I didn't realise your kind was so…insightful, is all," Toke finally got out.

"Oh, no, most of them definitely throw boulders at villagers and smash rocks in their spare time. I am an anomaly of sorts in that respect. As is most of my immediate family. Though I've definitely seen my father hurl a boulder or two," Vidar replied with a grunt. His mood soured as his voice trailed off.

"I see," Toke said, recovering from his fit of laughter. He took a deep breath and puffed on his pipe, then glanced at Vidar stretched across the cavern floor. He could sense a change in topic was due and asked, "I imagine you don't intend on hauling anything out of here?"

"I hadn't planned on it. Certainly, not now that my spine will likely be shaped in a curve for the rest of my life," he replied.

"Oh, you're still young. You'll recover soon enough," Toke replied. Vidar stopped.

"Young? How old do you think I am? And no, I'm not fishing for a compliment," he pressed.

"You're around fifty human years, aren't ye? But that's nothing for a giant! You're barely out of nappies, aye?" Toke replied with a chuckle. Vidar lay quietly.

"Been around my kind, have you? I thought you had more sense than that," he asked.

"Not as frequent as I'd prefer and more often than I'd like," Toke replied. Vidar flashed his brow.

"I again find myself sympathising with the sentiment," Vidar replied.

"Since we're becoming familiar, mind me asking what exactly yer looking for? You don't strike me as the type to swipe candle holders and fancy plates," Toke asked. Vidar swung upwards into a seated position.

"I thought you'd never ask," he said with a smirk on his face. "It's called a Uridar…"

"Aye, yes. The totem," Toke interjected. Vidar frowned, his explanation cut short.

"It's more than a totem," he said.

"Oh? I'd just assumed the legends were a bunch of malarkey. You know…fairy tales and such told to keep the lads in line. To fear the divine 'n' all," Toke mused.

"Quite the contrary. They are sacred devices left here by those who came before. Before the gods. And they're still active," Vidar said, his tone inspired.

"I see. And what's a fella to do with it if you don't intend to take it with you? Are you just curious to see if it's there? Perhaps come back at a later time and take it away?" Toke asked, peering at him. Vidar wore a frustrated expression.

"No, no, that would be impossible. No one can lift, let alone move, the Uridar. Most of them are said to be unapproachable even if you could," he replied. Toke's expression of confusion grew deeper.

"So, what are ye going to do with it?" he asked again.

"We'll talk with it, naturally," Vidar explained. Toke's nod was exaggerated.

"I see. So, you're a poet…and a crazy person," he retorted, laughing. Vidar could not find the humour.

"Ain't it a great big rock? How are you going to talk *with* it? You know, I suppose you're not considered crazy unless it talks back," he continued.

"It's not a rock. It is a device, an object far beyond our understanding," Vidar argued.

"So, it's a totem?" Toke asked again.

"It is not a totem. A totem represents a thing. This *is* a thing. It is *the* thing, much like the mountain. The Uridar is like the doorway we passed through in order to get *inside* the mountain. But it is, at the same time, *also* the mountain." He was losing patience.

"So…there's someone inside the Uridar?" Toke asked, now genuinely engaged.

"I'm beginning to believe so," Vidar replied after a brief pause.

"And so, you aim to break into the Uridar? As we did this mountain?" Toke asked. Vidar began nodding.

"You're beginning to understand," Vidar replied with a grin.

CHAPTER TWENTY-THREE

RITES OF PASSAGE

YURI

A fine mist permeated the air within the temple, enhancing the glow of the vast array of candles that filled it. Darros stood at the altar before a long procession, crowned and dressed in crimson and gold robes. His oiled chestnut hair framed either side of his golden death mask, an intricately carved skull with a star embossed above the brow line and a deep purple gem affixed above it. And still, his eyes pierced beyond the façade. Gentle, inviting, emotionless, and devoid of life. Behind him, a chorus of men and women, their faces concealed under featureless masks, chanted a song in the ancient Khazmyrian tongue.

"Who approaches the altar? Who is it that has been found amidst those who are lost? Who has broken the chains of bondage and become deserving of ascension?" Darros called out. His voice echoed, silencing the chants and whispers.

"Hera, daughter of Herod and Lucidia, fourth generation bearers of the court of Darros," Yuri called out as the crowd parted to make room for her advance.

"Let her approach," he replied. Yuri extended her arm behind her as an invitation for Hera to approach, promptly stepping aside and coming to stand next to Merith, who seemed awkwardly out of place as he clung to the shadow.

Hera appeared at the opposite end of the carpeted walkway, her parents standing proudly behind her. She began her approach towards Darros in a slow and deliberate manner, her face aimed towards the ground. She wore only a thick golden collar affixed to her neck with two large, gold chains welded to either side and dragging on the ground behind her. Her hair, still braided, was pinned high and out of the way, leaving every inch of her dark, oiled skin on full display as it glistened in the candlelight, leaving nothing to the imagination. Those closest to the aisle extended their arms, indiscriminately touching any part of her body they could reach, no matter how intimate, although they were careful not to step into the aisle themselves. She suppressed the desire to react to the prodding and probing fingers that gave no heed to pressure or consideration of her tolerances. The closer she was, the deeper and more painful the prodding became.

A man by the name of Fennec, a statesman and sworn enemy of her father, saw the prime opportunity to exact his revenge – his response to an earlier dispute regarding unrelated matters often argued between men. As she approached his row, she caught a glimpse of him out of the corner of her eye. Her body tensed. His hand extended, sliding down her stomach and inserting a digit, first into her navel, then lower and deeper still. He squeezed her buttocks as she continued past him, and she clinched, anticipating his next move. He did not disappoint. The force with which his digit probed elicited a wince out of the corner of her left eye, but she recovered quickly. Fennec smiled and waved to her father, gesturing as if he took a whiff. Her parents did their best to ignore him lest they ruin their daughter's moment, but their complexions grew red as the blood rushed to their faces. Though she didn't break, he still counted it as a victory.

Caught up in his moment of pride, he failed to see who had been watching.

She climbed three small steps and waited. A trio of faceless men approached from in front of her, standing in a line. The first lifted her head, inspecting he face for tears. There were none.

Merith looked on in bridled horror.

"If you can imagine, it's even worse for men," Yuri whispered with a devious smile and gesturing hands, observing his discomfort. "They've got more to grab on to."

"Your journey, though at times an uncomfortable and painful one, has made you strong," Darros declared.

The first man smacked her across the face with all his force. She held her breath, hoping to numb the pain. Save for a passing grimace, she recovered her stance, and the man stepped aside.

"Enduring…" Darros continued.

The second faceless man backhanded her in the opposite direction. A quiet grunt escaped from her throat.

"…and powerful," Darros concluded.

The third man punched her square in the face, rupturing the skin on the bridge of her nose. She stumbled backwards two steps but returned to her position promptly. A small trickle of blood ran down her face. The men returned to their formation and walked back to the corner of the room. Darros approached her with an obsidian-coloured key in his hands. He unlocked the collar around her neck, being sure not to meet her gaze as it would cause her to break, ruining her ceremony. The impact of the metal and chains hitting the stone floor of the temple echoed.

"Your chains have now been removed," he said. Yuri approached with a folded white and gold tunic. Darros took the garment and presented it to Hera. Unable to contain herself any longer, she took it and dressed herself with rabid enthusiasm. Darros laughed quietly. She looked up at him, the candlelight illuminating the edges of his hair, and the gold of his robes and crown seemed to beam with light. She gasped. In that moment, he looked to be more than a man, but his eyes anchored her visions. She stared deeply into his eyes and broke down in tears. He wrapped his arms around her as the crowd erupted into cheers and applause.

"What did I just witness?" Merith shouted to Yuri over the roar.

"A birth." She smiled at him, feeling nostalgic for her own ceremony. Merith barely had time to ponder her words before she pulled him along to go see Darros. A group of enthusiastic women, all wearing tunics, rushed Hera and placed a crown of flowers upon her head, eventually pulling her away from Darros and into the crowd.

"Merith…glad to see you're still with us…" he said, glancing at Yuri.

"I chose the former…for now," she replied, offering a brief smile.

"Ah," Darros offered, returning his focus to Merith. "Actually, I'm glad you're here. See that fat, pitiful excuse for a man? The one who was previously a statesman…" he paused to see if Yuri had received her orders. She nodded in acknowledgement. Darros rested his arm on Merith's shoulder and leaned in. Merith took a breath, inhaling Darros' overpowering but pleasant smell. His hair was perfumed and wafted its aroma about when he moved. Merith came to.

"Yeah, there in the white coat?" he replied. He'd actually taken a second or two to locate the man in question, but he somehow already knew who Darros had been referring to.

"Yes. It appears he likes to smell things that don't belong to him. See to it he is never tempted to smell his fingers again," he snarled. Yuri furrowed her brow and stared at Darros. He'd deviated from his typical firm but passive tone. He seemed angry – irate, at the least.

"Yes, Darros," Merith replied. Darros gave a sharp nod and left, again by way of a hidden door at the back of the room. Yuri took a step closer to Merith, her hands folded behind her back. He was visibly still trying to decipher his meaning. Yuri smiled.

"He means to stick his own fingers up—" she began.

"I get it, I get it," he interrupted her, adjusting his collar.

"And then his nose," she continued. He turned to face her, slightly disturbed.

"Detached from his hand," she continued in a low whisper, folding her arms behind her back, "If that wasn't clear,"

"You gathered all that? By god, woman, how long have you been doing this?" he asked exasperatedly. Her response was an introspective stare into the crowd coupled with the flare of her brows.

Merith and Yuri intentionally lagged behind the crowd exiting the temple, keeping tabs on their target, the portly statesman known as Fennec Leroy. They crossed the street and found a pillar to post up against, observing…waiting.

"So, what's the plan?" Merith asked, rubbing his hands together.

"You seem a little anxious. Aren't you the tenacious would-be assassin who tried to kill the most powerful man in the world?" she asked mockingly.

"I'm more of a stick-the-sharp-end-into-the-bad-guy-and-walk-away kind of assassin. Not the torture-and-punish kind. I do what needs to be done, but I don't enjoy it," he replied. She nodded with a pout of her bottom lip.

"I see. Well, consider this something that needs to be done. Fennec has shown disrespect to Hera, and by extension, to Darros. The ceremony is sacred, and to try and force her to fail it, let alone over issues that do not concern her…it's just not acceptable," she said with a tinge of frustration.

"We must have observed two different ceremonies," he replied, folding his arms and leaning against the same pillar.

"How so?"

"The entire show was disrespectful. Arranging the assault of the poor girl, then for the very organiser to portray himself as the saviour from the abuse he orchestrated? It's a bit performative to the extreme, don't you think?" he asked. She faced him with a frown.

"*Show?* You've grown quite comfortable in your captivity, haven't you?" she eloquently reminded him.

Merith stiffened and cleared his throat, turning his attention to the crowd. He took the intended offence and remained quiet.

She broke the silence, feeling ever-so-slightly bad for shaming his predicament and choosing to explain, "The ceremony is performative to a degree, yes. It wouldn't be a ceremony otherwise, would it? Those chosen to receive it in their honour have already proven themselves to Darros. You don't prove yourself by undergoing the ceremony, if that makes any sense."

He nodded quietly, still stewing internally.

"It represents the…" She paused, finding herself unsatisfied with the common-tongue options for the words she was looking for. The only options she could think of had negative connotations. He turned to look at her during the pause.

"Abuse?" he offered, still intending to drive his point home.

"Growth," she quickly rebutted with a look of irritation, "we experience in life. The trials that life presents have no boundaries. There is nothing sacred, not your thoughts or feelings," she continued to a pause. "And definitely not what is in between your legs."

His expression argued her logic, but his lips remained closed.

"And yet we must be strong and persevere. Darros shows us the way…" Her volume increased. She again paused as Merith rolled his eyes and turned away, fussing at him, "Excuse you!"

"What? I'm listening," he said.

"I saw your face," she replied.

"Just because I am being respectful and listening to your beliefs doesn't mean I buy into what you're saying, and neither am I required to," he replied.

"Are you quite sure about that? You'll find your perception has little to do with your reality. You would be wise to remember on whose graces you so thinly tread," she replied, folding her arms.

He flared his eyes at her veiled threat.

"What?!" she demanded, growing ever impatient with his resistance.

"Nothing. You're absolutely right. I should bridle my tongue," he replied, feigning submission.

"Say it, you coward!" she yelled at him, her fists balled. He faced her with a fading smirk as he realised there was a certain attraction when she was angry.

"I'm just asking the question…wouldn't it be easier to destroy evil than accept its presence as a part of life? Destroy the corruption at its roots rather than trim or hide the unsightly leaves on occasion?" he offered. She worked through rebuttals and translations of rebuttals in her mind, all the while processing his words. After some time, her face softened.

"I don't think we're too far off from one another," she said.

He scoffed. Her frown returned.

"We accept that evil exists and that it should be destroyed. But how do you suppose you should arm yourself when the only tools available are the very ones the enemy uses to break you? How is that any different from soldiers who train in environments and conditions foreign to their own? Who punish their bodies to strengthen their minds and spirits?" she argued.

He began to speak but stopped short several times. She smirked, feeling victorious for stumping him.

"Choice," he said plainly. "They have a choice. Whether to be a soldier, a farmer, or a fisherman."

Her victory faded, leaving behind nothing. He looked her up and down, stopping at her eyes.

"Did you have a choice?" he asked solemnly.

Her gaze dropped to the ground, then shifted quickly to the crowd in the distance. She remained quiet as she rapidly blinked away the uncontrollable watering that had accumulated in her eyes.

"I'm sorry," he apologised quickly, realising that he, much like Fennec, had probed too deeply. She wore an angry expression.

"Prepare yourself; Fennec is leaving," she said, nodding towards the man as he exited the crowd. She stepped away from Merith in pursuit of their target. Merith delayed a moment, feeling remorseful for his choice of words, but quickly caught up to her before slowing to her walking speed.

"I don't have a weapon. How am I supposed to sever this offending finger?" he asked, looking at the sword affixed to her hip.

"Fingers, not finger. The pointer and its neighbour. Or perhaps you would like to ask Hera which they were he dug into—"

She began to scold him, but he raised his palm to stop her graphic words. She looked around as they walked and took notice of an axe lodged into a chopping block. She briefly diverted from their path and retrieved it.

"I will beat this prudery out of you, even if it's the last thing I do." She shook the axe in his direction as she handed it to him.

"It's a good thing you're enduring, then, isn't it?" he smirked. She did not look amused. He pressed on, joking, "Aren't you afraid I'll escape now that you've handed me a weapon?"

"No." Her reply was concise, and her tone filled in the blanks. Grabbing his arm and pushing him forward, she asked exasperatedly, "What is it about your enlightened sense of morality that is preventing you from carrying out justice? Didn't you say cut the root? Am I to believe you would rather kill everything than attempt to reform it? How does that reach your moral high ground?"

"I absolutely agree with reforming, if it's an option, but this isn't about justice. It has nothing to do with an entitled bureaucrat burying his digits in Hera, violating her free will; we're just doing the dirty work of a self-appointed god because someone touched one of his playthings in a way he didn't care for. Mind you, the hundreds of other hands didn't seem to bother him as much as they did her," he replied.

"That's not what it's about – you've missed the point entirely," she replied irritably. "Besides, what does it matter? Punish the man for Hera's sake, for his actions. A course of action we both agree is the correct one. Or would you rather just 'stick the point in him and walk away'? In the end, it doesn't matter what Darro's reasons are for commissioning this punishment. The end result is the same."

His eyes opened, the dots rushed to connect for him, and his tongue slipped as he murmured, "So that's how you cope."

"Cope? What does this word mean?" she asked, jerking her neck backwards.

"It means you're a conflicted soul. It jades you," he replied.

"I'm not conflicted about anything," she replied defensively, taking on a scolding tone. "You're stalling. Get it done."

A slightly inebriated Fennec unlocked the front door of his home and sauntered inside. Yuri and Merith followed just a few steps behind him.

"Do we knock?" he asked. She sighed loudly.

"If Hera were your daughter, how would you approach this situation?" she asked, having grown tired of his delays.

The explosive force with which Fennec's front door was kicked in, ripping it from its hinges, sent the chubby fellow to the ground. He tried to gather himself, but Merith had already rushed in, grabbed him by the collar, and dragged him to a nearby table. He began to fight back until he saw Yuri standing in the doorway, her arms folded, at which point he failed to block Merith's incoming blow to the gut.

"Yuri," Fennec wheezed through stolen wind. "I didn't know it was you."

Merith tightened his grip on his collar.

"In your blind quest for vengeance, you have disrespected He Who Sees All," she announced.

"Darros," Fennec cried out, "please give Darros my—"

"Save it. It is too late. You are hereby stripped of your title and authority. This is the last night you will lay your head in a bed. Darros gives, and Darros takes away. If you are found here in the morning, you will be put to death. You will sleep with the animals, as you are so keen to act like one – that is, unless Darros has a change of heart." She paused.

Merith's eyes widened, some of his enthusiasm to mete out punishment waning.

"But I wouldn't count on it," she remarked.

"Blessed be Darros for his generosity and…" The pathetic man cried, attempting to bow to her. Merith's reasserted grip on his collar prevented him.

"Oh, you will still be punished for your actions. Like for like…multiplied," she assured him. Fennec whimpered.

"Make it quick," she instructed Merith, turning to leave before pausing. Glancing back over her shoulder, she corrected, "On second thought, make it…memorable."

She exited to stand outside the doorway. Merith, having lost the steam that drove him through the door, regained his composure briefly – only to lose it again, taking notice that the man had pissed himself.

"What is the sentence, my lord?" Fennec asked, still whimpering.

Merith was overwhelmed by what had transpired in front of him. He had difficulty processing it all – processing the fact that this large man had immediately given up the will to fight, even for himself, at the sight of Yuri, a small-framed woman he could have easily overpowered. It was chilling. A low-pitched cry in the corner sharply caught Merith's attention. Children were watching: a young girl under the age of ten and a teenage boy easily of the age to assist his father. Merith's colour vanished. He looked behind him to where Yuri had stood. She was out of sight. He looked back at the children.

"Leave!" he whispered aggressively. They hesitated but shuffled out of the room, their weeping intensifying.

"Like for like, multiplied. I am to take your fingers. I am sure you are aware to which I refer," he replied hesitantly.

Fennec nodded in acknowledgement.

"There, rest your hand on the table. I will make this quick," he continued.

Fennec complied, resting his hand on the table and meekly muttering, "Thank you, milord."

"Don't look; it will only make it worse," Merith whispered to the man as he retrieved the axe from his waistband. Fennec nodded nervously in agreement and looked away.

Merith adjusted his angle of approach and took a few practice swings. He mumbled out disbelief of the moment to himself and swung with all of his might. A loud, sharp impact of metal against wood rang out, quickly subsumed by Fennec's scream.

"Oh, fuck!" Merith shouted, having realised he'd taken all four main digits, not just the two. Fennec's screaming increased before being muted by his other, unmutilated hand.

"Fuck! Fuck! Fuck!" Merith continued to shout as a small bout of chaos ensued. He looked for Yuri to come running back into the house, but she did not.

"Is that all, my lord?" Fennec asked through gritted teeth, sweat beading as he struggled to gain some modicum of composure. Merith bared his teeth nervously.

"Like for like," he said again, motioning towards the bloody, severed fingers lying on the table.

Fennec flared a look of disbelief as he nursed his bloody hand, quickly submitting to further punishment.

"Across the table, I suppose," Merith said, swallowing back an acute desire to vomit. Fennec bent over the table and dropped trou, exposing his large, hairy backside. Merith picked up two of the four fingers from off the table and disgustedly examined them. He walked to Fennec's backside and held his breath, first trying to insert one with delicacy before resorting to more forceful means.

The explosivity with which excrement vacated Fennec's bowels caused a sound Merith would not soon forget. Merith stood there, defeated, covered in faeces.

"Take it out and put it in your nose, and we will conclude this," Merith said at a low volume.

"I am sorry, my lord…my nerves…" a mortified Fennec tried to apologise.

"Into your fucking nose!" Merith shouted, absent the remainder of his patience.

Fennec rushed to oblige, causing himself to begin spewing vomit. Merith shook his head and dropped his axe to the floor, immediately walking out of the home.

Yuri was leaning against the building. She took stock of him with wide eyes, then began walking. Merith followed.

"Is it done?" she asked.

"What does it look like?" he asked. She couldn't help but laugh.

"I suppose it's too late to tell you, but you could have ordered him to do it all himself. We aren't always the weapon; sometimes, we're just the hand…pun intended. For that matter, you could have charged someone else to do it," she said.

"About twenty minutes too late. And what do you mean we? I didn't sign up to be Darros' lackey," he replied.

"On the contrary, you did – when you exchanged your life for his mercy," she replied sharply.

"You really don't understand the concept of choice, do you?" he responded, and not without some bitterness.

"I understand fully: your values have a price…" She stopped walking and met his gaze, pointedly declaring, "…and Darros paid it in full."

His eyes dropped as he lagged behind momentarily before catching up to her.

"What of the children? Were they made to watch? The last thing we need is another generation of Fennecs, just as he mimicked his own father's reign of terror and entitlement. They were already accused of beating up orphans who were just trying to make a wage." Her tone shifted coldly. His face flattened, somewhat understanding the logic.

"Yes…of course," he said in quiet contemplation.

"Good. Darros will reward you for your due diligence and efforts. Come, let's get you to the showers…and I'm getting hungry. What are you in the mood for? Sky's the limit in the court of Darros," she replied.

"A tall cliff and a running start," he replied.

She laughed again.

CHAPTER TWENTY-FOUR

VESPER

LYSAND

Her eyes wandered over his incandescent, pallid face. Powdery white skin dusted the same dimples she'd gotten lost in since she was a hatchling, his face having been the first she saw. He was loyal and kind, stalwart in his friendship and one of the few who could still stir the rigid muscles in her cheeks to form a smile.

He was a constant in a chaotic world of change that was once as still as mountains.

Most referred to him by an alias, such as Moon or Luna, but she knew him only by his true name – Nyctore, the eternal light in the night sky.

Her feet floated a few metres above the ground, hands barely spread, offering only the appearance of aid in maintaining her balance. Nyctore's light amplified the white of her hair where it wandered through the air as if she were at the bottom of the ocean. Her tonals were open, glowing with a blue bioluminescence. She grinned as she communed with the orbital body.

Suddenly, the streams slowed, the insects grew quiet, and the creatures retreated to their beds and burrows. They all felt the need to rest. Even Lysand felt the gentle pull of comfort.

There were few whose presence brought about such calming warmth, but even among them, none were like Oroben. The irony lay in that most

191

mortals found his appearance rather unsettling, be it his gaunt features, leathery skin, or opalescent green eyes. He didn't change his appearance to provide comfort, as Lysand did. He neither needed nor cared to.

'*I figured I'd find you here, conspiring with him,*' Oroben spoke to Lysand's mind. His cheeks dimpled lightly, and his departure from the forest clearing made no sound. Elderharts moved with a subtle grace few could mimic, like footsteps made in another world propelled their bodies forward in this one. A smirk graced Lysand's features. Her head turned as she looked back at her mate, who approached still on foot. Oroben gazed up at Nyctore, greeting him with a bow.

'*Join us?*' Lysand asked, extending her hand to Oroben. He declined with a brief jostle of his head.

'*I am on my way to see Galathir and his kin,*' he replied.

'*You speak as if you are bound by time. Stay with me a while, and I will go with you,*' she replied. He sighed.

'*What are you two up to now? Does Nyctore still have your ear regarding Elarion? We should not bother with such things,*' Oroben scolded kindly.

'*Nyctore and I have a different perspective,*' she retorted just as gently.

'*As did Reh'gara, and now the winds have changed, thankfully near the end of our watch. You must let go, as it is time to go. These forms are at the end of their measure, but our journey continues onwards,*' he replied.

'*I am not ready to go. Soon, but not yet,*' she replied. His stiff brow arched, and she continued, '*He is like us, you know.*'

'*A fragment, yes…*' he agreed.

'*More than a fragment,*' she countered. Her hair lay straight as she descended to the ground, rotating towards Oroben. Her eyes blinked, opening to meet his locked gaze. '*I would not expect you to understand.*'

His brows flattened as his eyes rolled to one side.

'*The blood does not matter; it is his mind that is attuned for this course. His spirit will follow,*' she assured.

'*He suffers from the same fondness for perishables as you do. You both long to sire one. This is just your way,*' Oroben replied. She glanced at the ground.

'*I do not deny it, as if I could. I can't explain it,*' she said, drifting into an empty gaze.

'*As did Reh'gara and the others,*' he said.

'*It is because of Reh'gara and the others that I…feel…this way,*' she replied. Her brow furrowed at the word *feel*. It was foreign but seemed fitting. Oroben frowned.

'*Identifying blame doesn't change consequence,*' he replied.

'*They broke the order; I simply aim to right a wrong,*' she said.

He grunted, asking, '*Do you really believe his ascendance will satiate your maternal desire? Is the Forest not enough?*'

Her focus snapped to the trees. '*Belief is such a frail word. The Forest feels more a part* of *me than it does something* from *me,*' she said, using the word again.

'*I sense these emotions within you, yet they are foreign to me. I feel them as you do, and while we are bonded, I am isolated in understanding,*' he said, frowning at the paradox. Her eyes lowered as a muscle in her right cheek raised. He was trying, but it was not his way.

'*I will not force it upon you. Would you leave me behind so I may rejoin you in time?*' she asked.

'*No, I do not wish it,*' he said.

'*Then stay with me a while, and we will leave together,*' she implored, her gaze returning to him. His lungs filled with air for the first time in a long time, puffing out his chest. His deep sigh was audible.

'*As I always have,*' he replied after a pause.

'*Elarion is almost ready, I can see it,*' she said as her tonals awakened. He looked at her curiously, and she offered, '*Nyctore can see him, even amidst the sea of lights in this world. That has to account for something.*'

Oroben's eyes widened.

'*We cannot leave him like this,*' she continued, her eyes longing.

Lysand reached out for Oroben's hand. He gave it to her. The purple veins under the skin of his tonals coursed with life and light as his pupils faded to white. Their toes were the last to lift off the ground as they did, their eyes raised.

'*I see,*' he said, bathed in Nyctore's light.

CHAPTER TWENTY-FIVE

WATER AND SALINE

CONNERH

It was a chilly day, yet he found himself sweaty and uncomfortable. He'd removed his armour in hopes of finding some relief but had yet to acquire it. Connerh sat on the ground, slumped against a stone pillar, and nursing an empty pipe. It was the last remaining mark of where his house had once stood, other than a still-smoking carcass of charred wood and melted nails. The dead men were beginning to smell, causing his nose to wrinkle whenever the breeze caught him off guard. He prided himself on having at least a streak of humanity left, though at times, it felt fleeting. He smirked.

Haim's boots still stood where he had last departed them.

"Who sent you?" he shouted. His voice carried. Metal-reinforced wooden wheels came to a steady stop over the gravelled path in front of him, concealed behind a wall of dried stalks. His voice was weary but determined. He'd been waiting, sorting the chaos of thought in his mind as the wind blew solemn gusts of air.

"Do we have permission to step onto your land? We have pressing matters to discuss with you," the voice shouted back. Connerh smirked.

"And if I decline? Won't you trespass anyway?"

"I should hope not, sir," the man replied. Connerh's brow raised at the formality.

"You should have been here at least an hour or so ago. Why did you delay?"

"We threw a wheel and needed to repair it, sir," he replied surprisingly quickly. Connerh could sense the truth being spoken. It would buy them a few minutes of his time. He sighed and took a deep breath, realising he would have to stand. He'd grown rather comfortable in his discomfort, fearing the painful reminder he would soon receive due to his inappropriate sitting position. He winced at the pain his muscles released as he rose to his feet.

"Get on with it," he said, looking up to see if he could spot his spear, shielding his eyes with his hand. It was somewhere up there, watching, waiting, feeding him information on how many were on the other side of the wall. There were two carriages: one empty, the other with a single man in it. He'd gotten out to relieve himself back when they had stopped to fix the wheel. Each carriage had two men at the box, with another three each pretending to wander near them. That made six on foot, four at the wheel, one cheeky bastard in the first carriage, and then this lad. Twelve wasn't a small number, but it surely wasn't enough, he thought.

…Or was it thirteen? It was too early for arithmetic.

"Very good, sir," the voice replied, kicking off a cacophony of sounds that set off Connerh's headache — especially the wooden wheels rolling over gravel. His senses were still overtly amplified by the inka. He opened his wincing eyes to inspect the group as they came into view, counting them. They were dressed as commoners but were very much *not*, by Connerh's observation anyway. Twelve poorly disguised soldiers. What intrigued him most was that they'd maintained this charade for miles, at least since Connerh could track them. They flinched at the sight of him and his surroundings. Thirty bodies littered the ground like lawn ornaments in varying poses, some standard, others less flattering. Amidst the chaos, Connerh stood with his pipe in his mouth, like he'd just stepped out for a morning stretch.

"Does this work for you often?" Connerh asked with a humorous expression, gesturing towards the troupe.

"Sorry, sir?" the lead man on horseback asked.

"This is the worst bunch of fake villagers I've seen in a while. It's so very, very bad. What's your name, soldier?" he replied, shaking his head. They all exchanged shamed glances.

"The name is Quo, sir. Jaraquo in full. If you could spare a moment of your time, there is someone who wishes to speak with you inside," the man replied, motioning towards the carriage.

Connerh nodded and looked around. He paused, then pretended to lunge forward, grabbing at his hilt. The men responded by drawing their swords, discarding their facade with ease. The scraping unison tugged at Connerh's ears. He erupted in a deep chuckle.

"Well, Quo, I'm not setting foot in your little carriage there. And the only reason I didn't dispatch the lot of you hours ago was for pure curiosity and entertainment purposes. So, I repeat, get on with it; I find you less interesting by the second," he warned.

He felt the request. His eyes glanced upwards with a shake of his head. The door of the lead carriage swung open, its metallic joints creaking in the wind, and a familiar face sat forward, knocking him off his pedestal of confidence. His expression betrayed that fact.

"It will only take a few minutes, I assure you. Then you can return to your company of dead men," the older, accented voice said.

Connerh froze in the moment, a spectre startled by a ghost of his past.

He walked forward and climbed into the carriage.

Rose's cheeks were still wet with trails that stained her face. She gripped the rope leading Aeryk's horse with white knuckles, trudging forward on knees that desperately wanted to give way. She tripped over half-exposed rocks and uneven terrain, her blood igniting with each occurrence but driving her to press on. She had to. Aeryk's small frame shivered as he gasped for breath, the result of his abated cry. He clutched at straws by way of incessant questions as a way to cope, to understand, to feel safe. No matter how just his intent, they scornfully triggered resurgent streams of hot tears to flow down her cheeks. She wanted the questions to stop. For him to stop. To just let her think for a moment.

There'd not been time to think.

She shook her head as she struggled to remain quiet, hoping her head covering would shield him from her unpleasant grief. Her chest was sore. Her eyes were wide, staring onwards with waning focus.

"Will he be okay?" Aeryk asked. Her face pruned as she bit down on her tongue, attempting to suppress the anguish, the irritation, the anger. It wasn't his fault.

"Physically," she said with a broken voice. It was unintentionally cryptic, providing only subtle reassurances to herself, for she, too, wondered the same; it'd been gnawing at her for hours. He would be okay, in a way. Wouldn't he? You obtained peace in death, did you not? Would the death of the spirit be the same if the body persevered?

"I don't understand. Why couldn't he come with us?" the child persisted.

The back and forth had grown tiresome. He didn't even seem to process her replies. He consumed them whole, immediately extending his hand for more, like a dog having long skipped a meal. It was frustrating and overwhelming, and she had *nothing* left to give. She felt his questions sharp and prying, seeking to upend her efforts to be strong for him, to expose that she was too afraid, too hurt, too vulnerable. But he would not relent, in the way that little ones often did not. An innocent defiance bundled in honest transparency.

"Because he could not run any longer!" she shouted. The boy recoiled with wet eyes and pouty lips. A surge of water pooled in his lids. "And because he did not wish for *us* to have to," she continued with realisation and reclaimed grace.

It was a good thought to hold on to. She would try. Her tears absorbed into her sleeve. One last sniffle for good measure.

"Will we see him again?" he asked. Her head shot up, stiffening her neck. She blinked rapidly, holding a deep breath. It was the one question she'd been avoiding. Her feet came to a stop as she was cemented in place, walking requiring too much focus at that moment. Her lungs compressed as she expelled the air. Her ribs tightened and stomach hardened. If she held on long enough, tears would abandon her. Her face flushed, alongside a gentle bulge of the eyes. Seconds felt like hours as she began to feel lightheaded – a cue for her mind to refocus. A funnelled exhale would provide the strength needed to speak a few words. She closed her eyes.

"I should think…I hope so," she said. The wind tossed her outer garment around. She looked inwards, hoping to find validation.

Walking would suffice.

Connerh looked over his counterpart with an aching desire to embrace him. A delicate shame he was unaware he stored prevented him, eventually pulling his gaze to the floor. Mormere was a stout dwarf, his greying beard and moustache enshrouding most of his face. He looked at Connerh with consoling eyes but struggled to accept that he was real. It was a complicated mixture of joy, relief, and bitterness. He, too, eventually found solace in the floorboards. They were dirty, mud-ridden, and embarrassingly far from the soles of his feet. He often stopped himself from swinging them when in the presence of others. It was degrading in front of *them*, but alone…to him, it was comforting. He fought the urge.

The silence did not feel awkward or out of place but, in some ways, appropriate. Connerh waited to be yelled at, perhaps assaulted in a brotherly way. It would be a just response, he thought. Mormere, on the other hand, waited for an explanation, an apology, or perhaps both. Anything, at this point.

"Oh, mate," he said as his voice broke. The sharp grunts of two men repeatedly clearing their throats filled the cabin. They both reached forward and rested their heads against each other's, arms extending to the other's shoulder. They would avoid eye contact, as it was the considerate thing to do in this scenario. There were others within earshot, after all.

"I hope you brought something strong…" Connerh asked, clearing his throat once more and pulling away.

"Shit me not," Mormere scoffed, reaching beside him to retrieve a leather cask and two small wooden cups. It was an easy path to laughter. He poured shots that vanished no sooner than he had finished the pour. A second was assured. The third was more, but to be sipped with measure.

"You look terrible, mate," he finally said after a brief exchange of stares. His lips were barely visible in the great tuft of hair surrounding them.

They chuckled, and Connerh's gaze fell to the bridge of his nose and back again. He felt the sunbeam lingering above his head. It was his moment to talk, to part his lips and offer…something. Anything. But where to begin?

"Are you at least alright?" Mormere asked, interrupting his faltering attempt to speak. "Considering…" he added, looking out at the bodies, the remains.

Connerh could only nod as he rushed to compartmentalise the deluge he was about to unleash.

"Bloody fucking hell, what happened to *that* lad?!" he shouted, catching sight of Heim's boots, still figuratively smoking with charred stumps protruding beyond them.

"Door-to-door salesman," Connerh replied with a dark grin. Mormere turned red with bursting laughter.

"A simple *not interested* would have sufficed," Mormere replied.

"I tried!" Connerh replied, throwing his hands in the air.

"I don't suppose you know who sent them?" Mormere asked, pausing to brace for his next thought.

"I now conclude that it was *not* the same person who sent you," he said, clearing his throat once more.

"You'd think right. Ioelena sent me, figuring I was one of the only ones you wouldn't try to kill," Mormere replied with a subtle chuckle. Connerh's eyes discreetly widened. He glanced upwards.

"We'd wanted to do this differently…to find you, if you were to be found, before anyone else did. And, well…too many people know you're alive who shouldn't. Where you are, where you've been, that sort of thing," he continued, filtering himself as he spoke. Connerh frowned. "They beat us to it, unfortunately. If it were anyone else, I would've wished I was able to get here sooner." Mormere looked out at the carnage again. Then, with an abrupt shout, he declared, "God damn it, man! They're just sitting there, staring at me! Where's the rest of him?!"

He was referring to Haim's stumps. He looked back at Connerh with humoured disbelief, then stood and pummelled the roof.

"Canan, go cover up those bloody stumps! I don't want to see 'em staring at me anymore!" he shouted. Canan's shuffling oblige shook the cabin. Connerh smiled. He took in air as his lips parted.

"Just tell me you did it for good reason. That it was the right thing to do, as you saw it," Mormere pressed, intervening once more as he raised his hand to stop him. Connerh deflated. He stretched his fingers on both hands; they felt restricted. He went to speak but paused, internally verifying his statement.

"It was…at the time," Connerh said, looking down briefly, then up to lock eyes. It didn't quite encapsulate what he was feeling, and in some ways, it sounded more regretful than perhaps it should have. His brow furrowed in irritation with himself. Mormere's nodding became more pronounced as he ruminated.

"That's good enough for me, then. There'll be time for us to talk more, but we're on a timeline of haste. Ol' stumpy out there is likely the first of many, especially now. This only adds fuel to an already raging fire," he replied.

Connerh couldn't help but gaze at his house – what was left of it.

"That, and I didn't bring anywhere near the amount of spirit we'd need," he continued with a smile.

Connerh grinned, disappointed. The honest truth suddenly burned within him, and the desire to release it was tormenting. Perhaps he deserved it.

"Ioelena wants to start anew, but others have something to say about it, and the more who find out, the worse it'll be. I'm not going to lie to you, lad; what you did," Mormere began, stopping to inhale, "caused ripples. Hurricanes, if I'm to be honest. But even then, that storm was already brewing. You do have some supporters, but you know how it goes," he added.

Connerh agreed, although his mind was still fixated on those first words... She wanted to start anew. Could such a thing be possible?

"What about you? Have you been good?" Connerh asked. He'd been wanting to ask for a while now, coupled with how tired he was of being the centre of attention. There was a tinge of guilt in his ask.

"Of course, of course. We missed you...but there was plenty of liquid delight and women to pass the time." His laughter rumbled.

Connerh smirked.

"I knew in my heart of hearts you were still alive; it was only a matter of time before we'd meet again," he said with recollection and a grin. Connerh's attention vanished as it focused and stuck within himself. The absence of their anger, of frustration, of screaming and yelling made his guilt towards his shame deepen, becoming overtly and overwhelmingly burdensome. Mormere noticed his internal struggle.

"So, the plan says you'll be carried to the castle in this disguised caravan pretending to haul goods. If they're able to keep you under wraps, you'll be taken to a safe location within the castle, hidden until things can be sorted," he said.

There was a noticeable pause.

"And if not?" Connerh asked, snapping out of his daze. Mormere focused his eyes.

"You'll be taken to the prison *below* the castle, and a fake spectacle will unfold and play out. Two options for the same end. One private, one…humiliating." He found displeasure in putting it bluntly.

"She should have just opted for the second. It's the only way to avoid suspicion of…" Connerh began to reply with a hint of frustration, ready to accept penance at a moment's notice. Mormere looked at him as if he were protesting unnecessarily. He was.

"I gave up trying to talk sense into both of you long ago," he replied instead. Connerh attempted to focus his thoughts, rubbing his eyes with his fingertips.

"Okay…okay," he surrendered. Then, looking hopeful, he asked, "At least you'll be keeping me company, I suppose?"

"Oh, I'm afraid not. I've another mission before I can head back. I'm splitting off from here. Got to see a man about a horse, as the saying goes," he replied, leaning forward to embrace Connerh before hopping out of the carriage.

"There's enough juice in there to last a normal man a few days. Try to make it last, eh?" Mormere joked. Connerh grabbed the cask and weighed it in his hand.

"I won't make any promises," he chuckled. They lingered on one lasting glance.

"It was good to see you, lad," Mormere said.

"And you, old friend," Connerh replied.

He plopped down in his seat as the door closed. There was a relief that was freeing — and a lingering guilt in the pit of his stomach that was binding. The sounds of Mormere shouting orders were muffled, even his internal dialogue seemed submerged. Was it that easy to start again? Could all things truly be forgiven?

The cabin felt smaller.

The undercurrent of thought pulled him in opposite directions, adding to his confusion a surge of emotions.

He felt as if he were forgetting something.

CHAPTER TWENTY-SIX

Eagles and Heiresses

Egress

Egress stared at the open sea through a small porthole, its round pane of glass encircled by a frame of gold and black. The water was turbulent, but its violence was subdued by the ship's mass. The halo of light that shone through illuminated the surface of the writing desk in front of her, despite making the interior of her cabin feel darker. When she grew tired of the smell of pine board and lacquer, she reached over to release the latches holding the window closed. A sigh escaped. *Was it the sea that smelt of fish, or did fish smell of the sea?* she wondered. A draft of air quickly stole her warmth, but despite the chill and the smell, she would not retreat. She pulled her favourite blanket tighter around her shoulders.

It was a gift from her aunt that she'd cherished since birth. Io, Lena's mother, had personally made one for each of the children in the family, and though they all generally looked the same, each had its own subtle variance. Even lined up to one another, the children could easily identify their own. It was made from a fine knit of cotton, hand-dyed in a purple only obtained from combining the rarest of berries with the black of squid ink. In memory, Io was a kind woman, soft and small. Fiery to outsiders but kind to her own. Her button nose had a tilt, and it wrinkled when she smiled. Egress smirked as her scent somehow still lingered within the threads, in just the right spot, after all these years. She wondered if it was

202

the same for all the others…

Io's mark persevered, just as Egress would have to.

The door to her cabin opened abruptly. A familiar gait and a heavy-heeled boot vibrated the floorboards. She felt inclined to correct her posture.

"Why is it so dark in here?" Hargatha asked, hinting at impatience. Her eyes drifted down. The knit emblem of raven wings confronted her. Her head raised, gaze held forward.

"Still clinging on to that *ratty* old thing?" she asked.

Egress dropped her head, staring back in her mother's direction but failing to provide a reply. The question wasn't worthy of it. Hargatha retrieved a blanket neatly folded atop the bed. Crimson in colour, it bore the family sigil of a Golden Eagle. She opened it and grunted with satisfaction. Her hoof-like steps resonated as she approached to drape the heavy blanket over Egress's shoulders.

"This will actually keep you warm," she added. Her hands lingered on Egress' shoulders.

Egress delayed a moment before reaching up and grabbing Hargatha's hand. She held it to her cheek, then kissed it. Hargatha's dimple creased. She ran her fingers through Egress' scalp, collecting her long, pale blonde hair into a bunch, just as she'd done when she was a little girl. It hadn't quite turned white yet, but it soon would.

"I like it when you wear it down. You were gifted with my mother's long hair. Oh, I could never get mine to grow to such lengths. And once it turns…it will shine like the sun," she offered, gently releasing her hair before she walked over to the curtains, ripping them open – much to Egress's dismay. She recoiled at the luminous assault.

"The view is better top side, you know. Besides, I want you to get to know the crew and meet the others from our delegation who are accompanying us on our travels to the Rim. It will be good to begin familiarising yourself with our allies," she asked. Egress blinked through her heavy brow, lifting her gaze to her mother.

"You know I don't like the sea, and I like socialising even less. This is as close as I wish to be to either," she replied, gently rolling her eyes.

"You don't intend to hide in here the entire time, do you?" Hargatha asked.

"That depends on how much longer it's going to take," she replied.

"At least two weeks. It depends on whether conditions stay

favourable," Hargatha explained with a frown. Egress nodded quietly.

"Then I will be hiding here the entire time," she replied, returning her gaze to her porthole. Her brow sunk.

Hargatha's arms folded as she mounted a reply.

"Why is she sending us away?" Egress asked promptly, her gaze lagging as she turned to face her mother. The question was partly a strategic change of topic, partly genuine. Hargatha's focus averted, forced as she was to provide either a strategic answer or the cold truth. She noticed a brush on the table. She took it, walked behind Egress, and began brushing her hair.

"It would seem your cousin is eager to stretch her wings, as it were," she said, quickly losing herself in the act of hair brushing.

"Is that really such a bad thing? Perhaps she felt your grasp was too tight," Egress asked. Her head lurched backwards. Hargatha had momentarily become too enthusiastic in her task.

"Children reach a point when they believe they are ready to face the world, and often much earlier than they are actually ready to do so," Hargatha replied.

"She's a grown woman," Egress fussed.

"By human standards, perhaps, but the sentiment remains," she quipped. "She's ill-equipped and has no idea what I shielded her from…what the wolves will do now that she wades into the open."

"Perhaps she uncovered your plot and felt threatened by it," Egress replied.

"The weak are often fearful of the strong. And *uncovered?*" Hargatha stressed. "That's a polite way to avoid incriminating your brother."

"You don't really think Vidar had anything to do with this?" she rejected the thought in question form.

"I think we underestimated the lengths your brother would go to satiate his own desires. To make a name for himself. Look around: who of us are missing from this little journey?" she asked.

Egress dropped her gaze and pondered a moment. She frowned. The implication was clear.

"Why am I lumped in with this?" she asked.

"I already told you. The weak fear the strong," Hargatha replied. "But worry not. This does little but delay the inevitable. A different path leading to the same outcome. In some ways, it saves me a few steps. That is why you must be ready."

Her head canted as she took more delicate strokes with the brush.

Egress's gaze focused on the ocean.

"What will you do when the time comes for you to wear the crown?" Hargatha asked. "Will you learn from the mistakes of the past? Or, like your cousin, repeat them?" she continued, pulling the old, knitted quilt from beneath the crimson blanket that covered it. She held it out between pinched fingers and dropped it in Egress's lap. "Learn from it. Observe it often. But leave it there," she concluded sharply.

Egress took the blanket in her grasp and stared at it. Io's scent was masked by the ocean breeze. Hargatha resumed brushing her hair, refocusing her attention on her mother's touch. Egress was listening, quietly pondering. Her mother watched as she worked through her thoughts. That was Egress' way. Unlike Vidar, who spoke his mind freely and often, Egress thought more than she spoke. Hargatha could tell she was fighting a lingering thought.

"Your uncle made a grave mistake putting Io on the throne. Humans aren't cut out for the job. Look around; in just a short time, Hildeheim has already been stripped of its identity, reduced to a sliver of its former self. Marred by scandal and embarrassment…by weakness. I shudder to think what will come next if left unchecked. Even now, she marches us towards war…and for what?" she began.

Egress's posture began to stiffen but halted as her mother continued to speak. Hargatha sighed.

"But she was a lovely woman in private moments. She was a terrible ruler but a wonderful aunt. Sometimes too wonderful, if I am to be transparent. I'd be lying if I said I didn't struggle with bouts of jealousy, especially with how the children flocked to her," she continued, her voice softening progressively. Egress spun around in her chair, her shoulders relaxed.

"Why would you be jealous? She was the fun relative. She got to enjoy spoiling us while you and Father raised us. That was her job. That's nothing to be jealous of; she wasn't there for us in the moments that formed who we are…for the important moments. That was you. So, put it out of your mind. I'll hear nothing of the sort," she replied, turning back around in her chair. Hargatha grinned with a low brow.

"Perhaps that is where I went wrong: I didn't spoil Lena enough. I wasn't the *fun* aunt for her," she offered.

"Perhaps you spoiled her too much. She forgot who was by her side when it mattered," Egress replied. Hargatha smiled, pulling away and facing the door, brush still in hand. Her head dropped. Egress turned to look at her, pity in her eyes.

"I'll not forget," Egress quietly reassured. Hargatha turned with a hopeful smile.

"Don't be too hard on your cousin. That is the way of humans, my love. Guided and controlled by emotion. Doing what feels right over doing what *is* right…for sometimes doing what is right does not feel good," Hargatha mused. Egress glanced at the floor and turned back around.

"You're right," she said plainly.

Hargatha looked on, waiting for her to continue. Egress stretched her back in the chair.

"Will it blow in the wind, or should I put it in a bun?" she asked.

Hargatha's grin deepened.

"I think, in this instance, a low ponytail would suffice," she replied with a chuckle.

"Come, now; I must look good for my sailors," Egress pushed.

CHAPTER TWENTY-SEVEN

FEAR AND LOATHING

VIDAR

There was a smell. Vidar fell just short of identifying it. His nose wrinkled. It wasn't overly offensive, just…persistent. Only moments had passed since he'd made short work of the brittle door separating them from the heart of the subterranean temple. Both men stood with their torches held high, peering blindly into the darkness.

"Why does it feel like someone is out there, staring back?" Vidar whispered. Toke's eyes would have widened if they weren't already stretched to capacity, trying to pick up hints of light. The darkness was thick, like a soup with too much starch.

"Aye. The dead quiet doesn't help matters," Toke replied.

"Now's not the time for puns, Toke," Vidar reprimanded in a serious tone despite joking along with him. He pushed past Toke, who shot him a bewildered glance. Vidar looked around for something on the ground. The flames of his torch roared. Toke chuckled, finally connecting the dots.

"At least our light hasn't gone out. That means there's fresh air in here still," Vidar said.

Vidar bent over and retrieved a piece of stone. He examined it. Checked its heft. His large arm swung backwards and snapped forward. The stone was hurled into the void, audibly resisting the air.

"Remind me never to get on your bad side," Toke joked, mildly impressed.

"Okay," Vidar replied. A distant crack and tumble echoed. "That was the floor. This place is massive. Much larger than I had anticipated."

"There should be pitch pool lines along the walls. As long as nothing's damned them up, they should still be flowing," Toke said as he wandered in a chosen direction.

"You're speaking Dwarvish; you'll have to translate," Vidar muttered, waving his torch around in search of what he did not understand.

"Aye. Pitch pools, you know… Tar, is it? There's a godly river of pitch running through the mountain. The olde kin tapped it and ran troughs or lines down and across the walls. It's how we lit great rooms back then," Toke replied. Vidar nodded as it became clear.

"That explains the smell," he said.

"It's mostly self-sustaining. Course, it smells something fierce once it's burning. They had a liquid they'd pour on top to help, but…you can only do so much," he continued.

"I don't suppose you have any of that with you?" Vidar asked.

Toke shook his head and replied, "No, unfortunately not. "

He tossed his satchel on the ground and began fishing through it.

"I found 'em. It looks like the *out* was stopped up, but there's a good amount of pitch in the line still," he shouted before he dipped his finger in the sticky, viscous substance, then immediately regretted the decision, unsure of where to wipe it. Vidar turned back and walked in his direction as he retrieved a vial from his bag, desperately trying to budge the cork with his thumb.

"I'll hold that," Vidar offered, taking Toke's torch. He cautiously looked at the troughs etched into the wall. There were three lines with roughly two feet between them and a stone reservoir extending out from the wall for each.

"You may want to take a few steps backwards. The pitch burns hot once it's lit, but it needs a little help. I'm adding what we call Dragon's Jelly…" he explained.

Vidar's face pruned at the nomenclature. Toke thoroughly spread the gelatinous liquid across the surface of the bottom trough, it being the only one he could reach.

"It burns quick and fast, just like my mother's temper," he continued with a grin and stood quickly after finishing his task.

"Go ahead and give her a tilt," he said, motioning towards the torches still in Vidar's grasp. Vidar cautiously tilted the torch atop the thin layer of jelly. A rapid flash of light marked an audibly loud hissing, bubbling, and searing sound. Both men instinctively recoiled at the abrupt combustion. As designed, the trail of flame immediately began to crawl like a glowing snake winding across the forest floor of darkness. The interior of the cavernous temple slowly became illuminated with the rose and orange billowy flame of the pitch lines. Vidar's head dropped backwards as he examined the lines diverging and twisting upwards into the immense cylindrical ceiling before running back to the far reaches of the room.

"Toke, this is incredible," he murmured in awe.

"Legend says the totem barrelled through the sky, burrowed through the mountain, and rolled down to where it lies. We later came and expanded the chamber to what it is today," Toke said.

Vidar's eyes tracked the path. A thick, ornate wall of golden chainmail in the distance obscured his view of what lay behind it, in the direction of the *eyes* he felt staring at them. The room seemed virtually untouched, save for a thick layer of dust and a few cluttered piles of fallen stone and rubble. Golden candlestands throughout the space still held spindles of partially melted wax, as if they had been put out just the day prior. There were three sections of chairs split in two by a walkway that traversed them, each section further divided by a curtain of mail. These curtains appeared even more reddish and brilliant in the warm glow of the pitch line flames, the second being silver and the third bronze.

Vidar concluded his observations and lowered his gaze upon Toke.

"And what does legend say happened to this place?" he asked as he began to walk slowly forward. Toke rushed to keep pace.

"Legend says the priests went mad and sealed themselves in here. Allegedly, the sky totem is an evil object that makes you lose your marbles," he joked, growing increasingly uneasy as they slowly walked towards the golden section.

"And what do you believe?" Vidar asked. They crossed into the bronze section. The chairs still looked deceptively strong. They were thick, made of wood with silver joints.

"I think it's a story designed to keep people from pilfering. But then, we were different back then. Our focus was just like our taller cousins, always outward. Upwards. Now it's just inwards," Toke replied. His gaze wandered.

"Is that what you really believe?" Vidar asked. His tone was low and deciphering. Toke stopped and began to shake his head, trying to rid himself of an onset headache.

"Are you alright?" Vidar asked. He stopped and turned to face Toke.

"Yes, sure… It's probably the smell of burning. Just giving me a spin for the whirl," he said.

"Do you want to know the truth? Or does this version suit you?" Vidar asked. He took a few steps forward and gently prodded Toke backwards until his head pain seemed to lighten.

"I suppose…" he replied.

"As best I can put it, the Uridar contain…a presence. Or they are some other type of creature entirely, either not from here or here all along. It really doesn't matter in the grand scheme, though the thought exercise is intriguing, just the same," he began. "There are many, and so far, I have found one. That one was quite…angry. Its effect on those sensitive to its energy would cause them to combust into flame, as if they were coated in your Dragon's Jelly," he continued.

Toke lurched backwards.

"This one is said to have a very different effect. It wasn't the priests who sealed themselves in; it was your leaders who did it. Despite the clerics having a higher tolerance to the Uridar's effects, they had indeed gone mad, killing and sacrificing those who ventured in to pay respects…or to worship." His focus shifted. Vidar turned to face the bronze curtain. A walkway of tiles and gems stretched outward before him.

"This Uridar has a different emotion to share: fear. After all these years, its power is still potent, probably as strong as it was then. Even now, I can feel it tugging at the frayed threads in my mind," he spoke with intrigued delight.

There was no answer.

He turned to see Toke glaring into space, his eyes bloodshot. Vidar frowned and ran to guide him back to where they started.

"Sit. If you feel it getting worse, go back the way we came, and I will rejoin you in time," he demanded.

"Don't you… Why you…you can't…alone?" Toke mumbled.

"Don't worry, I seem to have some immunity to…well, at least the last one. We'll see now, won't we?" he asked rhetorically, standing erect.

"Why?" Toke asked.

"Because they ask me to," Vidar replied, resuming his approach with a respectful gait.

Vidar's finger slid across the back of each chair as he walked. The journey seemed short initially, but now it felt like an eternity. The metal felt cold, the wood brittle, frail, and hollow. The silver section. Just past the demarcation, the air felt thicker, even for a man of the mountain. It was cooler than before, a welcome but contrasting change from his last encounter with a Uridar. He looked behind to check on Toke. He was still there, rubbing his temples but watching Vidar intently. Vidar's attention snapped forward, having thought he heard someone. He froze, tilting his head and raising his ear.

Surely it's a bat, he thought, quick to dismiss the natural inclination of his nerves. There was no other sound for some seconds, so he pushed forward. The chairs in this section were different, being made almost entirely of silver. The layer of dust that covered them made them look frosted, and they were also quite cold to the touch. The were small skeletons lying on the ground in between rows, the fabric of the deceased's robes still covering them. Some were purple and yellow; others were black and grey. He started when he saw the first one. Their jaws were in a stretched position, either yelling or gasping for air – he couldn't be sure. Toke extended his head, seeing Vidar's reaction.

"What do you see?" he shouted.

Vidar looked down, refusing to turn. He thought about lying.

"Just remnants of the past," he offered, continuing his walk. It wasn't a lie.

Toke grunted.

The gold section.

These seats were white, like bone or ivory, embossed with gold accents. They were warm. The air was at its thickest, requiring effort to fully expand his lungs. There was a heat source emanating from beyond the golden veil. It was like feeling the direction of the sun from beyond closed eyelids, except on the skin. It was pulling Vidar closer. There was a noticeable pressure in his head, with an inclination to dwell on specific memories. He frowned. The pressure was stronger than the effect it produced. It was an overt imbalance that left him curious. The walkway split in both directions, leading around the curtain. He looked back once more. Toke mouthed something to him that he couldn't understand, but the dwarf followed up with a raised thumb to make it clear. Vidar nodded, being sure not to give away that he was hearing something shifting. Something was definitely back there. He chose the path to the left; a few steps removed him from Toke's view. He rested his right hand on the hilt of his sheathed blade and proceeded, slowing his steps even further. There was more than one veil –

there were several, in fact, with large slits to walk through. It was a creative way to isolate the Uridar without needing to maintain a sustained presence like building actual walls would require, thus limiting the exposure of those charged with the task. It was growing darker the farther he progressed. An all-too-familiar blue hue was glowing in front of him, as was the scar on his cheek.

There appeared to be a final section.

"My god," he uttered as he saw it: a massive pile of bones as tall as he and twice as high as the average dwarf, laid out in three or four connected mounds.

"They really had gone mad," he muttered. Carefully navigating the deceased, he saw one last veil that barely concealed the Uridar's glow. He slid through the opening of the final curtain, and there it was: large, perfectly round, and made of a material resembling slate. There were shapes and writing carved around its entire circumference, and it hovered off the ground just like the other Uridar as it emitted its signature eerie luminosity. His curiosity negated his cautionary approach as he rushed to examine it, almost ignoring the figure that stood behind it…staring at him. Vidar was startled, shouting and taking a few steps backwards. He slid his sword out of its sheath a few inches, then paused.

It was his mother, Hargatha…and she looked angry.

He visibly wrestled with questions. His head turned and rotated as he observed from a safe distance. Recognition bridled his concern. His sudden laughter reverberated and increased in volume.

"This is extremely fascinating," he mumbled with a smile. Then, tapping his temple, he asked, "Been poking around here, have you?"

No response.

"I didn't know you were capable of such a thing. That's what she looked like years ago. But why then? Why this version in time?" he asked.

The facsimile looked away, still scowling. Vidar resecured his blade and walked towards it. She slowly walked in the opposite direction, maintaining the Uridar between them.

"Don't run now; you called me here. Didn't you?" he asked.

It said nothing but returned its gaze to him.

"Now I know for sure you're not her. I don't think that woman has stopped talking since she was born; I'm pretty sure she talks in her sleep." He laughed to himself. "Why that one? Is that all you could gather? Is my resistance preventing you from delving further?" he chuckled. "You'll have to do better than that if you want to frighten me."

The facsimile transformed into a giant yeti and towered over Vidar, its sharp fangs dripping blood. Its pawed hands raised in the air, and its ferocious growl was loud to Vidar. It was just as he remembered it.

"My father came just in time to separate the creature's head from the rest of its body. I was scared then…but I was a boy. I am a man now. Beasts don't frighten me," he said, confused, shaking his head slightly.

The yeti returned to its form resembling Hargatha. She continued to scowl at him.

"Wait…this is connected. Yes…yes, I remember," Vidar said. He felt a rush of excitement. She yelled at him in a familiar cadence, the voice similar but warped, the words unintelligible.

"I snuck out of our den one night to go exploring. That was when I stumbled onto the Yeti. My father didn't say much, but I could tell he was…disappointed. Back when that meant something to me," he scoffed. "But it wouldn't matter. My mother would say enough for the both of them."

He squinted as he focused on the facsimile's mouth. It was still shouting nonsense.

"I can still remember what she said…most of it anyway," he recalled.

"Damn you, Vidar!" it said amongst the garbled words. His head canted.

"Is that how this works?" he asked. "What was it she said?"

He thought hard, averting his gaze for a moment. The harder he thought, the more legible her words became. She was berating him. It was incessant. The emotion was raw. She was speaking out of…out of fear. Her tone was irrational. She paused. Galabrand had intervened, but the Uridar wasn't showing him that. She'd just stopped. *A limitation, perhaps?*

"If you want to sneak around like a rat, perhaps you'll enjoy living like one!" he announced in unison with the facsimile.

Her words were clear and understandable. Forcibly calm and sinister. Her gaze matched the tone.

"She locked me in a cave for two weeks. I roamed around in the dark, ironically eating rats to survive. I was scared. Terrified, even. But soon my anger took hold. It persevered…it sustains me," he said, looking downwards into blending memories.

Hargatha smiled at him. He nodded as if he understood, then frowned and shook his head.

"I don't understand," he declared, throwing up his hands in frustration.

Toke woke up to find he was leaning against a pillar. He could hear Vidar still arguing to himself. He figured that it must have been hours, based on the amount of drool accumulated in his beard. The natural ventilation had done a good job of helping to ward off the vapour and smoke caused by the burning pitch, but it wasn't perfect. A light fog permeated the cavern, granting the corners of everything a blue-red edge.

"Must not be working at full capacity. We've got to take a break," he mumbled to himself as he rose to his feet. He felt dizzy. He heard whispers – a chorus of whispers – and they were aimed at him from above. Judging him. He looked up cautiously, curious to find the source but hesitant to confirm it. A slow walk progressed into a light jog as he ran to Vidar.

"None of this makes any sense!" Vidar shouted from where he sat on the ground, rocking back and forth. "I get it. You're not actually trying to scare me. You're trying to tell me *something*, but what?!"

The Uridar's projection transformed several times into different variations of his mother in different wardrobes, shouting or talking about various things in various tones and pitches.

"The other Uridar could connect with my mind. It brought me comfort, in this euphoric...kind of..." He struggled to describe it. Hargatha stopped. Her head canted sharply.

"It was the deepest rest I've ever felt. It was angry at first, but so am I. We kind of connected in this mutual..." he mumbled on, motioning with his hands as he stared at the ground.

"Where are you going, Vidar?" Hargatha asked. He stopped speaking and scoffed.

"See? What is this? What does that even mean?" he argued and stood.

"Where are you going, Vidar?" she asked again with an annoyed and exhausted tone.

"I'm not going anywhere until you start making sense. You'll not get rid of me that easily," he fussed. Hargatha stopped repeating the phrase.

"Maybe I've made a mistake, Brand," she said. Her voice was distant. He'd overheard his parents talking as he had spied from his bedroom.

He squinted his eyes with a smirk. He found the projections fascinating.

"What are you saying? Are you saying you've made a mistake? What mistake?" he asked.

"Maybe Egress is better suited," she said.

"Well, now you're just trying to piss me off," he growled with a turn of the head.

She laughed.

He grunted.

"You're a little shit, aren't you?"

"Where did you sneak off to this time, Vidar!?" she shouted. He shook his head with his mouth half open.

"I didn't sneak off anywhere!" he replied. She sighed.

"I told you he couldn't do it," she said. Her voice was rife with disappointment. Resignation. It triggered a twitch in his eye.

"Stop it!" he shouted in a burst of anger.

He expelled the air from his lungs, closing his eyes and trying to clear his mind.

"Where did you sneak off to this time, Vidar!?" she shouted again.

"I didn't go anywhere," he replied in defeat.

"No, you know where I went! You know already! I went to an old, abandoned dwarven mine out near Khalkhal. Insert the yeti, Galabrand the hero…blah, blah, blah, she locked me in there… We've covered this *at length* already," he sighed, his face sinking into his hands. "I'm starting to understand why the clerics went mad. I'm scared to think how much more of this it takes to get to the sacrificing part."

"Are you sure?" she questioned.

"Yes, I'm sure. The place had all kinds of stories of ghosts and otherworldly things. That's why I snuck up there to begin with. There's no way they'd let me go knowingly," he fussed.

"Were you alone? Did Muckmouth put you up to this?" she asked.

"That's a new one," he laughed. "Muckmouth…that incompetent fool." It was a humorous memory to recall. "In all fairness, it was Muckmouth who got me into cave diving. And his name wasn't

Muckmouth; that's just what we called him. Couldn't understand a damned thing he ever said," he chuckled.

"You expect me to believe you were alone?" she pressed.

"All by my lonesome. Every day was night. It took some time for my eyes to adapt when they finally let me out," he replied. He recalled the memories not with fondness but humble remembrance.

"Is that the story you're sticking with? You only get one more chance to tell me the truth," she said.

"I told you I was alone. For a time, I thought there was someone in the dark there with me, but it was surely just my mind playing tricks," he said. He stopped and raised his head. Rushing to his feet with sudden realisation, he asked, "Wait, are we talking?"

"You're a little shit, aren't you?" Hargatha transformed into a version of him. "Maybe Egress is better suited." It changed into Hargatha again.

"Very funny. I get it. So, start again. Start over," Vidar said, stretching his arms.

"The other Uridar could connect with my mind," his clone said.

"Yes. Do you know… Are you aware of the others? I hadn't thought of that," he said. Curiosity and confusion blended.

"Where did you sneak off to this time, Vidar?"

"You want to know where the other Uridar is?" he asked, excited at his connection.

"You're a little shit, aren't you?" it said.

"Can you recall memories of words? Or does…how does this work?" he struggled to figure out a solution.

"I told you he couldn't do it."

"What? Me? No… You…you couldn't do it. Couldn't do what?" he asked.

"Can you recall memories or words?" it said. Vidar shook his head as he connected the thoughts.

"You can't recall words…so it's just memories?" he said.

"You're a little shit, aren't you?" it said.

"We have to find you a new memory for acknowledgement," he chuckled. Then he exclaimed, "Wait. That's it!"

He faced it head-on.

"Yes," he said.

A pause, no more than a second or two.

"No," he said.

He looked upwards.

"I stood here, saying yes, then no," he whispered to himself, as if he needed to save the event in his mind.

"Yes. Yes. Yes," it said.

"So, you can only recall memories?" he asked.

"Yes," it replied. Vidar quietly congratulated himself.

"This is progress. Now I just have to act out an entire codex of words. At least form some sort of structure by which we can communicate," he plotted with himself.

"You're not going anywhere for a while. Maybe this will teach you a much-needed lesson," it said in Hargatha's image and voice. Vidar shook his head.

"That, it did. But what do you mean? I'm not going anywhere," he replied.

Toke wandered in. He looked intoxicated.

"We need to get some fresh air. Breathing in all this smoke isn't good. Oh, hello. I didn't know you weren't alone," he muttered with a genial smile upon noticing the facsimile next to him.

"Wait, you can see it?" Vidar replied as he turned to greet him. His eyes widened.

"Toke, your eyes are bloodshot. I suppose you're right; we should take a break and get some fresh air," he said as he moved to intercept Toke.

"You're not going anywhere for a while!" it declared.

"That's a little rude," Toke complained quietly, swaying from his mental inebriation.

"I'll be back; he just needs to get some fresh air," Vidar assured it.

"You're not going anywhere for a while!" it repeated over and over again. Vidar scoffed.

"Just ignore it. Let's go…" he said, lifting the dwarf over his shoulder.

"Speak of this to no one," Toke groaned, resisting in tone only. The nausea was getting to him.

Hargatha's voice grew deeper and in triplicate. She grew into a troll, a thunderous half-giant, half-creature hybrid. It looked down at Vidar. Its eyes were large and piercing, and two fangs protruded past its moist, rubbery lips. Mucus ran from its pierced nose.

"You're barely a snack, but you'll do!" it shouted.

"Run, lad!" Toke shouted.

Vidar promptly obliged the suggestion.

CHAPTER TWENTY-EIGHT

ENTANGLEMENT

CONNERH

He would not forget this day.

A relentless downpour assaulted the convoy for the better part of an hour, halting their journey towards the capital. The men drew straws. The winners found shelter stuffed inside one of the two cabins; the short ends took *the long shower*. As luck would have it, the smelliest of the bunch drew poorly – nature's way of intervening, perhaps. While it was less than preferable being shoulder to shoulder with one another in such confined spaces, especially those who had to manoeuvre around the food and supplies secured in the second cabin, it still beat being left in the elements.

There was an awkward silence, penetrated only by their jeering at their brethren caught in the rain. They stole glances at Connerh when he was distracted, comparing him to their mental expectations. They all knew who he was, who he was said to be, but this was their first time actually encountering him; most of them had been far too young when he was at the height of his celebrity. Coupled with the fact that he looked different now, aged, worn, and disconnected, his quiet and stoic nature made him seem more intriguing than perhaps he really was. They were all undecided, anticipating the time when they could discuss it freely with one another. Meanwhile, he mentally soared above the clouds with his spear, sorting through information about what lay ahead, who and what was nearby. There was no one. Empty, barren, and uneventful would define the journey

218

for the next few hours. He sighed.

Just when he thought to join the short ends, the rain ceased, quickly and unceremoniously. The air inside the cabin had grown warm and moist, made up of bad breath, body odours, and whatever the hell had been transported in the carriage prior to its current use. It was all amplified by his elevated senses. He now knew far too much about them. The men filed out one at a time, although Quo remained for a moment, hoping to have a memorable moment with him.

"We'll try to dry up our brother at arms as best we can, then we'll keep on. Let me know should you need anything," he said. Connerh nodded, watching his exit.

"Thank you, Quo," he said, drawing a smile to the young man's face.

The ambience grew loud with the sounds of camaraderie, muffled and distant to Connerh's ears. The sound of his isolation was sharp and ringing, never more apparent than now. *Perhaps before hadn't been so bad*, he thought. A sudden rush of frustration overwhelmed him. What was he doing? Why was he allowing himself to be transported like a delicate artefact, incapable of ensuring his own destination? He was deadly and feared, and that was even before the spear came into his life. They had no idea what he was capable of. A grin pulled at his cheek. He thought to show them.

A small voice grew loud, an internal rebuke. *That's what got him into this mess to begin with.* The grandiose demonstration of power often went overboard, where the line between justice and vengeance blurred, where causality became casualty. His expression blanked. Things would need to be different this time. Especially if they were to succeed, the voice reminded him. His eyes dropped at the thought of Rose and Aeryk. A fresh start had proven difficult to find, and the stars had just handed him one on a silver platter. He'd tried doing it his way, but it never lasted. Even *fleeting* felt too long a descriptor.

Things would be different this time. They had to. Perhaps that had always been the lesson in all of this suffering: the lion learning to be meek. Death, retribution, and the instant gratification of justification couldn't always be the answer. Perhaps there was more in store, buried beneath whatever made up his existence. That would explain the void. The one he could never describe and no sooner fill.

He frowned and shook his head in response to the voice.

No, he wasn't suggesting pacifism. Evil still needed to be held at bay. But perhaps, in order to receive mercy, he would first have to extend it. Set the stage and let it play out.

Yes.

He would detach the ego, become an observer. Let the stars drive for a while. It was the only way…the only way he hadn't tried yet.

And if it meant death?

Perhaps it was meant to be. Perhaps it was a door being held open for him – a portal to what lay in wait beyond. The answer for which he'd prayed.

You can't be serious?

He was.

Say it.

He took a moment, a daring grin on his face. His lips parted, teasing the words he would say aloud.

"Yes."

The pain was sharp, sudden, and encompassing, the ringing of his isolation now made real. A clawing at his mind. Twisting. Unravelling. A sudden rush of cold as his warmth left him. It was bitterly cold outside, but he couldn't find the metaphorical ladder to escape the spiral of agony he was experiencing to focus on it. His vision swam, the edges of his world blurring. Each breath was a fight, a shallow rasp against the crushing weight in his chest. He coughed, a wet sound that tore from his throat, tasting metallic. Panic clawed at him, and a primal fear threatened to consume him whole. He was alone. He could no longer sense beyond the carriage.

It had abandoned him.

CHAPTER TWENTY-NINE

THE GOLDEN PASS

LENA

Lena peeked impatiently through the white frilly curtains with a tug of the finger and a tilt of the head.

"Anything?" she asked aloud, rapping on the ceiling of the carriage with her fist.

"I'm afraid not, Your Majesty," a muffled exterior voice replied. She began to frown as the air grew still. It was cold, though not quite cold enough to see her own breath, and she was becoming impatient.

Surely Darros would not stand me up? Would he? she wondered. She was beginning to question her use of theatrics to garner his attention, but even he couldn't pass up an opportunity to honour an 'ancient' tradition.

"I stand corrected, Your Majesty; we have a flagman entering the field from the south. Stand by...we'll see if it checks out," the lookout said. She rushed to take another glance outside of her carriage, but the view was blocked by the rows of soldiers surrounding her. She let out a quiet growl of frustration and tapped her fingers on her lap. She looked up at the ceiling as if she could see the lookout on the other side, anticipating a follow-up report. Lena could hear rushing footsteps, the horses snorting and adjusting their hooves in place; she could hear them whispering. The men were tense and alert.

"Sending our flag now," the coachman said. She rubbed her hands together with a hopeful smirk. A few more shouts provided enough for her to paint the scene in her mind as it unfolded outside.

Minutes passed.

"It is Lord Darros, after all, Your Majesty. Do I have your command to proceed?" her coachman shouted. She shuffled in her seat, straightening her clothes and arranging her features into a nonchalant expression.

"Carry on," she said, doing her best to appear calm and composed. With a subtle jerk, the carriage moved forward. A soft glow of yellow began to illuminate the foggy glass, producing a smile. She resisted the painful urge to wipe the glass clean and press her face to it. She flexed her fingers in and out of her palm in an attempt to draw warm blood into them.

"About halfway there now…" the coachman said in a low tone.

"All is going accordingly," another horseback soldier reported to her right. The minutes were taking forever as the carriage travelled at the pre-ordained speed.

"Alright, just a moment. Once there, the lieutenant will jump down, and I'll take us to second position. We're all here should you need us, Your Majesty," the soldier whispered. Things progressed just as he said. The carriage came to a slow stop, and Darros' carriage cast a shadow against her window. Her coachman took a few steps and jumped. The abrasiveness of his impact echoed within the cabin, followed by the distant sound of galloping horses coming from either side of her. She sat frozen in place. Her eyes darted around and upwards as she waited for the sound to stop. It became quiet. She counted to herself before opening the window.

Darros did the same. And there their carriages sat, opposite one another with only a few feet between them, in an expansive field of yellow winter daffodils at the border of Hildeheim and Khazmyr, she on her side and he on his. His side profile of black and gold stood in his window, and she stood in hers, draped in a garb and gown of black furs and black feathers.

Merith and Yuri sat on their steeds along the tree line of the valley, observing the meeting of power taking place. Merith watched Yuri observe Hildeheim's soldiers intently. He raised his hand to his chin, twirling the hairs of his beard.

"Look at them. See how the weight of their armour is irrelevant? It doesn't even phase them," she said. She didn't hide the fact that she was enamoured with the men. Merith looked at them and back again.

"For what it's worth, I was perfectly fine," he began.

She looked up at him immediately; the disbelief saturated her expression, and a rebuttal prepared itself in her mouth.

"For an hour or so…I was perfectly fine," he broke into a smile as she laughed. He continued playfully, "It was all the damned walking that took the energy out of me. And in my defence, that bugger got me pretty good when we ambushed him. So, there was an injury to consider that I feel I'm not being given credit for."

She scoffed and replied, "It was a pathetic attempt. Own it and move on. A ninety-year-old Hildeheim soldier could wear the armour better than you did."

"Who knew someone so small could be so mean," he replied, pretending offence. She smirked.

"As part of their training, they march for days, through snowstorms of the highest mountain peaks, through the Forest of the Elves…and, when they had a peace treaty, through the deserts of the Far Sands," she rebutted. He studied her face, exchanging glances with the valley. He'd seen many looks, and this one was familiar.

"So, what's your connection to them? Too short to make try-outs?" he asked. She looked at him with an irritated smirk. The short jokes were coming dangerously close to her limit.

"If it weren't out of concern for the horse, I'd knock you to your arse," she said.

"Oh, I believe you," he laughed, rubbing the horse's side.

She went back to observing the meeting.

"So, what is it?" he pressed.

"What do you mean?" She broke her fixation, having some sense of where the conversation was going.

"You're practically drooling over 'em. I'm going to have to fetch you a baby's bib shortly here. Yet, you've not said one thing about your own soldiers down there. So, what's the rub? Have a little buyer's remorse? They not make armour your size?" he asked.

She shook her head, choosing not to reply. She had the patience for about one more short joke. In her mind, she replayed memories she had no intention of sharing, drawing a small sigh from her lungs.

"Ah, so she's not the open book she claims to be. Fair enough. Our relationship hasn't developed enough for secrets; I get it."

His attempt at childhood games had no effect. There was a pause while he continued to observe her. Her focus had shifted to Darros' carriage and the position of their men. The joy had sunk from her face. It was clear she was running through scenarios in her mind.

"On another topic, why are we out here and not down there with him? You're like his number two, aren't you?" he asked pointedly. She arched a brow and stared at him. He apologised with his hands, surrendering his attempts to pry, which had grown tiresome to her.

"You just asked the same question, but this time, under a different context," she snapped at him. He faux-pondered.

"No, I'm pretty sure I asked a different question. This one had nothing to do with Mountainfolk or your height," he said defensively.

Her patience had fully drained, and her fist balled.

"Sorry, I'm done. I'm done," he raised his palms. She took a moment to calm down.

"I was once one of them," she said after filtering her thoughts. His head snapped in her direction. She closed her eyes for a moment and shook her head, realising the statement was misleading.

"I mean…I am originally from Hildeheim. I…came…to Khazmyr as a child," she said hesitantly, still fixated on the valley.

He listened, anticipating the story to follow. She noticed his stare and looked back after a moment of it lasting.

"What?" she asked.

"Wait, that's it?" he questioned, sliding into a brief chuckle.

"Yes?" she replied.

"You are the worst storyteller I've ever met," he declared, changing his point of focus and readjusting himself in the saddle. She gave his protest no mind. He fussed, "You can't lead a story like that and end it there. That's like saying, 'The man lost control of the horse as it ran towards the edge of the cliff', end of story."

"He obviously fell to his death, and the horse along with him," she said in reply, purposely being difficult, then finally gave in and laughed. "Fine. I came to Khazmyr as a child. I once belonged to Hildeheim…but now I belong to Darros." She locked eyes with him briefly and said plainly, "End of story."

"Yes, ma'am." His brows flared. The message had been received.

"In answer to your second question, Darros does not have a number two like most rulers would employ. There is no number three, four, or so on. He has us all. There are many number twos; there's one with him now," she said.

"The Golden Pass…a ritual shared between Hildeheim and Khazmyr many generations ago…though long since abandoned," Darros began with an impressed nod. His soothing tone carried effortlessly over into her cabin. "I'll have to admit, it was not on my list of expectations for the year, but I am engaged. You have my attention."

Darros stretched his lower back, resetting his posture. His hand rested on the window seal, the golden covers adorning his fingertips glinting in the sunlight.

"Darros, you are as generous as you are gracious for indulging me," she began with a slight hint of sarcasm. He stared at her for a second and shook his head.

"Oh, knock it off, Lena. It doesn't make me the slightest bit stiff when you flatter me," he reprimanded disappointedly, inclining towards his lap with his head.

She smiled.

"If I remember my history accurately, this ritual began when King Archemond, your great former, met us here to ask that we indulge his lust for war. We obliged back then, but times have changed. Our focus is different now," Darros continued. Leaning into view, his long hair blowing with the breeze, he asked, "Surely you didn't make us come all this way for giggles and disappointment?"

She met his position and momentarily his gaze, then sighed loudly as she said, "I did not come all this way just to ask for war, Darros."

"We're off to a good start, then," he replied.

"I need more than that," she cut him off. His head canted to one side. "Oh?" he asked.

"I need gold. I need soldiers. I need to do what must be done. And I need you to stay out of it," she said as her back stiffened.

His head jerked smoothly backwards. For the first time, he was at a loss for words.

"They're going to come for gold and steel, and you will turn a blind eye. And when they come clawing at your gate, screaming and begging for aid," she paused, locking eyes with him.

"I'll turn a deaf ear?" he offered humorously.

"You'll pour the blue fire on them and watch them burn," she stated.

His brow raised under his mask. He sat speechless for a few moments. She could hear his muffled breath.

"And what if I don't want to get involved?" he asked. It was a weak counterpoint, but he wanted to see where it would lead.

"It would seem you're already involved, seeing as they came for your head. It wasn't the first, and it won't be the last. Thanks for the package, by the way; I will add it to my soon-to-be growing collection," she replied.

"Fair. But from an alleged neutral position, why would the leader of the world bank…deny his constituents? Show preferential treatment to only one?" he asked, once again leaning in to watch her expression. Her eyes dropped as she thought. She leaned in once she gathered her thoughts.

"Because I'm the only one that matters now, and…I'm closing their accounts," she said. He let out a shocked chuckle that paused and restarted a few times.

"You don't have that kind of coin…" he said in questionable disbelief.

"Even if I did, of what interest is coin to the man who owns it all?" she retorted. He nodded in humoured agreement.

"What I have, coin cannot purchase. I have land—" she began.

"All land can be purchased…or taken," he interrupted coyly.

"Not from me," she replied. "As a generous tribute for his victory, Darros gifted King Archemond the Emerald Chain, an archipelago just outside of the rim of his harbour. The Chain, as you are aware, gives me unfettered access to your rear…" She paused for effect and to leak a smirk. The pun was not lost on him. "Yours and that of every kingdom to my south, east, and west. The Chain is a valuable component of my naval power, allowing me access to strike anywhere, at any time." She concluded, "A force that, I admit, I have allowed to slumber…until now."

"And when you lose this battle, and the sounds clawing at my gate are replaced with horns, drums, and retribution as they march against my domain…what then?" he asked, titillated but not fully convinced.

"You wake up from the dreadful dream you're having, for it is only in your dreams that I am capable of losing. And don't feign impotence, dear…Khazmyr is more than capable of defending its borders," she countered.

He sat back in his seat and pondered for a long moment.

"It's more than capable, but that's not what concerns me," he assured her, raising his hand to caress his covered chin. After careful consideration, he decided, "It's a little early in the game to push all your chips to centre."

"On the contrary, from where I'm sitting, we are late in the game indeed, and I mean to end it with a checkmate," she said. He smiled beneath the mask. Darros enjoyed bantering with someone who could effectively wordsmith.

"Why would you sacrifice such a strategic advantage? Am I allowed to ask what brought this about?" he asked.

"Blood. I've conceded too much for far too long. They took my mother, and all I did was grieve. Then Connerh, and I was inconsolable…"

"And now?" he couldn't help but interject. She reached into a satchel in the cabin, retrieved Bjorn's warning, and handed it to him through the window. He took it and read it.

"I see," he nodded and handed it back to her.

"Besides, I have other ways of asserting my will across the kingdom. I need not rely on man and machine any longer. Peace was my grandfather's way; I gave it a try, and look where it has gotten me. Peace only works when you're the one in control. I am cramped and surrounded on all sides by those who would see my demise. These savages only understand one thing, and that is spilt blood, and I, the humble servant of the north…aim to please," she snarled.

He broke eye contact for the first time and looked ahead. She attempted to study him intently, but the mask frustratingly concealed his thoughts. It served him and one of its many purposes well. He looked at her, his eyes betraying his full smile.

"I could get used to this new and improved Ioelena. You remind me of your mother in her early years, anxious to break free from the shadow cast by her father. Except your ambition is of your own will, not driven by immaturity fuelled by piss and vinegar. Well, perhaps a small amount of piss and vinegar remains…but in a good way. By the end of this, I will have to fashion a new nickname for you," he said, impressed by her.

"What do you mean *new*? What is it now?" she demanded with a frown, caught unaware. He chuckled to himself.

"Send me what you need. I'll await the next steps," he said after a brief pause. Her brows relaxed as she tried not to give way to the burst of joy that exploded within her.

"Very well," she replied, overly nodding her head. He signalled for his driver to approach. She did the same. The quiet stampede of horses grew louder as either side rushed to collect their respective leader.

"This…" he said, waving his hand around the field. "Let's revive the Golden Pass. Perhaps some things that die deserve a resurrection."

"Perhaps," she concurred.

"Lena…don't fly too close to the sun," he offered.

"I am the sun," she replied sharply before pausing. He stared at her.

"There's that vinegar," he said. Her head lowered.

"Message received," she obliged as a wave of humility overcame her.

"Better," he replied.

He offered a small wave as the carriages slowly pulled away from each other.

Hera raised her head from his lap, wiping her wet mouth with a hand.

"I'm sorry, Darros. I…" she started. He silenced her with a raised hand.

"My mind is preoccupied; the fault is not yours to own," he assured her, though it was of no consolation.

"Perhaps if I…" she motioned to lower her tunic and expose herself to him. He stopped her by resting his hand on hers.

"You have earned your tunic. It is yours to offer, but I will not demand it," he said with true concern in his voice. She smiled.

"I offer it freely to you, Darros; it is the least I can do, considering all that you have done for me." She slid her tunic down, but his expression remained, causing concern to appear in her own.

"Of course, I can feign refusal if that pleases you," she continued. He remained quiet. She looked down at his lap and smiled, suddenly reassured. "I see that it does."

"When we return, you'll have seven days to see to your affairs. Khazmyr will be closing its doors until this passes. Confer with Yuri to expel all outsiders; this is not the time to keep our enemies closest," he replied. She acknowledged his order. With business concluded, she lowered her tunic and lay back. He reached for his mask to remove it, but he first pulled the window to his cabin closed.

PART TWO

CHAPTER THIRTY

WINTER BERRIES

CONNERH

Six days inside a lavish, luxurious carriage could do a number on one's backside. Sadly for Connerh, his was neither of those things; it was old and smelly. His mobile penitentiary was plain in appearance, hand-painted in a black lacquer that had begun to crack and fade three years prior. His accommodation was intentionally non-descript, not with maltreatment in mind but concealment. It was bad enough that a carriage was involved in his transport in the first place, but at least this one looked second-hand...or fourth-hand.

Townsfolk often repurposed the refuse of royals to suit their needs, meaning it wasn't entirely unusual to see one travelling along the roadside, especially in this condition. While it would be sure to catch a glance or two, they would be fleeting in nature at best; reclaimed carriages, much like this one, would be reused to haul goods or animals, allowing them to remain protected from the elements. Judging by the smell, this one had most assuredly hauled swine at some point in its service. Ridding a space of the smell of pig faeces was hard work seldom volunteered for by the commoners in these parts. Its pungent, ammonia-forward odour lingered in fabrics and wood, stinging the interior bridge of the nose. Regardless, they'd sooner learn to ignore the odour than spend the time to clean it, especially when that energy could be better suited for other tasks. Hildeheim's people were as stubborn as they were tolerant of discomfort.

The interior was no more impressive than its shell. The upholstery had been scavenged down to its studs and bolts long ago, along with anything else that had enough value for trade. All that remained were the wooden base of the seats, a floor, and a roof that surprisingly lacked any holes or signs of mould. Dry splintering wood aside, someone had managed to smuggle him two large, overfilled pillows for sitting or sleeping. It was a kind gesture that forced him to dwell on his younger days – days when a twenty-six-year-old Connerh would never have extended such courtesy to his prisoner.

Although this was something quite a bit more complicated.

Had it not been for the quiet he was afforded, along with regularly paced breaks to stretch his aching back, he would have gone mad, or so he was convinced. Routines had changed now that they were travelling through a more populated area of the countryside, meaning the breaks had lessened and ambient noise increased. To make matters worse, in order to maintain a low profile, they now wouldn't stop until nightfall, which was at least three hours away. All things considered, it had been a successful exfiltration with little-to-no abnormal attention raised, albeit other than the random cursing of pedestrians forced to whiff them passing. The oft-creative combinations of swear words made him smile and chuckle quietly. At this point, his nose had adjusted to the smell; he'd dealt with worse before, on more than one occasion.

The crude remarks, however, though temporarily humorous in nature, served as a reminder of the reality of his situation. He was, in fact, a prisoner being marched to an unknown fate at the hands of the love of a past life. Connerh was not one for theatrics, but there was something inescapably poetic about his plight that aided his resignation. Of course she would send for him in a carriage. The one place they had spent untold hours together, though their method of passing the time was vastly different from now – and preferable. His cheeks blushed as a smirk slid across his lips. The carriages that had carried them were vibrant and lush, with comfort-aiding accoutrements that catered to every whim and desire of its youthful and ambitious passengers. There would be nothing but the best for Princess Ioelena and her loyal guard, Connerh Manthil.

A quiet laugh gently jostled his head.

Funny how we can never imagine the ghosts of our future's past, he thought.

But things change, and like the carriage, he too was now old, splintered, and in many ways, smelled of shit. The irony was not lost on him. His gaze dropped at the moment's reflection, and with a sombre smile, he sighed.

Lost in time within the pool of his mind's eye, he hadn't noticed that his surroundings had gone quiet. Though Connerh used the word, he'd truly forgotten its meaning. Even in the dead of night, when not a sound could be heard, his spear always sang to him. Its voice was a deep, low, subtle vibration, always present in the back of his mind, and it had been missing for six days. In the moments they took roadside breaks, when the horses stopped galloping and the men dispersed to relieve their bowels…in the void that is silence on a winter's mountainside, he agonised and struggled to adapt to its absence. The first night was the worst. Thankfully, the men were respectful enough not to ask questions after he shrieked and writhed for hours. To him, the silence was like a high-pitched, torturous ringing sound in his inner ear. He later offered the men an excuse for his behaviour that he was convinced no one believed — and rightfully so; they did not, but such things were not their concern. The daylight hours were far better. As fortune would have it, the commotion of the horses provided a new rhythm for his subconscious mind to process. Day by day, the silence grew ever more bearable.

His eyes focused. His head turned as he listened for audible cues. The sounds he could hear were sharper, enhanced in the fidelity of their individual notes. The caravan must have taken a rest. He lifted a shutter to peek outside, confirming his suspicions.

"Aye?" he shouted.

"Aye, it's clear," a near-distant voice replied. The voice belonged to Quo. The only one who seemed to give a damn that Connerh existed.

"Thank the maker," he muttered to himself as he slowly opened the door and stepped out. He instinctively arched backwards as he rooted himself in the snow-covered ground. He gave a loud sigh of relief as the cracks and pops of air escaping his spine came and went. Quo observed him with a smirk, still unsure of what to make of the strange passenger. He reached out and offered Connerh a piece of dried meat. He declined with a soft shake of the head and a raised palm.

"I've got to drain my trousers first." Connerh replied. Quo laughed.

"Aye, sir. You're better off going that way. I'm afraid whatever my commander had for supper isn't agreeing with his stomach, if you catch my meaning," Quo replied, pointing to the west.

"Aye. Clearing out the critters, is he?" Connerh asked. Quo responded with a high-pitched belly laugh.

"None of the men are standing downwind of him, if that tells you anything," he eventually replied. "I think I saw a few worms doing their damndest to flee."

Connerh eventually broke into soft laughter of his own. The boy's amusement was infectious. He found the young soldier, who drowned in his fur and oversized armour, reminiscent of himself at the ripe old age of eighteen and a day. There were still fragments of a glint just behind his eyes. It was obvious he'd seen death, but not by his own hand…not yet. The sombre thought eased Connerh's laughter, leaving a sliver of a smile behind. He nodded to the boy and began to walk westward. Quo watched for a moment, still smiling, before returning to his task of attending to the horses. It was in these moments that Connerh didn't feel like a prisoner. The men were scattered, some starting a fire, others having a smoke from a pipe, huddled in small groups for warmth. All of them collectively were not paying any attention to Connerh unless, of course, he required it. He could scamper off to relieve himself without as much as a single soldier batting an eye. It was a bit unorthodox and unsettling for Connerh. In some ways, he was rather offended that they didn't even seem to carry on a conversation about him.

Who's running this operation? he sometimes wondered.

Perhaps they don't know who I am, he thought to himself. He was a glimmer of his former self, the clean-shaven, chiselled appearance he once maintained long gone. His head, no longer shaved low, was covered in unruly, curly brown hair. A full, greying beard covered his face, reaching almost down to his chest. The possible reality that the men thought he was mentally ill set in, overtaking his expression.

Oh.

He gave a passing glance behind him and nodded to Quo, who was still watching him, though he pretended not to. Quo waved in return. After a short walk, he found the perfect tree upon which to answer the call of nature. Mid-relief, a scent captured his nose, forcing his eyes closed and turning his face towards its origin. The sweet, tarty aroma made his mouth water and his mind wander. His eyes shot open. They were in Aragath, he realised, a province just outside of the capital. His mind was flooded with a rush of recollected memories. It meant they were a half a day's journey away from their destination. If they left at dawn, they would arrive at the city centre by midday. There was a warm rush in the pit of his stomach, and he suddenly felt self-conscious about his appearance. His rational side argued the absurdity of the revelation, though it made little difference. The powerful, sweet aroma demanded his attention again, pulling his focus. After concluding his business, he wandered through the patch of forest in search of the source of the smell.

"Ah," he said aloud with a modest smile, bending down to harvest a bright red-and-blue berry from a fruit-covered bush. He ran his hand down his face and through his beard.

Her hand ran down his face, stopping at his bare chest as he sat up to stare out of the carriage window.

"Do you smell that?" he asked. She giggled playfully.

"Connerh, are you serious?" Her laughter persisted.

"Don't be crass. Seriously, how can you not?" His shoulders relaxed, and his head canted with disappointment. She laughed again. Lena sat up, covering her chest with a fur. She wafted the air into her nose with her hand.

"Oh! I do! Go on, now, and don't eat one until you get back," she demanded, kicking at him with her feet. He shook his head and began to dress himself as best he could. These carriages weren't made to be dressing rooms, much less bedrooms, but that would not deter them.

"I can't believe it's the season already," she continued. He pulled his boots on and opened the door to the cabin.

"Perhaps, if you let me breathe every now and then, we could track the time better." He gave her a devious smirk.

"Don't count on it; the heart wants what it wants," she replied.

"I don't think that was your heart I just left," he bantered.

"Wasn't it?" she questioned. Her eyes squinted with a glint, and her cheeks became rosy as her lips curled into the crevice of her cheek. He stopped, taking a moment to process her reply. His eyes lowered into the void, then the ground, and finally back at her. He smiled and exited the cabin, stepping down into his boots and wiggling his feet one at a time. His gaze wandered again before looking back at her, flushing in the cheeks. Her gaze remained, her legs wide and exposed, her heart on full display. He quietly snorted and shook his head as he walked away, intentionally taking his time.

"It'll only be a minute, Johann…" Connerh said to the coachman who watched him. Connerh looked down at the sound of Lena's giggling, her fingers giving him a show.

"…maybe five…or twenty," he giggled.

"Aye, sir," the coachman replied. Connerh's show extended as she reacted to his passive threat.

"On second thought, why don't you come down here and take a look at this door? It feels like it's loose." A shit-eating grin overwhelmed his face, increasing as Lena shrieked in response, rushing to close it before her indecency could be discovered. Connerh maniacally giggled.

"Aye, sir," the coachman said as he began to descend from his bench.

"Ignore that!" Her muffled shout could be heard through the cabin.

"Very well, Your Highness," the coachman paused midway down the ladder and returned to his post.

A short jaunt through the brush revealed its hidden treasure. Connerh dove to his knees, rabidly clawing at the fruit, spilling most of it on the snow-covered ground. Dots of blue peppered and stained the white powder as they flew all over the place. He shoved as many as he could into his mouth, the only limitation being the speed at which he could retrieve them.

"I knew you couldn't be trusted!" Lena's voice shouted from behind him. He curled over to glance behind himself, looking like a crazed madman in the process. His guilty laughter spat half-consumed berries and saliva out of his mouth and into the snow. Lena's giggle echoed in the brush as she hobbled back and forth in the snow towards him, trying to remain covered under a large bear fur. She collapsed onto him. He rolled over as she lay on his chest, snatching the berries out of his hand. They stayed there a moment until their laughter subsided.

"We should get back before…" he began, rolling to sit up. She pushed and pulled him back down.

"No, lie here a moment with me," she beseeched, looking up at the sunlight piercing the icy, frosted tips of the tree limbs above them. He resisted initially but quickly gave in. She raised her hand, turning it back and forth like she was reaching for the sky.

"Should I do it? I know we've kidded about it, but should I do it?" she asked, staring into a trance.

"What are you going on about?" Connerh shook his head with a frown.

"I can renounce my role, and we can go away. Maybe travel to the Chain, see all the isles… We'd stop and explore Khazmyr on the way, of course. It could be like this every day," she explained.

"I don't think the Queen Mother would approve," he laughed dismissively.

"I don't care if she approves," she decreed, not fully believing it herself. "Besides, Bjorn will be of age soon; he can take my place. That is my right as firstborn, is it not?"

He quietly listened to her argue with herself. A flock of ravens flew overhead, breaking the sunbeams as they passed through them, casting a flickering shadow across the two of them.

"If it will make you happy, then yes, I will go with you," he said. He raised his hand to his stubbled chin and began stroking it.

"It is decided, then. They may make it difficult for you to leave; we'll have to find a way to sneak away."

"I'm just a soldier among many. There's nothing special about me. I wouldn't be missed if I disappeared… Hell, if I had to, I could fake my death. If that's what it would take," he laughed.

"That's grim. I don't like when you joke about such things," she disapproved.

He snorted.

"I mean it. Promise me you'll never leave me…not for long. And if you *should* have to, promise me you'll always find your way back?" she demanded.

"I promise," he said without hesitation.

A scampering of footprints startled them to their feet. She quickly twirled around him. His bare, chiselled chest emanated steam, and his hands extended towards the danger, shielding her behind him. A small, rabid grey wolf snarled at them, positioning itself between them and the winterberry bush.

"I think that's his bush. I think we offended it," she offered in a whisper, peering around him. She discovered newfound confidence when she caught sight of the creature. She stepped out of Connerh's shadow.

"I'm going to do more than offend it," he replied as he sized up his opponent. He reached for his sword, but it was missing, as was his shirt, most of his clothes, and his armour in its entirety. His pants barely held on, as he had forgotten his belt.

"I think he means for us to turn back," she said with a frown.

"There is no turning back. It ends here," he snarled.

"Calm down, we just need to go. We can get more winterberries whenever we want; let's go, just back away slowly," she insisted, pulling at his arm. His eyes were fixed on the beast's, and his ears heard only muffled noises. Connerh explosively dove onto the wolf, wrestling with it in the snow. The beast snarled and growled as it writhed back and forth, trying its best to escape his hold and devour him.

"Connerh, stop it! Release him!" she shouted over and over again to deaf ears. The wolf managed to briefly escape his chokehold and bite him in the arm. Connerh shouted in pain, then anger. He dove at the beast again but fell short by a second, hitting the snow and rolling to his side. He quickly recovered and threw his body on top of the creature, regaining his grip on it once more.

"Stop it!" her scream shrieked, breaking through to Connerh. He and the wolf froze.

"Get off him, damn you! You'll kill him!" she shouted again.

The wolf whimpered, breaking free of Connerh's grasp and putting some distance between them.

"I didn't realise you were such an animal lover," Connerh said, surprised, nursing his wound. Lena stared the beast down. The powerful gallop of Whisper, Connerh's loyal horse, approached with the sound of snow compressing and crunching underfoot. The massive beast positioned itself between Connerh and the wolf, snorting and kicking at the creature.

"Calm down, boys. I think it learned its lesson," she rebuked them both. Connerh patted Whisper's hind leg, helping Lena climb and mount him. Connerh fake lunged at the Wolf, scaring it off. The circling ravens landed on nearby branches and squawked loudly. Lena met the gaze of one of them.

"We're going," she said with irritation in her tone.

"Sure, against my better instincts…but sure," Connerh answered, guiding Whisper towards the carriage. Lena maintained her stare until she could no longer see them.

Connerh re-emerged from the brush, berries in hand but otherwise distracted. He paused upon realising his escort was under attack from bandits who had stumbled upon the preoccupied men, hoping to make an easy score. Connerh took stock, exchanging a glance with Quo as he warded off blows from their attackers. He seemed in a little danger but capable. Connerh looked away, then down at his feet, choosing to ignore the conflict. He walked to the carriage, entered, and promptly closed the door behind him.

CHAPTER THIRTY-ONE

TETHERED

YURI

Joriah's hand cupped his ear and cradled the door. Its grains were rippled and porous to the touch, and its smell of charred wood and fresh lacquer immediately filled his nose. He eavesdropped on the voices engaging in conversation just on the other side. It was a welcome change from counting the dust particles that floated in the beams of light shining through the window. It was supposed to feel more homely here. It was supposed to make him feel as if he were not a prisoner. But a prison was still a prison, no matter the name it assumed.

He had been moved from the palace to a modest in size but luxurious home within the walls of the inner city just a few days ago. It was a smaller, exclusive region of Khazmyr that circled the palace, and those with elevated status called it home. The residents there were the sort of people so encumbered by wealth and/or political power that they felt it necessary to detach from everyday society. Khazmyr may have been a citadel for love and expression, but the natural forces of corruption and excess, when married with time, predictably formed a two-tiered society. It was a rose-coloured gem of little value.

The voices just on the other side were loud enough for him to discern the words spoken, but he fell short of being able to understand them. Still,

239

the words were beautiful to listen to. Native Khazmyrian was a smooth, slow, but enunciated language. Its hypnotic cadence enticed even those unable to speak it to mimic its essence. He backed away as a feminine voice moved closer to the door, signalling a break in the conversation. A gentle rasp quickly escalated into one forceful in nature.

Yuri frowned.

"Open the door!" she yelled with humoured impatience. Joriah complied, peaking from a crack before swinging it open fully. She smirked with a confused look. It was nice to see him, but duty and professionalism would temper her interaction, especially in such a public setting.

"Are you here to kill me?" he joked.

"Not today. Darros is loosening your leash. You'll no longer require a posted guard," she explained, motioning towards the two guards next to her.

"So, I am a free man? Was the mighty Darros impressed with my good behaviour?" he asked. She squinted her eyes and wobbled her head slightly.

"In a manner of speaking, sure. If that's what you need to tell yourself," she replied.

"What shall I do with this newfound freedom? Where can I go? Or perhaps the question should be, where can't I go? Khazmyr has been such a vast, veritable feast for the eyes. So much to see…only an eternity to see it," he said sarcastically.

"You could be dead like your counterpart," she replied. His mouth pulled away from his nose with a tilt of the head.

"Fair."

"You can go anywhere unless it is someplace you are not allowed. And as long as it is within the city walls. And while not officially a stated rule, it is strongly advised against wandering around alone after sunset," she added. He frowned.

"How will I know if it's someplace I'm not supposed to go?" he asked.

"You will be given…sharp…reminders, no doubt," she smirked.

"So, I'm not really free. The jail has just gotten larger," he remarked.

"I said that already: Darros is loosening your leash. It means you have *more* freedom, but…" she replied.

"The leash remains."

"Exactly. Still more favourable conditions than being dead, if you ask me," she said.

"Still no news on when I shall be released?" he asked. She looked at him with curiosity.

"In a sense, Joriah died shortly after we first met in a failed assassination attempt. It was Merith who was born that day, and it is Merith who stands before me. A *permanent* resident of Khazmyr. You were given a new life, and yet you long to return to being Joriah. A dead man on the cold marble floor of the Coliseum, drowning in a pool of his blood," she observed with a frown.

He averted his eyes. Hers dropped to the corner, ensuring those who were in earshot were listening.

"You may return to your barracks," she said. The guards posted at the door acknowledged her command and marched away. Her gaze returned to Joriah.

"Come. Let us prepare for your exploration of Khazmyr," she said, pushing him inside and closing the door behind them. She rested her head on the door, tilting her ear against the grain. She abandoned her post when all went quiet.

"I'm sorry. Someone is always listening. Always watching. I must maintain appearances," she apologised.

He remained in a dazed state of reflection.

"What?" she asked, observing his stupor. He snapped out of it, looking at her.

"Did you mean it?" he asked.

"Of course," she responded unapologetically.

"So, what did you apologise for?" he asked, raising his voice, all the more confused.

"I very much meant the words. I just would have chosen different ones," she assured him. He was perplexed, and it showed.

He began to speak but stopped.

"I don't understand," she prompted.

"I don't see how rewording would change the sentiment. I am very much Joriah, and I will always be Joriah, regardless of what some entitled..." he fussed.

She raised her finger and flared her eyes to quiet him. He lowered his voice.

They were always listening.

"Regardless of what some entitled psychopath thinks," he continued, baring his teeth.

"You are who the higher power decrees you are. Was it not your mother who gave you your name? Did you choose it, or did she assign it to you? Darros is your higher power now, and he has chosen your new name," she said. His eyes squinted as he shook his head.

"That... What? No...I mean, yes, but I accepted it. I could have changed it later in life, but I accepted it, and so it remains!" he hissed with the intensity of a shout.

She disagreed.

"No."

"What do you mean, no?!" he fussed.

"If I wiped the records of Joriah, your original name, so no proof was left that it ever existed, and if I commanded the world to refer to you only as Merith, would not Merith be your name then?" she pressed, eyes squinting. He frowned.

"My name is Joriah, a name given to me by my mother and father. The name of his father before him. It will always be Joriah," he demanded, his face red with irritation.

She nodded slowly as he spoke. A grin crept onto her face.

"Always remember that," she instructed, catching him off guard.

His face softened as he understood the lesson.

"They will try to shape you, to mould you, into who they want you to be. And while we may play along for appearances so they are unaware of our true intent...never forget who you are," she continued.

He smiled gracefully, then walked over to a shelf. He retrieved a sharp fragment of clay that he'd hidden behind several random items. Its point was stained in red. He stared at it for a moment before handing it to her. She took it, smiling deeply as she inspected it.

"Good. Good," she nodded continually, handing it back to him. "Keep it. In case you forget where to look."

He accepted, returning it to its hidden place.

"Make sure you tend to it twice a day. You don't want it to get infected...otherwise, we'll have to chop it off," she said as a matter of fact. He grimaced, staring at her lack of emotion.

"Can you at least pretend that it would bother you to do so?" he asked.

She gave a half-hearted attempt. It was a look more comical than fearful. Even she eventually started laughing.

"We'll work on it," he said.

"Look, I have a lot to tend to today. You are free to roam, but try not to get in trouble on your first day of freedom."

"Not freedom," he quietly spoke over her, folding his arms. She rolled her eyes and continued.

"I put my neck out for you, and I'd like to keep it attached. Perhaps, later, I can give you a tour of what you have not seen by then?" she offered with a smile, her tone softening on the personal note.

"I would be delighted," he replied. She flashed a brief, tender smile.

"Try to avoid the markets. You'll get sucked in and end up spending all day there. There's a strategy to navigate it and get out while still retaining coin in your pocket," she said as she opened the door.

"But I don't have any coin," he said, motioning to his pockets.

"It was an expression. You are a guest of Darros; you don't need any coin," she replied.

"Noted. I guess I'll see you later, Yuri," he bid, waving with his fingers as she walked out.

"I will see you later…Merith," she replied with a devious smirk. He shook his head. He hated that fucking name. He didn't even *look* like a Merith. But, of course, it wasn't about suitability, was it? It was about control – the constant reminder of who had it and who did not.

It didn't matter, he thought as he stepped into the doorway and watched her leave.

It was only temporary.

He didn't linger in the inner city. It was plain, boring, and unnervingly quiet. Towering white buildings covered with gold accents and manicured ivy dominated the affluent quarter. While the structures varied in scale, they shared a sterile, cloned appearance. Even the meticulously crafted stone tiles beneath his feet were uniform, lacking any natural irregularity. The perfection was almost as unsettling as the eerie silence that persisted. Sure, there were servants carrying clay vessels of water from the wells to their masters' homes, but their dialogue was always brief, and their eyes rarely left the ground. Everything felt sanitised.

Where are the women and children? he questioned.

Much was known about Khazmyr, but even that did not scratch the surface of what was unknown. The outward appearance of opulence, excess, and fame dominated its public image, much to the financial delight of its monarchy, but underneath lay something ominous. It was a missing puzzle piece whose outline was carved into the picture. He just couldn't find where it was hiding.

Hours passed, and Joriah still found himself wandering the outer city, listening and observing. The buildings here were made of sandstone and displayed natural signs of wear, a departure from earlier. The busy streets varied per district, some made of cobblestone and others gravelled. They, too, were well-travelled but still clean. The low rumble of voices settled like a morning fog. The voices melded together, making the individuals near-indistinguishable except for the obvious tourists shouting in their native tongues. They were all the same. Blushed cheeks, extremely pale or dark-skinned. Loud, insistent in their expectations and inconsiderate of local customs. Joriah scoffed at them as if he were a local, even while he defiantly ate his plum. He had acquired the sweet, round fruit from a street vendor and had begun eating it immediately, much to the dismay of the man who had given it to him. He'd quickly learned that eating in the streets was frowned upon here, but he didn't own a care to lend. In transparency, a part of him found pride in his miniature rebellion.

More hours passed, and the sun began to set.

He'd been looking for the slums – where the real people must have been kept. Every city had slums. The poor, the unfortunate souls, the seedy, the underbelly. It went by many names, depending on the station of the person you asked. The higher their station, the more disconnected from reality they were, often projecting their own desperate need to display pity for *those less fortunate*. As if acknowledging their existence offered penance for being successful.

But he could not find them.

The start of his journey originated in the centre of the city: he travelled north, then in a clockwise pattern for the rest of the day. But there was no underprivileged class to be found. It was…unbelievable. Literally. He refused to accept that an entire city this large was that prosperous.

Had Khazmyr cracked the code?

And if it had, why wasn't every kingdom mirroring every ounce of what it took to get there?

It wasn't adding up. For that matter, where was the depravity Khazmyr was so known for? Where were the brothels? The whores and nightcrawlers? A day of walking and not a single catcall or proposition.

Where were the vendors providing delicate delights said to enhance one's experience of reality? What of the street vendors openly selling illicit concoctions or the laced alcohol said to enhance pleasure? He frowned. Perhaps it was the Darros-provided garb he was wearing? He thought. Was it a sign to them that he was an outsider? Not that his sunburnt white complexion had a chance to blend in with the sea of olive, but even if that were the case, the whole world knew of Khazmyr as the vice capital of the world. Why would they hide it from him? Let alone to such an extent…

He took notice of the sun setting and decided to double back. Yuri had warned him about staying out this late, and her voice played back in her mind. His pace slowed as her words came to a conclusion. He would be defiant in this, too. What would they do? Arrest him? A smirk graced his dimpled cheek.

It wasn't but thirty minutes before a dark purple sky shadowed the city. Torches and oil lamps activated, illuminating like fireflies in the forest. The number of people roaming the streets began to dwindle as the chilled sea breeze rolled in, dropping the temperature.

A child's voice startled him. He hadn't seen or heard one the entire day. It was distant, predictably coming from behind a dark street. He stood at the entrance, talking himself into it. Talking himself into doing the stupid thing. It was how every robbery or murder story started. Something enticing or prompting of chivalry lured the dumb man down the dark alley, and just as he got close, it all went black. He'd heard the stories before. Laughed at them. Insulted the intelligence of every last single one of them. And now he was that man.

His pace hurried as he scampered down the dark path. The voice multiplied into many. They were speaking the native tongue, attempting to be quiet but failing, as children do. Oh, how he wished he knew how to speak the language – to understand it, at least. He checked his surroundings often, not that there was much to see. The soft glow of orange light flickered against the dark buildings. Fortunately, the moon was high and bright; it aided his eyes but made the trek all the more terrifying. He could see his breath softly illuminated in the night air. Khazmyr was tropical by day, but the nights were cold at this time of year.

The voices were at their loudest. Only one more corner to round.

"Hey!" a man shouted at him, intercepting him from around the corner he sought to turn. The voices stopped.

"You shouldn't be out!" the man shouted. Joriah frowned. Most people tried to lower their voices at night, but this man seemed to be making an effort to be as loud as possible. Joriah's head canted.

"How, uhh…" he made a show of trying to translate his words. "Palace? I am guest of Darros. How find?" he continued.

He resisted shaking his head at himself. He sounded like an idiot on mental replay.

"Palace this way!" the man shouted again. A large door closed from around the corner.

"Come. I'll take you!" he continued, grabbing Joriah's arm and leading him away.

Joriah's eyes lingered at the corner.

The orange glow had gone.

CHAPTER THIRTY-TWO

DESTINY

LENA

Many years ago...

"Your hair is growing so long," Queen Ioelena remarked.

The brush in her hand was of sentimental value, its jade handle ornamented with gold that contrasts starkly against ebony bristles. It was far older than either of them, and its history made it more valuable than most of the items in the room combined.

"This brush has touched the scalps of some of the most famous and powerful women in our family. Queens, the whole lot of them," she continued with a reflective smile. Egress' white hair flowed through the bristles like water over a riverbed. Their gowns were nearly matching, though the queen's was smaller; even at seventeen, Egress towered over her. Added to it was the fact that the queen was on the shorter side for a human, though her often-fiery nature more than compensated for it. Still, Egress made every attempt to diminish her stature out of respect for her aunt. She sat on a small velvet-covered stool, knees nearly tucked under her chin, that brought her head to just the right height.

The mirror they both shared was made of glass. Its image was far more detailed and sharper than the polished brass to which Egress was accustomed. She felt odd seeing such an accurate reflection of herself...it made her feel bashful. Her eyes had never looked bluer and her skin never paler, like she'd just applied a fresh splash of powder with a hint of blush. She could barely maintain eye contact with herself, having never realised the intensity of her own stare.

"I want you to come live with me," the queen said as she brushed

Egress' hair calmly. "You belong here, not in a cave. I love your mother and father, but you are greater than this, yes? We are more than just what we were born as."

Egress stared at her reflection. The longer her gaze lingered, the more her image blended with the queen's in her own mental mirage. Her focus wandered as her eyes did.

"You could just command it so, and it would be," Egress said, lowering her head. Ioelena gently tugged on Egress' hair, pulling her head up. A correction of posture.

"I could, yes. This is true. But I want *you* to want it," she replied. Egress frowned and turned in place.

"But I do want it…it's just…" her voice trailed, her head again opting to sink. Ioelena lifted her face by the chin.

"But what?" she asked, looking into her eyes from the bridge of her nose. Egress' eyes shifted back and forth. Between the truth and the softened version. She could not find the strength to tell either.

Ioelena's hand transitioned from the girl's chin to her cheek. She caressed it and sighed, allowing her eyes to drift to Egress' chin.

A queen's gaze never touches the floor, she would always yell at her daughter, Lena. A lesson, it seemed, that she would also have to instil in Egress. Ioelena released her hair and set the brush down in front of the mirror. Egress stared at the back of her head. She looked just like Lena from behind, albeit shorter and older. Streaks of grey brilliantly painted her silken black hair.

"I know it can be difficult to choose between what you feel is expected of you and what you want to do," the queen began. She turned her head sideways, her gaze pointing upwards. "And I would be lying if I were to tell you that, at times, as queen, you must fulfil what is required of you over that which you desire. However, what do you do if there are two things that contradict one another, yet both are expected of you? How do you choose?" Ioelena asked.

She turned to face Egress, eager to watch her mind work it out. Her eyes tightened as she observed every wince, every arch and depression of the brow. She knew Egress' tells. A slight twitch above the cheek and a pinch of her right lid meant she knew the truth but didn't know what lie to tell. Ioelena chuckled.

"You have a terrible habit of trying to please, but that is not what I am asking you to do," she said, lifting the girl's face again.

Egress' mouth opened, paused, then closed.

"Your mother compels you under such guilt…" Ioelena said.

Egress nodded in agreement after a delay, and her head began to drop. She fought the desire in a losing battle. She quickly raised her head as Ioelena reached for her chin. The queen smirked.

"I'm not asking you to choose between me and her; I'm asking you to choose between your mother and your future," she said sharply. "Yes, it is true…the choice is yours. You can live the entirety of your existence a simple giant among the mountain peaks, doing it is what giant folk do…and will continue to do until the last one breathes," she continued, the muscle above her left cheek twitching. Egress tracked Ioelena's eyes. "Or you can usher all of Hildeheim, middle, little, and giant folk alike, into a new era. It is time for the old way to pass."

"But what of the princess? What of Lena?" Egress blurted out in confusion. She quickly raised her hand and covered her mouth, realising the impropriety. A jet of air rushed out of Ioelena's nose, then a smirk. Egress' gaze dropped rapidly to just below the horizon, but a blink restored it above. Her head shook before the words could come out of her mouth.

"Lena will be queen for a time. Perhaps. Perhaps not at all. Regardless, your natural lifespan will outstretch hers," Ioelena replied. Her head shifted back and forth, between reality and desire as she considered in a lower register, "We must be prepared for all outcomes. It is clear to me that my children have no desire to rule. They have too much of their father in them. They find comfort in *this* life." Ioelena gestured to their surroundings. "Complacency leads to being tossed around by the current, and that simply won't do for the future that is coming." A barely there sigh. "I suppose I should take part of the blame. In my effort to spare them from the life I had as a child…well, perhaps I over-provisioned when they were young, and their father, the King, was of no help in that regard. He was so enamoured by the little ones, he gave them whatever they wanted. It was no small feat for a giant to have middle folk for offspring. It is quite rare indeed. He used to fawn over them like I had gifted him a litter of pups." She released a scornful laugh. "I suppose I should be thankful they looked like him. I can only imagine the scandal…and he always could have dashed them on the rocks, as was the custom for his generation. He was a good father. You know, he could hold them in one hand when they came out. Especially Lena; she was so small," she giggled with a softer inflection.

Egress offered a smile.

"Come now, stand," she said, lifting Egress' hand. She took a good look at her niece. They held hands as they faced each other. "It's not wrong, you know. To desire comfort. It is a basic need, after all. Our bodies crave it, and our minds prefer it, but comfort should be transitory. It should come and go, like tides or breezes on the wind. Otherwise, both the body and mind atrophy, and you become weak." She motioned to her own head and chest. "A leader who is both perceived and proven weak is murdered in the streets for all to see." She made a slicing motion across Egress' stomach. "Be a leader whom they try to kill in secret. Because they are afraid to face you." Her upper lip tugged in the air. "You must remember where you came from, but always know where you are going. It's what my mother always told me. I never quite understood it when I was your age. I mean, I thought I did, but I didn't. Not really," she said, opting to run her hands through Egress' hair. "It means tradition and legacy are good to remember, to honour, just like this brush. It should remind you of the past," she explained as she retrieved it, holding it up for them both to focus on. "But you wouldn't let it make decisions for you, would you?"

Egress thought for a moment, then shook her head. Ioelena nodded.

"That's right," she whispered. Peering into Egress' wandering eyes, Ioelena asked, "Do you understand my words?"

She nodded.

"I do. My mind is just filled with conflict. I know your words are true, and they inspire me. I just…" Egress began, forming the sentences slowly.

"You need time. And that is understandable; I expected as such. Which is why I am not looking for an answer today. I only ask that you dwell on it," the queen replied, patting off the dust on the girl's dress with her hand.

Egress gave a sigh of relief, and her face softened into a smile.

"Speaking of time, I have something for you. Wait here just a minute," Ioelena requested, scampering off into an adjoining room. Egress took the moment of isolation to look at the ground, as if to ensure it was still there. Her eyes pulled towards the mirror. She was already examining herself as her eyes met their own reflection. She grew more comfortable with it by the moment. She looked like a royal portrait of herself, and she was growing fond of it.

Young laughter and mischief exploded into the room as the large white doors burst open. Lena's laughter quickly subsided as she caught sight of Egress. Her expression flashed between irritation and amusement.

"Playing dress up again?" she asked, a cold demeanour revealing itself before being suppressed. Egress' focus dropped from the mirror. Her expression blanked. Connerh laughed, unaware of the dialogue in the room as he entered.

"Hello, Egress," he greeted as he caught his breath. His hands naturally drew to Lena's waist as he approached her. "You look stunning."

Lena looked back at him from out of the side of her eyes, then back to Egress. Egress blushed, chuckled, and stared at the ground.

"Come on, it looks as if we're intruding," Connerh said to Lena.

"This is my home, therefore I could not be intruding, could I? I am not the guest here," she replied. Connerh's smile faded as he read the tension correctly. Their spines straightened as they caught a glimpse of Ioelena as she re-entered the room. Her jaw locked at the sight of Connerh. His hand fell from Lena's waist, quickly but discreetly, pulling him down into a kneel.

"Mother," Lena said, her eyes dropping below her mother's gaze but above the ground. She eventually gave in to the unspoken pressure and curtsied. Egress' head slowly raised as Ioelena's hand rested on her shoulder. Lena's brow furrowed. Another jab at her cousin sat comfortably on the tip of her tongue, but she held it in, instead electing to run her tongue over her gums.

"She looks beautiful, doesn't she?" Ioelena half-asked, half-demanded a compliment. Lena opened her mouth as a scoff escaped poorly disguised as a laugh. Her tongue traced her upper lip.

"She does," she offered. It was as insincere as it looked.

"Jealousy will be your undoing, child," Ioelena snapped back. Lena's focus dropped. She refused to let the comment sink in. She smiled instead.

"I'll add it to the list of my failures, Your Majesty," she rebutted with a smirk. Ioelena laughed aloud.

"That will be all," the queen replied as she presented a box to Egress. She paused as Lena and Connerh's departure delayed, then instructed, "Close the door behind you."

That one hurt. Lena's brow furrowed again as her head dropped fully.

"Come, my love. I will share the news with someone who cares," she said, grabbing Connerh's hand. Connerh quietly obliged, bowing once more before the queen.

Ioelena's jaw clenched as she glared at him.

The door closed with a slam, leaving an echo to reverberate in the room.

"Promise me one thing," she requested.

Egress quickly nodded.

"Don't let them marry you off. Not before you're ready," she concluded.

Egress frowned involuntarily but agreed while Ioelena stared at the door.

"She'll be killed in the streets," she added quietly.

CHAPTER THIRTY-THREE

In Holding

Connerh

It smelled like a blacksmith's workshop, a pungent mixture of rusty iron and rancid oil. The underground facility had not seen prisoners in over a century, let alone a groundskeeper.

It'd seen better days. Months. Decades, even.

Once an inescapable sanctuary for the condemned, its now-brittle hinges lacked the strength to support doors; mould and creatures occupied the places and spaces prisoners once did. Abandoned to time, deep below Castle Corvidae, it was truly an ideal location for a secret captive. Although it felt impromptu at best, judging by the lack of preparation of the site, or perhaps his celebrity hadn't retained its value. The possibility stung a little. Not for entitlement reasons, of course…it was just, he'd sacrificed everything for Hildeheim…for her. Still, the sting hurt less than his back. The mat he lay on, filled with decomposed straw, served little purpose now other than as a dust cover for its metal frame.

His eyes lingered on the thick, nearly opaque spiderwebs that clung tightly to darkened corners, still inhabited by their creators as they awaited a meal. Frayed edges paired with patches of dry rot, signalling the journey through time the linens had endured. Their sweet, mouldy aroma betrayed their disrepair, adding to the layered ambience of ruin that simply refused to be ignored.

And yet Connerh found a certain charm to it.

The absence of sound this far down left a ringing void in its wake, heightening his senses to near-uncomfortable levels. His heart beat like a ceremonial drum, his gastric activity and breath a windstorm over turbulent seas.

It was another reminder of how loud the quiet could be.

The hours of isolation were otherwise kind to him, allowing his mind to wander through time with no particular emotion as its guide, a sort of free thinking to which he was unaccustomed. He found it relaxing not to be driven by the tempo of the day's anxieties…or regret. To not seek a cure for indecision, nor have to consider the needs of others.

Was this what true freedom felt like? Death?

He couldn't be sure if he was unsettled by the parallel or drawn to the peace of it.

It was too early to tell. Isolation without the white noise of life was, indeed, different, but almost unpalatable. Even withstanding all that he'd been through – including being in the current moment, this penance of the last ten years, if it really was penance – felt too easy.

The remaining residue of sadness directed his thoughts to Rose, springing his body, hands, and head into action. He could no longer stand to lie down, opting to pace within his doorless cell instead. Being apart from her was not new, but the depths of his confinement made him feel powerless. Unable to come to her aid should she need it, deaf to her cries for help had he the power to hear over great distances.

What had he agreed to? She needed him. His instincts kicked in. It was time to break free. He'd broken out of prisons more sophisticated than this, and those weren't encumbered by rust and decay. He and Rose would need to come up with a new plan, one less…sudden. He would transition out of their lives.

But having ripped off the bandage, would reintegrating himself only make it worse in the long run? His head dropped into his hands.

A noise paused him in his tracks, turning him in place.

The sharp notes of metallic footsteps rang out like bells on a winter morning, growing ever louder with their approach. He needed a distraction, and it seemed the universe was aware. He'd thank the gods, or God, had he had the time to find faith. He used to say that hope was for those who could quietly count the hours of their misery. It was a luxury not afforded him – until now.

It didn't matter.

No god would claim him anyway.

He knew at least one existed. He felt the cold shoulder, the gaze of a disapproving parent watching from the corners of his life that he could not face. Always out of reach. Too busy to talk but not to take.

A man's voice with a formal cadence spoke words to the guard, pausing for a muffled reply. A door opened briefly, then closed. The footsteps continued towards him. Connerh peered through remnants of the bars to his cell, as if he was being contained by them, his eyes affixed to the last door that separated him from his visitor. His saviour…

From himself.

It was in an existential moment like this when his spear first appeared to him. When fear of losing grip in the absence of faith was at its peak. When even the impedance of death felt like torture instead of release. It was then, like a beacon over foggy seas, that the spear descended from the sky, filling the recesses of his mind with a warmth that made his eyes water.

Even it had abandoned him.

His gaze fell as his eyes streamed a steady flow of tears. He stood, limp. His internal symphony of chaos deafened Elarion's approach. His greeting. His run. The sound of his embrace. Connerh's heavy eyelids shuttered as the tears trekked down his cheeks, as Elarion's warmth engulfed him.

Elarion was tempted to use his abilities to take Connerh's sadness away, as he knew he could, but he did not sense agony. His soul was merely shedding the pain it had held on to, and so Elarion waited a few minutes before intervening.

Connerh smiled deeply as Elarion's abilities soothed him. An involuntary inhale took in the elf's signature scent, anchoring Connerh back in the moment.

"Thank you," he whispered. Elarion nodded in reply with a smile.

Connerh broke away to sit on his cot, his eyes fixated on the ground.

"I've laughed when I should have cried, felt nothing when I should have writhed… Who knew it was peace and quiet that would break me?" he laughed to himself. Elarion folded his lips into a mournful smirk.

"Sometimes, heavy hearts need to hear their own echo to know they still work," Elarion replied. Connerh snorted bursts of air out of his nose as he resumed quietly weeping.

"Always so damned philosophical," Connerh said, finally merging into laughter.

He took a deep breath, focusing on hatred and anger.

He exhaled.

His tears dried.

His composure returned with a smile.

Elarion frowned as he sensed Connerh's technique for self-regulation.

"That is a dangerous game you play," he lectured, now leaning against the wall. His arms folded up into his chest. "Secrets, though unacknowledged, still exist. As do their tolls."

"Couldn't you just tell a joke about passing wind from time to time?" Connerh replied, causing himself to laugh.

"I suppose I could learn a few," Elarion acknowledged after finally giving way to a smirk. "Sometimes it's easier to offer a phrase than to regale with stories of the lifetimes I've lived." Breaking his focus, he said, "I can understand how it could come across as a lecture."

Connerh internally kicked himself, wearing it on his face.

"No, I…I've always appreciated your comfort and words. It's just hard to remember how old you are when you look younger than…than me now," Connerh replied.

Elarion laughed as he dwelled on it and asked rhetorically, "When did that happen?"

"Wait, I thought you had to have skin contact to use your abilities," Connerh mentioned with his brow raised. His thoughts had independently chosen to relive the last few minutes.

"I used to, up until somewhat recently," Elarion replied.

Connerh's eyes widened.

"Not many know. I'd like to keep it that way," Elarion quickly appended.

"Of course," Connerh replied. His thoughts pulled his lips into a grin, and conjuring the most unsavoury thoughts possible, he continued, "So, can you read my mind now?"

"It is a door that I have to open; it does not flow freely. And judging by your expression, I will refrain from doing so," Elarion said, joining Connerh in deep laughter. Elarion watched his old friend bask in levity. It was good to see him again. He'd lost muscle. Thinner but still athletic. He looked like a wild man; his hair was unkempt, his beard was full, streaked with grey.

Still, he looked worn but strong. Like an ox bound to the plough.

"What's it like? I know I've asked before, but is it different now?" Connerh pressed. Elarion sat on the ground, folding his legs.

"A little, though it is no easier to put into words. It's like…your immediate thoughts are at the forefront. Anything else has to be found. Like a room with many doors leading to more rooms. Like a maze," he started.

Connerh focused on the concept.

"If you're not careful, you can literally lose yourself in someone's nightmares. That is why touch is so important – it creates a physical tether to the real world," he added reflectively. Connerh frowned at the assertion.

"Like swimming with a rope around your waist tied to the dock. That makes sense," Connerh added.

"Exactly," Elarion replied.

"Again, I am envious while at the same time…not. I'm already a prisoner of my own nightmares; I'm in no rush to add someone else's," he said, ending in a chuckle. They both quietly recalled separate memories. After a moment, Conner prodded, "I feel inclined to ask…are there any other new abilities?"

"A few," Elarion blushed with a nonchalant shrug.

"Any that could explain what the hell I'm doing here?"

"I'm afraid not. Though I have my suspicions," Elarion hedged as Connerh danced around asking about her. "Unfortunately, I have not been able to consult with Lena either. Her attendant reports that she is currently away from the castle and should return in the next few days. It would seem your arrival was earlier than expected, as she intended on receiving you herself."

Connerh acknowledged the response under his breath, looking at his hands, then verbally replied, "And how is she?"

"Many years have passed since we last spoke. She did not take well to your absence and, I fear, took comfort in the wrong individuals, orbited the wrong circles," he said, pausing. "My caution was also not well received."

"I'm sorry," Connerh offered.

"It's not needed," Elarion countered.

Connerh sighed loudly instead of protesting. It would've been a useless cause.

There was a moment of silence between them.

"How did you know I was here?" Connerh asked. Elarion squinted as he thought for a moment, wrestling with disclosure.

"There are those from afar who have an interest in your future. Those who do not recognise doors…or place such limitations upon themselves," he replied with a curl of upper lip. Connerh's head tilted.

"What?" was all he could manage to reply with, his face was covered with curious confusion.

"I wouldn't know where to begin other than to say you have investors in high places that would rather remain…anonymous," Elarion replied.

"So, all the power with no limitations other than the desire for…no accountability? Sounds about right," Connerh remarked.

"That would be a fair assessment," Elarion shrugged.

"It seems we have a lot to discuss when I am free of…this." Connerh tossed his hands up both physically and metaphorically. His voice dropped in volume for the morally grey suggestion, and he asked, "Can't you just read someone's thoughts to figure out what's going on?"

Elarion frowned and replied, standing, "Yes. I could."

Connerh made a show about his sigh.

"I don't believe you know what you're asking," Elarion countered.

"I could tether you to the physical world," Connerh pitched.

"It's not about fear," Elarion laughed.

"Then what is it? What if it were life or death? Or the enemy?" Connerh's rebuttal felt desperate. Elarion shook his head.

"These men are not my enemy. And it isn't," Elarion replied.

"I don't see what the issue is," Connerh argued.

"To share a telepathic connection…" Elarion began, pausing at his disbelief at Connerh's misunderstanding. He took for granted that humans had no true concept of the encounter. Continuing carefully with a gesture, "…is an intimate experience."

Connerh's expression of frustration began to fade.

"And to force an experience would be similar to…" Elarion paused mid-thought. There was a subtle horror that lingered in his expression. He shook his head.

"I…I didn't know…" Connerh quickly interjected.

"In your world, the effects of power are bound by mortality. Everything is always fleeting…continually reducing from where it started," Elarion replied. He shook his head again. Ensuring he was being clear, he continued, "In mine, there is a different connotation."

"I'm sorry…" Connerh offered.

"I understand your desire for reassurance; it is only natural. Fortunately, there are layers to such abilities…" Elarion replied. "There is something else, although I do not know a human word for it…but just as you display emotions despite not sharing the cause for them, there is a telepathic equivalent. The mind puts on a similar spectacle, and there is often much to gather. Even now, you mentally scream at me, with your fears, concerns, and desires." Elarion felt it cathartic to explain.

Connerh focused on him, overcome with curiosity.

"I feel I have enough information by means of this to say that there will be a trial of sorts. I would imagine for reasons purely rooted in appearances, but I can't know for sure until I am in Lena's presence," he conceded. Connerh's head tilted with a thought, and Elarion replied to Connerh's unuttered thoughts. "There are limitations of range with my abilities." He noticed Connerh's puzzled expression. "Humans are always screaming, like children lost in the dark. I could almost hear what it was you were going to say," he answered another unspoken question.

Connerh shook his head as he marvelled and said, "I don't know how it is I'm able to call you friend or brother. I hope you know that I view it as a special privilege, though even now, I cannot fully comprehend it."

"You flatter me," Elarion brushed off the compliment, thinking Connerh was only trying to butter him up.

"No, I'm serious. Sometimes I look at you as a traveller passing through a foreign land. You try so hard to blend in, but it's clear you don't belong here. You're better than us. You're destined for a future we will never see," Connerh continued, pulling first a frown to Elarion's face, then finally, his eyes towards the ground. "I do not know where it is you are going, but I know it is long after me. Just promise you'll remember your time here."

Connerh spoke with a reflective eloquence only the heart could conjure. Elarion's large eyes immediately watered. Connerh hadn't tried to elicit such a response and only spoke in the way he was moved.

Elarion thought on his words, finally nodding in agreement.

"We have a long journey together, after which I will continue to watch over your kin for as long as the aeons allow." Elarion frowned.

They leaned in, touching heads to one another.

"For all these years, I've maintained your innocence. Or at least concluded that you did what you felt must be done, so there must have been just cause for your actions. However, if there is to be a trial, then I will remain and aid your defence. But if I am to ensure…" he said, hesitating to ask the question directly. He finally looked up, realising Connerh had his hand held out towards him. His expression was blank. Cold. Resigned.

Elarion nodded. They were on the same page. Connerh smirked.

"I suppose you don't need this nowadays," Connerh observed, lowering his hand.

Elarion reached out and grabbed it.

"No, but I prefer it this way," he explained, cupping their hands with his remaining one.

"Go on. It's all there," Connerh nodded with a smirk.

There was a hidden cue of embarrassment wrapped in understanding. If thererewas anyone alive to share his most intimate emotions, thoughts, and memories with, there would be no better candidate. And suddenly it clicked.

"I understand," Connerh repeated.

Elarion offered a small smile of appreciation.

They locked eyes. Elarion took a deep breath and released a sigh that carried on longer than was considered normal. He stood motionless as Connerh melted in place. His muscles relaxed; his anxiousness faded. It was a unique feeling when Elarion used his gifts. The nature with which he used them was always delicate, but despite layers of caring insulation, it could not fully mask his mental probing. The skin-to-skin contact and the embraced hands added a physical grounding that amplified the sense of a skilled practitioner, like a surgeon who took the time to prepare, to sanitise, to discuss his methods with the patient before making the first incision.

Connerh studied Elarion's face. With no distinguishable pupils, it was hard to know if he was actually looking at Connerh, off to the side, or some other place. He thought to ask. It was an unknown variable that made Connerh smirk. The concept of a being exercising power like this from the shadows, unknown to their victim, was extremely unsettling. Connerh frowned at the thought.

Elarion's cheek and eyes twitched randomly as he perused Connerh's memories. The reaction washed Connerh's face of its expression, and he eventually looked away. In times past, he and Elarion viewed the memory together in a shared experience that seemed to be happening in real time. Now he watched as Elarion made the journey alone. He felt a wave of nausea overcome him. The feeling of not being in control was overwhelming, like being drained of your blood and unable to stop it, or falling into an endless pit while submerged in darkness.

"Enough!" Connerh shouted, ripping away from Elarion's grasp. It was a subconscious reaction burdened by fear.

He felt Elarion's grip weaken. He blinked.

"I'm sorry. For where we are headed, I needed you to understand that power comes with a price," he continued. His head dropped as he reflected on what he saw.

"A fitting metaphor for all of this, isn't it?" Elarion noted.

Connerh remained silent. His breathing pattern had increased in speed.

"I'm sorry," Elarion repeated. Connerh shook his head.

"No. I understand now," he replied.

"As do I," Elarion said. He added, "I am saddened for you." Elarion's eyes wandered, and his brows crumpled as he continued, "I should have stayed with you."

"Not even you could have stopped me that day," Connerh replied. Then, looking up, he added, "Not even I."

CHAPTER THIRTY-FOUR

BLOOD AND STONE

LENA

Elarion stood with his helm nestled firmly between his arms. He felt overdressed but was not ignorant of decorum. His rigid stature stood alone, dwarfed by his surroundings. A high, round pane of glass acted as a spotlight in a graveyard, and his polished armour reflected rays of the sun, casting thick, opaque shadows behind him. Porous pillars accented his surroundings as they whispered the stories of these ancient halls. They were older than the bloodlines who inhabited this place and would go on long after the remembrance of them was forgotten.

Elarion was old, but they were older. Even if they were torn down, crumbled and pulverised, and restored into a new form…

They would still remember…

They would still remember the floors that cradled pools of blood and tears, that echoed screams of joy and pain.

They would remember the walls where treaties were signed, conspiracies were shared, and wars were started.

Where kings died.

Where kings were murdered.

If only the pillars could speak…their wisdom might spare these people generations of agony, he thought, drawing a sigh from his lungs.

Men were so easily held captive by the present, rarely learning from the past. It was an endless loop of both enduring suffering and causing it. It drove him mad to be an observer of it. Year after year, generation after the next… He felt he had more in common with rocks and trees than people these days.

They understood what it was like.

His eyes traced the height of the closest pillar. Its body was like a fossilised trunk, making him long for the Forest – where the branches intertwined into blanketing canopies, and the peaks of the trees seemed to rest in the heavens. Where the colours were vibrant and warm, not cold and repellent to life like Hildeheim. Its dismal hues of greys, blacks, and flat blues sucked the joy out of…out of seeing. And the palette was only a minor reflection of the environment.

He suddenly remembered why he hated it there.

The sound of his armour shifting filled the empty spaces as he bent forward, taking stock of his reflection in the floor, between the ingrained dirt and scuff marks. He rarely saw his own likeness, save for distorted images morphing over polished ceremonial cuirasses and helms like the one he was wearing. Never something plain like a mirror. Elves didn't put stock in vanity. He didn't even own one.

The face looking back at him still looked familiar. It was a good sign, he reasoned.

He stood only a few feet off-centre from Lena's throne. Far closer than the formal distance for subjects, even closer than that of dignitaries and royalty, but he had reason for it. True, it was a minor gamble that his proximity could be misinterpreted – not in ways that would spark an international incident, but in the sense that it could be received as over-familiar or perhaps a blatant breach in protocol, especially if his presence was undesired. It had been a long while since they had been closely acquainted, after all.

These were the sort of things Elarion pondered.

The large doors rolled open, producing a sound as if the world had been split. It continued as they closed.

Elarion's back was to her as she entered, his white cape flowing nearly to the ground. Lena didn't need to see his face to know who it was. She recognised him instantly by his posture and his ears – not for any overt reasons, but for the small tufts of split hairs at their peaks. Having never encountered another elf with hair there, it was a minor feature she always noticed yet somehow forgot to ask him about.

His posture was equally as unique as his persona. She'd always described it like a parent playing along in a child's game. He was involved, present in the moment, but clearly beyond such things. Yet, he continued out of a sense of…well…he had his reasons. There were a million things she could think of as better ways to spend an eternity, but the choice was his, she supposed.

All that to say, he looked comfortable in his armour but uncomfortable being *in* armour.

That was it, wasn't it? That was the sum of Elarion, she thought. A smirk rushed to her face with the realisation.

"Elarion!" she shouted with surprise and warmth in her tone. His brow sunk for a brief moment before balancing as he turned to face her, her reaction unexpected but welcome.

The distance between them grew smaller as she approached. Her heeled boots clacked with fierce precision, each step measured and deliberate, hidden beneath a stunning black gown adorned with ornamental clasps along the bodice. It was tight enough to strangle a fly, drawing attention to all the round places on her figure.

It was a blatantly intentional choice, he thought. A humoured expression washed his face as he was reminded of the adolescent nature of her romance with Connerh. Even now, distanced by time and change, it turned out that she, in fact, hadn't changed at all in this regard. It brought him a moment of reassurance regarding Connerh's well-being. He estimated that if she had ill intent, then eroticism would not play a part. The desire to probe her mind was strong, but he resisted, opting to sigh instead. It was such a simple gesture, yet it could quickly reestablish balance, at least for a time.

"It's so good to see you. You are ageing delicately, as elves do," he said. She blushed. She looked the same, mostly, save for subtle wrinkles starting to develop in her upper cheek. Her eyes looked heavy underneath the makeup. Her burdens were clearly taking their toll, and she slept less than she should. There was also a certain level of animation that used to be in her step that was no longer visible. Her youth had faded. Otherwise, she appeared healthy and in good spirits. Perhaps a little too calm, a little too collected considering the circumstances.

But Elarion would opt for a compliment laced with a gentle fib.

He'd almost forgotten to offer a bow and quickly did so with a bend of the neck and head.

"You flatter me," she said with a smile. Her arms raised, anticipating an embrace as she closed the distance between them. Her hug was tight but brief, gently pulling away but holding on to his arms.

He finally gave a glance to the small entourage following her, immediately noticing Farrah's beaming smile. It caused a similar one to sprout on his face. She had such a high, happy energy, which he adored. Farrah reminded him of a much younger Thaetra trapped in a mortal's body. He returned a nod to her feminine curtsy. She was capable of so much more, deserving of better than the life of a handmaiden. He was fully convinced Lena would release Farrah had she desired it, but she was content in her indentured servitude. She was loyal to her friend, who also happened to be the queen.

"I came in late last night and didn't want to disturb you. I figured our reunion could wait a few hours," Lena explained to him.

"Of course," he replied, his voice trailing to a whisper as he prepared to unload his thoughts.

"I am so glad that you will be here for this; I wasn't sure you would find it appropriate," she said as her gaze drifted away.

He frowned at the suggestion.

"But you are family to us. I apologise that my indecision lingered for far too long," she went on, restoring a smile to her face. His expression mirrored his acceptance of the apology, but the moment was short-lived. A cloud of emotion and thoughts caught his attention just beyond the closed doors. His head lifted up and to the side, and his eyes dropped. It was a bombardment of a variety of emotions, all from the same vein. Nervousness, anger, frustration, concern. A crowd was gathering.

It was obvious he was using his telepathic ability, which caused her to frown. She quickly withdrew her hands from his grasp. The voices were growing by the moment, and he looked back at the entourage surrounding the queen. His eyes widened. Judges, counsellors, and various scholars versed in the law, judging by their attire and the books and scrolls they carried in their arms.

There *was* to be a trial, he realised.

"I was hoping we could speak privately," he said. His focus finally returned to the present.

"Private? Yes...yes, of course," she replied. She turned to her followers and shooed them away, lifting her gown and walking up the stairs to her throne. To Elarion, she instructed, "Come, dear."

He followed behind, carefully ensuring she didn't fall. She sat, took her boots off, and wiggled her toes.

"Sorry. I've been galloping around all day, and these boots have been killing me."

Farrah appeared out of nowhere and sat next to her. She grabbed Lena's foot and began rubbing the sole. Lena sighed in relief as she leaned back.

"You are a goddess," she praised to Farrah's laughter. With a twist of her lips, she joked darkly, "Out of all the doom and gloom and lectures of what it meant to be queen, all the dangers and warnings…my mother never warned me that fashion would be the death of me."

Farrah giggled.

Elarion smirked.

"What is it you want to discuss, old friend?" she asked, leaning on the arm of her chair.

He unintentionally frowned, glanced at his right hand, and then looked at her. *It might be easier to show her than tell her,* he thought. She noticed and shifted her body to the other side of the chair, resting her hands further away from him.

"I don't think that would be appropriate. Old-fashioned words and gestures will have to suffice," she said, her voice ripe in formality. "I know you're here to defend him, and I would expect nothing less. But it is important, more than ever right now, that I maintain the decorum as befitting my station."

Her words were official, but her tone was personal. There was a subtle anxiety behind her eyes, a desperation in her voice. Her eyes incrementally watered. Her expression pleaded with him to understand, but she could never read his face properly. His eyes squinted slightly with a smirk of recognition. That was her mother speaking. He remembered her saying something similar, oh-so-many years ago.

She misinterpreted his reaction.

"You don't think it pains me that he's been sitting in that cell, alone? As if I don't want to run to run to him, if it really is him?" Her brows furrowed. They held locked eyes. She asked, her nose held high, "Is it? They say it is, but…" she asked, her nose held high.

He nodded with the confirmation she desired. Her eyes fell shut with a sigh of relief, masked under the air that rushed out of her nose. Her forehead wrinkled.

"He needs me," she whispered as her eyes rushed open, unsure of what to focus on. Her vision was blurred on account of the pooled water and saline. Elarion listened quietly. Her emotions were broadcast telepathically like a blood-curdling scream in an empty room. If they were an indication of her internal struggle, then her mind was a cavalcade. It would be so easy to wade through the chaos and let himself into her mind, compartmentalise the anger, hurt, and sadness, to tidy up a bit and give her a reprieve she'd likely not had since childhood.

It was no secret that she had a distaste for his abilities. He had once tried to bring her comfort in her time of need – when her mother was murdered. Her reaction was volatile, to say the least. A complete shit-fit, as Connerh had described it. Lena appeared sensitive to telepaths, being keenly aware of the mental probing where most were not. It was an interesting physiology that he was never able to study.

"Wine!" she shouted, holding out her hand awaiting receipt of her cup. It was filled quickly by a chalice nearly spilling at the edges with her favourite blend. She consumed its contents with haste, as if it meant life or death. Her eyes locked with Elarion's. She finished it and promptly extended her hand in demand of a refill.

"How is he?" she asked. "I assume you have visited him."

He nodded, replying, "All things considered, he's well." He shifted his posture. Holding out his hand, he continued, "I've seen it all, as should you."

Her eyes focused on it. A few tears quickly escaped, quietly running down her face. She rubbed the now half-full chalice against her cheek, and her mouth hung open as she pondered the consequences. The allure of his power was tempting.

"It's all so simple for you, isn't it?" she asked, a private thought that escaped her lips as she drank. She wished it were a pipe in her hand. "Perhaps I don't want to know. Perhaps I'd rather the lie. How do you deal with knowing too much?"

Her cynicism drifted into anxiousness. He lowered his hand, his head moving along with it for a brief moment.

"When I figure it out, I'll let you know," he said.

She laughed unintentionally out of shock. His answer provided absolutely no assurances. Sure, he was trying to bring levity to an otherwise serious moment, but there was a detectable truth in his words that unsettled her.

"I used to envy you, but now I'm not so sure. Perhaps it is you that is cursed to remember, and we are the ones blessed to forget," she mused, her eyes wandering beyond. "I've made mistakes. Many I have forgotten. Some that will remain with me until I pass from this world. Hopefully," she added, pausing to remember. Her eyes slid to Elarion. With a frown, she concluded, "I could not imagine living with them forever."

Her words got to him for a brief second and lingered for what felt like days, but his expression recovered. His head canted with a nearly imperceivable smirk.

"Some people need forever in order to learn from their mistakes," he replied.

The large doors rumbled open as if on cue.

"The court has assembled," the footman announced with an echoing voice. Lena's spine stiffened. Farrah stood up and attended to Lena's face, wiping remnant tears and reapplying powder to Lena's cheeks.

"I think you should look," Elarion whispered with a furrowed brow, offering his outstretched hand again.

She glanced at it. Shook her head with increasing fluctuation.

"What's he doing here?" a voice asked a little too loudly. Elarion gave her a final glance, ignoring the gossip and slander behind him. Her stubbornness and pride would be her undoing, he thought.

He could make her see.

His gaze wandered beyond her.

He could make them all see how stupid and pointless this all was. He turned to look at the mob behind them.

Amethyst's words rang in the back of his mind with urgency, her measured accented voice laced with empathy.

Forcing them to see would not make them understand, and robbing them of that journey, no matter how painful or agonising it may be for us, is a very unjust thing to do indeed.

His pupils slid across their faces. A mix of pity and disappointment tinged with a dash of disgust.

A sigh escaped his nose as he turned to leave.

"Elarion," she said in her natural voice.

He froze in his tracks, lowering his head to listen.

"Please stay," she whispered.

His gaze lowered and moved towards her direction as he was immediately plunged into a potent memory. His cheeks tightened around his eyes.

The muscles in his face gradually released, loosening their tension and expelling the memory from the forefront of his thoughts.

"As you wish," he said eventually, turning to face her.

"Oh, it's the Elf Master. Why's he here?" someone shouted.

"Well, pull my tongue, I thought he got shown the door! When's the last time you've seen 'em?" an overanxious, ready-to-gossip-without-the-proper-volume-control voice said to someone else.

"Excuse me, Your Majesty, but will your Right Hand Hargatha be joining the assembly today?" the voice of Nikolas Hargrave elevated over the crowd's rumble. He pushed his way to the front.

Lena couldn't help the eye twitch when he spoke. She was still fighting to regain her composure, and as usual, his timing couldn't have been worse. She trusted Niko about as far as she could physically throw him, and her upper body strength was admittedly lacking. Despite his overt flaws and a general appearance that inspired one to clutch their valuables close, he was reliably blunt when he needed to be — a trait that was uncommon nowadays. Even in the depths of her own riches and the wealth of the kingdom, who would have thought the truth was the one thing money could not buy?

Her mother had taught her how to form her courtly circle. *Keep a few people who were reliably untrustworthy, a few who were comfortable lying to your face, a few who feared you, and even fewer who loved you. Somewhere in the middle would lie the truth.*

It wasn't a perfect science, but it worked most of the time.

Connerh was a mix of all those things. He was reliably a basket case, just like her. He was comfortable lying to her if it meant her safety. He feared losing her. And he loved her, explosively. It was almost as if she were programmed to need him. Despite her mother's disapproval, she almost ensured they would be together.

She scoffed internally, but it showed on her face. He knew she wasn't there. Lena hadn't formally announced Hargatha's new assignment, but it wasn't exactly a secret. Nikolas dusted off his long white overcoat, a habit Lena had long figured out was his nervous twitch mixed with a behavioural twitch. He was somewhat of a germaphobe.

"No, Niko, she will not be joining us today," she replied with subtle exasperation.

"Oh. Well, then, I believe that means the responsibility of officiating today's hearing falls on me," he proudly announced.

She didn't respond, only stared at him blankly.

"Unless, of course, that is why you asked the elf…uh…Master Elarion…to join us today?" he tried to recover, feigning respect for Elarion, although he truly had none. The crowd loudly grumbled at the suggestion.

"That won't be necessary, Niko; I will be officiating today… It is a matter of great sensitivity, and I want everyone focused," she replied, all too happy to burst his bubble.

"As you wish, but I don't recall seeing anything of the level of importance that would require your focused attention on the agenda today," Nikolas prodded, unrolling a small scroll and pretending to examine it.

His insistent and relentless nature was irritating. *Fucking hell*, she thought. If she were to respond to him, it would only drag things out longer than things needed to be, and she really wasn't in the mood to waste her breath with him any longer. She shook her head and changed her focus.

"I need everyone to shut their mouths for a moment," she announced loudly, bordering on a shout as she shed what little formality she had left coursing through her veins.

The room went quiet.

She looked up at Aethelstan, captain of her guard, giving him a discreet cue. He nodded after catching her gaze. Lena stood, clapped her hands together, and looked around,

"I must confess that the agenda you all received was a farce. We have something of a delicate issue to deliberate today, and it is imperative that it remain a secret," she continued to the soundtrack of gasps and whispers. "Don't be alarmed; you will shortly understand my desire for discretion."

The voices grew louder when a full detachment of soldiers marched into the room. Elarion felt his hand move towards his hilt but stopped short, resting his wrist there instead. He resisted the urge to insert himself. The crowd's volume lowered as the soldiers continued to grow in number. Servants rushed in to pull giant ropes that closed shutters high on the wall, dimming the room by a considerable amount. The doors shut loudly behind the soldiers, startling the court.

"She's going to kill us!" someone shouted, inciting some to panic.

Lena couldn't help but laugh. It was absurd.

Or was it?

It would certainly make life a little easier, she thought wickedly.

"What is the meaning of this?" Vaelen Graymane shouted indignantly. She always felt he spoke to her with less respect than he should, almost as if he were speaking to his oldest daughter. It made her blood rush and face bloom. But she knew better; it was just another subtle attempt to make her crack. To make her appear weak if she reacted negatively.

A familiar game for a new day.

Aghor Emberheart, another head of yet another opposing house, joined Vaelen in grievances.

"First you take our weapons, then you surround us with an army. What *is* the meaning of this? And why's *he* here?" Aghor shouted, then pointed to Elarion.

"I knew it, I bloody knew it!" another instigator shouted in the crowd. He was obviously under the employ of Vaelen or Aghor; the stupid bastard couldn't even play his part convincingly.

She sighed heavily. The crowd grew louder in their anger and confusion. She scanned their faces. They were so easy to ignite, so ready to revolt. Why did she even bother? *Perhaps I should walk away,* she thought.

No. Run away. Grab Connerh and run.

Just like they had always joked about doing. Now was the perfect time. The boys, Connerh and Elarion, were back in her life, just like old times. What was the point anymore?

"You should quell this quickly," she heard Elarion whisper behind her. It was a warning, not a suggestion, and she received it as such.

She cleared her throat.

Lena felt the words, but her mouth prevented her from uttering them. She had a speech prepared. She'd repeated the words so many times, both externally and internally. Up until this very moment, she could have quoted it on command. But now the room was spinning, and it felt warm and restrictive in her gown. Her ribs felt compressed. She glanced a look of fear at Elarion, but he hadn't noticed; he was still scanning the crowd. A deep breath would have to suffice.

"Connerh Manthil lives!" she shouted awkwardly, having forced the words out of her lungs. The crowd went dreadfully quiet. Aghor and Vaelen stood with their mouths open, exchanging glances with one another.

She heard her echo bounce and reverberate before it slowly ceased to exist.

"I see," Vaelen replied with diminished aggressiveness. His voice was small in these silent walls. Vaelen and Aghor exchanged lingering glances as they returned to their places within the crowd.

"Today we discuss what is to become of him," she added with a sense of finality, her composure regained. They remained silent, their focus on her pronounced. "I realise there is much to discover and even more to discuss. Normally, issues of this magnitude would be deliberated over days, even weeks. But this is a special situation, so a consensus must be made today, after which I will consider the evidence and make a ruling before we announce it to the kingdom." With an increased amount of bass in her tone, she asked, "Am I understood?"

She glanced at the faces of the court as they nodded in acknowledgement.

"Very well. Aethelstan, would you please?" she prompted, sitting back down on the throne. Butterflies engulfed her stomach. It was finally happening.

She barely heard the doors open as she imagined what he must look like now. The soldiers' march was like a soft drumbeat in the background of her daydream-locked gaze.

A sharp gasp snatched her back to the moment.

The familiar bouquet of aromatics triggered a rush of nostalgia: the overstated but neutral smell of stone sewn in with dried blood and the salty notes of the ocean. A smirk immediately commandeered his face. He dropped his head, allowing his thoughts to jog through fonder times without the stimuli of his surroundings. They were great times, some of them even legendary. He lingered in the milliseconds turned days that made up the experience of memory...

But dark clouds quickly filled empty spaces.

The dark times flattened and sapped his expression almost as quickly as it formed.

His recollection was a lifetime of shifting perspectives. First as a boy, visiting the castle for reasons just beyond memory. All he knew was that it was dark and creepy – and that ghosts perhaps roamed the halls. Even then, he knew more than he realised. It wasn't until he was a teenager, having met and unofficially begun courting Lena, that these walls felt like home. He was newly enlisted then, young, dumb, and full of spunk, as they said. Back then, he felt the court was just, that wars were noble, and death was like sleep.

Many years later, as a man deeply in love, a commander of men, and the bane of his enemies, he knew the court was corrupt, that wars were evil, and death was agony.

Heat originating from above ripped him from his thoughts. He looked up and around, full of suspicion, as though he was being watched. Not by the crowd, of course they were watching him, but by the shadows atop the pillars. From where they always watched. Invisible eyes with no faces, just bodies carved from the mountain's soul. Between them…empty spaces.

Let them watch, he thought, returning his gaze downwards. Now, they would see him as an older man, a decade or two shy of being an elder. A prisoner. Bound and shackled, resigned to an undesignated fate.

Fuck the court.

Fuck wars and fuck death.

He sighed.

Many things had changed, but this place hadn't.

His guard stopped, their feet snapping forward in deafening unison. He stopped with them, anticipating what came next. Their loud march echoed as they parted, some going left, others right, leaving him standing alone in the centre.

He laughed.

There were even scratches that were familiar, there on the floor. A suspected assassin had proved the theories surrounding him when he had lunged towards Lena, clutching a small blade. Connerh had ripped the man's chains in the opposite direction, then slammed his shortsword down and through the assassin's face as he had hit the ground, chipping the polished marble beneath. His blood stains still lingered now, colouring white streaks in the dark marble flooring, trapped under layers of polish. Connerh grimaced at the memory of how he had laughed as he'd unwedged his blade from flesh and bone. They were indeed darker times.

The smell of her perfume reached his nose. Clamping his eyes shut and flaring his nostrils, his eyelids barely raised, releasing a small collection of water. His lips were torn between smiling and frowning. His stomach turned, but his chest fluttered.

It was only ever this strong when she spritzed it on her chest in addition to her wrists and hair.

The smile won.

And in that moment, he could hear everything. The gasps faded, and the whispers were silent.

His eyes shot up, locking with hers. His brow cradled his eyes as his cheeks dimpled.

She stood there, illuminated by a shaft of soft light, as beautiful as an angel – though fallen and draped in black. She wore her hair like he'd liked, straight and flowing down her back. Her body was concealed under a tight gown, though the protrusion of her bust filled his mind with delicate memories of what lay underneath. An intentional touch, he could be sure.

She looked at him with hope and longing, tugging at his heartstrings. He was prepared for anger and shouting, not this.

It was in the moments that felt like forever that the dark times flattened and sapped his expression almost as quickly as it formed.

The doors erupted as they opened like explosions deep in the mines. She rose to her feet as soon as she saw just a fraction of his face. She'd recognise that hair anywhere…and the indent. He'd always had a small indent near his temple since he was a small boy.

He'd had battle scars before he had battle scars.

The hair was overgrown and wild, like the grin she wore on her face. He was still handsome from the sweet glimpses she caught every other second; her head bobbed and weaved as she tried to gain a new perspective, a clearer view. He had a long, greying beard, a change from the clean-shaven look he used to prefer. She rather liked him with it, though it was hard to accept as being real. He was thinner, still muscular in frame but with noticeably less heft than he used to carry.

He looks rather unwell, she thought, and her lips curled to a frown. Then her thoughts rushed to where he'd been. Likely captured, perhaps in a cave, given inappropriate access to food and water…yet he'd survived, just as she always knew he would. She'd always joked that not even death could keep them apart. The bias of her prophecy rang loudly, a resounding affirmation in the vacuum of her ego. She felt validated, vindicated, and vengeful.

Whoever did this to him would pay for their abandonment of mercy.

A glimpse of his smirk carved a deeper one into her own cheeks. His flickering glances quickened her heart. Her hands were clasped tightly together, making the tips of her fingers grow cold. His guard stopped in perfect coordination, parting like ripples in opposite directions.

She blinked. The time it took felt like hours before her eyes opened again.

His face had changed.

Had she imagined his grin?

He looked like an empty sack, still holding the shape of the contents it once held.

Her face pivoted downwards, but her eyes remained locked on him.

"Hello," he mouthed to her with a minor wave of his fingertips held low to his lap.

She wasn't sure how to take it. Those weren't the words she imagined he'd belt from his lungs upon seeing her again. A frown indented her smirk.

Not *'I love you'*, not *'I've missed you'*. No, nothing of the sort. Just a faint *'Hello'*?

As if he'd just been caught.

"Take those chains off of him!" she erupted in a loud, shrieking scream. The crowd started. The soldiers near him scrambled to find the key.

She took a few steps down from her throne. Her head canted as if she was trying to see the real him, lost in the brush of *somewhere*.

She needed answers.

The chains were loud when they hit the ground, but perhaps not as loud as his silence. His lack of movement.

Connerh stood there, solemnly awaiting judgment.

He didn't run to her. He didn't even exhibit a visible ounce of restraint, not a sign that he wanted to.

"What's wrong?" she mouthed. He glanced away. His eyes visibly watered. "What have you done?"

His gaze fell as he folded his hands in front of himself. Her head rotated in disbelief.

She took two steps backwards as her knees began to wobble. She felt rabidly for her throne behind her, urgently sitting upon receipt of it.

The decade of his absence, now perhaps reframed as willing, suddenly felt like an elephant standing on her chest.

"I don't understand," she whispered to Elarion, looking up at him. His expression was saddened…for her.

Her jaws bit at words that brought forth no sound. Elarion's warm hand on her shoulder anchored her back in the moment, reminding her of the faces that watched.

"How do you wish to proceed? Perhaps you should give yourself a moment to…gather your thoughts. I admire your bravery in handling this situation, but you should never let them see you like this," Niko suggested quietly, his back turned to the crowd. She hadn't heard or seen him approach, now just a few feet in front of her. She rapidly blinked away the tears welling in her ducts.

"I'm fine," she said with a pronounced sniffle. Her neck softened to allow for a small range of mobility. "And I disagree. Let them see. I'm not the cold-hearted, emotionless bitch my mother was." She rushed to stand, shouting, "We have before us today the accused! Accused of murdering five thousand innocent souls, on the basis of orders from the crown," she said, pausing to look at him.

The words felt absurd to utter, if only because they were meant to describe *him*. It felt unthinkable. He winced at the number.

"Orders that did not exist," she added, her tone softening. "Men, women…and children were lost that day. We would be wise to keep their memory in mind, as we deliberate this day. Let it be for naught."

She frowned and grimaced at the same time. Her thoughts were in a dark place. Having lost her bearings on truth and understanding, she couldn't tell up from down. The internal voice that didn't care about his charges and would proudly scream it with all her being to the masses was growing dimmer by the second. Sinking down into a black sea. His head lowered deeper into his chest. It was then that the crowd remembered they were there. Whispers became vocalised in normal registers. There was confusion, there was anger, only a few making way for rationality.

"Let him speak!" a voice shouted to a growing chorus of those who agreed.

Despite her defiance, her tears gathered in hot pools that burned as her anger built. Connerh lifted his head as if he were preparing to speak.

"No."

The simple word out of her mouth brought stillness and quiet. Connerh locked his focus on her, confusion plainly observable.

"We've reached the point where nothing can be believed. Not feelings. Not relationships and imaginary bonds…and most certainly not words," she continued. "We will not rely on words…instead, memories. Memories can't be debated…manipulated…or twisted into what we want them to be. What we believed them to be," she said proudly, including a coded message to him with the added words. She now regretted not speaking to him first before dragging them both there, in front of a crowd. She had her reasons, although in honesty, they had felt clearer then than they did now. "We have a receptor in our employ. A telepathic mediator, of sorts. We will see first-hand through Connerh's memories what led up to and ultimately transpired at the Rim."

"And on whose word will we take these visions?" Vaelen asked, stepping forward.

"Your own," she replied quickly. "His memories will be shared with the lords and ladies of every house present. His thoughts will be placed into your minds. Only then will we understand and be able to make a fair judgment," she decreed, losing the will to look at him. In the name of honour and truth, Vaelen's question was valid, but his intentions were always suspect. "In reality, Connerh is not the only one on trial today. My right to leadership is just as much on the line if I am implicated in this atrocity. If the truth is as my detractors say…I'll renounce my crown immediately."

There was an explosion of gasps and whispers.

"Are you sure you want to reveal such…intimate details?" Elarion asked, leaning over to whisper in her ear.

"It's the only way to end this and move on," she whispered back, tilting her head to lock eyes with him.

"And what if it isn't?" Aghor shouted. She smirked.

"Then those of you who questioned me will crawl on your stomachs and beg for my forgiveness," she announced, her teeth bared and jaw locked. Vaelen's head was canted as he studied her. He seemed intrigued, willing to play along.

"Very well. I am eager to face the cold stone. I think we've waited long enough," Vaelen asserted. With his chest puffed out, he continued, "I volunteer as the first witness to these so aptly put…atrocities…"

Connerh had been staring at her, waiting for the reciprocation of his desired attention. She finally noticed.

His expression called into serious question her plan of action. She smirked, finding some delight in his discomfort.

"Very well," Lena replied.

Elarion cleared his throat and started to remove his gloves. He took a step past Lena's peripheral vision. Vaelen's mouth opened as his scepticism mounted.

"That won't be necessary, Elarion. All things considered, I don't believe it would be appropriate…considering your known allegiance to Connerh," she said, looking at him past the bridge of her nose.

He stopped awkwardly in his tracks, frowning at Connerh, who was staring at him. A crooked smile washed over Vaelen's face.

"Aethelstan…bring in Creature," she said.

Elarion's confusion was overt. He moved to a nearby pillar, abandoning his position next to Lena. His eyes were squinted. The doors screeched open. The rattling of chains and snarling preceded *Creature*. Connerh tried to catch a glimpse as the crowd parted, but all he could see was the top of its hood and the rhythmic rising and falling of its posture that indicated it walked with a limp. Groans and whispers filled the air. As the final individuals parted, he noticed Balfour, a resident alchemist, leading what appeared to be a frail woman covered in in black robe and hood. She was chained at the hands and neck, and she smelled of something horrible, like rotted flesh and garlic. The odour intensified the closer she got to him. Connerh's face wrinkled at the odour. Aethelstan went and stood next to his queen, his hand at the ready.

Vaelen took a few steps back.

"Thank you, Balfour. You may begin," Lena said safely from her throne.

"As you wish, Your Majesty," Balfour said with his old, weary voice. He waved over a soldier and handed him the chain by which he led Creature. "She won't run, but…well…the process can cause her some discomfort."

His warning did little to comfort the soldier tasked with restraining her. It was apparent that Balfour was more concerned for Creature's well-being than the soldier, who was cautiously suspicious of it. Elarion tightened his grip on his hilt. Balfour calmly removed her hood while she growled and snapped at him. Her teeth were sharp and pointed. Groans of disgust could be heard as she was revealed, but Balfour was unfazed by both the crowd and her playful attempt to bite him. Lena gripped the sides of her throne. She could feel Elarion staring at her but refused to acknowledge him. At one time, Creature was a normal Tu'Chauri woman. Being cousins to the elves, they, too, could possess the Gift, though far reduced in scope and capability. Along with it, the experience greatly differed from when someone of Elarion's calibre utilised it. For Tu'Chauri receptors, the experience was…quite painful…for both the receptor and the vessel. With reduced capability of control and precision, there was an increased risk of losing oneself in the sea of thoughts, emotions, and memories shared from the vessel, each experience chipping away at the receptor's true self.

The woman once known as Madika was a local healer, a refuge from her Tu'Chauri homeland before Balfour found her. In his attempt to amplify her abilities with his tomes and potions, she went mad, consumed by the horde of memories and emotions of those she had once tried to help. Under the direction of Balfour, she was made into an interrogation tool used against criminals, no matter how sick, twisted, or deranged they may have been, under the guise of Balfour's promise to help her return to her old self. It didn't take long before Madika was no more.

After a few failed experiments in an attempt to cure rabid dogs, her desire for normal food faded, replaced with an insatiable craving for raw meat, flesh, and blood.

Creature was all that remained.

It wasn't the first time Elarion had seen such an abomination. The last time was eighty-three years prior, when he and the rest of his regiment had put to death every Tu'Chauri man and woman who forced the innocent cursed with the Gift into similar servitude.

His glare burned. Lena continued to ignore him, though it was beginning to prove difficult for her. Connerh found Creature interesting. His eyes wandered over her face, her physique, her hands. They were gaunt, and her nails were long, having not been cut in quite some time.

Easily years, he thought.

"Just one moment," Balfour said, retrieving a vial from his coat pocket. It was small and clear, as was the liquid inside it. Balfour smiled and shook the vial in front of Creature's face as if it were a dog treat. He removed the cork and pulled her thin, straggly hair back, forcing her head back before pouring the liquid into her gnawing mouth. Dragging out the words, he said, "Yes, there we go."

Lena and the crowd looked on in curious horror. It wasn't the first time she'd seen Creature, but it was no less fascinating. Creature let out a gag and a cough. She started dry heaving and retching, followed by a deep inhale as if it were her first breath. Her shoulders relaxed, and she became more passive as the seconds passed. Her posture straightened, and her pupils returned to their normal size. She looked around as if she'd just woken up.

"Hello, Madika," Balfour greeted, delighted with the success of his potion. Her initial acknowledgement of him and accompanying relief soon faded as she felt the metal collar around her neck and hands.

"No, no, no, no," she continually whispered to him, growing louder each time.

"I'm afraid Her Majesty will be requiring your services. Just briefly, I assure you," he replied to her. She looked at Ioelena with fear in her eyes.

"Please, Your Majesty!" she begged. Lena lost the strength to look at her, and she looked away, finally and unintentionally locking eyes with Elarion. The anger and disappointment in his gaze crushed her, and she looked away again, landing on Connerh. He nodded with an expression of acceptance. Her brow crumpled.

In her mind, the world went quiet. Before her, she saw two people who were, in the moment, one and the same. On face value, there was little difference between Creature and Connerh. They were both shells of their former selves, forced to carry out the will of a master for the benefit of others, with little value given to how it impacted them. It clicked for her.

The regret was debilitating, but it was too late to back out now. Doing so would jeopardise…everything.

It would be quick.

"Madika!" Balfour shouted, raising his hand in preparation to strike her. After wincing, she immediately stopped resisting. She stuck out her arm and waited patiently, quietly. Lena watched from the corner of her eye. He guided her next to Connerh and retrieved a long strip of cloth.

"I will need the accused…ahem…I will need Connerh to extend his…" he began. Connerh raised his arm without hesitation, interrupting the request. He laid Madika's arm atop Connerh's and wrapped them together with the strip of cloth.

"Madika, take us back to the events at the Rim. Who? What? Where? And most importantly…why?" Balfour announced.

"Yes, Balfour," she said. Her voice was sweet and delicate, not matching her appearance at all. She then mouthed to Connerh, "I'm sorry."

He looked into her eyes and suddenly felt afraid. A cool sensation washed over his skin, making the hair on his neck stand. She looked at him, but it was as if no one was there.

"Connerh, you should be aware that this will be…slightly…uncomfortable." Balfour chose his words wisely.

Connerh looked at Lena one last time. His confidence had escaped him.

"You should…brace yourself," Balfour added as he backed away.

His distancing concerned Connerh further. Madika held Connerh's hand, interlocking their fingers. She maintained eye contact with him as her grip tightened.

The visceral and raw guttural screams that came out of them silenced the room.

Lena's eyes watered as she tried her best to restrain the tears that desperately needed to escape.

Elarion's hand trickled blood, his knuckles white.

CHAPTER THIRTY-FIVE

WE ARE ALL JUST

CONNERH

The pain resonated, deep and unrelenting, like the rumble that lingered after lightning. It shifted unpredictably, a discomfort that alternated between mental and physical, phasing from a dull throbbing ache to sharp overreaching stabs. It refused to settle and gave no quarter, nor a single moment of reprieve. Even here, deep within the confines of his mind, their screams reached him – blurry and distant, they echoed like wailing spectres drifting through abandoned corridors. A reminder. A tether, fragile yet unbreakable, shackling him to the physical realm just beyond his current reach.

This was a different experience. When Elarion entered his mind, it was with care, a gentle surrender Connerh had come to trust. Elarion was a gracious guest, cautious and deliberate, doing everything within his power to make his presence as warm and unobtrusive as possible.

But Madika – she was nothing of the sort. She wasn't a guest; she was a parasite with sharp teeth, gnawing and biting, tearing through his thoughts and memories with a feral hunger. She searched with a disregard that bordered on cruelty, her motives clear yet merciless, swift but without prejudice. It wasn't personal. She had a job to do.

Connerh found himself lying on a surface that felt like wet glass. The sensation was concerning, the smooth, cold material bending faintly beneath the weight of his body as if threatening to shatter at a moment's notice. For a fleeting instant, he wondered if he would break through.

When he opened his eyes, his view was inverted. She hovered above him, her legs crossed, hands clasped neatly in her lap. The sight was almost serene, like she was adrift among the night sky. Together, they were suspended in a black expanse, emptier than the void between stars, yet there was the faintest suggestion of a horizon – a line that shouldn't have been but was.

He pushed himself upright, slow and deliberate, his movements cautious against uncertain footing. The void around them seemed to beckon him to drift towards sleep. It wanted him to relinquish control, inviting him to wander into its depths, but there was something out there, an unspoken suspicion that made his pulse quicken. It was vast and empty, yet alive with unseen eyes watching with keen interest.

Madika's gaze, however, was anything but still. Her eyes darted rapidly, scanning the void with a focused intensity. Then, abruptly, her movements stilled, and her gaze locked onto him with silent precision.

"Who are you really?" she asked, her voice cutting through the silence like a blade.

Connerh stood and brushed himself off, more out of habit than necessity.

"Is this where I give you my name, or do you want a commentary on my life?" he asked, his tone dry, his gaze never leaving hers.

She tilted her head slightly, the faintest hint of a smirk tugging at her lips.

"Your mind is shielded," she observed, her voice laced with a mix of curiosity and frustration. "At least, some of your memories are. I've never quite seen anything like this before from someone who is not a telepath."

Her attention returned to the void, her eyes once again scanning the darkness as she looked for answers. He studied her for a moment, the faint glimmer of light catching on the scars that adorned her face like forgotten stories etched into flesh.

"Why do you not change your appearance?" he asked, his voice casual despite his head tilting slightly as he studied her more closely. "You could be anything here. You know that."

She froze mid-scan, her gaze snapping back to him with a suddenness that made him pause. Her brow arched slightly, a mix of amusement and challenge sparking in her expression.

"And how do you know what 'here' is?" she asked.

"I practically live here…in my mind. I'd recognise it anywhere, though this time, it looks a little different," he replied, looking around and then down at his flexing hand. "The colours are different." Surprise tinted his tone as the realisation occurred. He spun around, inspecting what little he had for surroundings as he continued, "It is my solace, my solitude from out there."

She continued to stare. She thought his response was a sad commentary, but at the same time, she understood. Empathised, even…

"I don't change my appearance because I don't have an objection to it. Do you?" she countered.

"I think you're rather attractive beneath the scars," Connerh remarked, his words unguarded, spoken without hesitation. The corners of her mouth twitched, an involuntary smirk slipping free before she could catch it. The subconscious always had a way of speaking with a sharper honesty, cutting through the filters of decorum and pretence.

"I could say the same…" she replied, her voice light but edged with something unreadable. Offering a sarcastic smirk, she concluded, "I won't, but I could."

"And why the chains?" he pressed, tilting his head slightly as if studying her reaction.

"I think you forget whose mind we're in. We're not here for me." She tapped the side of her temple, a motion both dismissive and pointed.

"You think it's scary, is that it?" he asked, a faint hint of a challenge in his tone.

She rolled her eyes and returned her focus to the swirling depths of his thoughts, continuing her probing as if she hadn't heard him.

"I get it," he continued, undeterred. "It's like armour – or a mask. You think if you wear it with enough pride, no one will see the shame living underneath."

That made her stop. Slowly, her gaze returned to him, narrowing slightly as one of her small, bare feet touched the glass-like surface beneath them. She let it linger there a moment before the other followed, and she began circling him, each step deliberate and soft, like a predator considering its prey.

"And you talk too much," she decided, her voice sharp as she moved. "Is that *your* armour?"

"Sometimes," he admitted, his candour disarming. "Though, as of late, I've found it easier just to keep everyone at arm's length."

Her lips twitched again, this time in genuine amusement that led to laughter.

"We're a lot alike, you know," he went on, watching her movements.

"Oh?" she replied, arching a brow as she continued her slow orbit.

"Animals locked in a cage, only set free when it's time to perform," he said evenly, his words heavy with something unspoken.

Her eyes sharpened. "You think I'm a circus act? Is that what you think is going on?"

"Isn't it?" he frowned, without the faintest hint of doubt in his voice.

She stopped pacing, her head tilting slightly as her expression softened, though it wasn't with kindness.

"No," she said simply. "We're all playing a little game, doing what we can to gain a foothold while mitigating our losses. That's life, sweetie. It's not so scary once you accept it. Some of us, though, are still in denial. Too proud to accept what we've lost."

Her words hung heavy between them, and Connerh glanced away, his gaze drifting low.

"Denial?" he chuckled to himself. "Denial is what keeps some of us alive. I've seen men cheat death by refusing to acknowledge their injuries. I've watched soldiers keep fighting despite the loss of limbs, and dead men willingly march to their graves. It is as you would see it, the refusal of reality that allows us to survive…to do things we otherwise couldn't."

"And do things you otherwise wouldn't?" she cut him off.

Her words triggered him to pause and take a deep breath.

"I've met men like you before," she began, her voice cutting through the void. "Been intimately acquainted with their minds…always content with the same brittle philosophy: *the end justifies the means*. I suppose I should be envious of the bliss such levels of ignorance must provide. Maybe you did see those things, or perhaps you saw what you wanted to."

Her tone was dismissive, almost accusing.

Connerh didn't respond immediately. He let her words settle, folding his arms as his gaze drifted past her before he acknowledged, "Maybe. Or maybe I saw what I needed to."

He turned back to her, his expression hardening.

"That's the thing about justifying the end, isn't it?" Her words grew sharper, more deliberate in their delivery. "It gives people like you permission to twist the truth – to warp reality until it fits whatever makes their actions bearable. But what about the means? What about the choices you make every step of the way? The lives you ruin. The lives you *take*. Does the end wash the blood from your hands?"

"Not even death will wash it away," he replied, his expression fading into something unreadable as his focus trailed into a distant memory. His surprising candour caught her off guard for a second time. With a sigh, he continued, "No, I'm afraid we get to keep that stain, in this life and perhaps the next."

"Then why do it?"

"You take me for a glory hound?"

"Well, you wouldn't be the first of your kind," she replied.

He shook his head, answering, "We're made to believe we do it for others. For the weaker ones. For the ones who can't fight their own battles."

"And what do you believe?"

He thought on it, lowering his head for the duration before finally replying, "I don't know anymore. I suspect, ultimately, that's why we're here right now." Looking up at her, his shoulders slumped.

"Then why not shed your cowardice and embrace death's invitation?" she jabbed.

"It is nearly impossible to choose death when hope still remains – or, as you call it, denial. And were it so easy, I imagine you would not be here." His tone was deliberate now, each word carrying weight. She hesitated, her expression betraying the briefest flicker of acknowledgement. "I suppose to answer your earlier question…hope is my armour." He raised his head with positive reflection in his tone.

"How romantic," she sneered. She studied him for a moment, her gaze sharp but not unkind. There was a flicker of amusement in her tone when she said, "You're amazingly lucid for someone who is also, at the same time, desperately guarded."

Connerh acknowledged her words with a subtle raise of his brow. She smirked as the amusement took root.

"There's something unexplainably odd about you," she went on, stepping closer. "It's fascinating, yet I can't help but wonder if I've made a mistake by involving myself in this. Like something lingers under the surface, beyond my depth."

He remained silent, watching her.

"Normally, I interact with a reflection of the self," she continued, her tone shifting to one of genuine intrigue. "A less autonomous, unfiltered version of the person who operates the legs, fingers, and lips. But this is *you*, isn't it? The whole of you. As if your subconscious is…conscious. I bet the you out there is indistinguishable from the one in here," she concluded with a hint of amazement. "You really do live in your mind, don't you?"

It was a rhetorical question.

She paused, tilting her head as if trying to make sense of him.

"Oh, you're special for sure. Is that why she wants you back so badly?" she asked, her voice tinged with something between admiration and frustration. She stepped closer now, her eyes narrowing as they met his. "From what memories I've seen, you're not a monster – a manipulated, love-stricken fool with self-worth issues, yes, but not a monster. Your wounds are deep, but your secrets… They go even further. What exactly are you hiding?"

Her words hung in the air, charged with curiosity and tension. She peered into his eyes as if searching for something buried just beneath the surface.

"Do you mean it? Do you not think me a monster?" he asked, a sliver of vulnerability oozing through his cracks.

She was hesitant to give him what he wanted, unsure if he deserved such reassurance.

"No…monsters don't feel regret." She shook her head, a specific example coming to mind. "Bad men do, but not monsters. Even still, it's too early to tell. The darkest things are still trapped in this head of yours. For all I know, it's not true regret I sense, just more denial," she said, frowning. "Besides, it doesn't matter what I think – only the court of bloodthirsty politicians out there. I suppose you can't just conjure some of that hope to get yourself out of this one?" she jabbed after taking a deep breath.

He offered a tempered smirk.

"No? I thought not. Come on, lover boy, I'm on a timeline here. I don't need your shadow wandering around my mind for the rest of my life. I've got to get in and out. Don't get me wrong, I enjoy the banter…but…no." She paused to look him over. "We'll save the consideration of disappointment and sorrow for another day. She took his hand and led him forward. "Show me the events that led up to the Rim. Who, what, where, and when. All of it."

The bright yellow ball of the sun was the first to appear, rolling from one horizon to the next just as it was setting. The scenery quickly followed it.

The rain fell, heavy and relentless, the air thick with the harsh scent of black smoke. Madika grimaced as the mud encumbered her feet, forcing its way between her toes. She briefly thought to conjure shoes, but what would it matter? It wasn't real anyway, just Connerh's mental projection of a memory long passed. Still, the detail of his recollection was surprisingly intricate, overwhelming in its similarity to the real world.

Laid atop the earthy scents that rang familiar, there was another that clung to the air, sharp and foul. The abrasive bouquet of death crumpled her expression into one of disgust.

Lifeless bodies were scattered everywhere.

She turned to Connerh, but her gaze faltered as it lingered on the destruction. The city – or what remained of it – lay in ruin. Buildings, homes, and carriages, all consumed by a fire that burned too hot, too fast, a savage beast with a hunger that twisted its flames into shapes bordering on unnatural. It was more than fire – it was an appetite, a force that sought to devour everything, as though it had a mind of its own.

Even with such explicit detail, she wondered if his memory was tainted, coloured by emotions and degraded with the passage of time. She'd never seen a fire like this before. It was ominous, almost sentient in its desire to consume.

She heard the sobbing, but her eyes were reluctant to peel away despite her head beginning to turn in its direction.

They were all dead, most of them with their faces submerged in the thick mud.

There were so many.

Surely this memory was altered, she thought. Her own mind fought to accept his recollection as factual. It was beginning to feel gratuitous; she couldn't bear to look at another lifeless form, another shell of flesh and bone. With a slow, deliberate turn, her gaze finally fell to him.

Connerh was holding a dead child in his hands.

The sight was too much. She staggered back. Her movements felt sluggish, as though the weight of the scene pressed against her chest. When her hands hit the ground, the wet earth clung to her. Horror twisted her face, and her body jerked as she tried to crawl away. In an instant, she had accepted that he *was*, in fact, the monster that he claimed. The security of the illusion abandoned her, and in that moment, she felt in danger.

But then she froze.

Her brow furrowed.

It was Connerh who was weeping.

A woman – the mother, she presumed – sprinted towards him, her cries primal, raw, almost inhuman. Too guttural for anyone but a grieving mother to produce. Connerh leapt to his feet, his sword rising, the razor-sharp tip aimed at her throat. The threat should have been enough to freeze her in place, but it wasn't. She didn't flinch. Her gaze never left the child, her roving hands reaching wildly for it. She would have thrust the blade through herself if it meant getting to the boy, had Connerh connected the dots any slower. He dropped his sword without a word, its impact splashing into the mud with a heavy and final report.

He moved swiftly, closing the distance between them. In a motion too delicate for the chaos around them, he placed the child in her arms, his eyes darting over the boy's small, still form, searching for any sign of life. Madika could only watch, frozen in place, as the woman's hands moved with frantic precision. She rubbed the child's chest, skin against skin, then pounded his back, desperate to stir something – anything – alive. Connerh's gaze never left her, tracking every movement, every rhythm.

Then, amid the wailing and the rain and the distant crackle of burning wood…

Just a little, brittle cough sounded. In that moment, it was the only thing that mattered. The spark of life was brighter than any flame and louder than any sound. Madika's expression softened as she observed their silent celebration, even while they were overshadowed by a grief that was slow to fade. The wake of *what could have been* kept their tears in steady motion.

The woman held her child to her chest, rocking him back and forth, murmuring her thanks to Connerh through her sobs. Her joy and relief were raw, almost too much for her to bear.

But Madika saw it die. The spark in Connerh's eyes – once a fire – began to dim. Faint at first, then unmistakable. His soul, just as fragile as the child's life, began to wither.

His moment of humanity had passed.

His focus on the woman and child faded, and with it, the tears he had for them. The chaos, the smoke, and the ash were gone, relegated to noise in the background. The stillness around him deepened as he retrieved his sword, wiping it clean with his garment, his movements deliberate. His gaze swept across the wreckage, coldly assessing what needed to be done.

His transition from saviour to killer was effortless. Seamless, even, like closing one door and opening another. It was as natural as breathing. Madika watched him, her stomach twisting. There was something too easy about it. Too calm. It unsettled her, leaving her with undecided feelings about the spectacle. She frowned, swallowing against the dry lump that had settled in her throat.

His attention flicked back to the woman, and his sword rose, gleaming as it ascended to chest height. The look in his eyes had turned to stone, the chill unmistakable.

The woman, still cradling her child, squeezed her eyes shut, an acceptance of fate settling over her face, an understanding that death had already arrived even if she couldn't hear the blow fall. At least they were together now. She heard the whisper of his sword sliding into its sheath, but it was far too late. Her body shook violently, as though it fought to cling to life, but her protests went unheard. The world blurred and her vision dimmed, her final sight…Connerh's sudden approach.

They say the journey to Elysium feels like flying, carried in the arms of valkyries. She never could have imagined how true the words of legends were. The cold wind against her skin, the freezing raindrops that felt warm against her face, it all seemed so surreal. Her son was still in her arms, and she couldn't help but smile, even as the world slipped away.

She wondered how long it would take for them to reach the gates. The life she'd left behind – words left unsaid, regrets that festered – would soon be forgotten. It wouldn't matter anymore. Soon, she'd remember nothing at all, just pleasant afterthoughts of her life from before. She released a soft, restful sigh, even as the lingering sensations of her body began to distort, as though caught between worlds – her skin slick with acidic tears, her bones reverberating with a thunderous beat.

The air had cleared. The wilderness, the simple and familiar smells of life returned.

But there was something wrong. The scents weren't ethereal. Nor were they heavenly. They were…too real. Too plain.

Her brow furrowed as the sensation of floating ebbed away, replaced by the firm, undeniable weight of the earth beneath her. The syncopated jostling of her body, once detached and ghostly, now felt grounded in experience, not in the unknown. She was no longer drifting. She was here.

The power of Whisper's hooves jolted her awake; she was still alive.

Elarion glanced at his hand, the blood tracing thin streams down his fingers that gathered briefly before dripping to the floor. He tightened his fist around the self-inflicted wound, feeling the sting as a useful distraction. His tongue traced the roof of his mouth, restless, while his eyes scanned the crowd. He searched their faces for something – anything resembling humanity – but not even pity could be found among them. It saddened him in a way he hadn't anticipated, leaving an ache sharper than the pain in his hand.

Connerh and Madika writhed before them, caught in their private agony. More needless suffering. Time slowed for Elarion as each twitch of their suffering stretched, distilled into something unbearable. He could hear the muffled gasp of Connerh's breath, the pained arch of Madika's body, the rustling of her chains…all of it crawling like needles beneath his skin.

His mouth parted. His tongue roamed his teeth with hopes to sedate the rage that built.

It didn't help. He'd had his fill.

The sound of his armour rattling against itself as he lunged forward turned heads, breaking the heavy quiet. Lena's gaze snapped to him.

"I need to leave," he said, voice sharp and low, each word measured to hold back the fire rising within him. "Before I do something I'll regret for the next four hundred years."

He passed her throne without pausing, his stride aggressive, his presence cutting through the air like a raven. Lena barely had time to react, her lips parting to form a response that never came. He was already gone, vanishing into the crowd, swallowed by the array of bodies.

The doors opened, then closed. The room was colder for his absence, and a chill filled the spaces where his warmth had once been.

The room flickered with light and shadow; flames licked at the walls as perfectly pillowy plumes of smoke choked the air. The ceiling above was a paradisal hellscape, like painterly clouds smeared in soot and sulphur. Madika scanned the space anxiously, trying to override the natural desire to panic. His memories were so vivid.

Connerh appeared as a child now.

Wide-eyed, his face was frozen in terror. It was an expression she never would have thought to see on him. Fear rooted him to the ground, his small frame trembling, his breaths growing shallow. His high-pitched cough cut through the roar of the flames, each desperate draw battling for air against the acrid smoke.

The door exploded inwards, shearing off its hinges.

The young Connerh staggered backwards, every muscle in his body seizing to prevent much movement. A man filled the doorway. He was impossibly tall, his frame broad and strong, but there was something otherworldly about him. His features were sharp and striking, and his skin seemed to glow, untouched by the inferno raging around him. Madika's head canted, noting an interesting detail – that was, the lack of it. The man's face was a blur, as if he were being seen on the periphery. She stood to examine him closer, and she vanished in his silhouette.

His movements stilled when he spotted Connerh.

The boy's gaze darted past the man to the floor, where his mother lay crumpled in death. A pool of blood framed her like a shadow against a wall. Connerh's breath hitched as he tried to understand.

The man followed his gaze, his own expression softening.

"Oh," he said, his voice rough and unsteady. "You're not supposed to be here."

He leaned against the doorframe, looking at the boy as though the weight of the moment had hollowed him out.

"I'm sorry for it to go this way," he said quietly, glancing at the flames curling through the timbers. "But we don't always get what we want."

The ceiling groaned; a charred beam crashed somewhere behind them. The man didn't flinch. Instead, he studied the floor, no longer able to meet the boy's eyes.

"I don't know if we'll survive this, kid. I'd hoped for a different outcome…" His words faltered. He chuckled bitterly, biting down on his lower lip until his teeth drew a golden colour from it. His face crumpled, too many emotions fighting for dominance. "I didn't think you were possible, and yet here you are. You're my greatest accomplishment."

Connerh couldn't move, couldn't speak. His gaze stayed fixed on the man's face, desperate for an answer to a question he didn't yet know.

"I broke the rules because of love, and that is why I will be punished. Not because what I did was wrong, but because it needed to be done. I was one of the few strong enough to do it, and the strong always suffer for the weak. This needed to happen," the man said with assurance. His eyes met Connerh's again. "And I'd do it again. You were worth it." A smirk curled onto his cheek.

He straightened, looking up as if he had heard something.

"I'll be with you when you need me most," he concluded as a silver spear levitated into view. Its colour shifted into a shimmering aquamarine. Connerh felt a cooling sensation roll over him, the heat from the flames no longer nipping at his skin.

And with that, the man turned and walked into the black clouds.

The smoke thickened and filled the space where he stood, all but swallowing Connerh save for a sizable bubble by which he could breathe. The smog was dense, yet Connerh no longer felt it a challenge to fill his lungs.

The sonic boom came first, then the crack of wood and the roar of rupture. The protective cloud of smoke surrounding Connerh forcefully dissipated, but then it regenerated just as quickly. He caught glances of a hooded figure approaching the man, his father, just before his view was obfuscated again.

"What have you done?" the hooded figure shouted with a voice loud enough to shake the walls, if they but still stood.

"I've done what I must," the answer came, raw and heavy. "I would expect nothing less. Now you must do what you must."

The first voice softened, almost pleading. "I still loved you."

"If that were true, we wouldn't be here right now," came the bitter reply.

"That's not fair."

"But justice is."

The silence that followed stretched, thick with grief and finality. Connerh's eyes raced around the black fog.

His father laughed. "Is that what you're calling it now?" His voice was quieter now. "You're a cruel god, jealous but unloving. Weak and unimaginative." His voice crackled with cynicism.

"That's your problem! You think we're gods!" the hooded figure replied.

"Aren't we?"

"Curse the words on your tongue!"

A momentary silence lingered.

"You need to end this," his father said.

"Enough of this melodrama. You're going with the others for a while, at least until you cleanse your thoughts of these mortals…"

"No! I'll never let you lock me away again! End this, now!"

"Enough!"

"I'll never stop fighting you. There will never be a day, hour, or minute that I will not oppose you. Do it, you coward," he replied, his voice trailing to scornful whispers.

"I said, enough!"

A sizzling crackle like thunder erupted, the blue flickering lights illuminating through the cloud surrounding Connerh.

"I hate you!" his father's elongated scream began as he ran towards the hooded man.

The words were still hanging in the air when the wave of fire erupted as a brutal crescendo of flame and sound. Connerh flinched as the blaze rolled over him, licking up his protective cloud. A thunderous explosion punctuated the chaos, bringing with it death and quiet. Connerh's hands gripped his mouth as he held back the scream perched in his throat.

The hooded figure let out a lasting yell of both anger and regret. Thunder sounded instead of the pounding of flesh as his fists hit the ground.

Connerh's startled gasp brought a halt to the outburst.

The spear took on a gold appearance just as the stranger appeared, looking cautiously in Connerh's direction. He froze in fear at what the stranger might do, but he did nothing; he was unable to see Connerh. After a few passing moments, he retreated. Still minutes more, there was an air-splitting crack and a boom.

Madika stood there with her mouth open, eyes widened. She stared at Connerh as if he were an alien.

He might as well have been.

The spear floated closer to him, drawing his attention and pulling him into a deep slumber.

CHAPTER THIRTY-SIX

PERSPECTIVE

YURI

Joriah quietly opened his door before sliding inside and closing it behind him. The interior was lit only by the lamp he carried in his other hand.

"You're late!" Yuri's voice startled him. She sat in a chair nestled in the shadowed corner of the room. She stood quickly, causing the chair to make a fuss.

"I warned you about wandering after sunset," she pressed, walking closer to him.

"Oh, it wasn't so bad. You and I have very different opinions on what dangerous means," he dismissed, chuckling to himself. Her head canted, and her eyes squinted.

"Do we?" she asked, folding her arms.

"Indeed. I scoured almost every district, and there wasn't so much as a verbal disagreement, let alone a threat of violence. Though there was that one incident, near the trade quarter..." he mused, sitting.

"You were near the trade quarter?" she asked with particular interest.

"Yes," he sighed.

"And?" she moved closer. He looked at her, then away, sighing again.

"I nearly tripped on an uneven cobblestone. Almost died. You can be sure that Darros will hear of this," he said, feigning seriousness before

296

erupting into laughter. She rolled her eyes and scoffed.

"You are a fool," she replied, finally giving in to the smirk that pulled at her lips.

"I know. No, it was rather uneventful, in truth," he replied.

"You sound disappointed," she commented lightly, although her intrigue was evident.

"In a manner. Where is everything Khazmyr is supposedly known for? The excess, the drugs, the women?" he asked.

"You didn't strike me as the type," she said, this time a bit of disappointment leaking through. He noticed.

"No, no, that's not what I meant. I just expected to see a grand display that matches the grand legend of this place. And yet it seems concealed…and *that* is concerning to me," he said with a frown.

"Why is that?" she enquired, taking a seat in a chair across from him. He grabbed a plum from the fruit bowl on the table and began eating it.

"If a place that is known for its debauchery finds it prudent to hide it," he took another bite, then paused, "then how deep does the rabbit hole go?"

She stared at him plainly while he spoke.

"Yuri, where are the children?" he leaned in towards her.

Her eyes dropped.

"A city this size, they should be everywhere. I didn't see so much as one, though I heard the voices of some when night fell," he continued.

Her eyes snapped back up to him.

"It doesn't make any sense," he mused to himself. There was a long pause. She thought quietly to herself. It was evident a debate was unfolding in her mind, and a sigh punctuated its conclusion.

"There are quite literally two sides to Khazmyr," she said, standing.

His eyes tracked her.

"On this side, the day-to-day comings and goings occur. The docks are swarming, the markets receive visitors, and the artisans and craftsmen sell their wares…" she continued, pausing to second-guess herself. "But this is just the shell. The shell is for outsiders," she said, motioning around with her hands. With an arched brow, she continued, "After all, there is more to Khazmyr than spread legs and illicit concoctions, as you say."

"And what of the other side?" he pressed.

She stared, debating whether or not to answer. Eventually, she said, "It is better that you enjoy all else Khazmyr has to offer. I fear exposure to the underbelly would only make your time here…less enjoyable." Her eyes drifted away.

"What, are you worried for my eternal soul or something?" he laughed.

"Yes," she replied.

His laughing subsided.

After a moment, he replied, "I've seen some dark things in my life.".

"And you will find that somehow, it is worse down there!" She stepped towards him.

He stood.

"Underground…" he said to himself.

She scoffed.

"What are you so anxious to find?" she argued.

"Why are you so anxious to prevent me from finding it?" he snapped back.

"Do you want your freedom?"

"Of course."

"Then avoid that place. I've met men like you before. Good men with good hearts. Family men. Fathers, sons…it's all the same. They go into the Underbelly and come out forever changed. But that wouldn't be you – no, you're the other kind. The kind that go, see, and suddenly become overwhelmed with the desire to offer something you cannot…deliverance." She glared at him from low-slung eyes. "You cannot save that which does not want to be saved. But it will consume you…both the inability to provide that which you cannot and the beast itself, as you are already in its belly." She let out a sigh as she watched him stew on her words, standing to say, "I do not wish that for you, Joriah. But you are a free man capable of making your own decisions." She turned and headed for the door, stopping just in the frame. "To see the other side, you must be invited; that is the way of things. And before you ask, I will not do this for you. I will not out of my own free will and the desire not to see you destroyed. It's not that I think of you as a weak man… It's just…a thing that is larger, more primal, than any man can resist. I think of you as a strong man, and I wish to see you stay that way." She frowned again, averting her eyes.

"You never answered my question," he replied.

She chuckled. His insistent nature was humorous and frustrating. It also assured her of what his path would be.

"The children are kept inside, away from outsiders. There are paths and tunnels to get them where they need to go. Outsiders who come from the Belly find it difficult to differentiate between night from day, if you catch my meaning. We do this for the children's safety." Her brow raised.

He nodded slowly, his own brows arching. She fidgeted with her hands.

"You'll have to excuse me. I wish to reschedule our dinner plans; I've lost my appetite," she decided politely, with a small bow of the head.

"Yes…yes, of course. I'm sorry if my questions spoiled the evening," he said.

"I know what it is you will do, but my conscience will be clear. I just wanted you to know where I stand on the matter, if it means anything. We will see what kind of man you will become, Joriah of Hildeheim," she replied as she left.

He stood in the doorway and watched her vanish into the night.

CHAPTER THIRTY-SEVEN

...CREATURES

CONNERH

"Mouse!" a soldier barked, his voice cutting through the drone of the camp. Connerh jolted out of his daydream, his hands still unconsciously working the cloth over the long blade. The steel was nearly as long as his bony frame, but it didn't deter him. Polishing weapons was just another task assigned to him – the kind the regiment avoided. He didn't mind. Every blade was a new challenge, a small victory. Connerh wasn't old enough to fight, but the commander who'd pulled him from the wreckage had taken pity on him, offering what he could: a bed, a roof, and food in his belly. And work. Always work.

It kept his hands busy and his mind from lingering on the past.

The men looked after him well enough, and what they lacked in affection and tenderness, the nurses were all too ready to provide. Between their care and the soldiers' older-brother camaraderie, Connerh had learned to survive.

"One more minute!" he shouted back, giving the blade one last pass before turning it towards the light to inspect his handiwork.

"And who are you?" a voice asked.

It wasn't a soldier. He turned and saw her – a girl his age, it seemed. Dark curls spilt from beneath the hood of her thick winter coat, and the purple threads beneath the black fabric shimmered like a raven's feathers against the snow.

Connerh forgot how to speak. She was the prettiest thing he'd ever seen.

"Well?" she asked, waiting.

"Connerh," he stammered finally, "but they call me Mouse."

She tilted her head, studying him before, dismissing the nickname, she said simply, "Then it's Connerh."

He smiled shyly, suddenly aware of the pile of weapons still waiting to be polished.

"You're new," she said. "I've never seen an armourer so young."

"I'm not an armourer yet," he admitted reluctantly, his voice quieter. "Just helping out until I can enlist."

Her expression softened at that. "And is this what you want to do, or is that what they tell you to do?"

He paused, frowning. It was a question he'd never asked himself. He wasn't quite sure, in honesty. It was the only path that seemed viable for his situation.

"I don't know. Maybe. I haven't seen enough of the world to say otherwise."

"Mouse!" the soldier called again, closer this time, his laughter carrying.

Her head snapped towards the sound, and she said sharply, "His name is Connerh."

The soldier's grin faltered as he approached, but it wasn't until she lowered her hood that he understood. His face blanched.

"Princess," he stammered, bowing low.

"Kneel," she commanded, her voice cold and precise. Connerh moved to follow suit, his knees brushing the frozen ground before she caught his arm.

"No," she corrected, pulling him upright. "That's not for you."

When her gaze lingered on him, something in her eyes made his chest tighten.

"You're coming with me now," she said simply. "Let me introduce you to Mother."

She turned and walked away without waiting for a response.

Connerh blinked, caught between disbelief and a growing sense of excitement. The soldier, still kneeling, stared up at him, dumbfounded. Connerh handed him the polished blade and hurried after her, his thoughts swirling like the snow at his feet. Madika stood in the shadows, watching it all unfold. A quiet grin touched her lips. Above her, the sky seemed to shift as the world changed course.

The carriage was saturated with opulence. The walls were encrusted with gemstones and gold, while purple velvet draped and softened the edges of their cold splendour. Madika had never possessed the wealth required to become familiar with such a fabric – it was far beyond her reach. Even now, as she ran her hand across the ceiling, her mind had no reference to pull from and offered nothing to grasp. Just a flat, cold surface, with no tactile recollection to anchor it.

Her head lagged behind her eyes as they dropped, her gaze feeling predatory only to herself. Across from her, Connerh and Lena shared the same bench, exchanging quiet, intimate affections. They looked older now, standing at the border between their childhood and teen years – or perhaps just past it. The cradled opulence was invisible to them, much like she was. His subconscious no longer communicated openly with her as it did before, instead preferring to be delightedly engrossed in relieving the past, especially since the princess had entered the picture.

She folded her arms, leaning back as her thoughts drifted. She had stayed in his mind for longer than intended, ensuring a piece of him would remain trapped with her forever – just like the others. *But perhaps he would provide better company,* she thought. A bright spot among the horde, until she grew tired of his voice, too…

His dark clouds churned in the distance, leaving an unperceived tension in the air, but her anxious curiosity surrounding them had lessened. She'd witnessed many years with him, including moments that seemed otherwise small and insignificant to her, despite their mark obviously having left a lasting impression on him. So far, if he were to become the monster they claimed, there was little wonder what they thought would become of her.

They had similar beginnings, similar tragedies…thus, to some, a predictable end.

She sighed.

Time passed.

The carriage jolted to a halt, rousing Connerh with a soft snore.

"Your Highness," came a gentle rap on the roof, followed by the attendant's voice.

Lena stretched, stifling a yawn as she nudged Connerh and murmured, "We're here."

"Remember," she began, adjusting her gown, "to mind your tongue." Her tone turned wry. "And your eyes."

Connerh grinned through his sleepiness. "You act like I've never seen a woman before."

Lena shook her head, pushing him towards the door. "Just try not to embarrass me, and don't forget your mask," she muttered, laughing nervously before handing him the remainder of his costume.

He stepped out into a wave of foreign scents – labdanum, resinous and warm, mingled with the faint sweetness of crushed wildflowers. The air felt clean and pleasant. It roused Madika, and her mouth drifted open as she recognised the familiar cues; she'd experienced this moment before, though from a different perspective.

Connerh had never seen so many *tits* in his life, literally. The number up until this point had been at least three – a number once held in high personal regard now seemed comically insignificant compared to the vast array that stood before him. Like stepping into a prepubescent boy's fever dream, the sheer variety brought a smirk to his face that was hard to deny. Big ones, small ones, some round, some swooped in the shape of a teardrop, and everything conceivable in between. In the moment, their faces were a blur, just a sea of glistening bodies in loincloths amusing his unfiltered curiosity. There were hundreds of them standing at attention, women on the left and men somewhere *over there*. A red carpet rolled out to Lena's carriage, splitting them into two separate groups.

But it was the chains around their feet that sapped the guilty pleasure from his face.

It was the lifeless expression painting each face that both widened and averted his eyes.

It was the realisation of their reality that gave him heartburn.

Lena opened the door and looked out with the humoured expectation of Connerh choking on his own drool. But he wasn't. She was instead greeted by his raised hand to help her step down, his head focused on the ground. She began to peruse the volume of information his expression conveyed as she accepted his offer and lowered herself, quickly entwining her arm with his.

Before she could utter a word, the local attendant announced himself.

"Welcome to Khazmyr, Princess! I trust your journey was pleasant?"

Lena offered a polite smile and a nod.

"I trust your journey was a pleasant one. Well, what with such fine company as you have…" he continued, prompting Connerh's cocked brow and Lena's subsequent elbow to his ribs.

"It was, thank you," she replied.

Madika slipped from the carriage unnoticed, her eyes scanning the crowd. Slaves lined the walkway, men on one side and women on the other, their bare feet bound in chains.

Just as she remembered.

"Darros will see you now. Please take your time; we have prepared something special in light of your arrival," the attendant replied with a smile. He bowed and unexpectedly sprinted back towards the castle doors.

"This *friend* of yours owns slaves?" Connerh asked with literal masked displeasure. The music began as if to punctuate his question.

"*Friend* is a strong word. A word often used when mutually convenient, though honestly, never believed," she retorted, nodding towards the slaves now performing a ceremonial dance. "And if it weren't for who he was, his resources, and what he is capable of doing for us, he'd be…"

"Shackled in your deepest dungeon?" he interjected.

"Dead," she replied, offering a placating smile.

His brow raised, and Connerh's smirk faltered.

Lena's grip tightened.

"Friendships," she continued under her breath, "are not always pretty to look at. Sometimes we have to look the other way."

She struggled to retain his eye contact.

He frowned. "But at what cost?"

Her reply came sharp and quiet. "A temporary one that we must endure, for now."

Madika barely listened, her gaze locked on a particular face among the women. Younger, smaller, and trembling – the girl was herself from back then. Her lip pouted as she stared at her younger self. These weren't her worst days, nor were they the darkest. They were sad, though. She was frightened and alone. Abused and forgotten. She was ready to end it all. A blade glinted in the sun, trembling in her younger self's grasp.

Connerh saw it too. His brow furrowed as he strategised quickly.

Madika looked at her younger self, then at Connerh, then back again, connecting the dots.

"There's no way," she said in disbelief.

"I remember you now," she heard Connerh say, initially paying it no mind before finally realising he was staring at her.

She shrieked and fell backwards.

Time was frozen, save the two of them.

His subconscious had stirred, lucid and aware once more.

"As I do you," Madika replied, straightening herself with a sharp look. His eyes returned to Lena's frozen form, his curled finger brushing her cheek. His features softened with a slight dimple before he turned to Madika.

"You're there," he said, pointing towards the younger version of her standing twenty paces down the aisle. She followed his gaze, confirming the accuracy of his memory before averting her eyes.

"You saved my life that day," she stated plainly, pausing to gauge his response.

He shrugged away the gravity of her statement, explaining, "I only stopped you from making a mistake you wouldn't live to regret."

Her squint faded.

"I understood your reasons, empathised with them, even," he continued.

"Empathised? Funny, I don't recall ever seeing you adorn a nice pair of rust 'n' irons in these memories," she replied sarcastically.

"Literal ones? No," he replied. "I wish they had been. When you can see them, feel them against your skin…well, then there's never any doubt if you're wearing them or not. " He paused, and his expression grew shadowed. "Maybe I envied you for your courage to stop the haemorrhaging. To shed regret." He looked back at her. "I wanted to do more, but I lacked the agency," he admitted.

She frowned, softly replying, "I understand."

A faint smirk ghosted across his face. "Lucky for us both, your blade was dull, shiny, and far too short to reach anything vital."

Her lips curved into a dark, reminiscent smile as she retorted, "It was all I could muster at the time."

"I understand," he echoed, and his words carried weight despite their simplicity. The memory glimmered, and time resumed its forward cadence. Her reply died on the tip of her tongue as his subconscious merged with the memory once more.

She stifled a laugh as the sun caught the crude dagger of her younger self, its reflection flashing across Connerh's eyes. Her head shook at the amateur execution of her assassination attempt. Young Madika's trembling, glassy-eyed figure was barely holding itself together, the blade clutched tightly in her white-knuckled hands. It was Connerh who saw her first, thankfully, and not the guards — a split-second difference that likely saved her life.

He couldn't be sure if her intent was to spill her blood, his, or Lena's. The possibilities hung unspoken between them, narrowing into a single, silent exchange. None of them were acceptable terms. His head tilted in a slow, deliberate shake, his free hand lowering in a calming gesture.

Breathe, he mouthed.

His still reserve disarmed her. Her confusion in the face of both his words and demeanour incapacitated her. The chaos of music and dance surrounded them, but her focus tunnelled in on his face. Her breathing quickened, then hitched, struggling to slow. Her small figure remained rooted, stubborn yet fragile amid the frenzy.

Connerh disengaged from Lena and approached, shedding his coat as he moved. Madika's posture stiffened, her grip tightening further on the dagger as she aimed it forward. He didn't falter, draping the coat over her shoulders before anchoring her with firm hands. His whisper barely reached her ears before the music cut off, silence blanketing the onlookers.

Darros' attendant rushed forward, his face painted with alarm. Connerh's hands slipped down to take the dagger, tucking it discreetly into his sleeve with practised ease. Madika's gaze remained locked on him, unblinking.

"Is everything alright? Did she do something to offend you? Would you find joy in seeing her punished?" the attendant asked in near panic.

Connerh's eyes flicked towards him briefly before returning to her. "No offence has been taken. I was simply moved to give her a gift," he said evenly.

Madika's head tilted, confusion breaking through her tension.

"A gift?" The attendant's relief was palpable as he backpedalled. "Of course, my lord. Of course."

Connerh patted the coat lightly, a concealed dagger pressing against her.

"A gift from Hildeheim," he added with finality in his performance.

Then, as a whisper in Madika's ear, "Be smarter."

Lena yanked him away, annoyance thinly veiled beneath her poised smile, as she muttered bitingly, "And what was that about? Falling for the help already?"

"Saving your life," he replied under his breath.

An unexpected frown marred her pretty features, but before she could respond, Darros emerged.

Madika's breath hitched as he strode forward, his golden skull mask catching the light – a symbol designed to sear fear of what lay beneath into memory.

In Madika's case, it worked.

Both versions of her trembled.

One month later...

Layers of metal mesh and semi-opaque curtains divided Connerh and Lena.

He stood at the outer layers, one hand on his sword's hilt, the other resting on his hip, the fingers of both occasionally twitching with a yearning to spring into action. His restraint was eating away. Thankfully for everyone else around him, looks couldn't kill. Still, his gaze bore through the layered curtains, locking onto where Lena's silhouette was glimpsed only in fleeting fragments through the shifting weave. His jaw clenched tightly, flickering the muscles under his taut skin.

The curtains were a marvel of ingenuity – a blacksmith's creation. Interwoven layers of fine mesh with contrasting patterns hung from the ceiling between curtains of fabric, distorting faces and figures as they dampened spoken words, leaving the guards outside vigilant yet removed. It was called the Room With No Walls – a clever irony.

Inside, Lena lounged on a low couch, leaning close to whatever prince she entranced with whispers laced with poison. Her hand brushed against his shoulder in a caress intended to be misinterpreted, each touch calculated and deliberate, causing both discomfort and delight with each movement. She knew Connerh was watching; she could see his scattered shadow through the veil. The devilish grin she cast towards his silhouette pierced the metal and fabric, sharper than any blade and hotter than any branding iron. She tracked his shadow as it prowled in agitated loops, a predator caged by…no walls.

Connerh's face burned as though he was lit from within, heat pooling at his cheeks and crawling up to his ears. His mouth hung open slightly, his tongue pressing hard against the roof of his mouth — as if the technique had ever worked to suppress his bubbling rage. His chest rose and fell in shallow, arrhythmic beats, betraying a restraint fraying at the edges. He knew it was just a game, one where he was expected to turn a blind eye, to look the other way. But he could never.

She enjoyed these games — too much, perhaps. The thought was an ember that flared into something primal. Did she think he lacked the jealousy to act? Was she daring him to prove her wrong?

His hand tightened about the hilt, his thumb raising and lowering the blade within his scabbard. It would take one slash and twelve cuts to fit Prince Cassius into a barrel — counting conservatively, of course. She toyed with a beast she had never truly seen unleashed. She dangled prey before him, expecting him not to salivate, to suppress the hunger that lived in his marrow. Acid churned in his veins, and his mind grew heavy with darker impulses.

None of it felt normal, yet he'd been convinced otherwise.

"Why did you let her do this to you?" Madika's voice broke the air. She stepped to his side, her arms crossed and an overt tinge of disappointment apparent in her tone. Connerh's head tilted ever so slightly as if acknowledging her presence, though his response lagged. His gaze remained fixed on Lena. His subconscious avatar tore away from the memory of himself, manifesting beside it. His gaze lingered between Lena, shame, and guilt.

"I was convinced then, much like you, that it was just a game. Just a loss I'd have to mitigate," he began, his voice low but steady. His gaze flicked briefly to Madika. "I believed I was in control, not a pawn. That's the danger of having shackles you can't see."

Madika's eyes shifted up and away, no longer desiring to watch the scene unfold. Her inhale was in stages, her exhale pronounced.

"There are only two groups," he continued, his tone revealing his determined understanding. "Those who control…and those who are controlled. A game *is* being played, but not by those on the battlefield." He shook his head slowly, a bitter smile touching his lips. "We are the controlled."

Madika frowned, her mouth opening as if to speak, only to close again. She leaned closer, her voice brimming with frustration as she urged, "You should have let me kill her. It was meant for her, you know?"

Connerh turned his gaze to her briefly, the faintest twitch of a grimace on his lips, then back towards Lena.

"I never could have let you. Besides, it doesn't matter anymore," he replied, stiffening his posture.

"That's what you always say," she muttered, staring scornfully at the side of his head.

He faded away.

Another day, another month…

"I want you to take the Rim by force. There, I said it," Lena murmured in Connerh's ear. Her legs lay across his as they rested together, bare in her bed. She fiddled with his ear as he grinned and shook his head.

"You can't be serious?" he asked. Her fingers slid down his cheek, and his own hands traced the same path, his exasperation evident in the motion. "I'm so tired of the killing and the politics. Can you even understand that?"

She pouted as he shook his head repeatedly.

"I'm not starting an unsanctioned war just so you can, what? Buy your way into your mother's graces?" he asked.

"I knew a young soldier who would raze entire villages for me!" She grew loud as a smile overtook his face, and he rolled his eyes. "Of orphans, and…and injured kittens, no less!"

He erupted into laughter from the belly, joking, "No, not the orphans! The villages and kittens, sure, but never the children." He chuckled. "I was young and stupid then – and woefully unmatched in the face of your witchcraft," he said, kissing her shoulder.

"And now?" she asked, her face brightening.

He thought a moment, then declared to the tune of her laughter, "Now, I'm clearly older, just as stupid, and still equally unmatched."

"Don't be silly, that's not what I'm asking for. I just want heads…seven, to be precise," she attempted to reassure him. "And with the right ones – *only* the right ones – there will be no war," she replied.

"Only," she says, he thought as he scoffed.

"It's the only way," she quickly replied.

That word again, he thought.

"The only way for what!?" he asked, unable to keep the heat from his voice.

"She's going to replace me, you know?" she argued.

He rolled his eyes. "Here we go with that again. I'm still not convinced she would replace you, even if she could; you are her daughter. There are laws!" he replied.

She climbed up into his lap to face him. He wanted to push her away, but her touch was calming, her scent was intoxicating, and the way she looked at him…the way she looked at only him…

The combination sent him into delirium.

"You don't know what she's capable of. I swear she hates me," she confessed, playing with his chest hair.

"She doesn't hate you…she's old! That's what old parents do, especially royalty: they set unrealistic expectations for their children that are so high, they have no choice but to land somewhere still well above everyone else. It's your job as a daughter to…deal with it…until she's dead. And at this rate, you're nearly thirty, so that shouldn't be too much longer," he replied.

She frowned, coasting briskly beyond his reply to ask, "Have you lost your edge?"

He offered a frown, which broke into surprised laughter. His stare tightened as he wondered if she meant it or if it was purely provocation. His buttons were simple, but only she could reach them.

"Have you grown so cold, so desperate that the cost of her approval has no limits?" he prodded back.

"I wouldn't expect you to understand." Her temper flared, and her tongue ran away with her. She already knew she'd crossed the line as the words flowed, but they moved too quickly to delay them.

He went motionless, his jaw tightening.

"I'm sorry," she said with diminished volume, plunging her eyes closed and wrinkling her nose. Rubbing his chest with her hands, she repeated, "I'm sorry. That's not what I meant."

He nodded away the jab.

"I meant living the life of a princess, not…" she felt it necessary to clarify.

"I understand," he replied. She could be passionate about a great many things, and he was used to her speaking before thinking. She thanked him for his forgiveness with a smile and a kiss of his hand as she brought it to her face. With heavy sarcasm, he prompted, "Continue with your case for wanton murder."

She probed his face, hoping to gauge if he was still upset with her, although it was an unsuccessful endeavour.

"As you may know, the Rim has special significance to our family." She took a deep breath. "It belongs to us and has been under our rule for centuries – that is, until grandmother allowed them to rebel."

"What's significant about it, the land or the people?" he asked

"All of it," she snapped.

"But it's an independent nation now," he argued, the sarcasm still hinting at its presence, "mustn't you *acknowledge the will of the people*? And it's not enough that it has been independent for decades, but they are also isolated from Hildeheim. It's an island for all purposes, other than the small land bridge to Khazmyr," he argued with a hint of sarcasm.

"An independent nation? Founded by criminals? Are you serious?" she questioned. "Those are meaningless words spoken by men drunk on the illusion of power. It is a power that exists only because we allow it." She looked deeply into his eyes. "It only matters if I say it matters."

His head lurched backwards; his cheek twitched.

"And I say that it doesn't," she added for good measure.

"Spoken like a true tyrant. It must run in the family," he replied with a smirk. She shot him a glare.

"I've tried the diplomatic route, thinking that would win my mother over. Even just bringing him to the table would go a long way," she replied.

"The table where he surrenders, disbands his government, and ultimately ends up at the short end of a long rope? Whether by your mother's hand or that of his own people, that is the only way it ends. There's no way that works." He laughed as she frowned.

"Which is why I have been trying unconventional means of coaxing Cassius into compliance, but he won't budge."

"You mean flirting with him," he said plainly, without affectation. An irritated but humoured expression decorated his face.

"That beats the other option," she replied sharply.

"Oh? And what's the other option?" His eyes widened, head canted.

"My hand in marriage. His delusional gaze rests upon a perch he cannot reach." She adjusted her hair, moving it from in front of her bare chest, drawing his eyes. She let him stew in the thought for a few minutes. Lying her head on his chest, she asked, "Would you really thrust me into his arms instead of thrusting your sword through his chest? It would be so easy for you…"

Her perfumed hair wafted fragrance into his flaring nostrils, and his head twitched at the thought as he fought the barrage of replies that his mind wanted him to utter. Her chest expanded with air as she took a breath, then sighed.

"Even if I were to consider such a laughable suggestion, what message would that deliver to the kingdom? Hildeheim would be split into an amalgam of *independent nations* overnight. We would disappear from the map in less than a generation…and we'd be picked off, one by one, by our neighbours." She frowned as she sat up again, and his eyes opened wide.

"You do have a point. I suppose it's a good thing you're not considering it, then."

He said it as a statement…but it wasn't. She stared into the distance just left of his gaze.

"Right? Don't you think this is all a little much for Mum's seal of approval?" He sought clarification after her delay, adding a short chuckle. She gave him a disappointed look.

"Doesn't matter; Mother would kill me before I could utter the words *I do*. It makes no sense to save one to lose the nest," she laughed.

Connerh's expression flattened.

"But I suppose you're right…" she said as she began to pull away. "If you won't take it for me, I suppose there are other methods I can exhaust." She stood and began dressing herself, engulfed in her thoughts.

He frowned, tracking her bare bottom as she dressed.

"You know they're terrible people, right?" she paused to ask with serious disbelief on her face.

"What do you mean?" he asked.

"The rebels of the Rim. They're terrible people."

Madika stood in the corner, shaking her head repeatedly.

Three months later…

It began as any other day. A day with no particular relevance, no omens preceding dark hours, no foretold prophecies etched into far-away stone. He'd walked the path to Lena's quarters a number of times, too many to count, though maybe the walls knew. Surely the floors did, but this time, something was different. Off. Not in any overt or explainable way…but he just knew. It sat on his mind like a weight, pulling his focus inwards so thoroughly that he almost missed Prince Cassius walking by on the other side of the wide hallway, a deep grin etched into his face.

Connerh rounded the corner, still making sense of his intuitions as well as trying to process his distaste for the man. A scornful frown pushed at the corner of his lips, pulling his brow downwards. He paused upon noticing that Lena's guards were no longer stationed at their posts. His brow deepened; the moments between steps shortened.

He didn't knock.

The door swung open silently, the hinges recently oiled. Inside, the room was quiet but for the crackle of the hearth. Lena sat before it, her back to him, her slim figure silhouetted against the firelight. For a fleeting moment, relief washed over him. She was there, safe, as she often was.

But relief could often be a fickle thing. It ebbed as quickly as it came, replaced by unease.

His distaste for Cassius rushed in, reclaiming its place at the forefront of his thoughts.

"Why was he here?" he asked, giving it his best to sound humoured. As he approached her, he continued, "And where is your guard?"

She raised her head slowly, turning to look at him. Her makeup was running from the torrent of water and saline that streamed down her face, and his heart stuttered, the pit in his stomach deepening.

"Lena…"

Her name was barely a whisper from his lips.

He crossed the room in an instant, falling to his knees beside her. His hands hovered, unsure of where to land, as though the wrong touch might shatter her entirely.

"What's going on? What's wrong?" he asked, his voice softer now, seasoned with urgency. Each word was a plea for rushed clarification. It felt as if they were losing precious time for him to react. Her silence was unbearable, and as she lowered her head, his own fears rose – a flood of anger and dread crashed against reason. He grabbed her shoulders firmly.

"Did he hurt you?" his tone darkened with the demand, the dread draining from his voice until only the byproducts of anger remained.

"I dismissed them, the guard. I thought – I thought I could…" Her words were delayed; she found it difficult to relocate to the present, away from the moment in time she wanted to forget. Her eyes locked with Connerh's, her lips pouting and eyes welling with water. A blink. A new focus for her eyes and a clearing of her throat provided the focus she needed. "I invited him here." She glanced at him to gauge his reaction. His expression remained chiselled in place. "I assure you, under false pretences," she continued, and he finally blinked. There were words that took refuge, lumped in the centre of her throat, forcing her mouth to stay slightly open; her left brow raised and lowered as she attempted to coax them out. "I pushed him too far…and he took my advances as an invitation to take what he wanted…"

She barely got the words out before Connerh rushed to his feet, unsheathing his sword in what felt like a singular motion. Lena nearly fell over as she reached for his foot when he walked for the door. She grabbed hold of his ankle, tightly.

"Wait!" she screamed. Beginning to cry, she pleaded, "You mustn't. Exposing him would ruin me."

"Expose?" he asked in shock. "The only thing I'm going to expose are his innards."

She gathered her gown and stood.

"Connerh, please…" She rushed to embrace him, to hold him.

"This won't stand!" he shouted, and she turned her face to escape his ire.

"I just need time to think about what my next move will be."

She reached up to caress his face, hoping to soothe the rage that made his skin hot to the touch, but he ripped away, returning his sword to its place.

"This is not a game! And even if it were, then give it up; you've lost! This ends now! I will not stand by and remain idle while he continues to draw breath after he has…humiliated you!"

The word was difficult for him to say but generic enough to utter. He moved closer to her, holding her face in his hand. Her lips pouted, and rivulets of tears quietly rolled down her face.

"They'll write stories after what I'm going to do to him," he promised, stoned-faced. She just nodded, knowing there would be nothing she could say to deter him in that moment. She lay on his chest instead, inhaling his scent in large doses. He wrapped his arms around her, holding tightly, kissing the top of her head. They stood for a while as she continued to cry in silence.

"Just stay with me tonight…" she requested, her voice nearly a whisper as she swayed their bodies.

His jaw clenched.

"Please," she begged.

He finally agreed. "I'll stay…"

She let out a sigh with staggered breath.

"I never should have left you. I could have prevented it…stopped him. Killed him," he said, his gaze blank as he stared into his memories.

She shook her head and rebuked him. Her words fell on deaf ears.

"I'll stay tonight, but then, in the morning…I'll be gone for a little while," he said.

Her head tilted up, her eyes searching his face before his eyes.

"Don't make me lie to you," he replied to her unspoken query.

She nodded, resting her head back on his chest.

In the shadow of his neck, her lips curled ever so slightly – a fleeting smirk, gone before it could linger.

Madika had never witnessed a city under siege before, let alone from the inside. Her expression was marked by awe and shadowed by shock. The silent assassins moved with the cold precision of a blade sliding through flesh – quick, effortless, efficient. They scaled walls and slipped through alleyways, as comfortable in the labyrinth of stone as shadows in the dark. The few sounds they made were sharp and fleeting – dagger strikes, muffled gasps, the quiet finality of a life snuffed out like punctuation to the short-winded expression of death. They hunted with purpose, rooting out the loyalists to Prince Cassius identifiable by the brands they bore; some on the arm, others brazenly on the forehead. Little did they know, their badge of honour would soon become the promissory of their demise.

It all accelerated so quickly.

For nearly an hour, the slaughter unfolded in silence as blades, hammers, and arrows extinguished lives without so much as a whisper. Then came the screams – sharp, piercing, dragging the city from its restless slumber into chaos. Panic spilt hysteria into the narrow streets, but it offered no salvation.

There was no one to summon, no reinforcements en route. The barracks, garrisons, and watchposts had been the first to bleed out, their occupants drained before they could sound the alarm. The city gates were sealed, carts were overturned, and the few flickering lanterns that once held back the night were snuffed out, plunging everything into complete darkness. Even the full moon hid behind dark clouds.

There was nowhere to run, nowhere to flee. They could only barricade themselves while awaiting judgment – or whisper prayers to deaf gods and lifeless statues.

A man darted past Madika, his movements frantic but muted, like a hunted animal. He came close enough for her to see the mark on his forehead, four jagged lines like claw scratches, before he took his chances into the unknown. The soft swoosh of an arrow followed. His hurried footsteps ceased, replaced by a wet gurgle and the dull thud of his collapse.

Connerh emerged from a nearby house, busy wiping blood from his blade with a black cloth hung from his belt. A soldier approached, his steps sure despite the chaos.

"Most of them have the mark," he said.

Connerh nodded, his voice cold and certain, as he gave the order, "Burn it. All of it."

The soldier gave a curt bow and disappeared into the darkness. Another figure stepped forward, his face concealed behind a wild dog's mask.

"The path to the castle is clear," he said, his tone calm but purposeful. "They've barricaded themselves in, but we've found another ingress. I'll guide you when you're ready."

Connerh paused, his eyes scanning the burning ruins. He removed his mask, letting the chill night air fill his lungs. The light drizzle began to fall against his face. The soft droplets caught the glow of the spreading flames, turning to embers in the orange hues of the sky. Madika watched him with narrowed eyes, her brow furrowed as she studied his expression, a mask of its own. Cold. Detached.

As more men emerged from the shadows, the three quickly became twenty. Connerh replaced his mask, his voice low but commanding as he decreed, "Let it be done."

Together, they melted into the darkness, their silhouettes swallowed by the ruins as they advanced towards the castle. Madika followed at a distance, first trying to match their relentless pace on foot before her efforts proved futile. Closing her eyes, she bent the dream state to her will. Her feet lifted from the ground, and in moments, she was gliding at their heels like a haunting spirit. A frown marred her lips, but a faint smile tugged at the corners as she watched them cut through every obstacle with brutal efficiency.

If only I had these men at my command, she thought.

With each step, their numbers swelled, growing like vultures arriving at a fresh kill. When thunder rolled and lightning split the sky, Madika realised the Seventy had rejoined them.

They were all around, moving as one towards their final target.

Connerh stood at the mouth of the tunnel, steam rising faintly from his skin in the cool air. His rage was a living thing fed by the image of Lena's tear-streaked face looping endlessly in his mind. The storm outside intensified, its lightning carving jagged paths across the darkened sky.

"Are you sure you don't want us to go with you?" asked the lion-faced soldier.

The Seventy crowded close, their presence a wall of silent resolve.

"We can clear the way to the prince."

Connerh shook his head and removed his mask. His voice was calm, but his words carried the weight of finality.

"No. Let him know I'm coming." He handed the mask to one of the Seventy. "Seal off every entrance and exit but this one. Set it all ablaze."

The lion-faced soldier inclined his head with an, "Understood. Good hunting, brother."

One by one, the Seventy stepped forward, each pressing against his right shoulder with three taps of their fifth finger – their silent farewell. Connerh bowed his head to each, his fist resting against his palm.

"Good hunting," he murmured back.

Turning, he descended into the darkened path ahead. Just before the shadows consumed him, he paused.

"I'll see you in the after."

Their quiet roar of approval followed him as he vanished.

Madika watched the scene unfold, her lips parted in disbelief. She tracked their every movement, her mind racing. The Seventy weren't just a myth — they were here, alive and moving towards the heart of the storm. Men of legend. The ones mothers whispered about to instil respect in their children and which fathers spoke of with reverence, living vicariously through their exploits. Men who rode black horses — the Night Mares — and left no trace as they culled their enemies.

Somehow, not only had she found proof of their existence, but she had been in the mind of one of their leaders. As if she hadn't seen too much already, making herself a frayed end to a tightly woven pattern. A wave of uneasiness overtook her. She almost didn't want to see anymore, but there was a crowded throne room up there, waiting for her…for her report on the truth.

"What have I gotten myself into?" she muttered to herself.

Cassius, his kin, and their followers may have ruled the capital of Tidesreach and the port city of Greyshore for a few generations, but they had never grasped the full truth of the cities they claimed. The real knowledge — the secrets of their construction — belonged to the original builders of those cities, meaning Hildeheim. They were secrets that rested with Connerh and the Seventy. Among them were hidden pathways, winding unseen through the streets and beneath the castle, their entrances invisible to all but those who knew where to look.

Connerh emerged unnoticed into the heart of the chaos. They didn't see him — not because he was concealed but because they weren't looking for him. They thought themselves safe, barricaded against the evil they believed lay still outside the castle doors.

Like spearing fish in a barrel, his blade flashed in swift, silent arcs, the sound lost beneath the growing fury of the storm outside, which only grew more violent and turbulent with each passing minute. One by one, they fell, their cries swallowed by the oppressive weight of the night. Their false sense of security was shattered in an instant, but it was far too late. Connerh left none standing as he carved a path towards Cassius, cold and relentless, every movement an assurance of death.

He stopped in his tracks. The final door loomed ahead. The scent of burning wood hung heavy in the air, and thunder rattled the castle's stone as lightning streaked through the windows. For the first time in the twilight hours, his nerves surfaced – not from fear but from the weight of what had to unfold perfectly. He didn't want his rage to consume him, not yet. He wanted Cassius to feel it all, to savour every second before the end. He knelt, closed his eyes, and took slow, steadying breaths.

His mind drifted between the familiar battle hymns of his people, the Seventy, and a language which flowed that he didn't quite understand. The words swirled around him like the storm, grounding him in an aura that felt ancient.

He stood.

A calm reassurance wrapped around his shoulders.

His index finger extended, touching the door in front of him.

It exploded into dust particles and splinters – he was still too blinded by his bloodlust to notice.

Cassius fell to the ground, pleading for his life as he crawled, backing himself against a wall. Connerh approached, slow and evenly paced, the cowardice on display sapping a bit of pleasure from his approach.

"The world needs to be purged of men like you," Connerh stated, each step reverberating within the wood floor. "I will gladly take up the mantle of a coward slayer."

"But she asked for it…" Cassius managed to utter before Connerh lunged at him, grabbing his throat with his hands. His neck muscles flexed and contorted as he struggled to contain himself from crushing the man's windpipe in his grip. Connerh pushed away, laughing to himself as he paced in a circle.

"I've never felt this way before," Connerh admitted mid-laughter. "In truth, I'm a bit nervous, worried about overdoing it. I suppose that's where the expression overkill comes from." He chuckled to himself. "I wish I could restore your life after I've taken it thousands of times," he continued, canting his head while he examined his prey. "But we only have once to get it right," he added with a touch of finality, drawing both his sword and his dagger.

He dropped the sword at the door.

"We won't be needing that," he said.

Cassius wept profusely, begging for mercy.

It was when he repeated that Lena had asked for him to assault her that the first stab penetrated his gut. The effeminate scream caused the second, third, and fourth.

"Do you know how many cuts it takes to fit a body in a barrel?" Connerh asked, a gentle joy overtaking him.

Cassius choked on his own blood.

"Twelve," Connerh nodded to himself. "Conservatively, that is," he added. His dilated eyes reflected the candlelight ominously. "First, it's the hands...always the hands. Just so you can endure what's coming." He smirked before taking his prize from a reluctant vendor.

"Feet."

Thud.

"Forearms."

Splatter.

"Knees."

Something gurgled.

"Shoulders!" he shouted with a laugh.

He was losing time; Cassius was fading in and out of consciousness. He noticed, hastening his attack.

"Twelve, no...no, no, I misspoke," he declared, smacking his own forehead. "We forgot the bits that got you into this mess to begin with."

Cassius had no breath left to protest. He went limp before the cutting finished, nearly as it began. Connerh finished as the adrenaline started to fade, his senses overriding the remnants of rage. His thumping heartbeat clouded and distorted his hearing. His pupils began to constrict, returning to their normal size, and he panted loudly, heavily. His throat felt dry and chalked over. He swallowed vigorously in an attempt to saturate the symptoms.

And then he froze, his ears tilted upwards. There was noise like whimpering. He looked around, confused. There was a door leading to an adjacent room. He stumbled over to it as the fleeting rage left him tired but overwhelmed. He glanced at Cassius's remains and the bloody pool in which they lay.

He winced, frowned, and looked away.

There it was again. The whimpering. It was feminine. He raced to the door and ripped it open. There were two women who shrank back at his explosive entrance, screaming upon seeing Cassius. They had chains around their necks, feet, and hands.

A cold branding iron lay on the floor near the fireplace behind them.

Four scratches like those of creatures.

Connerh froze.

Their recognition worked faster than his, and their terror transformed into relief.

"Free us. Please!" they began to shout, overwhelming him.

"No…" Connerh whispered as his mind raced, his head shaking. His brow crumpled.

They all bore the mark. He heard his lieutenant's voice replay in the back of his mind, and it was as if his subconscious was pleading to justify their actions. The screams for help pierced his stupor as he rushed to free them. They scrambled away as soon as they were free.

He picked up the brand and inspected it. His eyes welled with tears as the crushing weight of the truth landed on his chest, pulling the air from his lungs.

Madika sobbed in the corner as she watched his reality crumble.

The smoke had thickened, had risen to cover the ceiling, and in that moment, he became the boy trapped in the burning closet.

He looked around, wishing to be saved.

But there would be no one to save him from himself, from the creation of his own hand. The thunder outside sounded like explosions, and the fire sizzled and crackled, searing in a manner that seemed unnatural.

The orange flames flickered in hues of blue and green.

He walked from the burning castle, its flames melting stone like wax.

A crack of thunder split the air.

A familiar protector flew threw a building on its way to Connerh, exploding it in its wake.

Its golden shaft reflected the chaos around it.

Bolts of lightning crackled through the sky, striking the ground around Connerh and sending mud and debris into the air.

He stood in awe, still struggling to comprehend the hours preceding him.

There was a desire to reach for it.

To grab hold.

But a child struggled to breathe in the near distance, choking on fumes as he emerged from a home still ablaze.

He was no older than three, maybe four.

Connerh's soul crumpled. His empathy backfilled the void of regret as he ran for the child, barely catching him before he lost consciousness.

The memory faded to black.

The story was told.

Connerh lay on the glass floor.

And he sobbed.

It was the longest fifteen minutes of Lena's life, feeling twice as long as Connerh had been away.

She lunged forward in an uncontrollable motion as Connerh and Madika's screams came to an abrupt end.

They crumbled to the floor before anyone could catch them.

CHAPTER THIRTY-EIGHT

MERCY

ELARION

The ring always felt cool against his chest.

It was forged from methylite, a rare metal ore that grew cold when it absorbed heat. Its uses in elven culture were many: blacksmiths wove it into armour, granting soldiers comfort even in the cruellest of deserts; builders laced it through roofs and floors to cool great halls in the height of summer; potters shaped it into vessels that kept wine chilled long after the pouring. Yet, for Elarion, its finest purpose was neither practical nor utilitarian. It was purely symbolic.

A ring for his betrothed.

Whether it circled his finger or hung against his chest on a delicate chain, the metal's cool touch was a constant reminder. It whispered of their love, unyielding and steadfast, even in the face of the sweltering trials of their lives. Pressed near his heart, the ring urged him to honour its purpose – to protect, to endure, and to cherish that which no fire could consume. Most of all, it was a reminder to use his heart…

As humans did.

Elarion lingered in the shadows of a narrow alleyway, his tall silhouette cloaked in darkness. A black mantle draped over his shoulders, concealing the glint of armour beneath. His fingers fidgeted with the ring, passing its cool metal between them as though the touch might quiet his restless mind.

Rain fell from the heavens in lazy, snow-like flakes, the kind that seemed to hesitate midair before surrendering to gravity. The scent of petrichor mingled with the crisp chill of wet cobblestones, filling the air with a bittersweet aroma. His breath billowed in faint plumes made visible in the cold, and somewhere deep inside, his body ached for the comfort of a hearth's warmth, the bite of hot tea against his lips. But not now. Not yet.

His eyes, sharp and discerning, swept over the shifting crowd. Each face was an opportunity, each step a possibility, yet none caused him to linger long in his scrutiny. Always the observer of the unobservant, he watched them pass without notice.

The ring span once more between his fingers before his hand rose, clenching it tight. The chain jostled faintly as he tucked it beneath his cuirass, letting the cool weight press against his chest. A sudden movement caught his attention: Balfour, his target, broke from the flow of bodies and disappeared into a small workshop, the door slamming shut behind him with a sharp splash of displaced rainwater.

Elarion stepped into the street, pulling the hood of his cloak tighter against the chill and drizzle. His boots echoed softly against the stones as he approached.

His knocks were pronounced against the thick oak door.

Balfour found it curious that the knocks came in only two sharp rasps – an unusual break from the customary three or more. His thick, furry brow rose as he shuffled towards the door, curiosity pricking at him. The warped hinges groaned like an old man complaining of the cold as he eased the door open. Surprise flickered across his face at the sight of Elarion standing there, his white-and-gold regalia peeking out from beyond his cloak, betraying his anonymity. Even under the pale wash of sunlight breaking through the overcast sky, Elarion seemed to glow. He looked otherworldly – out of place.

"Ah, Master Elf," Balfour greeted, his voice laced with equal parts respect and apprehension. "What brings you here?"

His gaze locked with Elarion's for a breath too long – those onyx eyes sent an involuntary shiver down his spine; had hairs traced it, they'd have bristled.

"Come in, come in," Balfour added hastily, dipping his head as though to shield himself from that unsettling gaze. He stepped back into the dim warmth of the workshop, gesturing absently. "I was just trying to get the fire going. It's a real pisser out there, isn't it? Even got me feeling the chill." He hobbled further inside, shoulders slumping beneath the thick layers of his coat.

Elarion paused at the threshold, his sharp eyes sweeping over the interior before he followed. He eased the heavy door shut behind him, the latch clicking into place with finality.

The room smelled of mouldy wood, parchment, and potions. In the corner, a squat fireplace struggled to kindle a proper flame, its stone facade darkened by years of soot. An engraved rocker sat before it, its legs creaking faintly against the floor – which had been worn bare to the grain beneath its weight. Books dominated the space, cramming every shelf in a chaotic sprawl of leather-bound spines and crumbling scrolls that teetered precariously, as if defying gravity out of sheer habit.

A large central table was no less cluttered, its surface a battlefield of strewn papers, toppled inkwells, and vials holding liquids of dubious origin. The room was an assault on Elarion's sensibilities, every disorganised corner grating against his preference. His fingers brushed the cool edge of his cuirass, a silent anchor to steady him in the storm of disorder.

There was another smell.

Elarion's nose twitched, his expression sharpening as he took a deliberate inhale. It cut through the stale aromas of the room, acrid and unmistakable. Vinegar – and something else. His eyes narrowed, flaring with recognition.

"Amber thistle acid mixed with vinegar produces toxic vapours. You should be more cautious with your tinctures." His voice was steady but edged with reprimand as he lifted the back of his hand to shield his nose and mouth.

"What's that?" Balfour called, straightening from his huddle near the fireplace where he had been celebrating the spark of reluctant flames.

Elarion gestured silently towards two vials sitting too comfortably side by side.

"Oh, yes…yes, of course," Balfour muttered, a sheepish chuckle bubbling out of him as he shuffled over to separate them with hurried hands. "Simply an oversight, I assure you. I always check my labels before mixing. I must've grabbed the colza oil instead." He let out another laugh, this one tinged with a nervous quaver.

Elarion's gaze swept the room with a pointed precision, his tone laced with dry disapproval as he said, "I can see how such a mistake could occur."

The old man giggled again, less heartily this time. "Well, yes… Now then, what was it you needed, Master Elf?"

"Please, my name is Elarion."

"As you wish," Balfour replied, bowing his head.

Elarion's posture shifted, and the air grew heavier. "Where is the woman you hold captive?"

His words landed bluntly, like stones dropped into still water.

"Who? Do you mean…Creature?" Balfour's voice pitched upwards at the name, like an ill-tuned string. He grinned devilishly. "Ah, you're here to solve your nightmares, perhaps? Add a few?"

Elarion's fist slammed against the cluttered table, rattling the vials and startling Balfour into a visible flinch. The elf leaned forward, his brow arching sharply over dark, narrowed eyes as he demanded, "Surely, she has a name."

"Oh," Balfour stammered, repeating the syllable like a chant as realisation dawned on his lined face. His head bobbed with hasty agreement, his mouth struggling to catch up to the motion. "Aye, she does. Madika is her name by birth."

"Then we shall call her by such," Elarion replied, his tone firm and final.

The shift in the room was palpable. Balfour's expression hardened, his head tilting, his mouth frozen mid-breath. When he finally spoke, his voice was softer, edged with careful correction.

"I'm afraid you misunderstand, Mas– Elarion." His head swayed, brows pulling low in a furrow. "Madika is not, as you say, held captive here…nor anywhere. Within full reason, she has complete autonomy. After all," he continued, his words gaining a measured cadence, "she suffers from a mental affliction. It would not do to confine her in such a state."

Elarion's gaze lingered, assessing. His fingers curled faintly against the table's edge, though he said nothing. Eventually, his voice rising from nearly a whisper, Elarion replied, "Those who are free do not wear chains around their necks."

"No, no, the chains…you misunderstand it all. The chains are for her protection. When she has an episode, she can get rather feisty. She's bitten off an ear or two, she has. And…I'd be lying if I said we didn't spice it up for a little bit of a theatre," he refuted, frustrated by Elarion's accusation. Balfour tried looking him in the eye but couldn't find the strength. He was very much vexed by the elf.

"Theatre?" Elarion repeated distastefully. "Those sound like the words of a man who has thoroughly convinced himself of a lie."

The light in the room felt dimmer, and Elarion's face grew brighter. Balfour shook his loose fists at his side; he writhed as he debated his disclosure. His eyes widened.

"No, no!" Balfour grunted, beyond agitated. He scurried off to find a particular journal amidst the paper-bound chaos. Elarion's brow spiked. "Give me a moment; all will be explained in detail shortly."

Balfour giggled in delight upon finding a particular red volume. He scoured the pages until he found *it*. He set it down on the table in front of him, traced the words with his fingers, and flashed a glance at his guest. His posture straightened as he stared at the words below his nose. A small smile wedged itself onto his face. He cleared his throat.

"Loth oehmen…braene…hoteph? No…yes, yes… Loth oehmen braene hoteph. By the ancient oak and the whispering wind, I bind your tongue and your mind. No word shall pass, no secret revealed, until this spell is broken or sealed," he declared.

Elarion's confusion may have been more apparent had his expression matched his thoughts. His head turned as he tried to figure out what language Balfour's words were supposed to be. As it stood, they sounded like gibberish. To Balfour, his blank expression was evidence enough that his spell had worked. Balfour closed the book and tugged the sides of his robe, rather impressed with himself.

"I hate that I had to do that to you, old boy. I just had to be sure of your secrecy. I do sense your good intent towards Madika, which is so rare these days! And I hate to say it, but I've been dying to let someone in on it, and for whatever reason, I feel it's you. I know you'll obey the blood oath. Damn well couldn't break if you wanted to! It's comforting to know your people are trustworthy, I know that much. No matter how…" his mouth lost track of his thoughts.

It was probably for the best.

"Madika had a very rough life," Balfour went on, mindless of his impropriety. "A very unfortunate life. Yes, a portion of what you have seen is mostly performative, but it's how they *want* to see her. They want to be afraid, shocked, and disgusted. It arouses them. It makes them feel superior. And then to see her bound…tethered, controlled…" he paused, staring into nothing with disgust. "Well, I imagine that's the only way some of those types get their knickers cramped and damp." He scowled, returning his attention to Elarion. He concluded, "And so, Madika obliges those expectations, if it'll loosen their grip on their coin."

"Are you implying that you coerce her to perform fake mind readings for money?" Elarion accused with an arched brow.

"Oh, no. I'm telling you that she is not only very much in control but also more the predator than the prey in these situations," he giggled. Lowering both his head and his volume, he continued, "And that's not to say the pain you see is fake. By no means! She very much endures a lot. That is why I say *mostly* performative." With a vulnerable admission, Balfour continued, "I need funds to fuel my research for a cure. Components aren't cheap, and stealing is a risky affair…and of low moral value, might I add. Of course, I won't lie and say I hadn't considered it."

Elarion finally nodded, understanding the reality of her situation as he enquired, "And how often is she in a feral state as opposed to normal consciousness?"

"It varies. It used to be all the time, but with years of trial and error, my potions have been able to keep her in full control only slightly less than half the time. Of course, I fear I might not live beyond my ability to fully cure her of this disease," he explained regretfully, becoming antsy and retreating to his rocking chair.

Elarion looked around the workshop again with different eyes. He could metaphorically see the ghost trails of Balfour frantically ravaging through and making new notes, emptying journals and starting new ones. The stained, messy shelves and tables had history and a story to tell.

His warm hand startled Balfour as it rested on his shoulder.

"If what you say is true, then you need not feel regret. You have done a good thing," Elarion said.

"*If* what I've said is true?" Balfour whispered to himself. He looked up at Elarion with confusion in his eyes. "I don't understand. Why would I compel you under the Blood Oath of Seme…Semeliron…" He tried to remember the name. "…of your Elder…if I were only to tell you a lie? That seems a bit absurd, wouldn't you say?" he asked, amused but dumbfounded.

Elarion smiled and said, "Semeliron is indeed a pillar in the annals of my people's history."

Balfour nodded.

"As a poet…the original founder of our theatrical arts…a very, very long time ago. Well before my time, and I am ancient by your standards," he recalled fondly. He leaned in, a smirk growing on his face, as he explained, "My people are not bound by blood oaths."

"I paid good money for that book," Balfour complained to himself before nervousness overtook his expression.

"You have no cause for worry; your secret is safe with me," Elarion assured Balfour before the other man could speak. "This is better than I could have hoped for. I have so many questions. First, I hope you are not getting your instructions for your potions from that book?"

Balfour began to reply but stopped himself. His head fell forward into a chuckle, and he replied mirthfully, "No, I should hope not. A bit of a laugh at my expense. I suppose I've earned it." His cheeks flushed over. "Failed incantations aside, I offer my apologies. Thank you for allowing me to get that off my chest despite looking like a fool."

"I understand the burden and danger you face; your apology is not necessary. I should hope I would have friends who would also go to such lengths to help me," Elarion replied.

Balfour felt a warmth fill his mind, and his anxiety began to melt away. His chair stopped mid-rock. He gasped.

"You have her abilities as well! But…but I didn't even feel…oh, you're much more advanced than she is!" he rushed to stand.

Elarion's gaze averted at the focused attention, and he said graciously, "I should have asked, but your willingness to help her moved me to help you. It can be forthcoming like that sometimes."

"You could be the one to help us," Balfour replied, brushing by Elarion's humility in favour of sinking into his own thoughts. He continued to rant to himself as he walked over to pore through the loose notes. Elarion tracked him. Without looking up, Balfour announced, "You should speak with her."

"Perhaps in time…" Elarion began to decline.

"No, you must! I insist. It is the only way I will accept your apology." He scampered over to Elarion and grabbed him by the arm, pulling him down the hallway. Stopping at the entrance, he pointed down the long hallway and instructed, "Second door on the left."

Elarion hesitated but ultimately acquiesced.

"Knock first; I don't know what state she's in. She's not swearing at me, so the odds are in your favour," Balfour explained before rushing back to his work.

His careful, stealthy steps brought him to the foot of her door. His ears twitched as he listened for any sign of life.

"Come in," she invited before he could knock.

His eyes dropped to the doorknob. He rotated it carefully and opened it, scanning the interior.

She sat in the darkened room in a white chair, rocking back and forth, staring in an empty direction. Clouds of her breath appeared in the soft white light beaming in through the small windows that lined the ceiling. It was a decently large room with a bed, nightstands, a trunk, and a chest of drawers against the wall. The lingering smell of burnt sage permeated the air, and a few dried bundles lay on the floor nearby. It was cold, past the point of comfort.

Elarion quickly removed his coat and began to walk towards her.

"I am not bothered and have no use for your chivalry. Come in," she said with a cracked voice.

He stopped short a few feet from her and took notice of the thick wool blanket wrapped around her figure. Her eyes pulled focus as she looked up at him.

"She's a damn lie. Don't let her charm put you off. He's not a customer, he's here to help. I can feel it," Balfour said as he brushed past Elarion with a lit bundle of branches. He knelt before the fireplace in her room and began to light a fire. Addressing Elarion, he fussed at Madika and said, "She forgets to mind her body, as she spends too much time in thoughts. It has its own separate needs, too."

An orange hue from the eager flames brought warmth to an otherwise pale blue environment. Elarion observed quietly.

"It needs far less than you think, Balfour," she said. Her tone was tired, exasperated.

Elarion looked at her when she spoke but dropped his gaze when she returned it. Her face was scarred and emaciated, covered in dark makeup that embellished her weary appearance even further. Still, her aura was calmer than her appearance let on. She smiled at Elarion's second-hand embarrassment.

"Gone and found another prince to save me, did you, Balfour?" she asked mockingly. He stood upon completion of his second fire.

"Don't be nasty. I didn't recruit him. He came looking for you. And he's not a prince… Or I don't think that he is, anyway?" Balfour flashed confusion and looked to Elarion.

Elarion diplomatically skirted the implied question, replying instead, "I'm not here to save you. Although I will offer my assistance if that is what you wish."

She stood as her eyes locked onto the growing fire, and she sauntered over to it. She rubbed her hands together in front of it before drawing them back under her blanket.

"That does feel nice. Thank you, Balfour." Her exterior broke for a moment of genuine gratitude, and Balfour giggled and kissed her forehead.

"You see, there's still a lady in there somewhere," Balfour announced before smiling. "I will leave you two, as you no doubt have much to discuss."

Elarion tracked his exit as Balfour closed the door with a smirk. His eyes trailed first to the floor and then to the back of Madika's head.

"You never did say much about yourself," she began.

"Pardon?" he said.

"You came full of questions but never really answered any," she explained, turning to face him. She knocked on a nearby wall. "Very thin walls. I heard most of it. Including Balfour's attempt to compel you." She gave a scornful laugh. "I told him that book was filled with nonsense."

Elarion flashed a smirk.

"You know I'm Tu'Chauri, right? You people may not have blood oaths, but you *do* hold grudges," she went on as she walked around him, maintaining a safe distance.

"I am well aware of your heritage," he assured her, keeping his eyes glued to her figure.

"And yet you still offer your help?" she asked.

"I do," he affirmed, finally locking his eyes with hers. She nodded and moved in closer.

"We could just cut to the point?" she asked, dropping her robe to expose her bare cleavage before moving in to caress his face. His eye contact remained steady; she gave him a wicked expression. He smiled and allowed her to touch him. She remembered being shocked by his lack of reaction, but the shock didn't come quickly enough to delay her touch.

The room went black as she was rapidly whisked away. She found herself falling. Her lungs filled with air as she woke up lying face down in a river. But she was not wet, nor was she wanting for air. She quickly cradled her chest. She could feel the clean linen between her fingers. The water was perfumed. It felt real enough, but her eyes doubted it. She looked up to see Elarion standing downstream with his foot propped up on a rock, his hands folded behind his back. His hair was long and abnormally dark for an elf.

"Who are you?" she asked, stopping to gasp. Her voice was no longer cracked but young, youthful.

He smiled modestly, glancing away, putting weight on his propped foot and then taking it off again.

"Assistance, if you want it," he replied, returning his gaze.

Her thoughts raced.

"Will you take the Gift from me?" she said fearfully.

His eyes wandered, returning only for him to shake his head.

"I will not; it is not mine to take," he replied.

Her posture straightened slightly. She stood and looked around.

There was a modest hut which looked more than vaguely familiar adjacent to the river. There were lush trees and vegetation, with animals far too comfortable and close to be real. She chuckled, exchanging glances with Elarion as he stared down at his fidgeting foot, still wearing a smile. Her smile faded as she saw them.

Just beyond the perimeter, in the shadows of her personal forest, there were figures absent of purpose. An endless horde of ghastly men and women swayed back and forth, seemingly with no desire to intrude. The ghosts trapped in her mind. Her posture stiffened, and she stumbled towards Elarion.

"They…they…" she stammered, looking up at him. She read his cues. Accepting the reality, she asked, breathless, "They can't bother me here?"

He shook his head and said, "They cannot."

She looked away as she pondered.

"Do you mean to trap me here?" she asked, frowning, her eyes becoming saturated with the tears that welled. His face crumpled as he reached for her hands. She sighed at his touch, and her fears subsided.

"No," he said.

"We're still in my room? I can sense it still," she said.

"They cannot enter if you do not wish them to. This place is your reprieve. They will be drawn to you, but here, *you* are in control," he affirmed.

She smiled, looking around as her confidence steadily built, and she remarked, "I could never manifest such a place for myself." She was drawn to look at him again. "My typical retreat is darkness…where they crowd and shout at me. They're always screaming…but they're so quiet here…" she murmured in disbelief.

Madika let out a restrained sigh through pursed lips as she wept quietly, fighting the desire to let go entirely. Her face grew pale, the bones seeming to protrude much as they did in reality, and her makeup ran. Elarion gave her the moment in silence, fighting the desire to offer comfort.

She sniffled after a few minutes, then closed her eyes as she took a deep breath. Her face restored itself to its youthful appearance with an exhale.

"This is beautiful," she said, sitting in the stream, crossing her legs, and resting her fingertips in the water. "Is it strange that sometimes, in the quiet moments, I can feel my own potential? Like I've barely scratched the surface?" she asked, repeating quiet breaths of relief.

Elarion smiled, shook his head, and replied, "No."

"I do not claim to rival your power, but why is it that you will not let me in?" she asked. "I only wish to know who it is that wanders my mind with such authority."

He continued to stare into the stream, his smile fading.

She gasped as he obliged her wish, allowing her a glimpse into his own subconscious. Madika's skin grew heavy, sagging from her face as her breath was pulled from her lungs, if only for a moment. She regained her composure with laboured breaths, as if she had just arisen from a loss of consciousness.

"I don't understand. Why would you waste your time on me?" She asked, still breathless, looking to him for answers.

"I have taken many lives, but I have never given one. I suppose it would be dishonest of me if I did not admit to some level of self-serving desire. But then, what good is an ability if it cannot be used for good? Evil is easy…and good is hard," he muttered, wavering in and out of reflection. Her gaze wandered as she processed his words.

"I understand," she acknowledged after a moment of stillness.

The water level had steadily increased up to her waist.

She looked around wildly, like she was tracking a new scent.

"Balfour is here," she announced.

Elarion turned to look at her, instantly rejoining the moment in reality. They simultaneously turned to acknowledge Balfour staring at them, his mouth hanging open.

She stood naked, her blanket having fallen to the floor, their hands cradling each other's faces.

"I…I…I brought something in case you were hungry," he said awkwardly, gesturing to a wooden tray of dried sausages and salted meats sitting on a nearby table.

"It's not what it looks like," she assured him, reaching down to rewrap herself in the blanket.

"Oh, I'm quite aware of that; I've been sitting here for ten minutes. You were both lifeless. It didn't seem either of you was breathing," he explained, not wanting to stare any longer. Instead, he asked, "So, it's true? He can help?"

Madika began to nod, her face beaming with joy.

"Perhaps," Elarion said.

Both Madika and Balfour wore looks of shock and disbelief at what seemed like overreaching modesty.

"I've not seen what you're up against, but my offer stands. I will try," he continued.

Balfour's gaze dropped, and with a sigh, he said, "Let's hope that you can."

With that, he backed out of the room. Madika sat on her bed as the door closed. Elarion glanced at her blanket. His face telegraphed more than he wished.

"I've had the unfortunate pleasure of being host to a few of your kin in my mind," she began. "Nasty pieces of work. They take pleasure in finding new ways to humiliate me in public when they fight for control. Tearing my clothes off is an old favourite." Her head lowered for a moment, letting out a forced laugh. "I'd just as soon not give them the opportunity when I can."

Elarion frowned, finding a place for his embarrassment somewhere in the grains of the floorboards.

"Don't apologise…for them," she continued, interrupting him as he went to speak. She studied him as he stood there, unsure of how to comment. "For what it's worth…I'm not embarrassed anymore," she said, dropping her blanket. His eyes were still averted.

"How long do you remain in control?" he asked, changing the topic the only way he could find to cope with the embarrassment, the guilt…and all the emotions in between.

"A few hours at a time, thanks to Balfour…and when I sleep…mostly. The trick is getting there," she replied, rewrapping herself again. He finally looked at her once more.

"Honestly, this is as long as it has ever been." She chuckled quietly. "Perhaps you'll be my good luck charm, then," she said, her gaze wandering. Her mouth suddenly opened as if she was distracted by another conversation, and with a hint of disappointment, she continued, "To be honest, I'm getting tired of…holding it together."

Her sigh was loud.

"I lied. I am a little embarrassed. I don't want you to see me like that."

She forced a smile as she fiddled with her hands.

"You will be okay. Rest. I will stay with you," he promised, taking a few steps towards her. Offering a smile, he continued, "I'll know where to find you."

"I *did* want to see what was in that hut. I think I know," she said, a hint of longing curled in her cheek. Finally, she asked, "Will I see you soon?"

He nodded.

The room went black.

She was whisked away from him as a crowd rushed towards him.

She was falling.

CHAPTER THIRTY-NINE

POWER AND KNOWLEDGE

VIDAR

Vidar sat cross-legged on the floor, his head heavy in his hands. The coarse stubble of his cheeks pressed against his palms, the bristles sharp against his calloused skin where they filled the spaces around his braided goatee, now loose and frayed from days of neglect. His eyes were closed, his breath steady, a faint snore vibrating through his nose. The chamber around him was still, save for the faint hum that emanated from the Uridar, which floated ominously at the far end of the temple.

The clatter of something hitting the floor pulled him from his half-sleep. The sound echoed through the massive chamber, bouncing off walls lined with ancient stone troughs. The air was thick with a persistent, tar-like smell, mingling with the faint smokiness of the burning lines snaking up the walls. Vidar twisted towards the sound, his movements deliberate, initially on the offensive.

His gaze settled on Toke, whose head poked into the chamber from the adjoining tunnel like a curious ferret, bringing with him a chilled current from above. Vidar blinked twice before his brain caught up, and a low chuckle rumbled from his chest.

"You've got a pair on you, don't you?"

"Big as melons," Toke shot back assuredly, smirking. His grin stretched wide as he puffed out his cheeks for emphasis. Vidar laughed, the sound rolling out of him in waves as it carried through the cavern and momentarily softened its haunting stillness.

"It's been days, lad. Are you alright? I was worried about you." Toke's tone softened, the echo of his voice melding with the faint hissing of the flames.

"Days?" Vidar muttered, rubbing a hand over his face. The word hung there, muddled in confusion, before he refocused on Toke. "Yes, I'm just…just a little tired, though if it's been days as you say, then that would explain the why part of it."

He took a deep breath. The acrid scent wasn't unpleasant anymore – it had become familiar.

"Why are you all the way back here?" Toke enquired, his brow arching as he hesitated at the chamber's mouth. Vidar waved him forward, encouraging him to step into the temple. The dwarf's hesitation was justified, based on his last experience.

"What happened to those melons?" Vidar teased, a crooked grin creeping across his face.

"Safely tucked away in my body!" Toke replied, not missing a beat. Vidar's chuckle reverberated again, filling the vast emptiness.

"Is it safe, d'you reckon?" Toke asked, his stance shifting as his gaze probed his limited view. The flames wound like fiery veins through the carved channels, dancing shadows across ornate carvings and stone reliefs along the walls.

"Yes, it's safe. Come on," Vidar entreated him. The timid dwarf stepped down and out of the mouth of the tunnel, his boots scuffing the dust-covered stone floor with a muted thud.

"I'm trusting you," Toke said, his voice unusually small.

Vidar nodded. "I should hope so."

He watched as Toke's gaze wandered and inevitably fixed upon the Uridar. It hovered near the far end of the temple, glowing faintly, its smooth surface seemingly carved from slate and etched with strange, indecipherable shapes. Its eerie blue luminescence contrasted with the golden light spilling from the burning channels, creating an otherworldly shimmer that played tricks on the eyes.

"You've torn the curtains down?" Toke asked, shocked. The golden chainmail curtain lay piled haphazardly near the side of the relic, its gleaming threads dull with dust and age.

Vidar nodded.

"What chased us away was an illusion," he continued, dusting off his hands as he stood, grunting with effort. "You'll be happy to know there's a limit – it can only travel so far from the Uridar before it vanishes."

"And this spot is just out of reach?" Toke asked as if solving the puzzle.

"It is," Vidar nodded, tracking Toke's small frame with a hint of amusement. "Actually, it's about there," he continued, pointing several hundred feet in front of them, where shadows met the final line of light.

"I knew you liked me," Toke replied, relaxing his stiff posture with newfound confidence.

He took a few steps forward, his boots thudding softly against the floor. The golden veil, crumpled but still shimmering faintly, caught his eye briefly before he looked back at Vidar.

"And what's it doing now?" Toke asked, pointing towards the relic with his thumb turned awkwardly.

Vidar followed his gaze as disappointment overtook his expression. The Uridar remained still, its glow faint, like a dying ember smothered by ash.

"Resting, I would imagine," he replied, his voice quieter now, as though speaking too loudly might disturb it. "Our last interaction was rather heated, so perhaps it has grown tired of me."

He sighed, staring at it for a moment before noticing Toke's fixated, glassy stare – it continued long enough to be concerning.

"Hey." Vidar snapped his fingers. Toke blinked, tearing his attention away. Brow furrowing, Vidar asked, "Are you alright?"

"Yes. It's just so…strange looking. Beautiful, yet haunting all the while." Toke replied, turning to look at Vidar. "Just like my ex-wives."

Vidar snorted, unable to resist a grin. "Wives, plural? As in more than one?"

"Aye. Four."

Vidar's brows shot up towards his hairline in shock, his head tilting back with surprise as he repeated, "Four!? And that's it? Just 'aye'?"

Toke shrugged. "They say I'm a free spirit. I'm just…I'm not the settling type. I've tried…gods know I've tried. It's just not for me."

For the first time, there was no smirk or grin but plain honesty.

Vidar's hand landed gently on Toke's shoulder. The gesture startled the dwarf slightly.

"I understand completely," Vidar said in a tone so genuine it left no room for jest. The two exchanged a slow nod of understanding, the warm flicker of the flames elongating their shadows behind them.

After a pause, Toke grinned. "Did we just have a moment right there? I'm feeling a little want for room in my britches."

"You're a fucking mess, you know that, right?" Vidar replied, barely resisting the urge to laugh.

"I do, I do," Toke admitted with mock pride.

Their laughter reverberated through the chamber, but as it faded, they both stared at the Uridar again. Its presence loomed, strange, alive, and utterly silent. The flames continued to ripple softly along the walls, their golden light bending around the relic's cold, blue glow.

"So, what now?" Toke finally asked, his voice quiet.

Vidar's gaze lingered on the Uridar.

"I don't know," he admitted with a sigh. "I figured I'd keep poking it until I've made a breakthrough."

Toke smiled as a joke came to mind, but he refrained from sharing.

"I'm wandering blind, to be straightforward with you," Vidar went on. "I know I'm supposed to be here, but what I'm supposed to do escapes me. It's like trying to communicate with someone who doesn't speak your language, you know? What do you do then?"

Toke shrugged.

"I usually just draw pictures in the snow and point. Food. Me. Now," Toke joked while gesturing.

Vidar's cheek dimpled at the comment as he processed it. His brow raised, tilted in the opposite direction, and his posture straightened as he gave it more thought.

"Did you at least catch a name?" Toke asked, his jovial nature fading.

"This one, no," Vidar sighed. "The other…I couldn't pronounce it even if I tried."

"Oh? Too long?"

"It's not spelt with any letters that exist in the Nine," Vidar frowned. "Or at least any I know of. I don't even know it to be a name. It just feels like it could be…" He shook his head with frustration. "The entire experience is…unique. The first Uridar showed me things – granted, I didn't know what half of it meant, but it showed me this place… It was inviting. It was anxious to share. It communed with me on a level I still can't fully explain," he said longingly, remembering. With irritation plastering itself over his expression, he continued, "This one, on the other hand, seems focused on keeping me at arm's length. As if it were looking for ways to distract me from reaching my goal."

"Which is?" Toke asked.

"Knowledge."

The word carried an echo.

"I don't know, perhaps I should go back and see if there's more to learn. It could be that I've missed something," Vidar continued with frustrated resignation.

"Wait, is this one of the first ones?" Toke enquired, pointing at the Uridar.

"The first one."

"And you said there's more? This is going to get confusing," Toke grumbled. "Do you think they know each other? Maybe…"

Vidar took a step forward. The scraping sound of his foot bounced off the walls, and his face pulled into a frown, the idea sticking like glue to his thoughts. *Could they know each other?* The first Uridar had led him here. Perhaps there was an obvious connection overlooked because of the spectacle of it all. A shared language. He grunted, his mind whirring with possibilities.

"What? Something I said?" Toke asked, assuming he had misspoken.

"That's a good question…a very good question," Vidar muttered, retrieving a book from his satchel. Toke suddenly became uneasy.

"Before you go and start your poking, I was thinking…maybe we could eat," Toke asked.

"I'm sorry?" Vidar's need for clarification was heavy in his tone of voice.

"It's been days, man. Don't you need food?" he replied, his tone more direct. "I went back to camp and brought more supplies. Aren't ya hungry?"

"I hadn't thought about it, actually." His stomach grumbled as if on cue. "But now that you mention it. Yes…yes, I am."

Toke happily retrieved a leaf-wrapped bundle from out of the satchel slung around his shoulder and handed it to Vidar.

"A foldling?" Vidar asked, amused, unwrapping the pastry. It looked a lot smaller in his broad hand. "I've not had one of these since I was…your size," he noted, chuckling as he took the two bites required to finish it.

"My size, eh?" Toke replied, eyebrows raised. "Fresh out of your mother's bush, were you?"

Vidar shook his head, smiling faintly. As he lowered himself back to the floor with a grunt, he muttered, "Something like that."

Toke stood near him with a raised brow. It was clear he didn't bring enough. He handed Vidar the rest, saving one more for himself as his wary eyes darted over to the Uridar.

"What are you going to do once I've safely returned to the surface?" Toke asked – though more accurately, informed. Vidar acknowledged his concern with a smile.

"I'm going to try and control the conversation. Ignore its attempts to derail me. If they're connected…if the first one trusted me enough to lead me here, then maybe this one just doesn't understand me yet. Maybe they…speak to each other in ways I can't see. What if I show it the drawings?" Vidar theorised while reaching into Toke's satchel, rifling through its contents. His hand stilled, and his eyes flicked up to meet Toke's, irritation flickering there. "You brought me sticky sweet bread filled with jam," he said, his tone incredulous, "but nothing to drink it with?"

Toke's mouth froze mid-chew.

"I forgot," he mumbled, cheeks still full. He swallowed hard, his eyes wide.

"You can't be serious," Vidar groaned, rising to his feet again. "Fuck. Let's go. There's no way I'm talking to that thing with tar mouth for the remainder of my time here."

Toke's laughter bubbled out, echoing faintly against the chamber walls.

"What about the relic?" he called, scurrying after Vidar as the larger man strode through the tunnel heading to the surface.

"It's not going anywhere, I assure you," Vidar replied, casting a final glance over his shoulder.

The chamber fell silent behind them, save for the fading echoes of their voices and the distant, steady hum of the Uridar.

CHAPTER FORTY

MODICUM

CONNERH

Connerh stirred quietly into consciousness, letting his eyes remain closed as his instincts took over, taking stock of his surroundings. Smells. Sounds. Vibrations and tactile sensations. His training had conditioned the survival habit into second nature, like recognising one's own reflection. The soft fabric beneath his cheek carried the unmistakable fragrance of rose oil and lavender as it curled around him like an embrace. The subtle imprint of her body still lingered in the bedding – a detail he was intimately familiar with and found difficult to ignore. He wished it were still warm.

A fire crackled nearby, its glow painting the edges of everything in the room. Of course there was a fire; there was always a fire, always ready like a faithful companion. The wood popped in its solitary inferno as if awaiting its cue, coalescing each detail into one complete picture – into everything he needed to know.

He could only maintain the frown on his face for so long before the centres of his brow pulled upwards. The conflict of competing urges was becoming too strong to resist, reducing his effort to unnecessary torment. His movements began subtle and slow, evolving into a controlled frenzy. He nuzzled his face against her pillow, vacating the breath from his lungs as if it were his last. In that moment, he accepted the terms if it was to be.

It was home.

It was where he belonged.

It was agony.

A dimple kissed Lena's cheek as she quietly stalked him, comfortably slouched in a wooden chair set just across the room. Watching his body meld into the shadow of their past sated some of her internal need for reassurance, giving her a modicum of hope.

A discreet adjustment in posture betrayed her anonymity, her chair releasing a modest creak that broke the quiet like shattering glass in the dead of night. Connerh's expression shifted as he straightened, his body no longer soft against the bed but tense and aware.

Lena cursed under her breath, frustrated at herself for disturbing the stillness. Her nose raised as his mouth parted, preparing to speak.

"I hope being a royal works out for you," he muttered, his eyes still closed. "You'd make for a terrible assassin."

She snorted, a sound both indelicate and charming.

"That makes two of us," she replied, her smirk blooming into a chuckle. He couldn't help but smile. He loved that laugh – high-pitched, unguarded, and dainty, though it sometimes rolled into a snort, a sound reserved only for those who knew her best. He clasped his hands together and rested them on his chest. His mind sprinted through the time spent with her, the scenes becoming ever-fleeting as they progressed. How it ended cast a shadow over how they began, over the good, better, and great times, like a thick canopy covering the forest. The waves of emotion gracing his face mirrored her own as she sat near the edge of her seat, wondering when and where his thoughts had taken him.

"How's Madika?" he asked as recollection faded, pinning it for another time. His voice was plain, calm but endearing.

His concern for Madika was centred, which sapped her grin all the more rapidly.

She glanced at the floor.

"Creature is fine. Alive…" Her eyes raised. There was a sharpness in her voice. "…well."

He could hear her leg shaking, the friction from the fabrics vibrating in place. He had no doubt it was crossed at her knee, her right hand folded under her left arm, and that hand holding a tall, slender pipe with an ivory bowl and a stem made of ashwood – judging by the sweet scent of burning rose petals, at least. He raised his head, peeked through one eye to confirm his suspicions, and chuckled quietly.

"Why do you ask? Still falling for the help?" she asked, the question cutting even though it was delivered with a smile.

He shook his head, saying, "What can I say? I go weak at the knees for a sad story."

The unexpected humour made her giggle.

He smiled.

"Is that what I am?" she mused.

"You were."

"And now?" she asked, intrigued.

He took a deep breath. His head rolled from side to side as he thought of something witty to say. Laughing, he offered, "A *tragic* story?"

"Takes a tragedy to know one," she shot back.

He chuckled, agreeing, "That's probably why I keep finding them."

His reply warranted a grin, eyes squinted. A delayed laugh. Affection was a silly little emotion, but its warmth could soften even anger to the point of being malleable. It allowed her to cope with the disconnected calm that seemed to imbibe him – and which frustrated her. They mentally paced like lions held and captured, longing to go home, but the way had been forgotten.

She'd prepared for this moment beyond the point of nausea, but already her rehearsed cues and segues dispersed like ink in water. Instead, her heart pushed her towards the predictable, demanding answers to the single question that had festered for so long.

Why?

She needed to ask, despite knowing there was no formation of words or incantation that would ever suffice. Could there ever be a good reason to abandon her? Her thoughts reset as if arguing the subject for the first time. She wanted to cry, to hit him, scream at him – to be held by him. Everything he'd been waiting for. He felt worthy of it, even while casting aside his own reasons to be angry.

"They say you're a hero," she said, pausing to take a drag, jets of creamy cloud jettisoning from her nose. "Saved slaves. A woman and child of note." His eyes opened, but he remained lying there, staring at the canopy above the bed. "Delivered retribution for crimes committed against the crown…" she continued, letting out a snort.

"Is that what they say?" he asked.

"It is… I didn't look," she replied.

He sat up.

"I've already lived one side of it. I couldn't bear to do it again," she continued. Her eyes shifted to his face.

"That's fair," he murmured.

They locked eyes and watched the other dance around the unspoken. It was too much. Her eyes watered, causing her to blink rapidly, as if the action would better tether her emotions.

"They say the reason you faked your death – abandoned your post, your kingdom, and your queen – was out of concern that your actions might look sanctioned by the crown," she took a puff, carefully dabbing below an eye. "They say many things, but I know a great deal more." She straightened her posture. "I know that some of those things are no doubt steeped in truth. After all, it fits the man. You were my hero…once." She smirked. "But I also know the sound of shit when it hits the floor. You never gave a damn about the crown. Fuck, it's one of the only things we ever fought about." She scowled.

He couldn't help but laugh.

"But there is one tiny little thing, one little detail that I don't know," she said, dusting her bodice before returning her focus to him.

"Oh?"

"What is it that you say?" she asked before taking a long drag, her gaze piercing.

His eyes were unfocused, staring into that indeterminate void we believe holds all the answers. His brow furrowed as he slid off the bed and stood, each movement slow and deliberate. He paced in front of the fire, its glow dancing across his figure. Her eyes followed him, tracing the contours of his body with quiet intensity.

"I'm many things, but a hero isn't one of them," he frowned. "Do such men even exist?"

"Only on parchment," she replied, turning his rhetorical question into a literal one. He didn't disagree, instead resting his arm along the mantle.

"I did save lives, but that doesn't make me anything more than a man in the right place at the right time. I did what any good man would do, even though…" He paused, brows crumpled. "…I am not. "

She stood, giving in to the desire to be closer to him; the combination of what he said and how he said it felt as if he had just shared something personal.

"You're a man surrounded by evil, doing what he must to survive.

Sometimes…" She stopped to correct herself. "…often…survival takes us to dark and familiar places."

She moved in closer and went to touch his hand just as he pulled it away. An unfortunate matter of timing. Their body language was awkward; what was once perfectly synchronised was now lopsided and rough around the edges. She cleared her throat to dismiss the embarrassment.

"And the woman?" she asked,

"I saved many women," he replied.

She placated him, understanding as she answered, "I see. You see, they…yes, hello, *they* again." She let out a small chuckle. "It was made to appear as if she was of some importance – being ever present in your collections of memory." She faked a smirk.

He looked up at her, and his reply was measured in response time but quick as he said, "Most likely Madika's visage."

She nodded, accepting the logic – it seemed sound, even if she didn't fully believe him. Liars often found difficulty believing the truth; there had never been any mention of a woman's lingering presence, only that he had saved her. Her own insecurities had filled in the missing details. Despite her efforts to break the ice, it still felt whole, solid, and slippery. She couldn't figure out why she found it so difficult to be transparent with him.

"Now what?" he asked, bluntly changing the subject, leaving the last and most important question on the table.

"You tell me," she shot back immediately. "I was hoping you could stay awhile before you trotted off into the wilderness to liberate slaves again."

She sighed, turning her back to him. It was a bit overdramatic, but it never used to matter. Perhaps this time it did; he remained where he was, returning his attention to the fire.

Her shoulders collapsed when he didn't run to her. Embrace her. Reassure her.

"I see," she whispered to herself.

The brief silence felt heavy.

"There'll be a formal convention of the assembly in three days to discuss what happens next. Despite your acts of bravery and defence of the nation's pride, there is still the subject of the legality of your actions and the fallout thereafter. As laughable as it may seem, some still believe you should be punished," she said, finally turning to look at him. A small frown graced her features as he continued to gaze into the fire, seemingly unfazed by her words.

"I should," he said in a low tone, plastering shock on her face.

"What?" she protested.

"I should," he repeated, nodding his head firmly as he looked at her.

"What happened to you out there?" she muttered after a long moment.

"Did they say how?" he asked.

"How what?"

"Did they say how I supposedly murdered five thousand?" he asked. She shook her head as she processed the question and subject change.

"Not exactly. Just some sellswords, most of whom succumbed to their injuries during battle. There was nothing left but charred remains. It's not like anything could be verified anyway," she answered, still confused. A smirk pulled from his lips as he nodded.

"You need to keep Madika safe. She knows a lot of things – things I don't believe anyone realises," he replied.

Her posture changed, and she affirmed, "I am keenly invested in her future."

Connerh closed the gap between them. She felt the warmth emanating from him, making her hair stand on end.

He reached down and gently took hold of her hand. Her shoulders dropped.

"I have a lot to explain," he said.

Her eyes watched his lips, suddenly drawn in like she was in a trance. She nodded uncontrollably.

"I just need some time to unpack it all, if that's not too much to ask?"

"Of course," she whispered. The brief contact with his skin made her body long for more, like a drunkard tormented by *just a taste*. She slowly pulled her hand away, despite her desire – as a show of strength, purely on the merit of appearance.

CHAPTER FORTY-ONE

UNDER NEW MANAGEMENT

HARGATHA

Hargatha sat, her legs crossed at the knee, the lower leg shaking violently against the floorboards. She stretched the rolling parchment apart to continue reading its contents, too entranced to notice the opening of the door to her quarters. Heavy footsteps entered the room ahead of their owner. The door closed as the floor creaked and groaned something awful as he approached, but it still wasn't enough to break her focus.

"What's wrong?" he asked, his gravelly voice finally peeling her attention away from the ink. She glanced up at his face, then away.

"It seems I… overestimated her. Lena, that is… Better than under, I suppose." She let out a brief laugh. "In her mind, she's still a little girl trying to hide the fact that she broke the candle holder," she continued, lifting the parchment to show him. "All this," she said, motioning to their surroundings, "because she didn't want me at Connerh's trial."

"She didn't want you to influence her…" he added.

"Or the court. As if I needed to be there to do it!" she replied with another scoff.

"Can you blame her?"

"Yes. Yes, I can. She *needs me*. She can barely walk, let alone run, without my arm keeping her stable. I've never seen a child more determined to destroy themselves so spectacularly," she mused. "Perhaps

348

that's what she desires, an exhibition."

He stood behind her and rubbed her shoulders.

"She'll never learn unless you let her fall. There's no greater reminder than pain," he said.

She thought on it, tracing her lips with a finger, before she finally replied, "There can be truth in old adages…"

"Speaking of self-destructing children, any word of Vidar?" Galabrand asked. She rifled through the dishevelled stack of parchments on the table in front of her, retrieving a particular one.

"Still gallivanting in search of treasure…or himself, I suppose," she answered as her eyes scanned the document.

He nodded quietly.

Hargatha sighed as her hands loudly searched the pile again, retrieving yet another. "Speaking of lost boys, Bjorn still begs for aid. Money and good-for-nothing men, to be precise. He claims to have a new lead on his mother's killer," she giggled with curious amusement. Then, frowning as the humour faded, she muttered, "They all just refuse to grow up."

He ran his fingers through her hair, scratching her scalp as he asked, "You're not worried he's going to do something reckless?"

"No. He still thinks it's his supportive sister behind the pen. I'll keep giving him seeds of hope and new dead ends to pursue, and he'll be old and grey before he figures it out. Besides, it won't matter soon enough."

He grunted. A quiet moment.

"Don't you ever get tired of all the politics and the games?" he asked, nuzzling his nose against her neck. He was there to provide comfort – for both of them. It was Galabrand's way of resetting things between them, especially when the playful bickering had lost its humour because of irritation at external matters. He somehow knew the perfect time for a romantic interlude…or perhaps, despite her armoured exterior shown to the world, he could always find the soft spots.

"Constantly," she replied, eyes closing as she turned her head, exposing more of her neck. "But it's necessary."

"We're just primal folk," he said, the puffs of air produced by his enunciation brushing against her neck, causing the hairs to stand and bumps to rise. "We take what we desire, smashing and crushing anything that stands in our way. It is a simple life…but it yields results. You should surrender to the old ways more often," he urged as his hands drifted down, unfastening her bodice. She bent forward, making it easier for him. Their bodies were already synchronising, though her mind lagged behind.

"Yes, but not everything can be smashed into submission, my love. The way I see it, she has three decisions, but there's only one which she'll make," she looked up at him. "She'll pardon him of his crimes and hail him a hero, all while erecting a statue in the city square," Hargatha shook her head. Her eyes drifted. "But we have contingencies for everything."

She came out of her ocular trance as he finished loosening her ties, and she instinctively stretched her back, lifting her arms in an awkward but temporary pose.

"Perhaps you're right…I should just let it all fall," she continued as she glared into nothing, removing the bodice and throwing it on the bed.

"Whatever you decide, you'll have an army behind you. We've heard back from the clans." He paused as she stood to face him with an anxious expression.

"And?" She could barely wait for his reply.

"Most of them will join us. The rest are either too old or too stubborn. A small minority; nothing to fuss over," he answered.

A rush of relief washed over her. She hoisted herself onto the table, lifting her legs and gown. He was already ready, waiting. He closed the gap between them.

"They'll arrive in waves, one after the other," he continued with a thrusting grunt. "The first hundred will be here within a month, and our numbers will continue to grow every two weeks thereafter."

She had a worried look on her face in between the moments of bliss.

"You're overthinking it. That's plenty. Most of these humans have rarely ever seen a giant, let alone fought one…never mind a hundred. We'll be gods to them," he assured her.

"I suppose you're right," she replied, her hands grabbing his arms.

"Of course I am," he affirmed as he gripped her waist tightly.

"Do you think Egress is ready?" she asked. He shrugged.

He shrugged, replying, "She'll adapt if she's not. She always does."

The table rumbled in a steady syncopation against the floor. Her thoughts lingered.

"She bothers you because she's quiet. Doesn't give in to emotion so easily like you and Vidar."

"She's hard to read, yes," she agreed, looking into his eyes as a matter of conversation before she got lost there, in the moment. He had the same lover's eyes as he did in their youth, just older now – and wiser. At times no more patient than he used to be, but somehow more considerate and aware of her…and her needs. "In this line of work, I depend on—"

He silenced her with his finger pressed to her lips.

She smiled as his finger was replaced with his mouth.

She took the hint and cleared her mind as best she could.

Hargatha, Galabrand, Egress, and the other giants – about thirty in number – lined the ship's side. Their haunting, towering figures loomed over the dock, casting shadows across the land like monuments at sundown, enveloping the thousands of assembled soldiers awaiting their arrival.

On land, there wasn't a comment or word to be heard. Just mouths slung open as the will to resist drained from their constitutions.

"Gods among men," Galabrand whispered in Hargatha's ear as they observed the soldiers below them. She smirked.

Her heeled boot hit the ramp nearly as soon as it touched the ground. She marched towards her new army, her burgundy cape flowing behind her stride. Hargatha towered over the tallest man, even as her taller husband and counterparts approached from behind.

"Who's in charge here?" she demanded. While still feminine in pitch and tone, her voice carried the bass common to female giants, abnormal to humans. The men closest to her flinched as she spoke. She walked the line, examining each in turn.

"That would be me, High Lady Hargatha," a man shouted as he rushed to her side. She stood still, looking him over from toe to head. "Commander Lingard at your service. I offer my apologies for running late, I…" he began.

She frowned. She reached out and grabbed him by the throat, halting the words that lingered there. She lifted him into the air, pausing in front of her face before throwing him to the ground several feet to the side of her. Galabrand grinned. The way his flowing white hair was backed by sunlight gave him an otherworldly glow.

"You are dismissed and hereby stripped of whatever decorative title you used to assume," she said, wiping her hand clean of his sweat.

The soldiers stiffened in posture. The sound of their armour shifting carried.

"Where are my sons of Hildeheim? Carved from Mount Eryndor? Hardened by the Caves of Aether? Forged by steel and tempered by snow?" she shouted.

She heard some call back to her.

"Sit down, the rest of you!" she shouted, growing impatient with their lack of ability to read her mind.

A cacophony of clanking armour filled the air as they rushed to sit, leaving only a handful remaining.

"You men are now with me," she said.

The twelve looked at each other, surprised and relieved but still unsure of what was transpiring. They took a second to gather their things and rush towards her.

"The eldest of you is now Commander of the Armies of the Rim. Which is it?" she asked.

The twelve whispered, deciphering which among them was the oldest.

"Aye, that'd be me," one of them declared, stepping forward.

"And your house?" she asked.

"Herrondale, your ladyship," he replied. She nodded, her gaze steady.

"An old family – trustworthy, stalwart. I've known many a Herrondale," she said, her voice cool and deliberate. "Pick two more of your brethren to be your first and second. Then you will build me an army, one worthy of Hildeheim's banner." She paused, watching his grin spread ear to ear. "You will report to Noose and Thea, who will then report to me. Don't ever make me break that chain of command. Do I make myself clear?"

Her finger shot forward, hovering just inches from his face.

"Yes, your ladyship," he stammered, bowing deeply.

Noose and Thea, two of the giants accompanying Hargatha, stepped forward. Though neither was the tallest among them, their presence alone demanded respect. Noose's massive frame and blank stare hinted at simplicity yet concealed the insatiable hunger that defined him. For Noose, combat was a calling and killing a joy. When death eluded him, fighting sufficed. His namesake was grimly earned: a thick rope, reinforced with chains, hung coiled at his belt, used to drag his victims across the battlefield like trophies.

Thea, by contrast, was his opposite in nearly every way. Where Noose embodied brute strength, Thea was defined by sharp cunning and lethal precision. Her weapon of choice was a bow standing nearly as tall as she was, its size granting her unparalleled range and power. She could let loose arrows that travelled vast distances, striking with terrifying force and accuracy. At close range, her towering ten-foot frame ruled out stealth, yet at a distance, she was no larger than a mouse. What made her an impossible target to miss up close rendered her almost invisible from afar.

"Go on, fuck off," Hargatha flicked her head, shooing him off with a gesture. She pointed to one of the remaining nine. "You. What's the meat in these lands?"

"We have some cattle, High Lady, but primarily it's anything that swims, and there's plenty of it to be found… Enough to feed a horde of your kind for a hundred years," he replied with a laugh that no one joined him in.

"Good. I'm glad to hear it," she replied, eyes widening before she frowned. Throwing a glance around, she asked, "Come to think of it, where's the governor?"

"Hiding in the castle," one of the twelve from Hildeheim replied.

Her eyes flared at the candid admission, a humoured smirk gracing her lips. She turned to face the man behind her and asked, "Your name?"

"Kaelthorn. No house, I'm afraid," he replied, a very slight hint of shame in the words.

"Every leader needs a good bastard," she replied.

He grinned.

"And why is your master hiding in the castle and not here before me, as he was so ordered?" she asked.

Kaelthorn looked at the ground as his mouth opened, then up at her.

"My master is addressing me, ma'am… But if I were a betting man, I'd say the governor is hiding because he knows what we all know," he replied.

She smirked and, wishing to be humoured, asked, "And that is?"

"There's new management in town," he replied. She chuckled as she turned to face the army.

"Damn right there is," she mumbled.

"Vaeloria, Torval, take my new attendant and relieve the governor of his duties. Perhaps see if he can swim." She ordered. Two giants stepped forward. "Kaelthorn, I need you to make preparations for a large gathering. I want everyone on this island in attendance." She turned to look at him, her tone sharp as she continued, "Do not let it be misunderstood; the invitation to this event is not a request."

"Aye. May I ask what kind of gathering you are looking to throw?" he asked.

"A coronation," she replied plainly as she turned to see Egress, who was late in arrival.

Egress stood, her form draped in a gown that seemed too regal for her demeanour. The heavy red fabric flowed around her, catching the light in patches of muted gold and silver as if reluctant to acknowledge its beauty. The gown clung to her like a stranger's skin, its intricate beading and embroidery at odds with the rawness that defined her, while thick chains of gemstones and precious metals draped her neck, each piece carrying a meaning she didn't even understand. A small crown, delicate but imposing, sat uneasily atop her head, its weight pulling at her composure. However, she did not falter.

She walked in front of her mother, her head held high.

CHAPTER FORTY-TWO

A Second Pair of Eyes

Joriah

Yuri was right about him, after all. He'd never denied it, though he couldn't have even if he'd wanted to. Joriah *was* the type to charge into a burning barn to save the horse. In fact, he was *unapologetically* that man. The world needed men like him, or so he was raised to believe and was thus thoroughly convinced. He believed that strong men made the calls others were afraid to make, performed the duties and took the risks others were too weak to take. It was beyond a code or creed and more complicated than a moral compass.

It was in his blood.

That horse was a symbol of livelihood to the family it served. It transported them to their destination over terrain that would otherwise see their ruin, then returned them home to a place of refuge. It provided protection from predators, offered companionship without prejudice, and carried the food that fed hungry mouths.

It meant life or death where he was from, and he would absolutely make that call over and over again.

He was a good man. Most of the time.

Even good men had to do bad things on occasion. Lie, steal, even kill – but never cheat.

355

He'd lied to Yuri.

He'd stolen the cloak he was wearing.

And the future would soon be written.

Joriah had spent the past few months getting to know the locals and memorising the routes of the lawmen – their habits, their patterns. They liked him well enough. Enough to begin teaching him the language a few words at a time. They were used to his presence, no longer leery about his intentions. They had even introduced him to a few of the older children. He knew what had to be done; he'd done it before, like putting on an old jacket. Except it wasn't that old, and the fit was perfect. It didn't matter where you were from, whatever your culture or beliefs. Everyone wanted to see what they wanted to see. It was a secret they kept, only betrayed by their behaviours and words. Once he'd learned the secret, the more he could acquiesce to their expectations, the more malleable he could make them; he was a master potter. With that skill, you could do anything, get anything…anywhere.

Like an underground cesspool whose water needed to be drained.

Yuri was right about him.

He would save them all.

The Underbelly was an appropriate name. It was large, not receiving much light, and it was full. A vast cavern of stone buildings illuminated by the light of the candle and the torch. The smell was pungent, pruning his fingers. Sweat, flesh, and body odour permeated the air along with an amalgam of varying incense. It accomplished little other than flavouring the stench. The audible cues of pleasure and pain echoed, bouncing off the cavern walls like the distant, desperate cries of trapped souls. His heart sank into the pit of his stomach. He lost the will to look ahead. His brow crumpled over his eyes as he averted his gaze.

But his courage prevailed, propelling one foot in front of the other.

The path before him descended into the small city it overlooked. A steady stream of visitors crowded the way forward. Cloaked bodies marched onwards with the hope of concealing their identities, their shame, and their excitement. He felt as if he were descending into the very bowels of the world, into a hellish landscape filled with sinners and their demons. He took one last look at the entrance behind him, ignoring calls from his heart to run. His resolve had other plans.

The barn was ablaze.

His cloak was black, his mask silver. The observer's garb. Blue was for the participants, red for the self-offerings, as it had been explained to him. And yellow…yellow had particular desires. Desires that boiled his blood, making it a strenuous task to stay his hidden blade.

There was a lot of red and far too much yellow, like a trail of tainted blood seeping into the dirt.

His hand trembled.

There were others like him dressed in black, but they were few, sprinkled within the array of disgraceful hues. He'd underestimated the task. This would require more hands than his own could provide, but it was too late to turn back now.

"Keep moving, you'll have plenty of time to sightsee," a large, pale, burly man shouted from the front. It was clear he hadn't seen the sun in a long time, his complexion having faded with the passage of time. He took the scrolls from the cloaks, inspected them, and looked for something on their persons.

Joriah's nerves spiked. He wasn't aware of a third step. He rummaged through his pocket to retrieve his invitation and held it in a white-knuckled grip. Within moments, it was his turn. The man was larger than he looked from back there. His towering physique eclipsed Joriah, while his breath betrayed his lack of hygiene. Joriah kept his focus forward as he handed the man his wrapped scroll, doing his best to act unbothered.

However, the man could smell his nerves. He grabbed Joriah's wrist and turned it. Joriah's focus snapped to the man. A deep smirk crossed the brute's lips as he exchanged a glance with his counterpart. His eyes squinted as he stared at Joriah.

Joriah dropped his other hand, forming it to match the shape of his hidden hilt. The next moment would decide everything. Whether his mission ended abruptly, dying on a mound of cloaked bodies, or something else entirely. He wasn't sure…

"Looks like we've got ourselves a *newcomer*!" the brute shouted, a raspy chuckle following.

The other guards rumbled with laughter.

"You go over there," he ordered, pointing to a man who was waving him over. Joriah relaxed his shoulders, though his nerves were still at a full sprint.

"This way, new blood," the man implored him. He led Joriah over to a small cave just off to the side. Inside were empty cloaks strewn across tables, and a raging fire burned in a large metal bowl. Three metal sticks were protruding out of the bowl.

"Are you satisfied with your colour? Now is when you can change it, if you wish. Understandably, most come in under the black, too ashamed to admit their proclivities to the one who extended the invitation," he laughed. "You'll soon shed such hesitation."

Joriah shook his head, remaining quiet.

"Very well, not sure what you like yet. I can respect that. This way," the man replied.

Joriah followed him slowly, taking notice of the other colours on the table. His imagination ran wild with what they could represent. He wanted to ask, but at the same time, he didn't want to know – and he was also concerned with admitting the same. Would it blow his cover? Was he supposed to know? He was overwhelmed by the depth of organisation he witnessed. He'd never encountered such wealthy and capable evil before. The enemy was embedded deep, like a tick on a dog's back. It would take serious effort to pry it loose.

"Alright, you know what comes next," the man said, staring at him while standing in front of the bowl.

Joriah nodded as he stood there, awkwardly awaiting…something. The man chuckled.

"Your arm, milord," he requested playfully while shuffling the metal sticks.

Joriah's panicked internally. He didn't know he would be branded. His thoughts flooded his mind, making it difficult to focus. He would bear a mark that would forever identify him with such depravity – depravity he had no intention of taking part in, but it would display his complicity. Perhaps he could hide it, or at least deal with it later. There wasn't enough time to think or plan, so he extended his arm, revealing his bare skin as he said the first thing that came to mind.

"Inside arm, above the wrist, if you would."

The man grabbed his hand and held it tight. His eyes lowered as he studied Joriah.

"Right," he said. He turned to the metal sticks, pausing before grabbing the one he'd reached for. He grabbed another instead. He locked eyes with Joriah, and he pulled out the glowing red brand.

"Are you ready?" he asked.

Joriah nodded.

"If you have a change of heart, now's the time. It'll be our little secret," the man pressed.

Joriah shook his head.

"Right," the man muttered. He rammed the brand into Joriah's arm, pressing hard.

Joriah bared his teeth as he fought the desire to scream. The smell of his burning, searing flesh rose to his nostrils. The man returned the brand to the fire before grabbing a handful of a slimy substance from another bowl that he slathered over Joriah's arm. It was cold to the touch and agonising on the fresh wound.

"Wait here," the man grumbled and walked off behind him.

Joriah's breathing was laboured. He stared at the symbol now etched into his flesh. It looked Khazmyrian but was subtly different. He couldn't decipher it. His thoughts raced as he wondered how he could conceal it from Yuri. From the world.

He heard several sets of footsteps behind him.

"You like it?" someone asked.

Joriah grimaced as he flexed his fingers and forearm, spiking the pain.

"There's gauze just on the table there. Go ahead and wrap it before you catch an infection," another voice said as it grew closer.

Joriah located it and reached forward.

And that's when it all went black.

The voices were warbled and distorted. A deeper voice replied to a smoother, more balanced one. He couldn't see. He resisted the urge to panic, to lunge forward, because doing so would alert them to his awareness. The back of his head felt wet but covered. He was lying down, and something was covering his eyes. He was bandaged. He flexed his wrists; they were restrained. A plume of light glowed through the bandage covering his eyes. A torch, perhaps.

His consciousness fully resumed. It was a good sign, despite the pulsing headache. He felt the coagulated blood sticking to his head and the wrapping.

"I see," the smooth voice said. His eyes widened. He knew that voice.

"Had he been anyone else, I'd have sent him back down draped in green," Darros mused to an eruption of laughter. There were many distinct voices around him. Darros continued, "But I've spared him for a purpose."

"Maybe a gelding for good measure?" a ratty voice implored.

Joriah tensed.

Darros chuckled, having noticed.

"No. But silence comes at a price," he said, the volume of his voice lowering, moving farther away, "so collect the payment, then set him loose."

A large door closed.

A cork popped.

"Whew, this stuff stinks," a man said.

"Hurry up before you smell up the whole place," another said.

"Good thing he's asleep."

"It doesn't matter; it still burns."

"Does it?"

"That's what I hear. They always shout, though I could never be sure if it was just the fear."

"Hurry up, the smell is spreading."

"Do I pour it on both or just one? Did he say both?"

"Just do the right one and let it trickle over."

"No, pour in the middle, just to be sure."

"Yes, but if he only wanted one done, then what?"

"Hurry up!" the voices piled on top of one another.

"Do his eyes need to be open? Or does it work when they're closed?"

"Well, don't look at me. He's never been this lenient before. I can't remember the last time we used this stuff."

Joriah's heart was thumping. He had no idea what was about to happen to him, but no matter what, he knew it would be unpleasant. His feet were restrained as well as his arms and hands. He didn't know how to react or how to proceed. It was a terrible predicament to be in.

His eyes rammed shut, and he prayed to the unknown for deliverance, for strength, for courage. He had denied the old gods but had yet to find a suitable replacement. He just knew something else was there. It had to be.

For their sake.

The images of the cloaks flooded his mind, enraging him. Blue. Red. Yellow. The anger quieted the fear.

The weakness abandoned him.

His eyes shot open. He tried to lunge forward but found a bestowed superhuman strength missing.

"Shit, he's awake! Quickly!" a voice cried out.

He should have kept his eyes closed.

The liquid was cold at first.

Then burning.

Searing.

He heard them bubbling.

CHAPTER FORTY-THREE

GRANITE

LENA

The smell of smoke jolted Connerh from a deep sleep. He tried to sit up, but his movements were restricted, his hands and legs bound by some kind of fabric. Straining his neck, he scanned his surroundings, a chuckle escaping his lips when he saw Lena bent over the fire, placing another log onto its dwindling flames. The faint orange glow of her pipe flickered intermittently as she exhaled. She turned towards him, her gaze sharp and head held high in silent contemplation. He smirked, a mix of curiosity and confusion swirling within him, then leaned back, waiting for the overdue explanation.

She approached, her heeled boots clacking against the floor. He lifted his head again. Lena set her pipe down on the table beside her and came a few steps closer. She wore a semi-transparent cloak decorated with raven feathers atop a black fabric that flowed around her. Heavy, dark eyeshadow accentuated her eyes, making them appear even sharper and more alluring. With deliberate movement, she began undoing the clasps around her neck, slowly peeling away the cloak to reveal what lay beneath. Connerh's gaze followed every movement until Lena stepped into the light, and he finally saw her clearly. Her eyes met his with a hint of mischief glinting in them as she blushed slightly under his intense scrutiny. Her eyes were glazed over, indicating she'd been indulging. Beneath the cloak, only a black corset and long loincloth remained, leaving little to the imagination.

The sound of small footsteps coming from behind him broke his focus. He quickly turned to place the source, feeling disoriented by the lack of visibility. A servant appeared, hurriedly moving in and out of his sight as they unfastened Lena's corset, hidden behind her figure as they did so. Connerh opened his mouth to speak, but Lena's finger shot up to her lips, silencing him with a gesture.

He raised an eyebrow in silent question.

The servant exited quickly, gently closing the door behind them. Connerh's heart sank, hoping it wasn't Farrah, as likely as it was. The embarrassment warmed his cheeks.

Lena pulled her corset off, dropping it next to the gown below. Her oiled skin glistened in the light of the fire. He looked away but kept his head up, stealing glances with increased repetition. He shook his head to himself, gently testing his restraints. She playfully scowled at him, squinting her eyes before walking to the edge of the bed. She slid his outer blanket off, inspected what waited beneath, and scoffed with a smirk, confirming what she already knew – he could never deny her, no matter how much he pretended he wanted to.

"What are you doing?" he finally protested, looking at her with an irritated expression.

"Mourning."

Her voice was low and husky, dripping with a mixture of lust and anger. She straddled him, denying him the privilege of seeing her own pleasure as he groaned quietly beneath her. Her eyes bore into his, brimming with resentment and unresolved tension. As she rocked her hips against him, each thrust growing more forceful than the last, she couldn't help but let out a sinister smirk. Her painted nails slid down his abdomen, leaving behind trails of white.

"Release my arms," he whispered in her ear, taking a voluntary sniff of her neck. Her perspiration mixed with her perfume, creating the all too familiar but unique scent that made his blood flow. She shook her head and pushed his head down into the pillow. The walls she had put up to hide her true feelings came crashing down, and she moaned in ecstasy. Her eyes closed as her head dropped backwards, her long hair flowing like a ribbon down her back. She lunged forward and opened her eyes. He was looking at her. She wrapped her hands around his neck, sneering playfully. He twisted his neck aggressively, shooing her hands away. She pinched his chest hard enough to get a reaction out of him, letting out a wicked laugh as she did. Somewhere in the struggle, they locked eyes. She got lost in the pools of his iris as he did in hers.

Suddenly, his expression flattened, and his gaze averted. She frowned, turning his face back to her. In that moment, all anger dissipated as they moved together in perfect harmony, their voices mingling into a symphony of passion. The quickening of movement and cacophony of their intertwining voices came to a sudden stop, and she collapsed onto his chest, avoiding eye contact as they both caught their breaths loudly. She lay on his chest as she caught her breath, unsure of what to say.

He looked away, speechless.

"I've never made love to a ghost before," she said in an attempt to be funny as she rose. She counted two breaths before he replied.

"Yes, you have," he said factually.

She slapped him as hard as she could. It was an involuntary reaction that she immediately regretted, but it was too late now. He smiled, not giving her the satisfaction of knowing how much it stung. She climbed off of him and draped herself with her cloak before sitting in a chair. He flexed his arms before ripping them from their restraints with little effort.

"I don't know what I did for you to hate me," she snarled.

"What didn't you do?" he mumbled to himself.

"Speak louder, or are you too cowardly to repeat yourself? Or maybe I should be the one to be careful. I wouldn't want to upset you and have you run away again," she replied sharply. He thought to verbally pounce on her but stopped himself. He snapped his neck away from her direction, swinging his feet out of the bed and retrieving stolen garments.

"My, my, haven't we changed? Have nothing to say?" she quipped, displeased with his lack of engagement.

"At least one of us has," he replied nonchalantly, then smirked to himself, knowing he'd just won the round.

Her mouth fell open as an excess of conflicting emotions flooded her chest. Anger won. He barely slid out of the way of the flying chalice that hit the wall behind him. Her eyes were bloodshot. Quiet tears burned her cheeks, carrying her already running makeup farther down her face.

"You promised," was all she could utter. Her voice cracked, and her chest shook as she held back her raw emotions. She took a deep drag of her pipe and used the exhale to expel the pent-up sadness. His smirk faded, and he suddenly lost the will to gloat, unable to find a place to focus his gaze. His instinct was to run to her…

But that's what she wanted, he thought.

He approached her and held out his hand, asking for the pipe. She turned her disdainful attention towards him but handed it to him eventually. He sat at her feet and took a few drags. Her face softened for a moment with the want to run her hands through his hair as she always did, but she resisted. The way her body yearned to surrender to him only frustrated her further.

"I did," he finally said, his voice affected by holding the smoke in his lungs. "But I also said I would return to you. And here I am," he continued matter-of-factly, exhaling and handing the pipe to her.

"Because I dragged you here! In chains! You don't get credit for that," she fussed at him. He turned to look at her.

"You really think I would be here if I didn't want to be? Do you think a detachment of men could stop me?" he asked, offended that she would think otherwise.

"You let me think you were dead…for ten years!" she exclaimed, half crying as her mind wandered over the lost years, eventually leading to her shaking her head repeatedly. He stared at the floor, noticing the grains and patterns contained within the marble. He imagined being so small that the floor was an endless span that stretched into the horizon.

Damn, the bugs would be massive then.

At least he wouldn't be here. Doing this. Right now.

He came to.

She was still fussing at him.

"Give me one reason. One fucking example of what I did to you that was *so* bad that you went on the run! For TEN FUCKING YEARS, CONNERH!"

She stood, pushing him out of her way and stopping him from inhibiting her movement. He was confining her, and she didn't want to be next to him anymore.

And why is it so hot in here!? she thought, fanning her rosy-cheeked face with her open palms.

She was on the edge of breaking.

Here's where he would stand, resting his hands on her shoulders, calming her down with his words, leading to a kiss, leading to his hands on her hips. His eyes trailed to the bed. He reimagined what they'd done there. How it felt. The chalice she'd thrown at him.

Not this time.

He sighed heavily, pulling himself up onto the chair. Her brow dropped into an angry frown. He was supposed to comfort her. He was supposed to cradle her face in his hands, the salty-sweet aroma of his sweat and musk was supposed to calm her, give her the release she desperately wanted. His reasons for leaving wouldn't matter then. But he didn't. And they still did.

Her angry scowl returned. Her eyes widened as intrusive thoughts flooded her mind, taking over and diving into the deep, dark void.

"Who is she!?" she demanded.

He had been internally congratulating himself on his composure, but it was shocking even to him. He'd gotten ahead of himself. Flashes of Rose's face assaulted his mind. What had he just done? The realisation of his unconscious acquiescence to their intimacy blanked his expression, and his mouth opened. The feeling of guilt filled the pit of his stomach like too much sand in a jar of water. She noticed, sending her into a cycle of head shaking as she nervously paced the room. She began to vibrate. He noticed the last straw snap in her mind and rushed to perform their familiar pain-to-comfort dance. She recoiled at his touch.

"Don't touch me!" she screamed with a snarled lip, the bass in her voice increasing.

He struggled to find a comfortable way to stand. His hands felt drawn to her, like filling a moulded imprint.

"Did you think I was sitting in a cave alone all this time?" he let slip with a boyish naivete. The tendency for sarcasm got the best of him.

Fuck.

That's not what I meant.

Terrible timing.

His eyes slammed closed as he shook his head. He shook his fist at himself. Her eyes shot wide in utter disbelief that he would be so blunt. He squinted, expecting a barrage of shouts, screams, and insults, but there was nothing.

A low rumble of laughter crackled from her throat, escaping from between her lips.

This is worse.

He peeked through one eye. She took a drag. The flare gave her a brief devilish glow in the darkened room.

"Is that it, is it?" she asked, smiling for no logical reason. She stood on her pile of flesh feeling vindicated, as if her wild guesses had paid out a handsome reward. The feeling was fleeting.

He sighed, cautiously looking to see what was throwable within her immediate reach.

She took a pronounced exhale. It was soothing to a degree, though it was like throwing a cup of water into an inferno. Sure, it helped, but…

"That's not what I meant," he interjected.

"What is that you meant, then?" she demanded in a mocking kind of way. Then, before he could respond, she exclaimed in a shout that almost startled her, "No, wait!"

She needed to figure it out herself first – as if she hadn't already spent a decade trying to figure it out. She rested one arm under the other, curling her hand to take another drag.

"Had you grown tired of me? I would have brought servants into our chamber if that was what you needed," she offered, her voice trailing, looking for any reason other than the obvious.

He cautiously approached her, his palms up and outward. She let him, releasing a torrent of tears as their skin met.

"You promised!" she repeated, pounding his chest as he came in closer. "Tell me it's *just* some random whore. Tell me, gods damn you!"

He said nothing. It was pointless at this stage. First, he had to endure the pain that he had caused.

It was fair, he thought.

He deserved it. After she came down from her rage…they would talk.

It was better this way.

Better not to say anything else to make it worse. Even a mince of words at this point could push her over the edge, he thought.

In her reality, his silence only confirmed the worst possible scenario. Every second of the last twenty minutes replayed in her mind in excruciating slow motion.

His casual dismissal of her feelings.

His refusal to touch her.

His smirks at the wrong time.

His casual use of *her.*

I've really lost him, she thought, the words uttered quietly.

He felt her rapid breathing increase to the point of being unsustainable. He tried to calm her, but her body went limp.

He rushed to pick her up and carried her to the bed.

CHAPTER FORTY-FOUR

MUTED WHISPERS

ELARION

It was wonderful to feel the dirt again.

The nearly frozen soil softened under his warmth, allowing his fingertips to sink an inch or two beneath the surface. He sat with his legs folded, perched between barren trees, swaying back and forth in rhythmic patterns. The nursery was quiet to human ears, save for the wind and creaking boughs. It was devoid of a gardener's ambience and would remain abandoned until spring. Thus, the senescent and saplings would have to fend for themselves, enduring the approaching ruthlessness of winter. While the roots of the elders could not reach deep enough to commune with the Forest, they still remembered most of the words to the great song. It was here they would pass it – and their wisdom – on to a new generation, teaching them to survive and sustain themselves through frost and snow. If successful, the young would one day be uprooted and planted in their final resting place. Those who remained, however, would continue to teach until they could no longer, until their voices faded into the dirt, and until their bark withered into dust.

It was an unnatural but noble life of self-sacrifice the humans had created for themselves, trapped behind a wall of glass and cut off from nature. But they were strong, adaptable, and rose to great heights and challenges. Still, even with trunks thicker than the width of a man and roots like arms, the toll of time and isolation was heavy. And so, his presence was a welcome interjection. His inner voice naturally synchronised with their humble chorus, filling the void of forgotten words and sharing dreams of summer…and the Forest.

Elarion's torso continued to sway in circular to oval patterns, submitting to the ebb and flow of the silent melody. He was accustomed to lasting gazes, especially ones believed to be cast in secret, but today, he had no appetite to become a spectacle.

"Good morning, Balfour."

His voice broke the silence. Balfour started where he was watching him intently from the other side of the glass. Elarion's eyes slid open as he watched Balfour enter reluctantly, his hat cradled against his chest.

"You are truly marvellous creatures. It is a shame you aren't more open to the world. There's so much knowledge you could share," he replied.

Elarion winced at the word choice. *Humans are closer to creatures than elves ever were.*

He immediately grimaced in self-rebuke.

Elven pride was a fiery one, but it had no place here. *We're all just creatures…in the end.*

"The Forest is an open book, and it welcomes all who wish to learn," he began, standing to reveal budding green grass under him.

Balfour took notice, arching his brow.

"You will find, however, that men often lose interest in what they cannot quickly control," he continued, stepping out of the soil and cleaning his hands with a small rag. Balfour's gaze was still affixed on the grass.

"Would I be welcomed?" he asked.

"Of course," Elarion replied. His bare feet pattered across the cobblestone as he walked towards a nearby chair where his boots awaited him.

"Could I learn this power?" Balfour mumbled as new buds protruded from the branches of the senescent trees.

Elarion shook his head, answering, "No."

His tone snapped Balfour out of his stupor.

"Not in the time you have remaining," he clarified.

"I promise, I'm a quick study," Balfour joked.

Elarion chuckled, stomping his foot into his boot and pulling it tightly as he replied, "How can I assist you?"

"Right, well, I followed your notes, and it will be no surprise to you that it worked. She seems more present, even when she's not in control. She even remarked on an improvement in the taste," he exclaimed, trailing into reflective laughter.

Elarion smiled and nodded, affirming, "I am pleased to hear it."

Balfour lit up with excitement, hoping to talk all things apothecary, but Elarion withdrew, barely offering a modest smile in return. There was more than a moment of quiet, but Balfour did not take the hint.

"She's weary. Fearful of the journey ahead but trying to remain strong for the others," Elarion explained as he stomped on his final boot.

Balfour nodded, assuming he was referring to Madika. Elarion stood, throwing his cloak over himself and fastening it in place. He walked over and rubbed his hand down the trunk of the tree he was referring to.

"There's stone and rubble blocking her path for growth, and she does not know the way around it," he continued. "It can be frightening to feel alone. When all you hear are the wrong voices instead of the one you know you should. The one you can hear echoes of, even when it's absent." His gaze went beyond what light could see. "We look for a way out and put faith in the first thing that gives us hope, only for it to fall short of our expectations. A failure by all accounts, but somehow better than the alternative. And so, we accept less than we should, fall back farther than we ought to allow, all so that we can make peace with being no closer than where we started," he continued, caressing a bud open. It was a beautiful white flower with shades of red and pink at its centre. Elarion's eyes lingered on the ground for a while before he turned his attention to Balfour, adding with a sigh, "The challenge is helping someone who has given up. Someone who no longer believes the goal even exists, let alone is attainable. The echoes of normalcy become a soundtrack of nightmares, and after a while, normalcy becomes frightening," he concluded with watery eyes.

Balfour was moved to tears himself, clearing his throat a few times before offering, "Please forgive her tendency to distrust. She has good reason to be that way, though she is getting better about it."

Elarion chuckled his tears away in near-silent puffs of air. It made sense that Balfour only applied his words to Madika, though slightly disappointing. Ultimately, Elarion was referring to both the trees and to her.

The tears were for her alone.

"I understand, and I do not fault her for it," he replied, pushing a smile to his face.

"So, you'll come back, then? With your knowledge, we'll surely make a lasting cure," Balfour begged.

"Madika does not need potions or elixirs to be cured," Elarion countered.

Balfour attempted to rationalise his confusion.

"I mean no disrespect," Elarion continued, "but the potions do nothing more than intoxicate her mind. It is not control, merely the illusion of it."

"I see. So, you will use your abilities to remove her malady?" Balfour reasoned aloud.

Elarion shook his head again, insisting, "She does not have a malady. She suffers from a lack of understanding, knowledge, balance, and faith. That is all."

"But I saw what you did for her…" Balfour argued.

"I merely showed her what balance looks like. Like a parent holding the arms of a child learning to walk. It is their faith that they will not be allowed to falter that gives them the confidence to propel themselves forward, but it is, in fact, the child that is doing the work," Elarion replied.

"I understand…" Balfour muttered as he mentally prepared a rebuttal, but Elarion shook his head and chuckled again. He didn't blame the man. Balfour just wanted to see his friend healed. His loyalty to her knew no bounds, ignored formality, and cared little for rules or processes. It was authentic. It was a heartfelt kind of love, the kind where selfishness was not only allowed but expected. Perhaps, sometimes, that was okay. After all, Balfour just wanted to see the same version of her that both of them knew existed somewhere in there. In this, Elarion found a lesson to be learned.

"Yes, I will come back with you," Elarion empathetically surrendered, saving Balfour his poorly constructed response.

Balfour's face immediately lit with excitement and relief, his cheeks growing flushed.

"I just need a moment," Elarion answered, tempering Balfour's enthusiasm with patience. The old man nodded and quickly scampered out of the nursery. Still, his curiosity froze his feet, drawing his eyes to watch again from the other side of the frosted glass.

Elarion's hand rested on the tree, and his eyes drifted closed. His mouth moved rapidly as he spoke, only uttering muted whispers. It took just a few minutes before he soon rejoined Balfour with a look of relief.

"Pardon the intrusion, Master Elarion, but what did you tell it?" he asked, ashamed to be so forward. Elarion stopped and turned to face him.

"You inspired me. I broke my rule; I told it how to reach the Forest. Sometimes in exodus, you walk through the front door," he said, taking a full look at the structure. "This nursery will be destroyed before spring. Glass will cover the dirt, and roots will cover every inch of its surface. I suppose I'll need to compensate Her Majesty for the damages."

"I won't tell her if you won't," Balfour replied.

They both chuckled modestly.

CHAPTER FORTY-FIVE

TWO BLIND MICE

YURI

The good news was that he was not completely without sight. He could still see the colour black and sometimes hues of red. Though colour lingered primarily in his left eye.

It was said the blind perceived nothing at all.

No yellows, reds, or blues. Not even black. Their eyes did not transmit an image to be translated by the mind.

And so, there was a void.

They could not feel empathy triggered by sight, be it anger or happiness. It would take something else to spark the emotions. Something more. It was a foreign concept – one he'd had plenty of time to ponder but could never fathom its meaning.

The eyes were there, seemingly perceiving everything yet communicating nothing. It was cruel and unpleasant and gave rise to a crippling anxiety when he thought about it for too long. There was no flexing of his hands, no tightening of fists to help the terror subside. His last episode resulted in him trying to pry open his eyes. An excruciating mistake. The tender, bubbled pustules welding his lids shut did not take kindly to forced manipulation.

The funny thing about healing is that pain often accompanies it.

He was alone, and that too hurt. His panicked flailing did little to help the feelings of isolation and helplessness. His power had been taken from him in the flash of an instant. Though he still retained his strength, his

373

knowledge, and his ability with a blade…he felt powerless. It was something that had seemed unthinkable just days ago.

He swung forcefully, looking for a surface to balance himself upon.

He grimaced as he felt his hand knock over a thin thing.

The sharp shatter of glass erupted from the floor.

"You're a fucking stupid man, you know that, right?" Yuri asked.

She'd be watching him for an hour now, unbeknownst to him. The glass had pushed her over the edge. Her eyes had been watering. He sighed loudly as he hung his head in embarrassment. The glass shattering sapped what little patience she had remaining.

"You don't know how lucky you are," she said. Her voice was coming from the left, so he oriented himself to face her.

"I can think of worse things," he retorted, reaching for his stones.

She was not in the mood for humour.

"Again, you don't know how lucky you are," she replied.

"Go ahead and say it. Say that you were right and I was wrong. I deserve no less," he said.

"Oh, I planned on it," she quipped. He heard her stand and walk towards him. He assumed her footsteps were intentional, as she'd had no issue breaking into his home in silence. Or had she been there already?

She pulled her punches but pummelled his chest.

"You stupid…stupid man," she repeated. He grimaced at the initial impact but relaxed, feeling that she meant them purely for emphasis. Her anger had subsided over the course of the hour that she'd observed him. "Did you find what you were looking for?"

"Yes," he replied quickly.

"How are you going to save them now?" she replied flippantly.

His head lurched sideways as he accepted the verbal blow. He was quiet for a moment, then asked, "How long did it take?"

"For?"

"For you to lose your soul. Your natural emotion? Your empathy? Or are you so brainwashed to think that…that is normal?" he shot back.

She said nothing initially, but he could feel her breath. He heard the air shoot out of her nose.

"I didn't know it was the victim's fault," she said pointedly. "Of course, that's what they say when they've pinned you down, isn't it? That you asked for it…begged for it?"

His brow crumpled. He attempted to speak multiple times but couldn't find a way to start. He thought he felt her staring, but her gaze was on the floor, locked in a memory. Her jaw flexed. She grabbed his wrist and turned it over.

"Do you know whose mark you bear?" she asked, her volume low, voice indignant in nature.

He'd forgotten about the mark. His lids raised painfully.

"Do you know what the colours of the cloaks mean?" she pressed.

"Most of them, I believe…" he began.

"Yellow! You bear the mark of the yellow cloak!" she shouted over him. "Yethsaren! The mark of the child!" she screamed the Elder Khazmyrian word. "Do you know what that means?!"

His head lowered, and he replied, "I have a sense."

"Wrong! You have no sense, and that is your problem! You are a ruined man. Do you realise that? You will be forever running from this mark. Do you know how powerful and wealthy you have to be before this mark becomes invisible to the naked eye? And you are surely lacking both, or you would not be here, flailing around in your self-imposed prison like an imbecile!" she shouted.

"You could kill him. You're constantly next to him," he said at a low volume.

His words cut through the noise, and her head lurched backwards.

"What?" she asked.

"Kill Darros," he began.

"And then what?" She frustratedly shook her head upon expecting a logical reply. "You think this ends because Darros dies? Darros is immortal."

He scoffed and replied, "He's only a man—"

"He is not a man," she cut him off.

They both paused.

His brow furrowed.

"He is evil, and evil transcends physical form," Yuri explained. "He is a scab."

She tapped gently on his eyes as a painful reminder. Joriah grimaced.

"A scab is an indication to others that a deep wound exists under it," she went on, her tone softening. "Yes, you could rip it off, finding its rigidness uncomfortable to both see and feel. But doing so, if done too early, can cause the wound to fester and become worse than it was before."

"So how do we heal the wound?" he asked. She scoffed. He turned his head, trying to gauge where she was. She pushed him forward, causing him to panic. He landed in a seat just behind him.

"You can't even walk without aid, and you want to kill a god-king?" she asked.

"He's not a god."

"Oh? He gave you a new identity, he imprisoned you against your will, he took your sight, and he will decide whether you live or die. And with this mark, you'd be better off dead," she sneered. "And to top it off…there's nothing you can do about it. What other qualifications is he lacking, Joriah? He doesn't need to be *a* god to be *your* god."

"He is not *my* god," he insisted.

"Who are you talking to?!"

She leaned in towards his face. He felt her warmth on his cheeks.

"Who is it that you are trying to impress?" she yelled in his face. "And since you cannot tell," the scorn was clear in her voice, "there is no one here but the two of us."

He frowned but remained still. She sighed and walked away to lean against a wall. Shafts of light separated them.

"I'm sorry, I didn't know," he said quietly.

"Those words carry no weight to me anymore. Empty words that are more helpless than the person they intend to comfort," she dismissed.

He could hear the distance between them.

"But I appreciate what I know you to mean by it," she continued after a moment of silence.

He offered a brief, humble smile and asked, "What should I say, then?"

She frowned, having been cornered in her thinking. She considered a moment.

"Perhaps…I'm angry with you," she offered.

The words sounded better with time. He nodded repeatedly.

"Right," he acknowledged, standing to his feet. She stepped forward, preparing to aid him. He walked calmly in her direction, stopping just in front of her, then reached out in search of her hand. She gave it to him.

"I'm angry with you. And I aim to do something about it," he said.

She smiled through her furrowed brow, expelling her frustration with a controlled breath. He had a kind face that made it hard to stay angry.

"I have to confess something…" he said as he moved to return to his seat. She helped him by the arm.

"That you're a terrible spy?" she giggled.

"I deserve that. I rushed my timeline. I should have taken more time to investigate and double-check my sources, but it's too late for that. Now I have even less time," he replied.

She smirked, asking, "What are you talking about? Your timeline?"

"I'm afraid I've not been completely honest with you," he replied.

She took a step backwards, her eyes lowering to a squint. Hesitant, she urged, "Go on."

"Help me take my boots off, would you?" He strained as he leaned forward to grab his leg. She looked at him with curiosity and caution before leaning over to remove his boots. He planted his bare feet on the ground.

"I am not Merith…and my name…is not Joriah," he said cautiously.

She stepped back. He counted the steps. His head raised until he could see the red of his eyelids. He bathed in the warmth of sunlight.

"I am Julian of House Graymane, one of the Brothers of Cree…" he began. Her mouth opened. "…and I am here to save you, Aiyana, daughter of Hildeheim. We have been searching for you."

She remained frozen, unable to swallow. He listened for her reaction with his head turned slightly, but there was nothing.

He lifted his foot and rested it on his knee. She took a step forward, leaning her head over to see what was on it. She saw the carving in his foot. Her eyes began to water. She moved closer.

There was a J.

She closed her eyes, ignoring the rest of the letters for a moment. She took a breath. She wanted to believe his words, but faith did not come easily to her. She wanted to burst into tears at hearing another human say her name, her real name, but she had forgotten how to cry. She wiped the tears that quietly saturated her eyes, blurring her vision…

CHAPTER FORTY-SIX

MY SELFISH DESIRES

CONNERH

He sat on the bearskin rug next to her bed. His knees were raised, hands cradling his lowered head as he rocked backwards and forward. It was the longest hour of his life, filled with unique anxieties…

…and regrets.

He was sure to check her breathing regularly – what felt like twice an hour was, in reality, closer to every three to five minutes, his curled finger resting gently beneath her nostrils. He'd never seen someone lose consciousness like that before, let alone at the mere thought of losing *him*. He'd never deemed his life worthy of such concern – it was an overwhelming concept to process. For the first time in his life, he'd spent those brief moments thinking he'd lost her and, in doing so, realised she was all he had left in this world.

It was a terrifying feeling, one that it so happened he was not prepared for…and did not want.

He offered futile prayers to those who could not listen, brewing a shame that could not overpower hope. There was no one to kill, threaten, or maim that could bring her back. Powerless to restore her to consciousness, his strength and ability were rendered inevitably useless.

"I should have been stronger," he whispered in self-pity.

She gasped loudly as she sprang back to life, her eyes wide and visibly startled, and they began watering instantly as she struggled to regain control

378

of her perception of reality. His heart sank into his stomach, leaving a burning trail in his throat as his eyes lingered upwards.

Had someone been listening?

"It's okay," he rushed to assure her as he turned around with a crumpled brow. He reached across the bed, cupping her hand between his own.

It took a moment for her to gather her bearings, then another to settle on the appropriate reaction to his touch. Her nostrils flared as she panted loudly, staring at him with hurt and encumbering sadness behind her eyes. Her vision blurred. She wanted to cry, but her mind was not aware enough to cooperate with her tear ducts. Her eyes strained as she struggled to produce a liquid that would not appear, leaving a gut-wrenching bleat to tear from her chest in its wake.

He moved up onto the bed with her, telegraphing each movement before taking it. His arms wrapped around her, holding her tightly until the panting and hitching stopped.

"I'm sorry," he apologised, kissing her scalp repeatedly. Her chest hitched again, randomly and longer still. She eventually pulled away — slowly, carefully so as to not misrepresent the reason.

She just wanted to look at his face.

"What are you sorry for?" she asked.

His tears were hot, his gaze focused somewhere just past the bridge of his nose. His mouth hung open, his controlled breathing the only thing keeping him together as he replied, "For being weak."

Her head canted and rapidly shook from side to side as her hand raised, futility wiping at his face.

She'd never seen him cry before. It filled her with incremental dread, like seeing the last light before death, but instead of acceptance, there was fear — and at that moment, her own tear ducts finally began to operate, producing a torrent of water and saline. She mimed words that never blossomed as her hands roved over his face, looking for holes to patch despite lacking the ability.

"You're still my hero," she finally offered, drawing a poorly constructed smile to his saddened face.

He dwelled in their synchronisation until comfort was sufficiently achieved.

She started, not expecting him to laugh at all, let alone so deeply even while their tears kept flowing. Confusion swept across her face.

"What's wrong with us?" he asked, still stuck somewhere within the amalgam of emotions. It was as if time was frozen.

Her gaze dropped. A chilled wave of sadness enwrapped her heart and expelled itself through a sigh. His armour had rehardened. It stung sharply, sapping her breath, yet she found herself laughing along with him. Her hand reached for his chest in gentle desperation, her soft clawing fading into a gentle caress. She wanted to tear through – to bring back what it was she'd only begun to perceive. Her head dropped, rapidly scanning the in-between spaces.

"It's my fault. I pushed you away…" she admitted. The words spewed out of her mouth uncontrollably, like a vomit of realisation. It was her soul's overriding attempt at reconnection.

His silence was loud, providing both clarity and confirmation in the span of just a few seconds. He had a passing thought to defend her, to cushion her admission of guilt, but he lacked both the inclination and the desire.

He thought it good for her to stew in it.

To suffer a little.

To feel the weight for once.

He watched her emotional knees begin to buckle.

"We failed each other," he offered instead.

She sighed through her nose. His hand on her shoulder pulled her eyes closed. She apologised, and it brought a small, genuine grin to his face.

"Tell me everything…please," she asked.

The sun was rising.

The fire had long died.

They still sat on the velvet couch that they had dragged in front of the fireplace some hours ago. Her head lay on his chest as they shared her pipe. A serious series of questions and answers often gave way to shared laughter, smirks, and glances.

And then there was quiet – not awkward or imposed, just the natural progression of self-reflection.

"Could you let them go so easily?" she asked, sliding down to lie in his lap, her face looking up at his.

"It was best," he answered with little thought while nodding his head.

She wasn't sure if his reply satisfied her question. He seemed sure of it...

"We never married, not that legality could interfere with love," he began.

She looked away, uncomfortable with the word in both its use and intended target.

"But ours was...different," he went on, grappling with trying to explain it, brows furrowed. "It's like a...saddle."

She sat up, immediately unimpressed by the illustration and fighting the urge to cross her arms.

"What?" he stopped to ask.

"Go on," she urged with a smirk.

"Never mind," he refused as he shook his head with a laugh.

"No, I insist. Please explain how your love for her was like a saddle," she replied, giving in to her arms' urge. Her tongue traced the rim of her lips as she smiled.

"We became what we needed for each other is all I'm trying to say," he replied in between laughs.

Her eyes squinted and her head canted. She closed her eyes and opened her mouth as she worked out her reply.

"Meaning it was a temporary arrangement," he explained, rushing to intercept her reply. "You make the best out of an otherwise uncomfortable situation. Without it, the horse is uncomfortable, you're uncomfortable...the saddle bridges the gap."

Her mouth closed, and after a moment, she asked, "And I presume this Rose is the horse?"

His head fell in defeat, his cheeks stinging from holding a smirk for so long.

"I think I actually understood what you meant," she murmured in a surprised fashion. "Your bond formed out of a necessity, need for comfort..."

"Exactly!" he was quick to agree.

"...so that the riding experience was mutually beneficial," she added, nodding to herself.

His embarrassment came out by way of a thunderous laugh and a strong blush. She eventually joined him.

"You're ridiculous," he replied.

She lay back down in his lap, grinning ear to ear. "I think I understand," she reassured him. "Do you think she feels the same? Or will I have to face her in combat one day?" she joked.

He sighed. "I believe she does."

"Do you want me to find them?" she asked, sitting up to face him. "It doesn't have to be under any royal decree or capacity. I have people to do this sort of thing now, you know? I can get them somewhere safe, let them start a new life. Being on the run is no place for a child…or a horse."

He rolled his eyes at her sarcasm, but as she gently caressed his face, he gave it thought – considered the consequence of merging his two worlds. It did not take long, as he felt an urgency to ensure their safety.

"Do it," he replied. "Thank you."

She smiled.

"You have a knack for saving lost little boys," he mused softly.

She thought fondly of when they first met. "Perhaps we're both saps for a sad story," she smirked, recalling his jab from earlier. "I'd heard of the orphan Commander Eregor had saved, and I just had to see him for myself," she recalled, taping his nose with her finger. A puff of air shot out in response. Then, choosing her words carefully, she asked, "You know, in all these years, you've not been able to recall the days before that time. Were you able to reflect during your…pilgrimage?"

His head immediately fell, and the smirk left. Feeling compelled to speak the truth, he said, "I've never been completely honest about that."

She frowned. Using the best words she could conjure in her shock, she simply asked, "Oh?"

"I've always remembered. Like it happened yesterday," he explained, his brows lifting as his eyes lost focus.

"Why the secrecy, then? There's nothing to be ashamed about…" she offered, moving in to touch his face again.

"It's not shame," he cut her off.

The confusion on her face was easy to read.

"I don't think my father was…" he paused to look at her.

Her curiosity was overwhelming and, anxious to solve the mystery of his reservation, she blurted out, "A good man?"

"Human," he replied instead.

She erupted into a chuckle, thinking he was pulling one over on her. His gaze fell, and his head turned a half second later.

"Okay? So, you're a half-breed… What's the big deal? I'm a half-breed, as is Elarion. It should seem right, as we are all nearly inseparable. Perhaps that explains our bond." Her mind connected all the dots, needing little confirmation. She scanned his face and features as she spoke, pausing as the unspoken became clearer. "What do you think he was?" she asked, tugging at his ears. "Surely not an elf?"

"I don't know. I feel like I do, but I can't recall, if that makes any sense?" he replied. "My recollection is sharp, seemingly abnormally so, but certain things seem walled off…kept out of reach." His wandering gaze finally met hers. "I remember most childhood memories rather vividly, except for him. He's a blur. I remember how I felt when I was around him. I felt loved, safe…but there's one emotion that doesn't make sense," he said. "Awe."

Lena smiled, excusing the mystique away with, "All little boys look up to their fathers; that's perfectly natural."

"No…it was a different type of awe. Remember when we saw Galabrand rip that man's face in two by the jaw?" he asked.

Her eyes shot wide, and she replied with a canted nod, "I do."

"A hundred times greater than that," he replied.

"Oh."

"I've gone my whole life trying to ignore it…but it's just one of those things that won't go away…" He paused to watch her nod. "Like you." He laughed as she punched his arm. "You giant half-bloods are so violent."

"You'd think you'd be smarter around us, then," she smirked. Her gaze returned to her internal thoughts, and after a moment, she insisted, "Have you ever thought to use Elarion's Gift to find out? Surely he would acquiesce."

"I don't know that I want to know. There's a certain enjoyment in the mystery," he answered.

"Comfort, even…" she added.

"Yeah," he acknowledged.

She slid closer and lay on his shoulder, offering, "Would you like me to see what I can find? Hildeheim has some of the most expansive archives in the world – surely we can dig something up on him… I can review it first and let you know if it's bad or not?"

He nodded in agreement, then joked, "This new Lena is so gracious."

"It's kind of addictive, if I'm to be honest," she laughed. "We can all change, you know…" she continued, slightly quieter. Then, in a sudden segue, as if it had been weighing on her mind, she murmured, "I'm sorry if

I made you become someone you did not want to be."

"You didn't force me; I had to agree to it," he refuted.

"Damn it, would you let me apologise?" she fussed, sitting up to look at him. He silenced himself, and she continued, "I was a spoiled, castle-bred brat who placed little value on the lives of others, let alone on the impacts of my own actions. I drove you into darkness, and in doing so, away from me." She shook her head. "I'll never forgive myself for it... You did what you had to do. I'm just sorry that I put you there," she concluded.

He smiled, grabbed her hand, and kissed it repeatedly. Tenderly.

He pulled her in close as her eyes watered.

"I forgive you," he promised, kissing her head.

She inhaled with a hitch and exhaled loudly.

After a glorious, silent moment, she asked, "Will you stay when it's over?"

Night had fallen.

Lena gracefully glided past the towering doors, her bare feet barely touching the polished floors as she nearly sprinted past her throne. Her nightgown billowed around her, catching the breeze that swept through from the balcony. With rushed movement, she placed the parchment on top of the railing and secured it in place with the inkwell. She paused for only a moment to consider how to begin, decided upon with a snort.

"Many questions," she wrote, dotting the period with a swooping motion. The ink seeped into the page and slowly faded, vanishing letter by letter. She refreshed her quill in the ink in preparation for a reply. Her impatience was exposed by the way she bit on her lower lip.

"About?" appeared on the page.

"Where to begin?" Lena murmured to herself. After a brief moment, she opted for direct simplicity. As she wrote, "Connerh," she signed his name with the same precision as if it were her own. As expected, it also faded in due time.

Seconds turned into minutes without a reply. Her anxiousness got the better of her; she paced along the balcony, doing her best to contain her frustration.

"Don't be a coward," she muttered under her breath.

Unable to keep still, she returned to the railing and began writing his name again.

A low rumble and a sudden drizzle of rain interrupted her thoughts.

"I suppose I've been called worse," came a worn, older voice from behind her.

Lena gasped in surprise, accidentally knocking her inkwell over the edge and into the sea below. Running towards the figure with open arms, she exclaimed in delight, "Reh'gara!"

He chuckled as he caught her and pulled her close, one silver lock of hair tickling her cheek. He pulled away slightly to get a good look at her face. His face folded into a deep smile, and he remarked, "You've aged."

CHAPTER FORTY-SEVEN

IN SLUMBER

LENA

Many years ago…

It may have been spring, but it was still cold at this elevation. The grass dampened Whisper's stride, and Lena carefully held on as she sat behind Connerh, her flowing dress bunched up in her lap. The view was breathtaking. Vibrant green grass covered the peaks as far as the eye could see, some harbouring stubborn and sporadic patches of white snow like islands in a vast sea…

But the attention of young love could not be drawn away.

Never mind the variety of wildlife too engulfed in play to mind their intrusion, and never mind the perfect panorama and visibility highlighting the crown jewel of Hildeheim in the distance, her walls and spires so clearly observed. All he could think about was her smell and soft touch; she, his ruggedness and the way he handled such a ferocious creature with ease.

"I can't believe you've convinced me to come here," Connerh complained with a frowning smile.

"I can't believe you're a grown man still afraid of giants," she replied rapidly.

"I'm not afraid of them. They just make me feel…I don't know…"

"Small? Squishable?" she asked.

He laughed, "No…they just don't seem right, as if they shouldn't be real. That and the stories and legends are less than favourable, you'd have to admit."

"They're just stories. Besides, I'm half-giant – am I not real enough for you?" she asked, sliding her hands down his sides.

"Yes, but you're…different," he offered, struggling to find the right words.

She shook her head then, light-heartedly pressing, "Were you going to say normal?"

"Well…yes. You're not taller than some homes. And you don't throw boulders when you're angry…thank the gods," he chuckled.

"Only because I choose not to…so don't make me change my mind," she teased as they both laughed. "What? You don't like the idea of my towering over you…squishing you between my large toes?" she asked, lifting her bare foot up and onto his thigh before wiggling her toes.

His brow raised. He thought about it…

"Actually, on second thought, you may be on to something," he agreed as he looked back at her, interrupted by her devious cackle.

Whisper whinnied, and Connerh's attention snapped to the road. Vidar stood there with his hands up.

"It's only me…no reason to startle," he called out as he resumed his approach.

"Vi!" Lena shouted with giddiness.

A smirk crossed Vidar's face, and his ponytail jostled as he continued to stomp downhill.

"Vidar," Connerh acknowledged, nodding.

Vidar replied with a nod of his. He knew how his aunt, the queen, felt about the boy, as well as his mother's personal sentiments, but he was indifferent. He had neither great nor bad things to say about the man. He seemed alright for a human, and if he made his cousin happy, then that was enough.

"Where are you two troublemakers off to?" Vidar asked.

"To talk to the only person that listens to me," she complained with a frown. Both young men looked at her from below raised eyebrows, and she defended herself with, "Well, besides you two, obviously."

"Whatever keeps her out of my ear, I'm all the more grateful for it," Vidar replied.

"Oh, that's harsh. Don't talk about my Gatty like that!" she teased.

"Gatty…" Vidar scoffed. "Well, you can have her. I don't know why you hang around this one," Vidar joked with Connerh, gesturing towards Lena. "If you were smart, you'd flee nine days past the horizon. You know, she may be small, but she's still half-giant, right? That means she's a little you-know-what." Vidar made a twirling motion next to his temple, and Connerh smirked.

"And he loves me for it," she interjected, reaching around to shoo Vidar away.

"I see," he nodded seriously. "Then I suppose I'm beginning to question his judgement, too." Breaking into laughter, Vidar gave a small, sarcastic bow as he declared, "Well, I'm off. Don't let me interrupt any further."

"Where to?" Lena asked.

He made a show of looking around before focusing on a spot in the distance. "I don't know, maybe over there? Anywhere but here, really. Well, not here with *you*, specifically… You know what I mean," he dismissed, giving up and continuing on with his trek.

Connerh gave two short tugs of the harness, and Whisper continued on.

"I like Vidar," Connerh mused.

"That's good to hear since you will be related to him one day," she replied with a smile.

Connerh looked around Hargatha's home. The sheer scale of everything was unsettling to him. He felt like a child next to such oversized pillows, yet somehow, Lena paid it no mind. She laid on his lap, loose-lipped, venting to her aunt without mind. Of course, he'd interacted with giants before, but typically only in public settings. There, it wouldn't be abnormal to see a larger-than-average chalice here or a sword made from masses of steel there, but they were always the exceptions in a room of all things normal.

Here, he was the exception.

His eyes settled on Hargatha. She was a lovely-looking woman. She had a strong jawline, but she maintained a very soft, feminine air about her – the soft splash of vermilion on her cheeks provided a warmth to her otherwise pale skin. She wore a smirk as she listened to Lena's diatribe, complete with impressions as it was. He'd never seen her this close before. Her eyes were stunningly piercing, ruthless with potential but wrapped under brows of wisdom and caring. Her white hair was only another expression of it. She looked to be a woman in her forties, but he knew her to be much older, at least doubly so.

She glanced at him, the heat of his stare deepening her smirk. He noticed the subtle wrinkle straddling her lips and focused on it. Lena paused, an amused frown decorating her face as she stared up at him. She made a comment, but it was a haze to him. Hargatha laughed, switching which leg crossed the other and exposing one of her feet in the process. His expression blanked. He'd half expected it to be large, hairy, and unwieldy, but it looked soft and was perfectly arched…

Lena gasped.

"Do you need a moment?" she asked him, a bit too loudly for his preference. She sat up and threw a pillow into his lap. His flushed cheeks dropped with his head.

"I just think sometimes you're too harsh. She just wants the best for you, and sometimes she has a hard time making it obvious," he recovered.

Hargatha nodded, and Lena gave him a playful, evil eye. It was a good recovery.

"Being overprotective comes naturally to a mother," Hargatha replied, drawing Lena back into the conversation, "though it must be tempered with patience and love. There is a difference between wanting what's best and demanding it."

"Exactly!" Lena added, flailing her hands in the air.

"I never said it was a good thing, but it helps to understand where a person's heart lies. Sometimes it can get lost in translation," he added.

Hargatha protruded her bottom lip, raised her brows and nodded, agreeing, "Intent can be a fickle thing. They say there are mountains of bodies buried under good intent."

The valid point took control of his head movement, shifting it with a twitch.

"But he's right," she continued. "You can tell a lot about a person but the content of their heart. You are intelligent and insightful, and your promotion was well deserved. I'm sorry my sister-in-law could not find the time to congratulate you."

Lena looked at him with a hint of accomplishment and pride, then scoffed, throwing herself back into Connerh's lap as she declared, "She was too busy training my replacement."

"Oh? What do you mean?" Hargatha asked, quickly moving from accepting it as a jest to taking more noted interest in the words.

"It is as I say, Gatty. She's training a replacement princess," Lena pouted.

Hargatha's laughter was still unsure as she replied, "She can't replace you, and not just because you're adorable. There's the matter of birthright and laws…customs."

"I have seen it with my own eyes," Lena continued with a flare of faux distress.

"Who is it?" Hargatha quickly asked, her tone reflecting a seriousness that her face yet did not. Her fingers rubbed past her thumb. Connerh attempted to glance discreetly at Lena, unsure if she would be transparent or not. Hargatha noticed and, displeased with the intimation of secrecy, prodded, "Well? What's this for? Who is it?"

"A pretender. It doesn't matter; I will not let her," Lena dismissed, staring up at the ceiling.

Hargatha glared. She stood, her frustration with not knowing becoming too much as she pressed, "You would be wise to learn to put into practice what we discussed. What we always discuss. You don't always have to say what is on your mind or, more importantly, *how* it resides in your mind. Even wood can be made malleable with warmth." She folded her hands in front of herself.

Connerh's face clearly agreed, and Lena playfully shook her fist at him before replying, "I know you're right, but she doesn't make it easy."

"I suggest you find some endurance, then. At nineteen years, you've still a way to go before you inherit the crown, especially as your mother remains in good health – and spirits no less," Hargatha instructed.

"The latter is debatable."

"Be that as it may, politically, you look like spoiled goods. You're two years past when your hand should have been given in marriage to some pretentious royal prick – apologies," Hargatha replied, pausing to acknowledge Connerh in the room. He nodded away the comment. She went on, "Instead, not only do you refuse tradition, but you rebel against the status quo by running around with a bastard footman, then flaunt that rebellion not only in your mother's face but in front of the entire world. Again, apologies."

He offered a forced smile this time, curling his lips into his mouth. Lena sighed loudly and folded her arms in front of her chest.

"As a mother, I can't say that I blame her for being concerned," Hargatha continued. "Understanding the pressures of a queen, doubly so. Entire kingdoms and dynasties have crumbled at the hands of a single leader who missed the mark." Lena's shoulders dropped. Hargatha observed how she looked away for a moment and back again before she added, "But perhaps, if she were a better mother, she would have less to worry about as a queen."

It pulled Lena's lips into an appreciative grin.

"Trust me when I say, Little Bird, that you cannot win both battles. You will either have to concede your hand or start playing the game," she insisted.

Connerh and Lena exchanged glances.

"Be honest with yourself, what is it that you're even wanting? Either you don't want the crown or you do," Hargatha continued.

"I don't want the pressure. Is that so much to ask?" Lena argued. "Why is it that I feel like I'm asking the impossible? To marry who it is I want, when it is I want?"

"Life often thrusts us upon—" Hargatha began.

"I understand that!" Lena argued, closing her eyes and pushing the air away with her hands. "I just…I understand that life thrusts us towards our destiny, but we're not there right now, are we? Even you say that Mother is in good health. What is the rush? Can't I just live for a while?" Lena pressed in an exasperated tone.

Hargatha chuckled quietly, finding herself momentarily wishing she could go back to when innocence clouded knowledge. Before she understood that evil lurked in every corner and murder only existed in cautionary tales. It was a simpler time. To be so naïve was both a curse and a blessing.

"And why does it matter who I marry? Sure, he's a bastard, but that's not his fault…and he's…he's *my* bastard." Her fuss broke down into gentle reflection. Connerh smirked. "Just because things have always been a certain way…does not mean so they should remain. Is my happiness and the success of the kingdom really dependent on a series of aligned opinions?" she continued with an animated brow.

"Some would argue that your happiness is irrelevant in the sum of things," Hargatha interjected bluntly.

Lena frowned, snarking, "I'd just as soon burn it all down – and any who would count themselves as *some* along with it,"

"A queen could," Hargatha replied without missing a beat.

Lena froze. Her gaze dropped, and her brow crumpled.

"I see," she uttered after a moment of quiet. Her head tilted after a delay as if to punctuate the thought. Her mouth opened as her tongue slid over her teeth. Hargatha smiled deeply. It was clear the seed was beginning to sprout.

"Pull the reins," Hargatha said. It jolted Lena from her deep reflection. "Your first thought is misplaced. You lack the experience and precision to execute what you see yourself accomplishing so clearly," she continued, breaking into laughter. There was no mistake: She was proud of Lena for finally understanding, but she was not ready to fly solo. "Remember, change comes with time, and conspiracy blossoms overnight. You cannot walk into your mother's chambers within the next hours or days, suddenly seeing the light of her wisdom. She would never accept it as truth," Hargatha continued, deflating Lena's pride.

It was in these times that Lena readily took the lesser position, understanding how her aunt's wisdom preceded her own. She was reminded that the heart was loud, insistent, and often capable of embarrassingly terrible blunders, but only when Gatty spoke to her. The giant woman held a special place in her heart, and she wielded that position carefully, with love and authority. It was in these moments that Lena felt like a child again in her presence, and she found it acceptable.

"Trust. That is all I ask of you," Hargatha continued. "With enough care and planning…perhaps you can have both." Pivoting to Connerh, she insisted, "But you'll have to help; she can't do this alone."

He nodded quickly in agreement.

Gatty paced as she thought, murmuring, "Do not dwell on this pretender to the throne… She does this only to provoke you into action."

Lena's brows raised.

"Even then, a little competition doesn't hurt," she continued. "Most people fight for this opportunity. Some kill. You should prepare for both."

She locked eyes with Lena, and Lena's gaze quickly fell.

"Perhaps you should let her believe that her prodding has worked. That would be the quickest path," Hargatha said, pausing to reflect on her own words. "Yes…yes. Don't fret, Little Bird; your happiness is just beyond the horizon. Besides, there are worse fates than being queen."

CHAPTER FORTY-EIGHT

Under Advisement

Lena

"We have a guest," Elarion uttered, his voice piercing the calm stillness. He sat on the ground, legs crossed, hands resting on his knees with his palms upturned – a small bronze sphere still levitated before him, its surface etched deeply with symbols self-illuminated with a warm hue.

Thaetra sat waxing the strings of her bow across from him, a pipe clinging to the edge of her lips, the puffs of smoke imitating the cadence of her thoughts. Her wavy red hair and pale skin juxtaposed with the darkened interior. She pulled her extended leg closer, making the dagger hidden in her boot readily accessible.

Elarion stood, rolling his hand over the sphere to claim it before sliding it into a small black sack set on a nearby wooden table. He stood at the door, listening for a moment before revealing who stood behind it. Lena was on the other side, surrounded by guards. Her expression betrayed her discomfort, but her folded hands signalled a humble intent where they rested in her lap. Elarion straightened his back, bowing at the hip.

"Your Majesty," he offered a formal greeting on behalf of the onlookers. She gazed at him with familiar eyes, as if his formal gesture embarrassed her.

"Do you mind if I come in?" she asked, as though there might be a chance he would decline.

"Of course," he replied quickly, his brow furrowing at the suggestion.

She removed her hood, releasing the torrent of hair it concealed as she crossed the threshold.

"I'll be fine, Athelstan. Wait for me here," she instructed, inhibiting his movement forward with her hand on his shoulder.

Elarion nodded, assuring him, "There is no one here other than my ward and me."

Athelstan nodded, albeit reluctantly. Thaetra stood and curtsied despite not wearing a dress, but the garb of an elven assassin, thin layers of black cloth and leather embroidered with Elvish runes.

"I'll be nearby should you need me, Master," she offered.

Elarion began to nod.

"No," Lena interrupted. "If he trusts your companionship, then so should I." She looked at Elarion, seeking his agreement. "Besides, what I offer will be public knowledge shortly anyway," she continued.

Thaetra exchanged glances with Elarion, who nodded. She sat again and returned to tending to her bow, mentally excusing herself from the conversation before it began.

"You built it, I presume?" Lena asked of Thaetra, moving closer to inspect it – delaying an uncomfortable discussion.

"I can only wish I were capable of such craftsmanship. I am quite young; I have yet to delve into such secondary endeavours," she refuted with a smile. "It is, in fact, an heirloom bestowed upon me," Thaetra explained, glancing at Elarion and then back at Lena.

It was a fine bow made of an ancient wood, black like tar and shimmering under any amount of light as if the stars themselves were stuck to its surface. Each limb ended in carvings of a lion's paw, each knuckle granularly carved with the finest string clasped between them.

"May I?" Lena enquired, and Thaetra nodded, handing the weapon to her.

Elarion smirked as she inspected it, his pride shining like beams of the sun. He cleared his throat. "It was my great forefathers' bow…" he began, stopping himself before he regurgitated his full ancestry alongside all the many other details he rationalised would bore her. He settled for a grin to himself. "Thaetra will carry it through a time I will not see." He paused to sigh. "And then she will pass it down, thus carrying on the tradition."

Lena's expression saddened as she handed the bow back to Thaetra. She next approached Elarion, resting her hand on his chest.

"Have you really given up on love? Could you not pass it down to your own offspring one day?" she asked in a low voice, her brows crumpled with disbelief.

Elarion's eyes widened, but his expression remained the same.

"I'm sorry, that was incredibly inconsiderate," she reprimanded herself, covering her mouth with her hand. "I only speak out of turn because…well, because I envy you," Lena went on, her expression further saddened. "So full of story and wisdom, you must think so little of us and our collective crisis of existence. Our lives must seem like the days of summer, gone in the blink of an eye."

His gaze disengaged as he thought.

"The days are like minutes, the months like days, the years like weeks…" he corrected her perspective. Her head rotated. "It's not so much that time passes, though that is the easy thing to say. It is more like…a stretching." He gestured with his hands. "Sometimes I wake up and forget where I am in the stream of time. I continue conversations as if I've just taken a pause, yet at least a hundred years have passed. My memories are forever alive…only the people they involve are not."

"Will you tell stories about me?" she blurted in a moment of vulnerability. It was a sincere plea dipped in vanity, and it caught him off guard. Her tone made him frown.

"Of course," he replied, "but it is not up to us what story we tell."

"But of course it is," she rebutted. "Elarion, could it really be possible that you do not truly understand the power you wield?" she asked in disbelief. "From your lips, you can both shape and end dynasties." She looked around, nervously giving in to laughter. "Do you know what is more powerful than ink? The living word. We fight wars, claim land, and carve our likeness into stone." She paused to shake her head. "But what good is it if you can rewrite history?" Her face tugged into a portrayal of humoured frustration. "In the spaces between life and death lie both our differences and commonalities. Where you seek meaning, we seek desire. Where you value longevity, we bask in impermanence. In your world, decisions can be rewritten. But in mine…they are all-too-often permanent." Her eyes remained locked with his.

"What you describe is a selfish desire for control, for power, for immortality," he corrected her. "The reasons for such a pursuit, no matter how humble the approach may be framed, do not change the fact that it is…inappropriate. How will future generations learn authentically from a past that has been altered?"

She looked disappointed, and her focus changed as she turned away.

Elarion knew it wasn't what she wanted to hear; she would have preferred to be even only mildly humoured. However, it was a sore topic for him, and he was used to being the bearer of bad news – especially to those inwardly inclined.

"But what of the good you could do? You could erase the memory…" she began.

"Of what? My enemies? Yours? The bad times…the horrid ones? Things we regret? It would be a disservice to those who endured them. Would you rob them of their stories to better your own?" he asked. She stared high and away as she listened. He retrieved and lit his pipe. "Do you think yourself the first to wish for the erasure of their mistakes?" His tone changed, softened, as if he were now using his real voice rather than the tone of the formal teacher to which she was accustomed. She met his gaze just as he exhaled, an opaque puff of smoke dividing them briefly.

He took a deep inhale and billowed smoke through his nose, his head canted slightly.

"What is it that you've come to discuss?" he asked, seemingly privately perturbed.

Her head dropped with a hint of shame. She took a breath before saying, "The assembly has convened. Half want him punished…or worse. The other half…want that which I tell them to want." Her eyes glazed over, and there was embarrassment over her admission of her influence.

"And what is it that you want?" he asked.

She expected the reply but still had no good answer for it. "To have my way with no consequence." She laughed quietly to herself through the honesty. Her hands found comfort fidgeting with one another. "But rarely do such things work out in my favour." Her head rolled with the absurdity.

"You are the queen, are you not? What you say is law, and that is commonly accepted practice. What makes this decision any different?" he asked.

"Because what I want and what I need do not align." She shifted her weight so that she could shake her leg. "What I need…is permission to be selfish."

"Both accomplish the same result, only one is taken and the other gifted," he replied. "But it is not mine to give."

"I say that it is!" she countered.

"That is not how this works," he smiled.

"You said it yourself: I am the queen, am I not?"

"You are…"

"Then I say that it is, and you will accept it as truth," she demanded.

"Impermanent words spoken by an impermanent being," he said, dismissing her with a shake of his head. "You barely have control over your own emotions, let alone my fate."

Thaetra smirked.

"Spoken like a god. I know you don't care what happens to us, Elarion, but would it kill you to pretend from time to time?" Lena shot back.

He sighed.

"You wouldn't know a god if you saw one. They walk among you every day, yet you mistake them for beggars, always so focused on yourselves. It's not permission that you seek to find; it is accountability that you seek to evade. And that is impossible…even for a god," he replied, his complexion having reddened.

She was ready to reply but stopped. It felt odd to spar verbally with Elarion; no matter your passion, you knew that you were somehow wrong. It was like they were having two separate arguments in the same conversation.

They were.

Her expression re-hardened just as quickly as it fell. There was a forced silence on account of all the things left unsaid.

"Why is it that I feel judged whenever you're around?" Lena asked sarcastically.

Elarion glanced away, replying in a murmur, "The guilty often do."

Her jaw stiffened, and her eyes rolled. She thought to make another cutting remark but hesitated, knowing he would return it in full.

"I'm sorry…" she began, her eyes fluttering. "For the other day," she offered after a moment of silence. "I've never seen with my own eyes the Gift…like that." Her gaze shifted through memory. "You were always…kind, gentle," she explained, shaking her head to dislodge the image of Connerh writhing. "I didn't know…but I can't say the outcome would have been different if I had. I must avoid the appearance of impropriety." Her tone stiffened, her demand for the acknowledgement of justice sounding like a plea for validation.

"Madika's ability with the Gift comes at the price of inexperience. Like handing a sharp knife to a child," he replied.

"Will you help her?"

"I will try."

"I knew as much…" she breathed, folding her arms and dwelling on a thought. It faded, and her eyes wandered the house where they stood. "I wish you would have let me accommodate you in the castle," Lena said as she continued to look around, displeasure in her tone.

"Your graciousness is appreciated but unnecessary. This is more than sufficient," he insisted.

"But the gardens," she protested. "There are no gardens here. You must come and see the new greenhouses… They are no comparison to the Forest, but I think you would find them lovely," she insisted.

Elarion nodded, and she smiled, her head drifting downwards. He could sense her hesitation like a thick blanket on a warm day.

'Give us a moment,' Elarion put the words into Thaetra's mind. She nodded and excused herself. Lena followed her with her eyes, quickly discerning what had transpired. She waited for the door to close behind Thaetra.

"Did you ever allow yourself to be selfish?" she asked.

"Once," he answered, his tone quiet but firm, as though the memory were held behind lock and key. She turned in a hurry, amazed by his admission, but he deflated her curiosity with a look, insisting, "This isn't the time or place. Your decision is to either make him suffer or allow him to be murdered under the guise of justice."

"To punish and humiliate him, to take on the role of the tyrant and will it all away…or to bury him…again. Any decision I make is the wrong one," she lamented.

"You're not here for political advice," he objected.

"I'm looking for forgiveness," she countered, looking up at him.

"You're looking for a god. And that, I am not…nor can I offer you absolution," he answered finally. "Perhaps our worlds should not co-exist, and that is the unfairness that burdens you. Yet they do cohabitate. You look to me as conscience embodied," he said, shaking his head. "But that is not my purpose. I am nothing more than a man cursed with the inability to grab hold of the moment before it slips through my fingers. You call it wisdom, but it's really called perspective."

Her bottom lip puffed out with a frown.

"He was your friend, too…once."

She regretted the words as they left her mouth. His face contorted, angered. It seemed as if the room had darkened and his face had brightened.

"You don't understand what I keep at bay." He stepped closer to her. "There is no one here who could stop me from saving him from this if I so chose." He scowled. She felt a hint of fear as he spoke. "Intervention is a choice loaded with consequences…and I would not rob the stories of others to better my own," he went on, beginning to pace. "I even considered cowardice – to not be faced with the worst outcome for him, if even for a moment as brief as lightning. And for someone like me, that is an agonising eternity." His eye refocused, watered. "I am the only one who will keep his memory alive. What is it that you offer him? You couldn't fathom the care I have for him…of him," he remarked, his words biting with intention.

Her mouth hung open, a reflection of her shock. She was, for once, speechless.

His anger eventually subsided, and his shame over the outburst guided his gaze to the floor. His sigh was long and pronounced. Thaetra walked in shoulder first, her expression heavy with suspicion and distrust. She glared at Lena, not shying away from eye contact until Lena broke first.

"Is everything alright?" Thaetra asked, her tone sharp as she moved to Elarion's side, having sensed his emotional shift. His hand rested on her shoulder, calming her defensive reaction. Lena watched as they exchanged glances, an obviously private conversation going on to which she was not privy. Lena glared enviously at them.

"You're not always going to get it right, and that's okay," he said, snapping Lena out of her mental fog and drawing her focus. "Be resistant to the waves that take you off course but never to change," he instructed as if he were reluctantly granting a wish, like a djinn bound by service.

Her head canted as she stared at him, and her eyes eventually fell as she pondered the words.

His nose flared as he breathed heavily.

She nodded.

"I understand," she acknowledged.

He nodded.

"You should go. You have some that are looking for you," he replied. It was more than a suggestion. He blinked more than normal.

She nodded, walked to the door, and opened it.

"I should hope your stay will be an extended one…" she said as she looked back. "I've missed you."

"The future isn't written," he replied.

She scoffed and shook her head.

"I wish you would just lie to me sometimes."

He smirked as she closed the door behind herself.

CHAPTER FORTY-NINE

FORGIVENESS

CONNERH

He was nearly invisible in the vacant hall, surrounded by antiquities and forgotten relics. He was imagining his bones one day resting here, hidden behind ornamental walls of glass and gold – his life reduced to a mere footnote in a story, retold only by those still alive to remember it. Though some valued these objects more than life itself, he found their reverence hollow – nothing more than a fleeting novelty, a spark of relevance that disappeared too quickly given the weight of their history. At its core, this place was just another prison, awe and praise shouted in the place of curses and jeers, rare gems and gilding for decoration instead of rust and iron.

A longing for…remembrance instead of freedom.

Connerh sighed.

He picked up a sword that appealed to him, lifting it off its horizontal stand and violating nearly every rule the curator had very recently reminded him of. It was a gift from the Far Sands, well-decorated and bearing a name with entirely too many awkward syllables for him to pronounce. The sound it made exiting its sheath betrayed its age; the metal of its blade was becoming brittle, much like his soul.

"You shouldn't touch that," a voice said from behind, startling him, shaking his body.

"Damn it, Elarion," Connerh scolded upon recognising it.

Elarion's chuckle was clear in the absence of ambient noise. "I couldn't resist."

"You pointy-eared bastard," Connerh whispered, eventually giving way to a grin. After a moment of silence, he asked, "I suppose you were there when this first arrived?"

Elarion's brow raised, and he smiled, "I'm not *that* old."

Connerh shrugged, losing interest and returning the sword to where he'd found it.

"O'san mehaleovichnic siris," Elarion said. Connerh looked at him with a furrowed brow. "It means *the setting sun*…in Sanderin. The sword was a gift from the then-Three Princes of the Far Sands," he continued.

Connerh's laughter interrupted him.

"What?" Elarion asked.

Connerh excused his laughter with a head shake, his face still holding on to a grin as he dismissed, "Nothing."

"I wasn't there, but I—" Elarion began his rebuttal, but Connerh's laugh interrupted him yet again. After the humour faded, Elarion asked, "What brought you here?" His gaze wandered around the room dubbed the Hall of Reflection.

"I don't know," Connerh mused, continuing his slow wandering as if looking for the reason. "I felt a pull to be with other things no longer needed and long forgotten, I suppose."

Elarion's face mirrored the absurdity he heard, and his head dropped as he asked, "Is this about the sentence?"

Connerh shrugged. "No…I've been whipped before. It's not the worst thing to happen to me." His chest hitched, his pitch affected as he concealed a yawn. "A couple of lashings, a few dozen cups of wine…and I'll be back to normal in a day or two," he said through the forced exhale. "I'm not even sure I'll feel it. There are so many scars already…but if it solves Lena's political crisis and I get a fresh start out of it, then it's more than worth it."

"I see. So, it's your presumed fall from grace, then?" Elarion shot back.

Connerh locked eyes with him for a second and frowned, perceiving the line of questioning as aggressive. His gaze dropped as he found a new relic to investigate – a large tome with unfamiliar inscriptions.

"You have to have grace in order to fall from it," Connerh retorted, his tone sour.

"I would guess it depends on your definition of the word."

"Whatever it is, I didn't have it then, and I sure as shit don't have it now," Connerh bit out.

Elarion smirked as he grew impatient with Connerh's negativity.

"I came here thinking you were a man, either dead or soon to be sentenced as such. Now you'll leave here, should you choose to do so, with little more than a few scratches and a bruised ego. But before you lies the chance to start over again…an opportunity few enjoy." Elarion's brow raised. "By that understanding, I would say that you indeed have been given grace. Some would argue an abundance of it," he replied.

Connerh's gaze locked with his again, although his head still aimed towards the tome. He let out a loud sigh.

"Is this not what you desire? Are the terms not agreeable?" Elarion asked, tilting his head in question.

"I don't know what I want, and perhaps that's the problem," Connerh replied, wiping his face with his hands. He let out a sudden laugh and reached for the sword again. "I once thought of myself as a weapon. I wore that sigil with honour and pride. Then I committed unspeakable things and realised that I was right," Connerh continued, lifting the sword and examining it before throwing it to the ground. It shattered. Elarion's eyes tracked the priceless relic as it fell, and though he could not see where it landed, the noise it made did not instil confidence.

"Swords can be melted down…reforged for a new battle, or even a new purpose," Elarion replied.

"Eventually, they all end up in a place like this," Connerh countered, raising his hands to highlight his surroundings. "A graveyard. You can't reforge rust, my friend," he dismissed, his tone diminished but confident.

Elarion frowned as he thought for a moment.

"Then why are you here? Neither this castle nor its queen has ever been able to contain you in the past, so why now?" he asked, drawing Connerh's gaze and silence. "Sometimes our heart knows what we really want…what we need…but we're just too afraid to say it."

Connerh's eyes watered modestly. His tongue jammed behind his teeth. He cleared his throat and asked, "And why's that, do you think?"

"Because rejection hurts," Elarion answered as if the answer were obvious.

Connerh stared a moment longer before looking away. His quiet tears were met with equal silence that only Connerh's hitched inhale broke. A smooth exhale through pursed lips and puffed cheeks followed. He stared at the ground, his head finally canted to look at the broken sword.

"They're going to add some lashings for breaking this thing, aren't they?" he asked, eventually chuckling in between his sniffles.

Elarion let out a laugh that resonated in his chest.

"Oh, most definitely," he replied, reigniting their laughter.

Once the weight of seriousness returned, Connerh replied, "You're half-right."

Elarion met his glance.

"I don't say it…I don't…ask for it, because…" Connerh struggled with the admission, his head shaking in resistance. "I don't deserve it." His shoulders shrugged. A deep breath. "I see their faces…still." His face contorted, ending in a frown. "I thought I'd moved past it…but…" He continued shaking his head.

"Your experience with Madika must have broken through my barrier," Elarion murmured in a low voice, his thoughts made audible.

Accidentally.

"What?" Connerh replied quickly, his confusion apparent. Elarion glanced away for a moment.

"You—" he began but stopped. His brows crumpled. "You weren't doing so well, my friend…after what happened." He looked away again. "I took liberties I should not have, and in the process, I broke my rule. But I couldn't stand to watch you unravel," he continued, his head moving from left to right as he mentally relived the past, refacing the decision he'd once made.

Connerh frowned, mostly out of confusion, and he muttered, "I don't understand."

He walked towards his friend as the other man became increasingly emotional – that was to say, emotional for elven standards.

"I took it from you." Elarion's eyelids rested on his cheeks. "I hid the worst parts so you could…breathe. You were irrational, inconsolable." His face mirrored his past self's frustration. He noticed Connerh's confusion, and his eyes closed as he rewound time in his head. "I sensed something was wrong with you, and so…I sought you out," Elarion began.

Connerh looked away as he tried to recall it for himself.

"We crossed paths on your way to Utreden with the woman and child. You were doing your best to conceal the chaos contained within you…" Elarion shook his head. "But you were bursting at the seams. Once I knew what had transpired, I felt I had no choice," he explained, his words arrested.

"You had no choice but to do what?" Connerh pressed.

"I shielded you. Not from the pain altogether…just the sharpest parts. The parts that drove you to madness and our encounter, so that your mind didn't question the absence of memory," he pleaded for understanding, his hands animated.

Connerh's face explored a variety of emotions. Confusion, amusement, concern, amazement, and bewilderment.

"Elarion…" he began, locking eyes with the distraught elf. "You were supposedly in the Westwood when that happened," he continued, his eyes widening. With a shout of excitement, he exclaimed, "How powerful have you become?!"

Elarion froze like a deer caught in lamplight.

"That has to be a record, right?" Connerh pressed. Elarion's silhouette compressed in his embarrassment and humility. "Oh, how I envy you," Connerh added.

Elarion shook his head, insisting, "There's nothing to envy, I assure you."

"He who has not—" Connerh recited.

"That's a stupid saying," Elarion shot back, cutting him off, his tone scornful. "Defining envy doesn't make it any more profound than just expressing it plainly," he continued with a furrowed brow.

Connerh smirked, canting his head with curiosity.

"I knew the alleged poet personally," Elarion scoffed. "He was a fucking imbecile. Three hundred years later, and his overly simplistic sayings are still being repeated as if they ever held any sort of merit."

Connerh cackled, and it softened into a smirk as he took in his friend's face, reminding himself of how old Elarion actually was. He looked so youthful that it was easy to forget how long he had lived – that one day, he too would be a sentiment…a story for Elarion to tell someone, someday. His smile faded with his gaze.

Elarion noticed.

"Do you forgive me for robbing you of your free will…even if but for a moment?" he asked.

Connerh's eyes trailed away for a second before returning.

"Of course. You're foolish to ask. Foolish to wonder if you somehow committed a wrong," Connerh frowned with humoured brows. "Does salvation require permission?" he asked. "Sometimes we make mistakes in pursuit of what's right. Your heart was in the right place, and you did what you felt was best in the moment. Flawed reasons or not..."

Connerh's voice trailed off. Lips parted slightly as words sat heavily on his tongue. He looked at Elarion again, really looked at him, and his perception shifted.

The carefully placed words. The deliberate pacing. The way Elarion had let him arrive at the answer to his personal dilemma himself.

A quiet, breathless chuckle left him – half amused, half disbelieving. He muttered something under his breath, shaking his head.

Elarion simply nodded, a barely audible grunt expressing his satisfaction. His bottom lip pressed forward, he folded his hands behind his back, and he wandered out of the room.

CHAPTER FIFTY

More than a Memento

Elarion

The sleep was so good that her mouth was open, dripping petite trails of drool, although she was still aware of her surroundings. The birdsong kept her awake enough to find it rhythmically soothing. She lay with her back to the ground, embraced by dirt, silky grass, tulips, lilies, and daisies, the combination of which could not be found in nature. However, it was what she wanted, and she wasn't bound by those rules here. Still, she'd only ever seen the flowers from a distance, meaning they were at best an approximation of the real thing and, thus, near the limits of what she could conjure.

She was closer than she knew.

The breeze chilled the air a few degrees below her body temperature, helping her float in and out of consciousness. She embraced the waves of existence, keeping an eye on the shore. The light from the sun, which looked like quartz, beamed through her closed eyelids to create fractal patterns she'd never seen before. This place was magical, and to think it came from her own mind, something that typically dwelt in such darkness.

His footsteps broke a branch, fully rousing her, except she couldn't remember creating branches on the ground. Madika smirked.

"You're considerate even in dreamlands? I'm beginning to wonder if

I've conjured you as well," she remarked, sitting up.

Elarion walked towards her slowly, hands folded behind his back as they had been before. He wore a warm smile on his face. His regalia had been discarded in favour of a tunic and trousers the colour of earth tones. He was barefoot. She'd never seen an elf's feet before. She thought it curious, somehow imagining they would look…different. Her thoughts embarrassingly lingered on the subject before she patted the ground in front of her. He nodded and sat once he drew close enough, folding his legs.

"Promise me you're not here to bring me back," she said.

He shook his head. "No. You can leave whenever you wish. You're sleeping right now, and it will be that way until you're ready."

"I can stay here forever?" she joked.

He thought for a moment, then replied, "I suppose for as long as your body will allow, yes, I don't see why not."

Her hand raised to her chest. She started to stand but froze to look at him. Was he joking? She finished standing and paced for a moment. She glanced around, investigating her surroundings, then back to him.

"I don't know why, but I suddenly don't think I like the sound of that," she replied.

"I had hoped not, but that is your decision to make," he explained with a quiet chuckle. "Though, if I am to be honest, this doesn't have to be like…this."

Standing to his feet, he paused. His face betrayed his conflict.

"What is it?" she asked as her curiosity grew.

"It's better if I show you," he ventured. With a wave of his palm, the scenery changed. "You could live here."

They were now standing in an affluent quarter of a far-off land she'd never visited.

"You could have a normal life, the way you want it to be. Full of possibility and people who would never know that you were the architect of their being," he explained, nodding to a man walking by. She looked around in awe, shaded by fear.

"They wouldn't know that they are figments of my imagination…" she murmured. "…but I would."

He thought about it and conceded with a nod. He returned them to her secret garden.

"I suppose you are right. I could offer you something more," he said reluctantly.

She didn't respond but looked at him. His gaze fell to the ground.

"I could send you to a place where you could start over, living the life you should have had. Having no recollection of your experiences up until now," he began, his gaze intense.

"I can't start over, I'm a grown—"

She began to refute him but fell silent when she heard her own voice. It was young again, about ten years if she had to guess. Her stature had changed; Elarion towered over her even more than he already had. She raised her palms to investigate. They were small. The scenery changed again. The smells, the sounds, her mother's voice calling to her from in the distance. She instinctively began to run towards the voice but stopped. She kept her back to him.

"And where would this place be?" she asked, turning to face him. He looked away. With disbelief and a frown, she asked, "In your mind?"

He nodded bashfully, maintaining his wayward gaze.

"You can do that?" she pressed.

He did not respond at first. His brow sunk as he heard her weeping, but he replied, "If you asked me to."

She turned and ran a few steps at the sound of her being called again, then stopped for a second time and turned back to Elarion. He watched her from behind lowered eyelids.

"But you don't think I should?" she half-asked, half-stated.

He shook his head, refuting, "It doesn't matter what I want."

"Why are you being so kind to me?" she asked as her face crumpled.

"Because you deserved better."

Her name was called again. She looked in the direction but stayed where she stood. There were a few moments of quiet.

"Are we all just figments of someone else's imagination?" she asked.

His bottom lip pushed out as his head tilted, giving the matter some real thought before he replied, "Perhaps. That is a very real possibility. Theoretically, by the very offer I just made, I could really never say for sure." He was surprised he hadn't thought about it before.

Her eyes shot wide, and she ignored another call. It was in a panic, flailing her hands, that she declared, "I don't like this anymore."

She resumed her original adult form, and her garden returned. They exchanged glances as she noticed the transformation.

"All of it!" she shouted, waking up in the real world with a loud gasp.

He'd told her the truth. She was, in fact, lying in her bed, neatly tucked under a blanket. He was sitting next to her in a chair, his face covered in scratches and dried blood. She sat up in a rush at the sight of it and ripped the blanket off, but she stopped again upon noticing his blood under her nails. She froze. His eyes dropped.

"It's not your fault," he offered.

"I'm sorry," she replied. Her eyes darted back and forth as she sorted through her thoughts. She tried to recall what had happened in the real world while she was sleeping, to engage with the others that occupied her mind, but there was a wall. Something was preventing their communication.

"Get out of here!" she screamed at Elarion, pounding her own head with her hand.

His warmth left her mind, causing her to wince as the chorus of thoughts and voices suddenly amplified. She wrestled with gaining control, finding it more difficult without Elarion's assistance. It took a minute, but she managed it. Balfour ran over, handing her a vial; he'd been observing from the corner. She took the vial willingly and poured it down her throat with haste. It was a putrid concoction, but it worked.

"You don't need those," Elarion couldn't help but speak up.

"What do you want from me?" she demanded, splattering confusion across his face.

"I don't want anything," he assured her. She scoffed, opting to stand and cross her arms, although not before wiping a smear of potion from her lips.

"I'm sorry, but my experience doesn't allow me to believe that," she snarled. "No matter how much I'd like to," Her brow lowered.

"I understand," he said.

She squinted and shook her head. "I look at you, here with me. An elf helping one of the Tu'Chauri…as unbelievable as that already seems. Every time you speak and offer your perfect kindness, free of charge…you assure me that either I really have lost the plot or…you're lying." Turning away, she mumbled, "Maybe I am a loon, and I've conjured my own personal hell."

"They always want something," she whispered to herself in a different voice and tone.

"They do, don't they?" she replied in yet another.

"Truth be told, Master Elf…" she started with her own voice.

Elarion frowned at her choice of words.

"Everything in my being is telling me to trust you. And for that…I don't trust it. How do I know you didn't plant those thoughts there? No one is ever so generous without wanting. I've seen it for myself," she decided, pointing to her own head.

Elarion nodded quietly. She turned to look at him as he stood. She didn't expect him to do that. His shoes scuffed against the floor. He tucked his necklace under his shirt and retrieved a folded piece of paper from his pocket, handing it to Balfour.

"Perhaps I have been too forward. I now see how this could be overwhelming for you," Elarion admitted in a humble tone.

He offered a small bow and excused himself.

Balfour and Madika stood there in silence for a few moments as they watched him leave.

"What is it?" she enquired, motioning towards the paper. Balfour's focus returned, and he rushed to unravel it, reading it from the bridge of his nose. He let out a half-chuckle.

"It's notes on how to improve the tincture, inclusive of ingredients and detailed instructions," he announced with a laugh of disbelief. She snatched the paper from him and read over it herself.

"I don't understand," she muttered, tone muted.

"You don't have to understand everything," Balfour replied.

She locked eyes with him.

"For example, I don't understand why you let him leave. You've been sleeping for days, you look and sound better than I've ever seen you, and you're shouting at him?" he chuckled to himself. She grabbed his robe.

"For how long?!" she demanded.

"Days…three, maybe four, depending on how you count 'em," he replied.

She looked up, lost in her own thoughts for only a moment before she bolted after Elarion, stopping just short of the door to Balfour's workshop. She swung it open and scanned for him.

He was nowhere to be found, just a loose crowd of passersby now staring at her.

CHAPTER FIFTY-ONE

RECONCILIATION

CONNERH

The sky was drab and swathed in grey, the air heavy with the scent of winter – an almost sterile aroma that triggered the memory of nothing in particular, just a general feeling of something specific.

A distant time, a familiar place.

Time spent with a familiar person.

Bitter gusts of wind cut through layers of wool with little effort, while snow flurries wandered to the ground, absent of urgency and powerless to cling on – to linger beyond their moment of impact. Yet despite nature's insistent push to seek warmth by a hearth or roaring fire, the streets were densely lined with people too high in number to count: a sea of monochromatic melancholy pressing in around him. He could smell their breath. They stood silently watching, waiting, as if they knew something he didn't.

If honesty were a priority, it was all just a little overwhelming for Connerh, forcing his curiosity to run wild.

Were they there in support of him?

Or of his sentence?

Their expressions were hollow – far too plain and emotionless to determine their thoughts or intent. They looked at him as if they were observing a ghost, a scene beyond what was normal. On the surface, being the centre of attention drifted through familiar territory, though never comfortable; the resulting sensation prickled against his skin. It was the sheer size of the procession that propelled the situation into uncharted waters, more akin to a royal wedding…or funeral.

His brow crumpled. The chains binding his feet and hands rattled with every step upon the cobblestone streets, an audible reminder of his shame…a physical cue of his captivity. Their soft ring masked the sounds of the soldiers escorting him, all while denying him the freedom to ignore the makings of his own spectacle.

The path was familiar; he'd taken it several times as a free man. It was a nearly direct route to the city centre, cutting through a few streets of homes and shops along the way.

Only now had it ever felt so long.

So distant.

Less travelled.

And suddenly, he wished for rain – like a blanket he could use to obscure himself.

Never in his life had he seen so many people turn out for what should be a standard exercise in public humiliation, by flogging. Standard procedure for a deserter.

Wasn't it?

"This way, Commander," he heard one of his escorts say to him, the soldier's hand extended just off centre, his voice soft but calloused with embarrassment.

The sound of his former rank filled Connerh's face with confusion as the hand on his shoulder guided his movement, competing for his focus. He hadn't been addressed that way in what felt like a lifetime, though reality had a way of making recollection feel stretched and diluted.

Something felt off.

Wrong.

A foreboding sensation tightened his chest, making it difficult to ignore.

His lungs felt only half as capable, his eyes no longer able to hold focus. His feet felt heavier, larger. He stumbled, tripping over his own steps, and his escorts hurried to stabilise him just as they rounded the street corner where Old Man Hegg's bakery still resided.

And there she was.

Amidst the cacophony that only existed in his mind, he felt Lena's gaze from a hundred metres away like a rush of wind in a still room.

Their pupils locked.

She rushed to her feet.

On what should have been the saddest day of her life, it rained – an abnormal and relentless downpour that puddled the streets. She remembered the hours with resounding clarity: a waking nightmare that remained at the back of her mind until she learned to avoid it, to look the other way. It was the middle of the week, on a day that held no particular significance. Ordinary and predictable in almost every way, yet when she awoke that morning, she felt something was amiss. But, true to form, she ignored it. It was like waking up in the wrong home – one nearly identical to her own but subtly off. The signs lay in the fine details, imperceptible to an outsider who wasn't searching for them, like a nick in a tapestry. She noticed a frayed edge within her reality, seeing it only as a loose thread that could be disregarded – believing it to be something that could be unseen and thus rendered inert.

After all, it seemed to work elsewhere in life.

But she was wrong, and by the end – lingering in the depths of her loss – she had become thoroughly convinced that she possessed a sixth sense, a way of perceiving bad omens when others could not. Even when her intuition failed her, she would later persuade herself into believing she had simply overlooked something she regarded as minor. Back then, everything mattered, no detail too small or too insignificant if it meant trusting her alleged extrasensory perception. Alas, with age came wisdom; in her heart, she knew there was only her, her five senses, and a deep desire to control uncertainty.

But in the shadow of the most uncertain times, old habits resurrect.

Today happened to be the middle of the week. The sky loomed ominously, heavy with the threat of rain, though it was far too cold for it; snowflakes fell in its place. The bed she woke up in this morning was her own. Everything was as it should be. After all, winter had arrived, and a day like today wasn't uncommon.

And yet...

Her eyes scanned the clouds as if searching for droplets or a sign they might appear. A modicum of peace settled over her thoughts when she found none, though she still fiddled in her seat. She blinked rapidly, pulling herself back into the moment.

The murmurs of the crowd roared in a low rumble, loud enough to hear but too indistinct to discern.

Word regarding Connerh's sentencing spread like wildfire through the dead brush. She expected a crowd, but not this large. They crammed together, shoulder to shoulder, with no patch of ground visible as far as the eye could see.

Her eyes widened when she realised she had no idea whose side they were on.

Would they riot? Or cheer?

The fact that she couldn't answer her own question filled her with doubt.

There were three elevated platforms in total. At the centre, Lena sat in a throne-like chair on the largest of the three, surrounded by no fewer than sixty guards. Athelstan stood beside her, Farrah just off to her right and behind, where she was accompanied by a handful of handmaidens and forgettable bureaucrats – political vampires biting at the chance to be seen next to her, hoping to propel their own careers.

In front of her, Niko paced with his hands behind his back, a smirk creasing the corners of his lips as he scanned the crowd. His black overcoat, laced in silver, bore not a single wrinkle or speck of dust, while his hair, beard, and moustache were coated in a layer of the finest perfumed oil, as they always were. To him, no attention was of the bad sort.

'A man seen is a man remembered' was the kind of bullshit creed he lived by – much to the ire of Lena and generally anyone who had to deal with him. But in politics, it was better to be reliably consistent than inconsistently unreliable.

"What are they saying, Niko?" Lena asked, her voice muffled under the ornate, white opalescent mask. He immediately spun in place at the sound of her voice.

"I'm sorry, I could not discern your words, Your Majesty," he replied.

She repeated herself but grew frustrated by his expression upon him still not understanding her. She ripped the mask from her face, taking a deep breath. A quarter of the crowd cheered upon seeing her face, freezing her in place.

It was a good sign, she eventually reasoned.

"I said, what are they saying? The crowd, that is," she asked, doing her best to whisper and not point, her frustration fading. Niko nodded and returned his gaze to the crowd.

"There is confusion among the people..." he began. Her expression blanked as she also looked out at the random sea of faces looking right back at her. "Some of them don't understand why you would punish your once-quite-public lover." He looked back at her, his grin still strewn across his face, although his gaze diverted as her eyes met his. "Others quite frankly despise you for doing so." He moved closer, lowering his voice. "We understood that the truth regarding what transpired at the Rim would get out," he reaffirmed, and she nodded. "As a result, many view him as a hero. A protector of the realm. They don't care about formality or military rules; they see him as someone who did what needed to be done, no matter the cost."

The smirk faded.

She looked worried, and a tinge of horror crept in. She swallowed.

"I was assured this spectacle would satiate any uprising, any..." She shook her head, searching for the right word. "...any...thing...that could be perceived as, uhh, improper," she argued in a low tone.

His eyes flared as his head canted, and he replied bluntly, "It would seem you were advised...wrongly, Majesty."

Her head cocked backwards.

"Don't get me wrong, there are those out there," he began, turning to look at the crowd briefly, "that would indeed consider the lack of punishment for desertion..." He paused and protruded his lips. "...a mistake. Especially seeing as it goes against everything Hildeheim stands for. We're a fighting nation, bred from the loins of warriors." His brows closed in. "Desertion is..." he paused, shaking his head as his eyes wandered, then dropped. "However, there must always be room for exception," he added, meeting her gaze once more with a small smile. "The very thing I voted for in chambers."

"I know...Niko, I know," she cut him off. He bowed his head quickly.

"I draw attention to this matter only that I may not incur your impending wrath, should this turn...unsightly," he said.

Her gaze snapped to the smaller platform to her left, where members of her court stood, Vaelen Graymane among them. It was where her wrath always should have been unleashed. His eyes were narrowed, as if trying to read her lips from afar, and he jerked slightly upon realising he'd been caught, offering a bow that felt insincere — or at least, that was how she took it. The more she reflected on Vaelen's assurances, the more she hated herself for even entertaining them. She thought herself the fool.

Her mother would have punished Connerh just the same, but with no regard to what anyone thought. Not the court, not her counsel, and most assuredly not commoners. It was the law, and that was that. Lena, however, in an effort to depart from her mother's style of rule, thought that the inclusion of all parties would in some way reframe her decision in a positive light. Wrong or right, ideally, it would make her seem like the *people's ruler* instead of *just another tyrant*. But now, in hindsight, it seemed so simple.

Laws didn't empathise with people; they only sought to maintain order. Caring was the job of the people enforcing those laws.

She sighed.

A small, nagging part of her missed Gatty, longed for the warmth of her wisdom radiating from above her shoulder. However, the time of finding refuge under someone else's wings had passed — she had her own pair.

Lena's head pivoted to the other platform, where her esteemed guests stood. Elarion felt her gaze and met it. He looked disappointed, his expression vague and devoid of emotion, lingering for only a few seconds before his focus returned to Thaetra without so much as an acknowledgement. Not even a nod. It stung a little. Next to them were representatives from the three provinces of the Far Sands, Khazmyr, and Utreden, as well as the Dwarven Nation. Among these representatives was Mormere, one of Connerh's closest friends from the old days. He avoided eye contact with everyone, his head canted as he stared into nothingness beyond the ground. He massaged his fingers with his other hand as his brow grew heavier. She could tell he was clearing his throat often. He always jutted out his lower lip just beyond his bushy moustache when he did it.

Her frown deepened. She wanted to join them, but it would break decorum — and surely, they would want nothing to do with her, she thought. Suddenly, Mormere hopped down from his chair and stood at full attention. She rose immediately as her head turned to see what it was he saw.

It was Connerh rounding the corner with a look in his eyes that perhaps only she saw. He was anxious, worried despite a mostly collected exterior. Elarion stole his attention without fanfare or an outward display, only an intense stare that made it seem as if he weren't even breathing. She tracked their eyes. The elf was obviously communicating with him. Her jealousy squinted her eyes as she sat dramatically, returning her mask to her face. If only she had such a power, she thought.

The silence was excruciatingly loud. Under normal circumstances, the crowd would roar – there would have been a call to order, and soldiers and guards would have been dispersed to corral the chaos. Not this time. They parted quietly as Connerh descended into the square, towards the centre stage.

"What is going on, Niko?" she asked in awed confusion. His head shook before he spoke.

"History," was all he replied as he observed curiously, a smirk developing.

"Pardon me for saying, but I believe you have surpassed your mother…" he began. Her spine straightened; a smile began to form. "…as the most hated Queen of Hildeheim."

His words sapped her strength, punching her in the gut. She curled forward.

"Can I stop it?" she asked, rushing to refill her lungs with air.

"I'm sorry?" he queried, turning to face her.

"Can I stop it?" she repeated.

He looked confused.

"All of it, the proceeding, the sentence, all of it," she replied, desperation sinking in.

His mouth opened, and his brows crumpled, lingering for a moment before closing. His eyes dropped, and he replied, "You are the queen. You can do…anything,"

She looked at the crowd again. Her tone softened, and her pitch lowered as she asked, "Should I?"

He looked away.

"I cannot answer your question." His eyes met hers, although his head remained lowered. "That is to say…I *should not* answer *that* question. I will do as you command, Your Majesty."

She tried to keep her tears quiet underneath the priceless artefact covering her face, but he heard her quiet, hitched breaths. He awkwardly diverted his attention to give her metaphorical space to process her emotions, instead observing as Farrah rushed to her side, positioning her body between Lena and the crowd and whispering into her ear.

"If I may?" Niko asked.

Lena nodded.

He approached and lowered his voice, asking, "What kind of queen do you want to be?"

She looked at him for a moment, then away as she pondered the question.

"If you were to stop it…I fear it would do more damage than allowing it to proceed. Better to be feared by the weak and respected by the strong than viewed as weak and destroyed by them together," he said, nodding in agreement with himself.

She was quiet for a few moments before clearing her throat, a forced cold overtaking her tone as she instructed, "Continue with the proceedings."

Farrah frowned and returned to her place.

"As you wish," he replied, but not before taking a bow. "I admire your strength," he added. Her head snapped in his direction.

Connerh walked up the steps of the centre stage, guards both in front of and behind him.

"We are gathered here today with heavy hearts and bittersweet emotions. Today's events serve not only as a reminder of the innocent lives lost at the Rim," Niko paused, allowing his declaration to trigger the memory of the past. If Connerh's gaze could kill, it would have. "But it also marks the return of one of Hildeheim's favourite sons," he continued. The crowd instantly erupted into a deafening cheer, causing Niko to take a step backwards. An encroaching fear paused his speech as they continued for nearly a full minute. He looked back at Lena, who was equally caught off guard.

Connerh's head dropped, and the attention became more and more uncomfortable. Niko's eyes wandered as he mentally rearranged his rehearsed speech.

"I'll be blunt with you: I didn't want to do this," Lena declared, appearing next to Niko.

The crowd was silenced when she spoke.

"As I am so often reminded, I hold all the power in this land." She tore the mask off her face. She heard whispers and murmuring. "It would be all too easy to will this away. To silence my detractors, by force if I needed to, wanted to…" Her eyes glazed over. "But what would that say about me?

That I am weak? A coward? That there are rules for you but not for me? Not for us?" Her voice grew sharper, louder. She scowled at Vaelen and his cohorts, who whispered to one another.

"Free him!" the crowd interrupted her. Their shouts and screams were impatient and angry. She went to continue speaking, but they had no use for her words.

"Guards," Niko quietly gave the order to begin quelling the disruptors.

"Wait," Lena interjected.

"Your Majesty, we must *control* this crowd. We are sitting amidst numbers that are easily a hundred to one. There is no one who could save us if they chose to raise arms," he replied, his eyes locked onto hers. There was fear in them.

Lena looked around, and panic began to swell within her.

"No," Connerh shouted. The crowd was silenced. He felt the eyes of everyone on him. It was a hot sensation that prickled his skin. "Her Majesty is right. The sentence is just, and I accept it...willingly. I knew the consequences of my actions," he continued, shaking his head as a memory poured into his mind. "And no matter how just the cause...I entered into the same contract, much like many of you... This is our way...and the law is the law." Taking a deep breath and marching himself over to the post that protruded from the stage, he leaned against it and announced, "Let's get on with it."

His guards unfastened his chains. Formality would see that his hands and feet were bound around the post so he couldn't run, but they chose to ignore it. Instead of guarding him, they guarded the stage.

Niko cleared his throat.

"We shall commence with the sentence as set forth in the law. The crime: desertion."

The crowd erupted into jeers and booing that lasted only a few seconds. Niko cleared his throat.

"The punishment set forth...is forty lashes by whip," he said hesitantly.

Lena gripped his arm tightly and suddenly with a quiet gasp of, "Forty?!"

He attempted to downplay her grasp.

"I was not told it would be so many."

"Yes, Your Majesty, the law has not been changed in over three hundred years. Perhaps it was an oversight not to mention the specifics..."

he replied, pausing as her nails dug into him.

"I have to stop this." Her voice was a whispered plea.

"You cannot." He turned to her, his eyes demanding and voice forceful, "To reward a rebellious spirit would most certainly ensure our deaths here this day."

Her grip grew tighter, somehow.

"Then so be it; I cannot allow this to proceed. It will kill him," she whispered urgently. "I will not watch him bleed to death for Vaelen's amusement."

"Perhaps there is another way," he replied, his tone still a whisper. His hand rushed to calm her grip. "Allow things to begin, and when you wish for it to stop, excuse yourself; I will stop it once you are to safety."

It took a moment, but she agreed, releasing him and returning to her seat.

Connerh stared into the crowd, his body leaning against the splintered post. He counted the faces, many familiar, about seventy in particular. They looked at him, waiting for the command. He smirked first, then shook his head.

They nodded and disappeared into the crowd one by one, like the spectres they were.

Like the sound of wind rushing from the mouth of a cave, he heard and felt his spear calling to him. His excitement easily drowned out the mental anguish of its screams filling the spaces in his mind as it once did. He looked wildly up at the sky, turning to find it.

"What is he doing?" Aghor Emberheart asked Vaelen, who smiled.

"What they all do before death. Communing with his maker," Vaelen replied. They both chuckled.

Lena watched them.

"I wish to see them gutted like pigs sooner or later," she unintentionally uttered.

"I will see it done," Niko replied quickly, catching her off guard. She rushed to look at him as if to confirm what she'd heard.

He bowed.

Connerh didn't hear the rest of Niko's speech – only the distorted ebb and flow of the crowd's reaction. He drifted in a strange euphoria, a blissful detachment. The thought of so many willing to intervene on his behalf brought a smile to his lips, filling a void he had long accepted as permanent, never to be mended. He wasn't sure how to process it. He only knew that, for the first time, he felt justified…in everything. Or at least almost everything.

His sacrifices hadn't gone unnoticed. They hadn't been in vain.

He barely registered the soldier's murmured apology before the fabric of his tunic was ripped away, exposing his back. The air was cold, the snowfall brushing against his skin like delicate kisses. His gaze drifted over the crowd where no three expressions were exactly alike – shock, horror, disapproval, anger, and frustration all merging, mixing, twisting.

He didn't feel the first impact, only the jolt of his body shifting in place. Neither did he feel the second or third. His only indication that the lashes were landing came from the crowd's reactions – some flinching, others turning their backs in silent protest. It was the fifth blow when he began to smell the leather.

With a slow, lingering blink, he opened his eyes and found Lena writhing in her seat, her shoulders trembling as she raised a hand to cover her masked mouth. His gaze shifted to Elarion, whose expression remained as unreadable as ever. Connerh exhaled sharply, now keenly aware of why he felt no pain. Another strike sent him lurching forward.

It's alright, he thought.

Elarion's head tilted slightly, his brow lifting in a silent question. He hesitated, delaying the next blow.

It will all have been for nothing if I do not face this truly, Connerh pressed, his resolve hardening.

Elarion took a deep breath, his nostrils flaring, his tongue tracing the edge of his teeth. Another strike landed. More of the crowd turned their backs.

The tenth blow came with the sharp tang of copper in the air.

"Please…" Connerh whispered. His voice barely carried, but Elarion heard.

The elf lifted his head defiantly. Without a word, he uncurled a single finger from his clenched fist, allowing Connerh to feel the pain in stages.

A dull impact, though stronger than before. No real pain, just the sensation of something connecting. Blood was running down his back now, warm against the cold.

A second finger.

The next strike stung, more than discomfort — a deep, bruising ache beneath torn flesh. Dread curled around his ribs.

A third.

Connerh squeezed his eyes shut and grunted. A burning sensation traced along his spine, radiating from his raw, bleeding wounds. His heart pounded against his ribs. The pain was real now, and it was only beginning.

Another strike wrenched a grimace from his face, his teeth bared as the wind was forcibly driven from his chest.

He felt the sun peak through the clouds with increasing frequency, as if it were curious about his plight. The next sent a sharp sting through his ribs, his eyes welling with tears as a loud grunt tore from his throat.

He turned to Elarion just as the fourth finger uncurled.

He had been whipped before — many times, in fact. But those had been makeshift, fashioned in haste from leather straps. This was different. Whips designed for capital punishment were meant to do more than hurt; they were crafted to *dissuade* repeat offence…or torture. Knotted, their ends embedded with shards of bone or metal, they did not simply punish. They carved their lessons into flesh, lessons that would one day scar — if the recipient were lucky — and leave a lasting memory. There was a gap between the blows, the executioner of the sentence likely changing hands.

The reprieve felt like a welcome eternity.

As did the rain as it began to fall, the snow having melted in its descent.

But just like the pause came to an end, so too did the relief the droplets initially provided, now more akin to acid splattering into his open wounds. His vision blurred at the unrelenting torrent of tears that filled his eyes, though he wasn't crying — not out of pain, anyway. It was a release of the darkness escaping his body. The guilt.

Lena caught his attention as she abruptly stood to her feet, her movement frantic, chaotic — he squinted, trying to figure out what was happening in between the blows and his own screams. She whispered something to Niko and left in a hurry, her figure descending the stairs at the back of the platform, her guards and Farrah along with her. Everyone else had turned their backs, save for Niko, Vaelen, Aghor, and those with him, as well as a sprinkling of individuals in the crowd. The smirk of accomplishment lingered on their faces.

It was the last thing he remembered seeing before it all went black. There wasn't even a gradual fade, just an instant disconnection from reality as abrupt as his introduction into the world as a newborn.

He awoke with a loud scream followed by a grimace. He was slumped over on the back of a horse – a warrior's horse, to be specific. He fought to open his eyes; it felt like weights were attached to the lids. The crowd that had previously watched his torment now shouted in cheer at his rousing, but the overwhelming pain he felt collapsed his face. He held his breath in an attempt to contain the discomfort, though with little success. There were so many hands reaching out for him, trying to console him through the agony.

He let out a scream at a sudden, sharp pain in his side.

"Where do you wish to go, my lord?" he heard someone ask.

"Lena…Lena…" he kept repeating, though he didn't know who he was answering. He heard a commotion before his horse began to trot.

CHAPTER FIFTY-TWO

APOLOGIES

LENA

Lena sat on the stairs leading to her throne, her remaining unbitten fingernail resting on the pillow of her lips. It was a nasty adolescent habit, but routine, stress, and the relief it provided made it hard to kick, like curling into the foetal position while in pain or sucking one's thumb. Thankfully, she'd never been a thumb-sucker.

Her thoughts wrestled with regret and second-guessing — an unforgiving tumble that never seemed to end, leaving room for guilt to slide its rusty blade between her ribs. She felt regret for leaving Connerh's sentencing early, fearing he might see her as a coward for having done so. She regretted having considered the public's opinion over her own, handing him over to her enemies to be publicly humiliated. He always seemed to suffer on her behalf.

Yet she couldn't even bear to endure watching it unfold.

She wondered if her mother had been right about her.

I am unfit, she thought, resigning herself to her failure as a queen, a lover, and everything in between. She crumpled, and her eyes were quickly overrun with water. She wiped it away with her arm, sniffling all the while. Her gaze snapped in the direction of random sounds before returning to her mental tunnelling. There were so many things she would do differently, had she the power and strength to relive the past once more.

But after today, they would be free of that burden — able to reset and restart, picking up not where they left off but where they should have begun. She rushed to her feet as the doors began to open, thundering in the cavernous hall. The hinges groaned as if they shared his pain. His contrastingly small frame entered the room, his hand still gripping the door. The scuffing from his limped steps bounced between the pillars and into her ears.

She gasped.

"Len—" Connerh attempted to call, his echo but a gentle whisper in the vastness surrounding him. His eyes clamped shut, and he stumbled forward, falling to his knees.

He only called her that when something was wrong. Typically, it was when she patched him up after battle – after he had seen death and lived to tell her about it. The air was expelled from her chest. Her eyes squinted with curious fear, a flicker of dread crossing her face as her body stiffened. She immediately ran to him, her heartbeat thundering in her ears.

"Len…something's wrong." He made an effort to breathe, tightening his face to contain that which he felt. Somehow, somewhere, she found the strength to run faster, the world blurring as her body surged. He gripped his right side, baring his teeth. His face was pale and drawn with pain. Her panicked hands trembled and fumbled, desperately pulling at the layers of his clothing, her tattered nails catching the fabric in her urgency. His cheek muscles tightened as he grimaced, jaw clenched.

He coughed blood onto the floor, freezing her in place.

Her eyes locked on the puddle of crimson, wide and unblinking, a sickened flutter of her throat betraying the panic now clawing at her chest.

"Get this off him!" she shrieked, the anxiety reaching its peak, her voice raw and strangled.

Her hands tore at his clothes again, shaking with violent determination. The nearby guards, once inanimate statues, burst into life, their movements sharp and alert – although they couldn't reach her in time.

"No, no, no, no! I don't understand!"

She panicked as she found the layers closest to his body damp…and red. The cloth was sticking to his skin, to his freshly whipped back. He screamed as she peeled it away and over his head. His breathing became laboured, his ribs heaving with the effort to draw breath, and a wet, gurgling sound filled the air. She noticed the two puncture wounds on his side as soon as she rolled him off his back. They leaked a steady flow.

"You've been stabbed!" she shouted. "When!?"

"Stop, no, no, it's okay. It's okay."

He hurried to stop her as she tried to pack her gown into the wounds, but they were too small. His voice was thick with exhaustion. His eyes, half-lidded and strained, found hers. His irises fought to remain focused on her, and as he smiled – weakly, tenderly – his lips quivered slightly, as if the effort alone was a battle. He rammed his eyes closed again, his features contorted for a moment. A grunted sigh produced a smile, as if he didn't want her to remember him grimacing in pain.

He had seen death, but this time, it had caught him.

"I'm sorry. I'm sorry. I'm…"

He stopped, his voice breaking. Hot liquid poured from his tear ducts. His body trembled beneath her hands, his entire figure vibrating with the intensity of his final breaths. His face twisted in a strange expression of acceptance, but the agony still bled through. His last sigh was deep, a sound that reverberated through her chest, hollow and guttural. It drew a groan from her throat, her chest aching with the release of air.

"Please don't leave me!" she cried, her head shaking violently.

The motion was sharp, as if trying to deny the reality as it played out in front of her. Her breath was uneven, coming in jagged sobs, her hand clutching at his chest as if to force him to stay, her fingers desperate but powerless. His limp shell quivered freely with her movement, his body made into little more than a hollow vessel.

"Uruk-khashûr, dak-dûsh az-gan!" she screamed in native Giant, the words tearing from her throat like a primal wail.

"Nai arwenyallo, ú-yanar!" she pleaded in Elvish. Her lips trembled as she whispered the words, but they rang out in the silence that had swallowed them whole.

In Dwarvish.

In the tongue of the old gods and the new.

In the ancient one she had been taught.

In the gestures across her chest, in the air, and in her heart.

It was the absence of relief that stung the loudest.

Her surrender had her eyes buried into the tops of her cheeks, her face crumpling beneath the weight of grief. Tears spilt freely, her body shaking with sobs that rattled through her limbs. Her breath came in a choked gasp, a final surrender as the weight of her despair grew too heavy to bear.

Reh'gara stood nearby, in the realm she could not perceive, his back turned to her and eyes held shut. His chest heaved with the effort to hold himself together, his face pale with the weight of her sorrow. His tears dripped, slow and steady, like icicles melting with the first touch of spring. He no longer desired to witness her pain. His shoulders hunched with the burden of it, the space between them vast and unbreachable.

She opened her eyes, blinking rapidly to clear the blur of tears. Farrah's face, previously tense, was now empty of expression, her mouth slightly parted in disbelief. She was devoid of the ability to provide words of comfort; nothing she could utter could possibly matter. However, the fear slowly started to build in Farrah's eyes, a shift from worry to horror as Lena's movements became more automatic.

Lena stood, the numbness creeping in as her grip mechanically released Connerh's body into the waiting hands of the physicians. Her lips trembled, though her face betrayed no expression, her movements so deliberate and detached that they seemed alien. Farrah reached out to touch her, but Lena's gaze was already somewhere else, her hand brushing past Farrah's without a second glance. Farrah's face slowly crumbled, the fear turning to outright panic.

Lena kissed Farrah's forehead – soft, almost tender, but with finality. It was an action full of meaning she could not express in words, a gesture that said all without a sound. And then, she swiftly made for the balcony.

She climbed onto the railing, her fingers stiff as they gripped the cold stone, her body trembling with a mix of exhaustion and determination. Her eyes, swollen and red from weeping, fixed on the horizon. The cries and pleas calling out to her barely registered.

She was sure his embrace lay just beyond the waves, though turbulent and violent they seemed. The weight of it felt like the price of admission to rejoin him.

There was one final curl of her stomach, like the last tightening of a fist before release. The breeze caught her hair, whipping it around her face and tugging at her. Her heart pounded, then slowed. The waves crashing in the distance seemed to beckon. She felt them drawing closer, closer, as though they were calling her, promising the end of this unbearable ache.

And then, with a final exhale, she let herself go.

Her body pitched forward, the cold air rushing around her like a violent embrace and stealing the tears from her face as she plunged towards the waves below.

She smiled and closed her eyes.

Her impact was indistinguishable amongst the crashing of the waves.

CHAPTER FIFTY-THREE

SALVE

YURI

"What is the last thing you remember? Of home, that is," he asked.

Yuri's movements slowed as she looked at him, slowly unravelling the bandages wrapped around his head and covering his eyes.

"I don't even know what to call you anymore," she replied in lieu of an answer.

He smirked and remarked, "I should very much like you to call me Julian."

"Only when we can be sure that no one will hear it," she retorted, shaking her head a little. Her lip briefly hitched with a frown when the remaining bandage fell to his shoulder, revealing his scarred eyes; the healing salve underneath had created an unsightly, sticky mess dyed a pinkish brown by his blood and sweat.

He nodded with disappointment.

"You know, you don't look like a Julian," she continued. His smile returned. His head had begun to drop, but she lifted it with her hand. Joriah winced as she slowly blotted at his eyes with a cold, wet rag.

"And yet it, it *is* my name," he replied, reading between the lines.

"Says the man with many names," she murmured.

"And what do I look like to you?" he asked. She backed away to get a

429

good look at him.

"I don't know… A Bernard, perhaps?" she laughed, deepening his grin.

He nodded as he thought on it, grinning, "I'll have to remember that one for my next suicide mission."

She smirked but raised a brow. He grunted as she pressed a little too enthusiastically, and apologised quickly with a quiet, "Sorry."

"You didn't answer the question," he replied instead, taking them back to the start of the conversation. She glanced away briefly, remaining quiet as she soaked the rag in a bowl of water before wringing it dry.

"Not much. I was quite young when I…left," she replied, returning to the task of cleaning his face.

"Any memory of family? Siblings? Parents?" he asked.

Her expression grew saddened.

"No," she replied, shaking her head. "I suppose that's why I've never tried to… Well…I struggle to say escape, as this is my home. Brace yourself; I'm applying new ointment," she said as she stood in front of him. His hands raised and felt for her, resting on her hips. She paused. She looked at them, then at him. A frowning smirk dug into her cheek.

"I'm sorry," he said as if he saw or sensed her reaction, quickly dropping his hands.

She chuckled quietly, guiding one of his hands back to her hip as she assured him, "No, it's alright."

His hands were noticeably larger than her own. The callouses on his palms matched the patterns left by a hilt and reins. They told a story without uttering a single word. She turned her head as she quietly studied his face for the first time. It was charming. Aged, but not old.

"I'm ready," he said, unsure of what she was doing that had caused a delay.

She snapped out of it and gently pressed her salve-covered fingers to his eyes, wincing with him as she applied it.

"Oh, this is horrible," he groaned with a forced laugh. He exhaled as she retracted her hand to recoat her fingers, then returned to the subject at hand by asking, "Do you really believe that? That this is your home?"

"I do."

"But it isn't."

"If I say that it is, then is it not?"

"But you do so against your will."

"That is *your* opinion. I do not recall giving you permission to speak for me," she replied with a tinge of indignation. "Besides, how could home be a place where you are not wanted?"

"Why would you say such a thing?" he asked, genuinely confused.

"Because I have been here my entire life, cast out and forgotten." She frowned. "Again," she added, applying another layer to his eyes. "Darros is the only family I need," she concluded.

"You speak like a captive defending their captor," he replied.

She smacked him across the face, at full force and without hesitation. His head turned violently. The sound reverberated. His tongue shot out of his mouth, tucked into the corner of his lips as he carefully bit down, seeking to contain the words he wanted to say.

"Go on, say it!" she challenged him.

He retracted his tongue, folding his bottom lip into his mouth instead. He lowered his head, then shook it. Rubbing his jaw with his hand, he offered, "I chose the wrong words."

He was lying.

"You did," she confirmed.

He erupted into laughter at her brazenness before patiently waiting for her to continue attending to him. She eventually smirked, frown gone as her surge of anger faded.

"You strike like a man," he commented, intending it as a compliment.

"And you dream like a child," she retorted.

"Was that the last time you dreamt?" he asked, immediately bracing for another slap.

She froze first, then asked, "Are you trying to provoke me?"

"No… Inspire, perhaps, but not provoke," he replied.

She stared as her mind raced before she finally settled on a scoff, asking, "Tell me, how will the blind man save me? And where will he take me?"

"My sight will recover."

"You should hope. Pray, even, if you believe in such a thing."

"I do."

"I'm not surprised." She took a few steps back. "Only foolish men cling to…*blind* hope," she emphasised, laughing at the irony. "I suppose it was meant to be after all."

He grinned in response.

"I would imagine you view this…" She motioned towards his face but stopped upon remembering he couldn't see her. "…as a penance, of sorts. A sacrifice for the greater good?"

His scabbed-over eyes looked down before his head followed suit. He finally answered, "Yes."

Her head lurched backwards, and she fussed, "To what end, *Julian*?"

He smiled at hearing his name, to the point of baring his teeth.

"What good will this accomplish?"

He just sat there, grinning.

"I can't deal with you," she huffed, punching him in the arm.

"Sometimes you just have to go with it and allow things to take their course. But we all follow a great purpose, even if we don't know it," he finally replied.

"I've been 'going along with' my entire life…" she mumbled, an unintentional admission. His smile faded.

"And now I'm here," he said.

She squinted at him, pursed her lips, and scolded, "Yes, you are…wasting my time, having me care for a grown man like a suckling baby."

With that, she moved in closer to continue applying salve to his eyes. His hands raised to reach for her waist again, but she smacked them away. He laughed.

"My Shoo'naan warned me about men like you," she reprimanded.

"And what exactly is a Shoo'naan?" he asked.

She thought for a moment and eventually translated, "In Khazmyr, it is like…ah, a woman who cares for children. Who teaches them when they are young, like a mother when there is none."

He nodded in understanding, a brief smile playing around his lips as he pressed, "I see. And what did your Shoo'naan teach you about handsome men?"

She giggled as she answered, "To be wary of the ones who say things you want to hear." Her smile faded quickly. His head canted. "That no matter how good looking or charismatic they may be, to keep my guard up…because they will become anything or anyone…to secure their desires," she continued, a frown forming.

There was a moment of quiet.

"Tell me, what is it that *you* desire?" she asked.

He immediately stood, his hands reaching blindly for her face. Upon finding it, he cradled it gently, and she met his touch with her own.

"To bring you *home*," he whispered, his voice trailing off, his brows furrowing. For a brief second, sadness flickered across her face as she stared into his closed eyes.

A deep knock at the door jarred them both. She pulled away quickly as he felt around for the chair, sinking back into it. He sighed to himself, knowing the moment had been lost.

Yuri moved quickly to the door, giving him one last look before opening it.

"Hera?" she said, shocked. Her counterpart stood outside the door, surrounded by Darros' personal guard. Her gown was stunning, made of shimmering emerald and gold. Yuri's mouth drifted open for a moment as she took notice of the wardrobe, the men.

"Come in," she called, moving out of the way as the door swung open.

"Remain here," Hera instructed as she entered, closing the door behind her.

"I see that Darros has taken you under his wing…" Yuri remarked.

Hera lifted the palms of her hands, pleading, "Please don't hate me for it. You know how he is; he takes what he wants. Today it is me. Tomorrow is another adventure for him."

"I am aware," Yuri replied, "and I do not hate you for it." Her voice softened as she sighed. "He has sent you here to flaunt his choice under the guise of checking in on Merith?"

Hera nodded, a hint of shame colouring her expression before she asked, "Please, use his name…his *real* name. We do enough for Darros; we need not carry his cruelty."

Yuri delayed but nodded. Julian's head elevated slightly, curious to hear how she would address him.

"Joriah is recovering well," Yuri replied as she returned to his side. "The salve that Darros provided is working as expected."

Julian's brow arched.

"I don't understand," Hera muttered, frowning as she leaned in to look at Julian's horrific scarring. "Why would he blind him only to heal him?"

"To teach me that he can both give and take away," Julian replied, catching Hera off guard. Yuri gave him a look of death, though he couldn't see it, hoping his reply ended there.

It did. He wasn't stupid.

"A lesson for him, and a reminder for the rest of us," Yuri concluded.

"I'm sorry, Joriah," Hera apologised.

"I brought this upon myself, although I appreciate the sentiment," he replied.

Hera lifted his hand and kissed it, turning to leave as she explained, "I only came here because I was told to. But I will not take up any more of your time… I believe my purpose here has been fulfilled."

Yuri waited until she had reached the door, then ventured, "Nicole…"

Hera froze and turned to look at her, absent the façade.

"Be sure to tell him the truth…" Yuri's head raised. "…that I didn't care."

Hera delayed, her gaze averting before she finally nodded.

"I will," she affirmed.

Julian stood at the sound of the door closing behind her.

"You play a dangerous game," he remarked.

"Look who's talking," she snarked back. "Sit, I have to rebandage you."

CHAPTER FIFTY-FOUR

Mother Root

Elarion

Elarion cradled a Velinmir in his hands, the symbols etched deeply into its round brass surface springing to life with a soft, warm luminescence – the sunset enriching it with shades of red and orange. He lifted his head, tracking its graceful ascent into the sky, its motion silent and undisturbed by the wind. The device appeared both ancient to this realm and foreign. Its behaviour defied the known laws of the world, yet its purpose was to amplify balance. Offered as gifts to those like Elarion, it allowed recipients to push the reach of their abilities – including internally.

His return to this nursery was bittersweet, although the quiet solace of abandonment and despair fell short of his desire for and expectation of isolation. While humans were nowhere to be found, the trees and saplings began to sing the forest's song loudly as they sensed his approach, excitedly wishing to commune with him once more. Their sentiment brought a smile to his face, a faint wrinkle dimpling his cheek, but it was quickly crushed by the sadness within. He felt a wave of guilt for wanting utter silence – to be unseen, forgotten for just a moment in time. Grief had been chasing him for over a hundred years, and not once had he permitted himself time…

…to be caught.

He stepped over the thick roots of the elder tree where it broke through stone tiles and grew over shattered panes of glass that crunched under his boots. A modest layer of fresh snow obscured the tree's hurried exodus from captivity. The air was crisp and clean smelling, an almost

435

complete return to nature – the smell of compost and people all but gone.

"You've been busy," he said, resting his hand on her bark with a light chuckle that quickly broke. He closed his eyes, whispering words and phrases that sounded like little more than wisps of air. Immediately, the Velinmir's light faded to purple, its brilliance intensifying momentarily before softening to that of a candle. He sat, crossing his legs and letting out a deep exhale as he prepared to retreat to the recesses of his own thoughts – but not before bringing the ring he wore as a necklace to the forefront. As it emitted a blue glow, he exhaled further…and further still, until he became as still as the tree trunks surrounding him. With time, his skin grew cold, the colour fading until it was pale. Without an audible sound or even the slightest hitch of his chest, quiet torrents of tears streamed down his face like a river breaking through a dam – inevitable and relentless.

The wind howled as it cut through the forlorn structure, its desolation feeling all the more permanent – all the more complete. But where his mind was now, he couldn't hear it. He could not see the light of the moon through his eyelids as it rose to watch over him in the twilight hours, nor could he see the sun as it took the morning shift. The two traded off in the evening again, and so on, many times over.

"Elarion."

Silence.

"Elarion, are you there?"

His eyes opened slowly, his breathing visibly deepening with violent hitching.

"There you are," Lysand greeted as her face appeared, metaphysically carved into the elder tree's trunk. "I've not seen within these walls in quite some time."

Elarion stiffly bowed his head to her as he waited to regain bodily function. His speech would be nearly the last to recover.

"This is no place for the young." Her voice was withered and strained.

He attempted to look around, his eyes stuck wide open.

"You're upset," she observed, a sharp and sudden departure from her train of thought. She looked him over in a rush of concern with an arch to her wooden brow.

The Velinmir grew brighter, its coloured light revealing the moisture that had accumulated under his eyes, wetting his skin.

"I saw your beacon and reached out as soon as I noticed your light fading," she went on. Her defensive nature revealed itself in her tone as she pressed, "What is the matter, and who is responsible for these tears?"

He sighed heavily, his eyes blinking with renewed moisture.

"The human?" she surmised.

He nodded, and his voice finally broke through, cracked and dry and given to anger – an emotion he had not succumbed to in decades – as he answered, "He was murdered."

Her eyes widened.

"I see. And your choice not to intervene troubles you?" she asked.

His shoulders compressed, and a rush of air expelled from his nostrils. "Yes," he replied, then cleared his throat. His tone balancing out as his face gave way to powerlessness, he continued, "It would seem the Candorians are involved."

"They're always involved," she replied, interrupting him, her scorn apparent.

"I sense one nearby, though who it is continues to elude me," he replied as he stretched out his limbs. Her eyes looked up and around.

"If it's Hildeheim, then there is no doubt Reh'gara is intertwined, but bring the *eye* closer," she instructed. Elarion nodded and reached out for the Velinmir with strained effort and a wince. It descended just a few metres, coming to rest above the tree. "Thank you," she replied, her face growing in detail the closer it came. She closed her eyes for just a brief minute, and when they opened again, she answered, "It is Reh'gara that you sense, but that is to be expected. These are his offspring, after all. The Candorian plays with fire, and it is best that we stay clear of his weaves…no matter how painful it may be. The price for his constant meddling will be paid soon." Elarion's brows were furrowed, but she ignored his expression to ask, "Who was it that sent you here?"

"Aenon, at the bidding of Amethyst, I would assume. He rarely acts of his own accord," he replied.

"And why do you believe this? What has she to do with this place?" she answered quickly.

"Initially, it was under the guise of news regarding Connerh. I thought it strange that he sought me out to provide what would be trivial to him, especially as Candorians offer nothing freely, let alone information." His brow furrowed as he spoke. "But ultimately I believe it was to find someone…who bears the Gift," he replied, his expression softening.

Lysand grew silent.

He noticed.

"Does this not please you?" he asked, his expression worried.

"Do you deem them worthy?" she returned.

"I deem her very worthy. Capable. There is much potential within her," he replied.

"Show me," she said. He closed his eyes for a moment, and the Velinmir's light turned yellow, its brightness increasing as he shared his thoughts with her.

"Yes, yes," she repeated, over and over. "Then bring her to me." Her voice creaked.

"Here?" he asked.

"No. To the *forest*. I wish to examine her with my own eyes, without the influence of *his* domain," she insisted.

"But that will require me to convince her to enter into our lands, and she does not trust our kind…justifiably so," he answered.

"You have achieved greater miracles, have you not?" she replied.

Elarion offered a hint of a smirk, sapped quickly by humility. "I just…" he began but stopped himself.

"You do not need to approach every interaction with them with such trepidation. Your delicate nature is so endearing." Her deep smile faded into a nurturing expression. "But there is a vast difference between Reh'gara's approach and yours," she continued.

His brows flared as he looked up at her, a heavy breath relaxing his shoulders.

"Showing them the way does not remove their ability to choose it," she continued. "More importantly, you are not required, even in your wisdom, to be perfect. Such a thing would be impossible, seeing as you are still so limited," she chided. "There are many ages of enlightenment between you and me. You are the morning sun, and I am the moon," she explained as a smile formed, and his head dropped.

"And yet I feel so capable, only to be restrained at every turn. Whether I aid, guide, or stand by and do nothing…it all ends the same," he lamented, sadness turned into anger.

"Oh, Elarion…" she sighed, empathy encompassing her tone. "I should wish to ask you something."

"Anything," he replied, putting aside the anger again.

"What is it that you want? What do you *really* want, distilled into a single wish?" she asked.

He frowned, giving it thought. His hand naturally drifted towards his necklace. "To be allowed to make a difference. To be the arbiter of change… Otherwise, they are only born to die, and we are condemned to watch," he replied, his eyes finally lifting to meet hers.

"And will this mend your broken heart?" she enquired.

"No," he replied quickly with a rapid head shake, the ring firmly pressed between his fingers. "But it will have made the sacrifice of playing along…count for something."

"Then I will do what I can to fulfil that wish," she smiled, "and then you will offer yourself to me? To your purpose?"

"I will," he confirmed.

Her chuckle was deep.

"You *are* a diamond in the rough, dear," she said, her face moulding into a smile. "A true reward lies in wait for you when the time is appropriate."

"And what of Connerh?" he asked. "Did he not deserve the same?"

"You still think of others?" she asked.

"He was caught in the same web as I," he replied.

"His existence defied what was natural," she countered.

"Was that his fault?"

"No, of course not. But it was his burden to bear," she replied.

His eyes became heavy atop his cheeks.

"No one said he had to do it alone. None of us do," she continued.

He looked up at her and nodded before his focus drifted away.

She noticed how he continued to fidget with the ring, sighing and dropping her gaze before she said, "She was very dear to us all. Even in the small details…like how she tenderly cared for you and nature."

His shoulders shook as he wept.

Thick roots traced up his legs and wrapped around his body, embracing him. His eyes drifted closed as he let go, releasing his weight into the thick branches that cradled him.

"I wish I were there to comfort you properly," she began. Elarion frowned, raising his hand to protest against her guilt. "But this will have to do, for now."

She clamped her eyes shut. The orb's brightness grew to the point it was painful to gaze upon, its colour changing to a hue of purple. Elarion gasped as air rushed into his lungs, his eyes expanding to the full. His exhale was sudden, and almost as loud as the orb was as it hit the ground – its runes absent, no longer etched onto its surface, its power all but drained. The detail of her face reduced, and they both fought to catch their breath.

"Thank you," he said. She smiled.

"Just…trust, Elarion," she instructed, calm and ·comforting as the branches surrounding him dispersed.

"I always have," he replied.

"With hesitation," she countered.

"Would you prefer blind allegiance?"

"No," she replied. "No, I would not."

They both dropped their gazes as a calm lingered for a few minutes.

"What has become of this place?" she asked, changing the subject and allowing him the dignity to regain his composure. He took a deep breath before speaking.

"This place is abandoned; it is but one of many nurseries within these walls. While it leaves little to wonder over, the rest of the city is…fairly impressive," he replied.

"Once upon a time, the then-Ice King grew paranoid of my power. He uprooted all of the trees within his kingdom's walls and lined the undersoil with stone, metal, and potions, severing my connection to my children," she continued, her frown still quite visible on the trunk, even with diminished power. Elarion listened patiently. "This was a time long before your little feet touched the dirt for the first time," she continued, a smirk of pride metaphorically beaming through the pores of the wood.

He smiled in return.

"They're afraid of what they cannot control. It is natural for them, being so fragile," she continued. "And that is why we are patient."

Her voice faded.

He looked up after she remained quiet for too long.

"Lysand!" he called for her.

The orb lay, depleted of its power, nothing but a plain sphere of burnished brass.

"Go. Bring Madika home," she urged with her remaining breath, her avatar fading away to leave only aged bark behind.

Oroben watched over Lysand, her body frozen in place where she reached out for the moon, encased by roots.

CHAPTER FIFTY-FIVE

CHOICE

LENA

Many years ago…

Lena often walked the castle barefoot, much to her mother's chagrin. With a worldview that bordered on *extreme* prudishness, something as simple as exposed feet was easily twisted into an overtly sexual display. Prancing about in such a manner was tantamount to flirting with every man who so much as glanced her way…according to Io.

She scoffed at her mother's voice echoing in the back of her mind every time she removed her boots. Lena cared little for such things – simply put, the shoes she was forced to wear were uncomfortable, and if there was one place where she refused to endure discomfort, it was in her own home. Besides, she had always believed that those who clung to such rigid rules were either hiding or compensating for something.

Her small frame kept her light on her feet. Even in the vast halls prone to echoing, her bare steps made little sound, allowing her to traverse the castle nearly undetected – save for the large, old doors that creaked something awful. But that was what hidden passages were for.

Perhaps that was what her mother truly hated, she mused. The loss of knowledge, control, and everything in between. Her entire existence revolved around power and control – the power to give and to take, to grant and deny.

Even now, she sought to take Lena's power and bestow it upon Egress. *As if it were hers to offer,* she mentally scowled.

She quietly watched from the shadows, observing through cracked doors that provided a complete picture. Her mother's ritual of brushing Egress's hair in front of a mirror made her sick to her stomach, like Egress were some damned pet. She envisioned herself walking in and giving in to dark thoughts and even darker desires, as if she had the guts to go through with it.

She didn't, despite possessing the ability to imagine it with such vivid and granular detail.

A sigh and an eye roll would have to suffice, just as they had for years. Another day, another opportunity for her mother to remind her of her failures – how she fell short of perfection, how she was something lesser. She couldn't understand why her mother despised her so much, what it was that fuelled such deep-seated disdain for her own offspring. Of course, she was far more patient and understanding with Bjorn, but perhaps that was because he held no aspirations for the throne. He lived a simple life, cushioned by luxury, opportunity, and privilege, making little to no waves in the political sphere – never given a platform to bring embarrassment to the crown. He didn't want one, and that was where they differed.

Lena felt born to rule. It was in her bones, the substance of her dreams – something she had known for as long as she could remember. It felt predestined, as if reaching that throne was only a matter of time. Time, however, was a currency she felt she was running low on.

Rumours swirled among those old enough to recall that, after the old bag suffered the miscarriage of what would have been Lena's older sibling, she had spiralled down a path of paranoia and self-loathing. Some claimed there had been multiple miscarriages, a known risk when giants bred with smaller, more fragile species. Regardless, by the time Lena and Bjorn were born – what should have been a personal triumph, a restoration of faith in her ability to conceive – the damage had already been done.

Lena realised how comfortable the darkness was – a saying Connerh often repeated but which had only recently begun to make sense to her. She heard him approaching, his cadence telling her he hadn't seen her yet. She knew everyone's walking patterns, from Farrah's quick, rodent-like scurry to Connerh's casual, heavy stride…and her mother's pronounced, measured clacking, like a *fucking horse* on parade.

She shook her head at the thought, raising a finger to her lips as he approached. He grinned as he caught sight of her silhouette, his eyes still adjusting to the darkness. Once he lowered his head to peer into the room she was observing, his smirk faded. His hand found her shoulder and rubbed it briefly. She glanced up, offered him a small smile, grasped his hand, and pulled him into a hidden passage behind them. The door sealed quietly — just as her mother poked her head into the darkened corridor, searching for the source of the sound.

"I can't a see a damned thing. I don't know how you manage," Connerh protested as she continued to pull him through the hidden labyrinth, her eyes aglow with a soft, eerie cyan.

"Lower your voice," she snapped with a whisper. "Giant blood has its benefits," she replied. "Just hold on to my hand, we're almost there."

"You know, we're not children anymore," Bjorn remarked as he rounded the corner, a small lantern in his hand, startling them both with his normally toned voice. "You don't need to sneak him into the castle like this."

"You're right. So, why haven't you grown up?" she bit back. "Shouldn't you be sucking on Mother's tit? Or, I don't know, doing something meaningful with your life?"

Bjorn lifted his lantern up to get a good look at her, a brow raised. "You know, one of these days, you're going to hurt my feelings," he mocked softly. He held the lantern higher to see Connerh's face. "What'd you do now?"

"It wasn't me," Connerh replied, his palms raised defensively.

Bjorn leaned down and stared into her eyes, asking, "Oh…is it that time of the week or that time of the month?" Lena scoffed. "Which is it? Leaking between your legs, or Mother's grooming of Egress?"

She crossed her arms and rolled her eyes, just like when they were teenagers.

"I see…Egress, then," he replied. "I could make excuses for our mother and draw your ire further, or…I could…fuck off?" he asked.

She stared at him with an irritated expression.

"It's not too late to run, you know?" he quipped to Connerh.

"Yes, it is," she interjected. The men laughed.

"I'm sorry," Bjorn offered with a sigh after the laughter subsided. "I still believe, deep down, she's just trying to protect you. She doesn't want you murdered like Father was. I'll not excuse her methods…but I know her intent to be good. Egress is…a safe option, as far as she's concerned," he said, maintaining eye contact with her.

"That used to stir something within me, make me feel special, wanted, loved," she mused, gazing into her own memory. "But then I turned six. Those days have long passed. She's but an obstacle in a path that has already been carved for me," she replied.

"Careful now. That sounds awfully seditionist of you," he replied with sarcasm in his tone.

"Why don't you go run and tell her?" she snarked back. Connerh's hand rested on her shoulder, although she only glanced at it.

"I'm not the enemy, big sister," he claimed, though he towered over her – their father's blood favoured Bjorn in the height department. Though he was not as tall as, say, Hargatha, he was taller than Connerh by about a head's worth.

"Perhaps, but I don't need more *friends*," she replied. Connerh discreetly squeezed her shoulder.

"Well, it's a good thing I'm your brother, then, isn't it?" he asked with a smirk. Bending over and extending his cheek in her direction, he urged, "Come on…give it up."

She reluctantly gave him a peck, causing him to chuckle.

"It really isn't too late," he said again to Connerh.

"She says that it is," Connerh replied, and they both laughed again.

"What are *you* doing in here, anyway?" she asked.

Bjorn looked at her, then at Connerh, a deep grin carving into his face.

"Come on…they're going to see you anyway," he announced.

Lena's head canted. Several women turned the corner, every single one scantily clad.

"Your Highness," each greeted in turn, bowing to her as they passed and giggling all the while.

"But *I'm* the whore?" Lena scoffed with disbelief.

"I take offence! I'm not the one with my feet exposed," Bjorn cackled as he walked off, hurrying to catch up with his guests. His glowing eyes faded into the darkened corridor.

"After a while, your scurrying sounds awfully similar to the rats, save for the giggling and banter," Hargatha called out. She smirked to herself. "Come in."

A façade of a brick wall scraped against the ground as it slid open. Lena and Connerh stepped through, and Lena continued on while Conner stopped to close it behind them. Hargatha sat lounging across a chair made specifically for her, a large chalice of wine in her hand as she reclined in front of a crackling fire. Her eyes were glazed over; she'd been there for a while.

"Aren't you a little old to be sneaking in boys?" she joked. "Hello, Connerh."

He nodded with an exasperated expression, then offered a bow as he greeted, "Hargatha."

Lena walked over to the cask and poured herself some wine, joining her aunt's ambience as she positioned herself on a chair next to her. She looked like a child in the oversized seat. Gatty's eyes tracked her with a humoured smirk.

"What are you two up to this evening?" she asked.

Lena sighed loudly.

"Uh-oh, let's hear it," Gatty invited, straightening her posture.

"I've not been entirely honest with you," Lena replied.

Gatty's head instinctively canted, and she took a sip of wine before she urged, "Go on."

Lena glanced at Connerh for reassurance…as if she needed it.

"My mother is actively replacing me in the line of succession," she began. Hargatha grinned. It was a familiar gripe from familiar lips. "But I never told you who it was that will be replacing me," Lena went on, taking a sip from her own cup for emphasis.

"I'm listening," Gatty replied, taking a sip of her own.

Lena looked into her chalice, her reflection in the pool of velvet cheering her on. "Even as we speak," her eyes raised and locked with her aunt's, "Egress is being groomed – quite literally, might I add."

Gatty's head rotated inwards, her sip deliberate and measured. Her gaze dropped as she stared into her thoughts, resting just above her cheeks.

"I see," she replied eventually, standing to face the fire. Her left arm folded under the right as her eyes darted around the room, her thoughts encumbering her focus. After some time, she asked, "You know I had nothing to do with this?"

"I do," Lena affirmed.

Hargatha nodded, returning her focus to the flames. She grunted, continuing, "This is unfortunate. And your feelings towards your cousin regarding this matter?"

"I don't place the blame with her," Lena replied.

Hargatha took a deep inhale, then released it slowly. "Glad to hear it. You know she wouldn't hurt an insect?"

"She'd apologise if she offended it," Lena huffed, causing her aunt to chuckle unexpectedly.

"You're not wrong," she confirmed.

"We should come up with a plan," Hargatha began, her mind racing with potential outcomes. "This won't work for so many reasons. Your mother isn't thinking clearly, she must be overwhelmed with—"

"I already have one," Lena replied, cutting her off.

She froze, her focus turning to her niece. She took a breath, or three, before she prompted, "Go on…"

"Just…trust me," Lena replied. "The less you know, the better. We need your authentic reaction to move it forward."

Gatty swallowed her spit, putting on a smile. She didn't care for the secrecy, but she also knew it wasn't the appropriate time to push back. She nodded in acknowledgement. Instead, in hopes of extrapolation information, she simply pressed, "And how will I know what I'm listening for?"

"You'll know," Lena replied. "Just act normal with Egress. Don't say anything or act any differently. She can't know anything if we are to ensure she is not implicated."

"I appreciate that," Gatty intoned.

"I meant what I said. I don't blame her."

Hargatha emptied her chalice with a large swig. Her posture straightening, she remarked, "I have to admit, I've underestimated your growth as of late. It fills my veins with pride."

"They all underestimate me," Lena replied, squeezing Connerh's hand where it lay draped over her shoulder.

CHAPTER FIFTY-SIX

ALL OF ME

LENA

She appeared with a warble and a high-pitched whistle.

Lena lifted her head, and for a brief moment, she locked eyes with him. He looked angry with her, though it was deflated by sadness. She hit the floor loudly, accompanied by the splash of the water surrounding her. He remained where he stood, staring at the back of her head while she vomited sea water so violently that it spewed from her nose. Her soaked hair draped over her pale face, her colour slow to return.

She took loud, deep breaths in an attempt to regain control of her body – a task that proved difficult. She stared at the floor as she came to and waited for him to start screaming.

But he did not.

"What must I do in order to sway you from this course?" Reh'gara asked, lowering his staff, his voice crackling with age and wisdom. The large gem at the centre of his staff still glowed with sparks of lightning. His tone was saturated with disappointment, resignation, and a hint of bitterness. She coughed loudly, clearing the salty brine from her throat.

"There's nothing you can do anymore. You had your chance…" She lifted her head and glared at him. "And you did nothing!" Her voice tore and scratched, her body shaking violently. Her outburst spurned a cough

448

that wracked her. He looked away, allowing her to continue processing her grief. The light from his staff faded. She worked up the will to stand, and her nose flared as her eyes widened.

"What good is an all-powerful wizard if he can't perform magic, I wonder?!" she shouted through the hoarseness.

"Is that what you see me as?" His brow furrowed. "A conjurer of cheap parlour tricks?"

His tone disarmed her; he seemed genuinely hurt by her words, though her disorientation lasted only seconds.

"I see you just as I see myself." Her nose lifted. "A coward. Powerful, maybe, but powerless to act when it matters. Always a step behind, a day too late, forever out of reach of your heart's true desire." Her focus wandered as her mind retreated into memories of her own misgivings. He didn't answer immediately, only stared at her plainly.

"Perhaps. Or perhaps you confuse restraint and control with weakness," he mused. She didn't have a reply at the ready. "It is easy to misinterpret that which our heart desires as the right thing to seek, if only because its demands are so clear, the reward for obeying so immediate."

"Are you saying what I did was the right thing?" she asked, her face wrinkled.

He shook his head before saying, "No. But the choice for me to not intervene…was." He frowned, anticipating her response as his eyes locked with hers upon speaking the last word.

"Then why am I not at the bottom of the sea?" she asked, anger creeping into her voice. He'd assumed wrongly, and he eventually chuckled.

"A gift of selfishness, perhaps?" he returned, maintaining her gaze.

"Then I do not accept," she replied with a scoff.

"You don't mean that," he retorted, shaking his head.

"Send me back," she demanded, a realisation of her own rights. "You have to send me back. I don't wish to be here if he is not!" she repeated. Her face contorted with anger, and she pushed away from him as she shrieked, "Send me back!"

"I will not." His own reply was small and diminished, and now he refused to look her in the eye.

"Then you will have to trap me here, in your place of endlessness!" she shouted.

He shooed her away with his hand and gently rocked back and forth, adjusting his robes.

"I'll never stop fighting you," she continued, the familiar words immediately drawing his focus. "I'll just jump tomorrow. Dash my head against the rocks or slice my wrist on something so simple, like pottery or a broken bottle." Her expression mirrored her fascination with all the ways available to her. She moved closer to him, her voice trailing into a whisper. "Maybe I'll fall on a sword, drink poison, or drive a stake through my heart." Her words became explosive, drawing from deep within, emptying her lungs of breath. "None of them could possibly hurt any worse!"

"Stop speaking in such a way!" he demanded, growing angry.

"Then kill me!" she shouted.

He twitched, yelling, "That is enough!"

"Kill me, you coward!" she screamed, lunging towards him with clenched fists held in the air.

His expression went blank, then twisted into something dark and unrecognisable. His body swelled as if he were returning to his natural size, his natural form. His eyes blazed with an unnatural, bluish light, cold and unrelenting, and the staff in his hand jerked upwards, its gem sparking violently as time seemed to warp, slowing to a dreadful crawl. Arcs of lightning burst from his fingers, surging into the staff with crackling ferocity, amplifying his power until the gem shone like a fractured star.

As the tendrils of electricity snaked through the air towards her, a flicker of hesitation passed over his face.

His chest heaved, his senses clawing him back from the abyss. The storm of anger in his eyes began to wane, and the darkness retreated – if only for a moment.

Looking at her from within calm eyes, she appeared hollow, as though her soul had been stripped away. Her frozen expression wavered between anger and hatred, making for a haunting mask of emotion carved into an empty husk. It was like her very essence was rejecting this realm, her mind and body fracturing under its weight – no longer tethered, already beginning to unravel, thread by thread, diffusing into a void. In the flicker of an instant, within the space between seconds, he turned his aim upwards, striking the stone-like ceiling above. Sparks of amber cascaded down, scattering around them like a fleeting, fiery rain.

With a steady cadence, he returned to his normal appearance, shrinking with a humility that weighed on him, his staff now as lifeless as the tree from which it was carved. As time resumed, he spread his arms around her, maintaining their embrace even as she pummelled his chest with her fists. The strength of her blows diminished by the second.

When her anger subsided and her blood cooled, when only her breath and thumping heartbeat remained, she found rest in his arms.

"Why does it hurt so badly?" she asked in a lowered tone, her chest quietly hitching. His brows crumpled.

"Because we were not meant to experience this type of pain…though we were built strong enough to endure it," he replied. "I am all too familiar with what you're feeling," he added.

She looked up at him, her eyes scanning his lips.

"I also live with regret and loss," he admitted, "most of which was created by my own hand. The same hands that are capable of a power so great that the mere temptation of wielding it corrupts mortal men. And yet, it seems incapable of preventing or mending this pain we feel."

"I don't understand," she complained. There was much she didn't know about Reh'gara, much that she hadn't even bothered to question over the years. He was a constant in her family history, as sure as the sun would set and the moon would rise – a mystical but paternal figure who offered knowledge and guidance, specifically to those who wore the crown.

More specifically, to her.

She had no concept of how fondly Reh'gara regarded her.

Lena backed away, her brow raised and gaze fallen to the ground.

"I suddenly realise there is much I don't know about you. Even, for that matter, who or…what you are," she continued, her focus returning.

He took a deep breath and answered, "You've never asked." His words were plain, simple, but layered – blunt but dismissive. "You were always very accepting of your circumstances. You knew where you wanted to be in the world." He laughed at the fond memory. "Never much cared for the why or the how – only the results, not the method."

Lena didn't care for the reply. It felt guarded, like an intentional misdirect. She frowned, her focus retreating to her surroundings – the ominous, fog-like surroundings with no start or end. The dense fog that, until now, she had ignored. She continued to back away slowly, toe over heel.

"What is this place?" she asked, her hands rushing to examine her own body. "Is this even real? Am I dreaming? Am I dead? Is this the afterlife?" She frowned, then asked solemnly, "The underworld?"

He shot her a smirk and asked, "And if I were to say yes?"

Lena's eyes widened, her panic taking little time to build. His chuckle barely delayed matters.

"Does it really matter?" he asked. "I intend to restore you as you were, as if your leap for death never happened. And you will continue on…as you were made to."

"As I was *made to*?" she repeated, frowning. "Am I your prisoner, then?" she asked with a tilt of her head. "Your pawn?"

He shook his head, ignoring her questions.

"Reh'gara, I meant my words. I will not go on without him," she continued.

He laughed out of contempt, dismissing her with, "You do not know what you say."

She lurched as his eyes began to glow; his staff activated.

"Wake up," he whispered.

She was forced to blink. Her eyes opened to see Connerh's limp, haemorrhaging body clutched in her arms. She frowned. It was as if time had rewound, though subtle differences stood out — like guards stationed between her and the balcony. There were more doctors rushing to take him from her arms than before. She caught glimpses of Reh'gara in between them. His smirk.

They couldn't see him.

Lena calmly walked to the balcony, tuning out the background. The guards parted but remained nearby.

"How many times have you done this?" she asked. The guards looked at one another, unsure of who she was talking to or what she was referring to. Reh'gara appeared behind her.

"Does it matter?" he replied. Her eyes shot open, fists balled. She looked at the crashing waves below them.

"They won't let you jump," he assured her. Lena shook her head, offering a chuckle.

"I wasn't going to," she replied.

"Good," he began, his tone oozing vindication.

She was quick with a blade; she was Connerh's prized student. Even Reh'gara was amazed by how quickly she pulled the dagger from one of the soldier's waistbands and drove it into her own chest. Over and over again.

The humour faded quickly from his face, and with a flash, he reset her again.

And again.

And again.

Again.

And again.

And continually, until he grew weary.

She found new ways to defy his will, to rejoin him in his foggy, grey place. To shed her tether. Some efforts were immediate, others hours apart. In all ways and methods, she remained true to her word.

She awoke with a gasp, once again in his foggy realm, a smirk strewn across her face.

"As I said, I may be your prisoner, but I will never stop fighting you," she replied, feeling victorious.

He sat on the ground, his head hung low as he faced away from her. She began to approach, her head craning for a better view of him.

"I have failed," he muttered to himself. "I just wanted what was best," he went on, loud enough for her to hear.

"That's what all tyrants say," she mocked, a scorned grin on her face.

He grunted, too tired to chuckle properly. He went to reply but stopped short, instead shaking his head. She was impossible at times, even as a child.

"And the only way you will go on…is if he is with you?" he asked, his tone saturated with defeat as he looked up at her. His eyes were damp.

"The only way," she affirmed.

He nodded and looked away.

"Why do you hate him so much?" she asked finally.

"I don't hate him. My dislike for your pairing…is beyond your comprehension," he decided on as an answer, rising to his feet.

"Try me!" she shouted at him, feeling bold.

"No." He grinned. "Besides…"

"It doesn't matter?" she inferred.

"It doesn't…not now," he confirmed. His smile caught her off guard.

"There is a way to do as you wish," he began. "To bring him back."

She nodded, feeling excitement at accepting her chosen fate.

"Do we just appear before he was stabbed? Days before? Hours?" she asked in a fervour, in her desire to understand. She rubbed her hands together slowly.

"No," he replied, shaking his head and reaching out his hand. His staff appeared in his grasp, his fingers wrapping around it slowly, one by one. "I will bring him back."

Her brows dropped with her lack of understanding.

"But first…there is a price. There is *always* a price for such power," he explained, eyes squinted.

"Do it!" she pleaded.

He held up his hand to stop her from interrupting, continuing, "I might never see or help you again. No letters, no advice. I will be…unreachable."

She thought on it, but the decision didn't take long.

"Do it," she replied.

It stung a bit more than he anticipated.

"I don't think you understand—" he began.

"What is there not to understand?" she cut in. "I never have to see the man that was never there for me in return for having the one who always was? Do it!"

His shoulders slumped, and he refuted, "You don't mean that."

"Valaë kin turai ven, lai kin velas áar turai—" she shouted in the Ancient Tongue.

He ran to her and covered her mouth before she could finish.

"Are you mad?" he demanded, eyes squinting as he began to think she might truly be. "You dare wish such a thing? What have I done so wickedly to you?" His eyes peered into her own. "I have been with you from the beginning and beyond! Everything I've done has been for you, for this moment in time. I have always been there when it mattered. No, I do not abuse my power for your benefit, but what good would that accomplish you anyway?"

She calmed as she listened to his reply.

"Just because you did not see me did not mean I was not there," he continued, vanishing before her. "I was the warmth on your shoulders when your father died." His voice was deep, sending a chill up the spine when he spoke. She spun around, looking for the source of his voice. "The invisible embrace when you needed it most. It was I who tucked you in at night when your mother had given way to wine during her encumbering grief," he said, his voice twirling around her. Her eyes clamped shut as she relived the memory. "It was I who drew you to Connerh to begin with, because you always felt alone," he concluded, reappearing next to her, his face saddened. "I was there in your darkest hour, when your anger and madness took control." His tone was vacant of feeling.

Her face contorted, embarrassed and horrified by his admission – her guilt.

"And I was there when you held his lifeless body," he continued.

Her nose wrinkled as she held back, gripping tightly to sanity, her teeth bared as she whispered, "And yet you did nothing."

He sighed.

"If I were to arrange every life event for you, you would then accuse me of stealing your right to choose," he laughed as his eyes leaked. "What shall you have me do? Spare you only from pain? How will you then learn joy? How would you learn of consequences? What is meaning without the potential for loss?" he scoffed, anger building. "Is this what you want? Say it, and I will curse you accordingly," he shouted.

She shrank back, her own anger fading. She shook her head in denial.

"Say it!" he demanded.

She didn't answer.

He turned his back and crossed his arms, releasing his staff to float in front of him. He sighed loudly after they sat a moment in silence.

"I will grant your wish…if it is what you truly desire. I have seen the handwriting on the wall. *Our* era is ending here, and I see now that I was a fool to try and delay it," he said, sitting down in mid-air as if there were a chair there; the air supported him as if there were. His hands crossed, and his thumbs rubbed against the knuckles of his other hand. Her brows arched as she attempted to hide her curious excitement. She moved in closer. He thought quietly.

"I will bring him back to you, but as I said, there is always a price," he said after a time, his voice deeper now as he stared.

"Name it," she urged, perking up.

"You need to listen carefully to what I say," he replied, shaking his head at her impetuousness. "The scales must be balanced, or we will all suffer," he continued, his voice tinged with worry.

Her head involuntarily canted. She'd never before considered the possibility that he could be inferior to someone or something else. He took a deep breath.

"By the rules of the old world, a life for a life," he said, pulling the words from deep within as if they took everything to utter.

"I don't understand. Whose?" she asked, shaking her head. She froze, assuming he meant his own, and guilt overcame her – yet it lasted only seconds. As she translated his words' meaning…she knew she would still choose Connerh.

His eyes were low, but they rose to meet hers briefly before settling on her womb. After a delay, his pointer finger raised; she followed his gaze. Her expression expanded and compressed, and her mouth slung open.

"A life for a life, and in this case…what you ask is worth many," he replied, hurt by the saying of it but bound by duty nonetheless.

She took a few steps back, feeling violated by his insinuation. Her hands instinctively layered atop her stomach.

"Would you give even your womb for him?" Reh'gara asked, his hand outstretched. Her eyes retreated for a moment, and her brows furrowed. But, again, it took only seconds.

"Is this your price? Or someone else's?" she asked.

He offered a sad grin. "I would need hundreds of years to explain to you how…" he smirked, looking up and around at things she could not see, "…how it all really works."

"Then I would rather die than bear another man's child," she replied. Reh'gara nodded, already expecting her reply.

"You understand, then, that this means…our story…it dies with him," he added, hoping to dissuade her.

"Then I can think of no better ending," she pressed, not fully grasping his or her own words. Still, they felt impactful, and that was good enough for her.

He nodded again, building up the courage to accept her decision. He dug his tongue into his upper gum for a second.

"Say the words," he instructed, holding his staff high.

She became momentarily overwhelmed by it all.

Could it be so simple? she wondered, swallowing deeply.

"Go on," he pressed. "Your wish, your offering. Say it clearly," he encouraged with nods of his head.

"Valaë kin turai ven," she began, pausing to accept the moment as it was happening, "lai kin velas áar turai, velan khe'ra whai…whai…" She paused, looking to Reh'gara for the wording.

"Va'khor ena… It means…all of me," he replied hesitantly. Her head lowered for a moment.

"Valaë kin turai ven, lai kin velas áar turai, velan khe'ra whai…va'khor ena," she recited.

The gem in his staff glowed brightly as a symbol etched into its surface…faded with time. He watched as it occurred, his eyes lagging as he returned his focus to her.

He sighed deeply, sitting on the ground with his legs crossed.

"May we sit here a moment, before we begin?" he asked.

She delayed, her nerves beginning to stir. She sat next to him, feeling the weight of his concern.

"I just want to see it once more…" he explained, an aching smile overtaking his face.

"See what?" she asked.

"My legacy," he replied as flashes of memories surrounded them, from her happiest moments as an adult to her childhood and before. In her mother's womb, through to the memories between her mother and those before. Together, they travelled through time, during and before the formation of the Golden Pass and still a millennium before. She saw moments and events she'd only read about. She broke her gaze away multiple times to look at him. His expression was saturated with pride, affection, and longing.

"Are the legends true? Are you my grandsire or something?" she asked with watered eyes, the realisation building and crushing.

He chuckled, lowering his gaze momentarily to reply, "Something to that effect."

"Why do you delay in telling me? Even now?" she asked.

"You were told what you needed to know. There are rules to everything." He pulled his watery-eyed grin away from the memories to look at her. "And I have broken so many for you, only that you might find your way. But in doing so, I find myself in a pit of my own design." His gaze returned.

She frowned as her eyes disengaged.

"I wish there was time to teach you all the things you do not yet know," he continued with regret. "But there are still ways I may teach…even after I'm gone," he continued.

She stared at him again. Sadness, confusion, despair, and…curiosity overtook her expression.

"It has begun," he said. With a blink, she appeared lying across a table with him standing over her. Her garments had been replaced with cloth covering her chest and pelvis, leaving her stomach exposed. A bright light blinded her.

"Formality prevents me from shielding you from the pain," he apologised, drawing her brow upwards. "Though I will do my best to minimise it," he continued, pausing to reflect. "I offer one last chance."

The silence extended as she struggled to comprehend.

"I wish to bring him back," she said finally.

He nodded with understanding and finality.

"May our sacrifices be forever understood," he replied.

He raised his hands, the skin upon them pale, his gaze fixed upon her womb.

"Reh'gara!" she shouted.

"Yes?" he asked, pausing.

"I'm scared," she replied.

He smirked and replied, "Good. So am I."

His hands lowered, their cold touch impacting her flesh and moving beyond.

The sensation was terrifying as they reached within her.

Her screams echoed.

CHAPTER FIFTY-SEVEN

LINE IN THE SAND

LENA

Her breath rushed into her lungs with a violent urgency, but it was interrupted by the sharp pain in her abdomen as she lunged forward. She caught sight of Reh'gara sitting at the foot of her bed just as he briefly turned to acknowledge her consciousness.

"Don't worry, you'll be alright," he assured her with no hint of worry or concern in his tone.

She looked down past the cloth wrapped around her chest, noticing a pair of runes etched into the flesh below her stomach – one on the left, another on the right. They hurt to touch, but she did so anyway. The skin was different there. Like a scab, but more rigid.

The moon was noticeably large, its brightness replacing the shadows in the room with a milky ambience – enough to see more than normal, but not enough to distinguish detail. It was the sort of lighting that made an overcoat look like a man when seen from out of the corner of the eye.

"The process of restoration has begun. I will return his body to you when it is ready," he pronounced, patting her feet overtop the blanket. Her face lit with excitement, only to be cut short again by a painful grunt. Her body felt warm, though she knew she should have been cold, nearly freezing.

"And he is alive? As he was before?" she hurried to ask. He nodded

459

but didn't speak a word. Her gaze wandered low, her breathing quickening. With her mind still racing, she insisted, "When can I see him?"

"Soon…soon. Not a moment longer than it needs to be, I assure you," Reh'gara chuckled.

Her joy abruptly faded, and she asked solemnly, "How can I ever repay you?"

He studied her face, a hint of a smirk creasing his cheek. "Don't waste it." His smirk deepened. "Make it count for something," he enunciated, a more serious expression replacing the humour.

"I will," she replied.

He nodded and returned his gaze forward.

"Reh'gara?"

"Yes?"

"I suppose it's too late to ask, but what's the catch to all this? Why did you offer this to me only now?" She frowned as he turned to her. "Why not my mother? My father?"

He squinted as he stared deeply into her eyes. He grinned and turned away briefly before swiftly returning his attention to her, his mind was toying with the consequences of honesty. Of disclosure. His gaze dropped.

"I wasn't there then," he replied plainly. "Besides, this isn't like fetching you a cup of water from the table," he fussed, becoming visibly irritated with her. "You don't know what I've done." He stood suddenly, walking to the wide-open doorway of her small balcony. He sighed as he crossed the threshold into the night air. "I fear the worst of it has only begun." His murmur barely drifted back into the room. "Not long, in the grand scheme. No, not much longer now. Perhaps it was for the better…or so I pray," he muttered to himself, looking upwards as if he were having a conversation.

She looked around to confirm they were alone, squinting her eyes to peer through the blackness, but there was nothing and no one. Just a cold, darkened bedroom fit for a queen, littered with…things. Her eyes lingered on the unlit fireplace, wishing it were otherwise. She was starting to feel the cold, and she could see her breath when she spoke.

"Are you speaking to me?" she asked, grimacing with each wave of discomfort, slowly standing and tugging her white wool robe to cover herself.

"Oh?" he asked as he looked back at her, a detached expression on his face. "Nothing. Only musing, as old men often do."

"I wasn't trying to act ungrateful…" she began, prompting him to glance at her, quickly diffused of frustration. "As it happens, I would very much like to know many things…" She paused and dropped her gaze, then concluded as she approached, "But you insist on keeping me at arm's length in that regard."

"I've told you a hundred times, it's not because of any lack of desire. You simply would not understand," he argued.

She threw her hands in the air.

He scoffed in reply.

"But you won't even try," she argued back.

He frowned, twirling his fingers through the air to conjure a lit pipe into his hand. He puffed on it with intense thought. After a few moments of quiet, he agreed with, "Alright. Imagine you are a chicken."

She quirked a brow with confusion and tossed him a smirk.

"Come, now, I said imagine!" he demanded after seeing her grin.

She quickly washed the expression from her face and nodded to appease him.

"You have a good life – siblings, parents. A caretaker who has protected and looked after you. This caretaker is an unbelievably large creature, and though he should be frightening to you, he's not. You trust him, as he has given you every reason to do so. He's kept you fed and warm, and no matter what's happened around you, he has kept *you* safe. And as far as you know, with your tiny little chicken brain…nothing exists beyond this arrangement." He inhaled deeply from his pipe, blowing the smoke out from between pursed lips after a long moment. Lena listened intently. "Now imagine that one day, you discover the odd sounds he makes are words – components of a complex system called language. He can speak several languages, seamlessly shifting between them depending on who or what he is speaking to. And with this ability, he can summon other animals you never knew existed, and he can command others just like himself. Big or small, it doesn't matter. He can make you feel things – happiness, sadness, anger, frustration…but even these words are just sounds you don't fully understand. Only the effect they have on you is clear."

She listened, an unintentional frown forming.

"Later, you learn that, like you, he has a family – children, a wife, parents, and so on. They all live in structures called homes, and these homes, much like them, are also unbelievably large, and they're filled with strange objects. And still, their homes are nothing more than specks among larger specks that form what is called a city. Oh, there's so much to do in a city – so much fun to be had, so much pleasure, but also terrible things. Very, very terrible things." His eyes wandered, drifting to the source of his illustration. "But there's more. There are many cities spread across vast distances that you and your little chicken legs could never traverse, even over many lifetimes. And still, together, they form a kingdom..." He paused, looking at her. "Are you beginning to understand?"

She nodded.

"Well," he continued, "as it happens, that kingdom is very unhappy with the unbelievably large creature who cares for you – and for reasons you can't yet comprehend. Because, as a chicken, you don't understand politics," he said, shaking his head. His tone deepened. "Let alone the type of politics where he comes from. And so, to appease the wrath of said kingdom...he has to make decisions. Decisions that will impact everyone he cares for..." He looked at her. "Family and chickens alike." He stopped speaking, his gaze drifting into nothing for a few moments. "Would you sacrifice sleep in order to learn the details, ones you can neither influence nor change, if they elucidated matters of death or freedom? Would you voluntarily live in terror in order to learn what really goes on in the dark? Or would you rather focus on your simple life, trusting that whatever the caretaker decides is in your best interests?"

He returned his focus to see her frown now fully formed.

"I suddenly feel like a burden," she replied.

He shook his head in disagreement, brow furrowed.

"If it weren't for me, you wouldn't be...here. Therefore, the burden is my own," he replied. "Together we have made a sacrifice in order to bring Connerh back to you, but in doing so, I have crossed a very deep line that has long been drawn in the sand, and there is no going back."

"But why?" she pressed, pulling on his sleeve like a child. Guilt was building in her stomach.

His eyes fell to rest just above his cheeks.

"A parting gift, perhaps...or stupidity, stubbornness, pride. Or all of those things."

"Parting? Don't speak like that; you're not going anywhere," she protested.

"Spoken or not, the truth remains. My affairs here are coming to an end," he retorted, walking to the railing and resting his hands upon it. She followed. "I'd sought to create a legacy, something new and improved…through you. And while some of us have found success, I have not been so fortunate. Irony, I suppose, for being the start of these chains of events. The knife driven further still, as you will be unable to continue your line," he said.

Her eyes watered, and she blinked rapidly, voice small in tone, low in volume, and laced in shame as she offered, "There's Bjorn."

His head snapped to her, eyes focused for a moment before drifting away, as did his consideration of her words.

She grabbed onto his arm and rested her head against it, asking, "What will I do without you here to guide me?"

"I wonder," he replied.

It wasn't the reply she'd hoped for.

"I still have a little while yet. I'll need to converse thoroughly with him when he awakens. For what lies ahead, you'll need him…more than you ever have," he replied.

She looked up at him and demanded, "Why is it that even when you speak plainly, I'm more concerned with what you leave unsaid?"

He smirked, a jet of air shooting out of his nose.

"You'll be fine. Just…live truly. Support the weak. Defend those who cannot defend themselves. Guard your heart and your trust. Love ferociously, but be slow to anger and hatred…all the familiar things you've always heard. Though the words grow repetitive, and their ring appears to fall flat, they never lose their potency…never less true from one day to the next," he decreed, kissing her forehead.

Her eyes watered again. She didn't care for the way he was speaking – as if he were preparing for goodbye.

"We'll talk many times again…we have time. Now go… You can see him now, though he won't wake for a while," he said.

Her eyes lit up as she wiped them dry.

"He's in your old room."

She sprinted for the door without giving it a second thought, although she paused in the doorway. When she looked back, he was gone.

PART THREE

ONE YEAR LATER

CHAPTER FIFTY-EIGHT

EMERGENCE

EGRESS

It had to be some kind of record.

Not only had they demolished the old keep, but they had also rebuilt a newer, vastly larger one in just over a year – nothing short of a miracle by human standards. Angry giants made quick work of the destruction, and moving obscenely large pieces of stone was their forte. It was as if they were made for it.

Everything felt new. An endless view of mountains had been exchanged for flatter lands and perpetual water. Snow was replaced by sand, grass, and trees, and warmth sprang up where there was only ice and cold. It was as if the entire world had been repainted.

Born anew.

"It looks fit for a queen." Hargatha's pride oozed through her words as she offered a small bow to Egress. Their family banner, having just been hung, unfurled from atop the castle. It made a noise like thunder as its thick, heavy fabric and steel cut through the wind to crash against the stone wall.

"No," Egress replied. "Queens die. And, just like ants, they're replaced by the next bitch with a different focus, different goals." she mused. "What we're building here is more than just another kingdom to be lost in some cobwebbed book upon the shelf of an old man's library. They will remember us long after our bones are dug up and ground into mortar. No, what we're building is an empire. Unchanging, like the mountains from which we were borne."

"Empress, then?" Hargatha replied, grinning.

"I like the sound of that," Egress approved.

"I don't know…*Empress Egress* sounds a bit long in the tooth," Hargatha pushed back.

"Then *Empress* alone will suffice," Egress replied, striding towards her new castle. Hargatha's brows raised, but she hurried to catch up.

"Hargatha!" Brüg, one of the tallest giants, called out, running up to approach.

"What is it?" Egress interjected before her mother could speak.

"You're not going to believe what we've found while digging the new tunnels!" he exclaimed, taking the redirection in stride.

"Show me," Egress responded and followed him without hesitation, her cape and mother following closely behind.

"We dug beyond the old tunnels that led from the castle to the coast, making it some fifteen metres or so…and then the humans hit it with their tools. Thankfully, one of us wasn't doing the work. We would've destroyed it if so," he continued with a hurried pace, near running.

"Destroyed what, exactly?" Egress replied.

He grinned, looking back at her.

"You wouldn't believe me if I told you."

They stood over a large hole in the ground that looked much like an old quarry. Egress stared, her mouth open and vacant of sound – as did everyone else around her, humans and giants alike. Her head whipped around to stare at Hargatha after a full three minutes.

"It can't be?" she asked with humoured confusion. The look of bewilderment on her mother's face, a rarity in its own right, washed the smile from her face. She looked back with furrowed brows. "How do I get down there? Get me a ladder."

Their movements were slow, still reeling in their disbelief.

"You heard Her Grace! Get her a ladder!" Hargatha shouted, startling them into action. Within moments, she was rapidly descending a set of wooden steps before her heavy footsteps planted solidly in moist dirt.

"Please be careful, Empress," the man stabilising the ladder begged. She smirked. It had a nice ring to it.

She lifted her crimson gown and began her approach.

"Egress, careful now," Hargatha pleaded as she slowly followed, making her way down.

"You're not afraid of bones, are you?" Egress shot back. Hargatha quickly caught up to her, wrapping her arm around her daughter and slowing her in the process. "You are afraid," Egress grinned. "I've not seen you like this."

"It's not often I feel insignificant," Hargatha replied, just shy of a whisper in her ear as her gaze stayed fixed on the behemoth ahead of them.

The skull was massive.

The bones looked strong, almost new, as if the creature might reanimate given a moment's notice.

Its teeth alone were the size of the humans present, and though not fully revealed, it was assuredly a fearsome monstrosity when blood had once pumped through its veins. Even half-buried, with only its top half exposed in dirt that was closer to mud, it looked as if it could consume giants with ease.

"I don't know…it's kind of exhilarating," Egress replied with a teeth-bearing grin.

She broke free from her mother's grasp, walking towards the skeleton with her hand outstretched.

"Egress!" her mother cautioned.

But she ignored her, pressing forward, her chest hitching as the flesh of her palm met the bone-dry surface of the fossil.

"How large are the remains?" she asked.

"Not sure yet. We're at thirty metres and still finding bone," Brüg replied.

"Any theories on what it is?" she asked, then gasped. "Do you think it's a sea serpent?"

"This far inland?" Hargatha added.

"Maybe it was brought here after washing up on the beach?" Egress pressed.

"It's possible," Brüg answered, shifting his weight from one foot to the other. "Your guess is better than mine. I was never one for legends or drunken stories. I only trust things I can see with my own eyes."

"Well, then, open them," Egress instructed a little more sharply. "Find some locals, wisemen, scholars – I don't care. It's time we learn more about our new home."

"Aye," he acknowledged, turning to leave.

"And divert all efforts from the tunnels to this. I want it dug out completely. Get an artist down here to capture it, and let me know when it's done," she said.

"Yes, Empress," he bowed and trotted off.

She stared at the skull, sliding her hand against it.

"No wonder we can't sail beyond the Great Sea," she murmured, her voice full of reverence. "Or can we?" She turned to her mother, eyes widened. "Do you think this was it? The creature taunting us all this time?"

"We don't know for sure what *this* even is yet," Hargatha pushed back.

"What else could it be?" Egress countered. "When was the last time we sent out a ship that far?"

"From Hildeheim?" Hargatha clarified, pausing to think. "Long before I was ever born. It's a death sentence. Besides, what would there be to gain?"

"Allies, land, resources," Egress listed.

"Enemies, monsters…absolutely nothing at all," her mother countered. "And who would you send? Would you really sacrifice our kind on a whim?"

"I'm not suggesting we send our own, Mother." Egress locked eyes with her. "Well, not at first. Send three ships, two full of locals and envoys. The third will be our own people, trailing far enough behind to monitor by spyglass but close enough to catch up if they succeed in passing the barrier."

"Even still, that's a waste of two ships," Hargatha argued.

"Not if they succeed."

"That's a large and unlikely 'if'."

"We could send fifty ships and still have the largest naval force in Aelthoria," Egress frowned, shaking her head. "Just imagine how many landmasses like Aelthoria exist out there. Maybe even larger ones!"

"And if they're empty?" Hargatha asked.

"Then we would have found a new home, where we will never be bothered again."

"I just…" Hargatha started to reply, hesitating only to organise her thoughts.

Egress' spine stiffened, and she interrupted, her eyes locked on her mother's, "I've made my decision."

Hargatha's head canted, and her silence stretched for a brief moment longer.

"I see."

Egress turned her back. "Inform me when they set sail."

Galabrand grunted, his arms outstretched as he hung a portrait larger than himself on the wall in their quarters. He looked sideways, taking notice of Hargatha's expression as she entered the room. She, in turn, took little notice of him as she removed her gloves, walking past.

"I've never been prouder of our people. This is a good castle. One day, this city will be larger than the one back home," he declared with a final grunt, stepping back to check the picture's alignment.

"This is our home now," she replied.

He frowned, detecting her tone, and asked, "Buyer's remorse?"

She shot a glance at him, then returned to removing her stuffy formal clothing.

"What did I do now?" he asked instead while approaching her. He went to grab her shoulders, but she pulled away. His head lurched. "Okay...you want to talk about it?"

She remained quiet. The sound of wine pouring into her chalice echoed through the room. He chuckled to himself. Hargatha licked her lips, holding the words she thought to say in her mouth. As he sat on the back of the couch, folding his arms with a smirk on his face, she sighed, took a swig, and then looked at him once more.

"Are we just terrible parents?" she asked. Her tone was absurd, well below her usual standard.

"Oh," he replied simply, flaring a brow. "Vidar or Egress?"

"Egress."

"I thought you said she was settling into her new role well?"

"A little too well."

"She's not a child, Hargatha. She might seem like it from our perspective, but our perspective is not the one that matters anymore. They belong to the world now. Old enough to make their own decisions…mistakes included," he replied with his natural gruff tone. "You can't hold her hand forever."

She looked at him, one quarter angry, another quarter disappointed, the remaining half left stranded somewhere between understanding and acknowledgement.

"Look, she's surrounded by her own people," he continued. "She has an army no one wants to fight with a navy no one can match. You couldn't ask for a better scenario for her to come into her own."

"The elves have a larger army and a larger navy."

"They don't count," he dismissed. "They live in their own world."

"Until the day they decide to be counted among one of us."

"We'll be long dead before that ever happens."

"We'll be dead either way," she quipped.

He burst into laughter, eyes shining with mirth as he asked, "Now you seek to control things you could never?"

"The world is about to change…"

"The world has already changed."

"No, I mean for us," she corrected waspishly. "The moment our succession is made public. Things change."

"What are you afraid of?"

"Why does everyone keep asking me that!?" she shouted before quickly regaining her composure.

He moved in, pulling her into an embrace as he murmured, "Is it guilt?"

"For what?" she asked. She knew.

"Connerh," he replied.

She pulled back a moment, looking at his eyes, then his lips, and finally back again before she replied, "No. I did what had to be done." She stopped short of finishing her thought. Her eyes wandered. "Without me, or him, Lena is a lost soul. And as this stupid, pointless war blows up in her face, she'll come running to me for help. And then I'll tell her what I should have said a long time ago: no," she continued, looking up at him once more. She grunted. "Connerh was just another consequence of her actions. She started this chapter of her life, and I finished it," she decreed as a frown formed. "With a little luck, Egress will never have to wage war against her cousin. As it is, it's a stalemate, but it'll never come to that. The people will turn on her, just as they did her mother, and she'll hang from her beloved balcony before it's over. Whether of her own accord or at the end of a rope."

She lay her head back against his chest, and his arms tightened around her.

"And let us never utter his name again," she continued.

Hargatha's heel echoed off of stone walls and through darkened corridors gasping for torchlight. Her cadence was urgent but not hurried. Purposeful. Focused.

She stopped and waited for the loud-hinged door to open. She ducked as she crossed under the doorway.

Before her, a man stood shackled to the wall.

Dirty.

Clothes tattered and in disrepair.

He was hungry, thirsty, and smelling of piss and shit.

"Hello, Governor," she greeted, a restrained smirk carving into her cheek. "Guard, get him some water; he's going to be doing a lot of talking," she shouted, ignoring the acknowledgement of her command. She pulled a chair away from the wall, dusting it off before sitting before him, carefully positioning herself into the epitome of composure.

He shrank back.

"I did you a favour by not letting my husband split your skull with his bare hands. It's like a party trick for him, did you know that?" she asked after a long moment.

The man said nothing, just stared nervously.

"Do you understand?" she shouted, her voice reverberating in the small cell, the illusion of composure crumbling. He nodded anxiously. "It'd be like you cracking an egg. I saved your life even while my daughter took over this place. And so, as I see it, you owe me."

The man agreed, anxiously nodding again.

"Good. I don't ask for much; I simply need a history lesson about this place. Legends, fairytales, all of it. I also want to know why there's a dead, *recently* decayed monster buried here, and why the *fuck* doesn't anyone in the mainland know about it!?" she demanded, her tone sharpening suddenly. She looked him over. "And then maybe we'll get rid of those chains, followed by a bath and a chamber pot. How's that sound?"

"Yes, Your Grace," the man replied nervously, begging for mercy with his tone.

CHAPTER FIFTY-NINE

CLARITY

VIDAR

It was…breathtaking.

The sky was clear, revealing the vivid, granular detail of every planet, constellation, and star – including those that blazed across the night with trails of fire. They were destined to be seen yet cursed to never know their watchers, too distant to understand their influence. Their presence seen as signs and portents, their existence evidence of the divine.

A life of isolation amongst the crowded expanse of infinity.

Toke lay on his back, arms crossed behind his head in the pose of a stargazer. His eyes were dilated, like onyx marbles trapped in a pool of topaz.

"You're not going to join me?" he asked. "You don't need to babysit the food, ya know?"

"No," Murnira replied, shuffling around. "And not everyone likes meat as black as your mother's beard," she grumbled.

Toke shrugged and replied, "That makes it your loss…twice!"

"How will I ever cope?" she intoned sarcastically.

"How often does your master come out of that cave?" asked Sevryn, a human man, as he exited one of the four tents.

"He's not our master," Murnira replied quickly, stirring the pot of stew suspended over one of the two fires roaring in their camp.

"Fine, employer…makes little difference."

"There's no setting the sun by it," Toke answered dismissively. "He comes and goes as he pleases. Could be a day, maybe two."

"I haven't seen him in four," Murnira added.

"You were sleeping last. If you'd smoked with me, you'd've been awake," Toke rebutted.

"I like my mind clear," she snipped.

"And you've been sitting up here, in the middle of nowhere…waiting?" Sevryn asked.

"And eating, and smoking in complete peace and quiet," Toke added with a chuckle. "Exploring the secrets of the cosmos."

Sevryn let out a quiet snort.

"She's rolling her eyes, isn't she?" Toke asked.

Sevryn confirmed with the inclination of his head, answering, "She is."

"He means lying on his back like a whore waiting to be bred," she added.

Sevryn's brows raised, and Toke's infectious laughter carried through the space as he quipped, "It's not too late to go home, Ranger; she's a mean one."

"I've suffered worse," he replied, walking closer to the edge of the camp, his hand coming to rest on the hilt of his sheathed sword as his eyes fixed on Vidar's manmade cave entrance. The pick he'd used to make it was still lodged into the ground where he'd left it. Sevryn looked back at the two dwarves. "And you said we can't go in?"

"Oh, you can go in, but I wouldn't advise it," Toke answered sincerely.

"You're being paid to secure the camp, not explore your curiosity," Murnira added.

"You're right." Sevryn's focus pulled away from the cave entrance. "She *is* mean."

Toke chuckled as Murnira grinned.

"When you offered me a sentry job, this wasn't what I imagined."

"We've had some randoms poking around the ledges from time to time, and Toke got scared. That's why you're here," Murnira replied.

"I did not!" Toke fussed.

She shrugged.

"You weren't here last year when that thing chased me out of the temple. Barely made it out!" Toke replied.

"Wait, is the threat out here or in *there*?" Sevryn asked.

"Yes," Toke and Murnira replied simultaneously.

"Come, lad, have a smoke with me," Toke invited.

Sevryn approached hesitantly as Murnira warned, "Don't do it."

"Oh, don't listen to the timid kitten. A grundor has never killed anybody."

"A *grundor*? Why does that sound like it has?" Sevryn said, grinning.

"Because it most certainly probably has," Murnira interjected.

"Well, it can't be both!" Toke sat up, turning to argue with her, his bushy brows elevated. "It can't be both certainly *and* probably!"

Murnira rolled her eyes, and Sevryn chuckled, asking, "What is it, exactly?"

"I thought you'd never ask."

He flashed a devilish grin, running into his tent and back out again, producing two brown tubes with a theatrical flourish. He ran them under his nose, inhaling their scent as his eyes rolled into the back of his head.

"Rolled in the finest moonleaf, it's made from a mixture of ground inka, briarthorne, and duskwort, with a little sprinkling of dwarven fairy dust!" Toke exclaimed. He finally looked up at Sevryn, anticipating his excitement but instead being met with a cocked brow and a frown.

"Someone has *definitely* died from a grundor," Sevryn replied, the look of concern chiselled into his expression. Toke's enthusiasm faded. "Do you even know what half those ingredients are? A moonleaf? From Tu'Chauria? The mist-making plant that drives you insane?" Sevryn asked in humoured disbelief.

"It's dried first," Toke rebutted pitifully, his volume dwindling.

"It makes you vomit, hallucinate, and want to kill yourself. And that's only if you manage to avoid passing out for days on end," Murnira added.

"Only the first time…" Toke replied, his sails devoid of wind.

"And that's only the first ingredient!" Sevryn added.

"A simple no would have sufficed, sir," Toke pouted, putting on a formal accent.

"Where I'm from, we keep it simple. Tobacco in a pipe. That's it."

"Sounds about as dreadfully boring as you would expect from Utreden," Toke snarked, plopping down on the ground next to the fire. He stowed the extra grundor in his pocket and began to light the other using the fire.

"Oh, come now, don't complain until you've tried it! There's whyte, grown in the north. It keeps you calm, relaxed. Good for the end of a long day, helps you to sleep if you so choose to but doesn't force it. Then there's brimble," Sevryn continued, taking a pouch and a pipe from his pocket, packing it with the very herb he was describing, "grown in the west. Sweet smelling and a nice, charred taste. Keeps your mind active and alert. Perfect for the hunt or a long watch." Lighting his pipe and taking rapid puffs to get it going, a gentle inhale was then followed by a pronounced exhale of semi-opaque clouds.

"Damn, you should sell the stuff with a pitch like that," Murnira remarked.

Sevryn smirked, and the pair stopped to stare at Toke, whose pupils seemed as large as horseshoes. He stared at them blankly, perhaps through them.

"By the gods, man!" Sevryn exclaimed.

"What?" Toke asked, oblivious.

Murnira shook her head, her usual response to his hijinks.

"What?" he asked again, looking back and forth at the both of them.

"How many fingers am I holding up?" Sevryn asked, holding up three.

Toke stared, though a bit harder than required. The wheels were turning, but his mouth wasn't cooperating.

He offered a non-verbal grunt and lay down on the ground in lieu of giving a reply.

"Enjoy your nap," she joked.

"I'm not napping!" Toke shouted.

It was a matter of minutes before his snore cut through the peaceful quiet.

Toke shot up, his mental faculties having mostly returned to normal by the time he was looking around to find an empty cam, the fires nearly reduced to embers, Murnira's subtle snores escaping her tent. Sevryn's tent was buttoned closed with not a sound coming from it. It was expected of a ranger. He sighed to himself as he stood, happily sauntering over to an unguarded pot of stew still simmering away in its chubby black pot. To his surprise, the spoon still sat in the pot, and with a satisfied smile, he kissed the tips of his fingers, savouring the quiet moment.

He blew on a freshly ladled spoon, pausing as a motion caught his attention from out of the corner of his eyes. It was a soft orange glow coming from the mouth of the cave. He frowned, putting the spoon back in the pot and moving around it to investigate what he thought he saw. It wasn't long before Vidar stepped out, foot and leg first.

"Ah!" Toke smiled, turning his attention back to food. "How goes it? I'm not ashamed to say I've missed ya, lad." With that, he stuffed his face happily, hot stew dripping down his beard.

"I'm both exhausted and wide awake at the same time," Vidar replied, letting out a sigh as he practically collapsed next to the dwarf. Toke chuckled.

"Sounds like you need a…" Toke began before shouting in alarm as he looked up at Vidar, dropping the spoon to the ground as he backed away.

"What's wrong?" Vidar asked.

"Your…your face," he replied, pointing with a hint of horror.

"You'll forgive me, but I'm in the mood," Vidar replied, the exhaustion oozing from his tone.

"I wish I were pulling your leg…but your hair…your eyes," he continued, now with curiosity.

Vidar's brow raised, his hand lifting to his head. It stopped upon discovering the absence of hair.

"Your hair's gone, lad!" Toke shouted.

Vidar grunted, quickly checking to make sure his beard was still intact. He let out a sigh of relief upon receiving confirmation.

"It seems the Uridar's effects are taking their toll."

"I'll say! Do you not feel it?" Toke asked.

"Feel what?"

"Your eyes! They're glowing!" His voice was tinged with disbelief.

Vidar frowned, lifting a hand to his face. His fingers brushed against his eyelids – nothing felt different, but then he saw the light pooling in his palm, a flickering orange glow. As he moved his hand away, the radiance faded; closer, it bloomed brighter again. He shook his head.

"No, they feel normal. Everything looks a little strange, but I was just blaming the exhaustion," he replied.

"What do you see?"

Vidar looked around, noticing illuminated swirls and distortions layered atop the physical world – sparkles and shadows that seemed to move with purpose, either unaware or unconcerned with his observation of them.

"I wouldn't make sense to you even if I tried to explain it, but I imagine it's far closer to the truth than we've been led to believe," Vidar replied, briefly getting lost in the spectacle of what he saw.

"It sounds like I'd be interested in whatever you're having…" Toke intoned with a grin.

"I'm not so sure," Vidar hedged, lying on his back, his hands interlocked at his chest.

"Are you hungry?" Toke asked instead, acknowledging his sudden shift in priorities as he walked back to the pot, reacquiring his spoon.

"No," he replied, quickly getting lost in the night sky. "You know, there are people like us out there. Different but similar, completely unaware we exist…and some who are. And still, we will never meet, coexisting like two remote islands in the same sea, both of them…just over the horizon in opposite directions," Vidar pontificated. Toke looked up as if to verify, a distrustful grin gracing his chubby cheeks.

"I see. And how did they get there?" Toke asked, sipping his broth louder than he should have.

"They were created, put there, like experiments…left to be watched, studied, allowed to grow…or die. Extinguished like candles when the wax runs out."

"And who created them?"

"I haven't gotten that far yet."

"What do you mean? Is that thing telling you all this?" Toke asked with a sharpness that felt out of character for him, suddenly realising he wasn't being teased. His beard dripped with broth and bits of meat.

"Yes," Vidar replied. "It found a new way to communicate with me. We've abandoned attempting to communicate with speech and my past… I lack the memories for it to make a proper analogy. The longer I'm in its presence, the stronger its ability to manipulate my mind has become. Now, it can deposit memories in my head, like flashes of events unfolding in the way they happened long ago. And I remember it as if I were there myself."

Toke wiped his mouth, his brow raised.

Vidar sat up, turning to face Toke. "And it's not a *thing*. It's a being…a person like us… It's trapped inside…" Vidar's focus wandered as he recalled. "…and I'm going to free them."

"And why exactly would you want to go and do that?" Toke pressed, an irritated but curious look on his face.

"Because they're all in agony."

Sevryn was, indeed, a skilled ranger able to evade detection even when he wasn't trying – it came naturally to him. So naturally that even Vidar and Toke, sharp as they were, failed to spot him in the near distance, a shadow against the mountain wall. He lay with ease, pipe resting between his fingers, the embers beneath his nose a smouldering hint of the same light trailing from Vidar's eyes. He listened, silent, tracing the constellations above as Vidar told of his stories, the stars and his words drifting together into the cold night air.

CHAPTER SIXTY

REMEMBRANCE

ELARION

Madika sat cross-legged on a floor of glass, a mirrored shadow of the world above. She bathed in the warmth of a light that had no source, enshrouded in darkness that stretched in every direction, where neither wall nor ceiling contained her.

Here, in the depths of her mind, a personal plane of solitude, she was free of the noise and distraction of the outside world. A place where few could enter, but she was always free to leave.

A dream within a dream.

Where she slept.

Where she maintained complete control.

She sat in a pose fit for meditation, a gentle stream of air exiting her nose as her thoughts faced no resistance. Her companion was a sole butterfly with wings of copper and white, its body as black as the absence of light. Its movement was silent as it watched over her, fluttering through the air before landing on her head. Its wings opened and closed in near-perfect synchronisation with her breathing.

She stirred as her mind processed his scent in the real world, her lips creasing into the hint of a smile.

"You're actually here?" she asked, her eyes opening tranquilly.

"In the flesh," Elarion replied, his palms outstretched, his cheek

481

dimpled.

She took his extended hand and stood, giving him a calm but tight embrace. Her butterfly took to flight, fluttering around him, landing on the bent finger he held out for it. She smirked, watching him observe her work.

"It's nearly indistinguishable," he remarked, holding it closer to inspect it more carefully. She beamed with pride as he asked, "Are you controlling it, or does it have free will?"

"Both. Sometimes I…well…I struggle to say *soar*…" They both laughed. "But I fly through its eyes. There's not much to see here, but the sensation is…like no other," she explained.

He nodded, his smile fading somewhat as he replied, "This is the foundation of a greater power."

She began to laugh but stopped, the realisation of his seriousness slow to set in.

"You mean I can do this in the real world?" she asked, a brow raised.

"With time, yes. You'll find there's little difference and nothing more than a weak barrier between in here and out there," he answered, gesturing with his head and hand. Her eyes got lost in the possibilities. "That's why it is important that we're strong…here," he continued, pointing to his head, "and here," pointing to his heart. "Just be mindful of whose mind you occupy. A lesson I need not teach you," he added, looking down.

Underneath their feet, trapped beneath the glass, were a horde of writhing bodies covered in black oil. They pounded against the divide, but it made no sound.

"I wanted them to know what it was like to suffer for a change," she added, her eyes resting above her cheeks as she looked down at them, barely lowering her head. Her eyes watered as her gaze lingered. Elarion rested his hand on her shoulder, snapping her out of a daze.

"They're just fragments of their former selves. Ghosts, shadows…they go by many names…" he said, drawing her focus. "But now, they are just as much a part of you as they were of their original owners. In the end, you're only torturing yourself."

Her frown was heavy, thick with anger and disappointment. She felt robbed of the satisfaction, as if her victory over her demons had been removed. Her footing, once stone, was now quicksand.

The floor cracked. It was loud, abrasive.

The split ran between them, running on into the dark void.

She began to shake, water welling in her eyes. Her breathing increased rapidly as she fixated on what lay beneath.

"If you wish to soar…owls, ravens, even magpies are often open to the bond. They have curious minds and often become quite attached afterwards. They make for fine companions," he offered. She refocused, looking at him with a confused expression. Her shaking calmed. "But be wary of gulls and crows. They are devious little creatures who cannot be trusted," he continued with a chuckle and a shake of the head.

She gave a small grin with a crumpled brow, accepting his distraction with grace.

"I once had an owl in my company. His name was…" He paused, chuckling to himself. "A fine companion he was."

"What was his name?" Madika asked, clearing her throat. Her head canted, a curious smirk deepening into her cheek.

He kept opening his mouth to speak but stopped himself. Eventually, with a chuckle, he admitted, "I was once told that I am rather bad at naming things. It has now occurred to me that it was an astute observation."

"It can't be that bad," she replied with a full grin.

He closed his eyes, shaking his head.

"His name was Owl."

She let out a loud, sudden laugh.

"Oh…oh, no. That's not bad, that's just lazy," she replied, trailing into laughter again. He shrugged.

"When you are linked at the mind, names have no use," he replied.

She stopped laughing, her brows raised.

"Oh," she said. "I suppose…that makes perfect sense."

She looked down. The crack had receded, although it was still present at the surface.

"Anger is useful in the moment…but sustained, its lasting effects only damage the wielder," he mused. She quickly looked up at him, then away, inwardly focused.

"It's been a long two months without you around," she said at last, sitting on the floor once again. He stepped over the crack and lowered himself to join her.

She noticed. Her face softened despite her attempts to hide it.

"Why are you so kind to me?" she asked, her voice briefly breaking.

"My answer will never change," he replied.

"No man has ever offered so freely without wanting something in return," she countered, wiping her eyes. "Surely there's something you want?"

He looked away briefly, and she sniffled.

When he finally said, "There is something," her spine stiffened.

"I see. And what is it?" she replied, clearing her throat.

He took a deep breath and exhaled.

"I wish to take you from this place. I wish for you to meet Lysand, an elder of our people and an ancient being with untold wisdom and knowledge. We wish to teach you how to free yourself of all this…" He gestured around them. Her eyes widened every moment he spoke. "…to unlock your power and true potential for no other reason than…you are worthy of it."

His head dropped for a moment as he awaited her reply. He looked up at her after a few moments of silence. Her eyes ran streams of water, as she stared quietly at him.

"In my heart, I believe every word you just said, yet my mind resists," she replied.

"I understand," he said, standing. Just when she felt a slight panic that might leave her, he lowered his hand to her, continuing, "Come, I want to introduce you to someone."

She hesitated before she took it.

They awoke in the real world. He sat in a chair next to her bed. She rushed to sit up to ensure he was, in fact, there, and she smiled as he sat forward.

Elarion reached under his shirt, pulling out the ring necklace. It began to glow.

He took her hand and placed it on his temple.

"Come in," he invited.

And their eyes went black as she entered his mind.

CHAPTER SIXTY-ONE

MOTHS, PAPER & FLAME

NIKO

It was late.

A large candle flickered near the edge of Niko's desk, its original form long buried beneath decades of molten history. Layers of hardened wax, ridged and cascading in uneven drips, had built upon themselves, forming a gnarled, organic structure – far from its humble beginnings as an unremarkable cylinder.

His office, once Hargatha's, had been remoulded to fit his style and taste, though some things still remained. The desk, an heirloom passed down from their predecessors, was just as much a part of the room as the floors or pillars, its place permanent. He chose to keep Hargatha's chair, oversized for his own frame. It looked more like a throne than a simple seat, a coincidence perhaps, but he liked how it loomed over him. Dark steel framed the piece, complemented by chestnut-coloured leather. The cushion was thick and comfortable; designed to support a giant's weight, it was overkill for his eighty kilos, and the steel ensured a knife wouldn't quietly find its way to his back.

He dipped his quill in ink, then signed his name with practised elegance. Tilting his head, he examined the signature, recalling the hours he had once spent perfecting it at his mother's insistence. She had always known he was destined for greatness, for importance – or so she said. Satisfied, he set the letter aside and reached for a fresh sheet.

A knock at the door.

"Enter," he called, his eyes never leaving his work.

The doors parted, then closed. Measured, weighted footsteps followed, accompanied by the faint metallic shuffle of charms or trinkets.

"How can I help you, Vaelen?" Niko asked, glancing up to confirm his suspicions.

"How'd you know it was me?" Vaelen asked.

Niko smirked. "You're the only one who carts around…whatever those are. Good fortune charms? They make a unique sound when you walk, like a ring of keys."

"Ah," Vaelen replied.

"That, and the smell that precedes you."

Vaelen's gaze lingered on him. Niko met it with a measured look.

"Rum isn't a popular spirit in the North. Few enjoy it, and fewer still can afford its import," Niko elaborated with a forced grin.

Vaelen scoffed. "You've grown comfortable in your new title. I remember when you were a snivelling court jester, begging for lords like me to take notice – let alone speak to you. And now, you casually insult me to my face? Has it really been that long?" He pulled out a chair with an ear-piercing scrape across the floor, shattering Niko's focus.

"Times change – and in a hurry, don't they?"

"They do. Which is why it's important to maintain beneficial relationships. One day, you're on top. The next…" Vaelen smirked. "…you're bent over a table."

Niko leaned back in his chair, setting his quill in the inkwell. "And I suppose, for the right price, you'll be offering the spit?"

Vaelen chuckled, his voice deep and gravelly. "Best hope I'm not the one doing the bending."

"Oh, I'm not worried about that; your spine isn't what it used to be," Niko replied, folding his hands and leaning forward. "It's gotten soft, weak… You've gotten far too comfortable letting others do your dirty work. Plain and simple, you don't have the power to thrust. Not anymore." Niko shook his head with a hint of disgust, promptly returning to his letter.

Vaelen pounded the desk with his fist.

"Careful," Niko intoned, "this desk is worth more than the tribute your house offers each month – an issue I fully intend on raising with Her Majesty." He looked up, locking eyes with Vaelen. "You see, as it is, you are the one bent over the desk, and the next words to leave your drunken mouth will determine whether spit shall be offered for your benefit."

Vaelen grunted, looking around wildly as he worked to calm himself.

"I came with an offering," Vaelen said a beat later, his voice smoothing over the tension. "Perhaps my sense of humour has been…misunderstood."

Niko's brows flared.

"Mothers are wise. Even when we don't understand their wisdom in the moment, their words always find a way of manifesting," Niko replied neutrally. Again, he signed his name in big sweeping gestures, blew on the parchment, and set it aside. "Look, I understand; it can be hard to accept change…to let go of the past. This candle, for instance, has been a part of my mother's family for hundreds of years. It's ugly and has little to no value, yet we keep adding to it because it reminds us of where we came from. You see, I come from a long line of poor, uneducated people – commoners, the sort that greased the wheels of the kingdom, whether by sweat or blood. This candle was once the only source of light in the darkness for their small, dingy hut. They should have settled for something made of tallow, something cheaper, more affordable. But this, this is beeswax." He shook his head. "It was a luxury of sorts at the time, imported from the other side of the world as far as they were concerned. It burns slower, cleaner – and, being perfumed, it smelled like nothing they were accustomed to. Why, you might ask? Why would poor commoners waste what little money they had on something as silly as a perfumed candle?" Niko asked.

Vaelen shook his head, not knowing the answer.

"It was a symbol of what could be. Only the rich had beeswax candles. My family believed that even something so insignificant, something relegated to their subconscious like a smell at the end of a gruelling day of work, could drive them forward, to excel, to do better for themselves. And now look at me: here I am, the descendant of such people, sitting in the second-highest post in the largest kingdom of the known world."

Niko paused, retrieving his quill once more. Vaelen's lips curled into a thin smile, his eyebrows arching as he leaned back slightly, absorbing the weight of Niko's tale. He shifted in his chair, the creaking wood under him almost echoing the shift in his thoughts. For a brief moment, the old man seemed to soften, the harsh lines of his face momentarily slackening in what could have been admiration – or at least the semblance of it.

"That's what I tell people, anyway. It's what they want to hear. The poor, stupid court jester finally getting his moment in the light after decades of hard work and perseverance. Like a tale you tell children as they embrace their begrudging life of hard labour. Just a spark of hope to keep the slaves working just a little harder. The truth about it all, really, is that tallow candles smell like cooked meat when lit, and they found it torturous to be reminded of what they could not afford. Imagine smelling the finest roast as you begrudgingly ate onions and rice, just so you didn't die of starvation," he continued.

Vaelen's eyes widened, his grin fading quickly. Niko glanced at him.

"It was my great-grandmother's candle, and I was fond of her daughter, who gave it to me…so I kept it. It's that simple. And the moment I grow tired of it, I'll throw it on a trash heap, where all things from the past ultimately reside." Niko blinked, his face blank as he watched the ink smear across the parchment. His voice even, he finally asked, "What do you want, Vaelen?"

Vaelen hesitated. The smile he'd been wearing faded as he leaned forward, his words slow and deliberate, heavy with hesitation. "What if I were to tell you…there's another with a claim to the throne?"

Niko's quill dropped. Ink splashed across the paper, the damage immediate. With a sigh, he wiped his eyes and face with his hands, the frustration evident in the abrupt movement.

"So, let me get this straight," Niko began, his tone mockingly incredulous. "You come here, in the dead of the night, interrupting my work and making impotent threats as you cling to former glory…and your brilliant plan is to tempt me with treason?" He gave a short, dry laugh. "You really should control your drinking, sir."

Vaelen's face flushed with embarrassment, and he stammered out, "No, no – of course not. It was simply a hypothetical question based on information shared with me."

Niko grunted, his frustration palpable as he crumpled the ruined letter and tossed it to the floor. He let his gaze linger on the ball of paper, watching Vaelen track it with his eyes. Niko covered his untouched letters with a blank sheet before standing and retrieving the discarded parchment. He walked over to the fireplace, tossed the paper into the flames, and watched it burn to ash.

"I suppose, in some cultures, it's customary to listen to a fairy tale before bed," Niko mused, glancing back at Vaelen, who was now turned in his chair and watching him intently. "Continue."

"There are whispers concerning Her Late Majesty, Queen Io," Vaelen began, his voice dropping to a conspiratorial tone. "As you may or may not be aware, there was quite a controversy regarding her many miscarriages before Prince Bjorn's birth."

"I remember," Niko replied flatly.

Vaelen paused, his gaze flickering as if weighing the words. Niko's brow arched in quiet curiosity.

"What if I were to tell you," Vaelen finally said, voice barely above a whisper, "that the first…was not miscarried?"

Niko stepped closer, his expression growing sharper. "I don't understand."

"What if, instead of being miscarried, it was sent away?" Vaelen offered, his words hanging in the air.

"Why? Why would she do that?" Niko pressed, his mind racing, trying to connect the dots.

"A fear of rumours of infidelity, perhaps?" Vaelen offered.

"Which would have meant death," Niko interjected, the realisation dawning on him.

"The child was born small, like Lena, showing no visible signs of giant heritage from the father."

"His Late Majesty the King," Niko corrected.

"Aye."

Niko paced, his face going pale as the implications rushed to the forefront of his mind. "Are you suggesting she never had a *single* miscarriage?"

Vaelen nodded, the confirmation chilling.

"Bjorn has the King's traits…and was spared," Niko said aloud, almost to himself, the puzzle pieces slotting together in his mind.

"He was a large baby and an even larger child," Vaelen added, his voice cold and distant.

Niko stopped pacing. "Then why didn't she kill Lena?"

"The eyes," Vaelen replied, his voice almost reverent. "Giants' eyes glow in the dark. The story goes that Lena was born at midnight, in the dark of Her Majesty's chamber. Only a few hours later, and she likely would have joined the rest."

Niko's eyes wandered, his mind spinning as the pieces clicked together.

"And the firstborn?" he asked, his voice barely audible.

"Alive," Vaelen replied, his face shadowed by the weight of the truth. "Unaware of who they really are, of course."

Niko let out an audible exhale, the realisation settling like a stone in his stomach. "Where?"

Vaelen stood, moving towards the door. "If I told you that, then you'd have no use for me.”

Niko’s smile was cold, the words light but laced with menace. “I’m not that messy.”

“Your types never start out that way.”

Niko’s eyes glinted. “Fair. What is your plan?”

Vaelen’s posture straightened. “You know as well as I do, this war is horseshit. It’s going to lead to unnecessary deaths. This kingdom has suffered enough at the hands of Io and her daughter; the bloodshed must stop.”

Niko’s eyes narrowed. “And you plan to replace Lena with another of Ioelena’s children? By the way…what is it? Man or woman?”

“That stays with me for now,” Vaelen asserted, a slight smirk curling his lips. “And yes, it’s another family member, but this one isn’t tainted by giant blood. No influence from Io. It’s a fresh start…a clean slate for all of us.”

Niko considered this for a moment, his mind calculating the possibilities. “And what do you hope to gain from this? Coming after my job, are we?”

Vaelen’s smile faded, but his eyes remained steady. “No. I want to be like your candle, renewed until the time at which I’m thrown on a trash heap.”

Niko’s grin returned, sharp and knowing. “I like a man with realistic goals. I would meet with this alleged child of disregard. What do you need from me?”

Vaelen inclined his head in acknowledgement, his expression businesslike. “Nothing. I’ve efforts underway to bring the child here, but there may come a time when I need your help.”

Niko’s eyes flickered. “See to it, then.”

Vaelen nodded and went to take his leave, but Niko’s voice stopped him.

“Vaelen.”

Vaelen turned slowly, his face plain but curious.

“You are aware that I own you now, yes?” Niko asked, his tone casual despite the edge.

“I should hope I’ve earned the courtesy of your saliva,” Vaelen replied, nodding, his gaze steady.

Niko chuckled.

“We’ll see.”

CHAPTER SIXTY-TWO

INK BLOTS

YURI

Khazmyr was alive.

The high sun cast its proud rays over a sprawling city, reinvigorated and reborn through its self-enforced isolation. Shimmering ribbons of heat wavered on the horizon beyond its walls, distorting the distant landscape. Dust and sand rose in swirling clouds, not stirred by the wind but by the ceaseless trampling of feet along the bustling streets.

Since the city had sealed its doors, the masses had resurfaced from the underground, flooding the avenues like an anthill doused with water. The air was thick with moisture, where the briny tang of the ocean mingled with the spice-laden aroma of roasting meat. Beneath it all, the musk of sweat, the scent of leather, and the oil of well-worn wood formed an undercurrent, all combining into the amalgamated fragrance distinct to these lands.

"I didn't think I'd live to see such a day," Julian muttered as he and Yuri rode slowly through the crowd on horseback. She looked at him as he spoke. "Not long ago, there was not a child to be seen…now look at them," he said, pointing out groups of children laughing and playing in the streets. Some wore bands of cloth around their eyes, a sign distinguishing those from below who still struggled to adjust to the sunlight.

Yuri smiled, letting out a grunt.

"You'd never know the life they lived just by watching them. The horrid darkness they endured." Returning her focus to their path, she concluded, "Their minds wish to forget…but they won't, they never will."

"The question is, will Khazmyr revert to its old ways once those doors reopen?" he asked. "Will this mark change, or is it only a brief reprieve?"

They exchanged glances.

"The question is…why do you continue to wear that eye patch?" she smirked.

He lifted it, momentarily exposing his scarred right eye, its pupil now as white as snow.

"There are those who wish to see me as a broken and converted man. They want to see Darros' power as absolute…his mercy as divine. After all, that *is* why he continues to keep me alive, isn't it? To maintain the image of a merciful god? This isn't an eye patch; it is control. And by controlling what I allow them to see, I control them all," he said, his grin seasoning the pronouncement of his truth.

She stared at him, initially expressionless, but a brief frown flickered across her face before she glanced away.

"So, you're a man comfortable living in lies and half-truths?" she asked.

"A lie would be proclaiming that I am blind when I can, in fact, see. But if you draw your own conclusions, am I at fault for not correcting them?"

"We see things differently," she replied.

He laughed at the irony of her words.

"A wise man once asked me if I knew the difference between a martyr and a soldier," he said. "Both fight for a cause, knowing they are part of something greater than themselves, that their actions will inspire others. So, where does the difference lie?" he asked.

"The martyr does it knowing he will die. The soldier does it accepting that he might," she replied.

Julian nodded, holding his silence for a beat before a grin spread across his face.

"There is no difference…other than how they are remembered," he corrected.

Her eyes lowered for a moment as she thought before rising as she asked, "And how will you be remembered, Julian? Martyr or soldier?"

He blushed as his name was uttered from her lips, her accent adding a sensual flair. He took a deep breath, shaking his head.

"We won't know til the end, will we? For now…I'm just a man," he replied, his gaze falling, finally fixating on her eyes.

"Consider yourself lucky. Some men kill to live in such a world, detached from reality, seeing themselves as the hand that writes the future instead of the truth…that they are merely ink blots on parchment, written by someone else, forgotten as soon as the page turns," she said, a frown forming. "It's all lies, Julian. The lies that govern the world…and the lies we tell ourselves." Pulling ahead of him on her horse, she shouted as he lingered, "Keep up."

Night was approaching.

The sky was painted with purples and oranges, a speckle of stars bleeding through.

A chill swept over the city walls and through the streets, where the crowds began to dwindle.

"We'll leave our horses here and walk the rest of the way," Yuri barked, hopping off her mount and handing the reins to a stable attendant. Crossing her arms as she waited for Julian to catch up, she instructed, "We may be back late. Don't wait for me; I'll send someone in the morning if we're too long."

"Of course," the stablemaster said in reply.

"Where are you taking me?" Julian asked, dismounting.

"Are you hungry?"

"Starving."

"Then shut up and follow," she said, delaying in exposing her grin. He shook his head.

"We really need to work on your bedside manner."

"I'm not a physician."

"Clearly."

"I didn't see you complain when I was patching you up," she shot back.

He went to say something favouring sarcasm but stopped himself. A blushing smirk crossed his face.

She noticed.

"Careful," she warned, pointing at him. He raised his palms in surrender as they began to walk.

"Oh, no, I wouldn't want you to hit me again," he joked.

Her smile lessened into something between humility and regret.

"I'm sorry for that," she replied. "It was involuntary."

"There's no need to apologise…it didn't hurt," he replied with a shrug.

She squinted; a smile overtook her face despite trying to resist it, and she declared, "You're full of shit."

"Maybe. Probably," he chuckled. Her eyes rolled as his head shook.

They walked for about half an hour through parts of the city where luxury had faded, and the standard of living fell to just above the bare minimum required for survival. Cracked cobblestones lined the narrow streets, and the once-vibrant buildings now stood worn and weathered, their facades peeling. The air grew heavier, thick with the scent of damp stone and distant smoke, and the hum of the city seemed to fade into a dull murmur. Julian's head was on a swivel, his hand resting on the dagger in his waistband, eyes constantly scanning for any threat in the dimming light.

"You walk so carefreely," Julian remarked.

"What is it that I should be fearful of?" She raised a brow as she looked at him. "It's hard to believe, after all this time, that you still do not understand Darros' power."

He replied with a confused expression.

"I could walk naked, whether in the underbelly or above, and not a soul would look at me, let alone give thought to something improper," she said.

"That's the fear of consequences," he replied.

"And I have faith in the assurance of it. You were a part of that judgment once…for Hera. So, what's the difference?" she chuckled. "Is that not why you fear your gods? Fear of displeasing them? Fear of retribution?"

"But he's just a man hiding behind a mask," he answered lowly.

"Is he?" she asked. "Are your gods not hiding behind temples, idols, and hand-drawn paintings?"

His sigh was audible.

"I'm sorry, am I disturbing your mythos?" she asked. He frowned at her. "God is just a title. What matters is the power behind the name. And here…Darros is as good as divine, whether it be blood or the substance of stars that flow through his veins."

"God can't be killed," he argued. She stopped, abruptly interrupting his steps, before reaching into his waistband and retrieving the dagger he thought was a secret. She held it by the blade, a trickle of blood running across her palm, offering the hilt to him.

"Should I take you to Darros now?" she asked. "Will you slice his throat? Stab him in the heart? Are you sure he even has one? Perhaps the legends are true, and he has three? You only have one chance…so which one will you go for?" she demanded.

He stood, frozen in place, staring at her with concern. She laughed at him, shaking her head and tucking his dagger back in his waistband.

"You've come a long way for nothing, Joriah of Hildeheim," she replied, walking off. "Keep up."

"We're here," she said, walking into a nondescript building, its only delineation as a place of commerce being a small, poorly painted sign hanging above the doorway. Julian took a second glance before entering.

The place was dimly lit. There was a bar at the far end, tables in between there and the front door. Simple in design, even simpler in execution. Everything was made of wood, with little to no embellishment short of black iron. She picked an empty table in the corner and sat, motioning for Julian to join her as he lagged behind. He did so with caution, opting for a chair with a wall to its back. She watched his paranoia with humour.

She shook her head and asked, "What will it take?"

"What do you mean?" he replied.

"Nothing," she replied, sliding her arms out of the tunic and exposing her small but ample breasts. He turned away, his eyes widening as his cheeks blushed.

"Hello, Issara," she greeted as the barmaid approached.

"Yuri, good to see you." She nodded. "What's going on here?"

"Just acclimating poor Julian here to the ways of Khazmyr," she replied.

His mouth opened.

"I see…" Issara replied, sliding her arms out of her top, exposing her own chest. "Hey! Show some respect, we've got an outsider here!" she shouted, drawing everyone's eyes and attention. Within seconds, every diner, man or woman, had their chest exposed.

"What will you have, dear?" Issara asked.

"Lamb, wine, bread, and oil…the usual," she replied. "Julian…what'll you have?"

He stared at her uncomfortably, shrugging.

"He'll have the same with a side of acceptance," she replied, staring at him with an arched brow.

Issara chuckled.

"It'll be ready in a few, dear," she replied, walking away.

Yuri folded her arms.

"There is no crime here. Not the kind you're accustomed to," she said.

"I get it," he quickly replied.

"No, I don't think you do. I think you're just saying what you think I want to hear in order to put an end to your discomfort," she said, forcing him to lock eyes with her. "That's what you do, after all, isn't it? A bit of theatre to achieve the desired result?"

He watched her sheepishly.

"Even this is an act, isn't it?" she asked, laughing as she thought on it longer, her eyes wandering. She pulled her tunic back up. He stared at her, ensuring contact with her eyes, his embarrassment fading in silence.

"I believe the only truth that has come out of your mouth since you've been here…is your name," she said, her head switching sides to cant towards her other shoulder.

"How can you be so sure?" he asked.

"I know the look when you hear your own name. It's ingrained in you to acknowledge it, even if you hear it in regard to another. Faces betray truth…even in the most skilled of liars."

"Is that why Darros wears a mask?" Julian replied in his true tone and cadence.

"Perhaps," she replied, her honesty sweeping his sure footing out from under him. "But unlike you, he has no need to lie. He wants for nothing; he fears nothing. Personally, I think he enjoys the show of it… It elicits the response he desires."

"He has every reason to lie," he pushed back. "Everything here falls apart once his blood hits the floor."

She shook her head. His head canted, his expression mirroring his disbelief in her resistance.

"It will not, and it has not. You don't know what I've seen. Surely you don't believe you were the first to attempt killing Darros?" she asked.

"I'm sure there are legends covering scrolls that would reach the Westwood," he replied sarcastically.

"There are, but I don't rely on legends. I rely on what I see with my own two eyes. You weren't the first, and you won't be the last. Just in my lifetime, he's been stabbed with swords, daggers, and spears, shot with arrows and poisoned," she grinned in reply to the deep crease that formed between his brows, "and every time, he comes back as if nothing happened, without so much as a scratch."

She watched as the wheels turned in his head.

"And how does he come back?" he asked, his curiosity showing a crack in his determination, a hint of acceptance.

"You wouldn't believe me," she replied.

He leaned in, first looking around before he lowered his voice and challenged, "Try me."

"Okay…" she said, leaning in to meet him. "He sleeps it off."

He looked at her, waiting for a laugh, but there was none.

"What does that mean? Is that a metaphor, a double meaning?"

"No. It is as I said: he sleeps it off. Trust me when I say he cannot be killed," she insisted. He sat back in his chair, shaking his head once again.

"There is a trick at play. You said it yourself; it is merely theatre. Perhaps these attempts are staged…planned, all to convince those around him that he is, in fact, a god…when he is not," he said, his logical mind taking back control.

Her humoured expression faded, and she glanced away briefly.

"Have you seen him lose his head? Do you believe he could sleep that off, too?" Julian replied, still careful with his volume.

She glared at him.

"No," he continued. "He breathes because I allow it."

She giggled.

It annoyed him.

"Killing him too soon would have jeopardised everything," he went on, his brow wrinkled and heavy, eyes scanning back and forth.

"Jeopardise what? Saving me? I'm still waiting, by the way," she replied, her tone mocking. She leaned back as Issara set their plates of food and drink on the table. He did the same, maintaining eye contact, his annoyance still present.

"Let me know if there's anything else," Issara said as she walked away.

"Thank you," Julian replied. He watched as Yuri began eating, his mental stewing evident as he asked reproachfully, "Are there no manners in Khazmyr?"

Yuri grinned as she bit into her lamb shank.

"Do you think Darros says thank you? Please? May I? You judge this place with the eyes of an outsider. Do you see yourself as so pure? So righteous? Is it we who should be looking to you as a bar by which to measure? Or you, us?" she asked while chewing.

He scoffed.

"Khazmyr is a place…" he began aggressively, enthusiastically, amused but insulted…but pulled it all back again at a moment's notice.

"Go on…don't cower now. Khazmyr is a place of what?" she insisted.

"Governed by savages, for the pleasure of savages," he whispered, his tone final. Assured.

She leaned back, staring at him.

"There's the real Julian," she decreed, a scoff and half-chuckle escaping.

He frowned at her, his frustration with her lack of urgency and understanding broadly apparent. It was clear when a thought suddenly occurred to him; he looked at his food, then at her, and back again.

He pushed the plate away.

She watched, erupting into laughter.

"Again, you think I would walk all this way just to poison you?" She shook her head. "Why am I so important to you?"

"What?" he replied.

"Why am I so important to you? That you would risk your life to save someone who doesn't wish to be saved?" she rebutted.

A man approached, his steps light and deliberate. He bent close, murmuring something low against her ear. She didn't turn, didn't flinch — only angled her head slightly, her gaze still pinned on Julian. Her lips moved in a quiet reply, the native syllables slipping out like second nature — Julian's gaze shifted between them, his focus narrowing in on their lips. He subconsciously mimicked them with ever-so-small mouth movements.

Then, a shift. Her eyes flicked to the man, sharp, searching. The whispering continued, his voice steady, but something in it made her brows pull together. Slowly, her gaze drifted downwards, her fingers curling ever so slightly on the tabletop. She said something, a question. He shook his head.

There was a pause.

She dismissed him.

He nodded a little too deeply before he left. It was a discreet bow. Julian took a bite out of his food, observing Yuri intently.

Her mood had changed.

He looked around again, taking note of the individual faces.

Committing some to memory.

"I guess I'm a little confused. What is this place? What is it *actually*?" he asked.

She deliberately blinked.

"The best tavern for lamb in all of Khazmyr," she replied, resuming eating, her mind still preoccupied.

"I've had better," he said. "And so have you; you're a terrible liar."

"I'm sorry I'm out of practice," she replied. "Look, I don't mean to rush you, but…I need to see someone," she said.

"I can see myself home," he offered.

"No," she replied. "I want you to come with me."

CHAPTER SIXTY-THREE

PETRICHOR

CONNERH

He laughed. Consciousness filled his body like air rushing into freshly awakened lungs, but his eyes remained tightly shut. It was a raw, dry chuckle drawn from a throat that had almost forgotten how to vibrate. There was no rhyme or reason for it – just a reaction to the first emotion he genuinely felt in a long while. The voice was his own, but it rang foreign, strangely altered from what he remembered. A deep, lingering smirk settled on his face as his brow wrinkled, his mind carelessly floating in a thick, viscous pool of confusion.

Memories flickered, brief and disjointed, slipping through his mind like sand escaping panicked fingers. Lena at his bedside, her voice soft, her hands cool against his burning skin. Morning or night, it didn't matter – it was always her. Only her. No handmaidens, nurses, or physicians. Just her small, delicate touch pressing morsels of food to his lips in the morning, stretching his stiffened limbs by day, guiding water past his dry lips in the dead of night. He never saw her with his own eyes, never having the strength, only hearing her voice, feeling her ghost-like touch before the milky shadows swallowed him whole again. In those memories, his body had not been his own – he had drifted within it, a prisoner of flesh barely holding on to agency and consciousness.

Before long, the world bled back in like an all-consuming inkblot on a blank page of canvas. The scent of home – warm wood, embers, lavender, and beneath it all, her.

The eager chirping of robins, the distant, knowing call of a raven. It must have been spring.

Spring? The thought took hold in his mind, vacating any and everything else around it.

His eyes snapped open. He shot up, breath hitching, hands moving before thought could catch up, feeling his chest, his sides, searching for something – scars, wounds, pain, anything to anchor him in reason. But there was nothing.

Nothing.

He stilled. The room, which he quickly identified as hers, was empty.

Her scent still lingered, fresh, near. Beside him, the bed was still warm, as if she hadn't been gone long, but he couldn't remember lying with her. His fingers brushed his face and stopped. Rough. Coarse. Thick. A beard, long and unkempt. His lips parted, but no words came.

This made no sense.

The covers rustled as he tore them from his legs. He hesitated – only for a breath, no more – and then forced himself upright. His knees wavered beneath him, uncertain, untrusting, but in the end, they obeyed. His body remembered stillness, but it would learn to move again. It had to.

He felt drawn to the balcony. The air was thick with memory, so dense it felt suffocating, as if all the fresh air had been drained away. He rushed towards the linen curtains that veiled the sunlight, stumbling but catching himself. The distance was small, yet his legs struggled to remember how to move in harmony, making the journey agonisingly slow. As he pushed through the curtains, rolling clouds crept across the sky, dimming the sun's rich yellow into a pale, diffused glow.

His nose flared, an all too familiar scent rushing in and pulling with it the fresh air. His eyes closed, and his shoulders relaxed. He repeatedly inhaled through his nose, exhaling through an open mouth.

Her panic was evident in the way she burst into the room, the doors slamming against the walls that held them. Hurried footsteps came to a sudden stop.

"Connerh!?" she screamed, noticing he was missing from the bed.

His head peeked through the fabric divide. She saw him, instantly releasing a chaotic symphony of laughter, sorrow, and pain. She was overjoyed to see him, but the torment of his absence flooded her mind just as the first raindrops fell. She was a blithering mess, an embarrassing bleat vibrating in her chest – a noise that was both inhuman and the purest expression of humanity condensed into a single moment, a single sound.

Love, joy, pain, and anger.

All of them shades of agony.

He rushed to her, limping and stumbling along the way. Their embrace was so forceful that it hurt. Her eyes and hands roved about his face and body, careful but anxious. Delicate but ravenous, her mind in violent disbelief of her eyes. A deep smile settled on his face, and his eyes watered. He tried to frame her face with his hands, to establish and maintain eye contact, but she wouldn't keep still, as if she were avoiding it.

He gently shook her, forcing her to acquiesce.

"It's me," he said, his voice breaking the chaotic quiet. Her head bobbed wildly in agreement, tilting just before hot tears streamed from her eyes once more.

They sat together on her crimson chaise lounge, her head nestled into his embrace. He nuzzled the crown of her head, his lips and nose gently caressing her hair as he inhaled her soothing scent. The tears had dried, their heartbeats once again synchronised, and a serene calm settled over them. For the hour that had passed, the last eleven years felt like nothing more than a fleeting nightmare, distant and brief in hindsight. They shared a quiet longing for normalcy, a desire to move beyond the past, yet their thoughts lingered with unanswered questions.

He took a deep breath, a measured exhale. She sat up, understanding what it meant.

"Right," she said, turning to sit facing him, eager but cautious. Grabbing his hand and caressing it in her lap, she asked, "Where do we begin?"

"How?" he asked.

"Reh'gara brought you back to me," she explained, squeezing his hand as she spoke. He looked away, the predictable inclination to disbelieve arriving on cue.

"I was never sure what to think of the stories and supposed legends."

"Did you think I made them up?" she asked with a grin.

"No…yes…maybe a little embellished? I don't know," he replied. "I just thought they were tales your mother told you to keep you in line." He grinned.

"Well, it didn't work, if that was her intent," she laughed.

"I had no idea he was capable of such power." He frowned mildly.

"Nor I."

"But why didn't he…" he rushed to follow up.

Her gaze fell.

"I don't have all the answers, but when I asked about my father, he said that the reason was…because he wasn't there…" Her reply was laced with scepticism.

Connerh's brow briefly flattened; he was referring to her mother.

"Maybe his power has limits…or range, like an archer's arrow?" Connerh was quick to rationalise.

"Maybe," she acknowledged with an exasperated sigh. "Between you and me, it seems a little convenient of an answer. But then, it's hard to be selfish when I have you here in front of me, breathing, even though I held you when you took your last." She straightened her posture, spending a moment to take him in again. "I'd trade them both for you in a heartbeat." She looked him over, her expression flat. "Connerh, I want to get this next part out of the way. If I know you as well as I know that I do…then I fear this part will be harder for you to accept," she said, a frown crossing her face.

"Harder than coming back from the dead?" he quipped with a laugh, but her expression remained unchanged, snapping him into seriousness. Sensing the weight of the unknown, he prodded, "Okay?"

Slowly releasing his hand, she stood and began to pace.

"Well, now you're making me nervous," he joked, standing as well. "What is it?"

She finally met his gaze, stepping closer to take his hands back in hers.

"You've been unconscious for a year," she blurted out, deciding it was better to rip off the bandage than drag it out.

First, he laughed. Then came a frown, then a grin – an instinctive resistance to the truth she had so accurately predicted.

"It's okay to take some time to work it out," she assured him as he moved slowly away from her.

He suddenly couldn't stop thinking about Rose. A lot of things could happen in a year. Good things, yes, but there were a lot of bad.

"I don't want you to take this the wrong way, especially considering everything. And I don't mean…" he started.

"I haven't been able to find them. I checked every place you suggested five times spread out over months," she replied, cutting him off, already two steps ahead. She closed the distance between them, feeling the need to touch. "Especially after you were gone, I thought it only right, no matter whether Reh'gara's efforts were successful…" she explained in a hurry.

His gaze darted around the room.

"The way I see it…" She touched his face. "She's learned from the best, nothing more. It took me years to find you after all." She tried to console his racing thoughts, if only to keep him from running to her, pressing, "We'll find her and the child, I swear it."

He looked at her as her hands framed his face, her gaze scanning his eyes, his brow, his mouth, as if she were trying to read his thoughts.

"Please don't leave," she rushed to add with large, watery eyes. Plainly, directly. There would be nothing left unsaid. Not anymore.

"No, no, of course not," he assured her with a concerned expression. "I just wish I knew they were okay, and they, I," he continued, pulling her in and kissing her head. He was a man of his word, but she knew he'd thought it. The vision of going to find them himself had crossed his mind, even if only for a flash of a second – and to her, that flash was an eternity of rekindled romance with the woman of his past. That was far too long.

An *unacceptable* daydream.

"Why does the thought of losing one year feel longer than ten?" he asked, his hands rubbing her shoulders, now tense but trying to release.

"I lived it…and it was," she replied.

His cheeks ballooned as he released one last, controlled breath, and he asked, "What else has changed in the world?"

She shrugged, pulling him back to the chaise to sit.

"Well, we're at war…" she said nonchalantly.

"What!?" he replied in disbelief. She raised a brow.

"What? I suppose the word war *is* a bit alarmist…overkill, even. We're at odds with a few of the minor kingdoms. There, does that sound better?" she asked.

"For what?"

"Conspiring to kill my mother, conspiring to kill me, maybe even you… The list goes on," she replied. Connerh went to speak as his thoughts fought for priority.

"Here, all this time, I thought Bjorn was using his quest to find our mother's killer as an excuse to travel…but lo and behold, he solved the riddle," she mused, sounding thoroughly impressed. "This will get messy, no doubt, what with all of the intertangled alliances and secret agreements…but it will get properly sorted with time," she continued as he listened. "You know, I was worried about the truth getting out about Cassius," she said as her eyes glazed over, disengaged. "But it seems to have been in my favour. Never would I have imagined the rage it would instil in our people." She smirked. "And, yes, sentencing you was a grave mistake on my part, but your murder…well, it cemented an insatiable bloodlust. Hildeheim is no longer in the business of being kicked around, nibbled and prodded by those lesser than us. I didn't even have to suggest taking up arms; they all basically begged me." She laughed.

His frown remained.

"What do you mean…maybe?" he asked.

"I'm sorry?"

"You said 'maybe'. 'Maybe' they were responsible for my murder…" He paused and shook his head. "That feels odd to say…"

"Imagine burying you," she quipped.

His head sank, and he asked, "You had a funeral?"

"Yes," she replied, again with ease.

"Wait, does anyone know I'm alive?" he asked.

She squinted, replying hesitantly, "This feels like it's becoming too much for you."

"Oh, it's very well beyond that point, but answer the question anyway," he fussed.

She smirked.

"What?" he pressed.

"Nothing, it's just…we've not had a squabble in a while, and your nose is doing that thing it does when you're irritated," she chuckled.

"No, it's not, we're not squabbling, and you're changing the subject!" he argued.

"Fine, fine. Yes…I mean no… Well…Farrah knows…obviously, Reh'gara and I know…but that's it," she replied, grinning. "Even then, I just found you awake, so in that regard…only me."

"Farrah I understand, but how were you able to pull that off? The castle is massive, and it's filled with visitors and servants at all times."

"No one is allowed on this floor other than Farrah and those servants who are blind, visually impaired, or…equally bound to their oath to me," she replied. "Besides, I don't think you understand… The people practically worship me. If I say it, it is done." She stood to retrieve their wine. "At the moment, anyway. We all know loyalty is fickle and often for sale."

She looked at him, the struggle to process everything written clearly across his face.

"Reh'gara mentioned that it would take you some time to reacclimate. Perhaps we shouldn't push it. Remember, we're not catching you up on just a year, we're talking about eleven," she pointed out, handing him a full glass as she sat. "Try it. It's Renauld's wild red that you always loved."

She grinned, staring at him from over the rim of her cup. His mind was moving at a mile a minute, but her words cut through, simplifying the noise. He sipped from his cup, which turned into a longer swig. She watched intently, her head raising as his did. Her eyes settled on the drops that ran down his lips.

"Damn, it's been too long," he said, finally releasing the grin she had been building up.

She slid in closer, licking the wine off his lips as she agreed, "Yes…it has."

They lay naked under her sheets, her head on his chest, finger twirling his chest hairs. He stared aimlessly into her canopy, his thoughts roaming with no particular direction.

"Reh'gara wants to speak with you," she murmured, a thought seemingly from nowhere.

"Now?" he asked, curious but in good humour. She giggled.

"No…when you're ready. It doesn't have to be today, or tomorrow, or the next… He emphasised the need for your willingness," she replied.

He took a deep breath. She heard his heart rate increase a little.

"This sounds like a big deal," he prompted.

"I suppose," she replied.

"You take for granted your access to the unknown."

"Probably, but that doesn't change the fact that you should see him."

"What does he want?" he asked.

She laughed and propped herself up on her elbows to face him. "Are you afraid?" she asked, amused by his timidness.

It was a reaction that felt alien to him. He thought to lie, but he felt free of the desire to put on appearances.

"Perhaps… I'm not sure afraid is the right word, but maybe it is. Were you always this carefree about your relationship with him?" he asked.

She took a breath while giving it some thought.

"Yes, I suppose so. I've never actually given it much thought. To me, he is no different than a grandad…" she began, lying back on his chest.

"With cosmic powers," he added.

"With cosmic powers, yes," she chuckled.

"You're far too calm about this," he said.

She laughed again, scolding, "Stop being a baby and go in a few days. You'll be fine, he just wants to meet you formally…and explain a few things."

"That sounds ominous."

"It should," she replied.

He laughed.

She didn't.

He canted his head to the side in an attempt to gauge her expression, but her face remained hidden from him.

"Relax," she instructed, hearing his heart rate increase further. She rubbed his chest.

"What does he look like?" he asked.

"I don't know…an old man?" she replied, sitting up again. "He literally looks like he could be my grandfather."

His expression mirrored his heavy thoughts.

She smiled.

"You think and worry too much."

His focus shifted.

"The last time I stopped, I died," he replied.

CHAPTER SIXTY-FOUR

REPRIEVE

CONNERH

Connerh's fingers traced the cold ridges of limestone as he descended deeper into the ancient catacomb beneath Castle Corvidae. The lantern in his other hand rattled as he walked. Whispers of the long-forgotten kings and queens of Hildeheim echoed through the air, their presence felt yet unseen. The unsettling ambience deepened, shadows pooling darker than squid ink in ways only a cavernous graveyard could achieve. Tall mounds of beeswax candles lined the walls, their glow separating headstones from statues and carving a path for the living among the dead. Their flickering light was enough by which to navigate, yet it barely held back the encroaching darkness — an all-consuming cold seeking out its opportunity to devour…

…everything.

The scent of sage and pine resin mingled with the earthy musk of damp stone, struggling to mask the pervasive stench of death and decay. He hated graveyards — and, generally, all things dealing with the dead, ironically enough. The dealer avoiding his own wares was more than a familiar trope; it was a way of life.

And yet, he insisted that he wasn't superstitious.

Understanding — as a concept — was, after all, a matter of interpretation. He didn't cover mirrors, walk into rooms backwards, or participate in the form of theatre he often associated with the word. On the contrary, he prided himself on being practical, a cause-and-effect kind of man. Once upon a time, he believed the dead transitioned elsewhere after departing from this world. According to him, they became neither apparitions nor ghosts that haunted the living, especially having seen…or perhaps not seen…the other side for himself.

He stopped walking.

His stomach soured as his mouth began to water.

His vomit splattered the ground, echoing his convulsing shame.

He hadn't stopped to think about it.

Being dead.

It was odd to consider, even stranger to try and work out. He had no recollection of it, yet he knew it to be true. It was provable. Undeniable. It was the first time he'd thought about it since he had awakened, since the noise, Lena's distractions had left him. He was alive once more, rejoined to a world he had no memory of leaving, only having given in to the desire to sleep – to rest. The thought of being forgotten – whisked away in an instant, powerless to resist, unable to assert his will to stay – tightened his throat.

He risked burning his fingertips to extinguish the candle near him. He slumped on the ground, his back scraping against the jagged stone wall.

Now draped in shadow, he felt he'd received the permission that was needed, though it was truly neither needed nor required, to weep.

In that moment, he found solace in the darkness – preferring the company of monsters, ghosts, and the unseen over enduring another moment alone with himself.

Unkempt locks of white hair fell in front of Reh'gara's face as he paced back and forth. He brushed them away, tucking loose strands behind his ear. His hand ran down his cheek, coercing his wild beard into order. Pale blue eyes scanned around the circular stone table before him. Tall-backed, black chairs loomed over it – two of which were occupied.

He took a deep breath, the effort visibly expanding his chest.

"I remind you that once I commit to this…there will be no going back.

Only so that the natural order of things should unfold, as they should have from the beginning," he said. There was emotion sewn within his words.

Maybe fear, perhaps concern.

"And have you committed to this course? Are there no precautionary measures left to take?" an accented feminine voice replied. Her thick, red-and-white curly hair spilt from beneath her gold-trimmed, purple-hooded cloak. Reh'gara's eyes fell.

"I have. And there most certainly is not, Amethyst," he answered with a nod to himself. His eyes raised to find hers. "What will you do? Will you stay behind to look after them? They will need someone to maintain order," he enquired. She shook her head rapidly before she could muster her words.

"I will not, Reh'gara, nor will you ask this of me. I have supported, even indulged you with this little experiment, but I must draw the line somewhere. This is simply not my burden to bear. I have walked a tight line, that even that which started as a gentle rebellion ends with me having something good to show for it," she argued. "I'm sorry you are unable to say the same, but when I am finished here, I am finished for good," she replied, somewhat remorseful though mostly insulted by his request. There was no real way for her to sort it out, not easily. Not without making things worse for herself. "You knew the consequences, Reh'gara," she pleaded in the face of his expression, full of irritation. "Besides, even if I were to indulge you again...what good would it accomplish? Delay the inevitable any further? And at what cost? Will it please you to see me punished for *your* misdeeds? Is it company in misery you seek?" she pressed, hoping he would acknowledge his selfishness.

He shook his head, grumbling to himself as he raised his hand to stop her.

"This is for the better in the long run, I assure you. Let them sort it now. You've been in too deep for far too long. You cannot stop what has been set into motion...not even you. Not without killing every last single one of them and begging for mercy and banishment...at the least," she continued. He looked at her, expressionless, cold and detached but familiar with her suggestion.

She gasped.

"You jest!?" she demanded.

"I would be lying if I didn't admit that the thought had crossed my mind," he retorted.

She gave him a look of disgust, her tone laced with capable regret as she sneered, "I should've stopped you a long time ago. Your hubris knows no bounds."

"You sound like Ankhari." He scowled in frustration, releasing a laugh of contempt. Her brows raised.

"Have you stopped to consider that perhaps he was right?" she replied.

"I have considered that perhaps he has poisoned your mind and pivoted you against me, just like he did Torinir!" His mood quickly soured, as his face contorted.

Her eyes squinted as her head recoiled. She slid her chair back and stood. It made a horrible screeching noise, pulling his attention.

"You don't get to utter his name anymore!" she shot back.

They locked eyes, each waiting for the other to act, but Reh'gara's focus broke first.

"Do you think I live without regret?" he asked, his tone deflating.

"It's too late for that. Regret does not bring him back, nor repair the damage done to his child… No matter what laws against nature you break in order to appease your guilt, his blood will always stain you," she continued. "As does the blood of those you've imprisoned."

"Will you free them?" he asked.

"No," she replied. "They've surely gone mad by this point. A thousand years trapped in a Uridar. If they haven't taken their own lives, I can only imagine what they have become." She shook her head. "I will not let their desire for revenge upon you stain their record…or lower them to your standard. Balance will come. They will be restored in time. You, on the other hand…you should save yourself. Run. "Pray they don't break free beforehand, and that the child doesn't find out what you've done."

"Why? Will you tell him the truth to watch my undoing?!" Reh'gara shouted.

She smirked and shook her head, her grin deepening as she said, "That is not my way, darling – nor will I intervene when he seeks…and achieves…justice."

Reh'gara kept mumbling to himself – arguing, even. Eventually, he sighed, "Maybe I've not tried everything." His hair had broken free from his ears, and he looked tired, exhausted, and deprived of rest. Amethyst scoffed again, shaking her head at his stubbornness.

"Reh'gara…" she raised her voice, but he didn't hear her, trapped in his personal fervour.

"Reh'gara!" she shouted. "You cannot save them!"

His eyes widened dramatically; his nose flared.

"Yes, I can!" he shouted, dragging out the words.

Spit flew from his mouth as he violently shook. The room filled with sparks and bolts of lightning that struck every inch and surface…all but Amethyst and a second figure. A solemn silence settled between them. She lowered her hood once it stopped, revealing a sorrowful face and pale skin that glowed in the flickering torchlight. She approached to gently caress his face, the contrast of their skin tones stark against each other. His anger dissolved in her touch, leaving only desperation in its wake.

"I must," he whispered, his brow heavy with burden.

She sighed.

"I pity you. In your quest for legacy…for remembrance…you have assured your own erasure. But I will remember you…as you once were," she murmured. There was more she wanted to say, but the words felt futile now. Her fingers traced the contours of his face as if committing them to memory. His expression softened as he watched her, fear flickering in his gaze. He looked into her amethyst-coloured eyes – her namesake, always captivating. He had forgotten how beautiful she was.

"You look at me as you would the dead," he stated, his emotions becoming harder to balance. She offered a faint smile, kissed his forehead, and returned her hood to sit over her head.

"I'm not ready to go," he lamented, losing control over his sadness for a passing moment.

"We were never meant to be," she replied, walking away from him.

His eyes watered.

"And you, Aenon?" he asked, looking to the other hooded figure in the room.

Aenon stood motionless, remaining silent, his face obscured by black. Amethyst slowly returned to stand next to him.

"Yes, I suppose I already knew the answer," Reh'gara laughed lightly to himself. "Where there's one, the other is always nearby."

"Is it my fault that my thoughts lie with hers if the answer to this equation is always the same?" Aenon finally spoke, his voice shifting in pitch and tone as it always did. "You simply chose wrong."

Reh'gara stopped his reply, glancing downwards and behind him. He sensed Connerh's approach.

"Would you stay a while longer?" he begged Amethyst. "For me?"

Amethyst and Aenon both canted their heads and stared off into the distance, now sensing the stranger too. She looked first at Aenon, then Reh'gara.

"You would bring the *child* here?" she asked, surprised.

"He must be made aware. For Lena's sake…and the innocents'," he added.

Amethyst nodded cautiously.

"What's the harm in a little while longer…?" she replied softly. A sudden recollection.

"I've said that before…"

"This time will be brief," Reh'gara replied.

Connerh walked in near darkness for minutes, his lantern, the only source of light this far down the catacombs, held low at his side. Ahead, an ominous glow marked what he assumed was his destination. Voices seeped into the corridor, though he couldn't be sure if they were real or just conjurations of his mind grasping for distraction. That was, until one of them shouted, followed by what he refused to believe was thunder and lightning. It startled him, the echo shaking the walls and releasing a torrent of dust and pebbles from above.

He hadn't recognised the language being spoken, sounding beyond foreign to him. He wasn't even sure how to mimic it. He paused when the voices did, walking again only once their conversation resumed.

Finally, as the last corner approached, the conversation stopped. He could see shadows on the ground, standing, waiting, taunting him.

"Don't be alarmed; we're anxious to meet you," Reh'gara said in the common tongue.

Connerh's head cautiously peeked into the room before entering.

"There you are," Reh'gara greeted with a hint of enthusiasm. "I am Reh'gara. This is Amethyst, and beside her is Aenon," he continued, motioning towards them without looking.

"There are only two of you," Connerh replied sceptically.

Reh'gara's expression flashed with confusion, and he looked behind him to investigate.

"He does not wish to be seen by you, but he is there," Amethyst replied.

Reh'gara scowled.

"However, we are honoured to meet you; you have had quite the journey," she continued as she looked him up and down.

"*He looks just like Torinir*," Aenon remarked to Amethyst, only she and Reh'gara hearing him. She smiled, nodding in agreement. Reh'gara frowned.

"They were just about to depart when they heard you coming. There will be time to talk with them at length later…but for now, we have much to discuss," Reh'gara began, approaching Connerh despite staring at Amethyst all the while.

Connerh bowed with his head, maintaining a careful watch. Amethyst curtsied.

"Good luck," she offered, raising her brows before vanishing in a burst of green flame. As the fire flared upwards, Connerh caught a glimpse of Aenon's shadow stretching beside her, cast stark against the light. He lurched backwards, wincing from the heat.

Reh'gara took a good look at him, eventually prodding, "I realise the gravity of the situation from your perspective, and you most assuredly have more questions now than when you first came here. We are not pressed for time…so ask them."

"Am I still dead?" Connerh replied immediately. "Is *this* the after?"

Reh'gara shifted his weight, tilting his head towards Connerh. Standing taller, his proportions were just slightly larger than those of an above-average man.

"No. In fact, you have never been more alive than you are now," he answered.

"I see," Connerh murmured. He thought a moment, having nearly convinced himself otherwise. "Then I suppose my next question is, why me? What did I do to deserve a second chance?" Connerh asked. "I've heard the enemy cry for you as I approached their doorstep in battle. I've stood in your temples, watched women and men sob at the feet of your statues, offering money, cattle…even their own lives just so you might save their dying child." His gaze drifted past Reh'gara, unfocused, as if seeing those moments play out once more. His brow furrowed, lips pressing together before parting slightly, as though he might say more – might make sense of it. But nothing came. His jaw tightened. A slow breath passed through his nose. Then, his eyes snapped back, sharp and unwavering, pinning him in place. "But you looked the other way."

Reh'gara's chest expanded as he took a deep breath.

"I've been a good man at times, decent usually…and only evil when it was required… Hardly worthy of favour," Connerh continued, his focus wandering.

"I suppose I should destroy those places," Reh'gara replied. "I know it may seem hard to believe, but I am not…a god." He studied Connerh's face. "Those statues are lifeless blocks of stone. They don't even look like me," he tried to make a joke to lighten the mood, but Connerh's expression remained, and his own grin faded. "I did not give my permission for them to be made, nor the temples that contain them. They're just…buildings, empty things people put their faith in when there is little hope remaining." He threw his hands up in the air.

"But you have incredible power," Connerh rebutted.

"To you, it would seem so, yes."

"And how and when do you choose to use it?"

"As of late? …Selfishly," Reh'gara answered, his gaze falling.

"At least you're honest," Connerh replied. Reh'gara laughed.

"I haven't got much left *besides* honesty these days," he replied, sitting in his chair. He motioned for Connerh to join him at the table, which he did, albeit cautiously. "I was like you once, the good and loyal soldier. Willing to serve, happier to please. But after a while, it runs a little pale, doesn't it?"

Connerh grunted.

"And also like you, I saw an opportunity to do what my heart desired." His focus trailed to Connerh. "And so, I took it," Reh'gara's eyes flared before he ran his hands over his face. "As you are aware, the heart is a treacherous decision-maker, and there is always a cost." He spoke behind his hands. "We are all slaves to consequence." His hands lowered, his eyes focused. "Funny little expression, isn't it? We always blame the heart, as if it were something or someone else entirely, something more than what it really is: our purest selfish desire, expressed in another voice from the same body – free from the chained realms our minds inhabit."

"And what is it that your heart desired?" Connerh asked.

Reh'gara's expression softened.

"What every man wants." His lips curled into a smile. "To create. To have children. To have his actions count for something," he continued, his smile fading. "To be loved…feared…remembered."

He shook his head to himself.

"You can't have everything," Reh'gara nearly whispered, looking up at Connerh. His subsequent laugh was soft and subtle.

Connerh watched him quietly, studied him until he finally offered a nod of agreement.

"But I never answered your question, nor the ones you've yet to ask. Could I intervene in man's trivial affairs? Yes…but soon the cost of such interference would be more than any of us could pay. And to what end? Should you save all the grass from the sheep? And the sheep from the wolf?"

"They would all die," Connerh replied.

"Except the grass. The grass always grows. Even if it were to die, it would be reborn. It persists," Reh'gara said.

"And what is the grass?" Connerh asked.

"The grass is consequence…"

Connerh's brow grew heavy.

"…And I need your help to delay it…just a little while longer. She needs you…"

CHAPTER SIXTY-FIVE

AGENCY

ELARION

Madika's eyes were clenched shut. Elarion's mental world was loud – not in a sharp, piercing kind of way, but in ambience. Birds chirped, the echoes of their songs travelling through what sounded like a deep forest. Dogs and their pups barked and yipped as they chased each other, and the sounds of a brook bubbled nearby. The smells were rich, fresh, and alive. Her head moved to the curves of the scents as they traversed past her nose. A breeze blew, shuffling her clothes.

"What are you doing?" Elarion asked, his tone more natural and humoured, his stoic nature abandoned.

"I can't comprehend how it feels so real… No…truer than real, if such a thing were possible. I'm savouring this before adding what I'm sure to be absolute beauty and brilliance," she said, giggling.

"All things are possible in the mind," he replied. She felt him leave her side and walk onwards.

"You must be Madika." The words were simple, but they stung, like a punch in the gut. The voice was soothing, calm…feminine. Madika initially knew nothing of the originator, but her mind, intertangled with Elarion's, quickly sought information. His mind offered her answers with open arms and no reservation – the freedom of which made her sink into herself. She wished for a lie but only received the unfiltered truth in every spectrum of

517

thought and emotion. Her face wrinkled, her shoulders slowly dropped, and she became aware she was being watched. Her eyes drifted open as her head drifted downwards. She took a moment to marvel at the grass, the colour a rich, soft green. It was trimmed and looked soft, the perfect height to sit on. Of course it was. Her head raised, her eyes locking on the figure who spoke to her. Even in all the splendour of the world Elarion had created here…it paled in comparison…

"I was right," Madika murmured, her voice trailing into a small, shallow laugh.

Elarion stood behind a woman whose complexion resembled Madika's, but without blemish – perfectly sun-kissed and olive. Her cheekbones were subtly defined, and her lips lined her face with a soft, natural fullness. Her hair was the purest expression of white. A silver circlet shimmered around her forehead in the sunlight, and her dress was made of bleached linen.

She looked like a painting.

"She *was* beautiful, Elarion," she said, her voice cracking, dripping admiration and embarrassment for her private thoughts. Falling for Elarion was never a thought that crossed her mind until now. Or maybe it was, and she'd ignored it, shelved it in the back of her mind, only now for it to come rushing to the forefront in the face of inadequacy. Their bond was…intimate, unique…or so she thought. But that was the nature of telepathy, the melding of minds on a spiritual layer. She felt foolish. Even in the world of make-believe, she was one step behind.

"Was?" the woman asked, looking at Elarion and back again.

"She yet lives," Elarion replied.

"What?" Madika asked, not fully comprehending. She could've reached out mentally to seek the answer, but a part of her didn't want to know…to receive confirmation of it.

"She lives here, within me. Literally," he said. "Madika, I'd like you to meet Roselyn. I assure you, she is as real as you are," he explained, smiling. She bowed to her, approached, and kissed her hand.

"Here, we are not Tu'Chauri. Those customs are meaningless, but your intent is appreciated," Roselyn replied. She grabbed Madika's hand and kissed it in return.

"I…I don't know what to say," Madika stumbled over her words.

"It's okay. I understand. He's charming, good-looking, and lives through his heart," Roselyn continued. With a sigh, she continued, "That's why I fell for him, what must be hundreds of years ago by now."

Madika blushed.

"She has access to the link, and thus both of our thoughts. She's just a bit more…prone to prodding than I am," Elarion added with a grin.

"How?" Madika asked, her voice weak.

"You are witnessing the limits of power…in this stage of life, anyway," he replied, stretching out his hands. "The physical manifestation of thought is beyond me, currently."

"Meaning you can't bring her back to the real world?" Madika asked.

"No," he said slowly, as if it were an admission of his failure. "But your understanding of what is *real* will be adjusted…in time."

"But…how?" Madika asked again, her voice still unsteady.

Elarion took a deep breath, eyes closing briefly. He looked distant.

"There are rules," Roselyn added, her voice smooth – too calm.

"In the same way that a shadow of a person lingers when you link for too long…you can learn to capture all of it. Even the soul," Elarion replied.

"The physical is a privilege granted to us by something else…something higher."

Madika's brow furrowed. "By what?"

He shook his head slowly.

"You're not ready for the answer. Most aren't. Life in this world is still in its infancy stage, and what you enquire after…is beyond your capability to consume."

She narrowed her eyes.

"You speak as if you're external to it."

He paused, a faint smile tugging at the corners of his lips.

"Perhaps I am."

"But you choose to stay behind?"

"He does," Roselyn answered for him.

"Why?"

"I don't know yet," Elarion admitted, "but I'm compelled to."

Madika looked at Roselyn. "But what about Roselyn?"

"She's not going anywhere."

"But what if you die?" she pressed, her voice rising.

"In the physical realm?" Elarion tilted his head. His tone was gentle, almost amused.

Madika swallowed. "I don't understand, Elarion," she uttered, panic now threading through her words.

He laughed – softly, warmly.

"Lysand will make it clear," he assured her, as if speaking of an old friend.

"You mean I suffered for nothing? I could have just…ended it all, and still woke up…in a place like this?"

"No." His voice sharpened. "That's a lie told by charlatans. Even this – this space, this memory – is a privilege. But it is obtainable…by relatively simple means."

Barely above a whisper, she asked, "Why me?"

"That's the question, isn't it?" he replied. "Unfortunately, I cannot answer, as I do not have it to offer. I go where I am told. Find who it is I am to seek. Help those who are in need of assistance."

A long pause followed.

Then Roselyn stepped forward, her tone laced with a quiet empathy. "You've had a hard life. It's okay to feel with every fibre of your being. Hate what is bad, love what is good…even if it's my husband." She smirked at Madika. "He needs someone in your realm."

The sheer absurdity of it broke something loose in Madika. She laughed – suddenly, loudly – caught between hysteria and relief.

"This is a projection! By far the best attempt to pick up a woman I have ever seen!" she shouted, still laughing.

But Roselyn and Elarion didn't join her.

Roselyn walked over, silent and steady. She reached out and rested her palm on Madika's face.

The air escaped Madika's lungs with violent ferocity. She gasped, then froze as eighty years of Roselyn's life joined with her own memory in a single flash – a torrent of sorrow, joy, regret, and love.

Time collapsed.

Madika watched quietly from a distance as Elarion sat beside Roselyn's bedside. She lay there – frail, breath shallow, skin worn by time – yet her fingers remained interlocked with his, cupped gently between them.

"It's not fair. You look as old as the day I met you," Roselyn murmured, fighting for each word through ragged breaths.

Elarion smiled, the corners of his mouth twitching into a faint chuckle.

"Would you stop, you old fool?" she added, her voice light with humour despite the weight in the room. She laughed softly, but her eyes were glassy. She whispered, "It's okay to feel."

He looked away.

"Go on," she nudged him, her tone more of a plea than a command.

He nodded.

And then – without warning, without restraint – the tears came. They poured silently, cascading down his face while his expression remained fixed, calm but shattered. Only an occasional sigh betrayed the full force of what churned within.

Roselyn watched him, intrigued and pleased by what she saw. "In the end, it won't make you feel any better," she declared, her voice weak but steady. "But it makes me feel loved and cherished, knowing that losing me moves you in such a way. That grief... It's the most honest expression of love, my dear."

Elarion swallowed hard. "I would travel to the ends of the world if it meant keeping you." His voice cracked under the weight of the truth.

She smiled, pulling his trembling hands up to her lips and kissing them tenderly. "It's okay to let go."

"I can't," he confessed, and this time, his body broke with him. His face crumpled, and he sobbed – the kind of sobbing only known to those with nothing left to hold on to. Ugly, human, helpless. "What if there were a way..." he started, voice faltering. "But I fear it embraces the dark ways."

She narrowed her eyes gently. "What do you mean?"

"It robs you of your free will. You'd live on forever – a part of me – but only as long as I will it. You'd vanish the moment I let go, and you wouldn't have the power to stop it."

His shame was visible, each word tearing him apart further.

Roselyn blinked slowly. "How is that any different than now, my love?"

He sat in that question for several long moments, letting its simplicity strip him bare. She had a point.

"Just promise me one thing..." she urged, voice barely above a whisper.

"Anything."

"When I'm ready to go...you release me. No resistance. No guilt," she requested.

He sobbed again.

"Otherwise, you want me only for your own selfish desires…not for me to live on my own terms."

Eventually, he nodded – subdued but accepting.

"I understand," he whispered.

Then, with practised stillness, he turned off the tears as if flipping a switch – a gesture so human it hurt to witness. Roselyn smiled through her own exhaustion, shaking her head with jealous admiration of his ability.

"Well…go on…ask me," she teased, her tone rising just enough to cut through the grief.

He chuckled, despite everything.

"I would be honoured for you to join me through time," he invited.

"I would love to. What are you waiting for?" she replied, her eyes gleaming with mischief. With a painful chuckle, "Just promise me I won't look like this."

He laughed while he gazed at her – traced the lines of her aged face with reverence, her body still retaining its aged curves.

"It was a beautiful form," he said.

She blushed.

"For as long as it lasted."

He leaned in, pressing a gentle kiss to her forehead.

"It's the lips you'll miss," she joked, laughing.

He laughed too, his smile deepening.

And then, with love unspoken yet fully understood, they kissed for the last time.

The air filled Madika's lungs in a gasp. She struggled to catch her breath, even though the sensation was an illusion.

"I don't understand," she said. "What happens when you die? What happens to *her*?"

Roselyn smiled – soft, assured – before answering.

"Then together, we would both join a beautiful, violent array…of nothingness." Her voice was calm.

Certain.

Madika wept. The grief wasn't hers, not entirely. It surged from Elarion – raw, tidal, rushing through the link they shared and overwhelming her.

CHAPTER SIXTY-SIX

OUR LITTLE SECRET

LENA

Many years ago…

"Just breathe," Connerh said, a futile attempt to keep Lena from fidgeting. She picked at her nails, just as she did as a little girl. She'd kicked the habit as a pre-teen, when she met Connerh…but it came rushing back, like tidal waters crashing over parched sand. It wasn't the picking that provided comfort, it was the completion of it…the resolution of the problem. A mental reassurance that balance was in store, a hit of dopamine her reward.

But it wasn't working.

She repeatedly exhaled through her nose, her eyelids burning and watering with each occurrence. Her nerves were so inflamed that even looking at him – the very sight of comfort and reassurance – made her want to crumble, to come undone at the seams. But Mother always said, *Dignity before distress.* So, she avoided his eyes yet stayed close enough to feel the warmth of his orbit.

His brows smashed against his lids like dead weight. He hated seeing her spiral like this. He felt powerless to stop it, save for offering words that held little value – and even smaller impact. But they were programmed within him to utter, like legs to walking. His intent was pure, no matter how impotent…

Because taking the panic from her was never an option.

Had it been, he would've – every time, without a second thought.

Her embrace was desired, but her dignity was his priority.

The two guards posted at her mother's door stood motionless, wishing they could disappear from a moment that was never meant for them – and yet here they were.

"Give us a minute," she fussed, pinning the awkwardness on them. Her voice stayed restrained, no louder than a whisper. They obliged without hesitation.

"What's the worst she'll say?" Connerh asked.

"Say?" She stopped fidgeting and looked up at him. "I'm not worried about words. It's what she'll do that concerns me."

"She wouldn't do anything…not drastic, anyway," he offered, trying to reassure her.

"You don't know her like I do. She's liable to have me beheaded," she replied, dismissing his comfort without malice.

Connerh laughed.

"I'm glad you find it funny," she argued as a bead of sweat slipped down her forehead.

"Our men have tracked Tyreek as far south as the Wastes in the kingdom of the Far Sands. There have been some injuries, but as of the last report, no casualties. He's holed up in a cave of some sort, which is heavily guarded. With your blessing, I intend to send three detachments to end this and bring home the innocent," Hargatha reported.

"Like a snake to his den. Of course. Make them suffer," Io replied, brushing her hair in front of her mirror. She paused, lowering her hand.

"Any idea of the number of women and children they managed to kidnap this time?" Io asked.

"I can't be sure, but at least eighty that reached the caves. Only the gods know how many are inside," Hargatha answered. Io shook her head, her hands collapsing into her lap.

"Send *seven* detachments. End this once and for all…exterminate the vermin. Every single one of them. And if the Three Princes of the Far

Sands have anything to say about it, add their heads to the top of the pile," Queen Io replied.

"I'll see to it. Should we alert them to our activity in the area?" Hargatha asked.

"No. I don't recognise their authority, nor do I trust them. For all we know, they're involved."

There were gentle knocks at the door following a familiar cadence. Io smirked.

"Come in, Lena," she invited, returning to her brushing, watching the door through the reflection of the mirror. Her smile faded as Connerh entered.

"Hello, Mother," Lena greeted, nodding to Hargatha. Her tone was abnormal, having strayed from her normal, fiery and determined pitch and volume. Io frowned, pausing before turning to face her.

"What is it?" she asked, her intuition ringing familiar notes.

Lena feigned ignorance.

"You're either here to tell me something bad…or something terrible," she stared at Lena, her eyes trailing to her stomach. "You're not pregnant, are you?" she asked, her tone chilled. The follow-up course of action, had it been true, was primed on her tongue.

"No," Lena scoffed, a look of disgust flashing through her eyes in response to her mother's questioning.

"Oh," Io replied, looking her over once more. "I was going to say, I'm not paying that potion maker to keep your womb empty for nothing," she said with a chuckle – returning to her mirror-bound activity, her glare persisting. "He's still coming by with a little something for you to drink each week, yes?"

"Yes, Balfour is still delivering your poison," Lena replied, her eyes squinting. "And I drink it each time, hoping it overachieves and takes me." She feigned a smile. Connerh gently elbowed her with a frown, his head shaking forcefully, the only thing he could do without speaking.

Io stared, eventually breaking into a deep chuckle, her sarcasm at the ready as she quipped, "I'm sure he could adjust the recipe if you'd like."

"Funny you should mention it," Lena replied.

"You should really speak to me more respectfully. I am your mother, or have you forgotten?" Io asked.

"You would never let me, and there's no potion for that. I've checked."

A dense silence filled the room. Connerh and Hargatha exchanged uneasy glances as Io and Lena's gazes locked in silent confrontation. The unspoken dialogue between mother and daughter stretched tightly until finally, something subtle shifted in their expressions – a mutual understanding, a temporary truce.

Io's eyes softened. "How is the old man?"

Lena sighed; her shoulders relaxed.

"He's doing fine. He has some new pet, I hear," she answered, plopping herself into a velvet and gold chair.

"Oh? He never struck me as the animal type; he's far too skittish."

"This one doesn't have fur."

"What?" Io asked, turning in her seat again.

"Nothing."

Io grinned with confusion. "Well, go on. Out with it, girl. What have you two gone and done now that you fear my reaction to it?" she asked, her grin deepening confidently now.

"Connerh proposed," Lena replied, the words as precise as a knife's edge. She stared directly into her mother's eyes, allowing no chance for interruption. "And I said yes."

Her neck and back stiffened, muscles coiling tight as she braced herself for the inevitable storm of rage. Thrown things and violent screams, the usual accoutrement she was accustomed to in moments like this.

But there weren't any.

Connerh moved in closer, reaching down to hold her hand. Hargatha's eyes widened. Io's eyes tracked him for the moment, returning to Lena as her half-humoured, half-deliberating expression remained on her face.

Io's expression finally grew plain.

"Leave us, Hargatha. And take *him* with you," she commanded, her voice hardening to steel.

Hargatha complied without sound or acknowledgement; none was needed. Connerh instinctively dug his heels into the ground, ready to fight, to demand he remain by Lena's side – but her expression of resignation loosened his grip on the world. He became easy prey to Hargatha's purposeful stride as she ushered him out of the room, her hands resting on his shoulders.

She wasn't pushing him out of danger, she was pulling. He just hadn't realised it.

The doors thundered as they closed behind them.

Hargatha's gaze and hands lingered on the door for a moment, her mind racing.

"Very risky," she muttered, just before turning around to face him. "A good play…but risky. You should go…go to my home in the mountains. Tell Brand I sent you. Tell him you're there for safekeeping," she instructed in a hurried rush.

Connerh didn't understand.

"Go!" she shouted, sending him scurrying away as she remained by the door.

"I never wanted any of this, you know?" Io chuckled softly. "The gowns, the gold, the servants. I had no concept of this life at fourteen years of age, when I was taken…given to your father, as was the arrangement made by *my* father."

Lena's head swung to the left, low. She did everything not to roll her eyes. She'd heard these words before, her mother's sacrament. Guilt to disarm. Feigned sadness to garner sympathy. Maybe a few tears that bled into anger. Hurt. Withdrawal. By the time Lena was leaving, she'd feel guilty for…well, everything, though she was never quite sure why. Truth be told, she preferred the violent version.

"It bought peace between our families…between giants and men. It quelled a brewing rebellion that would have surely ended in a bloody civil war, possibly the extinction of our people." She paused to stand, her gown parting slightly. She wore nothing underneath.

Lena averted her eyes, no longer strong enough to deny them their rolling.

"But you know what? I didn't care…because I didn't ask for any of it. It wasn't my problem," she recalled. "Do you know who else didn't care? My cunt!"

Lena's eyes widened. She hadn't heard that one.

"Your father was kind, far kinder and gentler than any other giant man would have treated me. He waited until I stopped growing, believing that once I reached maturity, I'd be able to *comfortably* accommodate him inside of me." Her gaze wandered. Lena felt sunken in her chair, too embarrassed to move, to draw attention to herself – her eyes were still pinned wide. "Sadly, that day never came. But I'd begun to fall in love with him by then, and so I offered myself to him regularly. I became consumed with being enough for him…and then giving him children." Her brow crumpled. Lena's shock faded, a frown quickly replacing it. "Turns out I wasn't good for that either." She stopped to linger on a private memory, her eyes watering. Her gaze and focus were strong, deeply focused down and away. Her brows tried to pull her eyes upwards, but they refused to cooperate. "Only with Reh'gara's blessing could I have Bjorn, and then you." A smile broke through her trance, directing her attention to her daughter. Lena stared at her blankly, having identified the sacrament. "The gods know I tried to give him more…" Her eyes wandered again. "And then, when I loved…when I *actually* loved him, as I was meant to, those savages took him from me. They thought I'd run…not assume the throne, as was my right," she scowled.

Lena's eyes watered, and her gaze broke.

"They're not savages. Remember, they're my people too," Lena replied.

"You don't know them like I do. Make no mistake, all people can be savages. Giants are just capable of it…in far worse ways," Io corrected, her voice trailing to a whisper as a memory sapped her volume.

A few moments of silence passed, but it wasn't awkward. It was deserved. Io closed her gown, wrapping it tightly with a belt.

"I know you didn't ask for this either. Were the world truly yours, I know for a fact you'd wander to every edge…living a life of freedom, of choice."

Io's face softened, her eyes watching the internal fantasy, a smile forming as she imagined her daughter truly happy. Her expression suddenly blanked, and she looked around her massive room, with ceilings so high she'd never reach, with trappings and luxuries surrounding her. Her eyes fell.

"If I could go back to thirteen…I'd run," she whispered to herself, though it was still audible to Lena. She rapidly blinked away the water pooling in her eyes, and her head searched for something new to focus on. With one final sigh of resignation, she acknowledged, "But that's not an option, is it? We just have to deal with the lot chosen for us." Her posture straightened as she wiped her eyes. "And this is the lot chosen for you." Her voice steeled, a brow arched. "Did you think by forcing him to propose to you, you would somehow force my hand?"

Lena stood quickly, declaring, "I didn't force him to do anything!"

Io scoffed. "You really think I'm stupid, don't you? Or perhaps it's much simpler than that. Perhaps you are the stupid one. Men like that can't love people like us."

"Here we go again!" Lena shouted.

"Get over yourself, girl. Men like him only want two things: a warm cunt and a legacy. And you can barely provide one of those things!" Io scowled, her tone sharp.

Lena's mouth fell open, her complexion reddening before she remarked, "At least one of us is good for something."

It was quick, at full volume and strength. The gloves were off. Io approached her calmly, though her face was red. She smacked Lena with all the force she could muster, but Lena stiffened her neck moments before the impact landed. Her head barely moved.

She grinned through the pain as angry tears streaked down her mother's face.

"If you weren't so fucking unlovable, someone might have tried again," Lena continued her retaliation. "But you are incapable of receiving love, just as much as you are of giving it!" Her shouts echoed.

Io shifted her weight, swinging her palm again, but Lena caught it by the wrist. They locked eyes. Suddenly, Lena felt the acid drain from her veins, pushed out by clarity.

"We're not doing this anymore," Lena said, forcing Io to lower her hand to her side. The giant blood running through her veins gave her added strength – and something more. She felt alive, felt something awaken within her, fierce like anger but cool to the touch. "It's time to grow up, Mother."

Io looked at her, confused. Shocked, uncomfortable with Lena's iron grip on her wrist and her inability to move it. She tugged at Lena's grip.

"Connerh and I *will* marry. You *will* name me your successor, and maybe, just maybe, I'll forget how you've treated me my entire life – and perhaps I'll slow down a little as I hurl you from this pathetic carriage you call life," Lena decreed, devoid of emotion.

Io broke free from her grasp, falling backwards and to the ground. She looked up at Lena, the rims of her daughter's eyes glowing blue from the faint shadow cast by her hair. She reached for a hidden dagger nearby and aimed it at Lena, panic in her eyes. She stared at her daughter but saw a memory.

"You're just like them; your blood is corrupted," she gasped in disbelief, her aim hardening.

Lena's confusion overtook her expression. Io crawled backwards, grabbing a large candle holder to steady herself and stand, unwilling to turn her back on Lena. It fell with a loud crash, darkening the room. Lena's eyes were now glowing clearly.

"Oh, get up!" Lena shouted, her disdain on full display.

Io scrambled up as quickly as she could. She pointed the dagger at Lena, declaring, "You leave me no choice." Her words were rushed, pleading. "You will never see him again. I will command Hargatha to send him to the front lines in the Far Sands, where he will most certainly be killed within the hour," she began to rant.

Lena's mouth opened in preparation to protest as she took a step forward, a chill of fear tracing her spine.

"Back away from me, you savage!" Io screamed, her voice breaking as she continued to put distance between them. "I can't believe you struck me. I am your queen! I could have you hanged for this!" Her tone was beyond all reason. "Telling me what to do as if I were your servant!" She scoffed. "No! There will be no marriage, just as there will be no man. Egress will be named my successor, and she will care for you and your brother, though you do not deserve it. With my guidance, she will rid this kingdom of your kind, including the snake of a mother that birthed her. You are not fit to wear the crown, though chains are potentially in your future!" she screamed, spit flying from her mouth. "You ruined it! You ruined it all! If only you had kept your mouth shut and your legs closed! You discontented, small-minded whore!"

Lena stormed towards the doors, swinging them open. She saw Hargatha standing there…alone. Their blue eyes locked.

"Don't you dare walk away from me when I'm speaking to you, child!" her mother screamed. Lena slowly closed the doors and turned around, walking back towards her mother as the woman kept shouting at her, lost in her own rage. For a passing second, Io flinched, drawing back when Lena came to stand directly in front of her. Then she pressed forward again, puffing out her chest.

"Kneel!" she demanded, levelling the dagger at her.

Lena kneeled, slowly and deliberately, fighting every dark inclination racing through her mind.

"I could slice your neck and toss you over the balcony of *my* throne room, where you could join your brothers and sisters who never were. As dead as the day they were born," she hissed, shaking, eyes running with tears. "But I will show you mercy for the last time. And, if you are lucky, I'll only lock you in a tower for the rest of your miserable life," she shouted.

The dagger was silent as it entered Io's chest, the only sound being the gasp that escaped her lungs. Lena's hand was wrapped around her own — and the hilt.

It all happened so quickly.

Lena overpowered her and redirected the blade in what felt like a blink, an instant.

Lena was unsure of what to feel; her expression was an amalgam of emotions.

But she knew regret wasn't among them.

Io continually gasped as the blade was removed and reinserted.

Over and over again, as if Lena found new resolve with each stab, the cadence quickened with every second.

"It's the first time you've been speechless," Lena noted, an involuntary comment with an awkward scoff. "I loved you…once. If that counts for anything." She dropped her gaze, shaking her head in small back-and-forth movements. The dagger fell from her hands, ringing as it hit the floor, bouncing twice. "I'm going to be okay, I promise," she whispered in Io's ear.

Hargatha's hands rested on Lena's shoulders. She scowled at Io, observing the way her face still contorted in shock and pain.

"You need to get out of here. I'll take care of it," Hargatha instructed with cold precision. Lena snapped out of the calm that had wrapped around her like a warm blanket, now exposed to the cold reality of what had occurred. Her head and focus danced around, looking for a logical path forward.

"Better yet, wait," Hargatha continued. She moved to the door quickly, screaming for the guards. Within moments, two appeared.

"Get in here, Her Majesty has been attacked! Why weren't you at your posts!?" she shouted at them.

They panicked to come up with an explanation as they ran inside, Hargatha closing the doors behind them. One of the soldiers knelt by the queen, trying to figure out how to help her. Hargatha stole the sword from the other soldier's sheath and ran him through before he could react.

"What's going on?!" the other shouted.

Lena picked up the dagger and shoved it into his stomach quickly, just as he stood. Hargatha ran up and grabbed his head between her hands, the veins in her arms and neck bulging. His screams fell upon deaf ears, a whisper amidst the chaos.

And with a sudden jolt of her shoulders, his head imploded with a wet crunch, a bloody mess of bone shards and brain matter spilling out. She grunted as the adrenaline surged throughout her body, releasing his inanimate husk to the floor, reporting its descent with a loud thud. Hargatha stood hunched over, panting as she attempted to catch her breath. Lena sat on the ground in shock. In the suspended moment, she felt as if time itself had stalled: every heartbeat accounted for, a relentless reminder of life. Her breath came in shallow, rapid gasps, and her hands trembled uncontrollably.

"I'm sorry you had to see that," Hargatha replied, noticing. "As the story will go, this one killed that one, then the queen. We rushed in and I put a stop to it…but it was too late. The queen had already expired from her wounds."

Lena nodded in a frenzy, still not fully attached in the moment.

"Go! Take the hidden passages out of the castle, and go to Brand. Tell him…the little bird has found her wings. He'll know what to do," Hargatha spat, the command as sharp as a blade. She waved her hand, an impatient gesture.

Lena barely registered it, still stumbling to her feet, body moving on its own. Her gaze, though, locked one last time on her mother's body, sprawled in a pool of her own blood and the shattered remains of a man's skull. The sight hit her like a fist to the gut. Io, so small, yet so much blood. So much red pouring from her in waves, the venom of a lifetime spilling out. It burned on the floor, hot like it had always been inside her, hidden in the cracks of her skin.

Io's eyes met hers, slow and fading, as if reaching out one last time. There was no strength left in them, nor in her arms. Just hollow recognition. Nothing.

Lena's stomach twisted, and her head grew hot. A weight pressed against her chest, but her feet were already moving before she could drown in it. Her legs carried her forward, away from the room, away from the sight, but not fast enough to escape the image searing itself into her mind. She glanced back for one last moment. The faux wall opened before her, and as it closed behind her, the sound felt like a grave slamming shut. The reality she once knew now felt forever distant, slipping away.

"Why?" Io managed to utter with her final breaths.

Hargatha stood after relocating one of the soldiers' bodies.

"No one was ever good enough for you, Io. Not even me," she said, walking over to join her, standing over her. She kneeled. "That's what happens when you sit on an island alone. You're forgotten to the sea. Your sons marry and have children, your daughters breed kings, and your husband finds new love. And there you are, missing it all, on your throne of sand and emerald water," she sighed, shaking her head. "I loved him first; it should have been me next to him on the throne. He would've still been alive had he not been forced to marry you and turn his back on me. You thought children could quell what we had?" she scoffed. "You know that's why he even entertained the idea of you? He had difficulty getting me pregnant as well, but that was our secret… I thought it was me…turns out it was him after all," she laughed as Io's eyes widened, tears running, taking with them what heat remained in her body. "And now look, after all that, I'll be raising your children as my own, *for* you, and far better than you ever could. Funny how fate always wins, isn't it?" she looked up. "Throughout your life, you kept forcing my hand. If only you had just run away."

Io's breathing was reduced to forced gasps for air.

"Rest, friend. Now you are free," Hargatha whispered as she watched the light extinguish behind her eyes. "You'll get your wish. Lena will not be queen; I will," she promised, leaning into Io's ear. "And don't worry, I'll keep your little secret. No one will challenge my rule."

CHAPTER SIXTY-SEVEN

METHYLITE

ELARION

Madika and Elarion walked through the forest together, an awkward gap wedged between them. The city of Aylren unfolded in quiet layers between the trunks, where the trees thickened and the light broke apart into wandering strands. The scent of earth – rich, calming, and touched by crushed pine and the faint sting of tree sap – curled into every breath. Underfoot, the moss was thick enough to cradle bare feet, cool and damp, giving way just enough to remind the ground was also alive. Smoke drifted from low chimneys, carried by the slow, deliberate air that wandered with no urgency. The homes were modest, constructed with natural materials – living among nature, not disrupting it. Even the quiet had texture: a layered hush broken by the creak of a door, the rustle of leaves, the soft clink of a blacksmith's hammer in the distance.

And then fireflies littered the in between, just below the tree line but far above reach, gracefully creating light where the was shadow.

"I've never been to the Westwood. It's beautiful; I understand why the elves protect it so fiercely," she said, carefully stepping over a large, smooth stone on the ground.

"It is, but it doesn't quite look like this anymore. What you see here is one of my favourite eras…about five hundred years ago…give or take a few days," Elarion replied with a grin. She looked surprised. "Now, we've all but left the ground in most places. We live among the treetops with suspended bridges connecting it all," he went on. She looked up, trying to imagine it. He joined her, looking upwards as the scenery changed – a modern reflection of the present taking over.

"Wow…" They were the only words she could find to utter, the sound extended and nearly whispered. "And they treat you as they would their own there?"

His head lowered to look at her, his brow raising out of lack of understanding. "Why would they not?"

She looked at him, internally censoring her words. "Because you're different," she replied, briefly looking away.

"I believe…no, I *feel* they accept me because I'm different," he explained – a statement that was itself a riddle, needing context to truly grasp its meaning.

"There was a time when Tu'Chauri and elves were one people – a very long time ago. Back then, the Tu'Chauri looked different, spoke a different tongue…one quite similar to Elvish, I might add." He stroked his beard, eyes lifting as if peering through time. "I'd say they're all but extinct now. What remains is, I'm sorry to say, a diluted echo of what once was. And those who still claim the name? They bear little resemblance to it. What exists now is an amalgam – cultures and bloodlines blended over thousands of years. There's hardly any Tu'Chauri left." He stopped, focusing on her. "And that is why it all stopped. Why the line was drawn in the sand."

His gaze fell as the scenery began to change. Dark storm clouds gathered, a violent wind wiping everything away, leaving only grass and a dark, starry night. Madika watched with trepidation, convincing herself it wasn't real despite the way it very much felt otherwise.

"I suppose I should start from the beginning," he said, smiling, realising his rambling made little sense from an outside view. "Like all things, we have an origin. In the beginning, there were five original races – among them the elves, the giants, and the Tu'Chauri."

The words seemed to ripple outward, bending the quiet. Above them, the stars pulled apart like drifting ash. From the grass below, five towering silhouettes rose in solemn stillness, etched in dim light, undefined yet unmistakable. Each one stood apart, carved of different essence: one slender and graceful, another hulking and uneven, a third much like the first but with protrusions from the face. Madika stared intently at the third, finding it familiar but… She reached out just as they disappeared. The sky darkened slightly, and a thin wind stirred the grass, carrying the next words as the world began to listen.

"Back then, intermixing was allowed, even encouraged. As half-breeds bore children, and their children interbred in turn, a great mingling unfolded over a span of a thousand years. For a time, we were one large family. But, like all siblings, we began to drift apart. Some turned to nature, others to isolation, the sea, the mountains, or the deep refuge of caverns below the ground. And that's when everything began to change."

As he spoke, a horde of silhouettes appeared and began to move, slowly departing. Trails bloomed behind them – forest, ocean spray, curling stone, windblown tundra, and shadowed caverns. Each path unfurled and then dimmed, marking the birth of separation. Madika turned in place, following their dispersal with her eyes. There was no sound but Elarion's voice.

"Those who embraced nature became its caretakers, remaining close to the Architects of our existence and their allies. As faithful stewards of the land, they were gifted with exceptionally long lifespans. The others, preoccupied with themselves and caught in cycles of conflict, were not. And so, the divide between elves and all others grew wider." From the distant treeline that hadn't been there before, new shapes emerged – lithe and elegant, their outlines shone faintly with a green-white glow. Trees sprang up gently, slow and deliberate, branches forming over the grass like fingers folding over a secret. High above, the stars regrouped into orderly constellations.

"Even then, inbreeding had not fully ceased. The elves have always been a beautiful people – captivating in many ways, to many others. While some unions were born of love, others saw such pairings as a means to forge an everlasting legacy, breaking and bending the rules, hoping to steal that which was not rightfully theirs."

Two forms stood in the clearing, one glowing faintly like moonlight on water, the other heavier in posture, uncertain. The space around them flickered, unstable, as if the world itself couldn't decide whether their bond belonged. Madika's gaze lingered on the two, feeling a strange tension in their stillness.

"It was then that our Matron etched law into blood: any offspring born of an elf and another race would face one of two fates – either a mortal lifespan, or a long life stripped of the ability to produce an immortal heir."

A line of red light spread between the two figures. The grove around them shattered like glass struck by a whisper. Trees vanished. Light fell. The silhouettes dissolved into smoke, and once again, they were alone beneath the stars, only the grass beneath their feet remaining.

"A curse," she said.

"Especially for those unaware of its casting." He paused, and his head fell briefly. "The majority of elves see it as preventative tampering. Protecting a gift. It is a logical perspective," he added.

"So, they think they're better than us?" she asked, angered.

"Yes. In many ways, they are…but no one is perfect. Not even the elves," he replied.

"Tell them that," she argued. Taking a moment to think, she asked, "So, what do you consider yourself? Tu'Chauri or elf?"

His eyes fell to the middle of nothing.

"I try not to place emphasis on it. But what you see before you…is more elf than Tu'Chauri. So, if your judgment is based on sight…then I am elven. However, the part of me that is Tu'Chauri…is what makes me different from other elves…in more ways than one…including the Gift."

Her eyes lit up. He nodded.

"But by that token, I am more present here than I am out there… It's all about perception," he continued.

"No…go back," she pressed, her palms raised. He chuckled, intentionally torturing her by delaying.

"It is ancient Tu'Chauri blood which empowers our ability. Mine…is closer to the source, but it lies dormant even in your generation of offspring…occasionally springing to life as it has with you."

It took a few heartbeats for her to take it in. She shook her head as she glanced away.

"Did we all have it, once? And how old *are* you?" she asked.

He smiled and replied, "No, it wasn't rare, but neither was it standard."

She nodded, looking at him to continue.

He smiled instead.

"I'll get it out of you one day," she joked.

"Perhaps."

"I can't help but feel…"

"Overwhelmed?" he suggested.

"Useless…as if my life up until now had no purpose. Just drifting on the surface, waiting for the waves to take me under," she replied.

"You describe the feeling of most… So in that way, consider yourself normal," he offered.

"You'll forgive me for not rejoicing?" she asked sarcastically.

"Of course," he chuckled.

They shared a moment, their proximity reduced.

"What's it like…to live forever?"

"Honestly?"

"The only way I'd want from you…" she replied, moving closer.

He thought on the question, his gaze shifting, head in tow. "Agony." His eyes finally locked with hers, the joy having been sapped from his demeanour.

"Because of Roselyn?" she asked.

"No… Well, yes…partially." He grew frustrated with himself. "Agony comes in all shapes and shades, but in the end, it is all the same. It is what every person desires…the permission to be selfish. Permission to enact their will. But being denied it, though you are more than capable of expressing it," he remarked, irritation lingering in his tone. He sighed. "Being forced to watch the self-destructive behaviours of mortals, who do not desire to hear anything contrary to their hearts, who do not seek change, who repeat the mistakes made a hundred times over before them…and yet they never learn." He stopped, looking up at her, his mouth remaining open, hanging on a word. "It's maddening. But then…in the end, it's a battle of selfishness, is it not? Mine…versus theirs. So, in the end…aren't both wrong?"

"I imagine that's what the gods must feel like…" she said in a passing breath, her expression stuck in limbo as she thought on his words.

His head canted involuntarily.

"I never thought of it like that," he replied, his eyes shifting up and then down. She watched as he fiddled with the ring around his neck.

"What is that?" she asked plainly.

He looked at her, tracing the line of her eyes to his neck. He chuckled. "It goes by many names…but I much prefer the human term…totem. It kind of sounds like a heartbeat when you say it, doesn't it?" he replied. "It does many things." He laughed to himself again, burying his gaze in the ground. "When I am here…it tethers me to the physical world…and when I am there, it tethers me to her…here. Honestly, it's quite possible to get lost in both places. Does that make sense?" he asked, staring deeply into her eyes.

She nodded in understanding.

"Also…" he paused, his gaze falling away again. "I forgot to mention the other…curse…as you put it," he continued.

Madika's expression grew plain.

"Those of us with the Gift…*and* the blessing of eternal life… We often go mad…lost between the here and there. We quite literally lose ourselves." He stared at her again. "This is so I don't lose her…" His voice broke as he clung on to the ring.

He took several minutes to compose himself, and she rested her hand on his shoulder, her face crumpling.

"Because I grant her access to my mind…and thus my power…she can call to me through the ring… That's why it glows from time to time," he continued, a prideful grin etched into his cheek, forming dimples. "The metal is always cool to the touch…so I always feel it."

"That's beautiful, Elarion," she acknowledged.

He nodded, then blushed, insisting, "But enough about me."

"Is this what waits in store for me? Madness?" she asked.

"No…for two reasons… The first, you don't have the blessing…just the Gift. Secondly, you've already learned so much about controlling it…the voices. In time…you will be the master of it," he answered.

It was a relief for her, but it was also sad – the thought that she would die one day.

"So, the one you wish for me to meet is the…Matron, is it?" she asked.

"No…Lysand is not the Matron… That would be Amethyst. She does not make an appearance often, as she prefers working from unseen places so as to not be a distraction…unlike some of the other Architects. Though, in truth, they're called Candorians… I only substituted the word so that you might understand."

Madika shook her head, doing her best to remember the words and terms.

"As for me, I've maybe had the pleasure of meeting her a handful of times over my lifetime."

"I have a lot to learn…" she blurted out.

"Fortunately, the Gift allows us to slow time. You'll learn at exponential rates once you know how to perceive the lessons," he replied.

"I can…" she began.

He raised his hand to stop her, his expression souring as he said in a rush, "Someone is approaching, and it's not Balfour. I don't know who it is."

She panicked a little.

"Let's go," he said, grabbing her hand as they propelled into wakefulness.

Elarion opened the door to Madika's room just as the soldier raised his hand to knock.

"What?" Elarion asked, startling him.

"Her Majesty has requested the presence of Creature," he replied.

Elarion's expression darkened.

"What about?" Madika asked, pushing Elarion behind her, sensing his intent.

"That's not my concern, and nor should it be yours," the soldier barked.

She pushed Elarion again, fearing he'd kill the man. "Fine. I'll go…willingly." She looked back at Elarion, requesting, "Wait for me."

He took half a moment to calm himself…

…before finally nodding.

CHAPTER SIXTY-EIGHT

NO PITY FOR THE DEVIL

MADIKA

Madika glanced around Ioelena's throne room. It was grand.

Empty, dark.

Quiet.

She hadn't realised how hollow it could be in actuality, having only ever seen it packed with people. Yelling, shouting, screaming. They were always screaming. Her eyes lingered on the murals painted on the ceiling above. Various historical figures from Hildeheim's history were illustrated with masterful strokes in a heroic scene, vanquishing equally historic foes and rivals. The pillars that held the layers of stone, plaster, and paint high above made her feel small.

Have the paintings always been there? she wondered. Though she was modestly presentable, she felt underdressed.

"You wouldn't believe that the artist who painted that was as frail of an old man as he was. He hobbled up and down the scaffolding for months. My mother commissioned him when I was a little girl. I would sit in here for hours, watching him paint with an array of tiny little brushes with plain, wooden handles."

Lena's voice echoed from her throne as she gestured with her hands and fingers.

She'd been drinking. Heavily.

The cup was still sitting right next to her. The cask wasn't far off, judging by the painted drops of wine trailing into the shadows. She wore a gown of all black, with a train that flowed down the many steps leading to her royal seat. A sunbeam illuminated her silhouette in the darkened room, her eyes glowing in the comfort of darkness. She gently laughed to herself, recalling the memory. Madika's attention snapped to her, her head locked a quarter turn away. The image of her was unsettling, especially the eyes – even to Madika.

"He used to get quite stiff with me when I assaulted him with the meaningless curiosities of a child. If you look closely enough, there's a smudge just there, on Loadises' finger. I startled him one day, running in to show him a painting that I had made for him," she recalled, laughing once more. Still chuckling, she continued, "He yelled at me and called me a little shit. I was so upset I ran out of here like a wailing ghost, crying for my mother."

Madika continued to approach slowly, listening non-intently to her story. Her gentle footsteps barely made a sound.

"I could be a little shit…at times, yes," Lena mumbled, her gaze drifting into the void.

Madika reached a comfortable range and stood with her arms crossed, her hands holding her elbows. An unintentional scowl worked its way across her face.

"I ran to her, expecting to be comforted, but instead received a red bottom and orders to apologise for my selfish short-sightedness." Lena's smile faded. "True to form, I was then forced to clean his brushes and attend to his needs until the project was complete. Of course, he wanted nothing to do with me, so I sat facing the wall mostly. It's probably why I have such a distaste for art, come to think of it," she released a laugh, trying to lighten the mood, "but I wasn't being a little shit at the time, was I? I just wanted to show him my silly little picture, but he couldn't be bothered. I was only a child doing what children do."

She trailed off once more. Madika's brow raised as she patiently waited for the point of her diatribe. She snapped out of it, catching sight of Madika's expression.

"I'm sorry; that's not why I called you here. I swear, I didn't practise all that. To be honest, I hadn't looked up there in a while, and, well…seeing you do it triggered the memory," she confessed, looking up once more and straightening her gown.

Madika moved her head in a slow nod.

"I'm sure Her Late Majesty the Queen felt the punishment served a greater purpose…though seemingly heavy-handed, as you were a little one, after all. Parents are often locked in view of the future, whereas children only live in the present," Madika replied, her expression softening.

"You don't have to be polite to the dead. She was a stuffy old woman stuck in her ways and had children far too late in life," she scoffed. Madika's eyes widened, and she looked away, folding her arms behind her back. "Her womb was cursed. It seems we share a fate after all," she added, shrugging.

"On the contrary, Your Majesty, I feel that I do. Without the dead, how would we learn what to do? Or, perhaps, what not to do," Madika pushed back.

Lena's eyes rose at the supposed challenge as she responded, "Well, I suppose you *are* the expert on dead men, aren't you?"

It was a low blow that she instantly regretted; hearing her mother in her own tone spooked the sarcasm right out of her. She straightened her posture, retracting her fangs, as it were. Madika offered a humble smile, taking the jab with grace before lowering her gaze.

"I am sorry," Lena quickly apologised, recomposing herself.

"Apologies are not needed, Your Majesty. We can all be little shits…sometimes," Madika modestly quipped, folding her hands over her elbows again. Ioelena let out a loud half-laugh that echoed, and her lips folded inwards as she nodded.

"I deserved that," she offered.

Madika winked at her, signifying the subtle victory with a small nod. Lena leaned forward from the shadows, taking a moment to actually examine Madika. She'd put on a little weight; her cheekbones were no longer prominent. She looked…good. Healthy.

"Elarion sure has performed a miracle," she let slip, enamoured by the progress. Then, arguing with herself, she continued, "I'm having to apologise twice now, and it's not even been five minutes."

"I'm sure it won't be the last," Madika added quietly. "I'm used to it."

"What's it like now?" Ioelena let her intrusive thoughts win.

"What is what like, Your Majesty?" Madika asked, already having some idea but deciding to play coy. There was no sense in only one of them being uncomfortable right now.

Lena averted her eyes for a moment, thinking of the appropriate phrasing.

"First of all, please stop calling me that with every sentence," she huffed. "They say you heard voices all the time. A constant barrage of…of…different people?" she asked in shock.

Madika awkwardly nodded, not wanting to be pigeonholed into the past.

"And am I to believe that…that they are all gone?" she continued.

Madika nodded into a semi-shrug, her gaze trailing across the floor as she replied, "You're free to choose to believe what you want, Your…" She stopped herself from saying it. "However, they are very much still there. Just…a lot quieter now." Her eyes refocused, and she continued, "Thanks to Elarion, I can choose to…ignore them now."

Lena brought her hand to her chest and, as she drifted in thought, said, "Elarion… He is a powerful man. It's a shame he hoards it for himself."

"You must be speaking of another Elarion, as the one you speak of is not the same one that helped me," Madika pressed, lowering her arms. Her nose wrinkled when she spoke his name.

Lena noticed, and her brows lifted with a smirk.

"It was in jest," Lena defended herself. Then she jabbed, "I see you two have become rather well acquainted."

Madika took a step forward and snapped, "Must everything you say be forked in its meaning? Do you only find happiness in the distress of others? Of course, we know the answer to that. I've seen who you are." Having released the words burning inside her chest, she then recoiled, looking away as she held her other wrist. As Lena went to speak, she abruptly shouted, "Apologies are not needed!"

It was a strange thing to be unsure who was challenging her with Madika's mouth. Was it Connerh's memories? Elarion? Someone from her court? Or was it Madika herself? Reh'gara's handwriting had been proven right again. What a twisted, sordid affair she was in.

"Right." Lena course corrected, continuing awkwardly, "Look, as to why I called for you to join me… I don't know any other way to put it, but I have a request for you."

"Oh?"

"Yes…I need you to quiet some voices for me," Lena asked, resting back in her chair.

Madika's head canted, her expression mirroring her curiosity.

"I can't lose him again. I need you to enter his mind. Find a way to ensure he never leaves my side. Find out what made him leave, and then remove it…amputate it like a gangrenous limb," she demanded.

Madika's eyes widened, and she cautiously asked, "Enter whose mind?"

Lena delayed, looking her up and down.

"The gods have brought Connerh back to me," she replied.

Madika took a half step backwards, her mouth falling open, her face contorting with confusion and anger. "I want no part in this. I will not do it! I will not victimise him again for your sick pleasure."

Lena shot upright, then restrained her outburst by flexing her hands where they gripped the arms of her throne.

"You're really not used to seeing me without chains, are you?" Madika fired back.

Lena canted her head in disbelief.

"I'm not your little dog anymore! I'm sorry…that's not what you called me. I'm not your *creature* anymore! I will not rip away what belongs to him! His freedom to choose! It's not my place, and it damned sure ain't yours! You made me complicit in your crimes over the years…raping the minds of others…and I'll not be doing it again!" she shouted as spittle flew from her mouth, her cheeks vibrantly animated with colour.

"You don't understand—" Lena began, tossing aside Madika's refusal.

"It's not that I don't understand; it's that I don't care!" she shouted.

Lena climbed down the stairwell of her throne and headed towards her, lifting her gown so as not to fall. Madika intercepted her.

"You don't know what it's like! The ripping! Clawing! Pulling and shouting! Always shouting! They don't want to be there any more than I want them there! It's a terrible agony, and that's only half of what they go through!" she continued, her hands clenched into fists. "You don't understand what you do to people!" Madika shouted, trembling, loose tears losing their grip on her lids. "You don't know what you put him through," she continued, the strength in her voice weakening. She rushed to wipe her eyes dry. "But he's like me. We take the abuse. We remain. We'll always remain," she added, sniffling.

Lena stood, staring quietly.

"I am proud of you, I really am!" Lena grabbed her shoulders, pleading with her. "And I'm sorry for what you were put through – what I put you through. I know it's not any consolation, but because of you, lives have been saved! Don't you see how important that is? What a blessing that is?"

"A blessing?" Madika asked, shaking her head fervently.

"Who am I to question the will of the gods? It is my job as queen to ensure the scales of justice remain balanced. If that means making criminals a bit uncomfortable…then so be it," she mumbled.

"*Justice?* They weren't all criminals. Tell me, what is it like?" Madika asked. "What is it like to not give a damn about anyone else? Who lives? Who dies? What does it matter to you? Or to the gods? Just as long as you get your way, is that right?" Her accent and voice shifted as she snarled, "Well, damn you and the gods! I hope you suffer, and I hope he kills the lot of you! I'm damned sure you deserve it."

Lena looked saddened. She dropped her gaze for a moment, then pressed onwards, beseeching, "I simply need him to be as he was. Before the incident with Cassius…back when he was content in being my pillar…" She rambled on, half lost in memory, clinging to what was.

The shock and disbelief on Madika's face were tangible, and she backed away.

Lena grabbed Madika's arm, shouting in her face, softly crying, demanding, "You will bring him back to me." Pleading, "You must."

"I'm not doing a damned thing," Madika replied simply.

"You will!"

"Or what? You'll have me killed?" she snarled.

Lena pulled a concealed blade from her gown and held it towards Madika's neck, her darkness seeping out like a burst wound.

"I'm not that kind of queen. I do it myself."

Madika smirked, catching her off guard.

Lena was instantly teleported in time – to when she was on the other side of the blade. Madika leaned into the blade, drawing blood from her own neck before she took a half step forward, increasing the flow dramatically. Lena's expression twisted into horror as she flung the dagger to the ground as though it had seared her palm. Her gaze fell into herself – haunted, unblinking, her mother's body still vivid before her, as if the moment in history had just unfolded.

"That's all your kind ever does: talk. You're a predator, sure, but you're no killer. You just send someone numb enough like Connerh to do it for you, right? You wait to hear the job is done. Never have to see the bodies or smell the stench yourself."

Madika's voice and accent had now changed completely four different times.

Lena stared at her with a frown, bewildered and curious. When Madika saw Lena's face, she heard herself play back in her mind. She quickly covered her mouth, wide-eyed.

"They're more than just voices, aren't they?" Lena asked in morbid curiosity. "He couldn't get rid of them?"

Madika's expression flattened as she replied defensively, "Yes, he could have."

Lena looked confused.

"Then what would have been the point? What would I have learned? You can't just cut away the pain. After a while, there'd be nothing left," Madika continued.

"But you'll suffer," Lena replied.

"I don't suffer anymore. I live with the memories. The ones I want…the ones I don't. They all have a place, at times. But they are mine, and that means they are mine to live with. Who said I had to suffer because of it?" she asked reflectively. "I've learned to face my demons. Perhaps you should do the same."

Lena's eyes fell to the ground. The sound of the ocean in the distance filled the quiet moment.

"I already know why he left." Madika's voice broke the sound of the waves.

Lena's head snapped upwards, a desperation in her expression.

She continued, "And so do you."

With that, Madika turned to leave, but she paused halfway.

"I'm leaving Hildeheim – with your blessing, I am assured. I wish I could say I'll never see you again, but thanks to the memories of you, through his eyes…I'll see you for the rest of my life, as I do all my demons. I wish I could bring myself to bestow such cruelty on you…but I will not."

She glanced at the floor for a moment, then left.

There was a knock at Balfour's door. He stood from his chair abruptly, running to answer it, then paused upon seeing Madika standing there. She looked in a daze but snapped out of it once she caught sight of him. There was a pause as they locked eyes. She rushed to embrace him. Elarion stood from the table they were sitting at inside Balfour's home.

"Come, come," Balfour invited, leading her in and glancing around outside before closing the door. Full of questions, he promptly asked, "Well? Is everything alright?"

Elarion studied her face with anticipation. She reflected on the question for a moment before answering.

"Yes," she said, tilting her head upwards as if contemplating whether her reply was accurate. Then, repeating it more firmly, she said again, "Yes."

She looked at Elarion, who stood there awkwardly, not having the courage to do what she wished he would. She ran to him and collapsed, her head burrowing into his chest. He wrapped his arms around her and held on tightly. His scent was calming to her.

"I am free thanks to you," she whispered, looking up into his eyes.

His gaze drifted, landing on Balfour, who smiled from ear to ear in the background. He added, "Do not forget the efforts of Balfour. Without him, none of us would be here in this moment."

Balfour grew bashful and shooed them off. She pulled away slightly, resting a hand on both men.

"I could never," she declared as she held Balfour's hand.

He squeezed hers in return.

"I am leaving here, and I do not mean to return," she informed them both, referring to Hildeheim.

Balfour looked away as his eyes watered, and she winced at his sadness. Elarion remained silent, sensing her resolve.

"I'm coming with you, Elarion. I want to see the Forest. I need to meet all these wonderful people you've told me about," she continued, trying to move past her own sadness about leaving Balfour behind.

Balfour repeatedly cleared his throat as he looked at a wall in the opposite direction. She pulled at his shoulder.

"I am not safe here," she added, taking on a sombre tone, "nor most places. The secrets held in my head make me a liability, both to myself and those around me." She looked back at Elarion, realising the implication. Not having thought of it before, she asked, "Will that be a problem in the Forest?"

"No. The Forest will accept you and watch over you, as will I," he replied, nodding his head once as if confirming his words. She smiled.

"Balfour, you can come with us," she offered. Then, looking to Elarion, she asked, "Can't he?" Though it was framed as a question, in actuality, it was not. She frowned to ensure Elarion understood as much.

"Of course," Elarion replied, her message received.

"Oh?" Balfour asked, wiping his eyes and clearing his throat once more. The old man's mind raced, and his mood improved when she nodded affirmatively., "Well, I suppose…I suppose it is time for me to retire. I'd have to conclude some business dealings first, but yes…yes, that sounds wonderful." Then, realising it was perhaps not Madika's invitation to offer, he asked, "If…if you would have me, Master Elf?"

"There are a few to whom I would like to introduce you, for they also share your love of alchemy. I'm sure there are more than a few things you could yet learn," Elarion replied.

"Oh!" Balfour shouted as his cheeks flushed, and he grabbed at his chest, his mind wandering with the possibilities. "I hadn't even thought of that! I've got a few potions they could help me with that I've not been able to master." Lowering his head and promptly scampering around, he stopped abruptly and looked at them both when he noticed them smiling at him. Finally, he added, "But it would be a couple of days, a week or two at most, before I could leave."

"That won't be a problem, Balfour – relax your nerves. Right, Elarion?" she asked.

"That will not be a problem," Elarion replied despite the urge to leave sooner rather than later.

"Right!" Balfour declared, then paused. He quickly realised he'd sold short just how quickly he could be ready to leave, prompting him to urge, "No, no, you two go on. I'll meet you there. Just show me on a map what town or locale I am to go to." Then, seeing her about to object, he added, "No, no, I insist, don't start. I've got to make a few deliveries first, I just now remembered. That will only add…factoring in any emergency stops…a week and two days? Perhaps? Maximum…yes. Yes, that sounds about right," he concluded.

She moved in and hugged him again, instructing, "Two weeks and two days. I expect to be holding you again on the third."

A dimple formed in his cheek as he smiled.

"I demand it," she added.

He giggled, curtsying and dipping his head respectfully as he replied, "Yes, ma'am!"

She laughed. He held her shoulders and leaned back to look at her with admiration.

"What?" she smiled.

He lifted her hand and kissed it, telling her quietly, "I am very much proud of you."

Her bottom lip smushed up against the top as emotions welled up within her. She finally pushed him away and dusted off her dress as a distraction for herself.

"You're not going to make me cry, old man," she added.

Elarion and Balfour laughed.

"Do you need help gathering your things?" Elarion offered as another distraction.

The room went quiet. All smiles but Elarion's faded, and he wasn't quite sure why.

"All of my belongings are in that bag," she explained, pointing to a satchel resting on a bench in the corner. It was quite small, only being large enough to hold a few garments and rations. Elarion's smile washed off his face.

"You're going to need a larger satchel. We're going to pass through the markets on the way out and get you—" he began, defending her against the painful reminder.

"No," Madika interrupted, "that won't be necessary. I wear Creature's dress as a reminder. For them…and for me."

Elarion's eyes widened. He hadn't realised she was wearing the same version of the dress she had worn in the early days – only it was clean, not ripped and frayed. It was a dark blue with inlays of black, and mounting points for chains could be seen on the parts that covered her shoulders. She walked to her satchel and opened it.

"That reminds me," she murmured quietly as she reached in to retrieve a few items.

The rattling of chains filled the room. Elarion's eyes dropped. He connected the dots before the sight was revealed to his eyes.

"I had these made," she said, putting on earrings that looked like chain links. She reached into the bag once more and produced a necklace that also looked to be made of chains. She placed it over her head and fixed it around her neck so that it fit properly. Balfour looked away.

"Look at me," she instructed, sensing the shame they felt on her behalf.

They obliged reluctantly.

"I am not ashamed, so why should you be?" she asked. "They are a reminder…that I am free."

CHAPTER SIXTY-NINE

SCALES

EGRESS

Egress stared over the pit. Her crimson dress, sleeveless and embroidered with swirling patterns, clung to her frame. A single braid rested over her left shoulder, and a new crown of dark grey metal – its points jagged and spiked – sat atop her head. A resolute grin carved itself into her dimpled cheeks.

"It's so fucking hot here, I'm reconsidering the length of my stay," Hargatha joked as she approached, her tone sharp but laced with humour. She was still covered from head to toe in thick layers, leaving nearly no skin exposed. Egress glanced at her briefly, just long enough to let out a half-chuckle.

"You just need a new wardrobe, is all. You can't gallop around in the same attire you would on the mountain. It's not that bad, really... It's different," Egress replied.

Hargatha examined Egress as she came to a stop next to her, criticising, "You shouldn't have your shoulders exposed. It goes against—"

"Times change," she replied – a brief statement, but the glare that accompanied it said everything else that needed saying.

"But you're a queen now," Hargatha replied, her tone firming.

"Empress," Egress rebutted. "Even then, those are only words. It doesn't count until the world hears of my arrival." She tilted her head downwards and behind, not giving her mother her full attention. "How's the construction of my ships coming?"

Hargatha grinned to herself, her head dropping for a moment as she struggled to switch off the mother in her.

"They're good…coming along nicely," she replied after a brief delay, the grin refusing to vacate her expression.

"How many?"

"Seventy-five, but I want a hundred. At this point, we're waiting for Lena's next shipment of materials. I don't want to strip this land apart for lumber…we have to live here, after all."

"Seventy-five is already double the largest sea-faring fleet on the sea. Why a hundred? No one has a hundred," Egress fussed.

"That's why I want it," Hargatha replied quickly. "We're not talking about establishing a new kingdom from the dirt, we're talking about stealing an existing one. *Treason* is the word they call it, in case you've forgotten. We have to be prepared for anything…everything. You say it's near double the largest fleet, but we don't know what we don't know."

"What is that supposed to mean?"

"It means you don't prepare just for the worst; you prepare for the unimaginable. The elves are still a threat you need to consider, and they are as secretive as they come. We don't have a true idea of what power they sit on."

"The elves don't matter, they don't get involved…they never do."

"Someone once told me that times change," Hargatha replied calmly.

Egress stopped herself from answering, her head raised, finally turning to face her mother. A desperation clawing at her attempt to maintain resolve.

"I know you're eager to step out into the sunlight, but this is just a minor delay. Please trust me on this," Hargatha begged, resting her hands on her daughters' shoulders as her voice softened.

"How long?" Egress replied, allowing the moment to pass.

"Maybe another two to three weeks?"

Egress took a deep breath, sighing. It wasn't what she wanted to hear.

"And you don't think *this* changes anything?" she asked, motioning to the pit. Hargatha looked over the edge. The dragon's skeleton lay mostly uncovered, the bones of its wings fully spread, the tips still partially under the dirt. Men and giants alike continued working to unearth it.

It was enormous.

"Bones?" Hargatha replied.

"Don't play coy… It's more than bones," Egress replied. Hargatha grinned.

"What is it that you see, then?" she enquired, rubbing the sides of Egress' arms, the wind blowing their hair.

"Power."

Hargatha nodded slowly. Her hands fell from her daughter's arms. A deep breath punctuated the still.

"You're not wrong. But perhaps only in knowledge…and knowledge can be wielded as a weapon – the ownership of it and its manipulation. Knowledge can strike fear into our enemies…and maybe that is more important than ships…" She locked eyes with Egress. "But there's no reason we can't have both."

Egress agreed, but still didn't fully understand.

"I've not been completely forthcoming with you." She admitted.

Egress's head tilted, her brow slowly rising.

"I've been holding the ex-governor prisoner in secret…interrogating him when the need arises," Hargatha admitted.

"I know," Egress interrupted her, her gaze returning to the pit, a gentle tug of a dimple in her cheek.

Hargatha's mouth involuntarily opened.

"They really do see me as their empress. They tell me everything," she explained, turning to face her mother again. "And I need you to see the same…to do the same. Otherwise…*this* won't work," she continued.

Hargatha nodded, then asked, "How long were you going to keep it a secret? That you knew?"

"Until it was too late…"

Hargatha's head fell at her last word. It wasn't a threat; it was an understanding. Egress moved in, lifting her mother's head with her fingers.

"I'm sorry."

"Don't be. Change is difficult," Egress replied.

Hargatha's eyes widened, as if seeing her daughter as a woman for the first time. Her eyes traced the loose strands of Egress' hair down the sides of her face. She smiled as her mind drifted to memory. A few blinks pulled her back.

"How did I get so lucky? To birth an empress is a rare thing…" she murmured.

"An honour only befitting a rare woman," Egress replied, raising her mother's hand to kiss it. "Tell me…what have you learned?" she asked, shifting her posture and returning her attention to the men unearthing the dragon remains.

Hargatha needed a moment to compose herself, clearing her throat.

"For starters, your predecessor seems to enjoy a type of eroticism regarding giant women threatening to step on his chest… I'll need to find other ways to motivate him," she said, stretching her posture. Egress made a face, and Hargatha continued, "It's disgusting, I know."

"Regarding the dragon…it would seem this beast came from across the ocean… They've been coming every few years," she continued. Egress whipped back around, the excitement and curiosity overtaking her.

"There are more?" she asked in a hurry.

"Yes," Hargatha replied. "They're scattered everywhere. Apparently, this was one of the largest…and female." She paused to study Egress' reaction. "It would seem that when they arrive, they are drained of their energy…in a weakened state. Which would suggest…"

"Wherever they're coming from…is far," Egress interjected, turning around again, this time looking out to the ocean.

"Exactly."

"So, they die of exhaustion," Egress assumed.

"No. It's far worse. The people here surround and kill them. They carve them up and bury the bones. This one was lured to this spot; it was too large to bury on the beach. Too much of a risk of being spotted by boats in the area," she continued.

Egress's expression was one of disgust, horror.

"Why?!"

"Fear. Why else?" Hargatha replied, her tone casual. "After Con—" She stopped herself, her nose wrinkling. "After…the events that transpired here…some time ago…the last thing they wanted was to be the centre of attention again."

"They feared Lena more than a dragon? That's laughable," Egress remarked, fulfilling her own words.

"They suffered greatly…and had reason to be fearful." Hargatha's tone took a more serious note. "I've heard a new version of the events that differs greatly…from that which we have scribed into the history books."

"How absurd is it?" Egress asked, her smirk lingering.

"About as absurd as dragons…" she replied, her expression darkening.

She took a deep breath. "And that is why we prepare for the unimaginable."

"I see," Egress replied, losing her smile.

"The world is not as we've imagined it. And maybe…just maybe…that is the hidden weapon the elves covet." The wind blew a nearby banner, and the metal bar suspending it smacked against the castle, ringing like a bell, interrupting their discussion and drawing their attention to it.

Hargatha's eyes fell before her head did. She turned to Egress.

"Maybe it's time you forge your own sigil," she offered.

"But Father…" Egress rebutted.

"It's not his decision…or his future. The old lion has lost his bite. It doesn't strike fear into our enemies as it used to…" she murmured, looking into the pit from the bridge of her nose. "This is a new world we're entering…and we're going to need larger teeth."

"Any funny business, and I'll run you through," Hargatha ordered, a large sword forged for a giant pointed at the old governor's back. She hunched low, careful not to snag on the jagged rocks as they descended into the cavern, its tunnels never meant for someone of her size.

"Slow down!" she shouted, the nervous man moving too quickly for her – he also held their only source of light.

"I won't run off, I assure you," he answered, just happy to be free.

"You'd better not," she replied, her face scrunched with annoyance.

He waited for her to catch up, a fork in their path before them. He held up his finger, asking for patience, before cupping his mouth and letting out an absurd sound. It was a pitiful attempt at sounding like an animal…but it was distinct.

"You've got to be kidding me," she remarked, rolling her eyes. "*This* is your security?"

He looked up at her, momentarily getting lost in her eyes, her pale skin. She scowled at him.

"We think it's pretty clever," he replied.

"We clearly have different definitions of the word," she scoffed.

"If we don't follow the pattern, making the right turns, the right noises…then we pull levers and trap you inside with large boulders. The good news is, you'd suffocate before you starved to death. And this far in…no one would hear you scream," he explained with a smile. Her eyes shot wide.

"That actually *is* pretty clever," she remarked, her bottom lip pushed out.

"Now…you go right," he instructed, pointing to the fork.

She froze, her head held high as her eyes remained on him. She started and stopped her reply a few times, weighing her options. "You are a clever little bastard, aren't you? And why, pray tell, would I trust you?" she asked, looking down the corridor. "How do I know that's not my coffin I'd be walking into?" she asked, amused but cautious.

"Because I could've trapped you seven times by now. Besides, I wouldn't want to carry your body all the way back," he said, putting emphasis on the word *body*, eyes lingering a little too long. She raised the blade to his neck.

"Careful," she replied.

His smirk was devious, nasty.

She stared a little longer, convincing herself to ignore the warnings in her head.

"Alright," she finally announced, lowering her blade. "I'll play along." She sheathed her sword. "Just know, if I die…there'll be no one to step on your chest," she said, walking towards the entrance.

He giggled, shivering in place with giddy delight, all while licking his lips. He swore with urgency, "I'd never let anything happen to you."

She turned sideways and started down the right path, finding it cramped and narrow.

"Well, aren't you coming?" she asked, looking down at him.

"Once you're through, I'll follow… Just take the path to the end… There's light on the other side. There's no sense in both of us getting stuck if you panic," he said.

"Are you calling me fat?" she asked playfully.

"Never… You're just…a giant," he replied, logic chilling the temperature.

She took another moment to silence the voices warning her against continuing, ignored them against all reason. With a sigh, she pressed on. The deeper she slid, one step at a time, the more she doubted her decision.

Was some flirtation with hidden knowledge really worth this?

Worth death?

A humiliating one, no less…

Was she so desperate for leverage that she would risk it all?

She heard a noise, a screech…pausing her in her tracks.

It was unfamiliar, foreign…but quickly filled her veins with a surge of adrenaline, her movements increasing. Before long, she emerged on the other side, finding it dim on account of insufficient torchlight. A large, expansive cavern awaited, tall and wide enough to dwarf even herself. She smelled sea salt, sand, and rock. And something else…a stench like an animal, but different…stronger. There was a hint of something acrid in the air…but it, too, was unfamiliar.

Her prisoner emerged with much noise and grunting.

"Hurry up, Governor," she fussed, having been too distracted to internally rejoice that it hadn't been a trap.

"You know I have a name, right?" he asked, his torch revealing the sand under their feet.

"Do you?" she returned with a scornful smirk.

"Hey, now, you be nice to me," he said.

"I thought you liked it when I wasn't?" she replied.

He blushed.

"Go on…show me," she demanded.

He nodded, all too happy to please.

"It's about to get warm. You might want to shed a few layers," he suggested with a devious smirk.

"I'll survive," she replied, crossing her arms.

"Suit yourself," he said. Then, shouting, "Turning the light on!"

"Aye!" several voices echoed in reply, startling Hargatha.

"Stay here," he instructed, walking forward by about a hundred and twenty steps. He lowered his torch into a pool of something…that quickly lit fire, spreading, and revealing itself to be a pond of liquid. The cavern came alive as the light increased from the burning pool.

There was scaffolding everywhere. Rooms were carved into rocks. A makeshift nursery of sorts. The men and women who moved about in dim shadow stopped as they noticed Hargatha.

She returned their gazes…

Until a hiss startled her from behind.

CHAPTER SEVENTY

BEYOND THE PALE

VIDAR

The night's watch was often difficult. The hours dragged on, the weather could be inclement, and the isolation offered a type of silence that made one's own heartbeat audible.

But that wasn't the worst of it.

Idle minds. Simple games. Evil tricks.

It was seeing things that weren't real or defied reason, making the darkness all the more unwelcoming. It didn't matter how hardened the warrior, how fearless or practical; the eyes were a venerable opponent, an untrustworthy ally that easily rallied the other senses to promote a lie.

To make it seem reasonable.

To deify it.

Or demonise it.

The night air had cooled, the warmth of the day slipping beneath the horizon. In its absence, a stiff breeze rose, surging, gusting, unrelenting. Sevryn huddled beneath layers too thin to hold warmth, too flimsy to stand against the wind's assault. He kept watch over the camp, a quiet jealousy of his fast-asleep counterparts stirring in him – alongside his regret for leaving his overcoat behind in his tent. Leaving his post to retrieve it felt like surrender, a coward's admission of defeat.

And he was no coward.

558

Besides, it was far…

Though in truth, in distance, it was close enough. But in exposure – not counting the return trip – it seemed like a death march.

A strategic relocation, however…

Well, that seemed wise.

The manmade entrance to the temple was closer, shielded from the wind yet offering a clear view of the camp and the ridge beyond. But there was an eerie glow emanating from its mouth – something he swore he saw holding him in deliberation, a second's thought from action, each gust wearing down his better judgment. A rumble of thunder rolled in, drawn from clouds that crept forward, smooth and slow, uncertain of his existence. The sound brought a smirk to his cheek, a tilt to his head as he looked upwards as if to confirm its source – the unwritten, nonsensical rule we must all follow.

Had he manifested an excuse to satisfy his curiosity?

Or had one been provided to him?

The all-too-familiar smell instinctively thrust him into motion just before the first drops could fall. It was certain to rain – as sure as the sun would rise – and there was no sense in being cold…and wet.

He gathered his bow, sword, and effects, running towards the unknown with a sense of clarity at his heels, a hope for refuge in his sights.

It took a solid minute at full sprint before he crossed the threshold. The ominous red glow he'd seen from a distance was now nowhere to be found – never more absent than if he'd imagined it. He scoffed, chalking it up to a mirage caused by the dying campfire once flickering between them. Inside, the sound was dampened, the downpour reduced to an audible trickle. It stood in defiance of what he saw with his own eyes, but he ignored it, instead focusing on the most basic of needs. He rubbed his hands together to stir warmth, pausing to blow into them as if coaxing stubborn kindling.

The air was denser in the corridor, filled with the smell of burning pitch, and there at the end was the red, mist-like glow. His brow raised. Was something more at play? He pinched himself – physically and metaphorically – yet the mist remained.

He wondered what his employer was up to.

Remembrance of his duty pulled his gaze back to the camp. It hadn't moved, still weathering the onslaught of wind and rain, its tenants fast asleep and no enemy in sight. He sighed. Still, his curiosity lingered on the mist, pulling his eyes with it. He wondered if it were, in fact, beckoning him, or whether his mind simply preferred to deduce mystery rather than stare blankly into oblivion until sunrise.

An echo of a shout travelled from the depths of the corridor to his ears, piquing his interest.

Perhaps Vidar was in trouble, he thought.

He briefly looked at the camp before his feet propelled him into darkness, never a second thought to delay him further. He walked cautiously forward…

…towards the red glow.

"I'll need to warn my cousin first," Vidar said.

"Are you close?" a deeper voice replied, calm and authentic in its curiosity.

"Yes…I'd like to think so. I've always viewed her as the sister I should have had," Vidar replied. He kneeled on the ground before the Uridar, its surface aglow with activity. Chairs, candle holders, and curtains were levitating at varying heights, rotating on their own centred axis like the corpses of sailors being carried to the depths. "We're far from a normal family…though if I were to be completely honest, I couldn't point to an example of what is normal…so who am I to say?"

The voice laughed. It was layered with an oscillation that vibrated the walls.

"I could say the same about my own," it replied. Vidar chuckled, switching to sit flatly on his bottom. A white, mist-like aura seeped from the Uridar and into Vidar's head. He welcomed it, straightening his posture and leaning his head towards it.

"Which one? Sigherd?" it asked.

"Gods, no, that foul swine… Keep looking," Vidar mused. The voice chuckled again.

"Ioelena…? Lena…yes, this one resonates."

"That's the one…" he answered, his sarcasm and wit trading for rarely displayed tenderness.

"She has a brother, Bjorn…do you feel the same for him?"

"We were never that close, but sure, I suppose. We were both independent spirits, if you will… He had his quests…and I had my own. I don't feel strongly either way…but if you're pressing me, I would stop to give him food and water if I found him parched on the side of the road…if that answers your question?" Vidar joked, his signature smirk returning.

"It does. Are these the only relatives you care to save?" it asked. Vidar's expression flattened, his head dropping as his fingers fiddled with one another. He took a few moments to reflect.

"Yes," he replied, as if it brought him no pleasure to utter the words. "Oh…and Connerh… And, I guess, those dwarves out there…especially the one who's inebriated all the time."

"Understood," the voice replied. "What about the one peering from the shadows behind you?"

Vidar's eyes widened, and he rushed to his feet, every floating object falling to the ground in a loud echoing cacophony of chaos – spooking a startled Sevryn.

"I don't know who that is," Vidar declared, his eyes still glowing with the swirling white energy.

"Then let's find out," the voice said from out of Vidar's mouth. Vidar's hand raised, his arm outstretched. Sevryn was violently pulled forward through the air as if gripped by an invisible hand. He stopped moving after six or seven steps.

The voice grunted. "Well, that's different," it said.

"What's wrong?" Vidar asked, concerned.

"Your mind is matchless, but you lack the ability to express my full power."

Vidar frowned.

"Nothing to worry about; we *will* adapt," it said, shifting arms and hands, pulling Sevryn towards them again with alternating hands, like pulling a chain-bound anchor from the sea. Vidar raised the ranger high into the air once his neck fit into his grip.

"What name should I carve into your tombstone?" Vidar and the voice asked in unison.

"Sevryn! I work for you!" he shouted.

"I've never met you a day in my life," Vidar replied.

"Kill him," the voice insisted.

"Wait!" Sevryn screamed. "The dwarf hired me in your proxy! His name is Toke!"

"Likely story. We've been dealing with spies for some time now," Vidar replied.

"Let me look," it said.

The white energies trailed from Vidar's eyes and into Sevryn's head. The man's expression was full of fear and shock.

"He works for your mother," it said.

Vidar's spine straightened, his frown growing pronounced.

"Only as an information gatherer, and I've yet to send any type of report! I have no allegiance to her! I've never even met her personally!" Sevryn begged for mercy.

"He's telling the truth," it said.

"What do we do with him?" Vidar asked.

"I don't care. He poses no danger to us," it replied. Vidar dropped Sevryn to the ground. His body hit the floor with unexpected force. "Keep him around; we can steal his life force to heal you, should you sustain injury."

Sevryn's eyes widened. Vidar's brow raised.

"We can do that?"

"Yes."

"Wait…grab him," it said.

Vidar obliged, Sevryn trembling in his grasp. Vidar lifted his finger, pressing it against Sevryn's forehead. It made a sizzling, searing sound as he screamed. When complete, he lifted his finger away; a rune remained behind, etched into his flesh.

"What is that?" Vidar asked.

"A way to keep track of him. Now we'll know if he tries to betray us," it said.

"I didn't agree to any of this," Sevryn protested.

"You agreed to it when you obliged your curiosity," it replied, then sighed. "Let's go. As you can understand, I've grown a little tired of this place."

Vidar nodded, setting Sevryn down, albeit more gently this time.

The three of them stood at the opening – though only two bodies were present – as they watched lightning flash and thunder shake the ground.

"Step out into it…" it said.

Vidar hesitated.

"Please," it begged.

Vidar complied. His head lurched backwards, arms outstretched as the rain touched his skin. The voice let out a restful groan.

"It's been so long," it continued with a sigh.

Sevryn watched with fearful interest.

"Are you sure you'll survive gaining distance from the Uridar?" Vidar asked, the storm lashing him with a torrent.

"I've imprinted enough, though I may grow a little weaker the farther from my body we get. Still, we're talking elephants to ants in this world. Even reduced to a dog, you'll still be a god among them," it replied.

Vidar's head snapped towards the ridgeline.

"How many here do you claim?" it asked.

Vidar rushed to count. "Three. Two dwarves should be in their tents. And this one."

It grunted, reaching out with Vidar's arm. Four bolts of lightning fell like pillars, striking four previously hidden figures.

Vidar screamed in pain, cradling the hand it had just used. As the pain began to subside, he examined his fingers – singed, black at the tips.

"Interesting. That's a shame; I rather like that trick," it said.

Vidar grimaced.

"Don't worry," it continued, extending Vidar's other hand over Sevryn's head. A thin, white stream of energy began to leech from Sevryn's body. His face contorted, limbs twitching, a shriek of agony ripping from his lungs.

"See? All better," it said.

Vidar looked at his hand again. His mouth fell open. It was renewed.

"Who were those men?" Vidar asked.

"Useless sacks of flesh. Spies, the very type you mentioned before," it replied.

"How can you be sure from this distance?" Vidar demanded.

"They fit the profile."

"What's that supposed to mean?"

"It means that you should trust me."

"Why aren't you sharing the thoughts you absorb?" Vidar asked.

"That would require giving me more control, which would…make you the passenger," it said, pausing. "And that's not what we agreed upon."

Vidar stood in the rain for a moment, thinking.

"Right," he replied, recalling. He turned to Sevryn. "Are you alright?"
Sevryn nodded after a pause.

"Yes…just a little tired," he replied.

"He won't do that again without my permission," Vidar said.

"Sorry. I concede…within reason," it replied.

"Excuse me?"

"I'm not going to let you die. I've got skin in the game, too, you know? If I die out here, like this, then I'll never be strong enough to escape the Uridar. So, if that means we take a couple of nibbles from time to time…then that's what we're going to do. But I will always be straightforward and honest with you. No lies."

Vidar looked at Sevryn with a mix of awkwardness and helplessness.

"If you're so fond of this one, you can find us others," it added.

"What about the ones you just killed?" Vidar argued.

"That's not how it works. They have to be living," it replied.

Vidar threw his hands into the air.

"I'm not just some ration for you to take out of your satchel when you're impoverished!" Sevryn shouted.

"What purpose do you serve? What could you possibly offer us?" it asked.

Sevryn dusted himself off.

"I'm a damned good ranger…" he began.

"Debatable. Had you done your job well, you'd be dead right now – a singed corpse whose flesh would be picked apart in the morning," it replied, stepping back into the opening. A light sparkling of electricity flowed over Vidar's body, drying him. "But you failed at your job, and now you're here…our walking ration."

"Surely there will be a time when you require stealth. You can't just walk around striking people dead everywhere you go!" Sevryn argued.

It grunted.

"Perhaps you're right," it conceded.

"We'll keep him," Vidar decided.

"Thank you!" Sevryn replied, exasperated.

"You're welcome," they said in unison.

Sevryn tilted his head as he looked at Vidar.

"So, what is this, exactly?" he asked. "Are you some sort of a crazy demi-god?"

Vidar's brow rose.

"No…but perhaps one is sharing my body right now," he replied.

"Something like that," it added.

"Which one? Would I know your legends?" Sevryn asked, doing his best to push past the nerves.

It grunted again.

"Names are performative where I come from. They only mean something to your kind," it answered.

"So…what does our kind call you?"

It took a deep sigh, as if reluctant to admit the answer.

"Fear."

CHAPTER SEVENTY-ONE

WHISPERS

ELARION

Her body was as still and stoic as the stone gargoyles she stood between, her gaze as firmly fixed as theirs, together lining the semicircular balcony just one floor above her prey.

He sat barefoot on fresh grass, its blades still soft and tender, the scent of it drifting through the air. The hanging gardens were a quiet refuge built alongside Castle Corvidae yet still nestled within its walls, hidden from public reach. Lena refrained from visiting it in her spare time, and just as rarely used it formally, save to entertain dignitaries worth impressing but not liked enough to be invited into her favourite corners and spaces. Of the three gardens on the grounds, it was her least favourite – likely because it was her mother's. But she couldn't bring herself to demolish it, despite it being an annual consideration.

Connerh chose the space to meditate, knowing he could enjoy isolation here, perhaps even from her. In most moments, it was deathly quiet. The walls bordering the garden excelled at dampening exterior noise, and its groundskeepers were few and far between, drifting carelessly like leaves shaken from their limbs, clipping away dead foliage or gathering blooms for the castle's interior...

But where it really shone...was in its unobstructed view of the sun. His eyes were closed, his face colliding with the burning star's rays, his body absorbing its warmth. It was the first time he felt appreciation for it all, felt connected to something greater, something beyond the flesh and bones that contained him – liberating him from within, but exposing a fragile tether to the cosmic.

Lena frowned as Connerh's face dropped into his palms, his body gently rocking back and forth. It was unclear the cause or reason, seeming a sudden reaction without provocation.

Elarion's hand touched her shoulder, startling her into a muffled scream, hand over mouth. She rushed forward, away from the balcony's edge, so as to avoid detection from below. It hadn't been his first choice to get her attention, but he'd been calling to her for several moments by this point.

"Elarion!" she exclaimed quietly, rushing to embrace him. He was shocked by her reaction, delaying the return of his affection by a full half second. She eventually pulled away, her expression dimming as she observed his. It was flat, devoid of the joy she expressed. He walked passed her, his eyes quickly shifting to Connerh.

"By whose magick is this?" he asked, turning to face her.

She hesitated to reply, her gaze falling as her hands clasped.

"I am older than the construction of this very castle…" he paused. "And you think you're the only one who knows of beings like Reh'gara?"

Her eyes betrayed her shock.

"Is it true? Is this by his hand?" he asked.

She nodded hesitantly, her eyes retreating from his fiery gaze.

He shook his head, remaining quiet for a time.

"Do not think for a moment that I am not overjoyed to see him breathing again. To see his skin warm with life…" His voice shed its urgency, softening in intent. "But you do not understand…" He stopped himself from expounding further as his voice trailed to a whisper. After a moment, he demanded, "How?"

"What do you mean?"

"By what sacrifice?" he pressed, brow raised.

"I…I don't know…" she stuttered.

"These things always have a cost. Whether before, upon receipt, after…or all of the above. And you want me to believe you received this for free?" he asked, tilting his head in disbelief. He sighed loudly. "I could take from you every thought, every memory leading to this day since the day you were born, including crevices of your mind you can no longer explore…all from outside of these castle walls and without your knowing," he began. Her eyes widened. His head fell briefly. "But I do not, if only to extend respect to you. A fragment of which you cannot be bothered to return. Not to me, not to him…only yourself. And even then…I sometimes find that lacking," he replied with a frown.

She squinted as her face crumpled, blurring her vision.

"You could never learn to trust the right people," he continued with an involuntary admission of thought. "Reh'gara means to doom us all, and the temptation of power was just too much for you," he muttered, turning to watch Connerh again. "What stings the most is that it is Madika who told me of Connerh's return… A friend of a short time…and not the sister of a lifetime that I have held on to, counting every second, where others I've only counted the decades," he said, choosing to stay facing Connerh for his own emotional stability. "Your greatest weakness is that you allow others to shape you. And even in your gentle rebellion, you adhere to someone else's mould." He turned to face her. "You must learn to quiet the noise; to listen to the voices that utter the uncomfortable things you do not want to acknowledge yet know to be true. The ones that remain in even your darkest hours. Those that disregard convenience and comfort for truth," he pronounced, locking eyes with her.

She was reduced to tears.

"I leave in the morning. I hope one day to see you again…alive," he said with finality.

She rushed towards him, burying her head into his chest. His arms splayed from the impact, eventually wrapping tightly around her for what felt like the last time. Her voice breaking, she begged, "But I need you now, more than ever."

"It's too late for that now," he replied. His tone was cold but not unloving. He felt her vibrate in his embrace, and it crumpled his face for a full second, but his resignation refused to let it linger.

He broke free from her grasp and walked off.

She wept bitterly, the violence of which stole her breath.

"Connerh Manthil of Nyradhal, do you yet live?!" Elarion shouted, his voice thundering as he strode towards him.

Connerh rushed to his feet, the joy of hearing Elarion's voice suddenly sapped upon seeing the expression on his face. He seemed disturbed, worried. His voice was panicked.

"It's me," Connerh reassured, his voice cracking with uncertainty. Elarion's charge came to a stop, barely leaving enough room for a thin sheet of air to pass between them. His hands felt Connerh's face with earnestness, his fingers tracing every detail and contour until he was satisfied, the barrage finally ending with a sigh of relief.

"I thought I might have to find you," Connerh said, a near whisper.

"And I, you," Elarion replied, pulling his friend into a tight embrace by the back of his head.

"What's wrong?" Connerh asked, his voice muffled by fabric.

"I am in conflict. My heart is full regarding your return. Even as I temporarily allow myself to indulge in selfishness…" he replied, pulling away just enough to study Connerh's face, as if he still wasn't fully convinced.

"But?" Connerh interjected.

"You should not be here," Elarion replied as plainly as he could. "Your return only complicates a matter that had already ventured beyond the unnatural. But now this…this most assuredly marks this world for judgment," he continued.

"I didn't ask for this," Connerh replied with confusion. He felt himself grow worried, if only because Elarion seemed to be.

"Unfortunately, it does not matter. All things must eventually be returned to balance," he replied, looking away. "And they will," he continued, returning his attention to Connerh. "Tell me, what cost did you pay? Was there an arrangement with the Candorian in order to secure your return?"

"What do you mean? I didn't pay anything," Connerh asked. Elarion turned to look up at the balcony, but she wasn't there.

"Perhaps, you should ask *her*," he replied.

"Elarion, you're starting to worry me about something I was only just starting to accept," Connerh began, letting out a forced laugh. "I didn't pay, ask, or beg to be brought back. Honestly, in the final hours…I'd accepted my death…" he continued as both their brows grew heavy. "I'm strong enough to admit that I'd hoped for it…for a long while, actually."

Connerh grabbed Elarion's arm, drawing his attention.

"If I need to undo this, if…if that will bring balance, then so be it. I will prepare my goodbyes…properly, this time," Connerh insisted.

Elarion shook his head. "It is too late for that… An inconsequential action…a drop in a torrent of wrongs, no matter how noble your intent. Besides, you've suffered enough, have you not? Sacrificed everything… I would not wish a second death upon you."

"Then what am I supposed to do?"

"Live your life as you should have all along."

"Reh'gara seems to have other plans."

"Stop!" Elarion shouted, startling Connerh. "I do not wish to hear of this."

"Why?!" he demanded.

Elarion shook his head.

"Fine, then look at my memories," Connerh insisted, offering his hands, if only for display purposes. He knew the elf didn't require touch to peruse his thoughts…not anymore.

Elarion backed away quickly, putting space between them.

Connerh's head canted instinctively, and he grew angered, mostly out of fear. "Why won't you look?!" He pressed forward, and Elarion yet again backed away. "Look at what he plans to do!"

"No!"

"Why!?"

"Because…I might be inclined to stop it." Elarion stared at Connerh, just below the eyeline.

Connerh froze, and he asked, "You mean me?"

Elarion's eyes watered.

"I'm going away from this place…and I do not mean to return," he responded, the focus of his gaze preferring the ground.

Connerh's head tilted, and his mouth opened, brows crushing in on themselves.

"I brought you the gift that I was never able to deliver. It felt wrong to tell you about it until you were free…until you could receive it. But then, you accepted death." Elarion looked at the ground, a small grin escaping the sides of his lips. He concluded, "I can think of no one better suited…no one more loyal to be by your side in my stead for whatever comes."

Connerh's expression steadily brightened.

"He's still alive? Here?" Connerh exclaimed.

The royal stable was expansive, filled with iron and thick beams of wood, carved directly into the side of the mountain the castle stood upon – just off to the side of the courtyard. It was clean and perfumed by way of burning pine, but it still retained its musky scent of no less than a hundred horses.

The stable hands moved out of Connerh's way as he approached, mostly out of fear. Lena had made his resurrection public knowledge among those who lived and worked within the castle walls, fully aware the news would soon spread beyond their confines. Though she insisted it was both by the hand and will of Reh'gara, Hildeheim's chief deity, uncertainty still clung in the air. Even the people, devout as some were, found themselves unsure…of it all.

Of him.

His run slowed to a measured jog, noticing he was suddenly the centre of attention. Fortunately, his focus soon found itself a new home: the largest stall in the entire structure. A deep smirk carved its way into his cheek. He slowed even further, denying himself the instant gratification.

First, he saw the ears, perked and alert, rotating in place. However, they then fell as the beast lay down, a human-like sigh emanating upwards. Connerh hurried to the stall's gates, peering in with concern. He, too, offered a sigh, though it was with relief marred by sadness. His old companion looked as resigned as he felt – laid on dirt and hay, its head curled away.

Whisper was a rare breed – a one-of-a-kind mutation standing at seven-foot-two at the shoulder. Power radiated from him; his muscles were clearly defined beneath skin as black as the space between stars. From top to bottom, including the thick feathering that extended from his knees, he was shadow manifested into flesh. A monster to many, perhaps, but a gentle giant to those he loved…and grudgingly patient with those he tolerated. The two of them had been inseparable from the day Connerh adopted him. He had been a lot smaller then – both of them had. Although Whisper had been of normal frame in his newborn stage, the size of his hooves had hinted at his future rapid development.

His name…was a joke that Connerh found humorous. Like naming a bear Tiny, there was nothing remotely quiet about the beast, yet it fit him so perfectly. They fought wars together, crumbled cities, and explored the reaching edges of Aelthoria and everything in between…until the day Connerh left. The decision to leave him behind was painful, but those on the run couldn't have anything to identify them…let alone a unique monster in tow.

"Hello, sir," Connerh greeted, his brow carving a path around his eyes.

The creature's ears shot up, while its head delayed in investigating. His black eyes focused on Connerh, and out poured a dreadful whine and whinny that emptied its lungs. The commotion of the horse standing was loud and echoing, setting off the other horses. A crowd began to gather.

Connerh opened the gates and walked towards his friend.

"Be careful, my lord! That one's dangerous. He's killed several trying to saddle him," a stable hand rushed to warn him. Connerh ignored him as Whisper barraged him with nudges of his massive head, as if trying to communicate his desire for an embrace despite lacking the arms to do so. Connerh grabbed his face, meeting it with his own, their foreheads touching. He rubbed Whisper's face and calmed him with an elongated hushing sound.

"He remembers," Elarion noted, finally catching up.

"Of course he remembers. I raised him," Connerh said. Whisper whinnied.

"I have fond memories of riding in battle with you two," Elarion said with a smirk.

"Then don't leave," Connerh replied, turning to face him. "Perhaps we can make more before I leave this world for good."

"I must. Even if I were to abandon reason and follow you to the end of this…" He paused. "There are others who rely on me, who need me now."

"I understand. Elarion the wise, the keeper of others… I just wish you would live on your own terms for once."

Elarion grinned.

"And I, you," he replied.

Connerh locked eyes with him, a grin soon following.

"Will I see you again?"

"I'm sure of it," Elarion replied. Connerh nodded.

"That's funny; I was given a different response," Lena added, her entrance quiet and brooding. Both men grew silent, turning to look at her.

"You asked a different question, and so you received a different reply," Elarion replied, a frown and a raised brow accompanying it.

"Bring me his saddle!" Connerh shouted, turning his head to do so. Workers scurried to comply.

"Going somewhere?" she asked.

"Yes," Connerh responded.

"I don't think that's such a good idea," she insisted.

"I don't think there's anyone that could stop me," Connerh replied, holding out his hand.

A crack of thunder sounded off, the following explosion and scattered debris of dirt announcing his spear's arrival just beyond the threshold of the stable. It flew into his grasp, and she jumped backwards to get out of its way.

Elarion stepped back with measured paces.

"Yes...yes, I suppose so," she struggled to reply, an even stronger attempt to resist disputing the matter. "And...will you return?" she asked, her nose pointed upwards, her lids low.

"Don't I always?" he replied, releasing his spear to float on its own as he affixed his saddle to Whisper. Elarion's gaze never broke from it as he inched away. Lena released a forced chuckle.

"It's like old times, isn't it? The three of us?" she asked, pleading for a release of tension.

Connerh fastened a strap as he looked at her.

"I suppose so, yes," he replied with a smirk.

"I must go..." Elarion finally broke his gaze, though his frown remained. He took Lena's hand and kissed it before hugging Connerh.

"Please don't be a familiar stranger," she begged.

"I never was, and I don't intend to be now," Elarion replied, turning to leave. He delayed, taking a long moment to stare at the spear again before walking off.

Lena watched him leave, then turned her attention back to Connerh.

"How was your talk with Reh'gara? I feel like you're suddenly angry with me," she pressed. His eyes snapped to her, then squinted briefly.

"Angry? No...confused...yes. And that's why I'm going for a ride. To breathe...to think."

"What are you confused about? I mean, I'm sure it was a lot to grasp…but I thought you would be excited about it. A new perspective on life? People would kill for such an opportunity," she replied.

He walked up to her, standing face to face, and asked in disbelief, "There's a floating spear next to you that I called from the heavens with my hands and thoughts…and you're not the least bit distracted or disturbed by it?"

"Reh'gara said you may undergo changes after…" she began, but she paused.

"Are there no limits to what you will endure to be near me?" he asked.

"To be with you…? No." She stepped closer, a desperation in her movement as she tried to contain hands that sought to rove about his body. His eyes fell as he nodded.

"In truth…I could summon it before I was brought back. Only now, it is not agony to be in its presence. In fact, I've never felt such clarity."

"What? Since when? How?" she asked.

"I'm still learning the answers to those questions. I'm hoping that when I next speak with Reh'gara, he will shed some light on the matter," he answered. He turned to mount Whisper but waited for the horse to lower himself.

After a small grunt, he was mounted, his body rising high above Lena as Whisper stood. She held on to his foot.

"I will return. Give me a day or three to come to grips with…it all."

"I understand," she replied. She didn't want to let him go, but she couldn't stop him.

"I love you," he said, though he didn't look at her.

"I love you, too," she replied, her eyes watering.

"Come on," he said in a low tone. Whisper bolted, the power in his stride vibrating the ground like thunder, even long after he cleared the stable.

Connerh's spear lingered for a moment as if looking at her, then rushed to catch up, whisking through the air with a silent procession.

Two days passed.

The sky was dark, the stars as bright and brilliant as gemstones.

A crackling fire serenaded Whisper and Connerh as they sat next to each other, the man leaning against the horse. Whisper sighed in relaxation, letting out small noises as if he were telling a story, much to Connerh's amusement. The spear rotated eerily in place beside them.

A chill breeze blew in, prompting Connerh to pull his blanket higher around his body.

Whisper stood suddenly, grunting and snorting, alerting Connerh to someone's arrival.

But the spear had already told him.

"So, it's true."

He heard a voice in the distance, obscured by the darkness that surrounded the brightness of the campfire, standing between him and the voice. The voice was soothing. Calm, measured. Sly. Connerh rolled his eyes.

"What of it?" Connerh asked with a scoff.

There was a delay in response.

Connerh sat up.

"You can hear me?" the voice replied.

"Of course I can hear you; I'm not deaf," Connerh replied, his eyes now searching the darkness, looking for the origin.

"Well…" the voice began. The Red Wolf approached, sitting on his hind legs next to the fire. "You used to be."

CHAPTER SEVENTY-TWO

HEDGE

YURI

Going back always seemed faster than getting there the first time.

What initially felt like an hour seemed to pass in mere minutes. They had already returned to the stables and retrieved her horse, and they were now venturing deep into parts of the city he had never seen before. Julian sat behind Yuri while she held the reins, her focus unwavering. The route she had chosen was different. There were more guards in this part of the city, attentive yet weary. Even their garb was different, black and gold tunics in favour of the white linen Yuri and her counterparts wore. They watched Julian and Yuri's approach, their gazes fixed even as they passed – though it seemed clear their suspicions and lingering eyes were directed towards him, not her.

Yuri had been quiet most of the way, offering only grunts in response to his questions. Eventually, he took the hint. He held his tongue and focused instead on observing. Who, where, and when. A left turn here, a right turn there – this place seemed like a catacomb by design. A maze of intention. Yet her horse carved through sharp turns and tight corners with ease and aggressive force, angry and fierce like a hammer pounding an anvil in rapid succession. It wasn't just that Yuri knew the way; the horse did, too. She merely guided his cadence, calming him when he pushed too hard

576

and urging him past instinctual hesitation.

Suddenly, the path opened into a grand courtyard, and a wall of bushes lined up before them. Lampposts with candles near the end of their watch provided the only light in the area.

"We're here," she announced, lifting her head as a polite way of telling him to dismount. He took the hint and obliged. She followed behind him.

He looked around, his curiosity at full throttle while she quietly praised her steed.

"What's the Khazmyrian word for 'search'?" she asked, still facing away from Julian. He raised his brow as she turned to face him, smiling and shaking his head as he feigned ignorance.

She sighed.

"You're not the only one who watches. That's how I know for a fact you've been learning the language. You have tells, no matter how good you think you are at hiding them." She scoffed. "I don't blame you. You'd be a fool if you didn't. That is the first thing I would do if I were in a foreign land… It is what I did," she said.

His gaze dropped, a smirk tugging at his lips.

"Say it," she commanded.

"Oobonai," he murmured barely before her lips closed. She smirked, but not out of humour.

"Yes, that is correct," she replied, turning towards her horse. "Oobonai," she whispered, patting his face. The horse took off, vanishing into the night. "You want trust, yet you cannot extend it," she declared, shaking her head. "You want faith, yet you do not believe."

"What do you mean? You're the only person I trust," he replied.

She shook her head again, her laugh nothing more than a sharp snort of air.

"Always with the predictable sentiments. When there's no one else to trust, your words aren't loyalty. They're desperation."

"That's not true in the slightest. I could be like you and trust absolutely no one."

"It's quite simple," she said. "I trust no one because no one is trustworthy. I don't settle just because my options are few."

He didn't answer right away, eyes fixed on her as he weighed his next words.

"As I've said, beyond what it took to ensure my survival at the outset…I've never lied to you. Yes, I have a habit of under-sharing…but it's not out of malice. It's a survival instinct. I didn't think that was a crime."

"No, it's not. And thank you," she said, offering a mocking clap of her hands. "All I ask is that you extend in return that which you ask for."

He nodded. The grin he wore earlier was long gone.

"What is this place?" he asked after taking a deep breath.

"A hedge maze."

"I'm sorry, what is a hedge maze?"

"In this case, a deterrent. A cover for the unseen; a way to hide things in plain sight," she replied. "But plainly…it is a maze made out of tall bushes."

"Khazmyr is a strange place indeed," he remarked. "And…what exactly is being hidden?"

"An exit," she replied, pausing to observe his reaction. His eyes slowly widened, although he did his best to contain it. "What some see as freedom, others remember as the day they lost theirs."

"And we're meeting someone in there?" he asked.

"No. Come," she said, walking towards the entrance. He followed closely behind. Pointing, she instructed, "Grab that lamp." It was too tall for her to reach. "And save the jokes," she added, her suppressed smirk bleeding through. He chuckled, keeping his remarks to himself.

They'd walked for a while, countless turns in opposing directions that seemed to contradict one another.

"We're not lost, are we?" he asked.

"No," she replied. His brow raised. It was completely dark, save for the pathetic halo of light coming from the lantern – she'd pulled ahead, barely clinging to the edge of it.

"Either you can see in the dark, or you've memorised this place," he joked.

"Yes," she replied. His head canted with a grin. "It's about four thousand steps from the entrance; we're halfway there," she replied, turning to look at him.

He startled and froze.

Her eyes glowed a soft blue.

She chuckled.

"Is it really the first time you've noticed?" she asked. He held the lantern up to her face, the effect vanishing with little effort, and pulled it away again. He did it several times in amazement, like a small child.

"It was a gift from Darros when I was quite young. In fact, I barely remember. Not all his potions cause harm," she replied. "I learned to switch it on and off when I was younger; I grew tired of the other children being afraid of me…though it still slips out sometimes, when I'm angry."

Julian squinted. Torn between saying more and keeping his counsel, he muttered, "Right."

"What?" she asked, her grin slowly fading.

"I just had a thought," he said, holding the lantern up to open the door that shielded its flame. He reached out and took her hand. "I trust you," he said, blowing out the candle.

Her blue eyes were the only light remaining. She delayed, then chuckled loudly.

"Oh, that's good," she replied, giving in to rolling laughter.

"Even in the dark, I can see you blushing," he retorted as she continued.

"You're a fool, Julian," she replied, pulling him forward as she resumed walking.

"Must you disregard everything I say as a pickup line?" he asked, exacerbated but amused.

"Must everything you say sound like a pickup line?"

"You'd know if I were trying to seduce you," he replied.

"I have no doubt of that," she shot back, chuckling again. "Your grip is a little tight. Are you afraid of the dark?"

"I'd be lying if I said it didn't remind me of my days as a blind man. It wasn't the highlight of my life, to say the least," he remarked. She slowed her pace; he caught her looking back at him. Those eyes were hard to miss.

"I can't imagine what it was like," she murmured, her tone softened. He smiled in the dark.

"The frustrating part was knowing what things looked like…the toll of having something so precious taken from you…rendered helpless. The actual loss of vision was second to that feeling of being robbed. It strips you down to the foundation, and all that's left is who you are deep down inside."

"Darros excels at such games," she answered.

"I'm starting to see that."

"I'm just glad we have an understanding as to why I'm doing this," she said.

He smirked and canted his head – as she ripped her hand away from him.

"What are you doing?" he asked, concern feigned via a humorous tone.

But there was no reply.

She let him stand there for a few long moments in complete darkness. He turned in place, tracking shadows and trying to resist the ocular games his mind played with him, searching for her eyes. The panic began to set in, though he restrained any physical outburst.

"Do I have your attention?" she asked, her eyes activating.

He turned quickly to face her, following the sound of her voice.

"You do," he acknowledged, his voice dry with confusion and frustration.

"This is a part of the maze that we call the kill box," she explained, her eyes moving as she paced, though they remained locked on him.

"Charming," he replied.

"The hedge here isn't just overgrown," she said. "Over time, it's fused…woven so tightly together it formed a ceiling. Thick. Tangled. Alive." She tilted her head back, eyes scanning the invisible canopy above. "But that wasn't enough," she added. "Animal skins are layered throughout, stitched into the brush, draped across the arch. It ensures light doesn't get in and sound doesn't get out, nor anything else can find its way in…" She looked back at him. "There's no easy way out. It's nearly a hundred metres of perpetual darkness. A maze within a maze."

"You and I have different ideas of a first date," he remarked.

Her sudden outburst of laughter seemed sinister when accompanied by her eerie stare.

"Because of how the maze was designed…they always end up here – those who try to escape, that is," she said. "They get turned around, pulled deeper with every wrong turn. They wander for hours…sometimes days. No light. No direction. Just panic." She stepped closer, her voice low, almost a whisper. "Eventually, their feet give out. Blisters split open in the dark. Throats dry, minds unravel. And all because they heard the legend of *Surn'velthora*."

Her eyes narrowed.

"What does it mean?" she asked, sharp now. Demanding.

"Velthora means door. That's all I know," he replied.

"Good. It means the *Hidden* Door. The way out. A place so difficult to reach that it's left mostly unguarded. The truth is, there are guards who slowly sweep the maze in the morning hours, collecting those who tried to escape…something that is, without a doubt, a death sentence upon being discovered."

"But you could leave," he said. She stopped pacing, and he watched her eyes turn and focus on him.

"I could."

"So why are you telling me this?" he asked.

"Because, like me, you have a choice. You have two options: Tell me the truth…who you are and why you are here…or lie to me, and I leave you here to die, ironically mere steps from freedom," she said. Her eyes drifted downwards. "And we say goodbye to what was…a lovely distraction."

She watched through the dark as he frowned. His eyes snapped forward after a brief deliberation.

"My name is Julian Graymane, of House Graymane – one of the original Seven Houses of Hildeheim, and loyal still to its blood and honour. I am a knight sworn to the Brothers of Cree, a brotherhood older than kings, forged from the ashes of the first wars. We are bound to truth and justice, not to crowns and thrones. We do not kneel to power; we stand for what is right. We defend the weak, not the strong – the forgotten, those cast aside. There is a queen in Hildeheim, yes, but she was never meant to wear the crown. And because she rules without strength, without the will to lead, the innocent continue to suffer. Our enemies gather like vultures beyond the walls, drawn by the stench of decay. If we do nothing, they will feast. You are the forgotten firstborn of Queen Ioelena the Third, rightful heir by blood and birth. I have come to see you reclaim what is yours – not for conquest, not for pride, but for justice. For truth. If we fail to act, the realm will fall. And that, we cannot not allow."

He waited for a reply, but she remained quiet for a time. She was looking at the ground.

"Who says I would be any different, were I to want such a thing?" she asked.

"You offer a unique perspective that sets you apart from other royalty. Who among them has gone through the experiences you've gone through? The suffering, the pain? The ascension from such conditions?" he replied.

"I am not royalty," she scoffed.

"Your blood says otherwise," he argued.

"By your own admission, blood is not enough to rule."

"You're correct, but it is the foundation."

He watched her eyes blink rapidly, changing directions from time to time.

He heard a sniffle.

"Right."

"Darros did not impart your gift of night vision, Your Highness. Your father did."

"Is that so?" she asked, her tone uncertain.

"Yes. Your sister has it…as does your brother," he replied.

She approached, and he resisted the urge to recoil; her eyes were frightening to look at in such focused isolation.

He heard her chuckle to herself.

"Ioelena is my sister," she said to herself with amused realisation.

"Yes, and Prince Bjorn is your brother."

"He knows," she whispered.

"I'm sorry?"

"Darros knows. I've never been in the same room with her, never allowed, always given something else to do when she would visit, or when he travelled to see her. I always thought it strange, as I was present with every other king or queen, but…I never gave thought to it."

"So, you believe me?" he asked.

Her gaze returned to him.

"I do," she said, starting to pace.

"Then we leave tonight?" he asked.

"I can't…not yet."

"Why?" His tone grew in frustration.

She stopped pacing and grabbed his hand, replying, "I need to show you something," and pulling him forward.

They emerged into a hollow chamber deep within the maze – a clearing walled by thick brush and overhead vines, forming a natural dome. At the centre rose a stone platform, circular and ancient, its edges worn smooth by time. Eight rows of wide, shallow steps spiralled gently upwards, leading to a summit that held a singular feature: a massive, round door carved directly into the stone wall behind it. The door stood nearly twenty feet tall and two feet thick, its surface covered in etched symbols that pulsed faintly under the flicker of nearby lanterns. Two stone posts framed the door like silent sentinels, each supporting a hanging lantern that cast long, twitching shadows on the steps below.

There were no visible handles. No keyholes. Just the door, the wall, and the faint, nearly audible flicker of candlelight.

"This looks…ominous," he said, releasing her hand and walking up to run his hand across the door's surface.

"It is."

"How does this delay you? Do we need to find a key or cypher?" he asked, studying the etched symbols.

"I need to kill the last person who walked through it," she answered. He quickly turned around.

"When I arrived in Khazmyr, it was a different time. Our principles were much…looser," she began.

"I can't imagine how that could be possible," he added.

"Well, it was," she said, voice distant. "Khazmyr rose from between the legs of slaves." Julian's brow arched at the phrasing, but she didn't flinch. "Dragged from their homes in the dead of night – men, women, and children alike. Shipped across sea and sand like livestock, penned like beasts. They were bartered for, broken, and bound, their bodies used as currency to build a kingdom of silk and stone. It went on for generations, aided by slavers like a man named Tyreek. A man with no morals or conscience. A disfigured freak from the Far Sands, wanted dead or deader by most civilised kingdoms. It was men like that who kept Darros' court."

Her lip curled as if the memory soured her tongue.

"But when I arrived, I found favour in Darros' eye for reasons I am only now beginning to understand." Her voice dropped. "I suspect he knew what I was, who I was." She lowered her head for a moment, eyes half-closed as if watching ghosts drift past. "After learning how things worked here, after seeing such depravity, I made him promise me that things would change, and for a time, they did. We no longer purchased slaves from men like Tyreek. Those who offered their bodies did so of their own free will and under contract, in exchange for homes, money or favour. Our prisons were dismantled, the prisoners forced to work underground instead."

"What you're describing isn't any better," Julian interjected.

"It was progress!" she snapped back.

He bit his tongue.

"But Khazmyr's thirst for depravity cannot be held at bay for long. Sometime after, during one of Darros' drunken flesh parties, Tyreek showed up. After he was two sheets to the wind, he abused and murdered a friend close to me." She took a moment. "When I went to remove his heart from his chest…Darros stayed my blade, banishing him instead. A purely performative punishment, at best. It became clear that business had never stopped; it was only hidden from me. At that point, I pulled away from Darros…and things between us were never the same. Perhaps I should have told him that Tyreek tried to take me once…maybe then he would have done the job for me." She turned back to Julian. "You know, I always wondered why he tolerated me so. Allowed me to breach lines when others had been killed for less," she mused, walking up the stairs towards the door. "No matter. Tonight, I have come to learn that Tyreek has been smuggled back into the city, and he finds refuge here, under the order of Darros. That man has avoided death and the blade as if it holds no sway over him. However, I am to prove that theory incorrect. He dies, if it is the last thing I do," she declared, turning to Julian. "And I want you to help me,"

He thought for a minute before asking, "Then, we leave?"

She nodded, confirming, "Then we leave."

"Tonight, you will learn to navigate the maze, and when the time comes…" She paused, pressing against certain carvings on the door that gave way, recessing into stone. The door rattled to life and began a slow swing inwards. It was thick, roughly two feet, the sound it produced hinting at its weight.

Julian poked his head out the other side before eventually walking across the threshold. There was a large river, fit for a boat of a decent size, encased in a tunnel.

"It leads to a fork. To the left, inlets that run deep into Khazmyr. To the right, out to the great sea," she said, coming to stand behind him.

He looked out longingly. Freedom had never been so close. He thought to grab her and run, or even to run on his own. She stood on the other side of the door, waiting and watching.

"This is how the slaves are smuggled in," she added, drawing his attention. "Slavers bring them in by boat, all coming from the various water sources. This door is the last time they see freedom. Many never see daylight again, as they are sent immediately underground. It wasn't until recently, when the gates were closed, that many of them even came to know how large the city actually is."

He sighed heavily.

"When we leave…we'll need a boat," he replied.

"I'll have one waiting," she replied.

He fought his loud, better judgments.

"I may need more than one night to memorise this maze," he replied, stepping over to rejoin her. She smiled.

He painfully watched as the door closed, the scraping sound a mirror to his thoughts.

"We'll take as long as you need," she replied.

CHAPTER SEVENTY-THREE

THE RED WOLF

CONNERH

Whisper's snorts and grunts persisted, his body tense with agitation. He wanted it to be known: the Red Wolf did not have his permission to remain. He alternated between stomping his foot and feinting a charge, ears pinned flat against his skull. When it made no difference – his displays were entirely ignored – he instead opted to circle Connerh, each step deliberate, each breath sharp.

But the creature stood his ground. Unfazed. Undeniably striking.

He was beautiful in appearance – oversized yet understated. His orange fur, as bright as that of a fox, blended into an undercoat of tan, black, and white, while his feet appeared bloodstained. Though nearly half Whisper's size, his gaze held an added weight, ancient and unyielding.

Yet Connerh never felt threatened.

He remained seated on the ground, arms wrapped loosely around a raised knee, studying the beast with guarded curiosity.

"Well, you have my attention," Connerh said, his voice calm, though his brow arched slightly in intrigue.

"Ironic," the wolf replied, his words brushing against Connerh's mind in a voice both raw and steady, despite the panting that set his jaws trembling. "In all the years I wished to speak with you…I never bothered to rehearse what it was I might say." His tongue rolled slightly between the words, betraying the strain of effort it took to reach across the void between them. "I suppose I could start with the basics."

Connerh nodded once, slow and deliberate.

"My name is Ankhari," he began, pausing to exhale a heavy, almost bitter sigh. "And this...is not my true form." His ears twitched back momentarily, as if ashamed. "I was trapped in this visage by the man responsible for killing my brother. And that..." His amber eyes shifted, sharpening their focus. "...is my brother's spear."

Connerh jolted to his feet, instinct tightening every muscle.

The sudden motion excited Whisper, who stomped hard enough to send a spray of dirt flying, a surge of misplaced bravado filling the air.

Ankhari gave a short, soft laugh. Almost rueful.

"How's that for an introduction?"

"Brother?" Connerh asked, voice tight with disbelief. "You mean...you mean my father?"

"I do," Ankhari said, his muzzle dipping slightly in acknowledgement. "Though it's strange to hear you use those words."

"And the one who killed him?" Connerh pressed, a longing for rage flickering across his features – a slight tightening of the jaw, a hardening of the eyes.

"The very person whose stench," Ankhari replied, voice lowering to a growl, "still emanates from you. He is an evil man, born of selfishness and pride," Ankhari continued, voice steady but tinged with a raw bitterness. "He acknowledges no boundary, no line in the sand he would not cross...not if it means indulging his personal desires. Killing my brother is barely a page in his book of sins."

Connerh took a half-step back, his head turning slightly, mouth hanging open – involuntary movements, his body betraying him.

"You've always known his name," Ankhari continued plainly, standing tall on all fours, his tail flicking once. "It is the very one that comes to mind, yet you hesitate to utter it."

A heavy beat passed between them.

"His name is Reh'gara."

Connerh's gaze dropped to the ground, his stare boring into nothing, lost in thought. When he spoke again, his voice was low and brittle as he asked, "How do I know you're telling the truth?"

"Did you not see Torinir's murder?"

The blood drained from Connerh's face. His expression hollowed, and his eyes opened wider – not with understanding, but disbelief.

"That was his name, wasn't it?" he muttered, taking a moment to gather himself. His fingers flexed once at his sides. "I didn't see who did it…not directly. There was smoke, lightning, and thunder… The man was hooded," Connerh muttered, slowly pacing a tight circle. His hands moved in small, agitated gestures, like he could somehow reconstruct the memory if he tried hard enough. "Why would Reh'gara kill my father but then bring me back from the dead?"

Ankhari laughed – a deep, guttural sound that shook his chest.

"Is that what he told you? That he brought you back to the living?"

"Well, yes," Connerh answered defensively, "and that it was at great cost—"

Ankhari laughed again, a sharp, rough bark that cut through the air.

"I'm not following," Connerh said, his patience thinning, frustration tightening the corners of his mouth.

"You may want to sit down," Ankhari replied, his voice almost gentle now.

Connerh hesitated, pride flickering across his face, but his curiosity gnawed stronger than his pride.

And without warning – without the ritual steps he once believed necessary – he found himself *there* again.

In the Amber.

Glowing particles descended at a snail's pace, like frozen, illuminated raindrops caught mid-journey towards a ground adorned with smooth, black river stones. In the distance, a sea of black rippled out under an amber sky, while everything beneath was bathed in the burnished hues of a dying sun. Streaks of stars carved through the dark blue and violet heavens, and a sun-like star, bisected by the horizon, blazed intensely as ripples of heat distorted the ground beneath it. Yet, for all its fire, its light offered no warmth.

A deep, low hum reverberated in the background, audible and steady but never intrusive. It was as it always had been – except now, he could move, no longer a prisoner locked behind the bars of his own eyes.

Connerh looked down at his hands, rotating them slowly in place, feeling their weight. Their reality.

"You're responsible for this place?" Connerh asked, his voice muted in the heavy air.

"Yes. Prevented as I am from engaging directly with mortals…this was my attempt at bending the rules a little. After all, everyone else seems to find great pleasure in doing so," Ankhari replied.

Connerh turned and started slightly.

Ankhari stood before him now, not as a wolf but a man.

He wore a robe of faded burgundy, the edges trimmed with weathered bronze lacing, intricate symbols embroidered into the folds. Two ruby pendants dangled from a chain around his neck, catching the ambient light with a muted glow. His eyes, a deep and weary green, sat in an aged face lined with wrinkles and sharp contours – the map of a long, storied life. His dark brown hair, slicked neatly back, was streaked liberally with white, and his beard mirrored the same rich, timeworn pattern save for a single black stripe connecting his bottom lip to his chin.

Ankhari's hood was lowered, and his expression wore a seasoned, amused interest. His smile deepened by the second, forming a dimple on one cheek before, abruptly, he burst forward, grabbing Connerh's sides and pulling him into a tight embrace.

Connerh stiffened, incapable of returning the same warmth – confused but interested, wanting to reciprocate if only he could understand why. Ankhari pulled back just enough to stare into his eyes, searching for something beyond the surface.

"Anything? Do I look familiar?" he asked, his grin tugging wider with hope.

Connerh shook his head.

"Brilliant," Ankhari whispered, then straightened, a small laugh escaping. "I thought perhaps seeing me might trigger memories from before…but there's nothing, is there?"

"No," Connerh muttered, his brow furrowing. "At least, I don't believe so."

"Well, you'll be happy to know, I'm not the sort that finds enjoyment in riddles or ambiguity," Ankhari said. "I speak plainly, direct, just as I would expect in return.

And while this face may not ring familiar now…I would wish for nothing better than a familiar face to deliver the worst of news – or the best of it."

Connerh inhaled deeply and cleared his throat. "Which is it? Good news or bad?"

"That is for you to decide," Ankhari replied, nodding once.

"Go on," Connerh said.

Ankhari began to pace slowly, gathering his words. "You were raised to believe that Torinir was your father, and he was taken from you as a child. That…is not exactly true. Torinir is not your father."

Connerh's eyes widened, a lump forming in his throat as the foundation of his painful memories cracked, reshaped by the revelation.

"He is you," Ankhari said. "You did something new…something no one else had dared. You copied yourself. While the rest of us toyed with making offspring the old-fashioned way, you went straight to the source. A nearly perfect copy diminished only where necessary to optimise a genetic bond with mortals. Birthed by a human woman, the blanks were filled to produce a balanced template. Your children were to be purer – less prone to violence and madness, unlike the half-breeds so often born of our unsanctioned breeding."

Ankhari's voice grew sharper with every word.

"With every advantage – self-restoring life, connection to the natural world and beyond – your children would be gods among men. None would be their equal. It was this…that was unacceptable to some. Some like Reh'gara."

Ankhari circled Connerh now, his movements steady but intense.

"Your plan was nearly perfect. Even Reh'gara fell into it, killing you as you desired."

"Why would I *want* Reh'gara to kill me?" Connerh asked, voice trembling slightly.

"So you could start anew," Ankhari answered, his tone softening. "Live life, find love, have children – all for the first time…again. Together with your closest company, one gifted in the mental arts, you planned to transfer your original consciousness into the spear…and then into this new body when it came of age, but before a new spirit could fully take root."

Ankhari paused, his eyes narrowing.

"But something went wrong. Witnessing your own death – mistaking it for the death of a father – broke everything. You became *you*, a new individual, thus voiding the conditions your companion had set for the transfer. The slate had to be clean, and if it wasn't…the new life had to be allowed to progress on its own merit. And so, here you are."

Connerh clenched his jaw, fists tight at his sides.

"That motherfucker," he muttered under his breath, shaking his head.

"When you died…you didn't truly die," Ankhari continued. "In this diminished form, your body just takes longer to heal. Whatever interference Reh'gara provided…whatever he *did* to you, it could not have been good."

"What do you mean?" Connerh asked quickly, concern leaking into his voice.

Ankhari tilted his head.

"Well, for one, now you can understand me. Which means Reh'gara's tinkering has awoken your dormant abilities – your connection beyond this realm."

Connerh groaned, rubbing his face with both hands, lingering with his palms cupped over his features.

"I liked it better when I didn't know anything," he muttered.

"Don't we all?" Ankhari offered with a small smile.

"What am I supposed to do with this information? How do I summon the will for hate and vengeance without the memories…without the emotions that drive it?"

"That's not why I'm telling you," Ankhari corrected. "You couldn't act on it now, even if you wanted to. You're not ready. I tell you this because the time *will* come for you to join us when we move against Reh'gara. For now, the veil has been lifted, and that is good enough. Learn what you can about the enemy. Prepare."

Connerh straightened, steeling himself.

"How do I free you from this form?" he asked, urgency rising.

"You don't," Ankhari said simply. "Don't worry; things are already in motion to set me – and the others – free. I will rejoin you in time. And then…we will have a talk with Reh'gara."

"There are others?" Connerh asked.

"Of course. Reh'gara has trapped all who opposed him. But, like you, the tide is turning.
He did not account for all possibilities, and soon…we will all be free."

Connerh's hands clenched and unclenched as he fought the helplessness surging within him.

"I've struggled my whole life, feeling like a leaf blown by the wind," he said, "and just when I feel strong enough to resist…a storm comes."

Ankhari chuckled warmly.

"You're stronger than you realise," he said. "You just don't know it yet. That's why bullies like Reh'gara seem to win. They're strong when we are weak, powerful when we give them control. But no longer; today, his hold on power weakens."

Connerh's gaze shifted restlessly before falling against the spear.

"I'm still in there, aren't I?" he asked, his tone lingering in longing.

"Yes," Ankhari said.

"He…you," Ankhari corrected himself, "wish to apologise for abandoning you. Accepting his fate as an inanimate object…took time."

"I understand. But, wait – can he not speak to me directly?"

"No."

"Why?"

"It was part of the amended terms," Ankhari explained. "Only one person can alter that agreement."

"Don't worry," Connerh said, his tone sharp. "I know where to find him."

"There is more to reveal…but in time," he continued, his voice lowering into something almost reverent. "It is important now that you keep Reh'gara occupied. He must not know you're awakening. Be cautious, brother. Be wary. He is dangerous – and capable of anything."

He grabbed Connerh by the arms again, pulling him into a fierce embrace, one hand pressing at the back of Connerh's head.

"It's good to see you again," Ankhari whispered against his ear, chuckling. "Though you'll have to forgive me if I don't call you by this new name just yet."

Connerh hugged him back, still lacking emotion but compelled by a sense of something *almost* familiar.

"It's alright," he said, a small snort escaping his nose. "I understand."

And then he fell – backwards, through the amber world, the particles rushing past him like reversed rain.

He awoke with a jolt, rubbing his eyes.

Opening them, he saw Ankhari – once more in wolf form – sauntering away, his tail and legs moving with a casual, self-assured gait.

"Keep your head up, brother," the wolf called over his shoulder, vanishing into the absence of light.

CHAPTER SEVENTY-FOUR

VIOLENCE IN A BOTTLE

CONNERH

Connerh lingered in the stables, his back pressed against the cool stone wall at the rear of Whisper's stall.

A man, a horse, and his spear.

Whisper munched steadily from a fresh hay bale, one watchful eye fixed on Connerh, vocalising in low, familiar tones. The spear – Torinir – drifted nearby, his revolutions slow and deliberate, like he was watching and pacing. Waiting.

"I'm sorry I stole your body," Connerh murmured, casting a brief glance towards the floating weapon.

Torinir glided closer, brushing lightly against Connerh's shoulder before pulling back again.

His communication with Connerh was complex. Connerh heard no voice, nor any whisper – only intuition. A sense of truth, binary and precise, presented as fact or foreknowledge and inserted directly into his mind like a memory yet to pass. It bore no emotion, no personal sentiment, yet something clawed at the edges.

Like a man screaming behind glass, his cries silent, but his presence undeniable.

"We should find a workaround until we can make it to Elarion," Connerh said. He paused, then added, "It *is* Elarion, isn't it?"

Torinir's spin slowed. He bounced once, twice against the ground.

593

Connerh's eyes lit up. "I think you're onto something. Once for no, twice for yes?"

Two soft thuds. A yes.

"It's a bit primordial," Connerh offered with a short laugh, "but it's better than nothing. I was going to suggest you try writing in the dirt."

In answer, Torinir shifted his stance mid-air, the spearhead angling towards the floor. Then, with smooth, deliberate precision – like a brush guided by an unseen hand – he began to carve. Dirt scraped softly against metal, a quiet rhythm filling the space.

Connerh scrambled to his feet, startled by the sudden acceptance of his idea, unable to hide his curiosity.

Etched clearly into the earth: **You've had worse ideas.**

Connerh barked out a laugh.

"Not bad," Connerh said, folding his arms. With a dry smirk, he added, "Certainly better than my own handwriting." He began pacing in slow, concentric circles, his fingers tugging absently at his beard before he continued, "I don't know what I'm supposed to do." His voice was low. "How do I go on with this knowledge? How do I pretend to care about…" He stopped mid-step, brow furrowing as he searched for the words. A sigh escaped him. "…to care about things I'd already begun to drift from? Politics. Crowns. Wars. It's all pointless. Meaningless."

Torinir scratched through the previous message in the dirt, then floated back, waiting. Connerh arched a brow, trying to decipher the gesture. Realisation dawned.

He stepped forward and wiped the ground clean with his boot, offering a new canvas.

Torinir slid into position, spear tip gliding through the earth with graceful certainty.

Do it for her. We just need time.

Connerh's eyes lingered on the message. His jaw tensed, then slackened. A breath in – long and steady – was exhaled out through his mouth, nice and slow.

"Fine," he capitulated, voice quieter now. "What about Reh'gara? Does he know…about you?"

A single impact. No.

Connerh's brows lifted slightly, his head tilting.

"He thinks you're dead?"

Two soft taps. Yes.

"He knows of the spear?"

Again, two taps.

"Was it…somewhat sentient before? How does he not suspect something's wrong?"

Two more.

Connerh's brow creased, deepening as he stepped closer.

"Are you both in there?"

A pause. Then, two impacts.

His voice dropped, touched with sorrow. "Are you in agony?"

Two impacts. A pause.

Then – one more.

"Yes…and no?" Connerh asked.

When no answer was forthcoming, Connerh rushed to clear the dirt again. Torinir slid forward.

I'm fine, for now.

"You sound like me…" Connerh replied, trailing into laughter before he nodded and wiped the words away with a sweep of his hand. Pushing the thought aloud, he asked, "Can't we just share this body?"

One impact. A no.

Too dangerous.

Connerh's gaze dimmed, his eyes slipping out of focus.

"What would happen to me?" he asked, kneeling, dragging his hands across the earth to make space for the next truth.

Lost. Forever.

His eyes dropped. The weight of understanding etched itself into his features. Torinir pushed forward suddenly, bumping into Connerh and knocking him flat onto his rear.

No.

A firm response to a question Connerh hadn't given voice to – but had clearly thought.

Connerh scowled, not at the spear but at himself.

Patience.

"I'm afraid I'm running out," Connerh muttered, voice fraying at the edges.

Torinir drifted back, his spearhead brushing the ground, then leaning against the stable wall. He went suddenly still, as if he were nothing more than a weapon again.

Footsteps echoed from outside – quick, deliberate. Connerh hastily erased the dirt just as the sound rounded the corner.

Farrah.

Connerh jumped to his feet, catching the sharp restraint in her face before it crumbled.

"Connerh!" she choked out, her voice catching. Her eyes welled and fell as she bowed slightly. "She needs you," was all she managed before she turned and sprinted off.

He started to follow – then stopped, glancing back at Torinir and Whisper.

"Stay close, but out of sight," he said. "We have an advantage over Reh'gara; he doesn't know what we know. Let's keep it that way."

Two impacts. Yes.

Connerh took off.

Torinir's surface shimmered, shifting to a deep, iridescent violet – then faded as he slipped beyond the veil of mortal perception. A rush of air tore through the stables as he launched, silent at first before a crack sounded, like the sky itself had fractured. He streaked forward, trailing wind and dust. With a second, sharper burst, he ascended, vanishing into the clouds and sending a flock of birds scattering like torn parchment. All that remained was a trembling hush…and a spiral of dust twisting where he had been.

Connerh's pace towards the castle was quick, direct, his heels like thunder against the clouded stone. Farrah waited just beyond the entrance, gathering herself, suppressing her emotions. She joined his stride mid-step, matching his pace with ease.

"She's in the war room," she explained.

He frowned. That was never a good sign. He stopped; she followed suit a step or two later.

"Can I ask you a question?"

She closed the gap, orbiting him with the ease of someone familiar.

"Of course," she replied, drawing her hands up to her chest.

"What's actually going on?"

She glanced away, then pulled him into a side room, closing the door behind them.

"Actually?" she echoed, testing his intent. The pause before the storm.

"Openly. Honestly. Strictly between us, I assure you."

She breathed in, eyes closed.

"She calls it a war…" he continued, voice low. "But it isn't a war, is it? I see no signs of such a thing. No bannermen, no waves of troops preparing, nor being sent out in a cadence. No marching orders, no conscriptions."

"We're not at war," Farrah answered. "She's conducting an execution, and now it's blown up in her face."

She stepped closer, arms crossed.

"Her and Bjorn have been so distraught over the loss of Queen Io, they've made revenge their purpose. However, I don't think there's any sadness left. Only anger at the issue unresolved." Her eyes lifted to meet his. "And they found their excuse. Losing you sent her over the edge, her threshold for justification reduced to a razor's thinness. They feed off each other, and it doesn't take long for Bjorn to give her what she wants – anything. They've marched through every kingdom, every city, slaughtering anyone who ever stood against her. For a time, no one opposed them. No one dared. But now…now patience has run thin. People are beginning to see the truth. To understand what she's really doing. And they've had enough. Their uniting…against her."

She paused to let him process it all. His expression was grave. Mouth parted, brow heavy.

"All this time, Bjorn has been behind enemy lines, sending information and targets back to Lena. But now, he's been found, and they all want him dead. They want this to end. To them, she has become the Mad Queen – drunk with power, and at their expense. And they've had their fill."

Connerh's sigh was loud.

"I can't help but feel a certain level of responsibility for this mess," he finally replied.

"You had nothing to do with this," Farrah refuted. "Connerh, you were dead."

"Her descent started long before that," he replied.

Farrah's head fell towards the ground. She didn't disagree.

He started for the doors.

"Some say the elves are taking notice," Farrah blurted, as if it were her darkest secret and this her only opportunity for admission. Her eyes watered.

He stopped, looking back at her. He sighed again and then left.

Had it not already been known where the war room was, it was obvious now. A growing pile of servants anxiously peeked through the cracked double doors. Their whispers abruptly ceased as he approached.

"He's here! Make way, make way," they muttered, fussing and parting as he neared. His hands came to rest on the doors. He paused, peering through the crack to see what awaited him.

Lena stood among a crowd – military types, judging by their attire. He grunted at the familiar sight. Once, it would have stirred bloodlust. Now…it just felt sad. Withered. Pathetic.

He pushed open the doors and entered. The room quieted in unison, every eye turning towards him. He saw hope, disgust…indifference. Lena's expression shifted from anger and frustration to joy, even elation. She blushed but restrained herself, refusing to acknowledge him outright.

She looked as though she might speak, but she didn't. The discussion resumed, voices rising over the maps and figures strewn across the round table. Connerh clasped his hands behind his back and circled the room slowly, catching glances through gaps in the crowd. Lena discreetly waved him over to an empty place beside her. He declined with a subtle gesture.

Instead, he glanced back at the exit – blocked entirely by the mass of servants outside.

"Then it is agreed upon?" Lena asked the table, her voice seeking consensus.

They looked among themselves, murmuring brief exchanges. Connerh reversed course, pacing back the other way.

"I just want to state the obvious, again, before we agree to anything," General Oleander said, words chosen carefully, hands expressive.

Connerh's head tilted. Oleander, ever the rational one – sometimes too cautious, but rarely wrong.

"If we go through with this…it will escalate," Oleander went on, emphasising the word. "Everything. All the time and work spent slaughtering this cow, out the window. Precision be damned. The moment we march in with the numbers you're proposing…"

He flung his hands up in exasperation.

"It's Bjorn!" another general snapped.

That name made Connerh stop and turn towards the table, his hands drifting to his front. Lena watched him from the corner of her eye.

"I wouldn't care if it were Reh'gara himself – with all due respect," Oleander began, then raised his hands in pre-emptive defence. "The gods know every kingdom's been waiting for a reason. A reason to take a swing at the giant – at Hildeheim. The world's been teetering. Pressure's been building for generations, and we're the ones at the top of the pot."

Oleander's analogies were always food-related. Connerh smirked; some things never changed.

"Maybe this all started with Her Late Majesty the Queen Mother's death. Maybe that was the fuse – or maybe it started long before. Maybe the plan was always to remove us so they could thrive in our absence."

His voice rose, and his cheeks flushed. Connerh squinted. The truth of it stung. Fields. Bodies. The smell. It came rushing back.

What did we really gain, compared to what we lost?

"What matters is the chain reaction our actions will cause, dumping a barrel of wine into a cup already full. These lunatics have been itching for a pound of Hildeheim's flesh, and we'd look like the provocateurs."

Connerh mentally tallied the allegories. Three – no, four.

"Because we are!" Aghor Emberheart roared.

"Every rat-infested shithole between the Westwood and the Far Sands will jump at the chance to sink their teeth into us. They've been waiting for a spark to – burn…" Oleander stumbled. His metaphor broke.

Connerh grinned. The old bastard had lost his thread.

"Say it, Ole," Lena instructed, voice low and sharp.

"What he means," said Vaelen Graymane, ever biting, "is that your brother's recklessness could spark a world war. Millions will die for something none of them care about. Hell, I'm not sure even *we* do. With respect, Her Late Majesty the Queen Mother – lovely or not – was a recluse. She made as many enemies as she did bad decisions. The people loved her title, not her. And, frankly, you're not doing much better."

Of course she understood. Her mother hadn't exactly been popular.

"He means," Nikolas Hargrave added, stepping out from the shadows, "it could mark the end of your reign, Your Majesty."

Lena lowered her gaze. She wanted to look to Connerh, to seek a lifeline – but she resisted.

"Even if we extract the prince," Nikolas continued, shaking his head, "the chaos he's stirred in pursuit of justice… This is the moment, Lena.

The one I've been preparing for."

He didn't say it, but everyone knew: Nikolas was the kind of man who waited a lifetime to say the right thing at the right time.

"To quote the good general, the fuse is lit. It's no longer a matter of if but how this ends." He leaned in, speaking more softly. "Even if we win…you will still lose. War is the first thing kings want when people are unhappy, but it's the last thing the people want."

"So how many heads need to roll to save your brother – and for a grudge no one even remembers?" Torin Feather asked.

He rarely spoke, but when he did, it cut.

"It was fine when he was off causing trouble. A few skirmishes, keep the lads sharp – sure. No one misses pirates. But this?" posed Saleh Gryphon, an ambassador from the Dwarven Nation. "This is different. These are innocent people. Lots of them."

Lena listened, holding Saleh's gaze. She wanted to scream the truth – that none of it mattered. She would save her brother no matter what; he was all she had left.

Her eyes flicked to Connerh, who was watching her closely. Torin's words echoed in her mind.

How many heads?

All of them, she thought, looking away.

Connerh's head tilted. She was about to make the stupid choice. He needed to step in. Old Connerh would've encouraged her, but old Connerh was dead.

A soldier broke through the crowd at the door and approached Nikolas, whispering in his ear.

Nikolas turned, smiling.

"Your Majesty, if I may offer a brief reprieve from the tension…" He clasped his hands, expression mild. "I hope you'll forgive our ambition in acting without your consent. In these uncertain times, we felt it prudent to evolve your personal security. Athelstan is doing a fine job, of course – but we think more is warranted."

He glanced subtly at Connerh. It was a jab veiled in civility.

"There may be disagreement in this room – but on your protection, we stand united. We cannot lose another queen to senseless violence."

It sounded noble, but to Lena, it felt like she was just another object. Not kept for her worth, but because the owner was tired of losing things.

"We've retained the services of a skilled fighter, assassin, and former mercenary. A familiar face," Nikolas said, savouring the buildup.

Connerh leaned against the pillar, arms crossed, eyebrow raised. Lena interpreted his expression as jealous concern – it amused her.

Old Connerh was still in there after all.

Connerh ran through names. Niko wouldn't make an uninformed choice, and this had his fingerprints all over it.

But who?

"Niko, I'm exhausted. Skip the theatrics," Lena implored.

"Of course. I only meant to impress upon you the care given to the decision."

"And it's appreciated," she replied curtly.

"May I present – Dame Allister Winterbourne. A cousin on your father's side, if I'm not mistaken."

Connerh raised a brow. Lena's face softened. She remembered Allister – distant, yes, but familiar.

She had hoped for a burly man to parade in front of Connerh, but maybe it was for the best. He didn't need blood on his hands so early in the game.

All eyes turned to the door as Allister entered.

She was enormous – clearly giant-blooded, though diminished in stature. Over seven feet tall, platinum hair braided over loose curls, and grey eyes. Her armour was blackened plate, her cape a mantle of raven feathers. She looked like a fallen angel, yet her face was kind – if unsmiling. She had a job to do, and she wore that intent plainly.

She knelt before Lena, still nearly as tall as Lena was when she was standing.

"Your Majesty," Allister said. Her voice was deep and commanding, but still feminine.

"A disgraced knight? That's your idea of a 'careful choice'?" Connerh quipped.

Groans followed.

"I would be honoured if you accepted the post," Lena said, raising Allister to her feet. Her disapproving look was all for Connerh.

Allister stood, her armour rattling with the motion. She paid Connerh no mind, though her gaze briefly met his, disinterested.

"Are we to believe every rumour from out of the east?" Niko replied smoothly, but too fast. He'd fallen into Connerh's trap.

A personal pick. Interesting.

"Pay him no mind; he's only here to observe," Lena said. Her reminder carried weight.

Connerh smiled faintly and drifted into thought. Years ago, he'd have been at that table – arguing, fired up, eager to ride. Now? He watched the puppets pull each other's strings.

So easy to make people believe their choices were their own.

Dangerous, he thought, and smiled again.

"Are you caught up to speed?" Lena asked Allister.

"I am, Your Majesty."

Lena rolled her eyes at the title.

"Right. Then tell us – what would *you* do?"

Niko stepped forward, clearing his throat.

"I don't think Allister is qual—"

"Be still, Niko, and ever silent," Lena snapped.

He retreated, smiling tightly.

Allister stepped forward, avoiding every eye in the room to focus only on the maps.

"Mind?" she asked.

Lena gestured permission.

Connerh narrowed his eyes. It was all a dance. The same rhythm, new notes. The same old song. It gave him a headache.

Allister pored over the maps, scanning, calculating. Then she looked up.

"Why don't you sue for peace?"

The room stiffened.

She continued, calm and deliberate, "The prince is deep behind enemy lines – hunted, exposed. A small rescue force could be overwhelmed. A large one would ignite a war. So, we shift the approach. Propose peace talks. Your presence justifies a substantial delegation – large enough to move with strength, yet veiled in diplomacy. Whether those talks are genuine or merely a pretext is yours to decide. Either way, they grant us cover. We set the location – strategically chosen to give him the best chance to slip through and reach us under the guise of negotiation. Then, once the talks conclude, he returns with the delegation, and we quietly position twenty thousand troops just hours behind – out of sight, but ready. If it escalates, we're not caught flat-footed."

Silence. Then murmurs. Then stillness again.

They all turned to Connerh, waiting for his take.

He shook his head. No comment.

"I think it's a sad commentary," Oleander said in a sombre tone, "that it takes a warrior to suggest peace. But much like a feast, it's easy to overlook the simplest dish."

Connerh chuckled quietly.

"To pursue peace could—" he began, but Aghor cut him off.

"It only needs to *seem* that way. It'll be over my dead body before I ever ally with someone like Curzon," Aghor snapped.

A burst of cheers followed, loud and visceral. Connerh's gaze shifted to Niko, who didn't join in. His subtle smirk gave him away.

Then Connerh caught something: a glance exchanged between Niko and Allister, held just a moment too long. He stroked his beard, thoughtful.

Niko, sensing eyes on him, quickly erased all trace of expression. He took two careful steps to the right – just enough to land at the edge of Lena's peripheral vision. Just where she could notice him.

"Well?" Lena asked, her tone deceptively casual. "Niko? How did she do?"

Niko made a small show of reconsidering the proposal – hands behind his back, lips pursed – before finally conceding.

"I think she has great potential. This is, admittedly, one of our best options thus far. Apologies, Dame Allister, if I implied otherwise."

"I'll pay it no mind, Lord Hargrave," she replied coolly.

"My, my. If it isn't the little fisherman who could," Allister quipped. They stood shoulder to shoulder, facing opposite directions.

"And if it isn't the big bitch of the north," Connerh shot back.

Allister burst into laughter. Connerh joined in a beat later.

"That's your best one yet, little man," she conceded between chuckles.

"Thank you. I laughed hysterically when I thought of it," he replied, pleased with himself. "Though I did consider *giant cunt monster*. Had a certain ring to it."

"Well, that's lazy – and not terribly imaginative, might I add," she said, feigning seriousness.

"Oh, I disagree. There was *a lot* of imagining involved," he added with a grin.

She laughed again and punched his arm hard enough to knock him off balance. Their laughter tapered off.

"You look…good. Different, but good," she ventured, studying him. "Your fire doesn't seem to burn quite the same. It's a statement, for sure — though I'm not sure what it says yet."

He considered that, then shrugged. "It's more the *expression* of a statement than the statement itself. Or maybe I haven't found the words yet. So far, I'm going with *free*."

She wrinkled her forehead, amused. "Like I always say — whatever makes your cock hard."

He snorted before he asked, "What's got you roped in with the weasel?"

The humour drained from her face. "I'm very much aligned with what Nikolas said. She needs protection. Things are about to get very dark, and…better me than most. Didn't take much convincing."

She looked him over again, this time with quiet intensity. Connerh nodded in agreement. He had thoughts — lots of them — but this wasn't the place. He settled for a heavy sigh.

"Well, I'm glad it's you," he said.

"I'm glad it is, too," she replied with a small smile and a respectful bow of the head. After a moment, she nodded towards the table and asked, "So, do you miss it?"

"For what it *is?* No. For what it's supposed to *represent*…maybe," he answered, voice low and uncertain.

"It's certainly easier to just head out — blades swinging, heads falling," she said, adjusting her stance.

His eyes darkened, mind flaring at some unspoken memory.

"Maybe too easy," he murmured, locking eyes with her.

They lingered in silence, haunted by shared recollections of war.

"I'm glad you're okay," she offered softly.

He fidgeted. Here it came — the uncomfortable part.

"I was…not happy when we thought—" She smiled away the memory.

He looked down, brushing imaginary lint from his tunic. She punched him again, but this time it was more gently.

"We should catch up. When there's ale to fill the awkward moments," she offered, picking up on his cues.

"We will," he replied.

They nodded to each other, and she drifted back into Lena's orbit — but not before Lena exited it.

He blinked, opening his eyes to her standing there. So much on his tongue, so much held behind it.

"You came back," she said.

"I always do."

She grinned, a blush blossoming on her cheeks, her eyes falling.

"Yes, I suppose so." A moment passed, and she asked, "Are you up for one more adventure?"

Connerh looked around, a familiar energy coursing through the air. His eyes lowered, settling on her.

A breath escaped his nose.

CHAPTER SEVENTY-FIVE

WHEN THE BOTTLE BREAKS

LENA

The thunder of twenty thousand soldiers fell into instant silence as she approached – the kind of silence that doesn't follow a noise but *replaces* it. Like a single, unified crack of lightning through clouded skies, they rose as one, saluting their queen with discipline honed into instinct. Lena dismounted with the same composed grace that she wore like armour, her right fist pressing over her heart with two fingers and a thumb extended, the traditional Hildeheim salute. Across the field, voices answered her in unison, their chant of loyalty rippling across ranks in a deep, grounded cadence. Allister towered over her like a cloud blocking the sun, and Farrah was nearby, as she always was.

Her mind was elsewhere, yet their reverence reached her. It always did. A soldier's salute had a way of making it all feel like it meant something: the endless bureaucracy, the political dance, the delicate threading of power through halls and signatures. So much of it felt performative, distant and removed from the gravity of the real moments defined by blood, steel, and sacrifice. Her part was the foundation – the part no longer seen or acknowledged once the house stood on its own.

"Carry on," she instructed softly, eyes scanning the sea of blackened steel and bear pelts – not aimless but searching.

"Your Majesty?"

The voice cut cleanly through the renewed din. General Hyde. She spotted his tall, austere figure threading towards her, the chaos parting naturally in his wake. Without a word, she passed the reins of her horse to Farrah.

Hyde began to bow – but she crossed the space between them first and pulled him into a firm embrace.

He froze, startled, arms suspended in uncertainty before memory and affection caught up to him. A slow, genuine smile overtook his features as he returned the gesture.

"It's not my place to tell you where you belong…" he murmured, pulling back just enough to look at her, "…but I thought you'd remain with the delegation. It's safer there. Although I can't say I'm surprised to see you here, because that would be a lie."

The conflict in his feelings was written plainly across his face.

Hyde was an older man. He had served her mother before her, and he had watched Lena grow from a babe to a queen. In many ways, she was like an adopted child to him – and he, a quiet father figure in return. Yet decorum had long dictated their boundaries: he would never outright treat her as a daughter, nor she him as a father.

"They don't need me there. Niko is quite capable," she replied, her face buried into his chest.

She held him a moment longer, then stepped back to meet his eyes. He already had a sense of her state of mind, but her expression told him more than words ever could. Without speaking, he stepped aside and gestured towards a nearby tent. They walked together in silence, perhaps eight metres to the entrance – Hyde with his arms clasped behind his back, Lena with hers folded tightly across her chest. Allister intercepted them, walking inside first and holding the flap open for Lena.

"Leave us," Hyde thundered, his voice cutting through the tent before his body had fully entered.

The officers jumped, caught between instinct and protocol, unsure whether to salute both the queen and the general or to obey without hesitation. The lieutenants scattered quickly and quietly. The commanders, more seasoned, offered brief salutes before exiting. Allister moved closer to the centre of the tent, where the ceiling was its tallest, so she could stand fully. Her hands crossed at her centre, the right pulling her hilt forward slightly.

Hyde moved to the servants' table and poured two cups of wine. Lena draped her fur over the back of a nearby chair but didn't sit. Instead, she paced, absently picking at her nails.

"Join me?" he invited, sitting beside a small table and nodding towards the other seat with his head. She obliged, crossing the space to sit beside him, taking the cup he extended towards her and emptying it in a moment. Hyde raised an eyebrow, a grin tugging at the corners of his mouth. Noticing his gaze, she became suddenly aware of her impropriety – but the embarrassment soon gave way to her lack of care.

"Don't start," she said dryly, cutting him off before he could speak.

He gave a deep chuckle and lifted his palms in a gesture of surrender, the smile still faintly playing about his lips. For a moment, he considered delivering the expected speech – the one about her safety, her role, the danger of being this close to the front. However, he knew her far too well for that. She hadn't come all this way for a lecture.

She'd come for hope.

But he wasn't sure he could deliver the lasting sort that she needed. He took the empty chalice from her hand to replace it with his own, the wine untouched by his own lips, as if it were all planned from the pour.

She sighed, heavy and knowing.

"What is it? Give me the bad news," she pressed, swallowing.

"Bad news? There is no bad news. If nothing has changed between his last letter and now, Bjorn will arrive within the hour. We will intercept him at the border and make our merry way home. This is what we call child's play, my dear," he replied.

"And if he's followed?"

"Doesn't matter if he's followed by one or a hundred thousand. There's no army alive stupid enough to engage our forces. Our twenty thousand easily equate to forty or sixty in terms of strength, especially compared to any military in this region. It'd be like a dog fucking about, trying to snatch food from a cavern of bears, if you'll excuse my language," he replied, ending in a higher pitch. She grinned and batted his apology away with a shake of her head.

She set the chalice down, resting her hands in her lap as she acknowledged, "I'm glad to hear it. I'm also glad this is all soon to be over."

He nodded, blinking, before he asked, "The question is, what will you do next?"

Her head fell, her eyes tracking upwards.

"I don't know."

"Permission to speak freely?"

"Haven't you always?" she countered. He went to speak but stopped, and she corrected herself with, "Sorry, that came out wrong. Yes…please."

He leaned back in his chair, pulling his armour down from the waist to give his neck more mobility, crossing one leg over the other.

"I am but your humble servant. I turn the levers, I feed the meat grinder, and I serve it all on a platter. That is my purpose, and so it shall be until I'm too old to serve you or some lucky bastard gets the best of me. Hopefully, not while I'm on the privy. Either way…don't think I don't enjoy doing what it is we do best. However, you have three hundred thousand spread out across every kingdom surrounding Hildeheim, and your elite death squads march throughout the land like Death himself is on a mission, killing any and everyone who has so much as looked at you wrong. In the south, you've got Hargatha amassing a navy larger than she has the ports to support. You are very loudly telling the world that you are ready for war, but you've neither the cause nor the target for your aggression." He took a deep breath as she watched him speak. "You interpret this as strength…but to the contrary, it makes you look weak. Like you're trying to prove something. You're injured, nursing a wound, sword in hand, lashing out at someone weaker to make yourself seem strong. You're like a lion refusing to lie on his deathbed as the hyenas and vultures begin to circle, waiting for the right time to strike. Now, you could still pull back and gather yourself…but it must be done correctly. Too quickly, and you incite the chase. Too slowly, and they react out of fear. And, of course, there must be an enemy named by the end of this. Someone had to take the fall as the cause of your aggression – a head to hang from a pike as a warning to others. The topic of propaganda must proliferate throughout the streets for decades to come. Otherwise, you will be hated and targeted by so many that there is no army that could properly protect you." He paused, ensuring she was following.

Her eyes were glazed over, but she was listening.

"Do you know what happens to kings and queens who are hated and despised in such a way? Often earning the moniker of mad? Do you know how they die?"

"In their own beds," she nearly whispered, her eyes focusing on him.

He nodded in agreement.

"And usually at the hand of those closest to them," he added

Her head and focus shifted immediately. She cleared her throat, sitting back in her chair, her eyes trailing to her hands where they remained in her lap.

"There's a second option," he said, leaning forward. She looked up at him, her brows furrowing. He took it as a sign of her willingness to hear it. "You don't need to find a scapegoat. You already have one, and his name is Bjorn." His words seemed to echo in her mind, cutting like a finely sharpened blade. "And if I were to be so bold as to say…he is deserving of it. You and I both know that not a single man who has tasted Hildeheim steel over this is in any way responsible for your mother's death."

Her eyes widened.

"And what would you have me do, Kristoph?" she argued. "Leave him to die in enemy territory?!"

"That is *precisely* what you should do! You blame him for the bloodshed. You tell them he went too far without your informed consent. He abused his station, his power, and his command over the armies. You make a big show about his death, bolstering your presence in this region as you think about how you will respond to the murder of your brother, a prince of Hildeheim. Let them sweat a little…and then…you say that Reh'gara himself came to you in a dream and told you the bloodshed must stop. You accept his death as terms for peace, depart the fuck back to the mountain where you belong, and hope this blows over just long enough to salvage your reputation and your legacy. Having a few children often aids in that effort, might I add," he countered, still controlling the volume of his voice – although judging by his cadence and tone, he might as well have been shouting at her.

His head canted as she shook her head repeatedly.

"He chose this course of action, against all direction, against all guidance, and…against common sense! You practically ordered him not to go, and he did it anyway – if not just to spite you and all that you represent."

Kristoph failed at bridling himself.

"Order? He's not a soldier, Kristoph," she responded.

He snarled. Allister did a poor job of pretending not to listen; her eyes darted back and forth as they spoke.

"Damn right, he's not a soldier," he let slip before biting his tongue. "Behead me if you must." He looked at the ground, unable to defy her to her face, and his volume lowered drastically. "But I will not order a single man to cross that border to die for a *traitor*, let alone start a war that will cost the lives of countless innocents and *my* men. If he makes it across, so be it, and anyone who follows him will be first in line to enter the hereafter. If he does not… Well…" He closed his eyes as he finished his diatribe, expecting her to explode in return.

She grabbed the second drink and sipped it, then stood. A commotion of cheers erupted outside, distracting her for a moment.

"When this is all over, perhaps we should discuss your retirement," she snapped back.

"You don't mean that; you're just angry," he replied. "But you're angry at the wrong people. Again, you're lashing out in an attempt to protect the wound. Sooner or later, you'll need to realise who actually cares for you, and who is pretending to for their own gain. Usually, those are the ones telling you what you want to hear." Standing, he concluded, "But, when this is all over, if you still feel that way, then I'll hand-deliver my resignation."

She sighed at herself, her shoulders relaxing.

A soldier ran into the tent and saluted them before she could reply.

"Your Majesty. General. His Highness approaches with soldiers on his tail," the soldier announced hurriedly before he showed himself out of the tent.

Kristoph's eyes shot to Lena as she made worried eye contact with him.

"You're right," she started as she swigged the drink, setting the chalice back on the table. His head involuntarily cocked backwards. "I won't put that kind of burden upon you – or the men. It is not a fair request. We all must choose our own destiny."

He nodded in agreement, though he was thoroughly confused by the absence of her normal fiery disposition.

Lena walked to the tent entrance, and Allister followed.

"Go. Feed, and then we'll head back," she whispered to Allister, who nodded and left. "You're a good man, Kristoph; you have served me as well as you did my mother. Keep the men here at the border in the event my brother crosses safely."

She half smiled.

Kristoph offered a bow as she slipped out of the tent. His mind raced as he tried to piece together what had just occurred. Her reply was uncharacteristic and misplaced. However, his train of thought was interrupted by the growing commotion brewing outside the tent. The noise grew loud enough to inspire him to investigate.

As he stepped out of the tent, the sight of mass panic briefly incapacitated him. He looked at the soldiers who ran up to him, clearly yelling, but he couldn't make out the words. In those few minutes, time seemed to slow. Heartbeats later, his adrenaline lowered enough for the words to become clear.

"What are your orders!?" they screamed.

He looked around, trying to decipher the cause of panic for the now thousands surrounding him. Before he could utter any further words, his eyes followed the direction the soldiers were pointing. They then grew wide as he observed Lena in the distance, furiously riding a stolen soldier's horse over the border into enemy territory.

Alone.

Sheer terror overtook him. It felt like hours passed before his words found a voice to pour out of his mouth.

"Stop her!"

Like a blur, Whisper raced by him with Connerh on his back, sending Kristoph tumbling backwards. His hooves sounded like the march of a hundred men running at full speed.

In seconds, a torrent of horse-bound soldiers took up pursuit.

Bjorn finally caught sight of the thinning treeline. The border.

Close. So close.

Victory – or something like it – was within reach.

He glanced left, then right, at the few who had dared to follow him into this hell. They knew the cost. They knew the stakes. And yet, they'd come.

At the start, failure had felt like a distant possibility. Unthinkable, even.

After all, who would dare murder the brother of the Queen of Hildeheim? Who would risk war just to make a point?

Surely no one would be so bold. So reckless.

But now – now, with death howling behind him, failure no longer felt improbable.

It felt inevitable.

The Bajoreen horde roared through the jungle at their backs. Bjorn couldn't see them through the dense canopy, but he didn't need to.

He could hear them. He could feel them.

Thousands.

Thomas rode beside him. His jaw was tight, and a forced grin flickered on his lips. The kind that said, *I'm scared, but I don't want to be.*

He didn't know. None of them did.

Bjorn hadn't told them the truth.

Not all of it.

Not that the mission wasn't sanctioned – that it never had been. Not that their noble cause was laced with personal vendetta. That retribution, not justice, was what guided them.

He hadn't told them that death was always the most likely outcome.

The trees began to thin.

Almost there.

Then—

A wet slap. Then another. And another.

Arrows struck Thomas and his horse in rapid succession – nine, as fast as breath. They crumpled mid-gallop, disappearing into the brush with brutal finality.

The clearing ahead offered no sanctuary. No shelter. Just open ground and death.

Bjorn ducked low, veering as another arrow sliced the air beside him.

He pushed his horse harder, heart slamming against his ribs.

They broke through the trees – down the hillside, now. His enemies behind him poured down like an avalanche at his heels.

He squeezed his eyes shut.

Waited.

For the pain. The sharp pull of death.

But nothing.

He heard the pursuit, but…it stopped.

Bjorn risked a glance back. The enemy had halted, arguing amongst themselves amidst their pursuit.

He looked forward again – and saw her.

Lena. Riding towards him, an army at her back.

He laughed, wild and breathless. His shoulders shook with relief.

But then – snap.

A bowstring.

Then another. Then more until it became a chorus.

Pain exploded in his back. One arrow. Two. Three. Hundreds.

He screamed as the world cracked open.

Everything turned white.

No trees. No hooves. No other sound.

Only the echo of Lena's cries fading into silence.

"What are you doing?!" Connerh shouted as Whisper surged up beside Lena's horse.

"I'm saving him! I have to; this is all my fault," she shouted, voice cracking. Dirt kicked up in their wake under hooves, violent and intense.

"How?!" he shouted back.

"They wouldn't dare touch me!" she screamed back, spit flying. She drove the horse harder. Whisper matched pace, unbothered by the effort.

"Then let me retrieve him. Turn back!"

"No." Her voice dropped. Softer. Breaking. "I've already asked too much of you."

Her eyes watered, but the wind whipped them away. "Look – there he is!"

Bjorn had just appeared. Connerh's eyes found him. He said something low to Whisper – barely a breath – and the beast launched forward like lightning.

"Come on," Connerh muttered to himself.

The distance narrowed, but even with Whisper unrestrained, the gap wasn't closing fast enough. Not for his liking.

He got close enough to see the fear well in Bjorn's face – saw the panic – just as the arrows struck.

The horde peeled away, like a diverted current, heading back towards the cover of the forest.

"No!" Connerh screamed, the word drawn out until he lacked the breath to sustain it, continuing as he jumped from Whisper, catching Bjorn's body as it fell. He crumpled, arms trembling as grief and fury flooded through him. Lena arrived, dismounting, a scream already tearing from her throat. Her hysteria blurred the moment, her voice hitting a pitch so sharp it made him flinch.

"This has to stop," he whispered to himself.

He laid Bjorn gently in her arms.

"This has to stop," he repeated, louder forceful.

But his words fell on deaf ears. She didn't hear him. Or wouldn't.

Kristoph and his men arrived, circling them. A wall of men, swords, and shields. He dismounted slowly, taking only two steps before pausing, giving her space. His hands clenched around the hilt of his sheathed sword, jaw set.

He looked away. Disgusted. Disappointed. Grieving.

"This. Stops. Now!" Connerh's voice exploded like thunder, cutting through the moment and freezing every soldier in place.

He took a few steps away from Lena, arm raised. The sky responded. Torinir crashed from the clouds, a meteor wrapped in anger and fury. He slammed into Connerh's waiting grip, the ground quaking and parting beneath him.

The nearest men were thrown back, horses whinnying in fear. Even Lena was forced back onto her hands.

"Connerh, wait!" she shouted.

He turned to her, his eyes glowing a subtle white.

"Just remember, you asked for this," he declared.

He mounted Whisper and shot off with the report of a thunderclap.

"Grab the prince's body, and get her out of here!" Kristoph barked as it took to the forefront.

"No! Wait! What about Connerh?!" she protested.

Explosions boomed in the distance. The men surrounding her parted.

Through the smoke and light in the distance, they saw devastation. Bodies were flung skywards. Men and horses were torn apart, limb from limb. His aim – to leave no one breathing – was clear.

Pronounced.

Kristoph didn't flinch. "Don't worry. I've no doubt he's going to be just fine."

He extended his hand to her.

"But—" she choked.

"You're going to listen to me for once!" Kristoph snapped, grabbing her shoulders and jostling them enough to get her attention. Then, gently, his tone softened, as did his grip. "My job is to win your wars and keep you safe. Let me do my job!"

Lena stilled. Her expression went blank, although grief still trembled in the corners of her lips.

She went to nod but froze, catching subtle movement on the eastern hilltop overlooking them all – at the edge of another border.

Seven horsemen, their armour glistening in the sun, gold and ornate. Their helms, tall and slender. The white ribbons tied to their spears, flapping in the wind.

…Their tall ears, protruding.

They remained still. Watching.

"Shit," Kristoph muttered as he, too, caught sight of them.

CHAPTER SEVENTY-SIX

WESTWOOD

ELARION

Elarion had gone quiet an hour ago. Not withdrawn, exactly. Just still. Internalised, his fingers lingering beneath the collar of his armour. The treeline of the Westwood loomed ahead, slow in its approach as their horses began to falter, their breath misting in the cooling air – a result of long days and nights spent pressing forward, driven by urgency.

As the sun slipped beneath the horizon, fireflies sparked to life beneath the boughs, their soft pulse rhythmic, like a beacon drawing him home. Pale motes drifted around them, nearly glowing, remnants of a spell too slow to cast – magic suspended in the act of becoming.

And always, the roar of the great waterfall. Not violent, but constant, its rage made gentle by time, eroded down to duty.

A border between realms.

A separation by sound, stone, and water.

Elarion retracted his hand as the bridge came into full view before them – ancient stone half-swallowed by moss and twilight.

"*Virelen Thael,*" he murmured.

"What's it mean?" Madika's voice rose from the horse behind him, uncertain but curious.

"The Bridge of Last Light," Thaetra answered before he could. She sat just behind Madika, her voice soft and reverent – before it turned playful. "It's ancient. Something actually older than Elarion, for once."

Elarion smirked and gave a quiet shake of his head.

"He still won't tell me how old he is," Madika quipped, brow raised, a grin tugging at her cheek.

"It's like being young, but in reverse," Thaetra replied, eyes ahead. "When you tell someone how young you are, it's all they see. Everything you say and do gets measured against it. Judged for it…by it. Even when they don't mean to."

Madika nodded, the logic settling quickly. Elarion's brow ticked upwards, but he said nothing; she was right. There was nothing more worth adding.

He glanced back at them, then gave a brief nod. "We'll dismount here."

He swung down from the saddle as he spoke, loosening his pack with quiet efficiency. Thaetra followed without hesitation – graceful, composed, a series of actions followed thousands of times before.

Madika scrambled to imitate them, tugging her satchel free with both hands, fighting with the knots.

"Are we walking the rest of the way?" she asked, blinking between them, her brow pulled tight with confusion, her hurried pace unjustified.

"Just across the pass." Elarion allowed the corner of his mouth to lift – more memory than amusement. "There are…old friends waiting on the other side."

Thaetra's eyes flashed at that, urgency sparking in her limbs. She moved faster now, barely keeping herself from combusting with excitement. She leaned into her mount's neck, whispered something in Elvish – a farewell, a command. The beast gave a low grunt and turned back the way they'd come without protest. Elarion paused, pressing his forehead gently to that of his own horse. He murmured something low in his native tongue, then echoed Thaetra's phrase. The steed huffed once, then followed.

Madika looked between them, then at her own mount.

"Thank you," she muttered awkwardly. She gave its rear an unintentionally abrasive smack. The horse let out a screeching whinny and bolted, bucking all the way down the path as if it had been insulted.

Thaetra burst into laughter – bright, sudden, and unrestrained.

"Sorry!" Madika shouted after the poor creature, wincing.

"Come on," Thaetra said, already passing by. She reached out and gently tugged Madika by the arm, guiding her towards the bridge. Madika followed without protest, but she paused twelve steps past the chiselled stone span. Behind them, Elarion had lagged, kneeling at the threshold, one hand pressed to the worn surface as if in prayer – or memory. Its runes glowed into life.

"Is he not coming?" she asked, a sliver of panic threading into her voice.

"He'll join us momentarily." Thaetra's tone softened, then shifted – warmer. "Come; I want to introduce you to someone. But whatever you do…don't scream."

That last line caught her attention, pulling her from her concern. Madika blinked, uncertain whether to laugh or brace herself. Curiosity sparked alongside something colder. Maybe fear.

Maybe both.

Their footsteps echoed dully against the ancient wood as they crossed, the boards groaning beneath their weight. Mist clung low along the span, rising from the chasm below where the unseen waterfall roared. Elarion's form was barely visible now, shrouded in silver spray, obscured by the veil of fog leeching from the Westwood that drifted, ghostlike, across the bridge's span. Overhead, the warm hues of orange and gold surrendered to the advancing blanket of purple and dark blue. A celestial gradient. The stars began to appear, sharp and twinkling as brightly as the fireflies below them. The constellations began to assemble, their light awakening like a bear emerging from its den.

"Fareve en'vela, silme arda. Telamar, ananta nuin. Lome nauta i vilya – Virelen Thael, na vana. Telti i koa, sirna i londe…" Elarion began aloud, pausing upon sensing he was not alone. His eyes opened.

"Are you sure you want to go through with this?" Lysand's voice floated towards him, soft yet firm. She stood on the bridge, draped in mist and bathed in moonlight.

He sighed, finally standing. His gaze was distant as he spoke, still looking behind him. When he replied, his voice was low and weary.

"No."

"Then why are you going through with it?" Lysand asked, stepping closer, her eyes searching his.

"It's not my decision," Elarion answered, his tone heavy with the weight of inevitability.

Lysand raised a brow, the silence between them thick.

"The crown no longer sits on Galathir's head; it sits on yours. The forest obeys you now. That makes it very much your decision."

His face softened, a shadow passing over his features.

"My hand is not forced by any law of our land; it's forced by their actions — by their hearts."

She nodded in agreement. He understood she wasn't doubting him, nor was she encouraging him to doubt himself.

"The road to the Westwood will be narrowed to outsiders while they decide their fate — and while we prepare for our journey," he went on.

"That is wise," she replied. Her haggard voice remained clear, agreeable.

"Still…" Elarion's voice dropped, heavy with unspoken things. "I struggle to let go. I know this is best for them, but…a part of me still wants to help."

"As I told you," Lysand began, her tone edged with calm insistence, "accepting the role of King of the Forest will let you help in ways you never imagined. You've walked among them for far longer than any of them deserved. Now it's time to lead — on a grander scale. Push them towards greatness instead of pulling. In the end, no matter how much effort you give, they must choose to accept help. And they won't…not as long as they see you as a crutch, even though you've tried to distance yourself, to pull back in recent times." She chuckled quietly — a soft, knowing sound. "Besides, bridges can be rebuilt. Memories can be revisited."

His sigh was the only reply he could manage. He had long since learned the futility of debating her.

"Yes. Yes, they can," he murmured eventually, lifting his belongings from the ground.

The runes on the bridge flared to life — bright, almost blinding — as he stepped across the threshold. He and Lysand walked side by side, their footsteps soft and steady against the ancient wood.

"How is Galathir?" he asked after a moment, his voice breaking the silence between them.

"Still nursing his wounded pride for being removed from the throne," Lysand said, her tone light but edged with sadness.

"I still don't understand why you didn't pick one of his heirs."

"The council thought it the best time for change. And I agreed. We've come too far to descend backwards into meaningless pursuits and bloodshed. Your cousin had become corrupted…mirroring the attitudes of men. He will find a new purpose equally as fulfilling. Even more suited to his talents."

"But a half-blood elven king?"

Lysand's lips curved into a wry smile. "Those are meaningless words. They only carry weight if you will it."

"I suppose that's something else I'll have to learn to let go."

"Change comes with effort; the journey is just as important as the result," she replied.

As they neared the bridge's end, a swarm of fireflies descended upon him, merging with the glowing motes and wisps to form a crown above his head.

"It looks good on you," she remarked with a smirk.

He shook his head.

"Now, hurry; I grow tired of waiting. Your real crown awaits you here, with me…and I am anxious to meet this little one," she said, remaining on the bridge.

"Just promise me no fanfare," he begged.

She smiled, vanishing into the mist.

He took a deep breath and looked upwards. His gaze lingered on the source of pure light in the night's sky.

"Nyctorc, I request your aid."

The moon's light brightened.

"Fareve en'vela, silme arda. Telamar, ananta nuin. Lome nauta i vilya – Virelen Thael, na vana. Telti i koa, sirna i londe…" He paused once more. "Auta i ear, olendor hannon."

The words slid from his mouth like whispers released into a howling wind.

The waterfall surged with renewed fury, no longer the steady murmur of old memory but a force awakened. Its roar deepened as it swelled, rising like a tide of ancient judgment. Water crashed over the bridge, as strong as the stone it dismantled, devouring its span in a furious cascade. Rock groaned and split beneath the pressure, pried apart by the weight of the current, and its moss-covered blocks tumbled into the chasm one by one, vanishing into the mist below. The wooden boards twisted and snapped, ripped from their fittings as nature reclaimed what had always been hers.

He couldn't explain the rhyme or reason for the impulse, but he waved goodbye – his arm rising in an awkward, three-part motion, as if uncertain whether to commit or abort.

CHAPTER SEVENTY-SEVEN

A PINEBOX AND A SONG

LENA

Hymns were supposed to synchronise the individual to the hive…

To insulate the sting of grief.

To offer hope when there was none.

To provide warmth when the chill of darkness encroached.

Thousands of voices coalesced into a single current, requiring no music or instrument to remain melodic.

The power of song won battles. They marked their ends and preceded new ones.

They penetrated flesh, resonating in bone and mind.

And yet, Lena felt nothing.

Her eyes no longer seemed capable of releasing tears. The hollow in her stomach had stopped feeling unnatural, the emptiness no longer a signal her mind registered. She hadn't eaten in days and drank wine only out of reflex, an internal compulsion she didn't question. Her gaze drifted across the crowd, veiled and low. Their returned stares felt hollow – gawking, distant.

As if she were some caged animal, something meant to be observed from afar.

Perhaps she was.

Too dangerous to others to be allowed to roam. Or perhaps too dangerous to herself.

Her head turned slightly to the right.

Connerh's seat was empty.

She convinced herself his absence was…understandable, or at the very least, deserved. Though she wished he were there – maybe then, she could have allowed herself to be lost in the moment. Unfortunately, that particular outcome would be relegated to the land of wishes and regrets.

Farrah leaned in to whisper something. Lena met her eyes.

"The elven ambassador wishes to meet with you to—" Farrah began.

Lena's laughter erupted – sharp, guttural, raw. Farrah froze, as did half the crowd. Eyes turned. Mouths stilled.

"Yes…yes, I'm sure he does," Lena said aloud, not bothering to hush her voice, her eyes wandering in front of her.

"To offer his condolences privately," Farrah finished softly, embarrassed by Lena's outburst.

"Yes, of course," Lena replied, immediately regaining her composure, nodding.

She stood for a few moments before finally sighing loudly.

"Alright, I'm done with this," she announced abruptly, lifting her gown and walking away, Allister a half-step behind her. Farrah followed, a host of servants trailing in her wake.

The doors to the reception room opened. Allister entered first, making a slow circuit of the space and checking every corner – including the adjoining rooms.

Lena swept in behind her, ripping off her veil and gloves and tossing them onto the couch in front of her.

"Take this off of me," she demanded, referring to the train fastened to her shoulders with silver clasps.

Servants rushed in, detaching it and rolling it up with care.

"I need wine…and send for the ambassador. Let's get this over with," she snapped, draping herself across the couch.

"Do you need anything?" Aethelstan asked, standing just outside the doors with another of the Queen's Guard.

"No."

"Yes, Your Majesty," he acknowledged, closing the doors behind him.

The first cup went down with ease, immediately bringing civility to her nerves. She masked her eyes with her hand as she waited for her cup to be refilled. She lay back, wine arm extended over the floor, the other draped over her forehead, her eyes tracing the distant arch of the vaulted ceiling high above that dwarfed even Allister, ribs of dark oak soaring upwards like the inverted hull of a ship. Dust motes drifted through shafts of golden light slanting in from mullioned windows, catching on the weathered brass frames of ancestral portraits that loomed down, staring out through hollow eyes and fixed expressions. Floor-to-ceiling shelves lined the walls, packed with leather-bound tomes whose spines had cracked with age, their titles faded. The air was thick with the scent of old paper and burning kindling on account of the servants lighting the fireplace.

The view made her feel childlike again. She'd napped here before — truthfully, there wasn't a room in the castle where she hadn't once drifted off. Her lids hung low over her eyes, but they no longer burned, no longer fought for closure. Though the thought wished to tempt her, the meaning and enjoyment of rest had since slipped away. These days, she avoided it entirely, as if sleep belonged to a realm that no longer welcomed her. A realm that seemed darker than the absence of light, where uncomfortable truths and realities lay, like sea creatures waiting to drown her below the depths. They were formless in darkness, but their physical grip was undeniable.

She was safe up here, among the light and the living.

At least here she could be distracted.

Allister passed through the edge of her vision, still methodically checking the room, pulling her gaze back to the window — tall and wide, a bright halo blooming across the glass.

"It didn't rain…" she whispered to herself, frowning.

Three measured knocks immediately ripped Lena from her reflection. She shot up, nearly spilling her wine.

"Shit!" she fussed at herself, wiping at the fallen platelets of wine on the floor with her foot and setting her slow haemorrhaging cup on the table.

She rose to her feet just as the door opened, her hands whisking away moisture from her gown with abrasive patting.

"Your Majesty, the Ambassadors of the Westwood," Aethelstan announced.

Lena blinked.

There was something otherworldly about the elves. Something graceful, even as all three were draped in black. It was an uncommon sight; while they were normally adorned in a wide array of earth tones, they never wore black. It was haunting against pale skin and white hair, such a juxtaposed image. And still, it was as if rays of the sun remained fixed upon them, like a spotlight that followed their movements.

They bowed in unison, their long hair falling briefly in front of their saddened faces.

"Hello, Caelithor. Long time no see," she greeted, ignoring their gesture.

"Your Majesty," he responded, moving quickly to grab her hand, kissing it. Her head raised, turning half a quarter away.

"May I present my counterparts, Elyndra and Aelorin?" he continued.

The two of them approached and kissed her hand.

"A pleasure," she replied. She looked at Allister and Farrah. "Leave us."

Allister took a half-second delay, but she obliged once Lena did not waver in either her stare or her command; it was not a request. She nodded and left, closing the door after the last servant vacated.

"Please do not misinterpret my appreciation for your gesture of kindness and support in my time of loss," she began, refocusing her eyes on Caelithor. "But I know this isn't a mere call of pleasantries."

Her tone was balanced, avoiding the edge of self-loathing. She'd accepted the true reason for their visit.

Caelithor straightened his posture. His white hair rested against his chest and down his black gown — thin, form-fitting sleeves and a high collar. Simple, masculine, yet complex in its decoration.

"King Galathir sends his regards and was displeased that he could not be here himself. However, to reply to your sentiment…you are correct. It would be an understatement to say that the timing of our visit is…unfortunate." His tone was sanitised of grief.

"Go on," she pushed, crossing her hands in her lap as if awaiting sentencing.

He took a breath. She couldn't tell if he was losing patience with her or just found no desire to be there.

If it were true, then there was no love lost; she didn't want him here either.

"Your exploits abroad have not gone unnoticed, and they have given rise to some concern. We merely wanted to understand what your intentions are so we might determine if your desire for retribution has been fully satisfied," he replied.

They were words chosen carefully. Small in length, they communicated a great deal: a delicately woven rope with which to either hang oneself or escape a self-created pit of despair. The latter was not often afforded to offenders of this magnitude.

Not after this much bloodshed.

This was where she should have paced, maybe shed a tear or two, and pleaded her case with dignity and sound reserve…

Her head fell briefly.

But she had no tears left.

"Has my retribution been satisfied?" she asked, brow furrowing. Her breathing deepened, hastened. The elves noticed, their heads shifting sides. Her sigh was pronounced. "Yes."

They exchanged glances of relief.

She blinked.

Her eyes were stuck to the floor.

"My brother's grief spun out of control. I should've kept a closer eye – especially knowing the men under him were fiercely loyal. To him. To me. To the Late Queen Mother – rest her soul. But yes…it is over, and I will punish those responsible for failing the proper checks and balances before carrying out unsanctioned attacks. We will also financially reimburse where necessary, rebuild and reconstruct collateral damages where appropriate," she replied.

Caelithor clapped his hands, a deep inset smile on his face. A rippled dimple on his cheek.

"I am so glad to hear it," he replied.

"For the record, with regards to collateral damages, I am to understand that the loss of innocent life was a bare minimum," she continued, faux-lightly. "And those felled were…of the unscrupulous sort? Does your information match?"

Caelithor looked at his companions with an arched brow.

"That is…incorrect," Elyndra replied.

Lena's spine stiffened.

She swallowed. Her throat was dry, prompting her to clear it.

"I wish to be blunt with you," Caelithor interjected. His use of human phrasing caught Lena off guard. Waving his hand towards the chaise, he asked, "Perhaps we should sit?"

She opened her mouth and let it linger for a moment before nodding.

"Of course," she said, turning to sit. He joined her while the other two remained standing.

"What I say next, I speak in confidence. Is that acceptable?" he asked — as if it were an option.

"Yes. Yes, of course. You always have my confidence," she said, exchanging glances with the three of them, her face frowning.

Elyndra found the wine and poured them all full cups before handing them out.

Lena felt nervous for the first time in a long while, as if a lecture and spanked bottom were in her immediate future. Except she would not be stomping to her room, slamming the door out of anger. Those days were long gone.

Still, there was something cathartic about the violence of a door impacting the frame with such ferocity. The noise, the vibrations perfectly emulating the fury within her.

She sipped her wine slowly, deliberately.

Caelithor levelled her with a stare.

"Times are changing. The elves will not always remain in Aelthoria. In fact, our time here is running short."

"Where would you go?" Lena interrupted, confusion strewn across her face.

"To other lands. One in particular…quite some distance from here…far across the seas," he began, standing to look behind him. "I should hope to visit your balcony before we leave, if that's alright? It is such a splendid view," he trailed off.

"I'll take you myself," she added, a question of her survival masked within the brief statement.

"I would like that very much. I have spoken at great length with Elyndra concerning it on our travels here," he continued with a smirk.

Lena smiled. It was promising. She suddenly laughed.

"Jokes aside, what do you mean?" she asked.

He raised his brow.

"Oh, you were serious?"

"Yes. We will shortly begin leaving these shores until the time at which we are all gone," he answered, his gaze slipping into the future.

"How?" she nearly demanded, rushing to her feet. "No one crosses the Great Sea…"

"That is…incorrect," Elyndra added again.

Lena frowned. Her additions were growing tiresome.

"Our journey across the Great Sea is not under any threat of failure," Caelithor replied.

Again, small words, great meaning.

"I would hope that, in the future, you might feel so compelled to share how that is possible with us," she murmured, the request not a question.

He smiled.

"We do not have the authority to do so," he replied.

Lena grunted, slowly nodding her head.

"Be that as it may, before we depart, we desire this world to be…equitable. Balanced," he continued.

"Caelithor, you've known me for nearly two decades now. I know my life in your eyes is but a fraction – if even – of your own… But for the love of the gods, please speak plainly. My heart is empty, and my mind is, as of late…a blur," she replied, feeling bad for her rudeness. However, she just couldn't do it anymore. She couldn't continue playing the game of translation of intent.

He chuckled.

"I'm sorry," he replied.

"We want to ensure the world isn't burning when we depart, and you're holding the torch," Aelorin spoke, his voice gravelly.

"Is it anyone? Or just me you're worried about?" she returned.

"No one will be holding any torch," Caelithor replied.

"Even if that means removing the trees so they can't be made," Aelorin continued.

"Bringing balance to all *could* be a solution," Caelithor continued.

Lena thought for a moment. The implication was heavy. The suggestion of taking every kingdom back to the Stone Age passed far beyond the realm of threat.

It was an ultimatum.

"You are the largest kingdom with the most military might at its disposal. We can't have you raining fear and terror on the rest of the world every time something doesn't go your way. It's not just you; your mother and the generations before you have all teetered on the same edge. It has become a pattern…a pattern that is not sustainable by our accounting. This is not what strength looks like," Caelithor added, this time speaking plainly, as she requested.

Her head fell.

"I understand. And I agree. I've spoken with Reh'gara at great length concerning the need for change. He…he has impressed upon the need to stop the bloodshed. To right our wrongs to the best of our ability and to move forward with a unifying intent…not one of death and destruction," she began.

The three smiled at the mention of Reh'gara's name.

"Ah, Elder Reh'gara. I have not had the pleasure of being in his presence for several lifetimes. Is he well?" Caelithor asked, a large smile still carved into his cheeks.

"He is," she replied.

He nodded continually.

"Elder Amethyst has made us aware of…" He paused, taking a breath. "…his own exploits in connection with Connerh," he carefully continued.

Lena's eyes widened subtly.

"And while that is…well beyond our capability of commentary…it is also concerning," he concluded, his gaze lost in thought. "But those are issues for another day, to be handled by those more equipped for such a matter."

"And who might that be?" she asked.

He smiled.

"We'll have to see, won't we?" he said, standing. "Either way, I'm glad to hear you have a clear path forward. Your plans for corrective measures are admirable; please let us know how we can assist in facilitating such things. We have considerable time before our era fully ends…so if it is alright with you, I would like to check in from time to time to see how I can help. You've been under considerable stress and change. I know that can be difficult," he said.

It rankled. As if it were an option.

"You're always welcome, Caelithor. You know that," she replied.

"I would never impose. But thank you. The sentiment is appreciated," he returned. "I'm sorry you've suffered so much loss. You should come spend some quality time in the Forest. It would be good for your mind and body."

Her shoulders relaxed.

Her fears subsided.

"I will take you up on that," she replied. "But in the meantime, I do believe I have a balcony to show you. Perhaps we can take a few casks to catch up?"

"I would like that. I've brought several of your favourite reds from our master wine makers. I look forward to emptying them," he smiled, offering her his arm.

Many hours later…

She stumbled into her quarters nearly drunk. She should have been for the amount she had drunk, but elven wine was perfection. It was balanced, smooth. Intoxicating, but not violently so when overindulged in.

A delicacy in its own right.

The world wasn't quite spinning, but it seemed to lag as she moved.

She saw what she thought was Connerh's silhouette sitting in a chair cloaked in darkness. The soft white glow of his eyes, sitting there.

She exhaled with relief as she began to change her clothes, stepping behind a small wall.

"I'm glad to see you," she offered, layers of her clothes flying over the divide.

"We should talk," he said.

Her head popped out.

The voice was different.

She stopped, the potential for danger sobering her up with rapidity. She grabbed the sword she kept hidden near her wardrobe.

The man stood. He was much taller than Connerh, assuring her it was not he after all.

She stepped out, armed with sword in hand, though in her knickers. She frowned.

He walked into the light.

Her sword dropped, rattling loudly against the floor.

"Vidar?!" she screamed, running towards him.

"Maybe put some clothes on first," he replied, his voice now sounding as she remembered.

CHAPTER SEVENTY-EIGHT

LAMENT

LENA

'*Lena,*

First, I'm sorry about Bjorn.

He was a kind soul and a sweet boy who has most assuredly been taken from us too soon, and in such a dishonourable way. Not fighting like the warrior he could have been, but like an injured dog with his tail tucked between his legs. Such a disgraceful stain on the family name. I'm sorry we weren't there — not only to stop it, but to avenge him.

There are particularly colourful stories regarding what happened following his death in your arms.

Perhaps you'd be willing to provide some clarity.

I've heard the funeral was beautiful. Untouched by inclement weather, even. Brand sends his regards. Egress mourns. She's named a day of remembrance after him. Perhaps you should do the same on the mainland. It would seem only appropriate. A statue in the courtyard, perhaps? Please resist the urge to commission it in granite; brass would be more favourable. Yes, it will take longer, but it will offer his likeness true justice — its beauty will endure longer than any of us, especially as the patina begins to develop…granite is just so dull.

As for your…request.

We both know this has gone on far too long. I looked the other way for far too long.

631

But no longer.

We will not assist you in securing the seas, nor in rebuilding the damage you've caused — to your enemies, your allies, the world…your reputation.

You can't say I didn't warn you.

Today marks the end of an era. I hope you choose to mark its end with a pen, not a sword. It would be a shame to throw men into a meat grinder for the sake of pride.

You have no chance of retaking the Isles.

We have the advantage.

We have the ships.

And we have all the giants.

Those who remain on the mountain are old, and they deserve peace. Let them rest. They had no part in this; do not punish them.

And then there is the matter of my other assurance.

Our little secret remains buried with her.

Don't make me get a shovel.

When your legacy already hangs in the balance, it would be such an unfortunate conclusion to an otherwise short chapter in our history books.

Today marks the beginning of a new dynasty, with Egress at its head: Empress of Cindergarde.

She's renaming the Rim, declaring independence from Hildeheim once and for all, and withdrawing the clans from all accords and treaties — effective immediately.

Our loyalty and respect must be earned through time and action.

Not expected because of a muddled history.

Not demanded because it was once the way of things.

Time brings change.

Embrace it.

Don't be forgotten by it.

I always loved you, little bird.

—Gatty"

Lena's eyes burned — not with tears, but with anger and regret. She tossed the letter into the fire, watching it curl, blacken, and vanish into ash.

"What did it say?" Vidar asked from behind her.

She dipped her head in his direction, but her posture remained fixed towards the flames. Her response was delayed, arriving only after a dry, bitter scoff.

"Egress has named herself Empress of the Rim. She speaks for the giants now, or so I'm to understand."

Vidar's brow lifted.

"Sounds like my mother," he remarked, standing. "Sounds like treason."

Lena turned to face him.

"Do you want to take it back?" he offered.

She didn't answer at once. Instead, she walked to the window and stared out, eyes catching her own reflection in the glass. Her finger circled the rim of her chalice absentmindedly. Below, the scattered lights of the city drifted like fireflies in the night sky – silent, slow. Unaware of her royal gaze from on high. For once, clarity could not escape her grasp.

"No," she said at last, taking a measured sip and setting the cup down. "It's time we cut the Rim free. Besides, with your mission…with what's really coming…none of this seems to matter anymore."

"We could certainly start there, if you'd like," Fear offered.

"You're sure there's a Uridar there?"

"At least one."

Her head tilted. She let out a soft, amused laugh, dark thoughts flickering behind her eyes.

"No…no, I do love Egress. She's just caught in the same web I once was. I only hope her eyes open sooner than mine did…before it's too late." Her gaze dropped, then snapped up, locking on Vidar. "So, what happens to the rest of us when they're all free?"

"For most?" Fear replied. "Subjugation. The Mothers and Fathers will return to set their houses in order. The children have been at play long enough. Kingdoms will crumble overnight, the old ones will rise from their remains, and order will be restored. And, once Reh'gara's blood stains the earth, they'll come for his offspring. Hildeheim will be reduced to rubble, its people annihilated, the land divided among the strongest."

He stepped closer.

"But that needn't concern you. I will mark you as one of my own. You will be spared. Begrudgingly, perhaps, but none will dare cross me."

Her brows had long since fallen beneath the weight of his words, crumbling at the prospect of what was to come.

"Do I have to stay here?" she asked.

"Where would you go?" Vidar replied.

She turned back to the window.

"It's been a long time since I've visited the forest," she replied.

Fear laughed.

"Even the elves won't escape judgment. Amethyst is just as guilty – by association, at the least," Fear replied.

"I was told the elves are leaving," she replied.

Fear chuckled again.

"It seems no one is playing by the rules anymore. This will be entertaining. Amethyst moves to save her own creation…it's understandable. Cowardly, but I don't blame her. One day, an ocean between won't matter."

"He says they're going to a land beyond the great sea…" she began, turning to face Vidar. In calm desperation for knowledge, she asked, "How many lands are there?"

"Many," Fear replied. She looked back at the small figures at street level.

"Can't we warn them all? Move them elsewhere while this all unfolds? Can't you mark all the innocent?"

"What, like handing out rations?" He paused to laugh. "No. I could, but I won't. Sparing the rod is why things ended up this way to begin with," Fear replied. His tone taking a darker turn, he continued, "Besides, I have qualms with his offspring as well."

"And yet, you surround yourself and employ them," she replied boldly.

He chuckled ominously.

"You two are good kids. Controlled by forces stronger than you, trapped in a web more complex than you, yet you remain aware. Vigilant. You fight against the predator coming to devour you, while most accept it. We have a lot in common. Are you sure you're not one of mine?" he joked.

She smirked.

"Perhaps if not all of them, just a few more?" she asked – not pitiful, but pleading. "There are those close to me…"

He considered her for a long moment.

Then shook his head.

Her heart sank.

"You're lucky my recent exodus has put me in a good mood," he said, as if guided by exhaustion rather than mercy.

She exhaled. Smirked. Her fears, for now, subsided.

Vidar's head raised.

"Ah, your hopeless romantic approaches," Fear said, just as thunder cracked.

She quickly turned to face the door as it opened. Connerh entered, his pace steady, but he suddenly slowed as he saw Vidar.

"Vidar?" he asked, shocked. His head canted as he noticed Vidar's eyes, his own glowing.

"I have a lot to explain," Vidar answered.

"Come, sit; we have a lot to discuss," Fear invited, motioning towards the chairs in front of them.

Lena quickly closed the gap and grabbed his hand. He looked at her, concerned.

"It's okay…it's important," she entreated, leading him to the chair. She smiled as his grip on her hand firmed. The glow of his eyes dimmed, fading.

"What's going on?" Connerh asked.

"Change," Fear replied, then chuckled once more. "And, might I add, you look just like him. The resemblance is just uncanny."

Her throne, forged of iron and brass, seemed to vanish beneath her when she sat upon it, always swathed in crimson and gold. Her skin was radiant, sun-kissed but stubbornly pale, flushed with blood just under the skin. The seat hadn't been broken in yet, its cushion still rigid, resistant. Egress sat forward, her back untouched by the metal, posture impeccable. It only heightened her innate regality.

On either side of her sat a pair of juvenile dragons. Bound by chains, their bodies as large as a mountain lion, they were fully capable of devouring a man in several exquisitely painful bites. Their hisses echoed off the walls of her throne room, as dark and eerie as the creatures themselves.

The room was packed wall to wall with her subjects, men and giants alike. Their focus sharpened and tuned to the man kneeling before her.

"The accused stands before you, guilty of conspiring with the enemy. Here are the letters intercepted from his raven," Hargatha pronounced, standing at Egress' side. She tossed the raven towards the dragons – who briefly fought one another over it, before the winner devoured it in a single bite. Egress took the letters and reviewed them.

"The irony is you turned to the very person who did nothing as her pet destroyed these lands without care or consideration. You cry for salvation from your saviour, at the hands of your enslaver," she scoffed, shaking her head.

"I beg for mercy, Your Grace. I was just scared, is all, but I understand now!" the man begged.

Her face remained unwavering, uncaring.

"There is no room for fear here. Weakness must be purged from our blood. It is the corruption of living amongst men for so long," Egress declared, though she was talking to the room, to the giants. Not the pitiful man before her. "We were killers once. Hunters, warriors, conquerors. But we got comfortable being fed, cared for, fattened up like cattle. We allowed our servants to become our masters, and we their slaves," she continued, shaking her head. "That must never be allowed to happen again."

The cheers and grunts were deep, vibrating off the floors, walls, and columns.

"Is my navy complete?"

"It is, My Empress," Galabrand replied, at the forefront of the crowd.

"My new city?" she asked.

"It is, Your Grace," another shouted.

"Thank you, Master Builder," she replied, standing.

"Well, then…we don't need them anymore," she said.

Without hesitation, the carnage began. Every human in the room was murdered. Stabbed, pummelled, crushed, smashed with an assortment of blunt weaponry, a favourite of giants. The cries of fear and resistance were brief, sudden, fading.

"Take to the streets. Find them. Exterminate them. Spare only those working in the nursery. I want to see a pyre burning from my balcony," she continued.

The roars continued as they poured out of the room, like a torrent crashing against rock.

The man quietly wailed in front of her, hoping to be forgotten or spared.

"And as for you…it's the worst, I'm afraid," she replied. Turning to her dragon handlers, the only humans spared, she asked, "What's the word again?"

They swallowed heavily, looking at the man with pity, fear.

"*Vaskereth*, Your Grace," one whispered.

"Right…Vaskereth!" she shouted, the words slithering from her tongue like a serpent.

The dragons shrieked, their necks flaring as jets of acid spat from their mouths, engulfing the man in his own screams. Smoke rose from his sizzling flesh.

A sharp clicking erupted – rhythmic, rising – from deep in the dragons' throats. It grew harsher, faster.

A spark.

Flame.

The fluid ignited. His skin melted like wax from a candle. His cries faltered.

Then silence.

His blackened husk collapsed. The dragons lunged.

They tore into him with ravenous precision – chewing, crunching, slurping bone and steam.

Loud. Wet.

Egress watched with intrigue and curiosity.

Hargatha observed her in silence, the spectacle still echoing – louder than the cheers, heavier than the judgment cast. Her brow furrowed; her eyes slung low.

CHAPTER SEVENTY-NINE

SOMETHING BORROWED

FEAR

Connerh and Vidar stood at the border between Hildeheim and the Far Sands, in a place once known as Solmara. The once-thriving town was now gone, and its remnants lay buried deep beneath sharp, unforgiving sands. The flood had come without warning, without omen or storm – just a sudden, merciless surge from the high cliffs above, as if nature or the gods had revoked permission to dwell there, a permission never truly given.

What remained was desolation. The valley sloped gently downwards, where dark earth gave way to grains of sand in a transition so precise it looked painted. Wind-carved dunes loomed in the distance, their ridgelines glowing red beneath the low sun. Between them stood the husks of dead trees, twisted and skeletal, rising from cracked clay pans as monuments to what once was. The splattering of bushes that clung to the valley's edges – low, thorny, and stubborn – offered the only reminder that life had ever existed here.

The air shimmered with heat. Silence hung thick, broken only by the soft hiss of sand shifting in the wind. Solmara wasn't just abandoned; it had been erased, folded back into the land from which it was carved.

"And you don't remember anything?" Fear asked.

"As if it never were," Connerh replied.

"Fascinating," Fear murmured, a thread of curiosity laced through his voice. He tilted Vidar's head and continued. "Torinir always excelled at pushing boundaries. Thinking beyond conventional methodology."

Connerh said nothing. He watched as Vidar spoke in a voice that wasn't his – in Fear's voice – and then switched back again, the shift seamless. It unsettled him. Not just in concept, but in practice. Seeing it. Hearing it.

A lull settled between them as they waited for the others.

"So…what happens to Vidar? When this is all over?" Connerh asked.

"I go home to my freed form, and he enjoys life with a new perspective. Though he'll probably be sad for a while. He'll miss me…I think," Fear said, and Vidar laughed.

Connerh's expression didn't change.

"If there's anything I've learned," he mused quietly, "it's that nothing is ever that simple."

Fear smiled.

"And yet so many things are. Taking a life, for instance. It seems like it should take longer – be more drawn out, more involved than it actually is. But it's not. It's so easy, a child can do it. And they do. Gone, like blowing out a candle. That's all it takes to erase a lifetime of memories, of thoughts, of bonds between people and communities, strewn across time like…well, like the sands of this desert. All of it – snuffed out. And for what? A means to an end." He paused, then lifted Vidar's head slowly. "How many thousands fell to your hand, Connerh? To your blade? Was it hard? Was it difficult?"

Connerh shook his head and lowered it.

"I know you're used to being lied to, kid," Fear went on. "The truth twisted, bent into shape to make you act…or not act. To give you a reason to draw a line…or to cross it. But you're playing with the adults now, and I have no reason to lie. I'm told some find that reassuring about me. Others, though…not so much. I guess it's a little too overwhelming. Some need lies, but I…I have no use for them."

Vidar shifted his weight to the other leg.

"Vidar will be fine," Fear continued, his voice dipping, eyes flickering faintly. "There's a chance he might go mad – in the void my absence will create – but I'll take care of him. I'd never allow that to happen to someone who's been so gracious to me." He tilted his head, as if listening to something far away. "There'll be plenty to do in this…new world order, which is approaching like a fr—"

He stopped abruptly.

A crooked smile tugged at Vidar's mouth, but it was Fear who laughed first.

"I guess you don't know that word." He shook his head, amused. "It just wants to come out. Rolls off the tongue, doesn't it?" Then, softer – almost reverent – he added, "It's coming. I can smell it."

"The end?" Connerh asked.

"No. The dog, Ankhari. He smells *absolutely* terrible," Fear complained, wrinkling his nose in theatrical disgust.

Connerh turned, realigning himself towards the eastern rise, where Ankhari and Torinir were approaching. He blinked several times, trying to steady himself, torn from his thoughts too quickly.

"Well, look. A family reunion," Fear quipped. "Only ones missing are dear old Mom and Dad."

No one laughed.

Ankhari sat once within range, his eyes flicking between the group.

Connerh gave a slow nod to each of them.

"This is weird," he muttered.

"Welcome to the real world," Fear replied, rubbing his hands together like a merchant sealing a deal. "Ankhari, if you would. It'd make things go a lot faster."

Ankhari growled low in his throat.

"Excellent," Fear replied, clearly delighted.

Connerh plunged into the Amber like a body dragged under the ocean – abrupt, disorienting. Yet somehow, he remained calm.

Five men stood around a fire.

Vidar.

Fear – nearly as tall, bald as well, draped in dark grey robes threaded with red beneath. His age was impossible to place. A smirk clung to his face like a mask he never took off.

Ankhari stood to his right.

Next was Connerh.

And then…

Connerh froze.

It was like looking into a mirror — aged, sharpened, more deliberate. Torinir. Identical, save for longer, darker hair pulled back neatly to reveal a cleaner complexion, a well-groomed beard streaked with white.

"There. See? Told you. Uncanny," Fear remarked, slicing through the silence.

Torinir smirked.

"Tell him it's nice to be seen," he said.

Fear frowned. "He's right there." He gestured vaguely towards Connerh.

"I can't speak to him directly. I made a pact."

"Well, break it. That seems to be the trend lately," Fear shot back.

"I can't. Not this one."

Fear tilted his head.

"Sounds serious."

"The caster's known for it," Torinir answered, glancing at Connerh. "Who?"

"Elarion of the Westwood."

Fear's head jerked back in surprise, then shook slowly.

"Well, you walked straight into that one. You should've known better." He sighed. "I've been briefed on your little…idea. Swapping bodies. Brilliant, as always, but it pays to have friends with power — and fewer morals. No offence, Connerh; I'm glad we have you."

He offered a shrug that was half-sincere, half-showman.

"So, how do we restore you now that the experiment's done?" Fear asked.

"I don't know, but I need the pact nullified. If Connerh and I could operate more freely, we might find a solution."

"Can he not host you?"

"I'm not willing to risk it. He doesn't have the g—" He stopped, catching himself, eyes flicking to the others. He rephrased. "I don't believe he's capable of it."

Fear grunted.

"I just need one more to free my form, and then I just need time to get the rest on my own. I was hoping it would be you, but as usual…morality complicates things," Fear said, squinting his eyes.

Vidar and Connerh exchanged glances, like two children overhearing their parents argue.

"So, who's it going to be?" Ankhari asked at last.

Fear inhaled deeply.

"Desire is too far. Too messy to access without raising hell."

"Same with Life," Torinir added.

"Death?" Ankhari offered.

"Maybe. But the problem's the same with all of them. We need more hosts."

His eyes found Connerh again. "I just need one."

"Are you sure they can withstand it?" Torinir asked.

"I have a contingency to ensure they do," Fear said.

Torinir raised an eyebrow.

"I've tested it. It works. Don't give me that look," Fear snapped.

"Ankhari – none of your offspring carry the capability?" Torinir pressed.

"Possibly. But there are no Uridar left to test in the Far Sands."

"What's the closest?"

Fear smiled.

"Chaos. I didn't choose this location for fun." He pointed up towards the cliffs. "Vidar's already met my rambunctious little sister. Just didn't have what it took to contain her, I'm afraid."

"She's got a hot temper," Vidar muttered, grimacing.

"We'll need someone strong-willed. Maybe a little crazy," Fear said, chuckling as he stepped towards Connerh. He tapped him several times on the chest with a finger.

"Are you sure?" he asked, his tone almost sing-song, eyes sliding towards Torinir.

"We're concerned Reh'gara may have altered him," Ankhari answered. "But we don't know how. And none of us are at full strength – or in true form – to find out."

Fear rubbed his face with both hands, exasperated.

"Where are the other Candorians who came to this world?"

"Some are trapped with the Aspects. Some fled when they sensed his madness. Others stayed, but I don't know where – except for Amethyst and Aenon."

"Ah. The traitor and her pet," Fear sneered. "She's gathering her creation and trying to flee retribution. As if she could sit this one out."

"After what he's done, can you blame her?" Ankhari asked.

"Yes," Fear replied instantly, even before Ankhari had finished.

He paused. A brief flicker of uncertainty crossed his face.

"Maybe it's because the world's no longer balanced. Even Candorians can be affected…I suppose."

"It might not be too late to snap her out of it," Ankhari offered, "to sway her to our cause."

"Maybe." Fear faked a smile. "You'll forgive me if I don't hold his breath, I pray?" He loosely gestured to Vidar.

"So, what's the plan, then?" Torinir asked. He glanced at Connerh, who stared at him in silence. Torinir grinned. "You two – go deal with that pact. Tell the elf that if he doesn't comply, I'll pay him a visit." He turned to Ankhari. "Find me a host. Or five."

"And you two?" Ankhari asked.

"We're going to talk some sense into Chaos so she doesn't immolate all of Ankhari's children. We'll wait for their arrival."

"What about Reh'gara? What if he tries to flee?" Torinir asked.

Fear froze mid-step, tongue running along the inside of his cheek. He began to pace, visibly working through a thought.

"Yes…I hadn't considered that."

He stopped, straightened, and looked Connerh dead in the eyes.

"I have an idea," he said, "but you're just going to have to trust me."

Connerh looked to Torinir.

Torinir nodded.

CHAPTER EIGHTY

A Simple Prayer

Reh'gara

"I feel I must ask – not out of tradition, but out of concern. For a friend," Amethyst murmured softly, her gaze fixed on Reh'gara's face. "Are you certain you wish to go through with this?"

His head lowered, eyes flicking back and forth as if scanning a list of impossible alternatives.

Then stillness. A moment of clarity.

He shook his head.

"There are no other options. I've lost," he said at last, his voice faltering. His breath caught, his brow furrowing under the weight of it. "All…is lost."

She reached out, placing a steady hand on his shoulder. He offered a faint, grateful smile and glanced towards Aenon – ever silent, ever watching.

Reh'gara inhaled slowly.

They stood within a void shaped like a room, though no walls confined it. The space around them was the purest expression of white, not radiant, but *blank*, as if even light had been stripped of meaning and purpose. There was no sound other than their voices, not even a soft echo appropriate for such an expanse. The air held the sterile scent of cloud cover, cold and clean, like the sky before a storm.

"I can no longer keep our offspring hidden, walled away from the world, just as I can no longer meddle in its affairs. The scales must balance as they will…perhaps as they always should have."

"Does that include the freeing of the Aspects?" Amethyst asked, voice careful.

"No!" His reaction was sharp, pained, as if she had touched an open wound. "No…not yet. Perhaps balance can still be found without their…overcorrection." The fire faded from his voice, replaced by something wearier. Measured. "Not yet."

She exhaled, a sigh long-held. Her chest sank as she nodded.

"Very well."

"Where will you go?" he asked.

"North. To a land still unnamed. The people there are primal, still." She lifted her chin. "There are centuries of work to be done. The elves and I will begin again."

His face dimmed with sadness.

"And you?" she asked gently.

"I don't know… Perhaps I'll wander. Until I find a way to leave this world."

The resignation in his voice was unmistakable.

"I would hope," she said, managing the smallest smile, "you'll visit before then?"

He nodded. "Of course."

Amethyst reached into her robes and withdrew a small object – a key, though not a typical one. Octagonal and cylindrical, with her rune etched top and bottom, it gleamed like burnished iron. Aenon summoned his from the air, wordlessly.

Reh'gara gripped his staff and drew his own key from within its shaft.

"So…we drop the veil," he murmured.

Between them hovered a small sphere made of the same strange substance as the keys. Not quite metal. Not quite anything familiar.

Aenon went first. His key slid into the orb with no visible seam or slot – accepted, nonetheless. Amethyst followed.

Reh'gara held his a moment longer, then slowly inserted it halfway.

"May mercy be shown to our souls," he whispered – and inserted the key.

The moment it clicked into place, something shifted. A wrongness blossomed in his gut. His breath hitched. He hunched forward, clutching his chest.

"Reh'gara!" Amethyst called, rushing to his side. "Are you alright?!"

But he didn't answer her. He heard something else.

A voice — no, *voices* — rasping through shadow. Angry. Hungry. Everywhere at once.

He staggered, looking around wildly as they multiplied, pressing in.

"So soon?" he rasped, face crumpling.

And then, with a hiss like air tearing and sound collapsing into itself, he vanished.

CHAPTER EIGHTY-ONE

EYE FOR AN EYE

JULIAN

Her fingertips traced the stone wall with practised care, seeking a small, imperceptible divot that only she knew was there. Julian watched, one brow arched in quiet curiosity, his arms folded but loose.

She found it.

A grunt vibrated in her throat as she stepped back and pressed her palm into the hidden notch.

Click.

A heavy thud followed, like the release of a long-dormant mechanism.

Without hesitation, she pushed. The wall groaned forward and gave way, revealing a narrow passage shrouded in shadow. She slipped inside without looking back, vanishing into the dark.

Julian blinked. Then he moved – quickly, but cautiously. He ducked in after her, shoulders brushing the tight frame as he entered.

The hidden room was unlike anything he'd expected. Shelves of weapons lined the stone walls: gleaming swords, spears with intricate carvings, curved daggers, vials of dark liquid sealed in wax. Some bore the unmistakable design of distant kingdoms. Others were distinctly Khazmyrian – brutal, efficient, and familiar.

"I thought the mighty name of Darros was all you needed to wield," Julian teased, a crooked grin tugging at one corner of his mouth.

She glanced over her shoulder, expression unreadable for a second.

"This is for when I need something…basic," she responded. "You wear a sword at your hip, so it's always seen. In your world, order is maintained by the threat of retribution. I carry a dagger so it *cannot* be seen. When order collapses, predictable threats to chaos are the first to die. It is the unseen blade that stops the war before it begins…or brings it to an end in a sharp, sudden gasp."

She turned fully to face him, amused eyes squinting.

"A hidden blade is always more dangerous than the one you can see coming."

"So, you're an assassin *and* a poet?" he asked.

She widened her stance and slipped a hand up beneath her tunic.

"A warrior poet…I like that," she said as if nothing peculiar was happening. His eyes widened. Slowly, she drew a dagger from where it was strapped to the inside of her thigh. Her brow arched as she caught him staring.

"Settle down, soldier," she reprimanded lightly, and they both burst into childish laughter.

"I hope I never have to check you for weapons," he said.

"Liar," she replied, winking.

He smirked.

"Don't forget: without a sword to fight the battles, you may never know who your enemies are."

She grunted.

"Fair. I suppose everyone has their role," she replied, slipping off her sandals and pulling a small spike wrapped in leather out from the sole.

"How many more are you going to produce?" he asked, raising an eyebrow.

"You may have to turn around for the next one," she said, her expression serious for a lingering moment before her smile broke through.

Julian froze in place.

"I'm joking," she added, watching his shoulders relax.

"I almost don't believe you," he replied, rolling up his sleeves. "Maybe I should look."

He began stepping towards her, only for her to grab a shortblade from the shelf and hold it to his neck. Her grin deepened.

"Don't push your luck, Julian," she reprimanded, and he chuckled nervously. He smelled her breath, felt it on his neck. It was sweet-smelling, like honey and peaches. His eyes dropped to her lips. His grin deepened.

"You use my name as a dagger." His voice was low, trailing to a whisper.

She watched him stare at her. It made the hairs on the backs of her arms stand up.

"It gets your attention, just like the pointy end," she replied in an equal pitch, breaking away from his orbit.

He took a deep breath and shook his head.

"Find a dagger, preferably two. One we poison, the other we don't," she continued, shifting focus with ease as she replaced the spikes in her sandals. "When we find Tyreek, it will not be because we were looking; it will be sudden, and we'll need to act quickly. I usually have a few vials of the black stuff in my waistband, should fortune favour us with unwatched chalices," she continued.

"I'd hate to use the wrong one to cut my dinner," he remarked, holding up a dirk.

"Exactly. Poison on the left, no poison to the right."

"You ever get those mixed up?"

"I try not to, but I also don't touch my food with my concealed weapons."

"I would hope not, especially considering where you've been pulling them from," he replied with laughter.

"Remind me to hit you," she said, her tongue jammed into the corner of her mouth as she fought off a smile.

"You've never needed reminding," he shot back. She rolled her eyes.

A loud knock at the door cut through their moment. Yuri slid the dagger back into place along her thigh and adjusted her tunic before moving to investigate. Julian stayed behind, picking up a sword and examining it idly as he listened.

He heard the door open, then her voice – familiar, casual.

"Merith!" Yuri called. A coded signal.

He set the sword down, brushed himself off, and made his way out to join her.

"We're to hear a message," she said, eyes locking onto his, "together."

The messenger girl stood waiting. "Darros formally invites you both to dinner this evening – with a special guest. Attendance is required."

Julian and Yuri exchanged a glance. She squared her shoulders.

"Well," Julian muttered, "that doesn't sound much like an invitation."

"Oh," the girl added, eyes shifting to Yuri, "he also requests that you wear consort attire."

Yuri scoffed, then laughed aloud. "You misheard. I've ascended; I don't wear consort attire. Not to formal events. Not anymore."

"I assure you," the girl replied, one brow arching, "he was quite clear."

Then she turned and walked off.

Julian leaned in slightly. "What's consort attire?"

Yuri stared into the distance with a vacant expression. Then she looked at him.

"A message."

Julian stood in the corner of Darros' dining hall, clinging as close to shadow and obscurity as possible. Something was off. He could feel it despite not being able to describe it – a flutter in his stomach, a warmth at the back of his neck. He observed the servants setting placements at the table, cleaning well beyond what was necessary, a fear of disapproval fuelling their urgency.

No chairs. That was the first thing he noticed.

The dining hall stretched wide, a sea of colour and soft shapes. The floor was layered in overlapping carpets, deep reds and cobalt blues faded at the edges like a sunset. Pillows were strewn in deliberate excess, embroidered in thread-of-gold and silk too fine to touch without leaving fingerprints. They were as soft as they were decadent.

One low table, as long as seven horses and cut from singular beams of wood, sat at the centre. The tabletop gleamed with brass serving trays and crystal decanters sparkling in the abundance of candlelight. No torches here. Only lanterns – hundreds of them – suspended from above like stars frozen mid-fall, their stained-glass bellies painting the room in slow-moving colour.

At the far end of the chamber, a grand fireplace loomed, and servants fed the flames with bundles of rose and cedarwood. It was not merely for warmth or ambience but for memory. The fragrant smoke curled through the air, a lingering reminder that would cling to skin, hair, and fabric, ensuring Darros' presence followed his servants and visitors long after they departed.

Opposite the fireplace stood a wide doorway, its entrance shrouded by a cascade of curtains – some sheer as mist, others falling richly in deep colours. Layer upon layer, they concealed whatever lay beyond, a shifting, shimmering veil.

This wasn't a place to eat. It was a stage, every corner crafted to unsettle and captivate. A place to be seen eating.

First came the guards – one at each corner of the room, their stances rigid, shadows stretching beneath them. Next, the servants, draped head to toe in silk, each shrouded in a different hue: dark greens, liquid silvers, luminous blues, and deep, burnished reds. They moved like a living tapestry, silent and seamless.

Darros.

He entered like a star falling across a cloudy night sky – brilliant, unignorable. Draped in layers of white, he stood out, every step pulling attention towards him. A new mask clung to his face, a creation Julian had never seen before – polished silver, sculpted to wrap around his features like a second, gleaming skin. It wasn't a mask so much as a reflection, his face stripped bare, a silver skull sheathed in molten metal.

Julian felt his eyes squint as he stared.

It was theatrical, he knew – overtly so. Darros dressed, spoke, and carried himself not merely to impress but to unnerve, to disarm those outside his sphere of influence. The extravagance demanded notice, drawing the gaze even as it sowed unease.

And it worked.

Despite knowing a conman when he saw one, Julian couldn't help but feel a pull towards the man. Like a yearning to be shocked into some type of revelation. It was a sensation he couldn't quite name, pulsing just beneath his calm facade.

Everyone watched as he stood at the head of the table – and he knew it.

But Darros was not the only one who demanded attention. The room swelled with colour and motion – robes of deep crimson and emerald, silks that shimmered like liquid moonlight, and sheer veils embroidered with gold thread. Jewels flashed at wrists and throats, catching the glint of candlelight, while perfumed oils left shimmering traces along bare shoulders and collarbones.

Fabrics whispered against marble, rich brocades woven with silver and cobalt threads, velvet cloaks sweeping the floor like shadows. Gold bangles chimed softly with each graceful movement, and headpieces of polished copper, sapphire, and onyx gleamed beneath the warm light.

It was a glimpse into a world utterly alien to Julian. Every guest, every flourish of fabric and glint of jewel was part of the spectacle – ornament and opulence stitched together in human form. Yet amid the chaos, all eyes inevitably returned to Darros – his stark white robes and silver mask a cold, radiant beacon against the living tapestry.

But Julian wasn't the only outsider here.

Another figure entered, a smear of shadow across the canvas of colour – a man in drab, dust-stained trousers and a black leather cuirass, scuffed and battered. It was his only wardrobe, his second skin. He would never be caught dead leaving his chest or back exposed, not even here.

Julian's posture shifted, his back lifting off the wall as his gaze tracked the newcomer. The man was heavyset, bordering on obese, his skin marked with the pale remnants of acid burns across his neck and arms. Faded scars crisscrossed his exposed skin, the ghosts of old wounds: sword slashes, punctures, ragged tears. His dark hair was slick, either oiled or simply greasy – Julian couldn't be sure. His steps were pronounced and heavy, a direct interruption with every step.

He was a walking battlefield, a man who looked like he should have died several times over – yet, to Julian, he was the closest thing to reality in this place.

"Tyreek," Darros greeted, his voice commanding enough to still the air just as Julian mouthed the name. He gestured to the seat on his right. "Come, sit here."

"Merith."

The name sliced through the ambient murmurs like a hot knife searing flesh, snapping Julian's focus back to Darros. For an instant, he felt as if he were one of the servants – summoned, commanded.

"Sit," Darros repeated, pointing to the left side of the table.

Julian hesitated, a faint frown touching his face. He didn't understand what was happening, but a servant girl appeared at his side, her touch light but insistent as she guided him forward.

"Everyone, please be seated," Darros continued, lowering himself with a practised grace only after the others had settled on the cushions around the low table. "Now that the north's vengeance has cooled, I am glad to announce that business has resumed," he announced without the clink of glass or any external need to gather attention; he already had it.

The guests erupted into clapping and cheers, then naturally grew silent so he could continue.

"Our friend Tyreek is already bringing in new delights as we dine, and those who have enjoyed temporary respite are being gathered and returned underground, renewed, restored, and ready to serve," he declared, offering a single clap. The cheers resumed.

Tyreek and Julian exchanged a glance, the only two faces untouched by the feverish joy surrounding them. But Julian recognised the look in Tyreek's eye. It wasn't disgust or disdain; it was the flat, hollow gaze of shellshock. The relentless surge of noise, the shifting bodies pressing close – it wasn't a banquet to him. It was a battlefield of anxiety. Each laugh, each chorus of cheers was another assault, another chip at his composure. He held it well, but the emptiness in his stare was unmistakable – something that could never be hidden from another soldier. Julian couldn't help but nod to him, to offer acknowledgement. Tyreek nodded in reply, only slower.

"Tonight, we feast in celebration of Khazmyr's doors opening once more. May they never close again."

The guests stood and applauded. Julian watched them all, their expressions seeming genuine. It was an odd feeling brewing in his chest. He'd been surrounded by enemy soldiers on the battlefield, men who were responsible for great atrocities and crimes, yet he'd never felt more encircled by evil than now.

Without a signal, the feast began, musicians seemingly appearing from nowhere to play various instruments at a volume loud enough to ward off silence, yet sufficiently quiet for them to hold a conversation.

"Tyreek, I'm glad you could join us," Darros began.

"Thank you, Darros. I am honoured to be invited. I rarely get invited to such things," he said.

Julian was shocked. To be so repulsive, he spoke clearly, nearly eloquently in his pronunciation, though his words carried an extra breath behind them.

"I find that hard to believe. Surely this is not your first time here?" Darros asked.

Tyreek lowered his head and shook it.

"I'm afraid it is. Though per-perhaps I misplaced the invitation," Tyreek replied.

"Surely," Darros replied, his tone insistent. "Tyreek, this is Merith, an associate of ours. Merith is…" He paused, realising he didn't know how to finish the sentence. "Well…what are you, Merith? I can't believe, in all the time you've been here, I've not asked. What is it that you do, exactly? Obviously, you're not an assassin," he quipped to his and Tyreek's quiet laughter. "What's normal life look like for you? Back home."

Julian cleared his throat and looked back and forth at the two men.

"Originally? I started as a fisherman in the north. I captained a ship for a number of years," he paused, unsure of why he was being so candid. "Fishing is kind of what we're known for up there."

"Fascinating," Darros replied, contempt sewn into his faux interest.

"Started? What is it you do now?" Tyreek asked.

"He's still a fisherman. Only now, instead of chasing fish, it's lost causes," Darros interjected, drawing his own laughter.

Julian flashed a smile, imagining how Darros' blood might stain his mask. And then he wondered.

Did he eat with it on?

"What is that you do, Sir Tyreek?" Julian asked.

"I transport things for Darros."

"He's quite good at it, might I add," Darros added, turning to look at Julian. "Perhaps you've encountered something he's relocated for me?" he asked, an intentional jab that didn't quite land with Julian.

He smiled in reply, but only out of a sense of obligation.

They leaned backwards as servants brought in the first course – quiet, rehearsed, barefoot. Brass trays held pyramids of coloured fruits sliced with precision: figs soaked in orange blossom honey, blood oranges peeled so clean they glistened. Steam curled from saffron rice moulded into perfect domes, each crowned with gold. Beside them, meats roasted in a mix of glazes, their skins lacquered and gleaming, nestled beside bowls of yoghurt as thick as cream and dusted with a red spice. Everything had an intentional aroma, a spread designed for looks in equal measure to taste.

Servant girls leaned in with gold spoons and filled their plates with a variety, Darros' before all others.

Another pair ran over and quickly began to disassemble Darros' mask. It came apart in sections. Julian startled at the guards who stomped in place before they turned around to face the walls, as did those servants who were not attending to his mask. Julian cautiously returned his gaze to Darros, his head turned a half-quarter away, curiosity and confusion preventing him from turning his head fully.

His hair was let loose first, chestnut in colour, long and perfumed. The guests gasped in awe, like seeing a flower bloom for the first time. Julian's mouth opened as the man's face was revealed. The servants quickly ran off, joining the others against the wall, their faces turned. He made an involuntary noise that wasn't quite a grunt. It was…shock, with a mixture of pleasant surprise.

Darros was…rather attractive, enough for the most battle-hardened of men to admit. Even Tyreek stared. His features were striking, nearly carved into his face. His natural eye colour was pale blue, set against tanned, perfectly shaved skin. His gaze captured your attention, as if he both focused on you while at the same time looking through you.

Darros caught him staring and chuckled to himself.

"You're drooling," Darros joked.

Julian snapped out of his unintentional stupor, blinking his eyes as he refocused them.

"Shall we eat? I'm afraid I'm rather hungry after today's activities," he insisted. They nodded and began to eat. "You'll not be offended if I add to the scenery, I hope," he continued, clapping his hands before they could reply.

At least a hundred and twenty scantily clad men and women were led in, their eyes blindfolded. Guided with practised care, they settled around the table, bodies nearly overlapping, skin brushing against skin. The air thickened with the blend of their perfume, scented oils, and the faint hint of sweat – the distilled aroma of erotism.

"Much better, wouldn't you say?" Darros asked.

"Oh yes, I agree." Tyreek's tongue slid across his lips, hot breath reaching across the table, prickling Julian's face. For the first time, Tyreek's shoulders relaxed, his gaze locked on the glistening bodies and unable to look away, just like the others. His demeanour shifted – an intoxicated surrender, his restraint dissolving beneath the warm, perfumed air.

And suddenly, the fragile bond between soldiers snapped. Julian shook his head, a needed reminder of where he stood. He wasn't a guest among friends; he was a prisoner, just as much on display as the slaves.

"Excuse my question, Darros, but I didn't think you removed your mask," Julian ventured.

Darros' gaze settled on him with a hint of amused disbelief – the look of a man who had expected to hear something naïve anyway but still found it endearing, almost pitiful.

"Yes, well, sometimes it's good to embrace change. I've been thinking about a…rebirth, as of late."

Julian nodded, unsure how to respond. Darros' eyes remained on him, even while he ate slowly, keeping his eyes averted.

"What's the matter, Merith? Not up to your standard?" he pressed, his head turning as if examining beyond his face. "Speaking of, I'm afraid I'd forgotten about our special guest," he said, raising and clapping his hands twice.

Julian's head dropped, and his brows sunk.

He already knew.

Like a basic math problem or a premonition.

The drummers arrived first, their rhythm a slow, deliberate pulse that swelled like a heartbeat caught in a moment of anticipation. Then came the dancers, women adorned in silks, their bronzed skin shimmering beneath the glow of lanterns. They moved in unison, a living wall of peacock feathers held high, the vivid plumes arcing and swaying with each step. Beneath the forest of emerald and sapphire, a figure was concealed – hidden but hinted at, the briefest glimpses of a shadowed form flashing between the gaps. The dancers spun and stomped, their anklets of silver bells chiming in a hypnotic rhythm. Around the table they circled, feathers swaying like a vibrant tide, and the guests leaned forward, laughter and whispered anticipation mingling in the air. Nearing Darros, the drummers quickened their beat, each strike louder, faster, a thunderous crescendo. The dancers halted, the air quivering with tension – then, with a flourish, they cast the feathers aside, a jewelled wave falling to the floor, and the hidden figure stood revealed.

Her discomfort was visible first.

Her oiled, glistening skin shimmered beneath the light, dusted with flecks of gold that clung like molten stars. A delicate chain of interlinked gold wound around her neck, trailed between her breasts, dipped along her stomach, and vanished between her legs – a suggestion of modesty that concealed nothing. Her expression remained flat, a mask of indifference, but Julian saw through it – the rigid stillness in her shoulders, the faint tension at the corners of her eyes. The silent lethality of bridled rage.

She was stripped, and not only of dignity but of places to hide her weapons. No sandal spikes, no waistbands full of poisons, no thigh bands or tunics to conceal daggers. It was what angered her the most – what made her feel naked. But there was also sadness pooling at the interior of her eyes where tears usually gathered, a wet sheen betraying her stoic mask. Shame and humiliation clung to her like a damp shroud, made manifest by the thick metal collar encircling her neck, the heavy chain affixed.

"Go on. See if this is to your liking," Darros prodded.

Julian frowned even as he felt hundreds of eyes pressing on him. One of the dancers led Yuri forward, her chain pulling taut between them. Julian rose – slowly, awkwardly. The dancer extended the leash with a fluid, almost ceremonial motion, the chain links pooling into Julian's reluctant palm. He felt the chill of it, his grip resisting the instinct to tighten.

He focused on the chain itself, tracing the delicate links – anything but the woman they bound. But silence pressed in, heavy with expectation. Her oiled, gilded skin shimmered beneath the glow, each contour exposed, but his gaze skated across her in stilted flashes – the curve of a shoulder, the cruel descent of the chain. Relief came only when he found her eyes.

Dark, unwavering, and sharp enough to cut, she stared directly at him. Her expression was a fortress, but within that gaze, he saw the faintest shadow of something – defiance? Or solidarity?

In that singular exchange, they were alone, a moment of quiet in the spectacle's humiliating theatre.

"Well, go on…examine the merchandise." Darros' voice shattered the silence.

Julian blinked, confused.

"With your hands," Darros insisted, his tone laced with amusement, miming a squeeze. The guests tittered.

Julian's stomach tightened. He swallowed, the dry burn of shame crawling up his throat. His fingers moved to her shoulders, grazing her skin, a cold touch against warmth. Her nearly imperceptible smirk caught him off guard, a hint of sardonic amusement as her head tilted, urging him on. She was still staring at him, the weight of her gaze refusing to yield.

He brushed his knuckles against her chest, a ghost of a touch, and Darros' laughter cut through the room.

"Is this your first time with a woman?" Darros taunted, a fresh wave of laughter rippling through the guests.

Julian's jaw tightened, but he smiled – an empty, practised expression. He was beginning to imagine Darros' blood staining his perfect white gloves.

But then the approaching echo of footsteps pulled every gaze. The doors parted, and Hera entered.

Her gown was a cascade of emerald silk, shimmering with each step. Delicate gold traced the fabric's edges, and thin bands of gold wound around her arms like twisting vines. A golden crown sat like a halo atop her dark, lustrous hair — a circlet of leaves adorned with emeralds that shimmered beneath the chamber's glow. Around her, a host of servants followed. Women in silver robes carried the train of her gown with precise care, while others in muted greens scattered shimmering petals beneath her path.

Darros rose, spreading his arms wide.

"Hera, my queen," he declared, his voice carrying over the hall. He approached, embracing her, their lips meeting in a lingering display.

Yuri's gaze shifted, her face a mask, but her shoulders tensed beneath Julian's hands. Hera's eyes caught Yuri's — a fleeting glance, but in it, a world of unspoken words. Julian felt her muscles tighten beneath his touch, and he squeezed lightly, a silent attempt at comfort.

"I'm glad you're here," Darros announced, turning to the hall. "Everyone, I present to you the first Queen of Khazmyr. Tomorrow, we celebrate her coronation — followed by a month of festivities. And, yes…plenty of debauchery."

The hall erupted — gasps, applause, cheers. Even a few tears.

Yuri's gaze locked on Hera once more — a quiet, desperate plea answered only with a flicker of shame in the queen's eyes.

"Enough of this laughable display of virginity," Darros scoffed, turning. "Merith, take her to Tyreek. He'll know what to do."

Yuri's expression changed — an emotion too sharp, too raw to be hidden.

Julian's mind raced. He glanced towards the exit — one clear path.

"Hurry up now, and do it properly," Darros ordered. "The chain."

Julian took the chain, his grip tightening slightly. Each step he led her around the table felt deliberate, the rhythmic chime of silver anklets and the rustle of silks blending into the murmurs of the crowd. Her bare feet moved soundlessly, her gilded skin catching the light, yet her focus remained unwavering: fixed forward, her expression was a mask of distant calm. He avoided looking at her directly, his gaze tracing the floor, the walls. Anything but the woman bound to him.

When they neared Hera, Darros' voice cut through the low hum. "Have her bow before her queen."

Julian hesitated, feeling the weight of the chain in his hand, but a light tug seemed enough. Yuri's shoulders tensed before she lowered herself – slowly, with a deliberate grace that made the gesture feel less like submission and more like a calculated performance. Her forehead nearly brushed Hera's feet.

"Now kiss them."

Hera's expression shifted, her lips parting. "Darros – perhaps that isn't necessary."

"It is," Darros replied, his tone sharpening. "Kiss them."

Yuri leaned forward, her lips barely grazing Hera's toes. The contact was brief, a whisper of touch, but Julian saw the shadow cross her face. Humiliation weaponised as spectacle.

He guided her away, the tension between them taut, like a rope pulled tight against a sinking anchor. As they reached Tyreek, Julian's hand hovered at his waist, the chain swaying from his loose grip. Tyreek's thick fingers stretched forward, greedy, eager to seize control.

Yuri's eyes tracked Julian's movements, a question of his hesitation forming in the arch of her brow. His gaze drifted downwards, and she followed it, catching a faint, silvery glint peeking from his waistband. Her eyes widened, a sliver of clarity piercing the fog of humiliation. Their eyes met, and a silent understanding sparked between them.

Julian's jaw tightened. He said nothing only released the chain, letting it spill into Tyreek's grasp before turning away, his steps slow and deliberate.

Tyreek wasted no time. He yanked Yuri forward, her bare body colliding with his, the impact eliciting a round of drunken cheers and claps from the table. His hands roamed her with shameless greed, probing, groping – fingers tracing every exposed curve and crevice with brutish insistence. Hera's forced smile faltered, her gaze fixed but her discomfort obvious. Yuri's head turned, catching a gleam on the tabletop. Her attention was pulled briefly from Tyreek's fumbling hands to Julian's reddened face, anger etched into his features.

But she didn't let herself remain passive. With a swift, fluid motion, she straddled Tyreek's lap, taking control of the exchange. She leaned back, her head tipping over the table's edge, her body an arc beneath his touch. His tongue wagged, his hands rough on her gilded skin.

"I never did thank you, Darros," Julian's voice cut through the chaos, calm and almost conversational as he circled the table, nearing Darros.

"For what, exactly?" he barked, his tone laced with amusement, gaze barely tearing away from the spectacle.

"For opening my eyes. The least I could do is return the favour." Julian's words were a quiet promise, a blade disguised as gratitude.

His hand darted, shockingly fast for a man his age. The dagger slid free of his waistband, its tip blackened with poison, and plunged directly into Darros' eye socket. The burst of blood was violent, a crimson spray that streaked across the table. The force of its current was startling, as was the swift, high-pitched scream from Darros.

Julian twisted the blade, anchoring it. Leaving it in to let the poison seep.

Screams erupted, chaos swelling around them in a cacophony loud enough to drown out Tyreek's muffled, choking agony. It was hard to be heard with a dinner knife jammed up into your skull, through your soft palate, the golden hue of the utensil invisible through his blood. Her fingers seized another knife from the table, and she drove it into his body with ruthless precision, roving it about his body as he had done to hers.

Between his legs.

His chest.

His eyes, for good measure.

Julian's hand found her shoulder, yanking her free. Blood spattered across them both, but they were already moving.

She looked back at Hera as she was being pulled, but Hera was distracted, her focus fixed on Darros' body. The guards shouted orders, but their voices were drowned out by screams, ignored in the panic. They struggled to push through the crowd, while Julian and Yuri used the chaos as cover to slip away.

CHAPTER EIGHTY-TWO

CHAOS

LENA

They stood before the temple at Gryphon's Rest, where jagged peaks loomed high above the ruins of Solmara, giving way to deep valleys below – valleys that had once channelled the very floodwaters that had erased its existence. Gryphon's Rest was in little better shape. The few buildings that had once surrounded the temple had long been discarded into history. Frozen remnants of charred wood, blackened metal, and stone blocks littered the ground. The temple still stood, the only structure to be made of granite, but even it was dilapidated, struggling to remain intact – to cling to the memory.

Fear stood with Ankhari on the temple's steps as Sevryn approached, leading a hundred and fifty men on horseback, Toke and Murnira among them. Next to him, Connerh and Lena were saddled astride Whisper.

"Are you sure this is going to work?" Ankhari asked.

"Never second-guess; it doesn't do much to inspire faith," Fear replied, walking down the steps to greet the newcomers.

"Good, good. A hundred and fifty?" he asked Sevryn as he dismounted.

"To the very last hair," he replied.

"Excellent. It is so very good to see you again," Fear said, extending his hand to help Lena dismount. She smirked and took his hand.

"And how's Vidar today?" she asked.

"Good…resting," Fear replied, bowing and kissing her hand. "Fortunately for us, I don't need rest."

"Poor Vidar," Connerh joked as he landed on his feet.

Fear chuckled.

"You wound me, sir," he replied, pantomiming an arrow to the chest. "If you don't mind, I need to borrow your better halves to discuss a bit of family business."

Connerh nodded reluctantly.

"Sevryn, if you wouldn't mind…my effects, please," Fear requested, raising his hands to catch the tossed satchel. When Fear held out his other hand, Torinir slammed into his palm with a metallic tone that echoed. Connerh's eyes widened.

"Make sure the hundred don't let so much as a moth approach this place. As for the remaining fifty, position them outside the temple door. I'll call them in when we're ready," Fear instructed, leading Lena up the stairs and inside.

Connerh locked eyes of uncertainty with Ankhari, who stood for a few moments before finally wandering away.

"You happen to have a Grundor on you?" Sevryn asked Toke.

"Oh, no. I stopped touching the stuff since you-know-who's been around. Took a week to try and convince myself I hadn't hallucinated the entire thing," he replied.

"Imagine your surprise when he remained," Murnira added.

"I'm still not convinced I'm not hallucinating," Toke replied to Sevryn's laughter. Connerh approached.

"What was in the bag?" he asked Sevryn.

"Clothes," he shrugged.

Fear closed the temple doors behind them with a quiet thud.

"That Connerh – he's not a jealous man, is he?" Fear asked.

"Sometimes," Lena replied, her eyes drifting upwards as she took in the ruined interior. He grunted.

A steady stream of snowflakes drifted through breaches in the ceiling, caught in shafts of light that filtered down through the cracked stone. The delicate crystals shimmered as they descended, accumulating in soft, pale mounds across the ruined floor. Though the air inside was frigid, it remained still – an eerie, resolute calm amid the storm howling just beyond the walls.

Once a consecrated place of worship, the temple now served as a shelter for winged creatures huddled in the darkened corners of its vast, crumbling space. Scattered across the stone floor were loose bones and half-decayed skeletons, tangled in the broken wood and warped metal – relics of shattered pews and rusted tools, remnants of past looters and long-fled desperation.

But the ruin stopped thirty feet from the temple's centre.

There, in stark contrast to the decay, hovered a sphere – an immense black object encircled by immaculate ornaments of gold, silver, and brilliantly coloured gemstones. Notably, the nearest pile of bones halted at exactly twenty-nine feet, as though no living thing had dared venture closer.

The object floated just inches above the ground. Its surface was paradoxical – both liquid and solid, absorbing light at its edges yet reflecting nothing. It didn't just exist; it imposed itself. Though still, it radiated a presence – an echo of something real, yet untouchably other.

"What is that?" Lena asked, casually pointing towards it.

"A Uridar," Fear said, stepping past her. "I take it you've never seen one before?"

"No. Though Vidar has told me stories."

"Right…I remember," he recalled, glancing back at her. "What he didn't tell you is what a Uridar really is. But before I bore you with a history lesson, I have a few questions – if you don't mind."

"Of course. Go on," she said, sliding into a pew and sitting, her voice guarded.

"Why are you so comfortable betraying Reh'gara?" he asked, his tone sharpened with intent.

Her brows lifted in surprise. "Straight to the point, I see."

"That's kind of my thing."

"Well…" She hesitated. The answer wouldn't come. She wasn't prepared for the question.

"You see, it's rather important for me to know what kind of person I'm about to brand – to whom I'll offer my protection. There are no wrong answers. The only thing that matters is the truth, and your willingness to acknowledge it," he explained, spreading his hands in a brief, open gesture. "But take your time. I'm going to catch up with my little sister in hopes we won't both need what's in that satchel."

He turned towards the Uridar, and Lena's gaze flicked to the bag he'd left by the door.

"Torinir, if you wouldn't mind starting the conversation…" Fear released the weapon from his grip. Torinir floated ahead, glowing a hot orange as it neared the sphere. Fear followed closely, watching and waiting for a signal.

"This should only take a few minutes. Don't mind me," he added, glancing back at Lena. Then he approached the Uridar – slowly, cautiously. The hem of his garment began to singe, curling at the edges and sending faint trails of smoke into the air. He adjusted his posture and pressed on.

When he reached the Uridar, he inspected his robes. He smiled upon seeing they hadn't burned away completely.

"Good," he muttered, before resting both palms against the sphere's surface.

His head jerked back, and his eyes glowed with a steady, unnatural light.

When Fear snapped back to himself, Lena was still seated – still watching.

"All's well. She's onboard," he said, striding back. He took the pew in front of her, turned, and rested his arms on its back. "So," he prompted, "what's your answer?"

"I don't see it as betrayal," Lena replied. "That would suggest I held allegiance to him in the first place. I don't think I ever did. It's not like I was given a choice. And besides…he took something from me. Something I was willing to give, once – when I thought it was necessary. But now I know it wasn't. So, really, he betrayed me first."

Her voice was calm, but her expression tightened.

"What is it that he took?" Fear asked, his curiosity sharpened.

Lena lowered her head into her lap, silent for a moment, her hand instinctively rubbing across her stomach. His eyes tracked her action, his brows rose – and then she looked up.

"My womb." Her eyes squinted, the pain of remembrance clawing from within.

"Oh." Fear blinked, caught off guard. His brows crumpling, he asked, "Does Connerh know?"

Her head tilted, then shook. "No."

"Why haven't you told him?"

"I don't know what he might do."

"That's *exactly* why you should tell him," Fear replied, pointing at her. "If you learn anything, it is that you must stop hiding from the truth. It is the only way. I don't know, I couldn't, or I wasn't strong enough…are all always perfectly acceptable answers. You keep worrying about shame. Shame is not the acknowledgement of failure; it's what you feel when you believe you're not measuring up to someone else's expectations. So, focus on your own. Accept guilt, learn from it. But shame? Forget the spelling of the word."

She looked downwards from the bridge of her nose, her eyes beginning to water.

"So…" he began again, standing. "Why are you betraying Reh'gara?"

She looked up at him, down into her lap, and back again. She thought for a moment, her brows furrowing.

"Because I wasn't strong enough to let go. Because I've spent my entire life trying to balance what others expected of me, until I lost everything I tried to hold on to…watched it slip away from between my fingers," she said, looking down at them, a moment passed in reflection. "I'm tired of people dying in my arms," she mumbled to herself. When she stood, anger had seeped into her expression, and her clenched fists were trembling. Her eyes locking with his, she said, "And because he stole from me, and I want revenge."

Fear smirked, nodding.

"Welcome to the team," he welcomed, lifting his finger. "I present to you, my mark. Where would you like it? The forehead, perhaps?"

"No," she responded quickly, highlighting the absurdity of his suggestion. She looked over her own body as she thought, finally removing her coat of fur and exposing her arm.

"The arm," she said, offering it to him.

"Damn, I can never convince someone to willingly choose the forehead," he remarked.

"Will it hurt?" she asked.

"Yes," he replied, pressing his finger to her arm before she could reply.

Connerh heard her scream. He ran towards the door, but Ankhari intercepted him.

"She's fine," he assured telepathically, standing between Connerh and the steps.

"What's going on in there?" Connerh asked.

"Congratulations; she earned his mark," he replied. Connerh glanced at the door again, the fight draining far too slowly from his veins.

"Will we all need to do the same?" Connerh asked, his nose flaring.

"You don't need one," Ankhari replied, sauntering away.

"It only hurts initially," Sevryn added upon overhearing, rubbing his forehead.

"I still don't know why you chose the head. No one likes a braggart," Toke's laughter rumbled from his belly as he flexed his bicep, Fear's brand marking his muscle.

"Some of us didn't get to choose," Sevryn frowned, folding his arms.

"Now I present to you a choice, but first, I promised a history lesson. I'll try to keep brief," Fear explained, walking back towards the Uridar, his volume rising to account for the distance.

"Think of it as a vessel, or a boat. Except it's been beached. Its sails have been removed, its rudders stripped, and the paddles…well, let's just say they're missing," he continued. "Individuals like myself came here in Uridars, as did Reh'gara and his kind." He paused. Then, with a smirk, "Mine's bigger." He continued, "There are six like this one in total, including mine."

"There are more of you?" she asked.

"Oh, yes. Let's see – there's Desire, Order, Chaos, Life…and Death. We are six elemental forces personified. Connected, but separate. Unique, yet reflections of the same truth. I am an echo cast across countless worlds – different forms, the same essence. We all are. Together, we maintain the balance of existence…but Reh'gara has disrupted that balance. He sought to reshape the world in his image, with no regard for life – or those crushed beneath his arrogance. In other words, he seeks to play God."

"I don't understand. Chaos and death run rampant, children are still being born, and order still exists, the elves being the purest expression of such," she replied.

He grunted.

"The elves…" He scoffed. "Their homeland is where Life's prison lies. Her power seeps from the Uridar, warping the land – causing their forests to grow wild, unnatural, and unchecked. Those woods should stretch halfway across this continent, yet they do not. And because Death's influence has weakened, they live far longer than they should. All of you do. Immortality is a gift that is bestowed, not goods to be stolen."

She held her head, looking internally for a question that didn't sound completely encumbered by ignorance.

But none met the requirement.

Connerh moved through the crowd towards the source of the commotion. Four of the men met him, shoving bound prisoners forward, swords pressed to their backs.

"Who are they?" Connerh asked.

"They won't answer," one of the guards replied. "We caught them sneaking around the base of the mountain, trying to find a way around the patrols."

Connerh turned to one of the prisoners. His eyes lit up – white, crackling, merciless. He seized one of the men by the neck. A violent surge of electricity ripped from his palm, scorching the spy's face as screams twisted into static agony. Skin bubbled, blisters burst, and his eyes turned red with internal bleeding. The body dropped in a smouldering heap.

From a distance, Ankhari watched in silence.

Connerh stepped closer to the next man. "Who are you?" he asked, his voice low and dangerous.

"W-we're just tracking a man for Lady Hargatha!" the prisoner cried, stumbling back in desperation.

A soft, wet crunch cut through the moment – Elisceryn slid effortlessly between the man's ribs. He gasped, blinking once in disbelief before folding into the dirt. Connerh wiped the blade on the man's tunic and sheathed it with a sharp click. His jaw tightened at the mention of Hargatha – no words, just the flicker of recognition. There were no follow-up questions; none were required.

Ankhari stood and turned, his steps slow and deliberate as he walked towards the temple, Connerh's adulation roaring behind him.

"So, Reh'gara is something different?" she asked.

"Here, they call themselves Candorians – but they're little more than caretakers who've overstepped their mission. All of them. Their purpose is to guide life as it unfolds, stepping in only to ensure its course remains true. Over the course of hundreds of thousands of years, that life evolves, becomes aware, and ascends, eventually taking on the mantle of caretaker. Then, they are sent to another world, and the cycle begins anew. Sometimes sooner, sometimes later…sometimes never at all."

"What happens then?"

"Worlds collapse, fail, and life is erased – a clean slate from which it is restarted."

Her brows crumpled. She felt the question bubble up in the pit of her stomach. The answer felt predictable, though she wasn't sure she wanted to hear it.

"Has this world been…restarted?" she asked, her eyes fixed just below his eye line.

"Six times, to be precise."

She gasped – sharp, involuntary, her hand flying to her mouth. There was no logic to the feeling, no reason she could name, but suddenly her legacy – what little of it remained – felt irrelevant. A single dot on an endless canvas that could be wiped clean at any moment, painted over without a trace. No remnants. No records. No memory of what once was or what might have been. No history books. Just…nothing.

"Maybe he got tired of…seeing people get it wrong…tired of losing," she murmured, the words slipping out like a thought she hadn't meant to speak. Her brows pulled together, suddenly heavy as she once again looked at her hands.

Fear stared at her for a silent moment, his brow raising.

"Connerh!" a soldier shouted, urgency cutting through the noise.

He emerged from the crowd, a wall of bodies parting in reverence or fear.

"Look!" the soldier called, pointing down the winding mountain path.

Below them, ten thousand soldiers surged forward, their formation moving with the inevitability of the sea under a banner not yet discernible.

"Does a thief have the right to steal from you simply because he's hungry?"

"No," she admitted, stubbornly – already sensing where this was headed. "But…does that mean we kill the thief for giving in to instinct? Isn't that an overreaction?"

"Ask the wolf that circles a camp. Ask the bear drawn by the scent of food. Compassion doesn't make them less dangerous. Nor does your discomfort make the truth any less valid."

"Yes…yes, I suppose," she stammered, struggling to regain her ideological footing. "But is compassion not the acknowledgement, the understanding of guilt and shame?"

He took a deliberate breath, slow and sharp.

"How much compassion would you, or those responsible for you, extend to a cook who fed you poisoned berries hidden among fresh fruit? What would be his fate?"

She glanced away.

"Death."

"Why? What if it was a mistake? What if he misjudged the colours? Or perhaps it was intentional. Perhaps he believed you were a tyrant who needed to be removed. Perhaps your death would save others from injustice. By whose law is he wrong, and you right?"

She closed her eyes. Her head dropped.

"Does intent matter then? Does your elevated sense of compassion find its place?" he asked.

Her gaze drifted downwards, quietly.

"No."

"Then we have an understanding."

Connerh watched as a messenger broke free from the intruders' ranks. He waved a white flag as he, and he alone, traversed the mountain path towards them.

"Don't neglect the flank, but form up here. I want twenty-five in front with shields – tight formation. Behind them, fifty with swords, ready to rotate in. The last twenty-five, archers. When your quivers run dry, mount up and switch to spears. The path's narrow; they won't be able to overwhelm us with brute force. We'll bleed them out for as long as it takes."

"Why do they call you Fear? I don't feel particularly scared," she asked.

"Dare I say, I'm the most misunderstood of the bunch," he replied with a grin. "I'm far more complex – but, then again, don't we all claim that? I'm the one who keeps your hand from the flame. The one who gives you pause before leaping. The whisper in your gut that says something's wrong before your mind can name it. The little voice that says run...or fight.

I exist between life and death – leaning towards order, tempting chaos, tempering desire.

I am the definition of survival. And that is exactly why we're here today."

Her brows rose.

Ankhari nosed open the doors of the temple, drawing their attention.

Fear's gaze met his – a silent exchange, heavy and unbroken.

"It would seem time is no longer on our side. Ankhari, send in the men," Fear instructed, his movements urgent now, stripped of flair.

He straightened. One hand gripped the Uridar. The other, he extended towards her.

"A question remains," he posed. "Want to fix history?"

A gust of wind burst past her. Torinir flew forward, blowing her hair wildly as it rushed into Fear's waiting hand.

Connerh met the messenger halfway down the path.

"Who is it that comes to die today?" he asked, his tone assured.

"We are the Brothers of Cree. We know the Witch Queen is here, unguarded, and we intend to deliver justice…"

The rest of his proclamation never left his tongue. His head rolled down the path, severed cleanly from his body, Elisceryn already firm in Connerh's grasp.

The Hundred wasted no time, forming ranks behind him and guarding his flank as the Brotherhood charged.

"I don't know what sort of men you are," Connerh announced, addressing his men. "And this moment doesn't ask for allegiance – though if it did, I'd hope you're the worst kind. The kind who feels alive at the sight of blood. The kind who sleeps easily after a slaughter. There's no room for mercy here. No second-guessing. We're outnumbered, and some of you will die, so make it count. Unleash your hatred. It's the only thing that'll keep you alive."

They roared in a unified response.

"Don't let any of them pass," Connerh declared, walking forward – alone – his eyes glowing.

An explosion of light and sound thundered from the Temple, catching Connerh's attention for a flashing second. Long enough to distract him.

An arrow pierced his arm.

The broadhead slicing through his thin chainmail was the only sound he could focus on. It wasn't panic that coursed through his veins; it was survival.

It was fear.

Of losing.

He shouted as he ripped the arrow from his flesh, unaffected by the blow.

He felt no pain, only anger.

Ankhari lunged over him, tearing through the ranks like a shadow with fangs. His massive form crashed into men with the weight of a falling boulder, jaws snapping through bone, and claws raking armour like paper.

The already frail wooden doors to the temple blew apart and outward with violent force. The temple's walls began to crumble. Fear casually walked out as the rubble began to form.

Lena followed a half-step behind, changed.

The fifty lay unconscious, their lifeforce tethered to her like a chain.

Her naked body burned with its own radiance, a living sun given form. Her hair flowed as if caught in an unseen wind, each strand gleaming with celestial brilliance. Light itself cloaked her in modesty, shifting and alive, as though woven from divinity. Three orbs – whispers of raw energy – circled her in a rapid, hypnotic dance.

They both took stock of the chaos. Lena winced as Connerh took a blow – but before the thought had fully formed, she vanished.

In the blink of an eye, she was at the centre of the Brotherhood's charge. The orbs struck first, carving through armour and bone with searing precision, halving men before they hit the ground.

Lena followed with unrelenting brutality.

She grabbed whatever flesh or bone she could reach – necks, arms, ribs – and crushed them with impossible force. Bones shattered like glass in her hands, bodies crumpling before the orbs finished the rest. Her feet moved with merciless rhythm, slipping between blades, slamming knees, and tearing through lines like a living weapon of light.

Blood turned to steam on her radiant skin. Her face showed no emotion, only purpose. She tore through them, radiant and wrathful, a goddess of chaos wearing the mask of a queen.

The cries to retreat met Fear's ears. He clapped with approval.

She held her head, then let out a scream. Her voice spread like a shockwave.

Those in retreat stopped, confusion overtaking them. They turned on one another until one remained.

Connerh pointed to him.

A crack.

The sound of thunder and lightning.

Torinir split the sky, vaporising the coward where his last footstep lay.

In a brief moment that stretched out like an hour, Connerh stared at her. His face was an amalgam of emotion, unsure of what he was witnessing.

For a moment, he saw Lena looking back at him, a smile on her face. She looked younger, more youthful. Happier. But Chaos' expression was stronger, and she looked at him with recognition, but no familiarity.

"Fear, we're running out of time!" she shouted, vanishing.

"All those deemed non-disposable for the purpose of this mission, gather to the Uridar!" Fear shouted, garnering a wide array of expressions, mostly of confusion.

Toke and Sevryn flashed looks of concern at one another.

Ankhari, Connerh, Torinir, Chaos, and Fear stood in a loose circle around the Uridar, their gazes locked on Fear.

"Are you okay?" Connerh whispered to Lena.

Chaos looked at him instead, offering a faint smirk.

"This either will work, or it won't," Fear said. "Either way, we'll get our message across."

"What exactly are we doing?" Connerh asked.

"We're giving him a taste of his own medicine," Fear replied. "Reh'gara, that is."

"We're trapping him inside," Chaos added, "with me."

"I may have forgotten to mention — he has a rather annoying talent. The ability to turn back time. The stronger he is, the farther he can go. However, he's weakening. If we're fast enough, he won't have…time." Fear chuckled darkly.

"How do we stall him?" Ankhari asked.

"I'll handle that," Fear responded.

"And Lena?" Connerh's voice sharpened with urgency.

"In due time," Fear said briskly. Then he turned to the others. "Now, if everyone could place their hand…" He looked at Ankhari, then at Torinir. "…or whatever you've got…on the Uridar, I'll take care of the rest."

They obeyed.

Fear's head snapped back, and lightning split the sky, striking the Uridar. The air tore open with a screech of reality unravelling – and Reh'gara erupted from the breach, his face twisted in shock and dawning horror. Fear exhaled slowly, as though releasing the last breath from Vidar's body, a darkness emanating from his mouth to encircle Reh'gara, who screamed in pure horror.

From his perspective, the world contorted. He was surrounded by his own offspring – millions of them, pressing in. Their eyes bled. Their mouths dripped with anguish. They reached for him, a tide of judgment.

He stumbled backwards, mumbling apologies, clawing at the illusion.

Then Fear appeared before him, looming.

"Time's up," he said.

In perfect silence, Reh'gara vanished. The Uridar began to hum – a deep, resonant vibration, alive with its new prisoner.

Fear looked at Chaos.

"Back in…but only for a little while," Fear said.

Chaos hesitated, her brow raising, but she nodded.

Her form leapt from Lena into the Uridar.

Lena collapsed as the tether to the fifty severed, Chaos' grip over her expelled.

Connerh reached out to catch her but failed. His fingers grazed her warm skin as she fell.

She was human.

She was lifeless as she hit the floor.

THE EPILOGUES

CHAPTER EIGHTY-THREE

THE HIDDEN DOOR

ROSE

Rose held Aeryk close, her arms trembling under the weight of him, the pressure so intense that her muscles had gone numb.

She had yearned for normalcy – ached for it. But even with its promise brushing so close that she could almost taste it, she couldn't find the will to let her guard down. Her body ran on instinct now, her blood permanently thinned by adrenaline. Sleep had become a stranger, especially after Connerh's funeral. He had been her pillar, her calm in the storm. Seeing him laid out in a casket – skin pale, lips still – had split her world in two. Like a candle burning until the wick was ash, something essential in her had gone out with him.

She'd waited hours in the funeral procession, standing stiff and silent, clutching Aeryk's small hand as the line crawled forward. Now and then, her gaze had met the queen's. There was no recognition in Lena's eyes – only tears.

But when it was finally her turn, Rose couldn't help herself. She stepped forward and broke decorum, fingertips trembling as she brushed Connerh's cheek. Her hand cradled his face the way she used to when he came home late, bone-weary and wordless. Her shoulders shook with sobs, her grief too raw, her touch too intimate.

It was obvious: her pain was personal. And that was when Lena had noticed her.

The queen had been gracious. Unshaken. Gentle in a way that Rose hadn't expected. They had spoken for hours afterwards – quiet, measured conversation stretched thin by exhaustion but laced with something soft. Compassion, maybe.

At Lena's insistence, they were given rooms in the castle. Time to rest. She insisted, understanding how sleep could slip away from the grieving like sand through fingers.

She wasn't wrong. Rose initially resisted such graciousness, but Lena could be so persuasive. She wouldn't take no for an answer. When Rose felt steady enough to stand without shaking, Lena made sure they had everything – food, coin, and safe passage to a new home, which just so happened to be in Rose's country of origin.

The gentle murmur of conversation had faded nearly an hour ago, swallowed whole the moment their boat had slipped into the tunnels, just as the sun dipped below the horizon. Since then, silence had reigned, dense and oppressive – nothing but whispers and fragments of conversation.

The water seemed tranquil, its surface smooth as glass, but beneath ran a powerful, invisible current, tugging the boat forward with steady force. It was a false calm – serene above, surging below.

Only the flickering glow of torches and lanterns guided them now, casting long, wavering shadows that danced along the damp stone walls. Darkness clung to the edges of their vision, patient, watchful, and unyielding.

Then came a sudden jolt. A dull thud echoed through the hull as the boat lurched to a halt. Instinctively, heads turned. Passengers glanced at one another, eyes wide, expressions tight with anticipation.

"We've arrived," the captain called out, his voice echoing off the stone. "Grab your things and line up, fancy-like. We'll be disembarking shortly." Without waiting for a response, he strode towards the ramp, which began to creak and lower towards the platform ahead.

"I don't understand… It's just a wall," someone murmured, voice barely more than a whisper.

The captain stepped off the boat and approached the stone face. Behind him, shiphands barked orders, their voices sharp and urgent as they urged stragglers to move faster, to be ready.

Then – grinding, deep, and forceful – the wall began to shift. A low rumble echoed through the chamber, followed by the scraping of ancient mechanisms. From the stone emerged a massive circular door, its edges etched with symbols long faded by time. Slowly, it began to swing open.

The captain turned, a faint smile tugging at the corners of his mouth.

"Welcome to Khazmyr," he said.

CHAPTER EIGHTY-FOUR

CROWN OF GLASS

HARGATHA

Hargatha stood in the dim light, a floor above Egress and her dragons — listening as their screeches and trills mingled with her laughter, echoing through the rotunda. She played among them, unbothered, unafraid, as if the threat they posed didn't exist.

The air was sharp and acrid, veering towards putrid. Half-eaten corpses lay strewn near the dragons — slick with acid, their stench was so vile that it curled the nose and clung to the throat.

This structure, once a grand dining hall adorned in gold, copper, brass, and marble, had hosted royalty and dignitaries in its prime. Now, it served as a dragon's pen. The statues that once lined its interior — effigies of heroes and saints — had been pulled down, shattered into rubble to mimic the jagged terrain of the nursery where the beasts first hatched. An ode to home.

Hargatha had opposed the repurposing from the start. She saw the truth of it — not just what the place had been, but what it could still become. However, the choice hadn't been hers. Egress had insisted the creatures be kept close, declaring the original nursery too remote, too perilous for regular visits. She believed her presence was essential to their training, convinced that by staying near them, she could somehow imprint on them. She could shape them — not into pets, but into something fearsome.

Something loyal. Something monstrous.

Hargatha's gaze lingered high above her cheek, focused on Egress. Behind her stood the man who had once been a governor – now reduced to something else entirely. A thick brass band encircled his neck. The chains that bound him were metaphorical, yes, but no less real, held tightly in Hargatha's grasp.

"My girls and their pets," Galabrand remarked as he approached.

Hargatha offered the barest hint of a smirk, her gaze unmoving. Only when his arm slid around her waist, his lips brushing against her neck, did she finally look at him.

"Wait a minute," she requested, pushing him back to study him properly.

He was clad in black leather armour, chest piece bristling with buckles and ornamental clasps. Her brow furrowed in curiosity.

"What happened to the furs?" she asked, her expression softening. Her hands lifted to his face – his beard was neatly trimmed, his hair freshly cut. Still grey and white, but now…refined. A far cry from the haggard, weather-worn man of the mountain.

"What can I say? Our daughter can be rather persuasive. I wonder where she gets it from?" he chuckled, colour rising in his cheeks. He slid his hands to her waist and pulled her close, trying to shift the attention away from himself. "Do you not like the changes?"

Her brows arched, eyes widening slightly. A slow, thoughtful smile curved across her lips as she studied him.

But it didn't linger.

She wasn't sure.

Hargatha stepped into her quarters, the heavy double doors clicking shut behind her. For a moment, she rested her head against the wood, eyes closed, as if the day's weight had finally caught up to her.

The room was dimly lit. A soft breeze stirred the sheer curtains, making them dance like spectres. The air was thick with the scent of candle wax and crushed rose.

Then – something shifted.

A chill crawled across her skin as the hairs on the back of her neck rose. Her spine straightened. She turned slowly, her back still to the door, eyes scanning the room, expression sharp with aggression – then confusion.

She wasn't wrong. Her instincts never were.

The aggression melted away, leaving only shock. And beneath it…

A haunting need to survive.

She and the stranger locked eyes. The quiet moment felt like minutes turned to days.

A chair scraped softly across the floor, stopping after a few feet.

An invitation.

"I didn't expect to see you," she said carefully, her mind tripping over possible replies, denials, defences.

"I gathered as much," he replied.

"Are you going to kill me now?" Her voice was steady, almost resigned.

But she wasn't resigned. Not even close.

"Sit. We should talk."

Her gaze dropped, hands folding tightly in her lap.

"For what it's worth…I'm sorry, Connerh."

LIFE

MADIKA

"And then there's the matter of your training," Lysand said, her voice soft and measured, the kind one might use with a child. She paused mid-step, gently releasing Madika's hand.

Elarion and Oroben, who had been leading the way, stopped a few paces ahead, turning slightly to listen.

"As things stand," Lysand continued, "without intervention, your training will outlast your lifespan."

A shadow crossed her face – subtle, but unmistakable. Madika's brow furrowed. She had already known this, deep down, but hearing it aloud gave the truth weight she could no longer ignore.

"However," Lysand said, the corner of her lips curling into a hopeful smile, "having the Gift makes you eligible to petition for…an extension, of sorts."

Madika's curiosity piqued, and her brow lifted. Lysand glanced to Elarion and Oroben. They resumed walking, and Lysand, a hint of tension in her touch, reached once more for Madika's hand as they followed.

The forest was already stunning, but nothing could have prepared her for what lay ahead.

A radiant enclave appeared before them, protected by a living wall of luminous flowers and thick vines that rose high into the canopy before plunging back into the earth. A song, not sung but sensed, emanated from within – a resonance that thrummed softly through Madika's chest.

She leaned forward, instinctively trying to glimpse what lay beyond.

As they stepped through a curtain of willowy tendrils, her breath caught – then escaped her in a startled gasp.

Before her stood a Uridar: resplendent, green, and glowing. Alive. Ivy coiled around its surface, swaying gently despite the lack of wind. A delicate mist hugged the ground, swirling around her ankles. Animals roamed freely – birds wheeled overhead, while deer and goats grazed on foliage that regrew faster than it could be eaten. Near the base of the Uridar, a shallow pool of crystal-clear water shimmered, and a ring of small animals – foxes, rabbits, even a hedgehog – gathered around its edge to drink, unafraid and at peace with each other. Madika staggered a step forward, her eyes glassy with emotion. She didn't speak. She couldn't. The others watched her quietly, smiling. Savouring her awe, remembering their first encounter.

"I can hear it," she whispered. A single tear slipped down her cheek.

Elarion's smile deepened, rich with pride.

"What is it?" she asked, her voice barely audible.

He removed his crown, an elegant structure shaped like antlers of gold.

"Life," he said, "and together, we will petition her to grant you a gift. One that no amount of gold could buy."

He offered her his hand.

Madika hesitated – not out of fear, but self-doubt.

Did she deserve this? Was she worthy?

She took his hand anyway.

For a moment, she wondered if it was all real.

Was it a dream?

A fantasy world within her head?

An elaborate illusion of Elarion's?

But the warmth of his hand was real.

The pulse of the Uridar was real.

The song…the song was beautiful, nearly moving her to tears.

Lysand and Oroben walked forward, stopping on either side of the Uridar. Without a word, they placed their palms against it. Their feet rooted into the soil, bark-like skin spreading upwards from their toes. Their expressions turned serene as their limbs began to stretch towards the sphere, becoming one with the ancient life force.

"Come," Elarion said.

Together, they walked towards it.

Time passed.

Madika now sat alone before the Uridar.

Legs crossed. Arms outstretched. Palms open.

Her skin looked new – tighter, luminous. Her complexion glowed with clarity.

The markings on her face had vanished.

Beside her…

…her chains lay rusted, in a heap.

CHAPTER EIGHTY-SIX

DESIRE

DARROS

His golden sarcophagus bore his true likeness. No mask, no skulls, no grim symbols of death. Ironically – perhaps intentionally – it was the very opposite.

A mural of life.

Gold, onyx, and rare gemstones encrusted the surface, catching the flicker of torchlight in soft, shifting glints. The sculpted image was serene – his arms crossed in silent authority, a sceptre resting in his right hand and a small Uridar cradled in his left, it was as if he had never let it go.

At his feet bloomed intricately carved roses, their stone petals curling around the base as if frozen in the act of blooming. Beside them, small tablets were laid out, etched with symbols in a language too old, too foreign for any living tongue to decipher.

With a sudden jolt, the sarcophagus shifted, groaning forward on ropes thicker than a man's arm. The grinding of stone against stone filled the chamber, a deep rumble that vibrated through the floor and echoed off every wall. It was being pulled away from the mouth of Khazmyr's Uridar – which stirred in protest, its energy disturbed, reluctant to loosen the tendrils of light still clinging to the coffin.

The building that housed it was simple but beautiful. Tall sandstone pillars stood in solemn rows along the walls, weathered but unbowed. Translucent curtains fluttered gently with the wind, and a circular hole in the ceiling poured a single beam of sunlight directly onto the Uridar — a spotlight from the gods. In the adjoining room, silk and velvet pillows were scattered in careless luxury, a dining table long enough to seat a hundred. It was not a sanctuary; it was a playground. The kind of place where casual debauchery unfolded in the blanket of night — Darros' personal paradise.

After thirty feet, the sarcophagus came to a halt.

Servants rushed in, heads bowed and faces hidden, to carefully remove the lid. The moment it touched the ground, they sank to their knees.

A hand rose from within, fingers flexing as they gripped the edge of the sarcophagus, the tips covered in gold stalls.

Then his head emerged — his face whole again, features unmarred, expression unreadable.

Beside him sat a small table, and upon it, his mask.

He picked it up, turned it over in his hand, and studied it for a breath longer than necessary — then dropped it to the ground.

Darros rose again.

CHAPTER EIGHTY-SEVEN

DIAMONDS IN THE ROUGH

?

She always liked to watch the heat ripples emanate from the black sand. The granules sparkled like stars, and pearls of varying size were strewn across the surface like planets scattered through a night sky.

But the distortions were what held her; they reminded her of her father. His arrival, always marked by a similar mirage – but it was no illusion.

Sadly, he had not come to visit in a long while. Time seemed to pass slowly here, so she never truly knew how long he'd been gone or when he would return.

She just knew that he would.

One day.

Until then, she spent the start and end of each day waiting by the coastline.

"Rhe'a!" Quinn shouted.

She remained still, legs crossed, hovering just above the ground. She heard him but preferred being difficult, as siblings often did. A grin snuck onto her cheek.

"Rhe'a!" he shouted again, his rushed footsteps growing louder by the moment. Quinn stopped when he reached her, pausing to catch his breath. She hovered higher, allowing her legs to extend.

Rhe'a was half a head shorter than Quinn, but she never touched the ground when he was around. It kept them eye to eye.

"It's down!" he shouted, his tone a mix of enthusiasm and shock. "The barrier is down!"

Her eyes widened, swiftly turning towards the coast. Her breathing hastened.

"Then they should be here," she murmured, eyes sweeping the horizon. She looked over the sands with a confused expression – familiar ripples, but not the ones she'd hoped for.

Their excitement faded, gone too quickly with the wind.

"I don't understand…" Quinn muttered, his tone shifting.

She shook her head again.

"What does that mean?" she asked in a panic.

"I don't know… Let's ask Luc; he's about to send another dragon across the expanse," he replied.

"Why? They were never affected by the barrier," she asked, frustrated.

"Because he's riding it this time," Quinn replied with a smirk, taking off to run.

"Wait!" she shouted, stopping him in his tracks. "Where is he?"

Quinn looked up, his pupils disappearing before he replied, "He's still at the hatchery."

His pupils returned, only to find he was talking to no one.

"What?" he asked himself, turning to see Rhe'a floating, the echo of her giggles reaching him.

"You bitch!" he shouted, running to catch up.

Though he appeared their age, Lucien was, by far, the oldest.

Most of the children seemed to be in their twenties, though a few seemed younger – like Quinn and Rhe'a.

Old souls, suspended in time and bodies that refused to age. Though here, *age* was a sort of misnomer.

Lucien wore the face of a twenty-nine-year-old, with the faintest traces of where wrinkles might one day form framing his mouth. A sliver of experience in a sea of youth. They were like siblings, all of them – especially the ones who truly were. Brothers, sisters, cousins…bound by blood or something stranger.

In simple terms, they were kin, in one way or another.

As such, he felt a responsibility to watch over them, as a big brother would.

And so, he did.

He roamed the skies, day and night, on the backs of dragons, watching over his family and waiting for their parents to return – as they always had. But something had changed. The cart had arrived before the horse. Draeven's shadow slid across the black sands as they soared overhead, his massive wings concussing the air with every beat.

"Down there – land next to Rhe'a and Quinn," Lucien shouted. Draeven grunted, the sound vibrating through his body. They looked so small from this height. His graceful pivot cast a nearly undetectable shadow over the black beach as he turned. His silhouette compressed as he pulled his wings in tightly, hurling them towards the ground. Lucien leaned forward, lying against Draeven to avoid the drag, his wavy black hair whipping in the wind.

Draeven was massive but no less agile, especially when the wind cooperated. His wings flung open, engulfing Rhe'a and Quinn in sand and shadow as his body landed with report. Lucien hopped down, but not without praising Draeven. His hand raised, his hand balled, index finger pointed at Quinn.

"Stay out of my head! I told you I hate when you do that," he barked.

"It was just a little peek," Quinn replied in a small voice.

"One day, you're going to see something you're not going to like! Like me sticking my—"

"I get it!" Quinn interjected, his face contorting at the possibilities.

Lucien shook his head as he finished his approach.

"The veil has dropped, but my father has not returned. Have you seen uncle?" he asked, his voice calm and collected but with a note of concern. His pale green irises were piercing, nearly disappearing into the rest of the eye, though they darkened and became richer in colour when he was angry.

"No. I don't sense him, either," Rhe'a replied.

"I wonder if your other dragons will return now that the veil has dropped," Quinn added.

"Still running with that theory?" Luc asked.

"Why else would they not return?" Quinn asked. Luc looked at the horizon, finally releasing a sigh.

"Maybe you're right," he replied, looking around.

"Quinn said you're planning to cross the expanse?" Rhe'a asked. Lucien looked at her before nodding.

"I'm working on it… But first, we need to get to Serene. She's not been so well since it dropped…that's why I came to get you. That, and to get a break from the screaming," he said, turning to walk towards Draeven. Quinn and Rhe'a exchanged glances but hurried to keep pace.

Lucien pushed his way through the crowd, the other two in tow. Serene was sitting, seemingly calm now. Kora stood above her, her hand resting on Serene's temple. She looked up as Lucien approached, her purple eyes as brilliant as her mother's namesake.

"She's fine now," Kora assured.

"There were just so many voices, all at once and out of nowhere," Serene added, still trying to catch her breath. "So many… How could that be?" she asked. Luc's gaze fell briefly, but it rose with the building pressure of everyone looking for him to provide an answer.

"Then why haven't they come back?" someone shouted.

"I could sense some of the elders among them!" Serene interjected, sensing panic was soon to ensue.

Luc nodded to her, a silent thank you.

"Reh'gara, Amethyst, Aenon…" she continued, closing her eyes to reexamine. Lucien walked closer.

"What of my father?" he asked in nearly a whisper.

"Yes…and no… I don't understand, but yes…" she replied in kind. Her eyes opened; her brows furrowed. "But that is better than most…there are many missing." She whispered even lower, her face exposing a controlled fear. He bit his bottom lip. Still quieter, she continued, "There's also a new elder."

Luc frowned.

"What do you mean, *new*?" he replied.

"I don't know. Their light is different…dimmer, but it's there."

"Alright, I've had enough. I'm going to cross," he replied after deliberating, immediately turning to leave.

"How will you know where to go?" Quinn asked.

"We're coming with," Rhe'a demanded.

"Absolutely not. I'm not babysitting; this is for the adults. But you're right. Serene, you're coming – which means you're next up in the saddle, Kora. We'll need someone to soothe her mind in case she gets overwhelmed again. Coren and Ravi, you're up in the event we need to kill a lot of things… That, and I refuse to be outnumbered by women," he added with a smirk. The two men stepped out of the crowd, their figures imposing. "We'll send word for the rest of you once we ensure it's safe!" he shouted to a stirring crowd.

"Do you have dragons mature enough for them all?" Kora asked.

"I do," he replied.

"Good. That means Quinn and I are coming, then," Rhe'a insisted, grabbing her brother's hand and walking towards the hatchery.

Luc stared at the back of the twins' heads, unamused.

Seven dragons soared, casting long shadows over sapphire seas.

The island – their once-temporary home – faded into the horizon.

Beyond the veil of its protection, time resumed.

Their youth faded instantly, carried off by the wind.

<u>ACKNOWLEDGMENTS</u>

To my children — Thank you for the time you sacrificed during the times I couldn't always wait until you were asleep to write. Your patience and love made this possible. I hope this book stands as proof of what I've always told you: you can do anything if you set your mind to it.

To Bonnie — My editor, thank you for your sharp eye and your genuine belief in this story. Your thoughtful investment went far beyond grammar; you breathed new life into a manuscript I've lived with for four years, and made the process a joy. Here's to the next one!

To J.L - Thank you for the long nights spent unraveling the universe, mythology, and wild ideas. Your brotherhood and listening ear mean more than I can say. I don't know what I'd do without them. Now it's your turn!

To DMx2/MM - Thank you for kicking cancer's ass and showing us all that you don't need powers, swords, or magic spears to be a warrior—or a queen. And thank you for making us an Uncle and Aunt again, reminding us to savor these delicate moments as they linger.

To Chelsea - To our friend and beta reader, thank you for taking a chance on a genre outside your comfort zone. Your support means the world, and your reactions—full of surprise, laughter, and hilarity —made the journey even more rewarding.

About the Author

Anderson grew up on the eastern U.S. coast, in an era before the Netflix generation—when a wide variety of stories and adventures could only be found on the printed page. Led by literary classics and the imaginative worlds of *Star Wars* and *Star Trek*, a love of myth, meaning, and storytelling took root early. Surrounded by the works of Tolkien, Orson Scott Card, Michael Crichton, and Timothy Zahn, he developed a deep appreciation for epic narratives layered with emotion, wonder, and philosophical weight.

Now writing epic dark fantasy and speculative fiction, Anderson weaves classical influences with modern urgency—crafting fractured worlds, morally torn heroes, and the unseen forces that shape them. When not writing, he's most likely wandering secondhand bookstores alongside his wife.

You can find more about Anderson on his website:
www.andersonfrost.com

www.ingramcontent.com/pod-product-compliance
Lightning Source LLC
Chambersburg PA
CBHW031148310726
48969CB00001B/7